make me series

USA TODAY BESTSELLING AUTHOR
KENNEDY FOX

Copyright © 2017-2019 Kennedy Fox
www.kennedyfoxbooks.com

Make Me Series
The Complete Set

Includes: Make Me Forget,
Make Me Crazy, & Make Me Stay

Cover designer: Designs by Dana

All rights reserved. No parts of the book may be used or reproduced in any matter without written permission from the author, except for inclusion of brief quotations in a review. This book is a work of fiction. Names, characters, establishments, organizations, and incidents are either products of the author's imagination or are used fictitiously to give a sense of authenticity. Any resemblance to actual persons, living or dead, events, or locales is entirely coincidental.

MAKE ME SERIES READING ORDER

Make Me Forget
Ethan & Vada
An enemies to lovers,
summer fling romance

Make Me Crazy
Maverick & Olivia
An enemies to lovers,
road trip romance

Make Me Stay
Colton & Preston
An enemies to lovers,
small town romance

Each book can standalone, but suggested to read
in order for the best reading experience.

MAKE ME FORGET

make me series

USA TODAY BESTSELLING AUTHOR
KENNEDY FOX

CHAPTER ONE

VADA

The plane rattles and shakes as it prepares to make its landing. Cringing, I steady myself on the armrest, but when I place my hand down, it touches the guy sitting next to me.

"Oh, shit. Sorry." I jerk my hand back and wrap my arms around my body.

"It's okay. Take it," the older gentleman offers. I'm not afraid of flying, but I don't exactly love it either. Especially when it feels like we're about to fly straight into the ground.

"Are you sure?" I ask although he's already removed his arm. He nods, and I graciously wrap my fingers around it and squeeze. "Thank you."

We finally land, and once we deplane, I grab my carry-on and head for the baggage claim. I can already feel the heat and am completely overdressed in my black leggings, winter boots, and thick scarf. South Carolina feels like a sauna, and I can almost taste the heat and humidity.

I hail a taxi and inform the driver where I'm going. It's at least another two hours before we'll arrive at the house, but it'll be worth it. Quiet, solitary, peace. Just what I need to finish my novel. As soon as I open the car door, the scent of the ocean blows in the air. It smells like heaven.

"Thank you," I tell the driver when he pulls my luggage out of the trunk.

"You definitely aren't from around here, huh?" he comments, taking in my appearance and bad wardrobe choice. I furrow my brows, wondering if that's meant as a bad thing. "You have a midwestern accent." He confirms his suspicions.

"Oh, yes. Chicago," I tell him. "I'm definitely not in the city anymore." I laugh, grabbing for my wallet. Chicago has been home to me for years, but it's loud, attracts tourists all year round, and neighbors are so close, you can hear them pee. I can only drown out the noise for so long before it drives me insane, which led me to booking an Airbnb for a week.

"It's a whole different world out here," he tells me.

I hand him the money with a smile. "That's what I'm hoping for."

As the taxi drives away, I grab my luggage and take in the scenery. It's stunning. The Airbnb I rented is a small guesthouse with a garden view. The pictures were amazing, so I'm looking forward to staying in this little peaceful sanctuary for the next week.

Walking up the sidewalk to the main house, I notice a cute porch swing on the patio and some planters along the porch steps. The owner seemed very charming and kind by the pictures, description, and detailed information he wrote for the listing. Everything screams southern. I like it. In fact, I like it a lot.

I ring the bell, and when the door opens wide, my eyes scan up and down the man's body, and I'm shocked to see he's completely shirtless. He's wearing low-cut jeans that ride effortlessly on his hips.

He's maybe a couple years older than me. Dark hair is tousled across his forehead, piercings in his ears, facial hair grazes his hard jawline, and rock-hard abs line his stomach. I swallow as my eyes roam down to the deep V that disappears into his low-cut jeans. He's rugged and manly and definitely *not* what I expected to answer the door. He's the epitome of a heartbreaker I'd write about in one of my romance novels, and I'm not sure if that's a good or bad thing.

It's official. I'm undeniably not in Chicago anymore.

"Can I help you or do you plan to stand here and stare at me all evening?" he asks in a faint southern accent; his words take me completely off guard.

I snap my eyes back up and watch him as he studies my features. "That's a rather crass assumption."

"Not an assumption, ma'am."

"Don't call me ma'am. My name is Vada Collins. I rented the guesthouse," I explain, tilting my chin toward the backyard.

"Vada? Hm." He strokes his fingers along his scruff as he narrows his eyes at me.

"What?"

"I wouldn't have pegged you for a Vada. In fact, I read your name as *Vat*-ah."

"Yeah, that's happened all my life." I sigh. "Thanks, Mom and Dad," I mutter to myself, but he chuckles anyway.

"It's cute."

I narrow my eyes at him, annoyed that he just called my name *cute*.

"Don't call my name that. I'm not an eight-year-old girl."

"Fuck. You're feisty, aren't you? I like that in a woman." He winks, and it sends a shiver down my spine. What the hell is happening?

"Are you for real?" I ask.

"As real as my twenty-inch cock. Care to come in and see it?" He takes a step to the side and sweeps his arm from one side to the other, motioning for me to come in.

"Excuse me?" I nearly choke on my tongue and take a step back as I envision him pulling down his pants and whipping out his anaconda. "Are you insane or something?"

"Inviting you inside is what we folks down here call southern hospitality, sweetheart." He flashes me one of those smirks I'd write about in my novels where the girl's panties instantly combust, and although this man is sex on a stick, I'm not falling for it.

"I do not want to come inside and see your python-sized cock, okay? Just give me the keys, and I'll find my way around."

He starts laughing. *Laughing*. The asshole.

"Sweetheart, I wasn't talking about my python-sized cock—

although you aren't wrong on how big it is—but I was literally talking about my rooster, Henry."

Wait. *What?*

"You have a rooster?" My brows rise, and I can feel my cheeks starting to heat. I've just made a complete ass out of myself, and it's all his fault.

"That's what I said. He likes to wander around the backyard, so don't get freaked if you see him around the guesthouse."

I groan, closing my eyes to release the added stress. "Great, I'll be sure to watch for him." I hold my palm out flat in front of me. "The keys? Can I have them please?"

His hand reaches for his pocket but then stops. "Not so fast. I need to go over the rules and stipulations first."

"I read all of the rules online when I booked the place. I know what your *stipulations* are. I'm tired, I smell like airplane, and I just want to take a hot shower," I explain, but he ignores me.

"Follow me," he calls out, walking into the house and leaving me both confused and speechless on the porch.

I step inside with my rolling suitcase and follow behind him. The wheels from my luggage rattle against the hardwood floor, and before I can fix it, he turns around, grabs my suitcase, and carries it on his shoulder.

"Are you going to tell me your name?" I ask, realizing I only know him by his name on the Airbnb site—E. Rochester. Sounds made up now that I see him in the flesh. He looks more like a Mr. Robinson. Probably seduces young women and takes their youth and then bails. Or maybe the E stands for egotistical.

"No. Are you going to tell me your favorite position?"

"What?" I screech, certain I heard him wrong.

"Of baseball," he clarifies, looking over his other shoulder at me, sporting an infamous panty-melting smirk.

"I don't—"

"It feels like you're hoarding baseballs or bowling balls in here. Shit."

I narrow my brows, annoyed he continues to make sexual comments about normal things while knowing exactly what he's doing. And I'm giving him just the reaction he's hoping for.

Dammit.

"It's books actually," I correct him. "I'm a writer."

"A writer? Really?" He sets the luggage down in the middle of the kitchen that looks like it came straight from a *Country Living* magazine. "I wouldn't have pegged you as a writer either."

"What does that mean?" I ask, folding my arms over my chest defensively. I've known this guy for all of five minutes, and already he's labeling me and pissing me off.

"You look like a basic girl. I assumed you were a dancer or something. Maybe a gymnast. Or hell, even a model."

I'm not sure what the hell he's talking about, but I'm pretty certain that kind of sounded like a compliment?

"What's a basic girl?"

"You know, hair up in one of those ironic messy buns that probably took you at least ten minutes to get *just right*. You're wearing tight, black leggings with gray Ugg boots, and one of those scarfs that's more for fashion than it is useful." He shrugs, unapologetically. "All you're missing is a Starbucks Pumpkin Spice Latte in your hand and a pair of Gucci sunglasses."

"And that makes me a basic girl?"

"That's right, sweetheart."

I point a finger in the air at him. "Don't call me sweetheart," I tell him, annoyed. "And is that what they consider Southern hospitality down here because, if so, I gotta say—not impressed."

He laughs again, and it actually sounds real. "Just laying out the facts."

"Well, I mean, if that's what we do around here with someone you literally met minutes ago, I'd say it's my turn."

"Go for it. Give me your best." He crosses his muscular arms over his broad chest, and it takes me a moment to remind myself to stop looking at his incredible body. Getting a better view of him in the light, I see a layer of sweat or water covering his chest and torso. Either he was working out or just got out of the shower. But who the hell works out in jeans, especially in this gross humidity?

"Well, for starters, you answer the door shirtless. You have this whole edgy, heartbreaker look going on, which is probably because you think you're God's gift to women. Probably in a band and are used to sleeping with groupies every weekend. You flash that smirk around as if you know it gets you whatever you want, which if I were anything *like* a basic girl, I would fall head over heels for. You strut your body off as if it's the only way to grab my attention in hopes I'll just start stripping off all my clothes. Your hands look rugged and have calluses, so aside from playing in a band on Friday and Saturday nights, you work with your hands. A mechanic or builder, maybe."

He studies me as I continue to ramble, looking over his physique and handing out every stereotype he matches. If he wants to judge me based on five seconds of meeting me, then I have no choice but to do the same.

"So, how close am I?" I ask, feeling confident with my assumptions.

He purses his lips and nods. "I'm impressed."

"Well, I do have a knack for reading people. It's what makes me a great writer."

"Is that so?" He arches a brow, and I nod confidently. "Well, I'm sorry to disappoint you, sweetheart, but you couldn't be further from the truth," he says, matter-of-factly. "However," he continues in a low seductive tone, "you are right about one thing."

I roll my eyes and groan. "What's that, Casanova?"

"I was hoping you'd start stripping off all your clothes."

"You're so vain," I hiss at him. "I would never—"

"You're wearing six layers of clothing in ninety-degree weather," he cuts me off. "Stripping off your clothes is to make sure you don't pass out from a heatstroke on my newly remodeled kitchen floor."

I release a long-exaggerated breath, seriously over his sexual remarks and condescending attitude.

"If this is what southern men are like, count me out."

"Oh, I wouldn't worry about that. Your basic girl snark and sarcasm will scare them off for you."

I bite my tongue to keep from cursing him out. I don't have the energy to deal with this egotistical asshole.

"Can we just skip the rules and whatever else for now, and just give me the damn key, please? I've been traveling all day, I'm exhausted, and I need to wash the travel stench off me."

"I wasn't going to say anything but—"

"Can you just *please* stop being a dick for one minute?" I pinch my eyes shut and inhale deeply.

He raises his brows and then reaches into his pocket, revealing the keychain with a single key hanging from it. "Your wish is my command." He holds it out, and I quickly grab it before he can pull it away.

"Thank you," I say, firmly. He opens the back door for me and points me in the direction of the guesthouse.

He stays silent as I grab my suitcase and roll it behind me down the porch steps. The walkway to the guesthouse is lined with gorgeous flowers and bushes that I hadn't expected, especially after meeting the owner—who, by the way, I still didn't get his name.

I spin around, determined to make him tell me, but when I do, a swarm of bugs start biting the shit out of me.

"Oh my God!" I wave my hands around frantically, spinning and trying to get away. I scream, hoping he'll help me or at least get me out of here, but all I hear from his direction is laughter.

"What the fuck?" I shout, thrashing my arms around, trying to dodge them.

"If you had let me finish, I would've told you that your perfume was too strong. It attracts the mosquitoes. But so does travel body odor and sweat."

"You asshole," I mutter, knowing he'll hear me anyway.

"Tried to warn ya," he says casually, and when I look up at him, he's leaning against the doorway with his arms crossed like the smug asshole he is.

CHAPTER TWO

ETHAN

AFTER A LONG DAY OF WORK, I'm ready to call it a night. Windows paint the walls of the third-story tower room in my house that I use as a workspace. Although it's my favorite room, it gets hot as hell. Hotter than the rest of the house, especially in Charleston during the summer. But it's the only place I find inspiration anymore, so I work through it.

I jump in the shower and clean off the aftermath. This time of year, I usually wait for it to cool off and work in the evenings and night, but my schedule's jam packed between working and showings, that I need to squeeze it in when I can. Just as I'm putting on a pair of jeans, I hear doors slam outside, and when I peek out the window, I see a woman and a taxi driver talking on the sidewalk. Assuming it's my tenant for the week, I rush downstairs before putting on a shirt.

The moment she eyes me, I can read the judgment all over her face. I decide this can go two ways: I can dazzle her with my southern charm and prove she's wrong about me, or I can have some fun and mess with this unmistakable city girl.

I choose the latter.

She's attractive in an obvious way. Pretty face, long, lean legs, chocolate-brown hair—the type of girl who could get by on her looks alone. When I open the door and see her standing on my front porch, I notice that her eyes are a sparkling green, or perhaps that's just how they look when she's annoyed. Either way, she's got that girl-next-door mixed with a *Sex and the City* vibe. Innocent and classy, but could probably break me in more ways than one. Her sass proves that immediately.

Staring at me, her eyes continue to roam up and down my body. I smirk, knowing she's checking me out just as I was her. Though as soon as I speak, her attitude shifts and gives out a look of disgust. I find it humorous, really, because I know her type—uppity and snobbish. She pretends to be unaffected by me and then offended when I ask if she plans to stare at me all night.

And when she answers me, in that tone and scowl, I know I'm completely right about her.

The next morning, I wake up with Wilma's ass in my face. She's a feisty feline who doesn't give two shits about personal space or boundaries and wiggles her way under the covers until she's comfortable. She's purring softly, which means she's still sleeping, but that doesn't stop me from pushing her away.

"Nice work, Wilma," I groan. "Woke me up before my alarm, so I'll actually have time to make coffee this morning."

She stretches and meows before rolling onto her back and waits for me to pet her. I give in and then get dressed before I get too comfortable and fall back asleep.

"C'mon, Wilma. Let's get breakfast."

I slip on my jeans before heading downstairs. The sun is rising over the water and streaks of reds and oranges are shining through the bay windows. It's gorgeous. My favorite part of the day actually, but since I've been working more than usual lately, I'm usually getting up before the sunrise.

After refilling Wilma's food and water, I fill the coffee maker and pull out my mug. Just as I'm digging in the fridge for some creamer, a knock at the back door startles me.

"Shit," I curse when I see it's Vada. She looks like she literally just rolled out of bed with messy hair and sleepy eyes. It's actually kind of cute.

"You scared the living shit out of me," I tell her once I open the door. "What are you doing up so early?"

"Sorry," she apologizes, pulling her robe tighter around her waist. "I work best in the morning and was trying to get a head start, but…there's no coffee maker."

"And here I thought you were coming for another viewing." I cross my arms over my chest, emphasizing my biceps.

"Funny." She rolls her eyes, swallowing back a groan that tells me she's not in the mood for any games. "After letting me get swarmed with mosquitos, the least you could do is let me have some coffee," she tells me matter-of-factly.

I grin, leaning against the door. "Well…that's not the *least* I could do…"

"Oh, fuck it. I'll get dressed and go into town for coffee." She turns, but before she can walk away, I step forward and grab her arm.

"Oh, come on." I chuckle, finding everything about her amusing. "You don't need to go into town scaring the locals with your raccoon eyes and rat's nest. I made coffee."

She studies me for a moment, staying silent. Her eyes roam down to where my fingers are gripped around her wrist. I remove them and wait for her to say something. Her breath hitches and I wonder if it's because our bodies are so close—we're nearly chest to chest—or if it's from the loss of my touch. Either way, it doesn't go unnoticed.

"Fine," she grits between her teeth. "Only because I'm desperate."

I cough to cover up a smile as I widen the door and wave her inside.

Once she steps in, I shut the door behind her and point a finger to the cupboard near the fridge. "Coffee mugs are in there."

"Thank you." She walks over and reaches inside for one of my mugs, wrapping her fingers securely around it and studies it. "These are spectacular. Where did you find them?" She brushes her fingers across the markings and smooth surface. Tilting it over, she reads the bottom. "Paris?"

Clearing my throat, I adjust myself, so we're parallel from each other. I lean up against the island and watch as she admires the mug. "There's a shop in town that sells them. I probably have a dozen or so."

"Wow…I'm impressed."

I arch a brow and smile. "With the mug or that I actually own a piece like that?"

She grins. "Both."

The coffee maker beeps, signaling it's finished brewing. She pours herself a cup, reaches for the creamer in the fridge, and sits down at the breakfast bar. I follow suit, filling my own mug and then sit down on the stool across from her.

We study each other as she blows carefully in her mug, and before either of us speak up, Wilma makes herself known and rubs up against Vada's dangling legs.

"Oh, hello," she coos in a soft, sweet voice. "And who are you?" Wilma reaches up and paws at her, begging for attention as usual.

"That's Wilma," I tell her. She brings the mug to her lips and takes a small sip as I continue. "She's the only pussy allowed in my bed, so don't get any ideas."

Before I can react, hot coffee spews from her mouth and lands on my bare chest and face.

"Oh my God!" She covers her mouth and laughs. "Why would you say something like that?"

"Wasn't it obvious? To get your hot saliva all over me."

She tilts her head and narrows her eyes. "Do you ever stop?"

I purse my lips as if I'm truly contemplating her question. "Nah. I live for reactions like yours."

"For some reason, I don't doubt that for one second." She scowls, reaching for the paper towels on the counter and handing them to me.

"Aren't you going to at least clean me up? I mean, it was your fault and all."

Rolling her eyes, she takes the roll out of my hand and smacks me in the head with it. "Actually, you brought that on all by yourself. So nice try, Casanova."

After cleaning up the coffee mess, I sit back and watch as she pours herself another cup. "So what's with this term of endearment, Casanova? Does that mean you want to be seduced and bedded or you actually think I'm *that* kind of guy?"

"*Seduced and bedded*?" She laughs, walking back to the stool with her mug of hot coffee. I eye it, making sure she doesn't spontaneously trip and dump the entire thing on me.

"You sound like you've been reading historical romance or something."

"Not since I was fifteen and stealing the novels off my grandmother's bookshelf."

"You read romance novels when you were a teenager?"

"Only in hopes it came with pictures," I shamelessly admit, mocking the way she's throwing jabs at me. "That was before online porn, so I had to do what I had to do." I shrug, and she bursts out in laughter. I like the sound—a lot, actually. Although she's a bit uptight, I enjoy watching her laugh. The wrinkles in her face, the freckles that move along her cheeks, and the sweet sound that releases from her throat. It's adorable.

Once she controls her laughter, she straightens her posture and purses her lips. "And for the record, it's not a term of endearment."

I'm quick to press my palm flat against my chest, showing defeat. "Why must you break my heart?"

Her head falls back with laughter, louder than before and I can tell it's genuine. She's warming up to me even if she pretends she doesn't like me.

"As much as I'm enjoying this little early morning chat with you, I have to get back to my laptop and start writing. Otherwise, this entire trip will be a bust, and I'll never be able to write again."

"You just got here, so don't put too much pressure on yourself."

"Says the person who doesn't write." She rolls her eyes as she stands up and takes the mug with her. "There's no such thing as too much pressure. It's a part of the lifestyle. You're either writing, or you're not writing. There's no in-between."

"Fair enough." I shrug.

"Thanks again for the coffee." She holds up the mug in a peace-offering salute. "I'll be sure to bring it back in one piece."

"That's not even funny," I say seriously, pointing a finger at her. "I saw the way you stumbled to the guesthouse last night, so I'm not sure how trustworthy your word is."

She gasps, and her jaw drops in mock laughter. "I was nearly killed by a swarm of bugs while you just stood there and laughed!"

"I didn't laugh," I defend. "But it was pretty funny considering you were in the middle of scolding me."

She sighs and rolls her eyes, giving up the fight. Although we'd just met, I can actually read her quite well. She's snarky and quick-witted, just like me, except she knows when to give up. Me—not so much.

She opens the door, and just before stepping out, looks over her shoulder and smirks. "Have a good day, Casanova."

CHAPTER THREE

VADA

He kisses her softly, plucking his thumb along her lower lip, and when she releases a hungry, desperate moan, he slides his tongue in deeper. Helena arches her back, and Jordan wraps his arms around her waist, pressing her body tighter against his. She feels his growing erection against her flesh and can no longer resist the temptation to touch him. She's been waiting years for this moment...

Writing sex scenes is the hardest part of the writing process for me. Even though I usually have great feedback from my agent, it takes twice as long to write compared to other scenes. It doesn't help that I haven't been inspired due to my own pathetic love life.

Leaning back in my chair, I stretch my arms over my head and crack my neck from side to side. I can only write for a few hours at a time before I need to get up and walk around. I'm usually alternating between writing and social media, but I vowed to take a social media break while I'm on my mini writing retreat.

Casanova had mentioned downtown Charleston and all the quaint shops that line the streets. Chicago is covered in shops and malls, but there's just something about a new city that intrigues me. I close my laptop and decide a short break wouldn't hurt. Hell, it might inspire me for the first time in weeks.

After showering and getting dressed, I stop by the main house to ask for suggestions on where I should go, but he's not home. He must've left for work or something, so I schedule an Uber to take me downtown.

"Thank you," I tell the driver after he drops me off on the corner of King and Meeting Streets by Marion Square Park. He suggested this area once I told him I wasn't exactly sure where I wanted to go, and I'm happy to see he didn't let me down. I can already tell it's what I was needing.

"Enjoy yourself," he tells me with a smile before I shut the door behind me.

Shops are lined up and down both sides of King Street. The sun is shining brightly above, people are chatting as they walk past, and a high energy is in the air.

Usually being around a lot of people gives me anxiety, but today I plan to embrace it. Chicago's always crowded with tourists sight-seeing and locals walking to work, which is why I usually stay isolated in my shoebox apartment. But not here. I want to enjoy the fresh, warm air and all this city has to offer.

My first stop is a cute boutique with all kinds of handmade goodies. Jewelry and hair accessories, designer handbags, scarves, and sunglasses line the walls and storefront. I barely walk in ten feet before a woman approaches me.

"Well, hello there." She greets me with a sweet, southern drawl. "How ya doing?"

"Fine, thank you." I smile back. "Your shop is gorgeous."

"Thank you." She beams with pride. "It's actually my mama's, but my sister, Cherise and I do most of the customer service duties now that she's inching toward retirement. Although she still does all the accountin' and orderin'," she tells me, but I don't know why.

I smile and nod as I run my fingers through one of the scarves on display. "The fabric is so soft."

"Oh, that's because my Aunt Jeannie—she lives across Cooper River o'er there—washes all the fabric in baby oil before sewing the patterns together. Then she steams them, but only using distilled water, and once they dry, she sprays them with organic fabric softener. It's a process, she says, but she enjoys it, so she keeps doin' it." She rambles fast, making it hard to process everything she's saying.

Blinking, I bite my lip and nod. "Wow, that's very cool."

Oversharing must be common around here because you definitely won't get that in the Midwest.

Reading her nametag, I see her name is Cherry. Smiling, I walk around the shop as she continues telling me the backstory on every item I pick up. The pair of earrings her Aunt Mae designed, the sunglasses they found in Italy and can barely keep them in stock this time of year, the bracelet her Gram Gram redesigned from a bracelet her mama bought for her many years ago. With how much she talks, I could write an entire novel before I even get a chance to leave the store.

She asks my name and why I'm visiting. Once I tell her, she goes on and on about how she loved watching *My Girl* with her kids, who are named Christine and Caitlin, and then proceeds to tell me how she's read every single Nicholas Sparks novel to date after I tell her I'm a writer who's here on business.

By the time I make my way back to the front and checkout with a new scarf and pair of earrings—neither of which I really needed—I know all of Cherry's pets' names: Scruffy, Spinner, Spike, and Bella, as well as her thoughts on the annual Labor Day parade that's coming up. Granted, I was a little put off at first by a stranger telling me so many personal details, but by the time I leave, I've actually enjoyed the company—as weird as it was.

I continue walking down the street, the sun beaming down on me, and decide to tie my hair up into a ponytail. Once I've managed to get the hair off my neck, I bend down to pick up my bags when I see the store sign across the street—Paris Pottery & Studio. Recognizing the name from the bottom of Casanova's mugs, I walk there next.

I'm in complete awe as I walk inside and look around. Everything looks so clean and artistic. Lining a dark navy-blue accent wall are wooden shelves stocked with clay mugs, bowls, and plates. On the other wall is a display of mugs, similar to the ones in Casanova's cupboard. I walk toward that side of the store before anyone can stop and tell me their life story.

A sign on display reads Original Paris Mug, and I pick one up and look at the bottom to see the same Paris logo.

"Those are South Carolina's most popular mugs," a female's voice comes from behind. I spin around and see a young woman smiling at me. Her name tag reads, Hilary. "Made locally right here in Charleston." She politely folds her hands in front of her and waits for me to speak.

"I borrowed one this morning actually," I tell her. "I was hoping to find one for myself."

"Sure, darling. Ethan has a large variety of mugs. I'm sure we can find one you'll like." She winks, reaching for one on the shelf. "No two are the same."

"Ethan?"

"The potter. It all started with the Original Paris mug. At first, they were only available online, and it was more of a hobby than a career. He would do live videos of him throwing clay, and people just went crazy over it. Not to mention, he's not bad to look at either." She winks, and I'm starting to notice a pattern. "His videos and mugs started blowing up the internet, and soon he was selling out every week."

"Wow, that's amazing," I say in complete admiration.

"Oh, that's just the beginnin', darling. An investor swooped in so he could make this a career and throw clay full-time. He continued making his mugs and customers wanted more. The demand was so high, he opened up this studio and hired interns to run it."

"So you're an intern?"

"Yep, from the art institution," she proudly responds.

I smile and nod, appreciating the history behind the mugs and studio.

She starts talking about the process of each one, and it's all fascinating and overwhelming at the same time. By the way, she talks about him, I imagine this Ethan guy to be early-thirties give or take, obviously good with his hands and gorgeous. If he's anything like Casanova, probably an arrogant asshole, too.

"So do you see anything you like?" she asks me, and after taking another look, I pick out two of my favorite.

"Make sure to hand-wash only," she reminds me as she hands me a cream-colored bag with the word *Paris* written in script on both sides. I love all the cute touches this shop has from the personal customer service, the easy shopping experience, and the modern look mixed with the southern decor gives it a rustic vibe.

"Will do," I promise. "I can't wait to bring these back to Chicago with me."

"Enjoy, sweetheart."

After thanking her again and grabbing my bag, I start to head out. Before I open the door, a plaque on the wall grabs my attention. A plaque with Casanova's face on it.

CHAPTER FOUR

ETHAN

By the time the sun sets, I'm absolutely fucking exhausted. Running a business—a successful one, at that—isn't easy. Regardless if it's my passion or not, I want nothing more than to go home, pour a glass of scotch, and sit in the garden. Usually, when I'm anxious or worked up, viewing the flowers and listening to the cicadas in the late afternoon help me relax.

As soon as I get home and walk in, I go straight to the kitchen, throw some ice cubes in a glass and pour a double of Johnny Walker Double Black. Wilma comes trotting down the stairs and rubs her body against my legs. Bending down, I pet her and place some treats on the floor before walking outside. She's too busy eating to even notice me leave.

Finally, I let out a deep breath. I sit on a bench close to the fountain I had installed last summer and listen to the water trickle down the rocks. Just as I put the glass to my lips, Vada comes waltzing by, and I swear she's purposely shaking her round ass. As soon as she turns around, I'm halfway through an eyeroll. I'm actually kind of getting used to her death glare.

"No hello or anything?" Her hands fall to her hips, and I have a feeling she's used to addressing people this way.

This woman has no filter and calls it like she sees it. After only twenty-four hours, she calls my bullshit like she's known me for years. Not many people point out my antics; most just look at me with sorrow in their eyes. I push those thoughts away as quickly as they came. Giving a smile that doesn't affect her in the least way, I realize I may have met my match.

"Just sitting out here enjoying the *peace and quiet*." The sarcasm isn't lost on her, and she takes a few steps forward, closer to me, just as I take a sip of scotch.

"I was always told southern men were gentlemen. Going forward, I'm going to argue with anyone who believes that and let them know how entirely wrong they are." She pauses for a moment, glaring at me. When I don't respond, she continues. "So now who's the one gawking?" she asks as she crosses her arms over her breasts.

I didn't realize I was staring until she spoke, but I brush it off. "Just returning the favor from yesterday."

She grinds her teeth. "Let me set the record straight. I wasn't gawking at you. I was confused that you were shirtless and wet. Most people don't answer the door like that. At least not where I'm from." She takes a step closer.

"Really? Most people don't shower where you're from? Hmm. Thought it was a common practice, you know, around the world."

I can tell she's getting annoyed as she narrows her eyes at me.

To add fuel to the fire and to see how worked up I can really get her, I remind her of the deadline she's been so worked up about since she arrived. "Don't you have a book to write?"

She scoffs. "Well Casanova, I'm actually a little uninspired after going to this crappy pottery shop downtown today. It was absolutely awful in there. You must've heard of it, considering you have a few of their pieces. Paris Pottery & Studio?"

I don't know if it's the scotch that's sending a burning sensation through me or her words, but somehow, I force out a smirk. One of those that make me look like a bigger asshole than I really am.

"Really? That's a shame," I say, completely unamused. She has to know I own the place and she's trying to get under my skin, but she can't play the player. Realizing she's not getting to me, she continues on complaining about nonexisting issues.

"The walls were terrible. The art was sad. The lady working there was rude as hell…"

I lift my eyebrows, allowing her to finish, and that's when I realize she's carrying a bag with an Eiffel Tower logo and the Paris inscription. A devious smile touches my lips, and I nod my head and listen to her make a complete ass out of herself. Once she's finished, I stand, set my glass down on the bench and yank the bag from her hand.

"What are you doing?" she squeals, finally realizing she's been holding it the entire time.

"Just seeing which awful piece you decided to waste your hard-earned porn money on."

Her mouth falls open, and I can tell she's offended. "I do *not* write porn."

Nodding my head, I peek inside and see two items wrapped in brown paper. Mugs. It's the only thing she could have bought. "That's not what Google says about you."

"You *did not* Google me."

My eyes meet hers for a brief moment as I carefully unwrap the brown paper from one of the items. She chose one of the most recent pieces I made one early morning a month or so ago. After looking out the tall windows that surround my office, I painted it the color of the sky just as the sun was rising. As she opens her mouth to say something else, I pretend to almost drop the mug, and she gasps trying to catch it.

"Just what I thought," I tell her as I carefully wrap and place it back into the bag and hand it to her.

With puckered lips, she looks up at the sky as if she's trying to pluck her words from the clouds. "Fine. You busted me. I know you're the owner of Paris Pottery & Studio. Are you happy?"

"I bet that was painful to say." I'm smiling—a genuine smile—as she stands there defeated that she didn't win this round.

"So now you're going to truthfully tell me your opinion about the shop, right?"

It's almost as if she's trying to force the words off her tongue. Her voice is so low that whatever she says is completely inaudible.

"I'm sorry. I didn't hear you," I say, cupping a palm around my ear.

She huffs. "I said, I loved it. Everything about the place was perfect. The selection, the art. I was actually shocked when I saw your picture there. I don't know why you just didn't say yesterday morning when I was admiring your work."

My face softens, and I relax. "Because it's not a quick conversation, and it's easier if we don't get personal."

Almost instantly, her demeanor changes as if my words offended her, but it's the truth. Getting personal with my tenant only causes problems, and she'll only be here for a week anyway. What's the point?

"Well okay then, Casanova. My sincerest apologies for being an ass about your shop. I should probably get back to writing my porn now. Have a good night, *Ethan*."

It's the first time she's said my name, and it almost sounds sweet coming from her lips. Vada turns and walks away, and before she closes the door to the cottage, I speak across the garden to her. "Goodnight, Vada."

The door to the cottage clicks closed, and I grab my glass from the bench and walk inside. Before heading upstairs for a shower, I pour the melted ice and scotch down the drain and bend over to pet Wilma who's begging for more treats. I tell her no and go upstairs to my workspace on the third story to make sure the kilns are amping down.

Unbuttoning my shirt, I stand at the large windows that surround the tower room and look out at the garden. It's so high up above everything, that it helps me forget the worries that follow me throughout the day. I almost feel as if I'm in the clouds. After checking a few of my pieces on the wooden boards and just as I'm about to turn around, my eyes wander to the cottage.

Expecting to see Vada working at the small desk, I'm shocked when she walks from the bathroom with nothing more than a towel wrapped around her tight body. She snaps the sheer curtains shut, and the towel drops to the floor in a crumpled pile. As she crosses the room, I swallow hard at the outline of her naked body. Not able to turn away, completely magnetized to her, I watch through the large skylight that's conveniently positioned above the bed. When she lies down, I know exactly where this is going.

Her dark, wet brown hair cascades on the pillow, and she looks like pure perfection with her soft skin against the white comforter. Vada closes her eyes, allowing her hands to roam to her nipples, and I memorize every curve she has. If I concentrate hard enough, I can almost hear the soft sound of her moans and breaths as she pinches and pulls at her nipples. I shouldn't be watching her, but then she moves one hand down to her clit, and there's no way I'm walking away now. Taking her time, she teases herself with slow circular movements while palming one of her perky breasts. I halfway wonder if she can sense my eyes glued to her because she's putting on one hell of a show for me.

Watching her and imagining the way she feels is making my dick so goddamn hard, I'm going to have to take care of this sooner than later. The woman is teasing herself with such fervor that I'm getting worked up, which isn't something that typically happens to me. Then again, I've never experienced a beautiful woman masturbating in my cottage with every light on, giving no fucks about anything but her pussy.

I'm halfway tempted to go over there and ask if she needs any help. Just as the thought crosses my mind, she opens her legs wider and slowly inserts a finger. No, she doesn't need any help. She actually has it all taken care of. *Fuck.*

Vada is careful with herself, moving her fingers along her wet slit before inserting them back inside, over and over again. The rhythmic motions as she sinks deeper and deeper is driving me fucking insane. She's an expert at pleasing herself, and now I'm curious about the sex scenes in her books.

When her back arches and she picks up the pace, I know she's teetering on the edge. I wait with bated breath for her release as she continues to simultaneously finger fuck herself and rub her clit. Without slowing down, she gives her pussy exactly what it deserves, working herself to completion. She bites down on her bottom lip as the orgasm violently rushes through her, causing her body to buckle on the bed. Her mouth falls open, and I know she's moaning loudly, allowing the moment to take full control of her. Continuing to ride the euphoric wave until the very last moment, her body eventually relaxes, and it's the sexiest thing I've ever witnessed. I can only imagine how wet she is and the urge to want to taste her overcomes and shocks the shit out of me.

Her breasts rise and fall, and a small smile hits her lips as she exhales, completely satisfied with what she accomplished. With flushed cheeks and nipples as hard as pebbles, she lies there without a care in the world. Vada's beautiful and mesmerizing, and I can't seem to pull away from her. Though she doesn't have a filter on that mouth of hers, I find myself fantasizing about being inside her, giving her everything she can't possibly give herself sexually. My heart pounds so hard in my chest as her naked body stretches across the bed, and I can't deny this feeling inside me. It's raw. It's pure lust and hunger. Once her breathing steadies, she slides off the bed, puts on a robe then sits at the desk. Opening her laptop, she begins typing away with a shit-eating grin on her face. I can only imagine the words she's writing at this very moment. *Dirty girl.*

Somehow, I force myself away from the windows and walk downstairs to my bedroom, but the images of her and the look on her face as she came won't stop replaying in my head. My dick throbs so hard in my jeans that it's almost painful. Heading to the bathroom, I begin disrobing, dropping my clothes along the way. Once I turn on the water and step in, I close my eyes and grab my dick that's as hard as steel. As the water runs down my body, I grab myself in long strokes. Trying to steady myself, I place a hand on the wall, picking up the pace, feeling the orgasm ready to rip through me. Everything about her fills my mind. Moments later, my body is convulsing with the quickest orgasm I've had in years, and it's all because of that smart-mouthed writer and her perfect pussy. If only she could write about that.

CHAPTER FIVE

VADA

I WAKE up refreshed and happy with my word count for the night. It wasn't my personal best, but the few thousand words I was able to type bring me closer to my goal.

The morning starts off hectic with a call from my agent. Hannah is one of those ladies who is all business, and for most of the call, she hounds me for my manuscript, but it's still in draft mode, so I can't send her what she wants just yet. She really has my best interest in mind, but considering I'm already behind, it all adds to my stress level. I've never been late sending a book to my agent, and I don't plan on starting now. By the time I get off the phone, I'm a bit deflated and realize how badly I need coffee. The day just started, and I can tell it's going to be a long one.

After I brush my teeth, I head over to Ethan's house to grab a cup of coffee. Before opening the door, I look through the window and see he's standing at the stove scrambling eggs and frying bacon, and it smells so divine.

Unfortunately for me, he's wearing nothing but a pair of jogging pants that are hanging off his hips. Muscles cascade down his back, and I can't help but admire his biceps. Realizing I'm staring just a little too long, I make my presence known.

"I didn't realize you were so domestic," I say, entering like I own the place. He watches me as I walk to the cupboard, grabbing one of his beautiful mugs from the cabinet and pouring myself a hot cup of coffee. As soon as the caffeine hits my lips, I can't help but let out a moan. It's hot and strong, just the way I like the heroes in my books.

His brows shoot up as he continues studying me. "Do you always moan so loud in the morning or do you reserve that for when the sun goes down?"

I roll my eyes as I take a seat at the bar. I don't know what the hell he's referring to, but I'm not taking any of his crap this morning. Soon he's plating the food, sets it in front of me, then proceeds to cook himself more.

"You didn't have to. I was going to go out and grab some breakfast," I tell him, forcing myself not to devour it with my hands like a savage because it smells so good.

He looks over his shoulder and speaks. "Down here, we just say thank you. Now eat it. Swear it's not poisoned."

When he turns back around to flip the bacon, I can't help but smile. You don't have to tell me twice. "Fine." I swallow hard, forcing my eyes to look away from him. "Thank you."

The eggs practically melt in my mouth, and the bacon is the way I like it, not burnt but crisp. By the time I'm halfway done eating, he finishes cooking and sets his food down across from me at the table. As he walks over to pour himself a cup of coffee, his bare chest and the muscles on his stomach taunt me. Seriously, this man should be on the cover of a book. Hell, he should be *in* a book.

"So'd you have a late night last night?" Ethan asks as he takes a bite of his eggs. The tone of his voice makes me narrow my eyes at him. After being a complete ass yesterday, I'm trying to not let out every thought that's on my mind.

"Actually, I did. Finished a chapter I've been working on for a few days. I think the fresh air and country living atmosphere is really helping me," I say honestly, trying to keep it cordial.

"Hmm." Ethan snaps a piece of bacon in half and takes a bite. "Want to know what I think is helping you?"

I roll my eyes again, knowing some smart-ass comment is about to come from his mouth. "Please, Casanova. Enlighten me," I say, taking a big gulp of coffee.

"Maybe it was that intense orgasm you gave yourself that helped you write all night."

I almost spit my coffee out all over him and hurry to swallow it down. My eyes nearly bug out of my head, and I'm tempted to slap that smirk right off his face. I'm shocked and somewhat embarrassed.

"What?" I shake my head at him, trying to deny it. "What are you talking about?" I act dumb, hoping he's just messing with me and trying to get me all riled up like usual. I try to pretend last night never happened. But what the fuck? Does he have cameras in there or something? Sometimes when the words aren't flowing, having a release helps loosen me up. When I get tense or stressed, I tend to get blocked. So, last night it *really* helped.

"Come on, Vada. You don't have to get all uptight." He continues eating, his eyes meeting mine. "Honestly, I thought it was pure fucking perfection. So damn hot."

My body is on fire because no one has ever watched me touch myself. Often when it comes to sex, although I write about it all the time, I'm a private person. Heat rushes to my face. Ethan saw me completely exposed and vulnerable.

I stand, getting ready to walk away when he comes around the bar and grabs my hand. With strong arms, he spins me around until my body is close to his bare chest. He smells like vanilla and holds me in place, not allowing me to move.

"You're an asshole for watching. Do you have a spy cam in there or something? Are you some sort of perv who likes to watch his renters?"

Ethan tightens his grip on me, and his arms fall to his sides. "Did you feel the sun beat down on your body this morning?"

That's when the skylight above the bed dawns on me. "So you played Spider Man and was climbing on the roof? That's so creepy."

Shaking his head, he smiles. "My work area is in the tower on the third floor. There's a direct view into the cottage. I couldn't take my eyes away from you. The look on your face as you came; so fucking hot. But I couldn't help noticing that you could've used some help. There's nothing like the real deal, sweetheart."

"And what, you're the real deal?" I bark out a laugh. "You're a dickhead for watching." I glare at him and wait.

"Okay, I'm sorry," he finally says, sincerely. I can tell he means it, but it still doesn't take away what he saw. I never would've imagined I could be seen from a distance like that. Otherwise, there's no way I would've put on a show. Especially for *him*.

"That was private and not for you." I poke my finger hard into his chest to really get my point across. "Southern gentleman, my ass. A gentleman would've walked away."

He laughs out loud. "No way. No man would've turned a blind eye to that unless the ladies aren't his thing. That's the only way. So yes, even a gentleman would've watched. In fact, if I weren't a gentleman, I would've stalked over and joined in."

I gasp at his words, so bold and honest. Though I'm pissed that the moment wasn't as private as I thought, knowing he watched and enjoyed it is doing unusual things to my body. Tingles rush through me, and I feel exhilarated from it all, but even so, I want nothing more than to escape from his presence. He's way too close for comfort, and the way he's looking at me with soft eyes is…*different*.

"I said, I'm sorry. Accept it or not," he tells me before walking back to his breakfast.

I suck in a deep breath and go back to my plate of food and finish eating without saying a word while Ethan's eyes are glued to me. When I look up at him, he's smiling, chewing with his mouth open.

"Have some manners, at least. Not only are you an ass, but you're disgusting, too." As always, my words don't faze him. He stands and places his plate in the sink then walks around and grabs mine. His arm brushes against my skin and goose bumps trail up and down my body. Tucking my arms in my lap, I don't dare give him any fuel to add to his country bumpkin bonfire because he's enjoying this way too much.

I'm intrigued, but I don't say a word. Sometimes the silent treatment is more powerful than saying what's on my mind.

Turning around, he gives me a smirk as he leans against the counter. "So one more question for you. What time should I be in the tower tonight? Same as last night?"

"You're seriously one of the biggest douchebags I've ever met."

"Oh, come on. That can't be true. I'm sure you've met bigger ones." He grins, knowing he's getting under my skin.

"Sometimes I get anxious or restless, and I need a release to help me relax and concentrate so I can get back to work. It clears my mind, so I don't overthink while writing. There's nothing wrong with it. Nothing at all. So quit bringing it up. It happened, and it's over. Get over it. Next time, I'll make sure to take a nice long bath instead. There's no spy windows in there." I'm so annoyed, I walk across the kitchen to pour coffee in my cup that I plan on taking to-go.

"Shit, you must get yourself off several times during the day then, because uptight seems to be your middle name." Ethan chuckles.

I roll my eyes so hard they might actually fall right out of my head.

"Shut up, Ethan." There are too many words to write, and I'm wasting too much time with him. Just as I head to the door, he speaks up again.

"Vada." He walks to me, allowing himself into my personal space. I take a step backward, which only causes him to take another step forward. "Any time you need to be unwound, just let me know." His voice is low, rough, and so damn sexy that my mouth falls open.

I look into his eyes and can tell he's actually fucking serious. My face contorts, and I look at him like he's lost his damn mind. "Seriously? Is this the part where I'm supposed to fall on my knees for you?"

"You're the author here. Tell me how you'd write the story," he quips.

I pretend to throw up in my mouth.

"Goddamn, you're always so feisty. I kinda like that, you know."

I huff. "I don't know you, and you sure as hell don't know me. I'm not some whore at your service. That's not who I am. But then again, I'm paying you, so that'd make you my whore if we were to get technical here."

Slowly, Ethan brushes his fingers across my cheek and tucks my messy morning hair behind my ear. Those stupid tingles creep across my body, and it takes everything I have not to lean into his touch.

Leaning over, he whispers in my ear. "Sex doesn't have to be like one of those romantic scenes in your books. Sometimes it can be purely physical with no strings attached." His breath runs along my skin, and his mouth barely grazes the shell of my ear causing me to shiver. As he pulls away, I feel as if I'm unable to move, glued to the floor, holding my mug as tight as I can so I don't drop it. Swallowing hard, I try to catch the breath he somehow stole.

Snapping out of it and finally finding my words, I think of the perfect response. "So do you offer your dick to all the women who rent your cottage? If so, you should really update your Airbnb listing. *Country cottage comes with amenities, such as beautiful views, flower gardens, and gigolo services*. Probably could get double your rate."

Ethan crosses his strong arms over his chest and smirks. This time, the way he's looking at me with those honey-colored eyes practically make my panties melt off my body. Seriously, I'm surprised there's not a line of women waiting at his door. However, he's probably screwed and scared them all away.

"Actually, sweetheart," he starts, sucking in a breath. "You'd be the first." Ethan chews on his plump bottom lip before taking a sip of coffee.

Dead. I'm dead, but I have to pull it together before I do something stupid and spontaneous. *Like accept his ridiculous offer.*

"Right. I *really* believe that. It's been real fun, but I gotta go, Casanova. Try not to offer your dick to too many women today while you're out and about. It might fall off or something."

Before I close the door, I hear him loudly chuckling, and it drives me absolutely insane. He's enjoying this way too much, and it's bothering the shit out of me because nothing I say remotely affects him. It takes everything I have to not turn around and give him a piece of my mind, but he'd probably like it. Considering I've dealt with his type before, and I don't want to end up having rough, crazy sex on the kitchen floor with him, walking away is the best decision.

Once I'm in the cottage, I sip my coffee while sitting back at the desk and turn on my laptop. I reread the previous chapter, trying to get back into my headspace, but I'm drawing nothing. At this point, I've gone completely off my outline, and no words are coming to me. There's nothing but a cursor on a blank page. This chapter and two others have to be written today, which is thousands of words. I stare up at the ceiling, trying to concentrate then crack my fingers and place them back on the keyboard.

Blink. Blink. Blink.

That stupid cursor is mocking me.

A few hours pass and I write a lousy paragraph that I end up deleting. Hannah's words are repeating in my mind, and I remind myself that she's rooting for me and my career. Basically, I just need to get my shit together. My last book didn't sell as well as I had hoped, or my publisher expected, so if I don't knock it out of the park with this new project, my writing career may be doomed. There's no way I'm going back to the corporate world. Writing is my calling, my passion, and I have to make this work. Closing my eyes tight, I hope the words will just flow through my fingers like magic.

Blink. Blink. Blink. I'm two seconds away from banging my head against the desk, and after six long hours of getting nothing done, I'm becoming more desperate. This day cannot be wasted. I need words at this point like I need air.

All my anxiety and stress about this deadline is mixing with Casanova's words. He basically presented me his dick on a gold platter. *Probably all hard and thick with bulging veins and a velvet-soft shaft.* Fuck. Maybe he was kidding or baiting me, but when I looked into his eyes, I knew deep down he was serious.

There was no joking.

No animosity.

That man meant what he said with every fiber of his being. But the truth is, girls like me don't go for guys like him. Our types clash. Always.

CHAPTER SIX

ETHAN

Though Vada acted like my proposal disgusted her, I can read her like a newspaper. She's secretly thinking about my offer while trying to talk herself out of it.

I can't really blame her though. I've never done anything like this before, especially in my community where everyone knows of me, my family, and my studio. After Alana, everyone treated me like a broken soul. They weren't wrong. I was broken. Truthfully, I still feel broken from everything that was taken away from me.

Instead of dwelling on what happened, I buried myself into my work. Worked harder, faster, and longer. It was the only thing that kept me from falling apart most days, and even when I started to have success in my art, the fear of failing again never drifted.

One-night stands were strictly that—one night. I haven't committed to anyone since Alana, and I doubt I'll ever be able to.

The only priorities I have in life now are my work and family. I know my momma would like it if I settled down, but after getting the same response from me for the past few years, she's learned to stop asking.

After Vada stalks out and I clean up the kitchen, I head upstairs to the tower and start my morning work routine. I don't bother putting a shirt on because the sun is already beating down on me. With how the windows surround the tower, there's no way to escape the heat. I could wait till after the sun sets to work, but I'm feeling oddly inspired today.

I gather up my materials, tools, and block of clay. Once I've prepared the clay and wedged and smacked all the air bubbles out, I sit down at the potter's wheel and begin wetting my sponge. Pressing my foot down on the accelerator, I squeeze the sponge above the bat to wet the surface. I continue this until it's smooth and free of clay from the previous use.

Once that's all set, I throw my prepared block of clay as close to the middle of the bat as I can. This process used to take me a good half hour to get it centered correctly, but after doing it for years, it now only takes a few minutes. Wetting my hands, I begin centering by raising and lowering the clay as the wheel spins. Once it's ready to go, I start my process for making a Paris mug. I push my thumb down into the middle to form the opening, and once I have it just the way I like it, I use my tools to etch and design the outside.

Once it's ready to go, I use my cutting wire and slide it under the mug. I pick up the bat and set the entire thing on one of my shelves. Grabbing another bat, I repeat the entire process until I have twenty mugs complete. Next, I'll add the handles.

Standing up and stretching, I crack my neck and twist my waist from side to side. Working on the wheel and slouching over tends to make my lower back muscles stiff and achy, which is why I usually take a long, hot shower at night.

I head downstairs and make another pot of coffee. While waiting for it to brew, I whip together a quick sandwich and eat before I head back upstairs. Staring out the windows, I overlook the property while taking sips of my coffee. I notice movement in the cottage and see Vada sitting at the desk, but her fingers aren't flying across the keyboard like I expect. Instead, they're massaging her temples in slow circular movements. She's obviously frustrated. A moment later, she slams her laptop shut and leans back in the chair.

I imagine lots of cursing and groaning, and I anxiously wait to see if she'll come to her senses about my offer. Wondering if she'll take matters into her own hands again, I wait and watch as I finish off my coffee. She ends up grabbing a few things from her suitcase before locking herself in the bathroom.

Assuming she's going to be in there a while, enjoying the handheld shower head sprayer, I get back to work for a few hours. Once I've put handles on the mugs and inscribe my Paris logo onto the bottoms, I break to freshen up and grab some water. My chest and jeans are covered in wet clay, as usual, but before I head upstairs to shower, I hear a shriek from the back garden.

"Go away! Stop chasing me!" Vada screams, and as soon as I see who she's screaming at, I crack up and laugh my ass off.

"He's harmless," I tell her as soon as I open the back door and step out. "That's how Henry shows affection." I smirk, knowing she's not seeing the humor in any of this.

"A rooster who wanders around your yard pecking at my ankles is not affection!" She scowls. "I nearly fell on my face running from him."

"Stop running, and he'll stop chasing," I simply explain.

"Easy for you to say." She steps closer to the house to avoid Henry. "Do you have any idea how terrifying it is to have a rooster-creature terrorize you?"

Scratching my fingernails along my jawline, I suck in my lower lip to hold back what I really want to say. "And you call yourself a writer."

"Shut up. You know what I mean. Control your huge..." She lingers, and I don't miss the opportunity to fill in the word for her.

"Cock?" My eyebrows rise.

She groans and rolls her eyes at me. "Seriously. This is why I don't socialize with people."

"Yeah, I'm sure that's why you're an introvert."

"Hey, you don't know anything about me, okay?" she reminds me, and it's the truth, but I'm not going to let her off that easy.

"I might not know a lot about you, but I know some."

"Like what?" She crosses her arms, challenging me. "What could you possibly know about me in just three days?"

Leaning my body against the doorframe, I smirk and think back to last night and how her body sang after she got herself off. I haven't been able to get it out of my mind actually.

"I know you're as uptight as you look. City girl, isolated, with a lack of social skills. You have your guard up even when it's not merited. You don't let people in because of something that happened in your past, more than likely. You'd rather form relationships in your books than in real life."

"I'm not uptight." She tries defending herself, but I continue anyway.

"You're so uptight you have to touch yourself to relax. I know it took you approximately three minutes to get off. You know just where to touch and how you like it because it's the only relief you allow yourself to have. You arch your back just when you feel it coming, and I know you'd enjoy it more if you'd actually get fucked hard like you need."

Her jaw drops, her eyes narrowing as she stares intently at me. I can tell she's trying to find the words to respond, but she closes her mouth and swallows.

"Come in." I smile. "I'll make dinner."

I don't wait for her to reply and turn around to go back inside the house. She follows behind, silently, and when she closes the door, I glance back at her and can see her mind racing a million miles a minute.

Digging around the fridge, I pull out two chicken breasts. She watches me as I wash and cut them into cubes. We stay silent as I move around the kitchen and prepare dinner. Adding a box of rice to the cooked chicken, I cover the pan and let it simmer.

"Do you cook for all your tenants?" she blurts out as I grab two plates from the cupboard.

"No," I say, grabbing the utensils next. "I haven't cooked for someone in a long time."

"Why's that?" she urges.

"You really want to know?" I ask, directing my eyes at her in warning. She won't like what she hears, but I won't lie about it either.

"Yes."

Clearing my throat, I set the plates and forks on the table where she's sitting.

"Most tenants don't stay around the cottage all day. They're usually here to explore and go to the beach. They eat out, and I only see them at check-in and check-out."

"Okay?" she says as a question. "What about family or friends?"

"Not really. My mama and aunt are usually the ones to bring me food. Not a lot of time to socialize with friends."

"Which means you have none." She grins.

"I do. Most of them come over after dinnertime."

"Ohh…you mean, chicks. You could've just said that." She tries to keep a straight face, but I can tell it's close to breaking.

"I didn't think I needed to."

"So if you don't cook for tenants or booty calls, why do you cook for me?"

"Because even though you're an uptight city girl, I enjoy your company."

"That almost sounded like a compliment." She smiles.

I shrug with a smirk and get up to check on the chicken and rice. I turn the burner off and bring the pan to the table.

"Thank you," she says after I plate her food and set it down in front of her.

"You'd probably starve without me," I tease her.

She chuckles, not denying it. "Probably true. The writer's diet is no joke. I'm either eating everything in sight, or I forget to eat entirely."

"Sounds like my entire college career," I admit, remembering all the times I'd be scraping for change.

Halfway through dinner, I bring up my offer again. Mostly to taunt her, but also because I'm hoping she's changed her mind. I can't get the image of her touching herself out of my head, and I'd be lying if I said I wasn't curious about the way she tastes when she comes.

"Even if I was desperate enough to sleep with you, which I'm *not*, I don't have sex with guys I just met."

"Even good-looking ones?"

She starts choking on a mouthful of food, and that's all the answer I need.

"That's what I thought." I stab my last piece of chicken and shove it into my mouth as I watch her expression tighten.

"I was choking because you think so highly of yourself, not because I was agreeing," she clarifies, and though she's trying to sound serious, I see the corner of her lips tilt up.

Standing up, I take our plates to the sink and rinse them off. I feel her walk toward me and take the opportunity to spin around and face her.

"So how do you know if you've never done it before?" I ask, taking a step forward when she takes a step back.

"Know what?"

"How do you know you wouldn't enjoy yourself?"

"Because I know myself. I need to know someone to be intimate with them on a physical level," she explains, although I'm not convinced.

"You sure about that?" I ask, closing the gap between us until our bodies press against each other. Before she can respond, I cover her mouth with mine, and though she's taken off guard, only seconds pass before her body relaxes.

Slipping my tongue between her plump lips, she moans as I devour her. Cupping her cheek, I hold her in place as I taste her sweetness. Our bodies lean against each other, and a smirk forms on my lips when I feel her fingers digging into my hips, craving more.

I sink my tongue deeper, hearing another hungry moan release from her throat. I knew she'd taste good, but fuck, her moans and sweetness are better than I imagined. My cock throbs against the inside of my jeans, begging to be released.

Pulling back, I feel her heavy breathing against my chest. She looks up at me with swollen lips as her chest moves rapidly.

"If you change your mind, you know where to find me." I wink, releasing her body and walking out of the kitchen.

CHAPTER SEVEN

VADA

I'M PRETTY sure I need CPR or some kind of life-saving equipment.

I can't seem to catch my breath, even though I'm breathing just fine, but the way he just kissed me and then walked away has my mind reeling and my body confused as hell.

His lips were so warm and inviting, I couldn't stop. I didn't *want* to pull away, and that's even more confusing to me than I like admitting. However, I can't deny the way his kiss affected me. The way his body pressed against mine or how *my* body responded like I was some desperate sex-deprived woman.

I'm not, by the way. *Stupid, traitorous body.*

I'm still trying to catch my breath when I leave and walk out the back door. Quickly glancing around to make sure Henry isn't following me again, I walk the garden path and head inside the cottage.

I don't have time to think about Ethan and that kiss, I remind myself.

I don't have time to analyze the way that kiss made me feel, I also remind myself.

But fuck. It was a *really* good kiss.

But why did he kiss me? And why did I kiss him back?

Ugh! How dare he kiss me like that!

My mind is all over the place, and I can't keep up with my own thoughts. His proposal repeats in my head. I'm trying to forget his offer while talking myself into considering it. Contradiction plagues me. Would it really be so bad to have one night of fun while I'm here?

What am I even saying?

I palm my forehead, trying to smack the oxygen back into my brain.

This man is making me second-guess everything I believe, and it's driving me absolutely crazy! I write about heroines who have one-night stands or who fuck a guy after just meeting them, but that isn't real life. At least not for me. I've seen firsthand what jumping into a relationship based on sex can do to a couple, and it isn't pretty.

Deciding to march back over there, I don't bother knocking before letting myself in. I stomp my way upstairs even though I have no idea where he went, but I'm not thinking straight anymore. My heart is racing, and I'm determined to give him a piece of my mind. *Who does he think he is kissing me like that*?

There are two doors on each side of the hallway, and one is cracked halfway open, so I decide to try that one first.

"Ethan!" I shout. My bare feet thump against the hardwood floor as I try to find him. I peek around the barely open door, which ends up being the bathroom. "Ethan, where are you?" I raise my voice louder, not sure if I should try the other doors or not.

I step farther down the hallway and hear bass thumping along the ceiling. He must be in the tower.

Rounding the corner, I spot the stairs that lead up to the third floor. The music becomes louder as I quietly take the steps. When I reach the top, I see his bare muscular back hunched over slightly as his hands work a chunk of clay on his pottery wheel. It's loud and vibrates the floors, which is probably why his music is as loud as it is.

Wooden boards surround the room with clay mugs and bowls. Large white buckets are scattered around the room with *glaze* written on them, and it looks like a great working space. So peaceful and probably has a gorgeous view in the early mornings.

I watch him for a while, admiring the way his muscles contract in his biceps as he shifts in his seat between wetting the sponge and molding the clay between his fingers. I've never seen anyone make pottery before, but he makes it seem effortless. Actually, really fucking sexy. Studying him, I don't realize how long it's been, and when he shifts his body and glances at me, his face contorts. I expect him to scold me for watching when he didn't know, but instead, he scoots back on the seat and tilts his head.

"Come sit," he orders.

At first, I think I hear him wrong, the music must've jumbled his words, but when he jerks his head again, I know I didn't.

Licking my lips, I take a step and walk toward him. He sits back just enough to allow me to sit in front of him, basically *in* his lap, but I don't complain.

His arms wrap around mine, and he guides my hands to the clay in the middle of his wheel. Pressing his foot on the pedal, the wheel begins to spin again. His hands cover mine as we shape the clay, and he uses his finger to guide my thumb into the middle where a hole starts to form.

"I hope I don't mess up your piece," I turn my head slightly and tell him loud enough, so he can hear me.

His body maneuvers closer to mine, his chest against my back leaving no space between us. My body shivers at the close contact and how he's holding me in place with his thighs and shoulders.

"You probably will," he whispers, and even though his tone is serious, I feel his lips spread into a smirk against the shell of my ear.

I chuckle, leaning my body against his for support, not wanting to admit how good it feels to have him so close to me. I came up here to yell at him, and now his bare chest has captured my body, and unwillingly—my heart. He slowly removes his hands and slides them up my arms before reaching for his sponge. After wetting it, he squeezes it over my hands and clay.

Feeling his lips press softly against my neck, my eyes flutter as I lose focus. The scruff from his beard tickles my skin, and I feel myself unraveling. His hands slowly slide up my arms, leaving streaks of dirty clay water along them. My throat goes dry as his hand firmly wraps around my neck and tilts my face toward his. Warm lips capture my mouth, and I easily fall into his embrace. His tongue glides with mine, and soon the wheel is no longer spinning as my hands wrap around his wrists for support in a silent plea to not stop anytime soon.

His thumb rubs along my jawline as our kiss deepens, and as much as I don't want to, I know I should stop. Except I can't. His kiss is so fucking good, so controlled, yet desperate and eager. The way he holds me to him, the strength of his arms and body have me so entranced, I can't do anything except fall into his embrace.

"I've finally figured out what shuts you up," he teases against my mouth, a smirk playing on his lips. "Turns out it was keeping your tongue busy."

"If that's your version of sexy talk, I'm not impressed," I mock, barely audible.

"Your nipples say otherwise." He lowers his hand and plucks my taut nipple along the fabric of my shirt. "Hard and aroused. And I know it's not because of the weather."

"I really want to prove you wrong, but I know the farther your hand goes, the more right you'll be." The words bravely come out before I can stop them.

Leaning in, he bites down on my lower lip, causing a surge of electricity to spark through me. The last guy I briefly dated never made me feel this way, and Ethan has barely touched me.

A moan escapes my throat, and I feel him smile against my lips. *Fuck.* Now he definitely knows he's affecting me—not that I could really deny it anymore.

Keeping my face over my shoulder, he continues exploring my mouth as his hands pin my back to his chest. Even though the position is awkward, I don't make an effort to move. I love the way he's possessively holding me, my ass pressed between his thighs and rubbing against his cock.

Several moments pass of his lips and teeth teasing me before he presses his forehead to mine as we both try and catch our breaths. His hands roam my arms, neck, and face, and I now look like a living piece of art.

"We should clean up," he suggests, though not making an effort to move.

"That's probably a good idea," I agree, half-winded.

He backs off the stool and stretches his hand out for me to grab it. I place it in his, and he leads me downstairs. Following behind, I notice when he walks past the bathroom.

"I thought we were going to clean up," I say stupidly, assuming he was going to take us to the shower. I've let my guard down but am second-guessing myself now.

"We are," is all he says, leading me down the next set of stairs until we're on the main floor.

I can't deny how his mysterious tone sends butterflies straight to my stomach. I hardly know anything about this man, yet that doesn't stop me from following him.

We stay silent as we walk hand in hand to the front door and step out onto the wraparound porch. He continues leading me down the steps and onto the sidewalk, still giving me no indication of what he's up to.

Only walking a couple blocks, I finally see where he's taking me.

"What are we doing?" I ask, staring out at the creek.

He releases my hand and faces me. He smirks as he starts unbuttoning his jeans. "Cleaning up." He nods his head at me and continues, "Strip."

"Excuse me, what?" I gasp, taking a step back and thinking he must be crazy. "Out here?" Granted we're in an isolated area, surrounded by trees and water, but that doesn't mean other people couldn't be out here as well.

"C'mon, city girl. Afraid to get dirty in the country?" He arches a brow, challenging me.

I know he's mocking me, considering we're already both dirty, but by the way he's looking at me, I know he means it in an entirely different way.

I'm gettin' dirty in the south with Ethan Rochester.

"I see more of that southern charm is coming out," I tease, deciding to call his bluff and pull off my shirt. There's no way he's going to strip down to nothing.

"Down here we call it skinny dipping." He winks, kicking off his shoes before sliding his jeans down to his ankles and taking them off too.

"No," I say firmly, taking a step back. "I'm not going in there naked. With you."

"Why not? Afraid you'll actually have fun?"

I suck in a deep breath, my eyes gazing down his body—his beautiful, hard body. He's everything I write about in my books. Undeniably hot. Cocky attitude. Abs of steel that could cut my teeth. Hair shaggy on one side that makes me want to run my fingers through it as I straddle him. Mesmerizing eyes and lips that take over my senses every time I close my eyes. He's your typical womanizer, down to the ear piercings and rough scruff along his jawline that has me fantasizing how he'd feel between my legs.

Shit.

I've spent the last few years pushing men like him away, knowing they were bad news, yet here I'm standing in front of Mr. Bad News himself and not running away.

"Fine," I bite out. Two can play this game.

I unbutton my shorts and slide them down to my ankles before kicking them into the pile in front of us. Standing in only my bra and panties, I feel him studying me. His eyes slowly trace over my chest and move down my stomach and legs. When his eyes slide back up to mine, there's a knowing smirk taking place of his serious one.

His fingers wrap around the waistband of his boxer shorts, and I inhale deeply as he slowly peels them off. I tell myself to look away, but I can't. His eyes pin me to him, daring me to look away. Bending down, he pulls the shorts all the way to his ankles before standing back up and showing me the *whole* package.

Sweet fucking hell.

His ear isn't the only thing that's pierced.

Blinking, I swallow and try to act as if I am keeping it together. His cock should be packaged with a red ribbon tied around it because the way it hangs between his legs is like a gift to all women. Not to mention, I'm shamelessly curious how a piercing would feel inside me.

I want to make some kind of joke about it being cold outside and insinuate I'm not impressed by his size, but I'm fairly certain my voice would crack and completely blow my cover. My throat is so dry, I'm not sure I could form coherent words even if I tried.

His cock is thick. Thicker than I've ever seen and without

staring at it too long, I shift my eyes away. I hear him chuckle as if my reaction to his naked body is funny.

"What?" I snap my eyes back to his, although I can see his cock in my peripheral vision. It's there all thick and big, and it might as well have a huge neon sign on it that says *Look at me! I'm your wet fantasy!*

"You act like you've never seen a naked man before."

I glare at him, making sure to keep my eyes above his waist.

"Wait. You have, right?" he asks, stepping closer.

"I'm twenty-seven years old. I've seen a naked man before," I snap.

"Then why are you acting like I have a poisonous snake between my legs?"

"Snake," I repeat with a laugh. "Sounds appropriate," I mutter to myself, though I'm sure he heard me.

"You want to feel it?" he asks, palming his fingers around it as he takes another step closer.

"What?" I gasp, blinking my eyes back to his and making sure I heard him correctly.

"The creek," he clarifies, but I know his purpose was to shock me. "It's like bath water."

"Oh." I swallow again, wishing my throat would stop feeling so damn dry. This guy has turned me into an idiot.

"Are you going to go in like that?" He jerks his head down to my bra and panties.

Looking at him, I try and find the courage to follow suit. I've already had to give myself permission to have fun this week, but I'm not sure this is a good idea. In fact, I *know* it's not a good idea. A guy like him could ruin me, and that's something I've promised myself since I was a teenager that I'd never let happen since watching my father verbally and emotionally abuse my mother for years.

You're a worthless piece of shit, and maybe if you ever took that stick out of your ass, you'd actually be a joy to be around. My father's words repeat in my head for the hundredth time since he's said them to my mother years ago. I hate how I allow his words to get to me even after all this time. I force them away when they surface, but I don't know why they've surfaced now.

I push his ugly words away and wrap my arms behind my back, so I can unhook my bra. Ethan watches me, and when my bra slides down my arms, he arches a brow.

"What?"

He rubs along his scruffy jawline, a noticeable smile charming his lips. "Keep going," he tells me, having no shame as he stares intently at my breasts.

I hook my fingers in my panties then slide them down my legs before adding them to our clothes pile. Thank God I waxed before this trip, which was mostly because I had a gift certificate to use at the salon before it expired. A birthday present from Nora who gets on me for my lack of self-care since I've starting writing full-time.

"No carpet, huh? Interesting."

I roll my eyes, shaking my head and pinching my lips together, so he doesn't see me smiling. He's totally eye-fucking my body, and it feels good knowing someone appreciates it.

"Only during the winter months when we Midwesterners need to stay warm," I tease as he grabs my hand and walks us down to the water.

"Remind me to never visit during cold season."

"Oh my God," I say, bursting into laughter as the water hits my ankles. "Wow…it is warm."

"I told you." He turns and winks, pulling us deeper into the water until it's up to my breasts.

"I guess you did." I roll my eyes. "At least the view was worth it."

"I'd have to agree with you on that one actually." He pulls me close until our chests are pressed together.

"I meant the sunset," I correct him with fake annoyance in my tone. "You're so egotistical." I shake my head.

"So did I," he corrects with a knowing grin. He's such a fucking liar. "Now who's egotistical?"

"I'd believe you if you weren't staring so hard at my chest."

"Well, you have nice tits. They're distracting."

"My tits are distracting?" I ask with laughter. "You want to touch them?"

His eyebrows shoot up, probably wondering if it's a trick or not. When I don't waver, he licks his lips and clears his throat.

"What happened to you not being desperate enough to sleep with a man like me?"

Pinching my lips together, I try to think of the perfect comeback, but nothing clever comes to mind. Probably because every time I glance at him, his gorgeous pierced cock invades my brain.

So my tits are distracting to him, and his cock has me thinking all kinds of bad and inappropriate thoughts.

The irony isn't lost on me.

"I decided to throw out all my standards," I finally answer. It's not a complete lie, but it's not the whole truth either. I'd be a fool to not want to sleep with a man like him. He can probably do things to me I've only ever written about or dreamed about, and even then, I don't always write those scenes based on experience. Sometimes it's based on fantasy, pure imagination, or porn.

"Are you saying I don't meet your standards?" he asks, offended.

"Quite the opposite, actually. I didn't mean physical standards, I meant emotionally. I came back over to yell at you for kissing me and then when you kissed me again, I don't know…I didn't want to use the energy to fight it any longer."

Keeping his eyes focused on mine, he brushes his finger along my jawline and to my cheek before moving strands of hair behind my ear. My long hair sticks to my shoulders and back, but that doesn't stop his urge to touch me. Keeping his hand cupped along my jaw, he pulls me forward until our lips connect. My hands wrap around his waist and hold onto him as if I'll drown without his support.

It'd be worth it, though.

CHAPTER EIGHT

ETHAN

Kissing Vada admittedly does something to me, but I can't quite put my finger on it. These past few days of getting to know her and what makes her tick, has my body buzzing to touch and be near her, even when I should be pushing her the other way.

When our mouths touch and my tongue slides between her lips, my body reacts in a way I haven't felt in ages. This feeling is giving me a high—one that I don't want to come down from anytime soon. Her body against mine is making my cock unbearably hard, and every time a moan slips from her delicate lips, I want to push her legs apart and sink deep inside her.

Considering we're both completely naked in the creek and the sun is setting, I know I can't start anything we can't finish. Especially out here, but fuck do I want to. I want to so fucking badly that I have to talk myself down, so my body doesn't erupt before I even get the chance to feel how wet she is for me.

"Ah!" she squeals, pushing our bodies apart and twisting around. "I think something just touched me." She shifts her body, looking around as if it's going to jump out at her. "Are there alligators in here?" she asks, seriously.

Biting my lip, I try to stop the laughter that escapes my throat, but she hears it anyway.

"What?" She finally lifts her head.

I don't know how she hasn't noticed, perhaps my mouth was

keeping her mind too occupied, but it definitely wasn't a creature in the water that touched her.

"Vada…" I say softly, reaching for her and pulling her back to my chest.

"No, I'm serious. I felt it."

"Felt it?" I quirk a brow. "Something like this?"

I push my hips into her until my cock brushes against the lower part of her stomach. "It was that snake you were talking about earlier…"

"Oh my God!" She bursts out laughing. Her eyes lower but between the darkness of the sky and the water, she can't see anything below my chest. "How's that even possible?"

"Well, it's not rocket science, sweetheart. Hot naked girl kissing me and rubbing her tits against me is going to make me hard." I shrug, unapologetically.

"Even in water?"

"Sweetheart, my cock's been hard since the moment you walked up my steps, and when you opened your smart mouth, it got even harder. So yes, *even* in water."

"Jesus," she whispers, pulling her bottom lip between her teeth as if she has to stop herself from saying anything else.

I align our bodies so we're facing each other and my cock presses against her again. We lock eyes as I take one small step forward and feel my piercing rub against her clit. I hear a sharp inhale of breath as her shoulders tense, and her eyes flutter closed.

Palming my cock, I rub circles along her clit as she wraps her hands around my biceps, digging her nails into the muscle. Her breathing pattern quickens as I increase the pace, and when her head falls back, I know she's close.

"Does it feel this good when you touch yourself?" I ask roughly, wrapping my other hand around her neck and securing her body. I'm centimeters from being inside her, but I won't make the next move until she gives me permission. "Answer me, Vada."

"Fuck off," she finally responds, her eyelids barely open from the increased pressure.

"I know you're close," I say matter-of-factly. "So tell me," I demand, sliding my hand from her neck down to her breast and palming it with force. Squeezing her breast and rubbing her clit with my dick is going to unravel me any second, but I won't until I feel her body release.

"No!" she cries out, finally saying what I was hoping to hear.

"So you admit the real thing is better than doing it yourself?" I ask, rotating the tip of my cock in the other direction as I feel her body tensing up.

"No," she grits between her teeth, stubbornly—not that I'm really surprised. It makes me smile still.

"No? So I should stop then and let you finish yourself?" I ask, slowing my rhythm, as painful as it is for me. I won't let her win this battle without a fight.

"Fuck, no!" Her eyes blink open in a panic as her chest rises and falls while she tries to catch her breath. "Okay, fine. Yes! Your stupid pierced cock feels fucking amazing against my clit. There! Happy?"

A smile shines over my face because I know how salty those words must've tasted coming out. "Extremely."

She groans, shifting her body so she can slide her hand between her legs. "I'm so close, I can finish myself anyway."

"Fuck that." I quickly grab her hands and wrap them around my waist, securing them with only one of my hands. "You change your answer yet?"

"I thought I did already," she hisses, wiggling her hips to find relief. My cock is still standing at attention, but I tilt my body just enough so it doesn't touch her.

"I need to hear you say it, Vada," I tell her seriously. "I'll fuck your cunt harder than you could ever imagine, but I won't until you know exactly what you're getting into."

She's breathing heavier now, and I can tell I have her full attention.

"And what is that?" she asks, panting.

"I'm not those guys in your romance novels. I'm a gentleman, and I'll treat you real good in bed, but I'm not one of those guys who sends flowers and chocolate the next day, so I don't want you getting the wrong idea here. You're tense as hell, and the only way to get you to relax is to fuck you so good, you'll still be feeling me days later."

"I have no expectations from you, Ethan," she tells me honestly. "I'm only here for a few more days, and then I'm gone."

"Good," I say, releasing my grip around her wrists. "Right now, you should only concern yourself with how hard I can make you come, because sweetheart, after tonight your expectations are going to be a lot higher."

"Oh God," she whispers.

"So what's it going to be, Vada? Think one night with me will be enough for you?" I taunt, licking my lips as she looks up at me. Resisting the urge to kiss her, I wait impatiently for her response.

"I think the real question is…will one night with me be enough for *you*, Casanova?"

I nearly carry Vada back to the house, naked, but she makes me grab our clothes and get dressed before leading her the couple blocks back. I couldn't wait any longer. The way she makes me crave her is starting to become painful for my dick, and I know the only relief will come from her.

Wearing only my jeans, I rush us through the front door and immediately pin her against the door with my mouth. Before she can even finish moaning my name, my jeans are on the floor.

"I told you getting dressed was pointless," I say against her lips as I reach for her shirt and pull it over her head.

"You barely had any clothes on in the first place," she reminds me as I take her shorts off next. "I don't know if it's tradition to run naked outside in the south or something, but from where I'm from, public indecency gets you a misdemeanor."

"Good to know. Unshaved pussies should be fined," I tease, kneeling down between her legs as she holds onto the door for support.

"Yeah? What about guys who watch their tenants masturbate? Is there a law against that?" she asks with a condescending tone as I slide her panties down to her ankles. Once she steps out of them, I fling them behind me.

Before answering, I grab her thighs and spread them. She

squeals and rests her palms on my shoulders as she regains her balance. My mouth is on her before she can spit out another word.

Sliding my tongue along her slit, I circle her clit and taste all Vada's sweetness. She moans and digs her nails into my scalp as she pulls strands of my hair between her fingers.

Her body shakes as I sink my tongue deep inside her. She tastes so fucking good, I can't pull myself away.

"Holy fuck, Ethan…" she mutters, her hands roughly pulling at my hair, which feels surprisingly amazing when my mouth is on her.

My tongue devours her, sliding up and down her slit, sucking hard on her clit, and when I feel her body start to tense, I insert a finger inside her tight cunt.

"Oh my God," she says between gritted teeth, trying to keep herself together, but I know it's no use. She's going to unravel at any moment.

Speeding up the pace, I add a second finger as my tongue circles her clit faster. Her knees are seconds from buckling, and when she screams out my name, I push my fingers inside even deeper.

"Mm…" I groan against her pussy. Fuck, she tastes amazing. She's panting as I lick and clean her up, wanting to savor everything she gives me. Standing, I wrap my hand around her neck and without another word, pull her mouth to mine. She's reluctant at first, but it only takes her seconds to relax against me.

"Never tasted your own come before?" I pull back and ask. She licks her lips, and her eyes slowly trail up to mine, embarrassed by my question.

"I don't make it a habit."

I chuckle, figuring that's a no. "You should," I tell her. "Tastes like heaven, don't you think?" I smirk, brushing my tongue along my bottom lip.

She grinds her teeth down. "I wouldn't know. Guess I'll have to take your word for it."

"Smart girl." I wink. "Come on." I grab her hand before she can speak and lead her upstairs. We round the banister, and I walk us to the last door on the left.

Once we're inside, I shut the door behind us, and when she turns to face me, I know something's wrong.

"This is your room?" She raises her brows as she looks around the nearly empty space.

"No," I say, firmly. "I told you. No pussies in my bed except for Wilma."

"Oh, didn't realize you were serious."

"I'm always serious when it comes to pussy, Vada." I step closer, wrapping my hands around her and unhooking her bra. We both watch as it slides down her arms and falls to the floor. "You can change your mind, you know?" I reassure her, feeling uneasy about her mood shift.

"You don't sleep with women in your bed?"

"No."

"Why?"

I wrap my hand around my neck and squeeze. "That's not something I talk about. With anyone."

"So it's really just about the sex then?"

"Yes," I answer honestly. "That's all this is Vada. Can you handle that?"

"I already said yes," she reminds me, but she doesn't sound as certain as before.

"Good, because after tasting you once, I know I'm going to want to taste you again."

She looks up at me with wide eyes and smiles. I can tell her sex life was merely nonexistent before, which in a way makes me glad because I want to be the one to introduce her to all the amazing different ways I can make her feel fucking fantastic.

"So tell me what you like." I step forward, closing the gap between us. Wrapping my hand around her waist, I pull us chest to chest.

"What?"

"You write about sex for a living. You must have a preference."

"Uh…"

I smile, seeing the blush creep up her neck and cheeks. "How about this? If you're uncomfortable with anything I'm doing, you tell me, and I'll stop."

"Like a safe word?"

Chuckling, I say, "Sure. Is that what your characters do?"

She shrugs, her cheeks turning redder. "Sometimes."

"Okay. What's your safe word then?"

She chews the inside of her cheek as if she's really thinking about it. My cock is pressed against her stomach and the longer she takes, the more it aches.

"How about Henry?" she finally blurts out.

I blink. "Henry?"

"Yup."

"Big cock pun." I arch a brow, squeezing my fingers into her hip.

"I was thinking more along the lines of 'terrifying cock who chases after me,' but either one works." She's smiling and holding back laughter and fuck it's so goddamn adorable. If she wasn't standing in front of me completely naked, all wet with perky tits, I'd find all this talking before extremely annoying, but for some reason, it's not with her.

"Okay, so we're good now? You have your safe word, all the expectations are laid out, and my dick is rock hard and going to burst if you don't let me kiss you soon."

A smirk forms on her face as she grinds her body against my cock. "And who said chivalry was dead?"

I grin. "Probably a romance writer."

CHAPTER NINE

VADA

THE WORDS all but leave his lips before his mouth is back on mine. I take everything he gives me—his tongue, his hands, his body. I want it all. Even if it's temporary—a quick fix—I want it. I want *him*.

His touch consumes me, taking away my breath all in one motion. He palms my ass cheeks and lifts me up until my legs instinctively wrap around his waist. Feeling his erection against my leg, I rock my hips against him until I feel the tip of his cock against my clit. His piercing is giving me all kinds of curious and naughty thoughts.

"Vada, *fuck*," he growls against my ear. "Any time you do that, I want to bend you over and fuck that tight little ass."

I swallow, rotating my hips once again. "Would this be the appropriate time to say, *Henry*?" I joke, knowing that even if I wanted to use our safe word, I wouldn't unless I truly meant it.

"Oh, sweetheart," he drawls, walking us to the bed, "I haven't even started to make you question your decision to be with me yet. At least wait out the good stuff." He winks, laying me down once we reach the mattress.

"I've been questioning my decisions since the moment you opened the door."

He towers over my body with his hands firmly planted on both sides of me. Leaning down just enough to brush his lips against mine again with my legs still wrapped around his waist, he whispers, "It's freeing, isn't it? Once you stop overthinking and analyzing every little thing, you start learning how to have fun again."

"I think it's safe to say I haven't been thinking straight since I got here," I admit.

"So why start now?" He flashes his infamous panty-melting smirk that keeps me hypnotized.

I roll my eyes playfully, agreeing that being with him would indeed be freeing. Maybe even a little careless.

"So you're saying if I have sex with you, I'll magically get over my writer's block and finish my manuscript?" I tease, although the thought is intriguing.

"Baby, you have sex with me, and you won't be able to type fast enough." He feathers his kisses down my jawline and neck, landing on my earlobe.

My hair cascades around me as I laugh at his overconfidence. Although I have *zero* doubt the man's performance will be nothing short of amazing, I have to remind myself that this thing between us can only be physical.

"Sounds like a T-shirt slogan. *Have sex with Ethan Rochester and never have writer's block again*! You'd have a line of women around the block."

He lifts his head, the corner of his mouth tilts up as if he's giving it some real thought. "You willing to give me an editorial review? You know, to put on the website and all."

"You wouldn't need a review. Just a picture of your abs and python-sized cock, and they'd be running over each other faster than a sale on Black Friday."

"Okay, now you're just making me sound like a piece of meat. I have feelings, you know."

"There's no feelings in fucking," I remind him, although I'm the one who needs convincing.

"Fuck," he growls, the tip of his cock torturously brushing against my clit again as he roughly palms my breast. "I think that's the hottest thing I've ever heard a woman say."

"Yeah? Well, show me like you mean it then," I challenge, arching my hips because the way he's taunting me drives my body insane. His piercing rubs against my pussy again, and I'm two seconds away from flipping him over and riding him like the Raging Bull roller coaster at Six Flags—*hard and fast.*

He leans back briefly, reaching into the nightstand near the bed and opens the drawer. At first, I'm confused, but then I see he pulls out a strip of condoms. Jesus, does he buy them in bulk? Or perhaps he should just buy stock in the damn things. *He probably already does.*

He tears one off but doesn't open it. I watch as he kneels down between my legs and without saying another word, grabs my thighs and pushes my knees to my shoulders.

"Ah!" I yelp, surprised by his quick movements. My ass is hanging off the edge of the bed as he kneels on the floor and presses his mouth directly on my clit.

The moment his tongue sinks inside me, I feel my body floating. His hands palm my ass cheeks as he devours me like the starved man he is. He moans in pleasure as he licks up and down my slit, bringing me closer to the edge with every calculated movement.

"Holy fuck, Ethan," I blurt out, my head falling back as I arch my body and his tongue slides in deeper. My nails dig into the sheets, and I'm clawing at them with every long stroke he gives me. The way he rotates the tip of his tongue has me moaning and screaming, both wanting more and needing the release.

His mouth takes no prisoners.

A finger slides inside, and he fucks me as he tastes my arousal. I'm so close, but the moment I'm about to come, he teases me with another finger. I'm ready. I need it so fucking badly, and just as my body tightens, he slips one of his fingers into my tight ass.

"Oh my God!" I squeal, my nails digging deeper into the mattress.

It's so unexpected, and the feeling is so foreign, yet the moment my body relaxes, I know I've never come that hard from oral before.

"Hurts good, doesn't it, sweetheart?" Ethan towers over me, drinking me in as my eyelids flutter open.

It takes me a few moments to catch my breath, and while I do, he kisses my neck, shoulder, and chest. He wraps his lips around my nipple and playfully flicks it before moving onto the other.

"Now I see I was right about you..." I give him a dreamy look that proves just how completely smitten I am by him. Even before I saw the whole package, I knew there was something about him. Something *mysterious*.

"And what's that, darlin'?" He muses.

"That you're a heartbreaker," I tell him, at the same time reminding myself, *Don't get attached. Just sex.*

His smile deepens, and I know it's not because he finds me funny.

"Baby, I'm not." His tone is steady and honest, and although I want to believe that with every fiber of my being, deep down I know otherwise.

I pluck my bottom lip between my teeth as I gaze up and study him.

"Maybe not, but you'll definitely break me."

Without saying another word, he steps back and sheaths his cock before pressing his tip against my entrance.

"You still sure then?" he asks, wrapping a hand around my neck, so our mouths are only inches apart.

Swallowing, I nod. "Yes."

He slides into me in one smooth motion before sliding back out. God, he's so thick. His piercing rubs along my walls and brings an added sensation all together. I kind of like it.

As he presses our mouths together, he pushes back in, this time rocking his hips back and forth. My legs are tightly holding him against my body as if he'll get away. I want him. I *need* him. Everything he's giving me, *anything*, I'll take it.

"Fuck, you feel so good, Vada," he whispers, wrapping a fist in my hair and pulling. "Who knew a big-mouthed city girl would have such a tight little cunt?"

His words are so crass, yet my body gets hotter every time I hear him talk like that. The characters in my books aren't any better, but I never realized the words sounded as good on paper as they do in real life.

"You like when I talk like that?" he asks. When I don't respond, he continues, "I felt you tighten when I talked about your cunt. You liked it, didn't you?"

"I write about cunts and cocks all the time," I blurt out like it's an excuse for my body's response.

His brow arches, amused. "Well, I hope you're taking some good notes, baby. I'm about to show you just how bad I can be."

Before I can truly comprehend his words, he steps back, grabs my ankles from around his waist and places them on top of his shoulders. He nearly bends me in half when he leans back over my chest and roughly pushes inside.

"Shit," I curse, as I suck in a deep breath. "This sounds a lot easier in books."

"Not as flexible as your characters?" He winks, driving his cock in deeper.

"Not when I spend the majority of my time on my ass."

"Or back," he counters.

The laughter that releases is hijacked by a deep moan. He increases his pace, wraps his hand around my neck again, and pulls my face closer to his.

"I want you to watch, Vada. Watch my cock sliding inside you. Watch me fucking you because sweetheart, it's the hottest fucking thing I've seen in a long time."

Straining my neck to see where our bodies connect, I watch as he slowly pulls out—so slow it's torturous. His piercing pushes against the latex, and just as I'm about to beg him to take me out of my misery, he forcefully pushes back inside me.

"Ah, God!" My head starts to fall back in pleasure, but Ethan grips me harder.

"No. Watch," he demands.

Blinking, I do.

Fuck, it's so hot. I've written several sex scenes over the years, yet I've never actually watched with intention.

"See how our bodies stay in sync?" His eyes lower. "Like they were made to fuck each other."

"Wow…real Shakespeare shit right there," I tease, getting antsy because I need to come again. Just when I feel the orgasm building, he slows his pace.

"I'm a man of many qualities." He grins.

"I have no doubt."

"You need to come," he says—not a question.

I nod, eagerly.

"Show me how you rub your clit," he orders.

"Watching me once wasn't enough for you?" I fire back.

"I could watch you every day and never get bored. Rub your clit until you come. I want to watch you while I fuck you."

My cheeks redden at the memory of him seeing me. I know I shouldn't be embarrassed, but I can't help it, especially since his abs were the reason I came as hard as I did that night.

Obeying him, I slide my hand between us and circle my clit. His grip around my neck relaxes as the pressure builds.

"Jesus Christ. You squeeze my dick so fucking hard when you get close."

"I know." I smile. I have way more experience getting myself off than I care to admit. Trust issues, failed dating attempts, and lack of social skills is to blame.

"Open your eyes. Watch our bodies as you come."

"I don't think I can," I say, breathlessly. My fingers circle my clit faster and harder, and soon it's all too much to bare.

"Vada!" he growls, grabbing my attention. My eyes shoot open, and as soon as I see his intent stare, my body unravels.

He slows his pace as I ride out the wave, my hand falling slack against the mattress. My chest rises and falls as I feel him slide all the way out.

"I won't be surprised if I'm missing a layer of skin tomorrow," Ethan teases. "Your pussy's so fucking hungry."

Yeah, it's been a while. Tell me something I don't know. I roll my eyes at myself, not saying the words aloud.

"I'm not done with you yet." His words vibrate against the shell of my ear, and soon I'm being lifted into the air and flipped onto my stomach. "Ass up."

"My entire body is jelly," I try to explain, but when he slides his hand up my spine, I push my ass out for him.

"I warned you," he growls. "There's no way I'm fucking you without getting an ass view."

"You warned me?" I question, putting my body into position so

I can rest my head on the mattress while my ass is in the air, patiently waiting.

"I knew you were tense as hell, and the only way you'd relax was to fuck you so good, you'd be feeling me days later," he reminds me, repeating what he told me almost word for word.

"Right," I murmur to myself, but by the way he positions his cock against my pussy, I know he heard me.

"I think it's safe to say you're pretty relaxed now, but just in case, I plan to fuck you until we're both raw and bruised."

Raw and bruised? What does this man have planned for me? I wondered but didn't have time to dwell on it before his length was deep inside me.

My fingers dig into the sheets as he palms my ass cheeks and spreads them apart. He squeezes my hips and pushes me harder and faster into him as he speeds up his own pace.

"Fuck…fuck…" I moan, closing my eyes tightly as I take every brutal thrust. One of his hands release me, but within seconds, I feel it smack against my ass cheek. "Ah!" I yelp, jerking forward.

"That's for teasing me with this ass since the second you got here." He does it again and once more before tightening his grip on my hip and fucking me so hard, I fear I might break.

I smile although he can't see me, knowing that he's been lusting over me since the moment we met.

"Goddammit, Vada…" he hisses, anger and lust woven into his tone. "You feel too fucking good." Releasing his hold on me, he leans his body over my back and snakes a hand over my breast, squeezing roughly. I've always liked my breasts touched and played with, but by the way Ethan is handling them, you'd think they'd done him wrong in some way.

His hand slides down my stomach and lands on my pussy. Arching my back more, his cock moves in deeper while the pad of his finger rubs my clit.

"I love how tense you get before you come," he whispers into my ear. "Then a second before you do, your body relaxes, and you release everything out of your mind. For a moment, you have no thoughts, no concerns, no worries. It's pure fucking bliss."

"Yes," I moan in agreement. "Coming is the best high there is."

"Then I better make sure it's worth your while, huh?" His lips smile against my neck. "Your pussy is like heaven. I never want to vacate."

"Sorry, one-night stay per guest only." I grin.

"Fuck that," he growls, adding more pressure to my clit as he speeds up his pace. "The only guest allowed to check-in is my dick, sweetheart."

"Who knew you were so territorial?" I mock, knowing he hasn't been up to this point.

"Not me. Definitely not me," he says as if he's shocked by his own words. "However, that was before your cunt took over my brain."

Before I get the chance to make another joke about his southern charm, my body goes rigid, and his fingers continuously rub my clit as my body tightens all around him. Seconds later, he goes still, and I know he's not far behind.

Leaning back, he grabs my hips roughly and our bodies rock together. Our skin smacks together so hard and fast, I can barely keep up.

"Fuck, fuck, fuck," he hisses on a moan as he stills, our bodies shaking together as he releases inside me.

He groans as he pushes once more against me and curses. "Shit, Vada."

My entire body goes lax. I can't feel my arms or legs. Before sliding out and tossing the condom, he leans over me and presses a sweet kiss against my neck.

I flip over and settle into the bed, enjoying the warmth. Although the room is dark, there's a flicker of light coming from the moon outside the window. It glows against his tan skin, accentuating every part of him that was just mine. Stunning and beautiful, I can almost see right through him and the facade he hides behind.

"Mission accomplished," he says as he lies next to me in bed.

"Mission?" My brows arch. "I was a mission?"

"Rode my dick raw and yet…I want more." He turns and looks at me, waiting for my reaction.

I'm not quite sure how to react, but I smile in agreement.

"Yeah, I could get used to this," I say, dreamily. "Although, it feels like my pussy needs an ice pack and a cigarette." I squeeze my eyes shut the moment the words spew from my lips. "These scenes are way sexier in romance novels."

He chuckles, pulling the blankets that survived and covers us up. Even though I know he's not the flowers and chocolates kind of guy, I'm hoping this doesn't make things weird between us. I still have four days here, and if we can stick to the sexual stuff only, this will be the best writer's retreat of my life.

CHAPTER TEN

ETHAN

I HAVEN'T SLEPT with a woman since Alana. I've had plenty of one-night stands, but sleepovers weren't a thing I allowed. At least not until right now.

Having Vada sleeping against my chest feels intimate, yet I'm not pushing her away like I should—like I usually do. Her body heat feels nice, and for the first time, I'm not going to bed feeling empty and alone.

Even if that's exactly how I wanted it all these years.

Closing my eyes, flashes of Alana and the memory of the life we shared evades my mind. I manage to get a few hours' sleep before those memories wake me.

After a half hour of watching Vada sleep next to me, I decide to stop fighting it and get out of bed. I slide on my shorts, and before leaving the guest bedroom, I turn around and stare at her. I don't know what comes over me, but I walk to her side of the bed, pull off the covers, and wrap her in my arms. As quietly as I can, I carry her out of the room and walk us to my bedroom where I lay her down and cover her back up. She looks good in here. Looks right.

And that scares the shit out of me.

The guest room is the only bed I've let women be with me in, and the status of being a one-night only hookup doesn't fit right with Vada. I know I've set the rules for us, and we both know what to expect of this, but our connection isn't on the same level as a random one-night stand. Leaving her in there just didn't feel right.

Once I'm in the hallway, I shut the door and tiptoe down the stairs. I decide to make a pot of coffee since I know sleep won't be coming to me anytime soon.

After filling up my mug, I head upstairs and go to the tower. The sun should be rising shortly, and the tower has a perfect view of it.

Memories of Alana and I first looking at this house comes to mind. We met in a small town, high school sweethearts you could say, and were each other's firsts. Everyone expected us to get married, have kids, and live happily ever after.

Too bad life had other plans for us.

After living the apartment life for two years, we decided it was time to start house hunting. It just so happened we found the right one at just the right time. Alana was six months pregnant when we found our house.

"Babe, come check the view from up here!" she called from the third story when I was still climbing the stairs to the second floor. It was a traditional southern house with original wood, wraparound porch with three-bedrooms and two point five bathrooms. It even had a big yard, which was something we both wanted.

"Coming, hold on," I called back. "How'd you get up there so fast?"

Alana might've been pregnant, but she didn't let that stop her. She was as active as she'd always been. Both in and out of the bedroom.

"This is the part of the house I wanted to see the most. It's amazing," she said with adoration in her voice.

I finally caught up to her, taking the final steps into the tower. Windows surrounded it in a complete three-hundred-and-sixty-degree view. You could see for miles up here.

"Wow," I said as I wrapped my arms around her waist from behind. She covered my hands with hers as we stood in the middle of the tower and just stared out.

"I know," she whispered. "Imagine all the sunrises and sunsets we could watch from up here."

"And fireworks over the water," I added. "It's perfect."

"It's like being on the Eiffel Tower." She beamed, and I knew no other

house would even come close to this one. Alana had been obsessed with the Eiffel Tower since our honeymoon when we visited a couple years ago. The beauty of it inspired her to focus more on what made her happy.

"I could do all my pottery up here," she told me as we both glanced around the space. "Put my wheel in the middle, my wood shelves along that wall over there for all my mugs, and put the kiln on the other wall. What do you think?" She looked over her shoulder at me with pleading eyes. Alana loved pottery, and even more, loved creating it. I couldn't deny her of what made her truly happy, especially if it meant I got to see that beautiful smile every day.

"I think you're absolutely right. The space is perfect for it, and you really can't beat the view." I gave her a tight squeeze for emphasis. "You think you'll still have time after the baby arrives?"

"Probably not at first, but eventually when we have a schedule down," she explained, and I agreed.

"Good." I kissed the top of her head. "You're too talented not to."

"If you don't buy me this house, I'll divorce you," she teased with a laugh.

"It's pretty perfect," I agreed. I turned her around and knelt down. Rubbing a hand over her belly, I spoke softly, "What do you think, Paris? Do you want this to be your first home?" I looked up at Alana, smiling down at me as I talked to our daughter.

Seconds later, she kicked.

And that was all the confirmation we needed.

We put in an offer, and a month later, we moved in. I'd spent the following few weeks finishing up the nursery, knowing Alana wanted it perfect. The house needed some updating, but I knew we'd have to do a little here and there until it was complete. It was something we were supposed to do together.

At thirty-two weeks, Alana went into early labor and had no choice but to deliver. She was preeclamptic, and the doctor didn't want to risk waiting longer. As much as we were excited to finally be meeting our little girl, I was also scared. Becoming a father for the first time is something I've been thinking about for years. Especially with Alana.

Everything started out smoothly as they induced Alana, and it became a waiting game as she started getting contractions. The doctor warned us it could be awhile before she'd be ready to push, so in attempt to keep her distracted, we talked about all the remodeling plans we had for the new house.

The next several hours were spent getting Alana ice, rubbing her back and shoulders, and massaging her feet. The contractions became more intense and closer together. She was tough, always had been, and even though she wanted to have a natural birth as much as possible, she started to beg for an epidural.

"Alana," I said softly. "You're doing great, baby. Are you sure you want the epidural?" I asked because she had made me promise to not let her get one, even though I didn't see any reason not to when she was in this much pain.

"I can't bear the pain, E. It's like she's clawing her way out," she cried, and I winced. I couldn't stand watching her suffer any longer.

"Okay, baby." I grabbed her hand and kissed it. "I'll tell the doctor."

"Ah!" she screamed out and clenched my fingers in a forceful fist. She squeezed her eyes and lips, and I knew something was wrong.

I paged the nurse, and shortly after she came back in the room, she checked all of Alana's stats on the monitor and read the contractions record. The baby monitor that wrapped around her belly had shifted slightly.

Once the nurse retightened the strap and the stats flashed on the screen, a look of worry flashed across her face.

"Is everything okay?" I asked, concerned.

"The baby's heartbeat is slower than I'd like, so I'm just going to page the doctor and have him come check you out."

She rushed out before I could ask more questions.

"Is the baby going to be okay?" Alana's eyes watered, and I knew I had to keep her calm.

"I'm sure it's nothing, but the doctor will come and check," I reassured her, but I wasn't certain myself.

Within a few minutes, the doctor had arrived and checked hers and the baby's stats again. Two nurses followed.

"Alana, we're going to roll you to your side and see if that helps increase the heartbeat. Okay?"

The nurses helped Alana get comfortable on her side, and after a moment, the heart rate went back up.

"Perfect." The doctor smiled.

"Is she okay?" Alana asked.

"She is for now, but if the heart rate drops again, we'll have to deliver via C-section."

"What? Why?" Alana cried, looking panicked.

"Vaginal delivery is too risky if the baby is in distress. Her heart rate decreasing during birth could put her at risk for too many complications, and I'd like to avoid all that." His words come out rehearsed, and I wish he'd give us some closure that everything was going to be okay.

We waited an hour before the doctor returned and told us the bad news.

"I'm sorry, the heart rate isn't staying as steady as much as I'd like. I'd feel more confident if we did a C-section to avoid any other risks."

Since she was preeclamptic, she was already a high-risk case, so we had no choice but to follow the doctor's orders.

Everything happened so fast after that. The nurses prepped Alana for surgery, and I changed into scrubs. They gave us a briefing of what to expect, but no matter what they told us, none of it felt real.

They took Alana in first, and once the doctor was ready, the nurse escorted me inside by her.

"Baby," I whispered, kissing her cheek. She looked terrified and as scared as I was, I couldn't let her see that.

"E," she whispered back. "Please tell me she's going to be okay."

I kissed her again. "Everything's going to be fine. I promise, okay?" I flashed her a smile. I couldn't see much over the sheet they put between Alana and the doctor, but I could tell she felt some discomfort.

"You okay?"

"I can feel pressure, that's all. It feels weird."

"Well, in just a minute, we're going to have a daughter. Can you believe it?" I smiled so wide as I held her hand.

"Okay, Mom and Dad. Are you ready?" the doctor announced. I was anxious but so excited to meet my daughter. "Here she is." He lifted her up briefly giving us just a peek at her. "She's beautiful, congratulations," he said after handing her off to one of the nurses.

"Oh my God," Alana cried. I knew she was upset about not having a natural delivery, but having my two girls healthy and safe was the most important thing.

"She looks just like you," I said. "So beautiful." I kissed her softly on the lips. "Thank you."

Tears poured from her eyes and fell down her face. "For what?"

"For the greatest gift you could've ever given me."

I kissed her again.

"Can you go with her? She's going to be in the NICU, and I don't want her to be alone."

"I don't want to leave you, baby…" I was so damn torn. I needed to make sure Paris was okay, but at the same time, it felt like I was abandoning Alana.

"I'll be okay," she promised with a hand squeeze. "They have to finish putting my stomach back together and then set me up in a room anyway."

"Are you sure?" I looked around the room as the doctor continued working on Alana and the nurses tended to Paris.

"Yes. Go, please!"

I kissed her once more. "I love you, baby. I'll get an update on Paris as soon as I can, okay?"

"I love you, too, E." She smiled up at me, and we both stared into each other's eyes as I walked toward the nurses.

They cleaned Paris and were preparing to transfer her. She looked so small in the incubator, and I still couldn't believe she was ours.

"Is she okay?" I asked a nurse who was looking at her chart.

"Her breathing is unsteady, and she looks jaundiced, but everything else looks okay so far." She smiled up at me. "They'll take good care of her up in the NICU. Don't worry."

"Thank you."

Another nurse introduced herself as she arrived and explained she'd be the one bringing Paris down to the NICU. I followed her as she wheeled the little cart to the elevator and took us to the fifth floor. I wasn't prepared. I wasn't prepared for any of this, and I felt like a damn fool.

As we walked the quiet path down the hallway, I could see in the other rooms. Tiny, helpless babies all in incubators. I'd never witnessed anything like it in my life.

I was anxious to get back to Alana, but I knew she'd want me to stay with Paris until I had a solid update. My baby girl was covered in tubes. A breathing tube and feeding tube, along with a variety of monitors.

The scene broke me.

I felt incredibly helpless as I watched our newborn baby fighting to breathe. She was premature, weighing only four pounds, and I wanted nothing more than for her to stay strong and healthy.

About an hour later, the doctor who did Alana's C-section knocked on the door, and as soon as I saw his glum expression, I stood from my chair and walked toward him.

I waited for him to speak, but his eyes flickered to Paris and back to mine before he finally did.

"There were some complications with Alana," he began, and I felt my entire world ripped out from under me.

Those memories continue to haunt me in every aspect of my life. I blamed and beat myself over not being there for her when she needed me the most—completely vulnerable and exposed. To have to choose between being by my wife's side or my newborn baby was a game I couldn't win. I'd already felt guilty for leaving her in the operating room, but either choice would've been the wrong one. That's something I know I'll have to live with the rest of my life.

Just when I thought things couldn't get worse, after planning my wife's funeral and burying her, I watched helplessly as my baby girl fought for her life. Two weeks after I lost Alana, I lost Paris, too. She was too little, too sick, and I was heartbroken all over again.

I lost more than my wife and daughter—I'd also lost myself—and it's prevented me from ever wanting to fall in love again. At first, it was acceptable to grieve the way I did. I shut down, unable to step into the tower surrounded by her pottery and things, but when I heard a mouse up there one night, I went into a blind rage.

Being around her things that were left as if she were coming back to me, set me off. It mocked me, taunting me of everything I'd lost. All her clay and supplies. Her bowls and mugs. The old radio we bought at a rummage sale she'd play while working. The room still smelled like her.

The mouse squeaked as it ran across the room toward the other end, stealing my attention. Without thinking, I grabbed one of the empty buckets and threw it in his direction. I knew I'd miss, but the moment I released my grip, anger filled my body.

I grabbed the next bucket and threw that, too. Then another. Picking up and throwing anything I could get my hands on. For a solid minute, I destroyed everything in my way. By the time I stopped, I was out of breath and silently cursing myself. But releasing the anger felt necessary and overdue.

Aunt Millie found me sitting in the tower the next morning. She could see the mess I'd created and that I was self-destructing. She knew how much Alana meant to me and how her unexpected death derailed me.

"Ethan, hon, I know you're hurting. You have every right to be, but this isn't the man Alana would want you to be." Her voice was soft, but firm.

"What's it matter, Aunt Millie? My life is over. It's nothing without her."

"I know it feels that way right now, but you need to grieve and give yourself permission to move on and be happy again. Alana would want you to," she told me, although I've heard it all before. It'd be two years since her death and no matter what people said, time didn't heal all wounds. Not at fucking all.

"I'll never be able to move on from this," I said, confidently. "I lost my family, my entire world, and my only reason for living."

"Find a way to connect with her, Ethan. Instead of thinking about everything you lost, find a way to keep her spirit alive within you." Her words were wise, and I appreciated them, but it wouldn't change anything. She'd still be gone.

"How?" I asked, defeated. Exhaustion was setting in, and nothing made sense.

"Find something she loved," she began, waving her hand around the mess I made and continuing, "like pottery."

"I can't make what she did, Aunt Millie. Even if I did, it was her dream. It'd feel as if I were taking it away from her." Emotions filled my throat, and I swallowed down a sob. I'd never felt that vulnerable in my life, and there I was sitting on the floor of the tower, my wife's favorite place, surrounded by the destruction I created.

"Quite the opposite." She patted my leg, sympathetically. "You'll feel what she felt while she was creating her bowls and cups and connect with her through that. It could help give you closure, even if right now it feels like you'll never get it."

The only closure I could ever feel was knowing that Alana wasn't alone. She and Paris had each other, and until I'd see them again, I'd be dead inside.

"Healing is a process, and it takes time, but that doesn't mean you stop living in the meantime." I knew she was trying to comfort me, but I felt too empty inside to take her words to heart. I didn't want to heal. Pain was the only comfort I had anymore. Pain was the only emotion I felt.

"I don't know how to live without her," I explained. "It still feels like it all happened yesterday."

"Try it, honey." She handed me a block of clay from the floor that was a victim of the destruction. "You don't know till you try."

Aunt Millie's words repeated in my head for weeks after that. I knew my family was still worried sick about me, but depression sucked me into its black hole, and I wasn't looking for a way out.

That'd been my life for years.

Then came the anniversaries and birthdays.

Those days I ended up blacking out completely. I couldn't bare the pain anymore, so I drank until I was numb.

Until I picked up that block of clay. It was like Alana was saving me from myself, from the personal hell I created. Somehow, she was still here with me, helping me get through the hard times just as she always did over the years. Learning her craft was hard, and I was terrible. Each day I made lopsided mugs and crooked sculptures, I wanted to quit but didn't. It was almost as if Alana was pushing me to create, to live out the dream she always wanted for us. That day, I promised myself I'd never let her down. So I worked harder, hoping she'd be watching me from heaven with our baby girl in her arms.

Aunt Millie was right after all—this time.

I smile now when I think about Alana and the memories we shared all those years together. Though I'm completely disinterested in relationships in general, Aunt Millie likes to remind me of Alana and how she'd want me to be happy, even if that meant moving on. I've had no interest in anything more than a one-night stand or random fling, but for the first time in a long while, the woman sleeping in my bed right now has me rethinking everything.

The thoughts in my head take me off guard, though I can't deny they're true. Vada came barreling into my life, so unexpected, and yet, it's as if I'd been waiting for her all this time.

These feelings scare the shit out of me because this all happened so quickly, but knowing she's leaving in a few days has my mind spinning. I want to make the most out of our time together, but I can't stop the guilt that continues to eat at me every time I look down at my left hand and see the ghost of the wedding ring I once wore.

CHAPTER ELEVEN
VADA

Waking up with hard muscles against my body shocks the shit out of me. Making sure I'm not still dreaming, I slowly peel open my eyes. I don't recognize the room as the sun peeks through the windows, but I can tell it's early morning. This isn't the same room we started in last night. But I don't have much time to analyze it because when memories start flooding in, my cheeks heat. All the things he did to me, all the *ways* he molded my body, and the way I responded to them. *Holy shit. Yes*, we did that. *No*, I don't have any regrets.

Nerves take over as I think about sneaking out and doing the walk of shame. I haven't had to face a one-night stand since my early college days, so I feel completely disoriented. It's not like I can just leave and avoid him anyway, but the anxiety of facing him has me overthinking everything.

However, the weight of Ethan's bicep holds me in place. There's no way I can slip out of bed without waking him. As if he heard my thoughts, he hums against the shell of my ear and pulls me closer to him until my back presses against his warm, hard chest. Our bodies fit together like two jagged pieces of a puzzle that somehow line up perfectly. We both have our sharp edges, but somehow it works. His strong arms hold me like I'm his, and I can't help but smile at the fantasy of it all—because that's what it is

—make believe. We've both agreed that this isn't anything more than sex and a good time.

Though I write sex scenes in descriptive detail in my novels, this morning, I have no words. That's something that doesn't happen often. Me, speechless? Yep. Being with him was exhilarating, to say the least. We're adults who are obviously missing something in our lives. Last night, Ethan made me realize exactly *what* I've been missing, unadulterated sex with no attachments.

One-night stands are not in my sexual repertoire. Too many times I've overly romanticized relationships, but the men I've dated were basically worthless, so there's that. No man has been able to live up to the expectations as the ones I write—alpha males, smart, loyal, *perfect*. After all my failed relationships, I'm fairly certain my perfect real-life hero doesn't exist, and if he does, I'm sure he's taken.

"Morning," Ethan says in a husky, deep tone against the crook of my neck. Goose bumps travel along my skin as he slides his hand across my bare stomach. I turn my head as his honey-colored eyes flutter open.

"Morning," I say, happy it's not as awkward as I imagined it'd be. Then again, knowing this is purely physical without any strings attached helps. I can open my heart for a few days then seal it back tight before I get back to Chicago as if nothing ever happened. My secret will stay in South Carolina, and Ethan will be my perfect sexspiration.

"Coffee?" I ask, ready to get my day started. Just as I scoot away from him to place my feet on the floor, he pulls me back to face him.

"Not so fast," he says with a sexy smirk on his lips.

My heart feels as if it will beat right out of my chest. Ethan rolls over, his face hovering above mine.

"Don't think I'm going to stop giving you shit just because I fucked your brains out." He winks, and I know for certain nothing has changed.

I laugh at his blunt confession and go along with it. "Honestly, I wouldn't expect anything less," I mock, just before he places a sweet, lingering kiss on my lips as his hand slides up my body and cups my breast. Folgers has nothing on Ethan Rochester. Morning sex is now the best part of waking up.

I sink into the taste of him, his hands exploring my body as our legs intertwine together and a noise from the hallway has us parting.

"Shit," he whispers.

He turns his body just as the door swings open. Scrambling, I quickly pull the sheet up to my chin as I stare at an older woman with salt and pepper hair, and a soft, sweet face. Her cheekbones are high, and I can tell she was really beautiful when she was younger, but time has been good to her. She makes eye contact with me then looks over at Ethan who gives no fucks that he's naked. The sheet covers the lower half of his body and instead of trying to hide from her, he places his hands behind his head.

"Well, good morning to you, too," he says to her with a sly smile on his lips, and something about their expressions makes me think this isn't the first time this woman has caught him in bed with someone.

She crosses the room and smacks him across the head. "I know your mama taught you some manners. Now you gonna introduce us or what?"

My cheeks burn, and I'm shocked as she reaches her arm across Ethan's naked body to shake my hand.

"Honey, my name is Millie. I'm Ethan's favorite aunt."

"My only aunt." Ethan snorts.

I grab her hand in mine and shake it, making sure to keep my breasts covered. "I'm Vada."

"Well, it's nice to meet you, Vada. Sorry, my inconsiderate nephew forgot his manners this morning. Must have had a *late* night." She looks him up and down. "Get dressed. I'll meet you downstairs. Don't keep me waitin'."

Millie turns and gives me a sweet smile before leaving the room. I can hear the stairs creak with each step she takes.

"What the hell was that?" I ask with a nervous laugh, pulling the sheets tighter against my naked body.

He turns toward me and wraps an arm around my waist, pulling my body to his. "Sorry, that's Aunt Millie. She likes to come over unannounced sometimes. But usually there's not a woman in my bed, so I'm sure I'll have some explainin' to do." He grins, pressing a quick kiss against my cheek. "Get dressed and meet us downstairs. I'm pretty sure she'll be cooking something, and Aunt Millie doesn't like it when people let her food get cold. Don't get on her bad side this early in the day. She's a grudge holder." Ethan winks at me before slipping on a pair of jogging pants and leaving me alone in his room.

I sit quiet and still and can hear her muffled voice along with Ethan's. Scanning the room, I search for my clothes and remember they were in the other room. Wrapping the sheet around my body, I hurry down the hall, open the door, and find them in a crumpled pile on the floor. I tiptoe across the worn wooden boards and glance over and see Wilma staring at me with her judgmental cat eyes. Each time I look at her, I think of my Oliver at home. He's a long-haired Siamese I rescued a few years ago. Most of the time, he's the only thing I talk to during the day. He's pretentious, but I think Wilma may have him beat on many other levels.

"Don't look at me like that," I whisper-hiss at her. "I'm not peeing on your territory."

Her tail flicks a few times before she turns around and prances down the stairs. I can hear the bell on her collar ring out, almost mocking me.

After I slip on my clothes, I find the bathroom and wash my face and freshen up. I'm sure more than enough time has passed beyond just getting dressed, but I try to work up the courage to face them both downstairs as if nothing happened between us. But considering his aunt now saw us naked in his bed, there's no story that can cover up what happened last night. Oh, God. I wrinkle my nose. *Does his room smell like sex and shame?*

I run my fingers through my hair until it's halfway workable and throw it up into a messy knot before taking the stairs down and walking into the kitchen. Ethan's leaning against the counter showcasing his bare chest and hard muscles with a cup of coffee in his hand. His hair is a mess, but he easily swipes a hand through it, making it look as desirable as always. His lips move, flashing his perfect white teeth, and soon he's laughing at something and so is Millie.

"So, Vada," Millie drawls in a deeper accent than Ethan's. She pours coffee into one of his beautiful mugs and hands it to me. "Ethan tells me you're an author and write those romance books I like to read."

My cheeks heat and my eyes go wide. I met this woman ten minutes ago, naked in her nephew's bed, and now the only thing she knows about me is that I write steamy romance. Worst first impression ever.

"Actually, I told her you write smutty romance books," Ethan corrects with a grin. "But she knew what I was talking about. Millie's a dirty old woman, so don't let her sweet face and southern drawl fool you," he warns, teasing us both. "She probably even has one of those red rooms of pain in her house."

I narrow my eyes at him, and I'm halfway certain Millie is going to slap him upside the head again, but instead, she sets a plate in front of me with the breakfast works—bacon, eggs, and toast. Ethan sits next to me and smiles as Millie works around this kitchen like she owns the place, setting out salt, pepper, butter, and jelly in the middle of the table.

"I do like those romance books. An old woman like me can use as much loving she can get, even if it's through fiction. I love me some Danielle Steele and that E.L. James," she laughs, pretending to fan herself. "Ethan dear, you talk about the red room of pain as if you've read *Fifty Shades*."

He shuts up, which only causes me to burst into laughter.

"Did you really read it?" I ask, intrigued, and remember our safe word conversation from last night. He *totally* did.

"He likes to act like he's some hotshot, but I'm pretty sure I saw a few copies of it floating around the studio," Millie tells me matter-of-factly. "And, he has a *Fifty Shades of Grey* inspired mug, too."

"I was capitalizing, Aunt Millie. *Research.* And honestly, who hasn't read it? The FedEx guy told me he read it five times," he tells her, talking with his mouth full.

"Ethan Booker Rochester! I know your mama taught you better manners than talking with a mouth full of food." She scolds him like he's twelve, and it warms my heart that she doesn't take his shit either.

"Booker?" I arch a brow, teasingly.

"Family name," he explains, shrugging.

"Never would've taken you for a romance reader," I tease. "You seem more like the kind of guy who *prefers* pictures."

Millie smiles and sips her coffee, eyeing the two of us behind her mug. "So what's the story between you two anyway?"

I was waiting for her to ask. Actually, I'm surprised it took her this long. Curiosity fills her face, and I continue eating, focusing on my food, not really sure what to say.

"She's renting the cottage while she finishes her manuscript. Apparently, she's on a major deadline and came here for inspiration. I think she may have found it, Aunt Millie." Ethan pops an eyebrow up at me, and before I can even respond to his sexual innuendo, Millie continues with her questions.

"So you're one of Ethan's tenants?" Millie's trying to piece together the clues of why we were naked in bed this morning. She raises her eyebrows and waits for me to respond.

"Yes, that's correct." I clear my throat and speak up. "I'm from Chicago."

"Okay," she says, her smile not faltering a bit. "Well, you two look like you've hit it off pretty quick. Ethan is a good boy, though sometimes he can be...arrogant."

"Aunt Millie! I am most certainly *not*," Ethan protests as he laughs.

She playfully rolls her eyes at him. "You know, I don't like to use those swear words because it's not ladylike, but many people, especially those of the opposite sex, believe you are." She looks at me, then whispers, "The ladies are always chasing him, but he's too busy shooing them away."

"So you're gonna blast all my secrets to Vada, are you?" He pushes himself off the counter and pours himself more coffee. "I see how it's going to be."

Millie winks at me, and I can't help but smile as she removes my empty plate. I realize I do need to get to the cottage to write. My laptop is calling me, and inspiration is basically bursting from my fingertips. I'm still smiling thinking about all the words I'm about to write. I haven't felt this excited to work in weeks.

"I should probably get to the studio. I've got some things I need to take care of before lunch," Ethan says, giving Millie a sweet kiss on her cheek.

I stand, taking that as my cue to leave. "Thank you for breakfast. I really enjoyed it. It was nice to meet you."

"It was so nice meeting you, darling. Now, don't you be a stranger for the rest of the week. Remember to come out every once in a while to eat and give Ethan a dose of his own medicine." She walks over to me and opens her arms to pull me into a big hug. I'm not expecting this at all, so I awkwardly hug her back. Southerners —I seriously love their friendliness—but I'm not used to it. Before I head out, I grab my cup and refill it with coffee.

"Bye," I say with a small wave. "Thanks again for everything." I smile at Millie before glancing over at Ethan who's watching me with heat in his eyes.

His dark hair stacks on his head, and I have the urge to run my fingers through it. My body knows what it had and wants more— lots more. I swallow hard, a small smile playing on my lips as I replay last night before I turn around and leave.

Walking across the cobblestone that leads to the cottage, I hold my mug with a death grip and hope Ethan's huge cock doesn't come after me again. Just the thought makes me laugh.

I walk into the cottage and set my coffee down next to my closed laptop. I quickly change into something more comfortable and pull all my long hair up into a messy bun. Once I'm back in my writing uniform, I settle into the chair and prepare to kick my manuscript's ass.

After opening my laptop, I crack my fingers and read the last chapter I had written. Yesterday I struggled hard, and today I'm laughing at the cursor that's mocked me for the past few months.

As soon as my fingers hit the keys, the words fly out in sentences, paragraphs, then pages. Hours pass, and I can't seem to pull away from writing, not right now, when I'm pouring my heart and soul into the pages, but I know I need to take a break.

Considering I've been here for four days already, I know I need to call Nora and check on everything back home. It's been a while since I've left the house for longer than a weekend.

I stand up and stretch, allowing every vertebrae in my back to pop. That's when I realize how sore I actually am, and the only person to blame is Ethan. Pacing, trying to stretch my legs, I grab my phone and hit Nora's number.

The line rings over and over, and before I hang up, she picks up the phone.

"Hey, Nora," I say with a smile on my face, trying to be as friendly as possible because sometimes she can be a grump. But that's why I love her.

She groans then chuckles. "I was napping, Vada."

"At ten in the morning?" I know she's giving me shit, like usual.

"When you're retired, it's always nap time," she informs me. "So what can I help you with? And before you can even ask, the cat is still alive. I've been feeding him every day and following the psychotic instructions you left for me."

"Have you been giving him his treats? The beef ones in the plastic container by the coffee maker," I remind her for probably the fourth time. Oliver is particular with his treats and doesn't really care for the seafood ones. I'm pretty sure he can sniff out artificial fish flavor from a mile away.

"Yes, but he snubs me each time I walk in and realizes it isn't you. I'm pretty sure he hates me." I can hear Nora opening and closing cabinets. If I close my eyes, I can imagine her pulling one of her favorite mugs with some sarcastic saying on it from the cabinet and pouring a cup of coffee. When I hear her sip loudly, I know that's exactly what she was doing.

"He can just sense when an angry old lady walks into the room," I reply, trying to get a laugh from her.

"Oh, I'm sure he can." She groans. "What's up with you? You sound...*different*." She waits for me to speak, and I wonder if she can tell something's up. She's over thirty years older than me and has this crazy mother's intuition when it comes to my life. Though she's grumpy and sarcastic most of the time, I love her like a crazy aunt. When I'm lonely or need plot help, she listens and gives me advice when I need it. Now that I think about it, Nora may be my only friend at home. I really need to get out more.

"Uh..." I stare out the window toward the house and images of the night flash through my memory like photographs. "Actually," I begin, clearing my throat, "I had sex. And not just boring, old married couple missionary sex either. Really *good* sex."

"What? I didn't hear you. Old age, remember?" She snickers.

I roll my eyes and speak louder. "I had sex last night, and it was amazing."

"If I could figure out how to use this damn iPhone, I'd tell you to text me a picture of Mr. Wonderful."

I laugh. "He's actually the type I stay away from, which is shocking."

She knows exactly what type I'm talking about—that I'll dump-you-in-a-day type.

"Ahh," is all she offers. Nora knows intricate details about my past relationships, why they didn't work out, and how I've been unable to have a long-term relationship in years.

"It's a no-strings attached kind of thing," I explain, and can just imagine her shaking her head in disdain, giving me that salty look she's known for before she breaks into a knowing smile.

"I'm sure it would have to be considering you're due home in three days, but you're young and beautiful. It's about time you had a little fun. Just make sure to leave your heart at the door or on the floor, well, unless you were on the floor." She pauses as I release a chuckle. "Anyway, you know what I mean. Just don't get hurt, kid. You know I kinda like you like the daughter I never had."

"Kinda? Well thanks, Nora. It's just some adult fun. I mean, what could really happen in three days?"

She laughs. "Ask Cinderella. And just to be clear, you're staying on deadline, right? If your agent found out you weren't writing and was…"

"Hardy har har," I say. "Yes, I'm on track. But speaking of, I need to get back to work. Thanks for taking care of Oliver. Kiss him for me."

She makes a noise. "Yuck. And get cat hair all over me? No, thank you. Keep me updated, and call me if you need anything, okay?"

"Thanks, Nora. I will." We hang up, and I immediately get back to work. I write until I've finished five more chapters—a new personal record that I couldn't be prouder of. Over eight thousand words have been added to my manuscript, and if I have a few more days like this, I'll finally be on schedule. But I'm trying not to jinx myself or creativity. I suck in a deep breath and look out the window and realize it's almost four in the afternoon. Though I want to keep writing, I force myself to take a break because my stomach won't stop growling, and I need to eat. Instead of scheduling an Uber and going out, I decide to shower, then sneak over to Ethan's and raid his fridge. Surprisingly enough, I don't feel a bit guilty about it.

CHAPTER TWELVE

ETHAN

AFTER HOLDING a meeting with the interns at the studio and setting up for the live preview event I'm hosting this weekend, I decide to call it a day and head home. Admittedly, I'm anxious to see Vada again.

As soon as I walk in, I smell something coming from the kitchen. Once I walk down the hallway and round the corner, I hear sizzling food. Vada's working around the kitchen, completely lost in her own world only wearing a tight tank top and skimpy shorts. Not making her aware of my presence, I lean against the door and cross my arms as I watch her shuffling carefree in front of the stove. I can't help but think how different things might be between us if she didn't live hundreds of miles away and if I didn't have a closet of baggage.

She turns around and gasps when she sees I've been watching her.

"Jesus!" She presses a hand to her chest as she breathes heavily.

"I'm sorry," I say with a smile. "Not too often is there a beautiful woman in my kitchen cooking *me* dinner."

Vada places a hand on her hip with a spatula between her fingers. "I wasn't cooking dinner for you." Her cute laugh gives her away.

Crossing the room, I peek in the skillet and see several hamburger patties. "So you're going to eat a quadruple burger?" I raise my brows, knowing she's full of shit. "I'd actually like to watch that. Love a woman with an *appetite*."

She laughs. "Yeah, a *sexual* appetite."

"Obviously. Because I'm an all-you-can-eat buffet, babe." I look her up and down, taking my time on her curves and breasts before meeting her eyes. A smile touches her lips, and her eyebrow pops up.

"Really? How much does that cost?" She chuckles.

"Just one night." I'm tempted to lean her against the counter and devour her for dinner, but considering the macaroni is about to boil over, I wait. After turning off the burner, she finishes up and carefully places the food on two plates.

Before sitting down, I grab her cheeks in my palms, lean in, and brush my lips against hers. Closing my eyes, I focus on her mouth as I run my fingers through her hair noticing how much she smells like vanilla and coffee. Vada melts against my touch, and for a moment I'm lost in the sweet taste of her. Grabbing her bottom lip between my teeth, I tug and suck on it before barely inching away from her mouth. I steady her as she looks at my lips with hooded eyes.

"Sorry, I've been thinking about doing that all damn day."

"All right, Casanova. Let's eat," she whispers. "Before it gets cold, please."

"Only because you asked nicely. Maybe you'll end up learning some manners after all. I have to warn ya though, those damn yankees aren't used to it," I tease with a wink as I add mayonnaise to my bread.

We eat while making small talk, and I realize how much I need to have her, taste her again. I'm a greedy bastard, but our time is limited.

The hamburger basically melts in my mouth. I can't remember the last time someone, other than my mom or Aunt Millie, cooked for me. It's a nice surprise.

"Dinner is delicious, by the way. Who knew writers were decent in the kitchen, too?"

"We are a species of many talents," she gloats.

"Well, I appreciate it. Sure beats the PB&J sandwich I was going to make."

She flashes me a genuine smile while taking the smallest bite of macaroni and cheese.

"So did you get a lot written today?" I ask, honestly curious.

"Actually." She clears her throat and smiles. "I did."

"Well, that's why you came here, right?"

"Yeah, it must be the country livin' or something," she says without cracking a smile, although we both know the inside joke to that.

She grins, and I can't deny how excited I get when I see her smile.

"Glad to hear it." I smirk. "Mac 'n cheese, good choice."

"I would've cooked veggies or something healthy as a side, but you've got macaroni and cheese for days, probably months," she says, changing the subject.

"My mama likes to make sure I'm eating. Between her and Aunt Millie, I've got enough to feed a football team."

"Or an army," she adds, which causes me to chuckle. There were several dinners missed as I worked until the sun came up. I completely engulfed myself with learning and becoming better at my craft. Work became nonstop, which is why Aunt Millie continues to randomly bring me food. She was never able to have kids of her own, so she's always treated me like a son.

My mama and her both knew I was wasting away in this house. After I lost everything that ever meant a damn to me, what was I supposed to do? This was the home Alana and I shared and the last place we were together.

Though the smell of her has faded with the years, sometimes when I'm trying to fall asleep, I can hear her voice asking if everything is okay. Losing Alana broke me into a million different pieces that can never be put back together. Though years have passed, I'll never be the man I used to be. Life didn't prepare me for the day I lost my best friend, wife, and lover. Nothing could have. Where love once lived, there's nothing but emptiness. That old saying, *It's better to have loved and lost than to not have loved at all*, is total bullshit.

I'm lost in my thoughts, but Vada somehow pulls me from my mind fuck memories.

"Maybe you should give those who rent the cottage a box of mac 'n cheese as a rental warming gift?" She laughs.

"Might need to send them all home with you, because I wouldn't be surprised if you sit at your computer eating a jar of Nutella with your finger when you have a book due," I say, trying to finish my burger, recalling her bad eating habits when she's on deadline.

"Ha! That's pretty accurate actually. One time I finished an entire jar of peanut butter in a week. Kept it by my laptop, and each time I took a break, I'd eat a few spoonfuls."

"I didn't realize you loved nuts so much. Should've though." I chuckle, which earns me a playful, much deserved eyeroll.

After we're finished with dinner, Vada places our plates in the sink. As I stand, she looks at me over her shoulder with a smile as if she knows I'm about to claim her as mine for the night.

"I really have to finish this one chapter." She interrupts the dirty thoughts streaming through my head.

I run my tongue along my lower lip, and her eyes follow. She's officially under my trance. "How long do you need?"

As she glances down at my hardness, I adjust myself. My dick wants more of what it had last night, and I'm not protesting. In fact, I'm fucking dying to be back inside her.

"An hour," she says. "Then I think I'll need a refill of inspiration."

"You mean more of my cock?" I cross my arms over my chest and laugh when she squirms.

"Are you always so direct?" she asks, turning her body around to face me.

"What do you think?" I inch closer to her, my breath crawling over her skin, which causes her to shiver. Her mouth falls open when she feels my length against her leg.

"I can see the anaconda is back. Should probably get going before I get a snake bite." She chuckles.

"Oh, Vada," I drawl. "You've already been bitten, and there's no antivenom that can save you from me now." I hum against her ear, lightly brushing my fingers across the bare skin on her stomach.

"Holy shit…" she whispers, her eyes fluttering closed, and I can feel her melt against me.

I lean in, pinching the skin of her neck between my teeth then trace the shell of her ear with my mouth. "Go write your chapter." I glance at my phone, then set a timer. "One hour."

I know by the flush color of her cheeks and how her nipples stand at full attention, that she's forcing herself to go write, which makes me smile. She may only be here for a few more days, but I'm going to try to make the most of it. I'll give her an hour, but just one, then she'll get exactly what she wants and needs to finish that damn book.

Once Vada rushes to the cottage, Wilma pounces down the stairs, and I place some wet food in her bowl. She stretches as if she's playing hard to get with her food.

"Stop showing off," I tell her and receive a sweet meow in response. Bending over, I pet her before she walks to her bowl because she can't be bothered when she's eating. I climb the stairs two at a time and head for the shower because I'm sweaty from working so hard at the studio today. As soon as the warm water hits my body, I allow myself to relax. I understand what Vada means when she talks about being wound up real tight. We're more alike than she knows.

As I wash over my muscles, I think back to the conversation I had with Millie this morning.

"Didn't think you allowed women to stay the night. It was one of your unspoken bachelor rules or something." She pushed for confirmation as she pulled eggs and bacon from the fridge.

"Aunt Millie, please," I begged, pulling a coffee cup out of the cabinet. *It was weird talking about my sex life with my aunt, but she always liked to pry and keep up with me considering I haven't settled down after Alana. Don't plan on committing to anyone either and that drives her insane.*

"You know why I'm here, hon. I wanted to make sure you're doing okay." She looked at me with concern written on her face.

"I'm fine, seriously." Though I'm not, and she could see right through it.

I place my hand against the shower wall and stand there until the water runs cold, which forces me to get out and dry off. So much can happen in a short amount of time, and when my life was turned upside down, then completely destroyed, I realized that. Most people say time makes it easier, but that couldn't be more wrong. Usually, I try to stay busy, keep my head down, my heart guarded, and my mind somewhere else. This is why I planned a big live demo for this specific weekend at the studio because being around people helps keep my thoughts away from the darkness that tends to haunt me. Another reason why Vada is a Godsend. She's the perfect distraction and might be the only thing keeping me from self-destructing.

I try to push the thoughts out of my head and think of something else because my mood is turning sour quickly. Looking down at my phone, I notice I have thirty minutes before I can forget everything that's swirling through my head and focus purely on Vada. *And in Vada.*

After I'm dressed, I make the climb up the stairs to the tower. The warm glow from the lights reflect below, and from a distance, I'm sure the tower shines like a beacon in the darkness. I try to clean up a bit, but I can't seem to focus. The kiln is full of mugs I made earlier in the week and won't be ready for another twenty-four hours. However, as I look around the room, I can't help but feel a tug at my heart. So much has changed, but some things are exactly the same—this room being one of them.

Before I get too caught up, my phone vibrates in my pocket, and I know time's up. I turn it off, climb down both sets of stairs, and walk through the back door. As I cross the garden, I see Vada sitting at the desk in front of the window of the cottage. Her fingers are flying against the keys, and she barely stops. Chuckling, I wait until I see her fingers come to a halt. While she reads over what she wrote, her lips move, and when she finishes, she sits back and smiles. The look on her face is pure satisfaction. At this very moment, Vada is so happy, that it's contagious.

Taking this as my cue, I walk down the path leading to the cottage. Sucking in a deep breath, I knock three times on the door. I hear Vada rushing around inside, and when the door swings open, I give her a knowing smile.

"It's already been an hour?" she asks. The look on her face tells me she lost track of time.

I don't give her an answer but take a few steps forward, until our lips collide, causing waves of want to rush through me. Vada sighs against my mouth before coming in for more as I kick the door shut with my foot. Taking no time at all, she begins unbuttoning my pants, then unzipping them.

"I want you so fucking bad." She moans as she forces my shirt above my head.

"I'm supposed to be undressing you," I tell her, doing exactly that.

Within moments, our clothes are on the floor, and she's standing in front of me naked. Taking my time, I memorize her body with my hands and lips. Her head falls back on her shoulders as I place a perky nipple in my mouth. Kissing across her chest, I make sure to give the other the same attention. Threading her fingers through my hair, Vada lets out a greedy moan which only causes me to smile. She's ravenous, and I love it, especially when she pushes me down on the bed, like a savage, taking exactly what she wants. I pull the condom out of my pocket, and she takes it from my hand and rolls it down my shaft, then slides on top of me.

"Oh my fuck," I say, as she throws her head back, and rides me hard and long.

"Yes, yes," she mutters, taking full control. Her breasts bounce with each time she rocks from the tip down to the bottom of my shaft. Taking some sort of control back, I thumb her clit, which only drives her wilder.

I like this side of Vada, the woman who takes control and takes exactly what she wants.

She leans over, brushing her lips against mine. "Ethan, I'm about to come."

"Do it, babe. I love watching you."

Tossing her head back, her mouth falls open, and she rides me slow, rocking her hips in circles.

"Yes, don't stop," she begs sucking in air, enjoying every second as I circle her clit.

"Never," I whisper, secretly wishing this week wouldn't end as I watch her lose herself on top of me.

CHAPTER THIRTEEN

VADA

I FIND myself chasing the white rabbit, as curious as the young Alice from *Alice in Wonderland*, only to be transported to a world other than my own. I'm falling down a never-ending rabbit hole as Ethan forces me to forget all the beliefs I had about casual sex.

He has me second-guessing everything and doesn't even know it.

My eyes flutter open, and I watch him, watching me ride him. As I scratch my nails down his chest and let out moans loud enough the whole neighborhood can hear, I realize I've actually become the sex-crazed woman in my book. My body is fully his, in every sense, and with each thrust, I crumble to dust with him. The orgasm rocks and shakes me so greatly that it can't be measured on the Richter scale.

As I float back to reality, I topple on top of him. Ethan's lips trace mine, and I know by the soft look on his face, that he'll unravel at any moment. His heavy breaths in my ear combined with long, deep movements have my body screaming out in protest, but the problem is I want more of him, *all* of him. Knowing this will all end when I leave for Chicago, I try to memorize every inch of him. With my legs wrapped tightly around his hips, he grabs my ass and lifts me slightly, controlling every deep thrust, giving me everything he is.

"Harder," I whisper sinking on him, wanting him to rip me in two, so half of me can stay here while the other half returns home.

Without hesitation, he does exactly that.

"Fuck," Ethan pants. "Vada," he says one last time before his body seizes and finally relaxes. We briefly stay like that, the closest two human beings can possibly be, and oddly enough, it's comforting. Ethan gives me a long, needy kiss before pulling away.

Once we've cleaned up and caught our breaths, he crawls into bed and pulls me into his arms. The moment is so intimate that my heart does a quick flutter, which slightly confuses me. *Why am I feeling like this is becoming more than just sex?* I wrap my arm around his waist as his fingers draw circles on my bare skin. I try really hard to push the thoughts away, but it's like my mind wants to convince me that this feels different. It feels right. But it can't. As I rest my head on his chest with his arms wrapped tight around me, I'm fighting an internal battle that I'm not sure I'll win.

It's just sex. I try repeating it over and over, but my heart betrays me.

Swallowing hard, I look up into his honey-colored eyes, and smile. "I could get used to this, E," I admit, honestly, putting my heart out on the line.

As soon as the words leave my mouth, I regret them immediately. Ethan tenses and forces a smile, but I notice he's uneasy. His eyes narrow, saying so much, but hiding secrets. I can't tell if it's anger or sadness or a combination of the both, and it confuses me. I want to pry and ask questions, but instead, I offer an apology. Saying anything at all was stupid, especially when he's made it very clear that this is temporary and that he doesn't do relationships. Honestly, I don't know what I expected.

"I'm sorry," I whisper. "That came out wrong," is all I offer as an explanation. His heartbeat vibrates hard in his chest, and I feel like an idiot for saying those words aloud.

"Goodnight, Vada," he whispers, leaning over and turning off the lamp next to the bed, then pulling me back into position. Ethan holds me tight as if he doesn't want to let me go. I fall asleep in his arms, listening to the rhythmic beat of his heart.

I roll over and reach for Ethan, only to wake up to an empty, cold bed. There's nothing but crumpled sheets and a blanket where his body was just hours ago. Still half-asleep, I sit up and look around the room, hoping to see him here still. My clothes are exactly where I left them last night, but Ethan's aren't. I didn't realize waking up alone after a night like that would leave me feeling so empty. Instantly, my mind goes to a negative place, but I try not to allow my insecurities to get the best of me.

After I stretch, I head for the shower hoping it will relax my muscles and mind. It feels as if I did gymnastics all night, but I guess in a roundabout way I did. My body is definitely not used to this.

The water somewhat calms me and does exactly what I want, but I can't help but think about my past and all the bad relationships I've experienced over the years. Trying as hard as I can, I push those thoughts away while I dry off and get dressed.

Once I feel somewhat normal again, I work up the courage to head over to Ethan's just to make sure everything is okay. I mean, I know this is purely physical, and I shouldn't be concerned, but I am. Last night as we were falling asleep after I said what I was thinking, he immediately tensed up. It wasn't the first time my honesty has ruined a good moment and knowing me, I'm sure it won't be the last.

As I walk down the path that leads to his house, I see Henry coming at me at a full sprint.

"Shit. Go away, Henry!" I scream and run toward the back door, somehow making it in before he can attack me.

I look out the window of the back door, and he's standing there, looking straight into my eyes.

"You're an asshole," I say to him as he pecks around, agitating me.

I suck in a deep breath, turn around, and listen. The house is quiet, but coffee has been brewed, and there are dishes in the sink. I close my eyes tight and open them before I decide to make my way up the stairs. For some reason, my heart is pounding hard in my chest. My adrenaline spikes as I reach the second floor.

"Ethan?" I whisper and wait. I don't hear anything, so I walk to his room and open the door. The bed is perfectly made, so I doubt he came back and went to sleep. Just as I'm turning to walk up the second set of stairs that lead to the tower, I notice the door I've never gone through is partially open. I've been in the bathroom, guestroom, and bedroom, so this room has me intrigued. Knowing I should walk past it and respect his privacy, curiosity gets the best of me. Instead, I stop, place my fingers around the wooden door and slightly push it open until I can peek inside.

My mouth goes dry when I see a light pink painted room with a dark wooden baby crib on one side. The walls are decorated with pictures and vinyl cut-outs of Eiffel Towers, and when I look at the wall above the crib, I notice wooden-painted letters spelling the word, *Paris*. A rocking chair sits in the corner facing the big bay window with a cute nightstand next to it. There's a changing table and dresser on the other side. It's obvious this is a nursery and a gorgeous one at that, but confusion ripples through me because I know Ethan doesn't have a child.

"What the fuck are you doing?" an angry voice growls from behind and startles me.

I still and turn my body toward him. He moves around me, grabs the doorknob and slams the door shut.

"I'm sorry, I…" I begin, but I have no words to explain the reason why I opened that door other than being curious and wanting to know more about the man I'm sleeping with, but I know that's not a good enough reason. Seeing him look at me now, I feel like complete shit for invading his privacy and exposing a secret he's obviously been keeping.

"I think it's time for you to go back to the cottage, Vada." Ethan's voice is monotonous and firm, which pierces straight through my heart. The man standing in front of me isn't the same man I've come to know. The look in his eyes says everything his words don't. He's pissed. I try to reach out to him, but instead, he turns and walks to the stairs that lead to the tower without giving me a second glance.

Minutes pass, and I stand there completely shocked and upset. I want to tell him how sorry I am, but I've learned to give people their space and calm down, though it's not always an easy thing to do. Like a dog with its tail tucked between its legs, I walk down the stairs, through the back door, and across the path until I'm standing inside the cottage.

Emotions swirl through me, and I wish he weren't so upset.

I sit on the edge of the bed and thoughts from my past come rushing in full force.

The rain poured down in buckets as I walked the few blocks home from school. I'd taken a half day and skipped my afternoon classes to surprise my boyfriend for our one-year anniversary. Lucas and I had been living together for a few months, but I knew deep in my heart that at any moment he'd propose, and as soon as I graduated college, we'd get married and start the rest of our lives together. With a bag of Chinese food gripped in my hand and an umbrella in the other, I crossed the street and followed the sidewalk that led up to our apartment building. Once inside, I climbed the flights of stairs and walked down the hall with a cheesy grin on my face.

When I slid the key in the door, I thought I heard a woman's voice, but chalked it up to being exhausted. Once I opened the door, I noticed panties, a bra, a T-shirt, and blue jeans in a line on the floor. The Chinese food slipped from my grasp and slammed to the floor causing a mess. Moans echoed from our bedroom, and my first reaction was to leave, to pretend it wasn't happening because this had to be one big nightmare, but then the anger set in.

I walked down the hall until I was standing in the doorway watching my boyfriend fuck my best friend.

"Are you kidding me?" I screamed out. Horror and anger on my face.

Lucas pushed Emma from on top of him as she tried to hurry and hide her body. Guilt and shame covered them both.

"Get the fuck out," I said in an oddly calm voice. "Both of you, get out right now. I can't stand looking at either of you." I stood my ground, not allowing my emotions to take hold though I felt like I was dying inside. The two people I loved the most betrayed me in the bed I've slept in since I was a kid.

I watched Emma as she wrapped the sheet around her body, not making eye contact as she walked past me and picked up her clothes from the floor.

"Vada, baby. It's not what you think. Emma means nothing to me. I love you," Lucas begged with his dick in his hand—literally.

"So did Emma just fall on your dick or what? Because I'm a little

confused as to why you're fucking my best friend in our bed after everything I've done for you while you go to law school. You make me sick!" I hissed at him, years of trust issues coming full circle.

He walked over to me, pleading, telling me how much of a mistake it was, but I couldn't listen to his lies anymore. I turned around and walked away. After he realized I wasn't taking his bullshit, he packed a bag of clothes and left. I watched as the two of them walked in the rain together toward her car that was parked a few blocks away. I should've realized everything wasn't perfect like I had built in my head. Our relationship was based on lies and broken promises, and I was the stupid girl who believed it was going to be my happily ever after.

After that day, I promised myself I'd never let that happen to me again.

Lucas was smart, but also one of those bad boy types. He lured me in with his charm and hot body. He was also a big flirt, so I shouldn't have been surprised, but in my mind, I created this faux hope that he was different.

I've always been attracted to the wrong guys. Even though deep down, I knew they meant trouble and heartbreak. I'm sure Dr. Phil would have a field day psychoanalyzing my attraction to men who are most likely to cheat, lie, and break my heart. After watching the way my father lied and manipulated my mother, it's somehow the only thing I know. What would Freud say? Daddy issues, no doubt.

Lucas, Jason, Brett, Tyler, and Todd. Hell, my ex list is as long as Taylor Swift's.

Lucas was a cheater. *Bastard.*

Jason was a liar and thief. *Money from my wallet just miraculously vanished every time he was around.*

Brett was an alcoholic. *Jack Daniels was a better match for him anyway.*

Tyler was a womanizer. *Apparently charming and sexy are my weaknesses.*

Todd, well, he was gay. *At least he made a great shopping partner.*

I could probably write the lyrics to a breakup song with my track record.

I'll be the first to admit I have trust issues, but how could I not? From as far back as I could remember, he'd verbally abused my mother, and worse, she just took it. He'd drink and lie about it. I swore to myself, that no matter what if a man or anyone ever spoke to me or treated me the way he did her, I would stand up for myself.

And better—I'd fucking walk away.

That didn't leave a lot of room for a meaningful relationship to form.

Many nights I buried myself in books hoping I wouldn't hear him screaming. Reading saved my life. It helped transport me into a world that didn't include my father berating my mother. In books, I found adventure and love and kindness, everything I was missing in my everyday life. Ultimately, reading later inspired me to become a writer and create worlds far better than my own.

As an adult, words became my escape as well, but in a different way. Though the world may be filled with loveless assholes and men who can't give me a happy ending, at least in my books there's always love and happily ever afters.

I stand up, realizing I'm hungry but too embarrassed to go back over to Ethan's. Going to my suitcase, I dig for the extra protein bars I packed for this trip. Once I find one, I go to my laptop and turn it on. I'm in a bad mood. Inspiration has left, but I put my fingers on the keys anyway because these words aren't going to write themselves. I go up one paragraph and read what I wrote before Ethan barged in and stole my breath away.

He looks at her across the small room and moves to her in one quick motion.

"I love you," he whispers across the shell of her ear, causing her to shiver.

Smiling, she bites her bottom lip and whispers the words back to him. How could two star-crossed lovers find their way back to one another so easily? Knowing this might be her last chance to spill her heart before leaving, she goes to him, and presses her lips so softly against his and steals the words that were teetering on his tongue.

Is it possible to be jealous of fictional characters? I'm half-tempted to delete what I've written in this chapter and tear the two lovers apart, only to leave the reader as heartbroken and confused as I am. However, instead of doing something rash, I pick up my phone and schedule an Uber.

When I walk out of the cottage, I look up at the tower and see Ethan staring out the window on the other side. I'm glad his back is to me because I don't think I could look him in the eye without feeling some sort of guilt or awkwardness.

He never mentioned having a daughter, so a nursery was the last thing I expected to see when I opened the door. Having a child means he got someone pregnant and knowing his record, it could've been from a one-night stand, or maybe it was from an actual long-term relationship. If it's with an ex he loved, and they had a child together, maybe that relationship is strained, so he doesn't have custody? Or maybe he only sees his daughter every other week? Different scenarios play in my head, wondering how he could've never mentioned it to me. I know it's not as if he lied to me because we weren't supposed to get personal, but I crossed the line the moment I opened the door that led to his daughter's room. If I could take it back, I would. The look on his face is one I won't forget. His furrowed brows, his intense stare, and his cold tone. He was furious, and everything about his stance and words told me he couldn't trust me. That hurts the most.

Ethan's a broken soul, and while I want to dig deeper, I can't help but feel like I've worn out my welcome.

Dread washes over me as his body turns, and I rush through the garden and hop inside the car that's waiting by the curb.

I don't know where I'm going, but I need to get away and clear my mind.

The countdown until I leave for Chicago begins now.

CHAPTER FOURTEEN

ETHAN

She called me *E*, and it nearly destroyed me. I was seconds away from crumbling.

It's been too long since I heard the nickname Alana used. Considering the anniversary of her death is upon me, waiting to destroy me from the inside out, it was too much to hear coming from Vada's voice.

As soon as I tensed and turned to flick the lights off, I knew she could tell something was bothering me. She assumed it was what she said about getting used to this—us being together—hell, she even apologized for saying it, but I was too lost in my own head to speak.

She didn't know that being called E was the nickname my late wife had for me; she couldn't have, considering I haven't divulged that part of my life to her. It was nothing more than a coincidence, and I wish I could go back and tell her my reaction had nothing to do with her and everything to do with my past, but I was caught off guard.

After Vada falls asleep in my arms, I slide out of bed, put on my clothes, and quietly leave. For hours, I sit in the tower and replay my life and all the events that led me to this very moment. I sit long enough to watch the sun barely peek over the horizon. Pink and purple hues paint across the sky in long painters' wisps, and I feel like I'm smothering in my thoughts to the point where I need some fresh air.

Putting on my shoes, I grab the keys to my car because driving sometimes helps clear my mind. I head down familiar streets, but nothing looks the same. Though I have nowhere to go, I follow pavement until I'm driving under the Magnolia Cemetery archway. As soon as I pull in, a heavy weight presses on my chest.

Every year on this day I visit, even though it brings me back to all those memories and makes me miss them even more. It was hard to come here at first, especially that first year, but after a few times, it became a little easier. Though being here will never be considered easy.

Sucking in a deep breath, I park at the edge of the street and walk across the plush grass to the oak trees by the river. As soon as I see the black marble of Alana's headstone, I almost fall to my knees.

No matter how much time passes, seeing their names engraved in stone always brings me back to the moment in the hospital when I found out Alana was gone. The only sliver of happiness I felt was knowing I had a piece of Alana in Paris until my sweet baby girl passed away soon after.

The pain in my heart is almost too much to bear as I read their names, *Alana and Paris Rochester,* together. Burying my wife and child made me second guess everything about life, especially the *whys*.

"My girls," I whisper softly, tracing their names with my finger on the cool stone. It was never supposed to be like this. We were supposed to have a handful of kids and grow old and happy together in our house on the small hill by the creek. I was supposed to watch my daughter take her first steps, hear her say her first words, watch her play at the playground, and go to her first day of kindergarten.

So many things that were taken from me.

I'll forever be robbed of those memories and of ones I'll never be able to experience. Her walking across the stage to graduate high school, driving her to college, and eventually walking her down the aisle.

Covering my face with my hands, I try to get a hold of myself, but it's a losing battle. The *should-have-beens* are enough to drive me crazy.

Sitting here under the oak tree is the only time I allow myself to fully give in to what happened. At the funerals, I was in a perpetual state of shock. Hell, for the last five years I have been. Most of the time, I try to keep my pain and loss buried deep. But being here, like this, there's no escaping my reality. I'd give anything to be able to hold the two of them again.

The cool morning breeze brushes over my skin, and I wish it could take all the pain away, but it never does. When I'm here, it's as if time stands completely still.

"Aunt Millie says you'd want me to be happy." I wait as if I'm going to hear her voice speak back to me. Nothing but the wind rustling the leaves on the trees can be heard.

"I know deep in my heart you'd want me to be happy and continue living my life, but I don't know if I can. Every day, I think about you. I think about Paris. I think about what we could have had. Where the three of us would be right now at this very moment. The studio is everything you wished it would be. It's doing so well, and I know you'd be proud."

A single tear streams down my face and splashes on my hand. I didn't even realize I was crying. I tell myself that out here, it's okay to feel something. It's okay to let those emotions take ahold of me. I close my eyes and find what I'm trying to say.

"I met someone." I let out a stifled laugh. "And you'd love her. She doesn't take my shit or let me say whatever I want. Aunt Millie met her too and basically gave her approval, but you know how she is—she likes anyone who isn't afraid to call me out on my shit."

Many times, Aunt Millie and Alana would gang up against me, and I find myself smiling about it now. I know it's been five long years of trying to find a way to cope and heal the shattered pieces of my heart, but this is the first time I've ever spoken those words. Moving on—I've been against it. However, being here today, knowing Vada is back at the cottage waiting for me, feels different this time.

"I'll always love you and our baby, Alana." But I know she knew that. No matter what happens in my life, Alana and Paris will hold a special place in my heart—always and forever. Trying to pick up the pieces and move on doesn't mean I'll forget them. I have to remind myself this even though Mama has told me that a million times.

"I don't know what to do," I say, wishing she were here. "I just…I wish you could tell me that it was okay, that you'd want me to move on so I'd stop feeling guilty at the thought of it." I sit and wait, but not surprisingly, nothing miraculous happens. After a while, the sun beams down on my skin, and I know it's time to go. I look at the grave one more time before I walk back to my car.

By the time I make it home, I'm emotionally and physically exhausted. I sit on the couch and fall asleep thinking of her.

Alana walks through the kitchen with a smile on her face, leaning against the doorway. I rub my eyes, not believing what I'm seeing.

"I know I'm dreaming," I say.

Walking across the room, she sits next to me. I glance down and see the wedding ring on her finger, and somehow mine is there, too. Though I wore it for years after her death, I stopped wearing it when I almost lost it while working on a piece. I wanted to keep it close to me still, so I keep it in the drawer of my nightstand along with Paris' footprints.

She grabs my hand and gives me a wink. "Ethan," she says, in that tone I was so used to hearing.

I look into her blue eyes, pulling her into my arms, never wanting to wake, never wanting to let go.

She leans back, pulling us apart. "Vada seems like she's perfect for you. So what the hell are you waiting for, E? You have to live your life. You have to learn to be happy again, and you deserve to be."

"But…" I try to protest.

She places her finger on my lips and stops my words though I have so much to say. "You have to take a leap of faith."

I wake, my heart pounding rapidly in my chest. Sweat covers my brow, and I thought I heard her voice, here in the room with me. My throat is dry, and I replay the conversation so many times I feel like I'm losing my mind. I asked for a sign, or maybe my subconscious is playing tricks on me, but there it was, and it felt so real. This isn't the first time Alana has visited me in my dreams, but it's never been so vivid.

Needing a shower, I climb the stairs. As I round the corner, I'm shocked to see Vada in the hallway, staring into Paris' room. At first, I don't know what to say or do, so I stand there stunned. I'm not ready to talk about it just yet, not when I'm in this fragile state of mind.

As soon as the words fly out of my mouth and she turns around, it's obvious I took her by surprise. I slam the door shut and she immediately begins to apologize, but I shut her out and go to the tower. Closing myself tight doesn't solve anything, but I need this time to think. I need to find my words and tell her the truth, as hard as that's going to be, but I feel like she deserves to know. The only problem is, where do I even start?

Most people in the area know my backstory and how I was a widower before I turned twenty-five. Most of the women I bring home don't mention it or even allude they know. I was the talk of the town for a while, especially after Paris Pottery & Studio opened. It was my way of honoring my baby girl and wife. It was how I kept and continue to keep their spirit alive. People loved Alana's pottery, and before her belly got too big, she was quickly becoming a hometown sensation. Between Millie and Mama peddling Alana's mugs out of their trunks after church, the news of her work traveled quickly, but not as fast as her death. It rocked everyone who knew her.

It destroyed me.

After I have time to myself, I realize I acted like a complete asshole to Vada and guilt washes over me. Not that it's an excuse, but visiting the cemetery left my wounds freshly cut open, but that's not her fault. She has no idea how broken I've been over the years, and how she may be the glue that can put me back together. I feel that deep in my heart, so strongly, that it almost knocks me down. Vada came barreling into my life with that smart mouth and sass, and soon she'll be leaving to go back to Chicago. Time is running out, and like a dream, she'll be gone, too.

Just as I'm about to head to the cottage and apologize, I see Vada leave in a rush, and it wears on me. I don't want to seem crazy and call her since I have her number from the booking, so I wait. This is something that needs to be discussed in person anyway.

While she's gone, I take a shower and try to get some much-needed sleep. Once I'm rested, I brew some coffee then go back up into the tower, turn on some music, and busy myself in my work for hours.

Before dark, I hear a car door slam, and from the tower I see Vada walk across the sidewalk with a Starbucks cup in one hand and shopping bags in the other. I watch her go straight to the cottage, shut the door, and close the curtains. Feeling nervous, I wash the extra clay from my hands and find an ounce of courage as I go to her. Once I'm at the cottage door, I knock, but she doesn't answer.

"Okay then," I say, turning around and heading back to the house.

"Ethan?" I immediately turn around and notice a towel wrapped tightly around her body, accentuating her curves. The late summer breeze carries the smell of her strawberry soap, which causes me to smile.

I walk toward her, but she stands in the doorway with her arms holding the towel. Water drips from the tips of her hair, and she smells so damn good. Vada looks me up and down, noticing the clay on my pants and shirt, and she almost takes a step back.

"I've got a lot of explainin' to do," I tell her, hoping she'll hear me out.

"You don't owe me anything, Casanova. I was the one who violated your space," she says, timidly, and I hate I've made her feel that way.

"Well, I *do* owe you an apology. I'm sorry, Vada. I hope you forgive me for being a total and utter asshole today. There's a lot on my mind, but that's no excuse for how I treated you. You don't deserve that—ever," I reassure her because it's the truth.

Her shoulders relax, and she slightly smiles. "Apology accepted."

"Do you have plans tomorrow night?" I slyly ask.

She looks at me like I've lost my mind. "Other than trying to write a book, my schedule's wide open."

"I'd be obliged if you'd accompany me on a date tomorrow night around seven," I say over insinuating my drawl and tipping my imaginary hat in her direction.

Now she's really looking at me like I'm crazy. "Seriously?"

"Yes, ma'am. Serious as eating ribs on the Fourth of July."

Her laughter echoes through the garden. "Actually, I think I might need to wash my hair tomorrow night around that time."

I take a few steps closer; our bodies are almost touching. "I'm not the type of man to beg…"

"Bad boys never beg," she says right before our lips softly meet.

As she kisses me, the worry melts away. The anxiety of everything swirling in my head temporarily disappears. In this moment, it's just me and Vada, and I'm thankful she makes me forget that gut-wrenching pain, even if she has no idea.

CHAPTER FIFTEEN

VADA

"I haven't been on a real date in years. I don't know what to wear," I tell Nora over the phone because she's my go-to in situations like this. Actually, she's my only person considering I don't have anyone to ask.

"Go sassy with a touch of slutty. Guys love that," she says matter-of-factly.

"Oh my God. How do you know that?" I let out a laugh, emptying my suitcase on the bed. Nora doesn't do dates, and the only time she gets out of the house is to go to the grocery store or visit her best friend. Considering the woman is in her mid-sixties, I imagine her version of slutty and mine are two totally different things.

"I watch a lot of television shows. I'm sure it's the same in real life," she tells me, amused with herself.

I roll my eyes, and I'm glad she can't see me because she'd totally call me out for it. "Okay, well hug Oliver for me, and tell him I'll see him soon. I'll call you in the morning and let you know how it goes," I say, trying to piece clothes together to make some sort of outfit that doesn't look like I'm going to bed or to the gym.

"You already know how I feel about him. And you better call me. You know I'll be up all night worrying about you otherwise."

"I'm sure you will. I promise I'll call." And I will. Nora cares about my life more than my own mother, and I'm happy someone does, even if she pretends to hate Oliver. Usually, my life is monotonous, and I live the same schedule over and over. To have some sort of action has got to be entertaining for her.

We say our goodbyes, and I throw my cell phone on the bed, right next to a sundress I bought on a whim yesterday while I was out. Slipping it on, and seeing how it fits in the full-length mirror, I know I've found a winner. Considering it's late summer in Charleston, the evenings are still warm so this will have to do. Pinning my hair to the side and putting on a hint of makeup, I sit down at my computer and am able to type a few pages before a knock echoes through the cottage, pulling me away.

Instantly, my heart flutters as I cross the room and open the door. Ethan greets me with a sexy smile wearing a blue, button-up shirt and slacks.

"You clean up nicely, Casanova."

Pulling me into his arms, our lips crash together, causing the butterflies inside me to swarm in circles. Taking our time, we kiss until our lips are swollen, until I feel like I can't breathe. There was a moment when I didn't think we'd make it out of the cottage.

"You're beautiful, Vada," he whispers across my lips, setting the tone of this date. Blush hits my cheeks as soon as Ethan tucks loose hair behind my ear, his fingertips grazing the softness of my neck. Once I close the cottage door, Ethan leads me down the sidewalk.

After seeing him, I feel completely underdressed for the occasion, and my nerves start to get the best of me.

"What?" I ask as he looks over at me with a smirk on his lips. I wait for his answer as we continue walking forward.

"Just thinking about taking that dress off you later," he teases, opening the door to his car for me. "Hope it wasn't expensive." He winks.

His words make me laugh and slightly relax. Once I'm inside the car, I take the moment to suck in a deep breath.

Ethan climbs in and buckles then starts the engine. "Everything okay?"

"Just nervous, I guess," I say honestly, buckling myself in.

"Don't worry. I left my cock at home," he teases, and all the worry I had of the evening melts away just like that.

We drive through town, and I'm confused when Ethan doesn't

slow. I turn to him, ready to ask where we're going once we cross the second bridge.

"I thought we'd go somewhere on the outskirts of town that's more intimate, away from all the touristy stuff," he explains when he notices my perplexed expression. "You can do that any day of the week."

"Oh, so I'm getting the exclusive Rochester treatment tonight?"

Ethan chuckles. "Babe, you've been getting that all week."

Soon we're pulling into the parking lot of a restaurant that's decorated with parts from old boats. Oars, anchors, and ropes are hung on the building, and when we step inside, I realize it's the entire theme of the place. I immediately fall in love with it. We're swiftly escorted through the quaint dining area onto the patio. Our table overlooks the white sand and dark blue water, and in the distance, I hear the waves crashing against the shore. Glancing over the candle that lights Ethan's face, I find myself smiling.

"This is perfect," I whisper to him, admiring his messy hair and the smirk on his lips. Though there's a few couples on the patio, it feels like it's only Ethan and me in this moment.

The waitress walks up, and Ethan orders everything down to my favorite wine.

She returns with a bottle of Cabernet and a basket of hot bread.

"How'd you know about the wine?" I ask.

"Google," he jokes.

"Oh, stop. You didn't Google me."

"I did," he admits, shamelessly. "Even ordered a few copies of your books to put on the shelf in the cottage for the other guests who rent it. Might actually update the Airbnb listing and tell them the world-famous Vada Collins wrote her upcoming bestselling novel there. It'll be as popular as the Stanley Hotel lobby in Stephen King's *The Shining*."

I actually snort. "I hope that works out for you. Could actually become a little cash cow of sorts. People will drive by and stop to take pictures with the cottage. I'll send you a headshot to hang on the wall." I wink.

Being like this with him feels so easy and natural. It's strange how a person can meet someone, and within a few days, it feels like old friends who've known each other for years.

Soon our food arrives, and I can't wait to dig into the Etoufee Flounder Ethan ordered us both. Apparently, it's a southern favorite, and I actually let out a moan when I take the first bite of fish. The sauce, mashed potatoes, everything is simply delicious.

"Told you," he says, noticing how much I love it.

"I'm never leaving Charleston," I kid as I take another bite.

"I wish you wouldn't," Ethan says, his tone more serious than before.

His words catch me off guard, and I open my mouth then close it, not really knowing what to say. My whole life is back in Chicago, and I know it was inevitable that this week would end. We both knew.

"I love Charleston because it's a little bit of city and a whole lot of southern. But mainly because we have everything here, the history, culinary scene, and more. What's not to love about Charleston?" he asks, quickly changing the subject.

After we're finished eating, he pays, grabs a blanket from the car, then takes my hand and leads me down the wooden path that points to the beach. The sun dips below the horizon and twilight is upon us. The light breeze brushes over my skin, and soon we're touching sand. He bends over and removes his shoes, and I do too.

"I have a lot to tell you, Vada." The light breeze carries his voice.

"Actually, I want to apologize to you, Ethan. I didn't mean to snoop, and I'm really sorry for doing so." I look at him, trying to read his facial expression, hoping he understands. "Trust is such a big part of my life, and I felt like I broke that with you."

Ethan shakes his head at me. "No, no. You have nothing to apologize about."

We continue walking down the beach, allowing the sand to squish between our toes. Once we're away from the boardwalk, Ethan stops and lays the blanket on the ground, then sits. Looking up at me, he pats next to him, and I set my shoes down and join him. Our arms brush together, and goose bumps travel across my skin. I nervously laugh, and Ethan does, too, as he stares out at the rippling waves.

"I was married," he starts, his words catching me off guard. I suspected he had some kind of relationship previously, but I hadn't figured he was divorced.

"But you're not anymore, right?" Suddenly I realize I haven't asked this question. My mind starts playing out all these scenarios of him still being married, which would make me a homewrecker. He doesn't wear a wedding ring, but that doesn't mean anything considering his line of work. As I sit here, I realized how I trusted him so easily, that it makes me almost feel stupid for not making sure beforehand.

Letting out a light laugh, he reassures me by shaking his head. "No, I'm not. She passed away five years ago."

The blood rushes from my face, and the wine from earlier feels like it's finally kicking in.

"I'm so sorry." I try to offer some sort of condolence, but I'm at a loss.

"It was sudden and unexpected." His tone is somber, and I want nothing more than to comfort him. This explains so much about him, and I'm already getting emotional without even knowing the details.

I wait patiently, not wanting to rush him. He continues when he's ready and tells me about Alana and exactly what happened. As I sit next to him on the blanket, tears stream down my face. I can't imagine being so young and losing someone so close.

"So I'm sorry for pushing you away. I've got issues that I'm still working on. But after reacting the way I did, I felt you deserved to know the truth."

"Thank you." I weave my fingers through his. "For trusting me enough to tell me. I'm sure it wasn't easy."

"It's the first time I've told her story to anyone," he admits, my heart swelling. "Southern town, lots of gossips—didn't take long for everyone to hear."

"I appreciate you sharing it with me." I flash a small smile, realizing how big of a step this is for him. "So your daughter?" I swallow hard, not wanting to push my boundaries, but he knows I saw the room that was set up for her.

Ethan sucks in a deep breath as if he's finding the courage to speak.

"Paris came two months early and fought to breathe from the

moment she was born. The tubes, the beeping of the machines, sometimes when I'm sitting in a quiet room, I can still hear it all as if I'm there. I think she died of a broken heart though. Once Alana was gone, it seemed Paris' likelihood of surviving diminished greatly. It's like she knew her mama was gone. Ultimately, she was too little, too sick, too weak. She ended up getting meningitis, which came with its own set of complications, and passed away two weeks later."

Ethan swallows down tears, and I see him fighting his emotions, which completely ruins me from the inside out. There's something about watching a man be so vulnerable that breaks me down. I'm so upset over this, and I'm crying for him and everything he's lost. His life was flipped upside down in a matter of weeks.

Regardless, he continues. "The first time I held her was when they unhooked her small body from the machines after she was gone." He covers his face with his hands.

I place my hand on his back, and he falls into my arms. Ethan holds me as if he's falling, and I don't let go. I can't let go, not when I feel like he's breaking in my arms. The pain he feels streams through me, and I wish I could take it all away.

"I don't believe everything happens for a reason. It's a bullshit thing that doesn't bring comfort to anyone. No one should ever have to endure such loss—ever. I'm so sorry, Ethan. I'm sorry this happened to you. And I'm sorry you're having to talk to me about it."

He sits up and rubs his palms over his eyes. With a helpless shrug, he reiterates, "You deserved to know, Vada. Maybe I'm actually losing my mind, but…" He swallows hard. "You're not like everyone else. Being with you is different. I feel like when I'm with you, I can be myself again, and that's a feeling I haven't felt for a very, very long time."

I suck in air, and it almost hits me like a pound of bricks when the realization sets in that he's right. It *has* been different being with him.

"I know what you mean," I admit with a smile on my face, staring into his honey-colored eyes. For a moment, no words exchange between us but so much is being said. My heartbeat rushes, and I wonder if he can feel it, too. Ethan Rochester is more than what I ever bargained for, and after tonight, I see him in a completely different light. I truly understand him on a deeper level—something I haven't ever felt with anyone else.

Ethan leans back on the blanket and pulls me down with him. The light breeze drifts over our bodies as he holds me in his arms. We look up at the stars twinkling in the sky, and in this moment, I don't want to be anywhere else in the world. Our hearts, our bodies, everything is perfectly in sync, and the thought almost frightens me.

"Thank you," Ethan whispers after minutes of silence between us.

I sit up on my elbow and look at him, the moonlight casting a shadow on his beautiful features. "For what?"

"For listening, for allowing me to be myself. For not looking at me like I've grown a second head or anything."

I give him a sweet smile, and he pulls me close. His hot breath kisses my skin, and it's almost too much for me to handle. "You had me at hello, you know that?"

I wasn't expecting to hear that come from his lips. "Ethan—"

"Don't." He stops me, sitting up and pulling me to his chest. My mouth hovers above his until he slightly leans up and claims my lips as his, completely stealing my breath and heart in the flicker of a moment. His kiss is so raw that it almost reaches bone as he cuts me open with the emotion that's streaming from this kiss. The shift I feel is so powerful, it's almost as if the entire world tilts on its axis.

CHAPTER SIXTEEN

ETHAN

I wish I could capture Vada so she'd stay with me here in this moment—as the waves crash in the distance—forever. Right now, I don't feel sadness or pain. I only feel that strange sensation that what we have is bigger than either of us realize. I'm not one to fall for anyone so quickly. Hell, if anything, I've pushed plenty of opportunities away, but with Vada, it's different. She's got me under her spell, and I doubt she's going to let me go before she heads back to Chicago in a couple days. The realization of that completely rips through me, but I keep it to myself.

We lay on the blanket for a while, until I feel Vada shiver.

"Come on, let's go," I tell her, sitting up. "The night's still young. What do you want to do?"

Vada looks at me seductively, and I'm almost tempted to throw her over my shoulder and carry her back to the car because it would be faster.

"Say no more." Standing up, I grab my shoes and slip them back on. She follows my lead and tries to help me pop sand out of the blanket.

On the drive back to the house, I interlock Vada's fingers with mine. It's a simple, but intimate gesture. I haven't felt the need to hold hands with a woman in years, and now I don't want to let hers go.

"I've got a surprise for you," I say, unbuckling. She follows suit and meets me in front of the car.

Grabbing for her hand again, we walk up the steps to the house where I lead her up the stairs to my bathroom. I light candles and place them around the white iron claw-foot tub. Turning on the hot water until it's steaming, I take my time undressing her, kissing her collarbone and along her shoulder. Her head falls to one side, and she lets out a long sigh as my fingers sweep across the soft skin of her stomach. As I undo each button of my shirt, she watches me intently, not speaking a word.

"How would you write a scene like this?" I ask her, wanting to know the eloquent words she'd use.

She shakes her head. "You don't even want to know."

"I do; come on. I know you're probably a wordsmith."

Watching me for another moment, she begins speaking out the scene. "Carefully, button-by-button, the gorgeous man removes his shirt. His ab muscles are as hard as steel and scream out for her to touch them, but she doesn't. Instead, she stands silent and waits for his permission as he moves to take off his belt before unbuttoning his pants. He looks at her with a burning intensity in his eyes as if he knows all her secrets but doesn't care. And maybe he doesn't."

"So, Vada. What secrets do you have?" I ask her, wanting to know, realizing I've spilled my guts tonight, but I haven't learned much more about her than I already know.

"I'm an open book. Other than the trust issues I have. But that's because of all the pricks I've dated in the past. And…" She hesitates. I watch her, completely unsure of what she'll say next. "And from things in my childhood. But it's all in the past now. Without all the liars and cheaters, well I wouldn't be the woman I am today or be able to write strong women in my books. So it all worked out, I suppose."

"Did someone hurt you?" I nearly growl, realizing how territorial that sounded. "I might kill them if you say yes." Just the thought of someone laying a hand on Vada almost sends me into a fury.

"No, nothing like that. More emotional abuse than anything. Being able to trust someone fully is important to me because I tend to go all in when I'm dating someone. The past hasn't been kind to me, that's all I'm saying. Every relationship I've been in has ended badly, so I guess you could say I'm a bit jaded. Empty promises covered with lies, and stupidly, I believed them over and over again. It's probably why I'm *overly* single right now."

"I can understand that. But let me add, I'm an open book too, Vada. I'll always be truthful, even if it hurts. I don't have anything to hide. You know all my secrets." I take a few steps forward and hold her in my arms. Skin against skin and there's something so intimate about standing in nothing but candlelight.

"Get in first," I demand with a smile, watching our shadows dance against the wall.

"So bossy, I *like* it," she purrs, dipping a toe in the warm water, then stepping in, and slowly sitting in the tub. I follow her lead, slipping behind her, my legs holding her in place.

"Ouch, your snake's slithering against my back," she jokes.

"Watch out, you might get bitten," I tell her as I grab a bar of soap and gently wash over her breasts. Vada sinks into my touch, allowing me to put my hands wherever I want.

"The water's so warm, it's relaxing," she states in a dreamy-like tone.

I slip my hands down lower, and my fingers rub against her clit. Letting out a moan that echoes through the bathroom, Vada arches against me, creating more friction. Her head leans against my shoulder, and I devour her mouth with mine as I continue to pleasure her. Dipping a finger inside, I can feel how tight and ready she is for me.

"Fuck, Vada," I whisper in her ear, as she sinks deeper into my touch.

"If you keep doing that, I'm going to lose it," she says between moans.

"Good." With my other hand, I palm her breast, tugging at her nipple that's at full attention.

"God, Ethan." She moans louder, with more intensity in her voice as she places her palms on the porcelain tub, leaning harder into me. Her body tenses against my chest, and she closes her eyes as she allows the release to take over.

"You're so fucking sexy when you come," I whisper against her neck.

She laughs, leaning her head against me. "Didn't realize getting clean could be so dirty."

I take my time, washing her body and hair until she's completely clean. "You were right about the exclusive treatment. Can I bring you home with me?"

When she mentions leaving, my heart lurches forward. "I wish, Vada. But you'd need a bigger suitcase for me, Henry, and Wilma. My cock and pussy go everywhere with me."

Sitting up, she lets out the cutest laugh ever, causing the water to whoosh in the tub. Considering it's lukewarm and soapy, I take that as our cue to get out and stand. I hand her a towel, and we dry off, and I can't help but admire how beautiful she is, all the way down to her perfect toes.

When I think about her leaving, it just doesn't feel right. Not at all.

And that thought scares the ever living shit out of me.

Grabbing her hand, I lead her down the hallway to my bedroom. "On the bed."

She tilts her head at me but doesn't hesitate.

"How do you want me?" she asks looking over her shoulder.

"You're the guest of the hour; how about you choose." I drop the towel to the floor as she lies on her back. I walk to my bedside table and put on a condom. My dick throbs in my hand and I know this won't take long, but I promise to take my time.

"How's this?" she asks lying on her back, the moonlight casting shadows across the room.

I go to her and start at her feet, kissing her ankles, her legs, the inside of her thighs, until I reach my final destination. As I taste her arousal, she runs her fingers through my hair, letting out moans that sound like music.

"Ethan," she whispers, and my name has never sounded so good. Before she loses herself again, I move closer to her, hovering above her, my dick teasing the outside of her opening. I move slowly, taking my time as our ends meet. She gasps, her eyes closing tight.

"Oh, Vada," I whisper across her neck, and that's the moment I realize we're no longer fucking, but rather, making love. When her eyes open, I know she can feel it, too. The look on her face says it all. Her mouth falls open as I give her everything I have. Eventually, Vada crumbles beneath me, and I follow soon after.

After we clean up, we lie together, both struggling for air, trying to understand what just happened. It wasn't just sex; it was more intense, more emotional. It was like she had opened the Pandora's box that held my heart, pulled it from the shadows, and somehow, it's still beating.

Vada's head falls on my chest, and she's listening to the rapid thump of my heart. I hold her in my arms, trying to enjoy it as much as I can. I know this week is coming to an end, and the truth is, I'm going to miss this. Pulling the blankets over our bodies, I stare out at the moon that's high in the sky from the windows in my bedroom.

"I'd like you to come to the demo and showing at the studio tomorrow. It's from eleven to five. Aunt Millie and Mama will be there, and I'd love for you to be there, too."

She sits up and looks into my eyes. "Really? Like a public thing?"

I nod. "Of course."

"I don't like crowds. They make me nervous as hell," she admits.

"Then hang around Aunt Millie. Crowds don't like her because she's loud and has no filter." I laugh, but it's the truth.

She looks as if she's thinking about it, then gives me a big smile. "You know what, I'd love to go and watch you. I mean, if you really want me there," she says, brushing strands of hair out of her eyes.

"It wouldn't be the same without you. So be my guest of honor?"

She nods. "Of course. Wouldn't miss it for the world."

We lie in silence, tangled together like lovers, and it feels right. My eyes are heavy, and I might fall asleep at any moment because I'm so relaxed and happy. Just as I'm drifting away, I hear Vada say something.

"I'm going to miss this. Seriously," she mumbles softly against my chest.

"Then don't leave," I whisper, holding her just a little tighter. "Stay another week or month or I dunno, forever?"

She sighs, and I know she's halfway between sleep and being awake because the words that leave her lips are completely inaudible.

CHAPTER SEVENTEEN

VADA

"Good morning," Ethan says, handing me a cup of coffee while I'm still lying in his bed. Sitting up, I take it from his hands while trying to pat the hair down on my head because it's all crazy and wild. My eyes are barely open, and I feel like I could sleep for days. After last night, I could probably sleep for weeks, but that wouldn't work because I have a book to finish.

"I've been thinking about something," I admit, clearing my throat with a sip of steaming hot coffee.

"Yeah?" He perks up. "You'll walk around naked the rest of the time you're here?"

I playfully roll my eyes at him. "Not quite, but I *was* thinking about extending my stay."

Ethan takes the cup of coffee from my hand, sets it down on his nightstand, and within two seconds his lips are on mine. I'm moaning against his mouth before he releases me.

"That makes me so damn happy, Vada. You have no idea." He brushes the outside of his fingers against my cheek then stands and returns my coffee.

"I have to call my neighbor about feeding my cat and get in touch with the airline. Lots of stuff to do in so little time," I tell him, finally feeling awake and taking another sip of coffee. I'm going to need all the caffeine today.

"And you have to come to the studio today to watch the live show." He winks.

"I already told you I wouldn't miss that for the world. Plus, I need to stock up on mugs. I seriously need a hundred of them," I say holding a blue and purple handmade mug in my hand. "I love them so much."

Ethan grins at me proudly, then begins pulling clothes from a drawer and getting dressed. I watch his muscles flex as he puts on a shirt, and all I want to do is tear it off him. The man should walk around shirtless with a body like that, but then again, I'm good with keeping him all to myself.

"You said it starts at eleven, right?" I ask again, confirming.

"Yes, and lasts until five. So anytime today. I just want you to see everything. Maybe you can write it into one of your books one day," he suggests with a wink. I can tell he's in a good mood, and him being so damn happy is contagious.

"Okay, great. I'm going to try to get some words in and then I'll Uber down there." There's so much inspiration in me from last night that I have to get some writing in today, or I'll internally combust.

"I can ask Aunt Millie to pick you up," Ethan insists.

"That's sweet of you. But I have a feeling she'd ask me five thousand questions, and I don't know when I'll be finished with this chapter I'm working on."

He lets out a laugh then walks toward me. Leaning down, he places his hand around the back of my neck and kisses me. "I'll see you there, babe."

"Save me a seat," I tell him, not really sure how this demo thing works.

"I've always got a seat saved for you on my face." He kisses me again, before saying goodbye. Once I've finished my coffee, I slip on my dress and head downstairs. I refill my cup before heading to the cottage to get some words down after I take a shower.

Once I'm dried off, I put on one of my favorite A-line skirts and a tank top, then sit down at my computer and the paragraphs pour from me. The words won't stop coming. It's a high like no other.

I feel like I've ripped my soul open, and though I don't want to jinx myself, this might be the easiest book I've ever written. I've never been this inspired, and I'm pretty sure Ethan is to blame. Actually, I *know* he is.

Hours pass, and I know I've lost track of time again and my coffee has turned cold.

Looking at the time, I realize it's just past one. "Shit," I say aloud, grabbing my phone and scheduling an Uber. As I wait around, I call Nora.

"Oh, so you're alive," she says with a hint of accusation in her tone.

"Wow, no hello or anything? I see how it is." I laugh, used to her attitude. If she didn't act like that, I might actually think there's something wrong.

"Glad to know you weren't chopped up into a million pieces," she says.

"You're so dark and need to lay off those CSI shows. Geez. I'm alive, so there's that. Okay, nice chatting with you!" I kid.

"Not so fast young lady. You left me on a cliffhanger yesterday, so I'm going to need you to go ahead and let me know how the date of the century went."

"Well…" I begin, replaying last night in my head and grinning like an idiot.

Nora clears her throat.

"He was married," I explain.

"Is he still?" Her inflection raises.

"No, no. It's nothing like that. He's a widower, and seriously Nora, I was bawling like a baby. Just think of the saddest movie you've ever seen times a million then put it on crack. Ethan's wife was pregnant and had complications during the birth. The baby was premature and got really sick and didn't make it. They both passed away within two weeks of each other." My voice cracks and I realize I'm choking up.

"I don't know what to say," she mumbles. "That's much heavier than I was expecting."

"Believe me, I know." I suck in a deep breath. "Still, the date was perfect though. The best date I've ever had."

"Well, I'm happy for you." Her tone is raw.

"Thanks, Nora," I say with a smile. "Oh! So that brings me to the point of this call." I look at my phone and realize the Uber is outside, so I rush across the yard and continue the conversation when I get in the car. "I'm going to call the airline and try to reschedule my flight. I'm staying another week. I'm getting ahead with this impending deadline, and I think it would be good for me to utilize the inspiration that's coming to me now while I can." I bite down on my lower lip, thinking of all the ways Ethan can inspire me for the next week. "So I hope you won't mind taking care of Oliver for me for just a little bit longer?" I ask as sweetly as possible.

She sucks in a breath. "I guess." Her tone is unamused, but I know she's just giving me a hard time. She's probably thinking the same thing I am. *Inspiration* equals Ethan's cock.

"Thank you. I owe you. I'm on my way to watch Ethan do a live pottery demo at his studio, so I have to get going. I'll snap some photos though and text them to you."

"Good, because I need to see what this Prince Charming looks like." Her tone perks up, and I know she's not annoyed with watching Oliver another week like she pretends to be.

The Uber slows in front of Paris Pottery & Studio, and I hang up with Nora before thanking the driver. I stand outside and look up at the sign with a whole new perspective, and my heart lurches forward. It's so beautiful that he named the studio after his daughter, knowing it would've made his wife happy. I take in a slow breath as I see all the people packed into the building and try to push my anxiety to the side as I enter.

I move through hordes of women who are all looking in the same direction. From the back of the room, I see Ethan at the wheel, with his hands on the clay, and I can't help but admire him. Honestly, though, I think every woman in here is. He's smiling and explaining his methods as all eyes stay glued to him. He looks so good wearing black dress slacks and a solid, dark gray button-up shirt. His sleeves are rolled up his arms, and his top buttons are undone. He looks business-professional, but I know what's under all of that—eight-pack abs and a pierced cock that knows how to melt off panties.

Weaving my way through, I see Aunt Millie laughing and speaking loudly in the middle of the room while she brags about her nephew. As soon as she makes eye contact with me, she waves me over, and I feel slightly embarrassed, but I walk toward her anyway.

Ethan's head lifts, and his entire face brightens when he sees me.

"Hi," I mouth, and he winks at me. Women start searching around the room, trying to figure out who he's openly flirting with, and that's when heat hits my cheeks.

"There you are, Vada. Ethan told me you'd be showing up, and I've been waitin' for you. Want you to meet someone," Millie says, grabbing my hand and forcing her way past people.

"Vada, this is my sister, Mollie. Ethan's mama."

My mouth drops open when I see a spitting image of Millie standing in front of me. "I had no idea you were a twin; what a surprise!"

"Mollie, this is Vada, the girl I was telling you about who's staying with Ethan." Millie gives me a wink, and I instantly blush.

"It's so nice to meet you," I tell her, and she gives me a hug, a customary southern greeting I've come to expect.

"You too, honey. I've heard so much about you," she says, and I glance over her shoulder at Millie with a smile and can only imagine what she's said about me.

"Really?" I try not to be too embarrassed.

"Yeah, Millie told me about your books, and I downloaded a few onto my Kindle."

I instantly start stuttering. "I hope you enjoy them." All I can think about are these sweet older ladies reading those raunchy sex scenes.

"I'm sure I will, sweetie," she says, having no idea what she's about to read.

Ethan grabs the bat out of the wheel with a brand-new mug he's just made and hands it to one of the workers who sets it down on one of the shelves.

At that moment, I take a quick photo and send it to Nora. When I look back up, it's like we're the only two people in the crowded room. I can't stop staring at him. It's almost as if he can read my thoughts as his eyes meet mine. Swallowing hard, I snap out of it and feel like a room full of eyes are on me. I can almost feel the jealousy streaming off all the women who came here just to admire

Ethan—and not necessarily his work. But it doesn't hurt he's sexy as sin, so I'm sure that's good for business. Although he doesn't need it. His work speaks for itself all on its own.

Once he finishes molding a few more mugs, he goes to the sink and rinses off his hands and arms, then makes a beeline toward me as interns clean up the area and restock his clay. My mouth goes dry when he dips down and gives me a kiss in front of *everyone*. I feel like I'm falling as he completely steals my breath away. Ethan brushes his fingers against my cheek, and before he pulls away, he whispers in my ear. "Hopefully all these thirsty women will get the hint."

I burst out laughing, especially when I get eyerolls from a few ladies staring at us together. "Doubt it. Some look like they're trying real hard and now want to murder me."

He nods. "You have no idea. Oh, did you meet my mama?" Ethan asks, searching around for her. She and Millie are the life of the party on the opposite side of the room. It also helps the interns are serving wine, so many people are giggly and buying mugs like they're shopping with a no limit credit card.

"I have to say I was shocked when I saw two Millie's staring at me."

Ethan chuckles. "I guess I forgot to warn you about that. But trust me when I say Mom is the good cop and Millie is the bad one."

The smile on my face may be permanent. "I'm so proud of you, babe. You've got a full house, and it's all just perfect," I say, sincerely.

"Thanks, sweetheart. That means a lot to me. Really." He places his hand on my cheek and smirks. "Have time to go to the back real quick?" His voice drops low.

"Uhh," I say, as he grabs my hand and leads me away from everyone. We walk down a long hall, and Ethan opens a storage closet full of supplies. He pulls me inside with him, and once he locks the door, we're standing inches apart.

"Fuck, I need you right now," he growls against my lips before he kisses me.

I don't even wait before I'm grabbing at his pants. Ethan takes a step forward until my back is against the only bare wall in the closet. Roughly, he lifts my leg in the air and pushes my skirt up, then tears my panties from my body. The way he's handling me, so desperate with want and need, turns me on even more.

"Shit," he says.

I search his face. "What?"

"No condom," he admits.

"I'm on the pill, Ethan."

At first, he hesitates. So I readjust my skirt back down over my bare ass, and he shakes his head.

"Don't think so, babe." Ethan grabs my ass and lifts me in the air. My legs wrap around his hips as he fucks me against the wall. Small moans escape from my mouth as our tongues swirl together, and I feel so naughty knowing there's a room full of people who suspect something is going on or even hear us.

"Vada," Ethan groans against my mouth. "You feel so good. You always feel so fucking good."

"I want more of you, Ethan. All of you."

He continues to give me everything he can. "When I saw you walk in, all I could think about was this."

"Yes, yes, yes," I whisper, holding on to him for dear life, digging my nails into him harder.

Before I come, Ethan sets me down on the floor and drops to his knees, then pulls my leg over his shoulder. His mouth is in between my legs in seconds. As he devours me, it takes everything I have to hold back all the moans I want to release. He doesn't stop, even when he knows I'm close. I hold onto his arm that's wrapped around my thigh because I feel weak in the knees as I lose myself on his mouth.

"I need more of you," he says, dipping his tongue inside, tasting my orgasm.

"So good," I say between breaths, as he stands, kissing me, allowing me to taste myself on him. He gives me a smirk, then turns me around, and bends me over. I place my hands on the wall, giving me the much-needed support, and arch my ass toward him.

Taking his time, he rubs his rough palms on my ass before he grabs my hips and slowly slides into me. I gasp as the top of his piercing rubs against me, feeling his length in places he's already been and claimed as his own.

"I'm so fucking happy you're staying," he says as I feel him tense and his warmth fills me. After a moment, I turn around and search his face with a smile, and he kisses me, soft and sweet, pouring himself into me.

"Do you think anyone heard us?" I ask, grabbing a few towels on a shelf to clean us up.

"I hope they all did." He smirks, zipping up his pants, and I roll my eyes.

"Thank you for coming, Vada," he says. "On my mouth."

"So dirty," I say, adjusting my clothes. "Don't you think you should get back? Everyone is probably looking for you."

He tries to straighten his messy hair, and I laugh.

"How do I look?" he asks.

"Like you just had sex. Swollen lips and guilt written all over your face."

He dips down and kisses me again. "Good," he says before opening the door and pulling me out with him.

A few people saw us coming out of the closet, and I'm a bit self-conscious, but I decide to take pride in my walk of shame. We're both adults, enjoying each other's company.

Ethan's hand is leading me as we walk back into the main room and through the crowd. Women look over their shoulders at us and snicker, probably knowing what we were just doing. I'm sure I look as guilty as he does, but he wears it with no fucks given.

Hours pass as I sit in the front row and watch him, completely mesmerized by his amazing skills. Each time he throws me a wink, I playfully roll my eyes at him because I don't want to get shanked when I leave here. Before too long, I realize I need to get back to the house. At Ethan's next break, I tell him I need to leave.

"I understand, babe," he says.

"I still have to call the airline and make arrangements to reschedule my flight, but I'm going to do that once I get back to the house."

Once the Uber arrives, he walks me out and pulls me into his arms. "Bye, babe. I'll see you *very* soon."

"You will," I tell him, placing a quick kiss on his lips before getting into the car.

I wave at him and blow a sweet kiss that he tucks into his

pocket before he heads back inside the studio. Letting out a sigh, I decide I want to do something nice for him tonight and ask the Uber driver if she can take me to a grocery store instead. She agrees and drops me off at the door.

"I can wait for you if you'd like," she offers.

"That's okay. I might be a while. Thank you, though," I tell her, and she gives me a wave and drives off.

My phone vibrates, and I see a text from Nora. I guess she figured it out after all.

Nora: DOES HE HAVE AN OLDER SINGLE UNCLE?

I laugh and send her a text back.

Me: No. And your cap locks is on again :)

Nora: DAMMIT.

I swear to myself that when I get back home, I'm going to teach her how to use that damn phone. Laughing at her, I walk inside and grab a cart and go straight for the steaks. As I'm looking at ribeyes and sirloins, trying to decide which one to cook, a tall, Paris blonde woman stands close beside me. She has long, lean legs and a pretty face; the woman could be a model.

As soon as we make eye contact, she flashes a smile. "Oh hey, I recognize you," she says, matter-of-factly, though I've never seen her in my life.

I'm kind of confused. "Really?" I tilt my head, trying to figure out if I recognize her or not.

"Yeah, you were just at Ethan's studio, weren't you?" she asks, her smile never fading, yet her tone is giving off a weird vibe.

I smile back at her, not really wanting to make small talk but decide to be nice. "Oh right. Yeah, I was."

"So I have a somewhat personal question," she tells me, sliding her cart to one side, so we don't block the aisle.

I'm not really sure what to say, so I just nod.

"Are you seeing Ethan? Like, are you two a *thing*?" she asks, her nose wrinkling.

I open my mouth and close it, trying to draw my attention back to grocery shopping. "Something like that, but I'm sorry, who are you?"

"I'm Harmony. It's nice to meet you," she says in an overly sweet tone that sounds fake as she holds out her hand, but I don't take it. "Anyway, I know you're not from around here, so I thought I'd give you a warning about him."

I furrow my brows and look at her like she's lost her damn mind, but still, I'm intrigued to hear what she has to say. I already know about his past and secrets, about his wife and daughter; what else could she possibly have to tell me?

"He likes to make women think he's falling in love with them, especially ones who are just in town on vacation. He makes them believe that they're different from anyone else he's ever been with." My brows raise, shocked by her bold statements.

"You're lying." The words blurt out of my mouth before I can stop them.

She looks at me with pity before continuing. "He has the same MO with all of them, honey. Takes them out on *special* dates to the beach where he'll hold your hand, and you'll walk along the sand barefoot together. He'll bring a blanket for you both to sit on, and that's when he spills his guts to you, just to hook you in even more. Then, once he's gotten his fix of you, he drops you like a bad habit, as if you and he never happened. He'll make you believe you're something special, that he's falling hard, and can't get enough before moving on to the next. Then you're left to pick up the pieces of your broken heart."

I feel sick. My head is spinning because she just replayed the most intimate part of our date. There's no way she could know that. We weren't even in town. The only person I told was Nora, and I doubt he'd tell anyone outside of Aunt Millie. How the hell does she know all the details? I instantly feel like a fool, and my heart hurts.

She carefully studies me, twitching her lips as if she's happy with my response, before she continues. "He told you all about his late wife and baby down at the beach, didn't he?" she asks when she notices all the blood rushing out of my face. "That's his pity game, darling. He knows women can't resist him, but once he makes them think he's going all in, they become putty in his hands." She flashes a genuine, apologetic smile. "Hook, line, and sinker," she confirms, and I wish she'd just stop talking so I can process her words.

Ethan's avoided relationships for years, but I know that doesn't mean he hasn't had one-night stands or flings. Why would he need to manipulate them when he's the one who doesn't want anything more than a physical relationship? But then again, how would she know about our date on the beach and him sharing those intimate details with me? What if it really is his MO? Questions swirl around in my mind, but I can't make sense of them. Nothing is making sense, yet I feel my insides twisting.

Finally, I clear my throat and speak. "How do you know all this?"

"Because I've been in your shoes, hon. So have many other women in town. Once the news started to get around of his dating rituals and women were onto his scam, he moved to tourists only, which is no secret why he rents out the cottage." She purses her lips as if it should all be clicking in my head right about now. "Same old story, too. He says he only does one-night stands to make us feel like we're something special, but once he's bored, we're kicked to the curb." Her expression is firm as if she's warned others before. "I know it's none of my business, but I just felt like you should know. We women have to stay together, ya know? But you can do whatever you want. I just wouldn't feel right walking away and not giving you a warning, since, by the look on your face, no one else has."

I don't even reply or give her a chance to continue again before I walk away without my cart. As quickly as I can, I find a bathroom and close myself in a stall, and that's when the tears unleash. Is that all this is to him? *A game?* Was I stupid enough to believe someone like Ethan could really fall for someone like me, especially when he dates women who look like Harmony? Every trust issue I've had in the past surfaces full force as I think about how easy I let a guy like Ethan in. *What the hell was I thinking?*

Looking down at my phone, I see my hand shaking. Slowly, I'm crumbling and feel like everything I thought I knew was a lie.

I'm a fool.

I should've never trusted him so easily.

He made me believe he was different and that letting my guard down wouldn't come back to bite me, but it looks as if I was wrong. *Again.*

I'm drowning in emotions as I schedule another Uber to take me back to the cottage.

My heart is shattering into a million pieces, and I'm pissed off that I put myself in this situation once again.

I need to leave.

I need to pack my shit and get the hell out of here as soon as possible.

CHAPTER EIGHTEEN

ETHAN

AFTER I HELP CLEAN up the studio, I hug and thank Millie and Mama for all their support in this venture of mine.

"I really like your *friend*, Ethan," Mama says with a twinkle in her eye, and it's the first time she's really given her approval for a lady since Alana. It makes my smile grow even bigger.

"She's cute. Perfect for you. Seems real nice," she adds, smiling. I know she's being sincere, too.

"She is, but tell me what you think about her once you've read her book, the one Aunt Millie made you download." I laugh, knowing it's probably full of dirty, vulgar sex scenes, especially if Vada's words are anything like the Vada I know in bed.

Millie bursts out into evil laughter. After standing for a little while longer, we exchange big hugs then I walk them out to the car, making sure they leave safely.

"We had a record day in sales," Hilary says excitedly when I walk back in. I round the counter, and she points her finger to the screen, showing me the amount.

"That's great news. I can't wait to make the donation to the March of Dimes," I tell her with a smile. If there's a premature baby out there that has a fighting chance, I want to do everything I can to save a life and someone else from going through what I did. Jessica, who's in charge of scheduling and other maintenance, lets out a loud aww, but I try to ignore it. I don't do it for recognition. I do it to make a difference, as small as it may be.

"Do you need anything else before I head out?" I ask, trying to change the subject.

Several interns speak up all at once saying they've got it, and I know they do.

"Fine," I tell them with a smile and a wave before I leave for the day.

On the drive home, all I can think about is seeing Vada again, kissing Vada, being with Vada. My thoughts are consumed with her. She's on my mind every moment of the day, and when she's away, it's like a part of me is missing. That woman somehow stole a piece of my heart, and I don't want it back. Hell, she can keep it as long as she's here in Charleston with me.

I drive across town and replay the last week, and I'm so fucking happy Vada is extending her stay. We'll have more time to be together and see where this leads. In my heart, I know this is the real deal, but I need to make sure we haven't rushed into something crazy. Regardless, I'm already falling hard for her, and there's no rescue mission in place. Truthfully, I don't want to be saved. Just the thought of her smile, laugh, the way she says my name, or the look on her face when she loses herself with me, makes me feel things I haven't in a long-ass time.

Before I head home, I stop and pick up a dozen red roses and a bottle of Cabernet, since I know it's her favorite. There's a lot of celebrating to be done since my Vada is staying. Eventually, she'll have to leave, but hopefully only to pack her apartment and return back to me.

Tonight, I want to order in and spend the rest of the night showing her what she truly means to me. At the studio, when she walked in, it was like everything around me had faded to black, except her. Vada makes me feel something I never knew I'd feel again—whole.

When I park the car, my heart lurches forward, and I'm so damn excited to finally be home. It was the longest drive ever. I walk through the house, hurry and feed Wilma, then go through the back door with the roses and wine in hand. The smile on my face almost immediately fades when I see all the lights are off in the cottage and the door is locked. Thinking that she's probably trying to surprise me, I walk back to the house and immediately climb the stairs to my bedroom. Opening the door, I realize she's not there either.

"Vada?" I finally call her name.

I wait but don't hear a reply.

Going back downstairs, I set the flowers and wine down, and that's when I see a handwritten note on the counter.

Confused, I pick it up and read the scribbled words. With each sentence, I feel like I'm choking.

My heart is torn as I write this, but I'm leaving for Chicago tonight. By the time you get home, I'm sure I'll already be on the plane. After I left the studio today, I realized how stupid I was being. I can't be here, Ethan. I won't be played, and I won't allow myself to be that girl. It's better this way.

—Vada

I notice the splashes of ink on the paper and know she was crying as she wrote this, and it tears me apart. Immediately, I pull my phone from my pocket and call her, but it goes straight to voicemail.

My voice cracks when I speak. "Vada, please call me. I don't know what you're talking about or what happened since you left the studio. Please talk to me so we can figure this out."

I know I sound desperate, but the best thing that's happened to me in a long time just walked away with a half-ass explanation, and I need to know what triggered this. Everything was absolutely perfect when she left the studio. I think about the last words we exchanged, and it was goodbyes, surrounded by smiles. If I would've known she'd be leaving for good, I would've never let her get in that car earlier. Something happened, and I'm going to lose my mind until I know what.

Halfway hoping this is some sick joke, I walk back to the cottage with the key tightly grasped in my hand and almost lose it when I see all of her belongings are gone. Her suitcase, laptop, everything. It's as if it was all a dream and she never happened.

"No," I say, quietly to myself. "This isn't happening."

Instead of giving up, I keep calling her, hoping she'll answer, but she never does. After everything we've been through, after I ripped my heart open and poured myself out to her, after she made me forget—she leaves me. Vada saw my true, raw self, and she still left, and the thought of what I've lost cripples me.

It's been a week since Vada left, and it's like my whole world has shattered into shards again. She rejects my calls and sends me straight to voicemail. I'm pretty sure I'm blocked at this point because I've called and texted so much, begging her to talk to me. Regardless of what I say on those voice messages, she doesn't return them. I have zero control over this, and while I'm trying to be patient and give her time if that's what she needs, it's not in my nature, especially when I'm hurting so badly.

There's a hole in my heart, and I miss her so fucking much.

"Why don't you go to her?" Millie asks as we drive across town to pick up some plants for her front porch. She refused to let me stay home and wallow in my emotions and even pulled the old people card to force me to join her.

"Because she doesn't answer my calls, so why would she want to see me? All I want is an explanation of what the hell happened, some clarity on what changed from the time she left the studio to when she decided to bail. Everything was going so great, then she was gone." I ball my hands in fists, and I feel like I'm losing all the control I'd found when she was here.

"Tell me what the note said again," she insists. "Maybe I can read between the lines."

I repeat the note without even having to look at it because I've read it so many times and have the damn thing memorized. Millie sits silently while she thinks and parks the car.

"Something significant enough to make her change her mind must've happened after she left the studio. That's what you need to figure out," she tells me matter-of-factly as if I hadn't already been trying to put the pieces together. I've been driving myself insane thinking of different things, but nothing makes sense.

I roll my eyes as I unbuckle, then mumble more to myself as I get out of the car. "Leave it to detective Millie."

Not waiting for me, she grabs a cart and walks inside the store. This is the last thing I wish I were doing right now, especially considering I'm in such a pissy mood. By the time I find Millie, she's looking at an ugly bush and talking to someone who's even uglier–Harmony Hansen—an ex-fling I'd rather forget about.

"Oh, hey Ethan," she says in an over-the-top, high-pitched voice. "So nice seeing you last weekend at the studio."

"Yeah," is all I offer, and Millie elbows me in the ribs for being rude, but things didn't end well between us, and I'm not going to give her false hope by being polite.

Harmony knew the rules between us. One night, that was it, but she didn't get the hint until I kicked her out of bed the same night. From that point on, she's desperately tried to get back in bed with me, but I knew what she wanted and what I wanted were two different things. I wasn't ready for anything serious, but she made it very clear she wanted something long-term. *A husband*. I was in no emotional mindset for that.Though it's been years, she hasn't given up on the thought of us. Harmony is literally the epitome of stalker ex. After one night, she was *obsessed*. If I could go back in time, I'd erase the history between us. It was a stupid, liquor-influenced mistake.

"Don't mind him, hon. He's in a bad mood. So what have you been up to lately?" Millie genuinely asks. "Haven't seen you at the book club meetings in a while." I really have no reason to stay around, so I pretend to look at plants, hoping this isn't a long conversation.

Millie talks about the books she's been reading and mentions Vada's name. My heart sinks at the thought of her.

"Vada, right," she says as if saying her name is venom. "I ran into her at the grocery store after I left the studio last weekend. Real sweet girl," Harmony says, plastering the biggest deviant smile on her face.

I blink, realization setting in. "Wait. What did you say? When did you speak to her?" My jaw clenches, and I instantly realize what happened. No telling what Harmony told Vada, considering I ignored her at the restaurant the night of mine and Vada's date. It was easier to pretend she didn't exist when she looked at me from across the room with those come-hither eyes. Seeing me with a woman always drives her insane, but seeing me with the *same* woman at the studio probably set her off even more.

"Oh, nothing." Harmony realizes how much she fucked up by saying those words. She knew exactly what she was doing when she saw Vada. She was trying to sabotage what we had.

Millie notices my flaring nostrils and speaks for me. "So what did you two discuss, hon? Her books?"

After hesitating for an awkward moment, she gives me an evil smile. "Ethan."

"You *bitch*," I growl, anticipating Millie's reaction, but she doesn't scold me like I figured. Instead, she glares at Harmony and shakes her head before walking away without another word, leaving the two of us alone. Aunt Millie and the silent treatment together is a frightening pair.

Before walking away, I look Harmony dead in her eyes. My tone is serious, and I hope for once she gets the fucking hint. "I told you once before we'd never be anything, so get the fuck out of my life and stay out."

Millie is still shaking her head as she pushes her cart forward, leaving me alone with her.

"Ethan, baby. I didn't tell her anything she wouldn't have eventually figured out." Her words are laced in a condescending tone. "It was just too easy. It was obvious you two were getting close and it was easy to assume you were telling her all about your sad past. Once I saw you take her down to the beach on your little date, there was no way you hadn't told her and as soon as I brought it up, her face dropped faster than her panties could for you."

"Don't you fucking talk about her that way," I growl, taking a step toward her and giving no shits how loud I'm being.

She doesn't even flinch, her cold stone glare fuels my anger even more. "Too bad she left before you could lie your way out of this one." She flashes an evil grin before jerking her cart forward and walking away.

My blood is boiling at the revelation of what just happened. As soon as I saw Harmony at the restaurant, I should've left and taken

Vada somewhere else, but I didn't want to start our night on a bad note. Should've figured she'd watch us the entire time.

I inhale deeply before glancing around for Aunt Millie and jogging to catch up to her.

"I warned you about those random dates, Ethan. Those type of women are no good and now look what happened," she scolds.

Pinching the bridge of my nose with my fingers, I sigh. "I know. I wish I could take back *that* mistake. I'm beyond pissed about this. I don't even know what to do right now. No telling exactly what Harmony said to her, although I have a pretty good guess considering what she just told me. She's a goddamn liar and a jealous and petty bitch." I shake my head, growing angrier at the whole situation.

"Language, Ethan," she reminds me.

I follow Millie to the counter and pay for her plants then help her load them in the backseat of her car. After we get in and before she starts the engine, she turns and looks at me.

"You know what you have to do, hon. You're a fighter. You always have been and always will be. When you want something, you go after it. So, fight for what you love. Harmony was wrong to do that to you, and I'm going to have a chat with her Mama the next time I see her."

I give her a small smile. Millie may be a polite, southern woman, but that doesn't mean she doesn't have a dark side. She doesn't get back—she gets even—especially for her favorite nephew.

"So, I'll take care of things while you go to Chicago," she adds, trying to cheer me up.

"I don't know, Aunt Millie. What if it can't be repaired? Who knows what Vada thinks of me now, and I know I couldn't handle losing her all over again. I don't think I can get over her or ever will. Maybe she needs some space, and I'll give that to her, even if it kills me in the end." The words hurt coming out, but once you lose someone you love, you're constantly afraid you'll lose it again.

"Don't be stupid, boy." She slaps me with her harsh words. "You fight for her and don't stop until she listens to you. Harmony filled her head with lies, and you need to clear the air, even if she decides she doesn't want to be with you. You owe her that much at least."

God. Leave it to Aunt Millie to put me in my place.

Although she's right, Vada may not give me the opportunity to clear the air or make things right—so I just might have to go another route to grab her attention.

Even if it takes the rest of my life.

CHAPTER NINETEEN

VADA

ONE YEAR LATER

MEMORIES INVADE my mind as I walk past all the tourists on King Street.

I've been excited, anxious, nervous—*everything*—since I found out one of my book tour stops was in Charleston. My publisher arranged the schedule, and there was no changing it, although I wasn't completely sure I would've wanted to. However, being back is bringing a mixture of feelings, and I don't know what to make of them.

Especially with the way I left—the last time I saw Ethan.

I've heard his voice, but we haven't talked since that last day I was here.

Leaving Charleston in tears doesn't give this city the best feeling of returning, but I'm not running away. At least, not yet.

It'd be impossible to forget a guy like Ethan, especially when my latest novel was primarily inspired by him. As cliché as it sounds, he really did bring something out of me that had been missing all this time. My writer's block was gone, and I couldn't get the words out fast enough.

Who knew my week with Ethan Rochester would lead to writing the best novel of my life?

When I returned home, I couldn't write because I was so hurt and upset. But eventually, anytime I thought about Ethan and our time together, which seemed to be all the time, my inspiration fire would reignite. I tried to push away all the negative thoughts and only focus on the good that happened between us. It was the best week of my life until I ran into that witch of a woman, and she ruined everything. My trust had been broken, and I was too scared to start over, not knowing the difference between his truths and her lies. It was too much.

As soon as I presented the new book idea to my agent, she ate it up. The novel practically wrote itself, which, as a full-time writer, I can confidently say has never happened to me before. Once I finished the first draft, relief rushed through my veins. My agent insisted my characters get a full happily-ever-after, even if I didn't.

So of course, they did. Complete with a big southern wedding and lots of babies.

Ethan had done what he promised all along—helped me find my writing inspiration. It's safe to say it wasn't the southern air or lifestyle—it was all him.

Our story ended with my heart broken and me crying in the plane bathroom. I knew the moment I told Nora, she'd tell me to talk to him and find out what happened. And if what Harmony said was true, she'd say to give him a piece of my mind. Hell, she was ready to fly to Charleston and do it for me like the mama bear she is.

Suffice it to say, I didn't do either of those things. Everything from my past resurfaced, and it was the same issues and lies from all my failed relationships all over again. Fear, self-doubt, depression. It all kept me from making that step, from going back to Ethan.

He'd called and texted dozens of times. They were all left unheard and unread. I was being childish, and I knew that, but I couldn't bear to hear if everything Harmony said was actually true. I couldn't bear to hear him lie to me either. I needed more time to think, and I had major deadlines to worry about on top of that.

Until one night, I finally braved listening his voicemails. It took two bottles of wine, of course.

The sound of his voice crippled me. God, it was so sexy when he spoke, but I could hear the pain in his tone. It was evident, yet I couldn't bring myself to hit the call back button. I was pathetic and weak, I knew that.

In the beginning of his messages, he desperately begged me to tell him why I left and what happened. Those messages broke me down. I was the spitting image of Carrie Bradshaw crying in her wedding dress—except I was alone with an empty glass of wine and my cat.

Later, his messages changed because he had found out about Harmony and knew she'd said something to me. He pleaded with me to tell him what she said so he'd know how to fix it, but that was the thing. It couldn't be fixed. Even if her words were complete lies, the fact that I let a guy like him affect me in only a week scared the shit out of me, and a part of me was running. Running from the reality of what happened so quickly. I'd become too vulnerable, and it was a hard lesson in trusting another guy with my heart. The pain made it impossible for me to move forward.

Part of me wanted to go back to him, hear what he had to say, and fall back into our easy ways. However, the logical part of me knew it was a formula for disaster. My life is in Chicago and his is in South Carolina. We both knew this; yet he didn't give up.

After one bottle of wine was emptied, I continued to the other, listening to another handful of his messages. God, they made me hate myself. I wallowed in guilt and self-sabotage. Yet, I continued to convince myself that staying away was for the best. It'd be better to get over him now before I really fell hard because if it didn't work out the second time around, my heart would be destroyed beyond repair.

I lied to myself, even if I didn't want to admit I was. Eventually, I started believing those lies.

Nora's words from earlier repeated in my head. *Give the boy something, Vada. Whether it's an explanation for your silence or just to say you want him to stop calling, give him some kind of closure.*

I knew she was right, but I couldn't work up the courage. Until I'd emptied those two bottles of wine and that's when I finally hit the call back button.

He didn't answer, of course. It was well after two in the morning, which meant it was even later where he was.

The next morning, I woke with the worst headache of my life. I rarely drank, and when I did, it was one or two glasses max. I was certainly paying for it now.

A loud knock echoed through my apartment, and I groaned, unable to deal with anyone or anything. It was well into the afternoon, so it could only be Nora.

"Use your key," I hollered, hoping my words would make it to the front of my apartment. After a moment, the knocking continued. "Dammit, Nora," I grumbled, pulling myself from the bed and opening the front door.

"Miss Collins?" an older man's voice rang.

Blinking, I finally lifted my head and saw he was holding a large vase of red roses.

"Yes?"

"Floral delivery, miss. Here you go." He handed them to me with a smile.

"Oh, um, thank you."

"My pleasure, miss. Have a great day."

After closing the door with my foot, I walked the vase of flowers to my kitchen and set them down. Searching for a card, I found one after my vision cleared.

Dear Vada,

I miss you more than I can express, but I'm willing to give you space if that's what you need to think everything through. I'll wait for you until you're ready.

You know where to find me when you are.
-Ethan

P.S. Don't think I won't stop reminding you how much I care and miss you though.

P.S.S. Hope you're feeling okay this morning. Take an Ibuprofen and drink lots of water. Hangovers are the worst.

"What?" I gasped aloud. I racked my brain, saw the empty

wine bottles on my living room floor, and reached for my phone. I checked my calls, and that's when realization hit.

I called him nine times last night. Left him voicemail after voicemail, worst—*drunk voicemails.*

"Oh my God," I murmured. "Fuck."

Why in the world would he even want to talk or see me again after that? I probably mentioned his cock and how I wished I could fuck his brains out just to use him the way I felt used. *Oh my God.* This was fucking awful.

After telling Nora the story, she laughed her ass off. Completely at my expense, of course. She even said she heard me rambling through the walls, and when I cursed her out for not trying to stop me, she said it was for my own good.

One thing I know for sure is that I told him I needed space, which was true. It was why I didn't respond to his messages because I knew the minute I did, I'd throw everything out the door. I needed to stay focused, work on my novel, and not let a man chase away my dreams.

Space was good. He knew writing was important to me and respecting that made me fall for him even harder.

After that night, I stayed on track and kept writing. His calls and text messages stopped, but the flower deliveries didn't.

Every week like clockwork, a new bouquet showed up at my door. Every week, a new note.

I miss you, Vada.

You're beautiful. Just thought I'd remind you.

I'll wait for you. No matter what.

I was tempted to call him several times, but I didn't want to lead him on. Truthfully, I didn't know what I wanted. I hated to cause him more pain, not knowing if I'd ever be able to be who or what he needed. Space and time couldn't heal everything, and there was no guarantee when that would even be.

"You'll always have a deadline, Vada. Go to him," Nora insisted.

If I was being a hundred percent honest with myself, it was fear keeping me from making that step.

Fear of putting my heart back on the line.

Fear of losing my creativeness.

Fear of giving it all up for him.

Fear that I wouldn't be able to trust him even if he'd given me no reason not to.

Even after a year, I kept all the dried rose petals from dozens of flowers that sat in a box on my nightstand. I looked at them every day and tried to remember the way he smelled. He always smelled so damn good. Purely male mixed with a hint of amber. It was heaven.

Even though I essentially ignored him for months, he refused to let me forget him, as if I could. One note he sent hit me hard. It said he was giving me all the space I needed, knowing I was working on my book, and that he'd be there when I was ready. He wasn't giving up—no matter what.

Part of me wondered how long he was going to keep it up and if he was still thinking of me as much as I was thinking of him.

Then the flowers stopped coming a month ago. Right after the book's release.

First, a week went by, and I didn't think much of it. I'd been preparing for my book tour, but when another three weeks went by, I knew I'd run out of time. A million thoughts tumbled through my mind. Had he finally gotten over me? Did he meet someone else? Was he done trying? Had I fucked up by not giving him some kind of response that wasn't wine-induced?

Or worse. Did he see the book and now hate me for it, for sharing those intimate parts of our relationship?

I knew the only person I could blame was myself and admitting that brought more pain than anything else. I was heartbroken all over again, and it was my own damn fault.

"Vada!" Olivia, my new assistant shouts. She's been traveling with me and helping keep my schedule straight. The promotional tour for this new book is the biggest and longest I've ever done, so my agent suggested bringing someone to help me. Considering there'd be a lot of events and meetings to keep track of, I took her advice and went through an agency to find a highly-qualified assistant.

Blinking, I realize she's waving her hand in front of my face. "You need more caffeine," she mutters, pointing to the Styrofoam coffee cup on the table, silently telling me to chug it down.

"I'm fine," I finally reply, grabbing for the cup anyway. She catches me daydreaming all the time, so I know she's used to me zoning out on our conversations. "What is it?" I ask before taking a large sip.

"Which outfit do you want to wear?" She's holding up a dress in each hand. "You have the brunch meet-n-greet at eleven and then the signing from one to four."

I narrow my eyes, studying each one. They both work just fine, but being in Charleston has me thinking I could maybe—just *maybe*—see Ethan. As quickly as the thought enters, I push it back out.

"The navy blue one," I say, pointing to the one in her right hand. "With my cream-colored heels."

"Great." She hangs them up. "You can wear your new blazer over it for dinner."

"Dinner?" I rack my brain, but I can't remember.

"Yes. You have an intimate meet-n-greet from six to eight."

I put it in my mental calendar, although I know I'll forget. Every day of this tour has me so jam-packed that I have a hard time keeping track.

"Thank God you have a great memory." I sigh.

She turns around before grabbing something and walking toward me. With a loud plop, she tosses a fat notebook on the table.

"I have a great planner," she corrects. "This is your Bible."

I arch a brow, amused by her dramatics. "The Bible?"

"Yes, the Bible." She starts petting it. "Treat it as such, anyway. It has everything in here from your schedule, your coffee orders, your outfit options for each event, your flight itineraries, your sleep schedule." She pauses to blink up at me. *"Everything."*

"Jesus, Liv." I pull it toward me and start flipping through pages. "Surprised it doesn't have my menstrual cycle in here."

"Page twenty-two," she says, not missing a beat. I look up at her with an arched brow, and she winks. "You think I just know when to pack extra chocolate and pads?" She taps her temple with a finger. "My number one job—keep my author happy."

I smile. "Wow, I never realized how much you do behind the scenes. Thank you."

She blushes, and I know our little moment is over. "Okay, well you have twelve minutes to finish your breakfast." She gives me a pointed look that tells me I better eat.

Grabbing the planner off the table, she walks back to her makeshift office in the opposite corner of the hotel suite while I finish my breakfast.

Exactly twelve minutes later, Olivia is pushing me into the shower and reminding me to shave my legs.

I look down and realize she's right.

"How did you—" I shout from behind the curtain.

"The Bible!" she yells back, and I smile.

Less than two hours later, we're heading to one of the hotel's meeting rooms where a group of readers are waiting for me. No matter how many events I do, it still feels surreal. I'm completely humbled that people read my words and even want to meet me. It's an intoxicating feeling, and every time I leave one of these events, I have to pinch myself because this is my life.

"You have one hour and forty-five minutes, and then we have to get you to the bookstore for the signing. Ready?" Olivia asks as she brushes one of my flyaway hairs off my forehead. She really is my right-hand woman.

"Absolutely!" I say, confidently and smile.

She opens the doors for me, and I'm greeted by a dozen women who all smile and start clapping as soon as I walk in. It's so overwhelming, yet I can't deny how great it feels. They stand up from the table, so I can give them each a hug while they introduce themselves to me.

Meet-n-greets are intimate and personal, which is one of the reasons I love them so much. I meet a lot of readers online, but there's nothing like connecting with them in person.

Once we're all seated and settled with our plates of food, questions start flying. "So does Nathan know you wrote a novel about him?" Amelia, a woman around the same age as me, asks. "I mean, he'd have to, right?"

Everyone leans over the table, itching closer to hear my response.

The *New York Times* reached out to my publisher and requested an interview with me and printed it right before the book's release where I confirmed the rumors about this novel being inspired by true events. Considering this was a steamy romance novel, they were intrigued, along with thousands of readers. So, of course, the million-dollar question everyone wants to know—did "Nathan" know I wrote this book primarily based on our week together?

Of course, Nathan was *actually* Ethan, but I haven't confirmed whether or not he knew because honestly, I didn't. I had no idea if he followed my social media pages, but I haven't come out and told him personally. Hell, I haven't even spoken to him. Concern on how readers will react to that truth is why I haven't publicly revealed that. Part of me worries my readers would be upset if I told our story without his permission, and the other part of me stresses they wouldn't connect with the characters if they knew the real-life love story didn't end the same.

"I don't think so," is all I offer to Amelia.

"Do you think he'd be mad if he found out?" another woman asks. "Like now that the book is released, he could know, right?" There's hopefulness in her tone.

"Sure, he could. Not sure he follows romance books, but never say never," I say with a forced smile. I knew going on tour and having these meet-n-greets would bring up uncomfortable questions and memories of Ethan, but being in the same town as him and where the story took place is affecting me in more ways than one.

The brunch ends on a high note when I announce there'll be more standalone books in the series. My agent ended up getting me a three-book deal for the series once she sold the first one, and after I sent in summaries for books two and three.

"You did good," Olivia praises. "I am starting to wonder if this Nathan guy is real though." She flashes me a wink, and I roll my eyes.

"Sometimes I wonder the same thing," I say with a chuckle.

"The more you talk about him, the more he sounds too good to be true."

"If it sounds too good to be true, it probably is," I say, confirming what she already expected. Ethan's the full package, and anyone that meets him would probably agree. However, that doesn't void the fact that we were destined to end this way.

His emotional baggage mixed with my trust issues was a disaster waiting to happen. But I can confidently say that if I had to do it all over again, I undoubtedly would.

The afternoon and night go by fast. The signing is a huge success and meeting readers who want my autograph and picture has me floating on cloud nine. I'm not a social person by nature, but as soon as I enter that room filled with people whose eyes are all on me, something in my brain switches.

I'm suddenly the most social person ever, remembering to smile and hug people. I pose for pictures and thank them for coming. Nora calls it Vada 2.0.

I laugh, thinking back to the conversation. She knows how introverted I am and often teases me for all the food deliveries I get.

"You have more men coming and going from your apartment than the Playboy mansion," she mocked.

"Well, what can I say? Food is my weakness." I smirked, earning a groan from her.

"One of these days, I'm teaching you to cook a damn meal for yourself. How are you ever going to be able to cook dinner for your future husband?"

I gave her a look that told her that wasn't something I'd have to be concerned about anytime soon.

"You could go out every once in a while. Meet up with some friends," she encouraged.

"I don't have friends." I deadpanned. "Except you and Oliver."

"Oliver and I don't count, although I don't appreciate you putting me in the same category as your damn cat." She grunted. "I mean, real friends. Girlfriends the same age as you. Go out and have fun. You're always worried about the next deadline."

"Because I'm always on a deadline." I half-laughed, half-cried because it's the truth. Deadlines on deadlines. "Plus, I don't want to be that social anyway."

"How's it you can't socialize with people your own age, yet you go on tour and socialize with hundreds of strangers?"

I shrugged with a grin. "One of life's many mysteries I guess." I flashed a smug smile.

"It's like you have an alternate personality. Vada 2.0."

I laughed, rolling my head back because I'd never thought about it like that.

"You're absolutely right, Nora. But Vada OG is my comfort zone."

Considering my writing schedule and hectic lifestyle, cooking just isn't a priority right now. Neither is going out and socializing. I know I'll probably look back one day and wished I'd formed some close friendships, but people who don't read or write just don't understand the passion. I'm better off in my own bubble with online friends who share the same interests and night owl schedule.

"Okay, that's it for the day," Olivia says with a deep breath. "You're officially off-duty."

"I can finally take off these heels then." I sigh with a choked laugh. "My writer's uniform is so much better."

"Wearing the same clothes for a week isn't a uniform, Vada. It's right up there next to homelessness." She eyes me, daring me to challenge her. "Plus, you look *good* in a dress and heels. You should go out and show yourself off." Her eyes light up at her suggestion.

"Sorry, Vada 2.0 is officially down for the night. Plus, I should get some writing done tonight. My agent is already clawing at me for the next part."

Sighing, she nods, and we head toward the doors and walk out together. Charleston is beautiful this time of year; a warm breeze blows across us as the sun starts to set. I close my eyes briefly, letting all the memories soak in.

"You okay?" she asks, adjusting her purse on her shoulder.

I blink and inhale a deep breath. "Yeah. I'm good." I smile wide.

Stepping out onto the sidewalk, Olivia plays on her phone, and just as we round a corner, I hear someone calling my name.

"Vada!"

The voice is deep and recognizable.

Spinning around, my eyes search for him, and it doesn't take me long to spot him. His hands are shoved into the front pockets of his dark-washed jeans. Dark shaggy hair tamed to one side. Piercings in both ears. Scruffy jawline.

He's as gorgeous as I remember.

A single girl's wet dream.

Ethan.

CHAPTER TWENTY

ETHAN

It's been a year since I've seen Vada in the flesh, but she's just as stunningly beautiful as I remember. Her hair is a tad longer, but thick and just as gorgeous as before. Seeing her in a dress instantly starts doing things to me, but when I see the expression on her face the moment her eyes find mine, I know the feelings I had for her haven't wavered a bit.

Coming here was a risk. After sending her forty-five flower bouquets and never getting a response from her, I didn't know if she'd want to see me or not. However, when I heard she would be in Charleston, I couldn't pass up the opportunity to know once and for all if we still had a chance at making this work.

I haven't stopped thinking about her since she left. I've been a tortured soul since the moment she walked out of my life, and I haven't even looked at another woman since she's been gone. This was my last attempt to lay it all out there on the line.

"Ethan," she says, her tone soft, as she walks toward me. I see the surprise in her eyes and hope I'm not breaking the rules by coming here.

"Hey." I meet her halfway, unsure how to approach her. I try to read her body language, but she isn't giving much away.

"You're here," she says simply, almost as if she'd been anticipating seeing me, which makes me hopeful. She releases a breath, and I wonder if it'd be appropriate to hug her.

"Of course, I am," is all I say in return.

"I'm just surprised to see you here. I just got the feeling you were done waiting." I don't miss the hint of sadness in her tone.

I take another step toward her. "Oh fuck no."

My blunt words take her off guard, but she chuckles softly anyway.

"I wasn't sure I'd ever see you again."

"I wasn't sure you'd ever want to see me again," I admit. "After everything that happened with Harmony and your writing deadlines, but seeing as you didn't slap me across the face, I take it you don't hate me." I rock back on my feet, nervously.

She smiles, lowering her eyes to hide the blush that sweeps across her cheeks. "Well, I actually decided to stop hating you yesterday. So, good timing."

"Whew, glad I waited."

We both smile.

"So…what are you doing here, Ethan?" She sucks in her lower lip as she studies me.

"I came to see if you got my flowers," I tease, knowing damn well she did. I paid good money to make sure they were delivered directly to her.

"Um, ya know…I'm pretty sure I did." She puts a finger to her lips as if she's truly thinking about it.

I narrow my eyes, but she cracks a smile, giving me the reassurance I need.

"Of course, I did," she finally confesses. "They were all really gorgeous," she says sincerely, and the nerves begin to wash away. "However, it was quite ironic, don't you think?" Her lips tilt up in a mock grin.

"Why do you say that?" I narrow my eyes.

"I recall you specifically telling me you weren't a 'sending flowers' type of guy." She flashes a wide smile, knowing damn well she's right. "And yet, you sent me a bouquet every week for almost a year."

I run my hand along my jawline, covering up the guilty smirk that flashes across my face. "To be fair, I hadn't been that guy for years, so I didn't want you to have the wrong expectations." I pause, keeping my eyes locked on hers. "But meeting you changed everything."

"Well, thank you. I loved them all."

"You're welcome." I smile in return. "I wanted to make sure you always had fresh flowers to keep you inspired. I would've sent Henry, knowing how much you enjoyed his company, but I was worried you'd send him back in a bucket."

She bursts out laughing, and it eases everything inside me.

"I can honestly say I don't miss your cock chasing me." She pinches her lips together, preventing her from smiling.

"Well, that's really a shame, because he's sure missed you," I tell her sincerely.

"I bet he's had plenty of other visitors to attack."

Lowering my eyes, I shake my head. "I haven't rented the cottage out since you left."

"Oh." Her voice sounds surprised, although she really shouldn't be. I haven't wanted anyone else in there. To me, it'll always be hers.

Clearing my throat, I work up the courage to tell her why I'm really here. "I came for you, Vada." I look into her big green eyes. "I haven't stopped thinking about you. I couldn't miss the opportunity to finally see you."

She bites on her lower lip before popping it back out. "How'd you know I'd be in town?"

"Aunt Millie saw it in the paper and told me," I confirm. "She's your biggest fan now." I smile. "Once I found out, I thought about this moment over and over and decided that even if you were pissed to see me, I had to chance it."

She pauses a moment before smiling with a nod. "Well, I'm glad you did," she replies, her words taking me by surprise. "I've wondered what it'd be like to see you again."

"Yeah, it's…" I pause, unable to stop looking at her lips and thinking about the way she tastes. Screw formalities. "Fuck, Vada. I'm sorry." I step toward her.

"You don't have to—" she begins, but I'm quick to cut her off.

"That's not what I'm apologizing for." I'm quick to close the gap between us, wrap my hand around her neck, and pull her lips to mine. I kiss the fuck out of her and am relieved when she kisses me back.

A risk—to assume she'd want to kiss me—but one *so* worth it.

Her tongue dances with mine as her hands wrap around my waist and pull at the fabric of my shirt, desperate to deepen the kiss. My palms cup her cheeks and hold her closely. The world spins around us as if we're the only two people here, and in this moment, it's only Vada and me.

"I've missed you so fucking much," I breathe against her lips, leaning back just enough to whisper the words. "Did you miss me?" I bravely ask, needing to hear her say it.

She swallows then nods. "Yes, but—"

"But it's not enough," I finish for her, predicting her thoughts.

"We live completely different lives," she confirms.

"That's not a good enough reason to be apart, Vada."

"You stopped sending the flowers," she whispers. "I thought you were done waiting for me and the thought nearly sent me back to desperate levels." I furrow my brows in question. "Wine," she clarifies.

Brushing my finger along her jawline, I tilt her chin to look back up at me. "I stopped sending them because I knew you'd be on tour. I sent them because I wanted to give you the space and time, knowing you needed it, but without smothering you. I wanted you to know that I was still thinking about you and that I'd wait for you as long as you needed me to—as long as I knew there was still a chance for us."

"Oh, I didn't think of that," she says, chewing on her lip again. I can see how nervous she is to be around me. "Harmony's words really stung and affected me, and it made me really scared at how fast I was falling for you. Then I started second-guessing everything."

"I'm so sorry about her. Everything she told you was based on lies, and I'm sorry she put them in your head, but I can't undo that part of my life. As much as I wish I could." I groan, getting fired up just thinking about her and the shit she pulled.

"I know, and I wanted to believe you once I finally listened to your messages, but it felt like it was too late. I'd already left heartbroken, and I knew I wouldn't survive another broken heart if

I called you back or even returned. It felt inevitable that things would eventually end, so I knew it was for the best to stay away."

"How could you make that decision without actually talking to me first?" I ask, more anger in my tone than I'd meant. "You weren't the only one hurting and confused, Vada."

She swallows, her body tensing. "I know, but I felt like I couldn't trust you even if what she told me was a lie. I couldn't trust those feelings anymore, and I couldn't go through the pain all over again."

"I never lied to you, Vada. You had no reason not to trust me," I tell her.

"I don't trust easily," she reminds me. "I didn't know if the feelings I had for you were real either because they formed so fast. I'd hoped once I was back home and writing, I would get over you."

"And did you?" I ask, brushing strands of her hair behind her ear, feeling the goose bumps along her skin.

Her body stills as she thinks about her answer. "No," she says just above a whisper. "Not even close." I bring her mouth back to mine, feverishly kissing her.

"Thank fuck," I murmur against her lips. "I've been dying to kiss you for twelve long months. I was going to die if I had to hold back."

She laughs against my mouth and the sound sends tingles down my body. Her laugh is music to my soul, and it's the first true smile I've had in months.

"How inappropriate would it be to ask you to have dinner with me tonight?"

She chews her bottom lip as if she's really thinking about it. "Depends. Are you going to offer your cock to me again?"

"Henry?" My brows lift. "I knew you missed him." I smirk at all the memories of him chasing and scaring the shit out of her.

She chuckles again then shakes her head. "No, not *that* cock."

I choke on my words before I can even spit them out. "Shit. You're still as feisty as I remember."

Her lips spread into a wide, knowing grin. "C'mon, Casanova. Take me to your lair."

After Vada introduces her assistant to me and explains she'll be riding with me, we take off in my car. The woman looked at me like I was a figment of her imagination.

"Are you sure you didn't mean to say *riding me* instead?" Holding her hand as I drive back to my house, I press her knuckles to my lips as we fall right back into our old rhythm. "Or are you two not that close?" I flash her a cocky grin.

"Ha! Still as confident and arrogant as *I* remember." She squeezes her hand in mine. "Quite the opposite actually. She probably knows more about me than I do. She takes care of my schedule and everything, down to what underwear I wear that day."

"Really?" I arch a brow in her direction before sliding the material of her dress up her thigh and revealing red, lacy panties. "Remind me to send her a thank-you card."

She bursts out laughing. "Please don't. She'll take it to heart and frame it or something."

Once we arrive at the house, I study Vada's features, and I'm positive memories of us here together are flooding through her mind. She looks around, her face contorting into something unrecognizable.

"What's on your mind?" I ask once we're standing on the sidewalk in front of the house. Grabbing her hand, I pull her body toward mine. "I'm really happy you're here."

"It feels a little like déjà vu," she says, honestly. "And it scares me a little."

"Don't be scared, sweetheart." I press a soft kiss against her mouth. "I don't bite, unless requested of course."

"Why can't I get you out of my head, Ethan Rochester?" She tilts her head as she asks the question. "You're bad news."

"Probably because I'm the best sex you've ever had," I say, confidently.

Her eyes widen as the realization hits her. "Oh my God." She covers a hand over her mouth, laughing. "You read the book."

"Of course, I did." I smile in return. "It was the church's book club pick of the month. Very popular with the older ladies, by the way."

Her cheeks redden, and her eyes bug out in embarrassment. "Stop it!"

"I'm serious! I couldn't look Aunt Millie in the eyes for weeks once she learned of my cock piercing." I chuckle, shaking my head at the memory of her reading those parts.

Her face falls into her palms as she dies laughing. "Guess they read between the lines."

"Yeah, Nathan?" I quirk a brow.

She's still laughing. "Fuck. I honestly didn't think you'd even hear about it."

"Seriously? It's been in the local papers for weeks and in those 'anticipated reads' articles. Apparently, being with a Casanova excites a lot of people." I wink.

"Aunt Millie must think I'm a slut," she blurts out as I lead her down the path to the front of the house.

"No, but she thinks I'm a manwhore. So thanks for that," I tease, taking out my keys and unlocking the door.

"She thought that long before I came around." She laughs.

"True."

After walking into the house, I lead her into the kitchen and pin her against the wall. I know I should be taking it slow with her, considering we still have so much to discuss, but I can't pass up this opportunity. I have no idea what it'll lead to—if anything at all—and I've been miserably waiting for this day to come.

"What do you say we skip dinner and go right to dessert?" I ask against her neck, inhaling her sweet scent.

I feel her chest moving rapidly as she breathlessly responds, "*Yes.*" It's a whispered plea, and I don't waste any time. My lips on hers, her hands on me, our bodies pressed together as if we'll float away without the weight of the other.

"Tell me what you want, Vada," I murmur in her ear.

"You."

Wrapping my arms around her hips, I dig my nails into her ass and squeeze. Lifting her up, she circles her legs around me, and I carry her to the table.

"I can't wait any longer, I have to taste you." After setting her down, I kneel and part her legs just enough for my hand to slide up her leg and tug at her panties. "Red is officially my new favorite color." I smirk, looking up at her as she blushes.

Sliding her panties all the way down, I pull off her heels and toss them aside. "When I'm done devouring you for dessert, I want you bent over this table wearing only those heels."

"Oh my God…" She moans, leaning back on her elbows. "You're giving me way too much book material." She smiles, and I know she's not joking.

"I'd be happy to give you more inspiration…I have all night, sweetheart." I meet her eyes and wink before parting her legs farther. Hooking her knee over my shoulder, I kiss a line until I reach the sweetness in between her legs. "Goddammit, Vada," I growl, flattening my tongue against her slit. "I've been craving this for months. Fuck."

She releases a throaty moan as I find her clit and circle it with my tongue. Her fingers wrap around my biceps, and her nails dig in as I slide my tongue inside her.

"Vada…" I breathe out, desperately.

"Ethan…" she whimpers in return.

I bring my hand up her thigh and rub the pad of my thumb along her clit as I kiss along her inner thigh. My fingers slide down her pussy and push inside her tight cunt. Her hips buck at the intrusion, and she bellows out another moan.

"Do you know how fucking mad at you I was when you left me, Vada…" I slip a second finger inside her. She stretches her neck and looks at me with hooded eyes. I push in deeper. "I lost my shit when I realized you were really gone. Your luggage was gone. The drawers in the cottage were empty. You took the last sliver of hope I felt and ripped it to fucking shreds." I increase the pace, finger fucking her hard and fast.

"Ethan…" she begins, but she bites her bottom lip, and a moan slips through them.

"I called and texted you a hundred times. For the first time in years, I felt something. I hadn't realized it until you left, and my heart broke all over again."

"Ethan, stop talking…" she orders, and I spread her legs wider and sink in deeper. The more I think about it now, the angrier I get, knowing she could've called or texted me so we could've worked it out. I still would've given her space to finish her book, but I was left in limbo.

"Aunt Millie told me to go to you. She said to fight for you, Vada. I wanted to, tried to convince myself I should, but I couldn't bear the thought of you telling me to leave or that the feelings were no longer mutual. So I fucking chickened out. Sent you flowers instead. Tried telling myself it was for the best, that one week with you was enough."

"Ethan, please…" she begs, her eyes filling with tears.

I slow my rhythm but don't stop.

"I've been lying to myself for twelve fucking months, hoping you'd realize how much you meant to me and come back to me, but now that I have you here with me, all I want is for you to know how much you hurt me…"

"Ethan…" she begs louder. "I'm sorry!" I rotate my wrist and slide my finger in and out of her again. "Fuck. I'm sorry I left without saying goodbye. It's been torturing me ever since." Her honest words fuel my anger even more.

"Then why didn't you come back sooner and let me explain?" I fire back. "I needed you as much as you needed me."

She winces before her body tenses, and I feel her tighten around me. Her orgasm starts to build, and she's no longer in control as she arches her back and releases a deep, desperate moan. Desperate for more, desperate for me.

"I was scared," she finally admits. "I'm still scared."

Standing up, I push my fingers inside my mouth and taste her sweetness.

"Don't be, because, for the first time in six years, I'm not. I know exactly what I want."

She adjusts her body and sits up so she can look up into my eyes. Reaching for me, she wraps her petite hands in mine. "Isn't getting closure this time a much better ending to our story?"

"This isn't the end, baby. We're just beginning."

CHAPTER TWENTY-ONE

VADA

THE MOMENT his lips touched mine, I was transported back to the first time we kissed. He tasted so good and memories of our week together were front and center in my head. I'd been anticipating this moment, wondering if it'd ever happen, and now that it has, I'm more scared than ever.

"Vada…" he says my name in a pleading drawl. "Please tell me you want this as much as I do."

I do. I want it so bad.

"I don't want to hurt you again, Ethan," I say, softly. "I don't know what I can offer you."

"You." He presses his lips against mine again, silently pleading for me to give us a chance. "I only need you."

I release a moan as our bodies press together and his hand wraps around my neck and holds us there, waiting for my response.

"Say yes, Vada…" he begs as his mouth brushes against mine. "Let me love you."

God. This man was the full package, and I'd be a fool to walk away from him again. No guy has ever fought this hard for me and knowing he waited a year for me lets me know how serious he is about us, too. After a moment, I finally nod, giving him the approval he needs.

"Thank fuck," he mutters against my lips before taking my

mouth. He positions my body between his legs and kisses the hell out of me. My heels dig into his ass as he rubs his fingers over my hard nipples.

Without warning, he scoops me up and carries me down the hall. I squeal with a laugh and cling to him while he takes us upstairs. I know exactly where we're going, and the smile on my face never falters.

Once we're inside his bedroom, he kicks the door shut and flashes me an evil grin.

"I've imagined this for a long time," I admit because it's the truth. I've spent many times in my bed, getting off to thoughts of him.

"Yeah?" He sets me down on the bed, towering over me with hope in his eyes. His mouth lands on my collarbone before he brushes his lips along my exposed shoulder.

Deciding to mess with him first, I reply in all seriousness, "I want to use a strap-on and fuck you in the ass while stroking your dick until you come."

He immediately chokes and leans back to face me, reading my expression. "Just because Nathan's into that, doesn't mean I am."

I burst out laughing. "Dammit. You really did read the book."

Smiling, he presses his lips back to mine. "Of course. Several times."

I wrap my arms and legs around him, pressing his body to mine. "Several times?"

"Yup. Memorized it like the fucking Bible."

"Had I known you were going to read it, I wouldn't have gone into such grave detail about your cock," I tease, loving the way his body feels pressed to mine.

"Speaking of which, Henry's butt hurt that you gave him a chick name."

My head falls back, laughing, which I seem to be doing a lot around him. "I'll explain to him that it was for his privacy, and hopefully he'll forgive me."

"I'm sure you two can work out a deal." He winks, sending butterflies straight to my core.

Leaning back, his hands push up my dress until he's pulling it over my head, and I watch as he tosses it to the floor. His eyes widen as he stares at my bra, which happens to match the red, lacy panties I was wearing.

"I think your assistant needs a raise." He smirks, rubbing the pad of his thumb against my nipple.

"I can dress myself, you know. She just so happened to pack everything for this trip so I could work on edits."

"Another book?" His brows raise, intrigued.

I nod. "There's always another book."

"Does Nathan make an appearance in it?" He kneels back slightly to remove his shirt. My eyes trace down his chest and abs, wandering all the way down to his happy trail that leads right to *my* happy place.

"He doesn't, but don't worry, Nathan will always be my number one." I flash him a wink as I reach over and help him unbutton his jeans.

"Good. Now let me fuck you like in chapter thirteen, because I'm in the mood for some backdoor adventures." He grins, waiting for my reaction.

"Nice try, Casanova." I unzip his jeans.

"A man can dream." He shrugs, standing and removing the rest of his clothing.

I swallow as I take in his beautiful body. "Well, keep dreaming."

"I think I am," he says, genuinely, kneeling between my legs again and brushing his fingers along my cheek. "I still can't believe you're really here."

"Me either."

He presses his lips to mine, sweet and slow, then slides his tongue in just enough to part my lips. My hands hang around his hips before my fingertips trail along his deep V line that brings me to his erection, hard and solid. I'd be lying if I said I hadn't missed the feel of his cock, the way it tastes, the way it filled me so fucking deep, and that piercing.

I feel the warmth of his hands wrap around my body and unhook my bra. He slides it down my arms and tosses it, cupping my breasts and massaging my nipples with his fingertips. I groan at the contact, loving the way his hands feel on me.

"I told myself once I finally had you back in my bed, I'd take my time with you, but fuck, baby. I don't think I can." He groans, moving his lips along my jaw and neck.

"We have all night," I remind him. "I need you as much as you need me."

"Fucking hell," he growls, leaning back as he grabs the back of my knees and pulls me to the edge of the bed until my ass nearly hangs off.

I squeal, grasping onto his arms. My head falls back with laughter at his urgency. "You make me so horngry," he says with a devilish grin.

"Horngry?" I ask, amused. "What's that?"

"It's when I can't decide if I wanna fuck you or eat you first." The corner of his lips tilts up in a knowing smile.

I laugh as he brings his mouth to my pussy and sinks his tongue inside.

"Guess I know which one won," I say.

"Yeah, I decided to spend some quality time between your legs first."

Sinking a finger inside, his tongue circles my clit and works me up until I explode. I barely recover when he flips me over and takes me from behind.

His hand wraps around my neck, tilting my head back so he can stare into my eyes as I unravel around his length. I love the way he's looking at me as if he can't get enough of my body.

"Vada, *fuck*." He groans, pushing into me deeper and harder. "You feel so fucking good. So tight and wet, baby."

He pulls back slightly, the tip of his piercing rubbing against my pussy. God, I missed that piercing. Pushing back in, he increases his pace and sinks deep into me until I explode again. Fuck, he's so good at that.

Fisting my hair, he pulls my head back again until our lips collide. He continues his rhythm, fucking me so good and hard, I can barely keep up with my breathing. I feel his body tense, his kiss deepens, and then he moans against my mouth as he releases inside me.

"Vada…" he whispers after a minute, against my lips, so soft and sweet.

"Yes?"

"Stay with me," he pleads, running his tongue along my bottom lip. "Give us a second chance."

He kisses me before I can respond, which gives me the time I need to process his words.

"I have three more weeks of my promo tour," I begin to explain as he arches his hips.

"Baby, I've been waiting twelve long months for you. I can wait another three weeks as long as I know you'll come back to me."

His words send shivers down my spine because they're everything right and perfect; any girl would die to hear them.

"I want to…" I start, unsure of how to answer him.

"Then do. Take a leap of faith, Vada. I'm not like those other douchebags you've dated. I won't hurt you," he pleads with such promise, and I want to believe his words with every fiber of my being.

Before I can respond, he pulls out of me and lies down on the bed next to me. I turn my body, so we're facing each other, and he moves closer until our chests press together.

Cupping my cheeks, he stares directly into my eyes. "Vada, baby. I'm not proposing marriage here. I'm asking you to give us a second-chance at making this work. I gave you space because I knew you needed it till you finished your novel, but I'm only a man of so much patience. I can't keep putting my heart on the line if you aren't willing to meet me halfway."

His confession hits me like a ton of bricks. This man is too good to be true, and I'd be a fool to run away from him again.

My eyes begin to water because his words are so strikingly beautiful. No man has ever fought for me and definitely not this hard. I want to savor everything.

"How would we make this work? I live in Chicago," I remind him.

He gives me a look that says it's not a good enough reason, and deep down in my heart I know it's not. "Yes, and last I checked, you're a writer, who can literally do her job anywhere."

I swallow, realizing all the excuses I'm making.

"Vada, what is it? Tell me," he asks, noticing my hesitation.

"If I moved here, to be with you, it'd put a lot of pressure on us to make it work. I already have a mile-long list of relationship and anxiety issues. I don't know how it'd work with that kind of pressure on us."

"There'd be no pressure, babe. I know writing is important to you, and I have my pottery, so I'd never put you in a position to choose one over the other."

"Okay…" I finally respond with a nod, giving him the reassurance he needs.

Enthusiastically, he grabs my face, and our mouths collide together. I laugh against his lips at his eagerness, and he smiles in return.

"As long as Henry doesn't try to eat Oliver." I grin, weaving our legs together.

He presses a long kiss on my lips. "No promises." Winking, he pulls me off the bed and starts leading us down the hall, and before I can question what he's doing, he brings us to the bathroom.

"Showers just haven't been the same without you." The corner of his lips tilt as he runs the water.

"You know? I've been thinking the exact same thing." I grin, letting him lead me inside.

"Good, because I plan to make up for lost time." He pins me to the wall as the water cascades down on us. His fingers find their way to my pussy while I stroke his shaft. He wastes no time hooking my leg around his waist as he slides back inside me. "I don't know how I ever lived without this—without you—and now that I have it back, I'm not letting you go."

I love his possessive side, even when he's being overly sweet about it.

He fucks me into oblivion, my breaths coming out in heavy pants. I dig my nails into his arms, holding onto him for support as he rips me in two.

Every part of me tightens as another wave of pleasure surrounds me.

"God, I'm so fucking close," he mutters against my neck as my hand tangles in his hair. "But I want to be inside you all the damn time, every single minute possible. How's it I can't get enough of you?"

"I thought a lot about this over the past year," I admit.

"Oh yeah?" I feel him smile against me. "Did you think of me when you touched yourself? Did you get off on those thoughts?"

"Well, you read the book," I tease.

"Ah, yes. Chapters two, three, six, and fourteen," he responds without missing a single beat.

I chuckle, amused he really did memorize the damn book.

"Chapter six was my favorite, I think. The way you screamed so hard during your orgasm, you ended up taking a lamp out."

"Oh my God." I blush, laughing at him. "To be fair, the lamp wasn't supposed to be there."

Without replying, he pulls out, turns me around and pins my chest to the shower wall.

"Chapter thirteen," I blurt out.

"What?" He leans his head over my shoulder almost as if he needs clarifying he heard me correctly. "Are you sure?"

I look over my shoulder and grin widely. "Absolutely."

His eyes widen before scraping his teeth along my shoulder. "Fuck, Vada. You're trying to fucking ruin me tonight, aren't you?"

"Only in the best way possible."

I feel his cock press against the small of my back. Shaking my ass, he drags the tip up and down my cheeks before positioning himself against my opening. He moves the showerhead so it's not directly on us before leaning back and pressing a hand on my spine till my back is arched enough for him.

He takes me by surprise when he kneels down, spreads my legs, and starts stroking his tongue along my slit. "Relax, Vada," he demands, soothing his hands along my hip. "Do you trust me?" he asks, and I don't hesitate to nod because I do. I really do.

He slides a finger into my tight hole as his tongue works my clit. My body relaxes against his touch, although the feeling is foreign. He loosens me up until he thinks I'm ready and when he stands back up, he slowly eases inside me. At first, it's so tight, and the pressure is so uncomfortable, I'm not sure how I feel about it. Then he slides in a bit more and wraps a hand around my waist, holding me in place.

"Touch yourself, baby. It'll help you relax, so you don't tense up," he tells me, and I oblige.

Sliding a hand between my legs, I rub my clit and feel the buildup as he slides in some more.

"Holy fuck," I blurt out at the intense sensation. I'd never felt anything like it.

"You feel so goddamn good, Vada. Fuck, I won't be able to last much longer."

A few moments later, my orgasm builds and everything tenses.

"Vada! *Fuck*, oh my God." His strained voice echoes through the shower as his climax hits him hard.

Breathless, we stand under the water together, both sated and defeated. He spins me around and captures me with a kiss.

"If you can still walk after that, then we're not finished."

CHAPTER TWENTY-TWO

ETHAN

I can't remember a time where I ever felt the undeniable hunger to have someone as much as I crave Vada. There's an animalistic desire I can't ever seem to satisfy. Prior to Vada, those thoughts would've never crossed my mind, but now, that thought no longer scares me.

"I'm pretty sure my legs will fall off if I try walking right now."

Smiling, I reach for the soap and reposition the showerhead over us.

"Let me clean you up then." I wink, lathering the soap between my palms before carefully placing them over her soft skin. She moans at the contact, and her head falls to the side.

I cover every inch of her perfect body and gently rinse her off. Although compared to what we just did, this somehow seems more intimate. After leading her out of the shower and drying her off, I carry her back into my bed and tuck her under the covers.

"I have a confession to make," I say as I slide into bed next to her.

"Oh yeah?" She looks up at me with hooded eyes. "What's that, Casanova?"

"I didn't really invite you over for dinner." I grin.

She turns and leans up on her elbow. "Well, then I guess I also have a confession."

My brows raise.

"I already had dinner when you invited me over for dinner." She smiles, and it's the cutest fucking thing ever.

"Ahh...I knew it." Flashing a victorious smile, I wrap my arms around her and hold her. We lie like that for several moments, both clinging to each other as if we'll die without it.

"I know you didn't ask, but I just want you to know something."

She angles her head up toward me and waits.

"I haven't been with anyone since you left. Haven't *wanted* to be with anyone. In fact, Wilma's pissed she wasn't the only pussy I had in here, but once she calmed down and I explained everything to her, she got over it," I confess with a grin.

Vada wrinkles her nose and snorts. "Wilma gave me the stink eye the last time I was here, so she probably thought I was taking over her territory."

"Yeah, she's a territorial bitch, but she'll have to get used to sharing now." I wink.

"Maybe Oliver and her will hit it off," she says with fake amusement.

"Well, if Oliver loves pussy as much as I do, then I'd say he'll warm right up to her."

"Oh my God!" She grabs the pillow that's against the headboard and throws it directly at me. "You're so bad."

"Yes, but you love it," I say without thinking. Worried she'll analyze those words, I open my mouth to say something else, but she cuts me off before I can.

"I do," she says softly, but looking directly into my eyes. "Who knew I would?" She smirks, lowering her eyes as a blush forms on her cheeks.

"Well, I can't say I'm really surprised. I mean, I'm a catch."

"I swear to God," she says, laughing and throwing another pillow at me.

Finding her ticklish spot, I dig my nails under her arms then laugh as she squirms against me. She squeals and tells me to stop, but I can't get enough of this. Enough of her. Laughing and smiling. She's so fucking perfect.

"Ethan, please...I'm going to pee if you don't stop!" She's

giggling, and before I know it, I pull her face to mine and kiss the fuck out of her.

"I can't let you leave without telling you first." I inhale briefly, rubbing the pad of my thumb along her bottom lip. "I'm so in love with you, Vada Collins. I think I always have been, but having you back in my life, falling right back into our ways as if no time has passed, solidifies everything I've felt for you." I pause, studying her expression before continuing. "I love you."

She sucks in her lower lip, her eyes widening as she swallows and processes everything I've just said.

"Why are you so good to me, Ethan? I mean, seriously. I leave without saying goodbye, I drunk call you and leave you a bunch of crazy voicemails, you send me weekly flowers, and when you find out I'm going to be back in town, you don't let the opportunity slip by to see me."

Her words come off accusing, but I know they aren't meant to be.

"I told you. I'm a catch." I wink.

"Stop." She chuckles. "And now you've just told me the most beautiful thing in the world, and I'm still so terrified to repeat them, although I want to."

I brush the hair away from her face, staring into her eyes. "I didn't say those words because I expected you to say them back. I said them because I never thought I could love anyone after Alana—I never allowed myself to—but with you, I want to. It was freeing, finally feeling like it's okay to love someone else."

"You have no idea how much that means to me." She grabs my face and plants a deep kiss on my lips. "Seriously." She kisses me again. "You just melted all my fears away, Ethan Rochester."

The next morning comes too fast, and soon we're standing on the front porch, saying goodbye. We spent all night wrapped in each other's arms and talking. I also spent some time studying certain parts of her, and though neither of us got much sleep—because I wasn't about to waste the short amount of time I had with her sleeping—we were up bright and early drinking coffee and eating breakfast together like tradition.

"Come back to me," I whisper against her lips, gripping her cheeks between my palms.

"I will," she whispers back. "I promise."

Closing my eyes, I try to get ahold of my emotions before kissing her once more. Olivia came in an Uber to pick her up, and in Vada's words, "to make sure I actually get in the car" since they have another flight to catch.

I walk her to the door, and when Vada opens it, I pop my head in and smile at her assistant. "Hello, again." I flash my million-dollar smile.

"H-hi," Olivia stumbles, clearly blushing.

"You're just mean," Vada teases, reaching up to give me one last hug.

"I was saying hi," I defend. "It's called being polite down here in the south," I remind her, teasingly.

"Yeah, right…" She rolls her eyes. "With your shirt off."

I shrug, smirking.

"Text me after you land, okay? Or call me. Or just stay, I mean, whatever."

She chuckles before giving me one last peck on the lips. "I will."

As I watch them drive away, it feels like a knife drives directly into my heart. *I know this isn't the end; she'll be back; we'll get our second chance to do this right*, at least those are the words I tell myself.

"What's wrong with you?"

I spin around in my chair to Aunt Millie standing in the doorway of the tower.

"You scared the shit out of me," I say, releasing my foot off the accelerator and stopping the pottery wheel. I dip my hands in the bucket of water and quickly wipe them off.

"Watch your language," she scolds, giving me pointed look.

"Sorry, Aunt Millie. What are you doing here?"

"What am I doing here?" she asks as if she's offended. "Well, boy, if you ever answered your dang phone, I wouldn't have had to leave my church group early to come check on you."

Guilt surfaces and I feel awful for making her worry. "Sorry, I've been working."

"Yeah, I see that." She looks around the tower and eyes the stocked shelves with mugs that are ready to be glazed. "You've been working 'round the clock again?" She arches a brow, and I know that look.

"Yes, but I'm just trying to keep myself busy," I tell her, which is the truth.

Ever since Vada left a week ago, I think about her nonstop and the anxiousness to have her back drives me crazy. Drowning myself in work is the only way to keep myself sane.

"That doesn't mean you ignore my phone calls." She clicks her tongue.

"You're right. Well, I'm fine. Just working to keep my mind busy."

She flashes me one of her pity looks, which I fucking hate. "She'll be back in a couple weeks," she reminds me as if I don't already know that. "So while I'm glad you aren't wallowing around, I need to get you out of this house."

"I've been out," I retort, though she knows it's only a half-truth.

"To the studio is not going *out*. C'mon. Get cleaned up and dressed. You're taking me to the church dinner tonight."

Smiling, I nod.

I'd been working so much, I filled up every ounce of space on my shelves, which meant I had to start glazing them so I could put them in the kiln next. I loved every step of the process, but glazing was something I could do without much thought. Creatively, I just did what felt right for that piece, and no two were the same.

Per Aunt Millie's request, I cleaned up and dressed so I could take her to the monthly church dinner. It was good to get out of the house for a change, but just another reminder that I was missing my other half. I told Mama and Millie about her return and anticipated permanent return, yet they refused to allow me to stay cooped up while I waited for that moment.

"Oh, did you hear?" Katie, a girl I've known since kindergarten, leans over her chair.

"Hear what?" I ask, turning to face her. Her eyes widen as she licks her lips, and I know it must be something juicy.

"Harmony was caught having an affair with one of her daddy's best friends, and he cut her off, *completely*." Her eyes widen with a smirk on her face. "No more fancy clothes, expensive car, and getting her hair done every week."

"What a pity." I snort. "Guess she'll have to start hustling for her next sugar daddy."

"Well rumor has it she caught one of those STDs, so unless her sugar daddy doesn't mind double-wrapping every time, I doubt she'll find one who'll want to take care of her."

I choke back a laugh at her words but realize it's funny as hell.

"Well, karma's a bitch when you get caught fucking a married man," I say, not feeling the least bit of pity for her. It'd been a long time coming for karma to catch up to Harmony and her antics.

"The best part? The guy's wife had suspected something for quite some time and hid one of those nanny cams in their bedroom, so she got the entire show on camera." She arches a brow with a knowing grin. Yeah, that'll be somehow "leaked" out.

I leave the church dinner in a much better mood than when I arrived. Seeing familiar faces definitely helped.

"Thanks for dragging me out, Aunt Millie," I say, kissing her cheek before opening the car door.

"You're very welcome. Now stop ignoring my phone calls, so I don't have to do it again." She winks, and I nod.

Once I'm back inside the house, I'm not the least bit tired. I decide to walk around the back. Henry greets me out there as I wander around the garden and cottage. It's been quiet out here ever since guests stopped staying, which was probably for the best given my state of mind during those months.

Getting a new idea, I pull my key out and open the cottage door. I've only been in here to keep up with the dusting and cleaning, but now that I'm looking at it in a whole new light, I decide it could use a makeover. Something that'll actually get some use.

And when I think of Vada, I get the best idea yet.

CHAPTER TWENTY-THREE

VADA

"Vada!" I hear Olivia calling my name, but I roll over and ignore it, pleading for just ten more minutes of sleep. "Vada, I know you can hear me." Her tone is accusing and harsh.

"Go away," I mumble, covering my head with the pillow.

"You cannot just lie in bed all morning," she tells me, but I beg to differ. I'm exhausted and her being in here isn't helping.

"Yes, I can," I retort. "I'll skip breakfast and shower in a half hour. Now turn off the light."

"Nice try." I feel her rustling around, and soon the covers are whipped off me.

"Hey!" I shriek, quickly trying to cover myself up, but she's too fast. "I could've been naked under here."

"Considering you're on the phone until three a.m., I'm actually surprised you aren't."

"Ha-ha," I mock. "I was too tired for phone sex last night, so the joke's on you."

"Yeah, clearly." She rolls her eyes. "Now c'mon. You need to stay on your schedule." She slaps my ass, and I shriek.

"Okay, God. I'm up." I sit up and stretch against the headboard.

"Good. Another flower bouquet was delivered this morning." She points to the vase of red and white roses. "You two are sickening, by the way."

I burst out laughing, smiling at the gorgeous view. Sliding out of bed, I walk to the table they're on and pull out the card.

To my Vada,

When I think about what the future holds for us, I grin like an absolute idiot. But then again, how could I not when I know you're The One.

Good luck today—you're going to kill it!

Love you,
Ethan

I press the card to my chest and sigh.

"We get it," Olivia's words snap me out of my dreamy haze as she yanks the card out of my fingers and sets it back down. "Breakfast. Shower. Dress. *Go*."

I pout and scowl at her for ruining my moment. Girl needs to get laid or something. Geez.

My publisher has arranged for a podcast interview this morning and then another meet-n-greet before the book signing later this afternoon. It's another busy day, but I don't mind. The busier, the better so I can keep my mind occupied.

Ethan's been sending me flowers to every hotel we stay at since I left a couple weeks ago. He sends them with the sweetest of notes, too, and I find myself anxiously waiting for them. They're the only thing connecting us right now when the phone calls and text messages aren't enough.

Though the thought of uprooting everything I've ever known in Chicago still gives me anxiety, I know I'll only be happy being with Ethan. I haven't quite broken the news to Nora yet, which is something I need to do before it's too late.

Once the day is over and I'm back in my hotel room, I decide it's now or never.

Grabbing for my phone, I think about what I'm going to say before calling her.

"Your stupid cat got hair all over my favorite sweater," she says immediately when picking up the call.

"Oliver doesn't shed," I protest. "Are you sure it wasn't a different cat?"

"You think I have a parade of cats around here or something? It was yours," she says matter-of-factly. I grin, knowing she secretly loves Oliver as much as I do.

"Well, I'm sure he's very sorry. Plus, it's not really his fault. I'm sure you were picking him up and loving on him, and that's how he got hair on you."

"I would never," she retorts.

I laugh, but we both know the truth. "I'm sorry. I've been a little busier than usual. When I get back, I'll make sure he gets brushed every day, so he doesn't shed as much, or you could brush him?"

She huffs into the phone. "Now you want me to spend quality time with him? Oliver loves to play hard to get when I try to catch him, probably learned it from his mama."

I chuckle, shaking my head at her though she can't see me. "If only I had a camera in my apartment. I bet you two are the best of pals."

She grumbles.

"So how are things going? Where are you now?" she asks, changing the subject.

"Texas," I reply. "It's humid as fuck, too."

"Yeah, us northerners can't handle that kind of heat. Aren't you glad you'll be home in just a week? It's starting to get chilly here finally."

"Well, that's what I kind of wanted to talk to you about."

"You're not leaving me with this damn cat," she immediately blurts outs.

"No." I laugh. "Ethan asked me to stay in Charleston with him," I say the words aloud for the first time, which surprisingly doesn't give me as much anxiety as I thought. I told her the story of seeing Ethan and how we were talking again but hadn't gone into detail about the status of our relationship.

"Oh," is all she offers.

"Yeah."

"So, you'd be moving down there," she says the words as if she's ripping off a Band-Aid.

"I think so," I say softly. "I mean, that'd be the only way to know if a relationship between us could really work. The long-distance would always cause problems, so—"

"Well about damn time," she says, bluntly.

"What?" I ask, laughing. "What do you mean?"

"You've been pining after that boy for a whole damn year, and now that you've reconnected, you'd be a fool to not see where it can go. There's nothing up here for you, Vada," she reminds me, though Chicago is all I've ever known.

"But the thought of just packing everything up and moving for him worries me because what if—"

"What if, what?" she cuts me off. "What if it doesn't work out? But what if it does? Or what if you never take the risk and know for sure?" She fires out the questions as if she's challenging me to really come up with a response.

"But—"

"Vada, dear. Don't end up like me."

"What's that mean?" I ask, pulling my brows together.

"I missed out on the greatest love of my life, and now I'm in my sixties alone babysitting some ugly cat."

I chuckle at her admission. "What happened?"

"Well, back before smart phones and sexting," she begins, making me laugh even harder that she knows what *sexting* is. "I met a man in college who I fell in love with, and although we were madly in love with each other, once graduation rolled around, he deployed with the army. We wrote to each other as much as we could, but when he returned, he wasn't the same man I'd fallen for. He changed; or rather, the army changed him. I was heartbroken because he turned to drinking and I couldn't stand watching him self-destruct any longer. Fast forward to three years later, he had sobered up, got clean, and was starting his own business."

"Wow…what an achievement."

"Yeah, it was. I was so proud of him, but he had moved to Florida to start his business and begged me to move so we could be together again. I was hesitant because my family was all here, and I couldn't fully trust that he wouldn't slip up and start drinking again. I let those fears smother me to the point where I backed out from moving. Although he said he understood and would wait for me to decide, by the time I finally geared up the courage to do it, he had met someone else down there." I hear her breathing softly on the other end, wondering how I never knew this about her. "What's worse is, I flew down to surprise him when I saw them together. I knew she wasn't a fling or some random girl because you could see the love they had for each other in their eyes, and that's when I knew. I was too late."

"Wow, Nora…" is all I can muster up to say.

"Fate handed me a second chance, and I didn't take it, Vada. It's something I have to live with for the rest of my life, but that doesn't mean you do."

I don't know when I started crying, but I feel tears streaming down my cheeks. I don't know why, but I just feel so sad that Nora missed out on something as wonderful as love.

"So you never met someone after him?"

"Oh, I did. I eventually tried dating other men, even married one, but I always compared them to Adam. The connection and love between us never felt as strong or authentic as the one we had. So I had failed relationships, eventually a failed marriage, and well, here I am."

"Geez, Nora. Way to hit me right in the feels." I wipe away another tear. "You know it's not too late for you," I say with a hint of seriousness.

"Oh you know I'm too set in my ways," she tells me as if I had no idea.

"Well, if you ever found Adam again and get that third chance, you best invite me to the wedding." I chuckle.

"You got it, dear."

We chat for a few more minutes before hanging up. I see Olivia's Bible organizer on the table and flip to the current month to check out the rest of the schedule. There's only a week left before the tour's over, but I don't know if I can wait that long to see him again.

I'm not going to waste our second chance.

As the Uber drives through the Charleston streets, I can't wipe the smile off my face. Olivia nearly murdered me when I told her I was leaving early. I only had one signing event left. The rest of my schedule was filled with interviews that I had her reschedule as phone interviews instead. I'd fly out for the signing this weekend, but I couldn't wait any longer to see Ethan, so I flew from Texas right to Charleston.

I decided not to tell him I'm coming so I can surprise him; however, after arriving at the house and seeing a bunch of random supplies laying around, I'm not sure if surprising him was the right way to go.

"Ethan?" I call out, watching my step as I walk through the house.

I head out back where Henry is clucking around but luckily doesn't come charging at me. Noticing the cottage door is wide open, I step closer and hear music coming from inside.

"Ethan?" I call again, but the music's too loud.

As soon as I round the doorway, I see him inside wearing tight jeans and a handyman's belt. He's shirtless, and sweat drips down his muscular back. Leaning against the doorway, I admire how fucking good he looks right now. It takes a moment for me to realize what he's doing. All the furniture is gone, the walls have been repainted, and the carpet looks like it was steam-cleaned. That's when I notice the little reading nook in the corner he's currently hammering nails into.

What in the world is he doing?

The song playing through the speakers comes to an end, and that's when I take my opportunity to let it be known I'm here.

"Knock, knock," I say loud enough for him to hear.

He spins around, and when his eyes find mine, his lips transform into the biggest smile I've ever seen.

"Holy fuck," he gasps, charging for me. Wrapping his arms around me, he pulls me up and presses a deep kiss against my lips. "What are you doing here already?"

I tighten my arms around his neck and press my mouth back on his. "I had to see you," is all the explanation I give him.

"You came back to me." He smiles, looking me over as if to make sure I'm really here.

I nod, tears stinging my eyes at the realization of how much I love this man.

"I couldn't spend another day away from you," I tell him, his arms holding me in place against his chest.

"Well, I wanted to surprise you, but…" He turns slightly, glancing around the room. "I'm building you your dream office space."

"Wait, really?" I look around and am in awe at everything he's doing. "I can't believe you'd do that for me."

"Are you kidding? This is where it all happened, baby. You touching yourself, fantasizing about me, and—"

"Oh my God, shut up!" I blush, laughing. "It is a dream though." I look around again. "You even added shelves."

"Of course!" He smiles. "I have it all designed. You're going to love it."

I kiss him—hard and without reservation.

"That's the sweetest damn thing anyone's ever done for me."

"I'd do anything for you, Vada. Anything," he whispers, pressing his forehead against mine.

"You're too good to be true," I tell him, meaning every word. "That's why I had to come back."

"What do you mean?"

"I had to tell you…" I pause briefly, getting ahold of my nerves.

"What?" He looks nervous for a split-second.

"I had to come tell you how in love with you I am, and that I'd be a fool to walk away from someone as amazing as you. I'm not running away from love this time. I want you—*forever*. I love you, Ethan Rochester."

He plants his lips back on mine, taking steps until my back hits the wall and he pins me there with his hard body.

"Fuck, Vada…I don't think those words have ever sounded so sweet till they came from your lips. I love you so goddamn much. You have no idea how happy you just made me." He presses his mouth back down on mine before I can reply, which is totally okay with me because what came next didn't need words.

EPILOGUE
ETHAN

TWO YEARS LATER

I'M COVERED in clay and need to shower before heading in for the night, but I can't pass up the opportunity to sneak inside the nursery first.

My gorgeous wife is rocking our baby and humming as she nurses him. It's the most beautiful image in the entire world, everything I ever could've imagined. And more.

"How's it going?" I whisper, grabbing her attention as I lean against the doorway.

She smiles up at me, a noticeable glow circulating her face.

"He's just like his father. Gravitates to the left more than the right." She chuckles, holding his precious little hand.

"We Rochester men know what we like," I say with an unapologetic shrug. "Plus, the left one is bigger." I flash her a wide, knowing grin.

She rolls her eyes and looks back down at him. Pushing off the doorway, I walk over to them and press a kiss to her head.

"I still can't get over how much he looks like you," Vada says, rubbing her finger along his soft cheek.

"Yeah, but he's probably got his mama's sassy mouth."

She chuckles softly. "And his daddy's crass attitude."

"The kid's gonna be a spitfire, no doubt." I lean down and press a soft kiss on her lips. "I'm going to hop in the shower if you want to join me after he's asleep." I flash her a wink, telling her everything I need to.

"You know we can't have sex for six weeks after giving birth," she reminds me as if I could've forgotten that little detail.

"I know, but that doesn't mean I can't feast on other parts of you," I tease.

Shaking her head at me, she bites down on her lower lip to conceal her smile. "You're naughty."

"And you wrote a whole book telling everyone how much you love my naughty ways, so there's no turning back now," I remind her smirking, and she wrinkles her nose at me before I lean down and kiss the top of London's head. He barely fidgets from my contact—too busy eating.

I head to the shower with a toothy grin on my face. I can't help it. I'm happier than I ever thought possible.

When we found out Vada was pregnant, I panicked at first. Although I was excited to be starting a family with her, I couldn't help that fear inside that something was going to go wrong again, and I'd lose everything all over again. I knew Vada felt it too, but we leaned on each other for love and support, which helped get through those nine months.

Everything went great during her pregnancy, and even her labor was smooth without any complications. The relief that struck me when he was finally here was unlike anything I'd experienced before. Just knowing I could hold him brought me on an emotional roller coaster. London was born a whopping nine pounds and a head full of dark hair. It was an indescribable feeling and one I'll never forget.

As soon as we found out we were having a boy, I was flooded with memories of Alana and Paris. I hated that I felt like I was replacing them somehow, although I knew that was far from the truth. Vada knew how important it was for me to keep their memories alive. She didn't change much in the nursery, knowing I'd want to keep certain things. She never pressed me on it, and I loved her even more for that. She wanted to keep the memories of my family alive too, and that meant more to me than anything.

I'm on cloud nine as I begin rinsing off my body in the shower and hear Vada sneaking in behind me. Spinning around, I gasp when I see her kneeling down in front of me.

"What are you—"

"Taking care of my man." She smiles up at me, grabbing ahold of my shaft as the water cascades on my back and blocks her. "Unless you'd like to jerk off in the shower alone again?" she teases, feistier than usual.

"Fuck, Vada…" I groan as she swirls her tongue around my piercing, knowing just how much it turns me on. "And for the record, I don't jerk off in the shower." I pause before continuing, "*Anymore*."

She chuckles, releasing the tip. "Yeah, okay, Casanova. That's not what you inspired in chapter sixteen of my newest book," she reminds me with a wink.

"That was one time," I defend. "And only because you were being a cock tease."

She bursts out laughing. "I was six months pregnant and out of clothes to wear," she reminds me, and memories of her wearing my T-shirts starts getting me hot all over again.

"Yeah." I flash her a knowing smile. "You should *always* be pregnant, wearing my shirts, and *only* my shirts."

She waggles her brows as she licks the length of my shaft and begins pumping it. Fuck, she's so good at knowing exactly what I like. I wrap my hand in her hair and fist it as she works me all the way to orgasm.

Reaching down, I grab her hand and pull her up. I press my mouth against hers and kiss her until both our lips are swollen. I clean both of us, taking my time as I wash and rinse her off.

"God, you're so beautiful," I tell her along her ear as I inhale her fresh, sweet scent. "Perfect in every way."

"That's always a nice thing to hear after having baby spit-up and poop on your clothes all day," she says, choking back a laugh.

I smile, turning her around so I can look into her eyes. Cupping her cheeks, I press one more soft kiss against her lips. "I couldn't imagine life getting any better, baby. Starting a family and being truly happy is all that matters."

"Look at you, smooth talker," she teases, resting her lips against mine. "Guess my writing is starting to wear off on you."

"Oh, sweetheart," I drawl, pulling back slightly. "Gorgeous brunettes who suck my cock like that…" I glance down, smirking, "…are my kryptonite."

"I bet they are," she says, laughing at the seriousness of my tone.

I lead her out and dry us both off. As I wrap a towel around my waist, I hear London stirring in his crib. Vada starts heading for the nursery when I stop her and pull her back.

"I'll take this shift, babe. You get some sleep." I kiss her on the cheek before walking the rest of the way to the nursery.

Before opening the door, I glance down the hall and see Oliver and Wilma snuggled up together. Oliver's licking Wilma's face, and Wilma's purring loudly.

"Get a room you two," I mock, rolling my eyes at how much they love each other. Once Vada confirmed she was moving in, we flew up to Chicago together so I could help her pack and arrange for all her things to get shipped down here. Oliver didn't exactly warm up to me right away, which caused concern on how he'd react to Wilma.

Suffice it to say, he warmed up to Wilma much sooner.

After meeting Nora though, I could see why Oliver was hesitant about meeting new people. He was used to being around strong, hard-headed women and saw me as a threat. Eventually, we had a heart-to-heart and agreed to both be the men of the house.

Walking into the nursery, I peek in the crib and see London's fussing and unraveling from his swaddle. I pick him up, check his diaper, and wrap him back up in his blanket before seating us in the rocking chair.

"Listen, little guy," I begin, brushing my finger softly along his face. "Your mama hasn't slept in five weeks, and I'm going to need her to be as refreshed as possible in about the next week or so, which means you have to start sleeping for a few hours at a time. Now, I'm not above bribery and negotiations, so you just tell me what you want. A playset? Jordan High-tops? A Mustang when you turn sixteen? I mean, you name it, and I'll make it happen, okay? As long as you give me one hour alone with your mama. Well, let's just say two." I smile as he eyes me curiously as if I've lost my mind. "Do we have a deal?"

I press my finger to his little palm and high-five him.

"If I didn't think that was the cutest thing I ever saw, I'd call you pathetic for trying to bribe our newborn baby so we can have sex." Vada leans against the doorway, shaking her head at me and smiling.

"Not just any sex, though," I defend, and her smile widens. "Postpartum sex, which means as soon as the doctor gives the thumbs up, I'm stripping off all your clothes."

"We're not having sex in the doctor's office!" she warns.

"Babe…" I tease. "Never say never."

She rolls her eyes and shakes her head.

"C'mon. Think of all the good book inspiration." I grin.

"You're horrible," she quips. She walks over to us and presses a gentle kiss on London's head. "Your daddy is a bad influence for you."

"Yes, but a good, bad influence," I correct with a smile.

"For now." She winks.

After getting London back to sleep and in his crib, Vada and I head into our room. "Are you writing tonight?" I ask, knowing she's been gradually getting back to it.

"I think so. Olivia's been sending me some juicy details," she explains with a knowing grin.

"Really?"

"Yup. Apparently, the new author she's assisting is forcing her to road trip with a new cover model across the country for a book tour."

"Oh yeah? Is he a bad influence, too?" I wink.

"According to Olivia, he's worse."

"Worse? How?"

"He has quite the reputation and Olivia isn't happy about it."

I laugh. "I give them a week and they'll be doing it."

She winces. "Ethan!"

Chuckling, I shrug. "What? You know that's *exactly* what's going to happen."

"Well, in my book, of course. But Olivia is a bit uptight," she reminds me. "She's not one to sleep around." She told me all about Olivia when she worked for her before moving here. "He'll probably drive her crazy."

I smirk at my internal prediction. "I drove you crazy at first too, remember?"

"Trust me, you still do." She smiles. "But in the best way possible."

Read Maverick & Olivia's story in
Make Me Crazy

USA TODAY BESTSELLING AUTHOR
KENNEDY FOX

CHAPTER ONE

OLIVIA

Oh God. Oh God. *Oh God.*

Panting. Heavy breathing. Toes curling.

Yesssssss.

My teeth sink into my bottom lip as a wave of pleasure hits my core, and then…

The piercing sound of my alarm bellows out, and my body shoots straight up in a panic to turn it off. I look and see it's six a.m.

Ugh.

That's the most action I've had in a year, and it was all a damn dream.

I stretch and slide out of bed, mentally going over my to-do list for the day. Walking to my kitchenette, I grab my mug of coffee that's ready to go. I always program my Keurig the night before, so all I have to do is add creamer in the morning.

As I walk toward the bathroom, I blow into my cup and take a small sip. Just as I check my phone, I see Rachel has already left three messages.

Rachel: I need you here by 8 today.

Rachel: Make that 7. Coffee extra hot.

Rachel: Please.

I roll my eyes at her last text, knowing it probably pained her to use that word. Author Rachel Meadows is a #1 *New York Times* Bestselling Author who has hit the list more times than I can count and is known for being socially awkward and blunt. She's in her midforties, and although she writes about romance, she doesn't have a love life because she eats, sleeps, and breathes writing. She's the very definition of a workaholic, which is why *I* work sixty-hour weeks. I maintain her life so she can focus all her energy on her work.

Perhaps if she did have friends nearby or went out with a man once in a blue moon, she wouldn't be so damn uptight 24/7. However, most people could probably say the same thing about me, which is one reason Rachel and I work so well together. Well, that, and I have the tolerance and patience of a saint.

My previous author client, Vada Collins, found her happily ever after and moved to the East Coast, which is how I ended up working for Rachel. Her assistant quit, leaving her in a major bind, and I needed a new job stat. The cost of living in Chicago is too expensive to stay unemployed for long.

So when Rachel Meadows called me back for a second interview, I prayed to the gods for good voodoo because it was the only local job opportunity available at that time. Now, after a year of working for Rachel, I know nearly everything there is to know about her and cater to her every need.

For example, when she says to arrive at seven with extra hot coffee, that's code for come fifteen minutes early and have a protein shake ready to go. Which means I have exactly forty-five minutes to shower, get dressed, stop at the Starbucks half a mile from her apartment, and read through her emails so I can brief her while she sucks down her blended meal.

Or when she's four days away from her cycle, I know to stock up on Andes Mints and red wine. She has two microwavable rice bags that I rotate out, so she always has a hot one ready for her lower back when she needs to lie down after sitting for too long. Though, if she's on a major deadline, she'll lie in bed with a heating pad and dictate her words to me so she can work through the cramps.

This morning, I woke up early so I wouldn't have to rush, but now I'll be taking a five-minute shower—cold—since I don't have time to wait for the water to warm. All thanks to Rachel deciding at the last minute that I need to arrive an hour early.

I manage to finish my first cup of coffee in the shower, so while my hair is air-drying, I take a few seconds to dab concealer on the bags under my eyes. I'm a workaholic just like Rachel, except I run marathons around her while she carefully crafts her words for thousands of readers. Once I'm dressed in a pencil skirt and tuck in my blouse, I slide on my Chucks, grab my oversized bag with everything I'll need for the day, and rush out the door.

My Uber arrives as soon as I jog down my apartment building stairs. I fly into the back seat, asking him to step on it. He understands my urgency and guns it down the road. I quickly read over Rachel's emails on my phone until we drive up to the Starbucks closest to her place. Since I ordered ahead on the mobile app, I won't have to wait in line, but I'll still be rushing to Rachel's at this rate.

As I hurry inside to grab the coffees, I check my phone and realize I have less than five minutes to get there. We're only half a mile away, but we're on a one-way street, and her building is behind us. Which means instead of having my driver drop me off at her door, I'll have to jog there.

After letting the driver know my plans, I secure my bag over my shoulder and start running down the block. I wear Chucks for this very reason. Running in heels would result in a broken ankle or blisters for days, and I don't have time for that.

"Excuse me, sorry." Holding our cups tightly in my grip, I maneuver my arms up and over my head while I weave in and out of the crowd walking toward me. Glaring because I'm on the wrong side of the sidewalk, they aren't moving out of my way, but I ignore them and push through. For someone as isolated as Rachel, she lives on one of the busiest streets in downtown Chicago. Even though it's convenient when she needs a coffee break or sends me on a random errand, it's hell to get through.

I make it to her apartment building and am greeted by one of the doormen. They all know me by name and often crack jokes about how they aren't even sure a woman lives in the apartment I work in every day.

"Good morning, Sam," I say as I sprint through the lobby. The elevator doors are already open and set to the tenth floor for me. He nods and gives me a small smile. "Thank you! You're amazing!" I call out right just before the doors close.

Sam Evans is in his late fifties, and within my first couple of weeks of working for Rachel, he memorized my work schedule and how many times I come and go throughout the day. Rachel sends me for bagels often, and as soon as I get them for her, she'll decide she wants a smoothie too. Of course, she couldn't have told me that at the same time so I didn't have to run out twice, but that'd be way too convenient for Rachel Meadows. Sam notices these patterns and has picked up on them over the past year. He always makes sure the elevator doors are open and waiting for me every morning, even when I'm early. He's a good man.

I juggle the coffee cups between my elbow and side boob so I can grab the keys from my bag and have them ready to go as soon as I make it to her apartment. Quietly, I open her door and step inside, making sure to shut it with little to no sound at all.

Setting the cups down on the table, I reach into my bag for my ankle wedge booties that cost me a month and a half's worth of rent and change out of my Chucks. They're one of the most expensive things I own, but comfort costs money. If I want to be taken seriously in this business, Chucks won't cut it. Rachel might be a homebody and live in the same clothes for three days in a row, but she expects professionalism from me at all times.

I shove my Chucks inside my bag and reach for the stash of doggie treats I keep in there. Rachel has a dog who absolutely hates me, and as soon as I walk inside, she nearly gnaws on my ankles to let me know I'm not welcome in her home. Angel—ironically named considering she's the mini version of the devil—is a Toy Poodle, and although she's fluffy and has cute pink bows in her hair, she's a predator, and I'm her prey.

Angel trots in with the worst doggy stink eye I've ever seen. She lowers her front legs and sticks her ass up in the air as she releases the most pathetic growl. She still hasn't figured out she's only ten pounds, and half of that is from fur alone. I wouldn't hate her so much if she'd give me a chance, but after months of trying to get on her good side, she rewarded me with a nasty bite, so I gave up.

"Oh, I'm shakin' in my boots now. I might even pee myself." I glare at her and toss her a treat. "Hope you aren't allergic to rat poison."

Before I walk into Rachel's office, I put some vegan protein powder in the mixer, along with a banana. I have a feeling she's not going to want it immediately, so I don't add the ice or soy milk. Grabbing our coffees, I manage to walk to Rachel's office without Angel chasing me. I place hers down on her desk without a word and walk to my little desk in the corner. Once my coffee cup is in place, I set my bag down and dig out my laptop, then start it up.

"I'll take my protein shake in twenty," she informs me without a hello or even a thank you.

"Of course." I smile, feeling as if I can finally read her mind. As soon as my laptop turns on, I grab my book and place it on my desk. The *Bible* as I've coined the very large notebook planner has everything about Rachel to successfully be her personal assistant and to keep her happy. Every detail from her personal life and professional work life is included—schedules, deadlines, likes and dislikes—anything that helps me help her. Reaching for my coffee, I take a sip and relish in the hot liquid.

"Olivia."

"Yes?" I briefly look up from my cup like a deer in headlights.

"I need you to organize my schedule and plans for my upcoming tour. I have that book signing coming up in Dallas, and if I'm going to be traveling, I want other events to attend during that time before I hunker down and start writing the next one. Book two more city stops with three events—or more—at each. A meet and greet, after party, or whatever. Schedule some dinner meetings with bloggers or my PR firm. Just keep me busy. I don't want to be gone too long, so it needs to be within a two-week period of the first signing."

I nearly spit out my coffee as I put it back down on my desk and scramble for my pen. As she continues to ramble, I jot notes down in the "Rachel Bible" knowing she won't repeat herself even if I ask. The book signing is three months away, which doesn't give me much time to plan the rest. I'd already booked her flight and hotel for that event, but now I'll have to reschedule her flight and book additional accommodations to meet her requests.

"Any particular cities you have in mind?" I ask, my pen still flying over the paper.

"That's for you to decide. My readers are everywhere," she replies. "You'll also need to get in touch with the cover model for the Bayshore Coast series and let him know about the added travel dates for the other events."

"Of course," I say, rolling my eyes when I know she's not looking. Her cover model for that series is none other than the arrogant playboy, Maverick Kingston.

"He doesn't fly, so you'll have to drive with him and make sure—"

"What?" I blurt out louder than I mean to. This is the first time she's ever mentioned that to me. How was he planning to make it to Dallas in the first place?

I look up to see if she's serious. "Maverick doesn't do planes, so you'll have to fly to LA where he lives, then drive with him to each city. I'm paying him good money for his public appearances, and I expect him to be at every event—on time and on his best behavior."

"So, you want me to babysit him?" I pinch my brows together, reading between the lines.

"I want you to make sure my investment doesn't get out of control," she clarifies. "My readers are nuts about him, and they'd die for a chance to meet him, so I need you to make sure he gets to where he needs to be on time." She pins me with her eyes as if to dare me to protest. "Will that be a problem for you?"

Yes. "No, not at all."

"Excellent. I'll be flying to each event, and since you'll be driving, keep that in mind when you make plans to give yourselves enough time to travel."

That means I'll need to book a rental car, hotels while we road trip, additional flights to two other cities, and the event spaces. All within ninety days from now. *No pressure.*

Her book signing in Dallas has been planned for over a year, and now she decides to add this to her schedule? It's not like her, but not entirely out of character either. Rachel's impulsive most of the time. One minute, she wants a turkey and bacon sub, and the next, she's a vegetarian, but this is somewhat extreme and random.

"Okay, got it." I finish my notes and start thinking of cities that can realistically be driven to from Dallas. I don't have much time to nail this all down. If she wants to do two more signings with other events in each city, I'll need to call bookstores, her publisher, get the tickets organized, and start marketing for them pronto.

"Oh, and Olivia?"

I look at her, almost scared for what else she has for me.

"Yes?"

"I have a strict no fraternizing policy among my employees. I hope that won't be a problem."

I snort, covering my mouth once I realize the noise was audible. She gives me a disapproving look, but I can't help it. That she even felt the need to add that bit makes me want to burst out laughing. "Trust me. That won't even be an issue."

CHAPTER TWO

MAVERICK

Snap. Snap. Snap.

"Okay, now let's get a few shots of you standing shirtless in front of the skyline," Katie says, glancing out the window at the cloudless Los Angeles sky. It's late afternoon, so the sun is casting a warm glow through the hotel room. It's the perfect time of day for a shoot. As a newish photographer, she's still trying to build her portfolio, and I owed my friend Jacob a favor, which means allowing his little sister to take pictures of me. She's in her early twenties and cute in a girl-next-door kind of way with a short blond bob. Her lips are bright pink, and her black pants are so tight they look painted on. As I slowly undo each button of my dress shirt, I can tell she's growing more nervous and flushed.

I sometimes have that effect on women. *Well, maybe always.*

I look up at her and give her a smirk, which only causes her to blush. "What are you doin' after this?" I ask.

She shakes her head, watching me with a hesitant smile. "Nothing, really."

"Want to grab some food?" I don't typically hang out with professionals after a job, but she's not actually paying me, so I don't see any harm in it, other than her being my friend's sister.

"Umm..." She nervously shifts on her feet, and I let out a small laugh.

"You want me over here?" I ask, noticing the slight tremble of her hands, so I try to change the subject. It's cute that she's nervous.

She nods. I get into position, tucking my hands into my pockets, and she instantly hides behind the lens. Considering I've been modeling since I was sixteen and have a good decade under my belt, I know my marks, how to look at the camera, and how to position my body, making it pretty easy for photographers to get their money shot. My portfolio includes high paying gigs in a few fitness and fashion magazines and cover model for the *New York Times* bestselling romance series by the award-winning author Rachel Meadows. Recently, I filled my schedule until the end of the year for fitness shoots and even signed contracts, but right now, as far as book covers go, I'm exclusive to Rachel. The advance I was given not to be on other romance book covers was well worth it. Ninety days after her last book is released, my exclusivity ends. I'm living the dream, but I'm still waiting for my breakout moment when agents are fighting over me and six-figure deals are being made. I know it'll happen.

I undo the button and lower the zipper as I move my pants farther down my body, showing the V I've worked so hard to perfect and throw my shirt to the ground. I leave the tie around my neck. Katie gulps—loudly—but continues to take pictures like she's a paparazzi.

"Do you want to get on the bed?" she asks, nervously.

"Only if you join me."

Her eyes go wide.

"I'm kidding," I reassure before I go to the bed. Katie moves to different positions in the room, asks me to change poses, and after an hour of taking photos, she's finally done. I button my pants and pick up my shirt as she scrolls through the photos she's taken.

"So, get some good ones?" I ask, carefully buttoning up my shirt.

"Yeah, totally did. Oh, can I get you to sign this release? If I sell any of these photos, I'll make sure to give you a cut."

"It's not a big deal." I give her a wink. "I owed your brother big time for recommending me for a job. The only thing is, these photos can't be used in the publishing media as far as e-books and paperbacks until my exclusivity expires."

"Oh, I know. My brother told me you weren't going to be released for that stuff until after summer. He repeated himself about thirty times." She chuckles. "So, about dinner..." She hesitates, turning off her camera and kneeling to gently place it in her bag. Katie looks up at me and smiles. Seeing her on her knees like this makes my cock twitch. I glance away from her and study the room she booked for the night and think how it'd only be a waste to leave the bed unused. "I have about an hour before I have to be somewhere."

"There's a place a few blocks over that has amazing pasta," I tell her.

Katie watches me, and I realize how bad of an idea this really is. It'd be so easy to slip into her panties and show her a good time, but if Jacob found out, he'd murder me. As I'm fantasizing about rustling in the sheets with her, my phone goes off, pulling me away. I glance down and see it's Rachel, and one thing I've learned over the years is to answer her damn call—always. Otherwise, she's a terror to deal with because the woman has the patience of an angry tiger.

"Shit," I whisper and look up at Katie. "Sorry, I gotta take this."

She glances at her watch. "Maybe we can reschedule this for another time then?"

I give her a smile and a nod and answer the phone as she finishes packing her things.

"Maverick. It's Rachel."

I'm well aware, I want to say but don't.

She continues. "So you know the last book in my series releases in less than three months, and I have Olivia scheduling an extended city tour around the Dallas signing."

I wish she'd get to the point. I already confirmed with her assistant I'd be attending. "Yes, I've already cleared my schedule."

"Well, I wanted to call and reiterate a few things first to make sure we're on the same page." Though Rachel is less than friendly most of the time, the seriousness in her tone is almost frightening.

I chuckle, waiting for her to continue because the silence is deafening.

"I'm sure I don't have to explain to you how important it is not to fraternize with my readers or my assistant, Olivia."

Katie stands around, waiting for me to finish my conversation, but this is going to take longer than even I expected. Rachel keeps talking, and eventually, Katie waves goodbye, leaving me alone in the room.

Rachel Meadows has officially cockblocked me.

As she goes into detail about her expectations, I interrupt her.

"Rachel. Hold on. You don't have to keep going. None of that is going to happen. I know the do's and don'ts when it comes to traveling and being on the job. I'm sure you mean well, and I know how other models can be, but I understand the importance of being professional at all times, especially in public settings. I'm not going to arrive late to the events and don't plan on sleeping with anyone. You have nothing to worry about. Trust me."

"Good. That's exactly what I want to hear." She actually sounds relieved. I can only imagine how many different scenarios she's made up about this trip and all the things that could go wrong. I refuse to be an issue, especially considering how high-profile she is. I'm sure Rachel could ruin me.

"I'm still working out your compensation with my publisher, and once everything is confirmed, my assistant will finalize all the fine details with you. Okay?"

"Alright, that sounds great," I tell her.

"I'll see you soon. And Maverick, just remember to be on your best behavior."

I want to explain to her that she doesn't own me regardless of the contract I signed, but she's paid me well, and I'm grateful for the opportunity. So I just agree. We say our goodbyes, and I grab my suit jacket and slip it on. Rachel doesn't take bullshit from anyone, and she won't take it from me. She tends to be straightforward without a filter, and over the past few years, I've learned how to handle her. Pick your battles because you will always lose when going against Rachel.

Not everyone can deal with her no-bullshit attitude, but I'm used to it. She was very particular about which photos were used on her covers, and even though she has a major publisher, what she suggests pretty much goes. The perks of being a best seller, I suppose. Every photo shoot I've had, she's been there to give direction to the photographer. It's annoying, but I get it. She takes her job seriously and wants to be involved in every step.

I look around the empty hotel room, tuck my phone in my pocket, and head out the door, walking down the hallway toward the elevator. Katie's long gone by now, and I'm not one to look desperate. Truthfully, it's probably best we didn't have dinner—especially with the way she was looking at me. Over the years, I've learned how to read a woman like a book. Not to mention, her big brother would have kicked my ass from here to New York if I brought her back to my apartment because things would've inevitably escalated. Pasta, wine, and the next thing she'd be in my bed as I give her the time of her life. Not a good idea.

As soon as I step into the elevator, a long-legged brunette eyes me from head to toe. Women love a man in a fitted suit, and I use it to my advantage each time I wear it, though I really don't need to. Her skirt barely covers her ass, and the heels she's wearing put her at eye level with me. I flash her a sultry smirk before the doors close. Lust swirls around in the elevator, and I watch her breasts rise and fall as I stand next to her. Her breath hitches when I shove my hands into my front pockets.

"Big plans tonight?" I ask her, trying to be polite, though my thoughts are anything but.

Her pouty red lips slightly part then close as if she's trying to find her words.

"Just grabbing a few drinks." She looks over at me, in a cute, sexy way. "I'm Haley."

"Maverick." I smile, reaching a hand out to her. "Nice to meet you, Haley."

Her chocolate brown eyes meet mine, and as she shakes my hand, electricity flows between us. I don't believe in love at first sight, but lust? I definitely believe in lust at first sight.

"I know this sounds forward, but…" I watch as she bites her lower lip. "Would you like to join me?" she asks, bravely.

I chuckle, glancing down at her hand before releasing it to check for a wedding ring. I may enjoy having fun and meeting people, but I draw the line at unavailable women.

"Actually, I was supposed to have dinner with a friend, but my plans got canceled. So, why the hell not?" I give her another signature grin, so she knows I'm down to have a good time with whatever she has in mind.

The elevator reaches the lobby, and the doors slide open. Haley walks out and looks over her shoulder, catching me as I take a glimpse of her perfectly round ass. I swear she's purposely shaking her hips as I walk behind her. She walks to the hotel bar, her heels clicking on the marble floor. It's late afternoon, and the lights are already turned down low to set the mood. A beautiful woman mixed with alcohol is a dangerous concoction, but I go with the flow and pull out the stool next to her and sit.

"Old Fashioned, please," she politely tells the bartender.

"Same," I say. "So you like whiskey?" I turn to her.

"If I'm being honest, it's my kryptonite," she admits with a smirk.

I tilt my head at her. "A beautiful woman is mine."

She laughs as the bartender sets our drinks down. Immediately, she takes a sip. When she sets down the glass, she hooks her finger in and pulls the cherry out, then pops it between her ruby red lips before crushing it with her teeth.

Fuck. She's pulling out all the stops. Tease.

As I reposition my body, my knee brushes against hers. I place my hand on her thigh, and she scoots closer. The smell of her perfume is intoxicating as it surrounds me.

"So tell me about you, Haley." I take a swig of whiskey, allowing it to burn as it works its way down.

"I'm here for a business conference. Fly out tomorrow afternoon," she says. "I'm not married or anything either; in case you were wondering."

I burst out into laughter. "I wasn't." I'd already confirmed that much by no ring on her finger, but I've been involved with women who've purposely slipped their wedding ring off. I said I try not to sleep with married women; I didn't say I haven't—unintentionally, of course.

"What about you?" she asks, taking another drink of her Old Fashioned.

"I live here. Not married either, in case *you* were wondering. Absolutely one hundred percent single. I'm too focused on my career to get into a serious relationship. I like to have fun. Surf. Workout."

She smiles. "I can appreciate that." Haley narrows her eyes at me. "So, are you like some sort of player or something?"

Now I really laugh. "Truthfully, maybe a tad." I have no reason to lie to her, not when she's flying out tomorrow. Sometimes one-night stands like this are the easiest because there's no expectation of the next day, or ever.

She taps her glass against mine and smiles. "Same."

I kinda figured she was, just by how open she was in the elevator, asking me to join her, and being dressed like that. I've met women like her before; they're a certain breed, and they usually put my playboy tactics to shame. She's beautiful and could have any man she wants, but tonight she chose me. It's painfully obvious where the night is heading.

I finish my drink and order another one. Haley does the same. We make small talk, keeping what we share with each other general. Three whiskeys in, or maybe it's four, and I'm feeling the alcohol stream through my system. Probably should've eaten before we started hammering drinks down, but that would've been the responsible thing to do.

After an hour, Haley leans over and wraps my tie around her fist, pulling me closer to her. "I'd like to take this off you," she whispers in my ear.

Gently, I move the hair from her shoulders. "I'm pretty sure I can help make that happen."

My lips brush against the shell of her ear, which causes her to shiver. Haley removes her tight hold on my tie but continues to lean into me.

"You two want more drinks?" the bartender asks. By the look on his face, he knows where this is leading to as well. I glance at Haley, and she shakes her head and licks her lips.

I hand over my credit card and take care of the tab before standing.

"My room?" she asks with a seductive smile playing on her lips.

I nod, placing my hand on the small of her back, allowing her to lead the way. By the time we make it to the elevator, we're unable to keep our hands off each other.

"I knew from the moment I saw you, I wanted to fuck you," she admits, the whiskey making her lips loose. I grab her ass in my hands and crash my lips against hers as the elevator doors close, and we're shot to the top level. Sometimes it's not easy looking this good, but it definitely has its advantages. Tonight Haley happens to be one of them.

CHAPTER THREE

OLIVIA

THREE MONTHS LATER

"Olivia, repeat it to me again," Rachel insists. "From start to finish."

I force a smile and grab the "Bible" in front of me. Though I have her itinerary memorized and we've gone through this several times already, I flip open the planner and read it aloud.

"Friday night before the Dallas signing, you'll do a private meet and greet with members from your reader group. It's from six to eight, and appetizers will be served. Drinks will also be available at the bar. We have fifty giveaway bags that include a canvas tote with a book quote printed on the outside, a T-shirt in their size with your author logo, and other pieces of swag items from the Bayshore Coast series."

"And Maverick?" she asks without a beat.

"He'll be there to sign anything they have for him as well as take pictures with the readers. That's what most of them voted on aside from the striptease I vetoed."

The corner of Rachel's lips tilts just slightly. "They're a feisty bunch."

I hold back a snort. That's an understatement. They're certainly fun, though—I've been an admin in her social media Facebook group for a while now and schedule posts in there from time to time when Rachel is deep in edits.

"The signing starts at eleven on Saturday morning, so I'll come down an hour beforehand with Maverick to set up your table while you're getting your hair and makeup done. You'll need to be down by 10:45 for the author photo. The VIP ticket holders and volunteers are allowed early entrance at 11:00 to get their books signed and photographs taken before the event starts at noon. There isn't a lunch break, so I have room service scheduled to deliver brunch at ten."

"Don't forget about my dietary restrictions."

"I didn't. Low carb, gluten free. I double-checked with the concierge this morning to make sure it's prepared correctly."

To say Rachel Meadows is high maintenance is like saying water is wet. Obvious.

"I also packed snacks for the signing in case you get hungry."

"Great. I'll chow down on a protein bar in front of a line of readers." She inhales a sharp, unsatisfied breath.

"You can take a five-minute bathroom break and eat it then, if needed," I tell her, so she doesn't get anxious about it. "The signing goes until five. You'll get an hour to relax, and then you have a six o'clock dinner meeting with Queen B's Blog."

I continue with the rest of the ten-day schedule that consists of meet and greets, VIP parties, signings, and meetings between three cities. I worked my ass off to make sure she'd stay busy and get the most out of this trip.

Maybe a little of it was because the busier she is, the busier Maverick will be, and the less I'll have to "watch" him between events. It's already bad enough she's made him my responsibility. However, according to my photographer friend, Presley, who shoots at bookish events, the fans need to be watched just as much. She's told me some stories about women going wild over models and basically giving them lap dances.

I shudder at the image. Mostly because I can't imagine acting like that with a guy I just met. Sure, he has the classic, panty-melting look—chiseled jawline, six-pack (or hell, maybe even an eight-pack), dreamy eyes, and a come-hither smolder, but that doesn't mean I'd even remotely consider throwing myself at him. Nope. *Never*.

God. The more I think about all this, the more I want to start dry heaving and tell her I'm too sick to go. I suck in a deep breath and pretend to sniffle. Is that a cold I feel coming on?

I haven't been sick in three years. It'd be *way* too convenient to get something now. Maybe if I hang out in the emergency room for a weekend, I could catch a nice infection that would get me out of this trip. Summer flu is a real thing.

Would that be going too far?

Absolutely.

Shit, shit, shit.

Rushing around my apartment while yanking my shirt over my head, I trip over something and have to hop on one foot until I find my bearings.

Fuck me, that hurt.

I look at the shoe that nearly assaulted me, and instead of chucking it out the window into traffic like I want, I decide there's no time for that and grab my bags. I've been packed for this trip for the past week but had to add some of my toiletries this morning and nearly had to jump on my suitcase to get it to zip up all the way. Today I'm flying to Los Angeles to meet Maverick Kingston, and I'm already dreading it. *Fuck my life.*

As soon as I'm on the sidewalk, I reach for my phone and realize it's not in my back pocket.

Oh, come on. *Not today!*

I am never, *never* late, and I'm not about to start now. I might not be graceful getting from point A to point B, but I refuse to get off schedule. My Uber is already on the way to take me to the airport so I arrive at my gate on time.

Dragging my bags with me, I rush back up to my apartment, scramble to unlock my door, and look around for my cell.

"Ring, dammit! Ring!" My phone constantly goes off with texts and emails from Rachel, yet it's conveniently dead silent now.

I search the table, kitchen counter, and dig between the couch cushions, then rush to my bedroom and search the bed, chair, floor. Nothing. *Fuck.*

"Okay, I can figure this out…" I stop and remind myself because if I don't focus, I'm never going to find it and I'll end up missing my ride. "I just need to retrace my steps." I walk back down the hall, glare at the shoe I tripped over, look around the area where my bags were before leaving, and then go to the kitchen.

Wait…

I made coffee this morning before my shower. Opening the fridge door, I sigh in relief when I see my phone next to the bottle of creamer. Quickly grabbing it, I shut the door and grab my suitcases. By some miracle, I make it to the street just as my Uber pulls up.

Thank God.

The gentleman puts everything in the trunk. I'm thankful for his help because one of my suitcases weighs nearly fifty pounds. Preparing to be away from home for two weeks wasn't easy. I won't have much time to do laundry since I'll be catering to Rachel's every need, so I had to pack for every occasion and include a variety of shoes. This isn't a pleasure trip, which means I'll be expected to wear business attire until I'm finished for the day and can hide away in my room for the night.

Not only did I have to get my own things together, but I also spent the past three days packing Rachel's bags and triple-checking our itinerary and reservations. It took five twelve-hour days to nail down her tour events and dates. Considering she only gave me three months' notice meant I had to kiss ass and beg for locations to squeeze us in. On top of that, I had to find hotels that allowed animals since she plans to travel with Angel. Of course, when she's in meetings or too busy, she expects me to feed the little devil and take her outside.

Have I mentioned how I'm not looking forward to being the babysitter bitch during this trip?

Even though I had to plead for space and accommodations for each event and worked day and night to get it all situated, Rachel insisted on re-confirmations even after I assured her everything would go off without a hitch several times.

Once I repeated everything to her yesterday afternoon, I left early to get my things in order. I'd asked my neighbor across the hall to keep an eye on my place and let her know I'd be gone for a couple of weeks. As a retired school teacher in her sixties, Margie's always trying to hook me up with old guys from her book club. She nearly had a heart attack when I explained I'd be gone for that long and had to explain it was a work trip. Just another reminder I should probably get out more.

I make it to O'Hare International Airport and arrive at my gate with plenty of time to spare. I made sure to arrive early just in case security was backed up. Even after stopping for coffee and a pastry, I had an hour to work on my laptop before I boarded.

The flight was four hours long, and considering I stayed up late to finish packing and cleaning my apartment, I slept for the final two hours of the trip. I was able to read for a bit, but I was too anxious about having to meet Maverick Kingston in person to really focus on the words.

Playboy. Arrogant. Cocky and full of himself.

Those are just a few of the traits I'd heard from Presley. She's well known in the book community for her photography skills and for having a huge following on Instagram. She takes extravagant bookish pictures and travels a ton. Presley knows everything there is to know about the drama between authors, readers, bloggers, and models. Anytime I need insider info, I just text her, and she has the full details within twenty minutes.

As soon as I land in LA, I text Maverick to let him know I'm here and that we need to meet up before we start our road trip to Dallas tomorrow.

Olivia: I just arrived at LAX. Can you meet at 4?

That gives me just enough time to check in to my hotel and freshen up.

Maverick: Sure, babe. Wear black leather pants and a red G-string. Don't forget the whip.

What in the ever-loving fuck? I narrow my eyes as I read his message and am certain he meant that for someone else.

Olivia: I sincerely hope you're joking. This is Olivia Carpenter, Rachel's assistant. I'm here to pick you up for her tour...

Maverick: So...you want me to bring the whip instead?

I groan internally.
This is going to be a fucking nightmare.

CHAPTER FOUR

MAVERICK

I'M NOT PARTICULARLY LOOKING FORWARD to meeting Miss Uptight Goody-Two-shoes, but she insists on meeting face-to-face before we leave tomorrow, as if I need to know how serious she is about this damn schedule. I offered to pick her up from the airport this morning, but she refused, stating she had rented a car and was more than capable of taking care of herself. Truthfully, Olivia is already rubbing my balls raw, and I've only spoken with her on the phone and through email. She's warned and threatened me in a passive-aggressive way several times about being on my best behavior. I roll my eyes just thinking about the conversations we've had since I confirmed I'd be attending Rachel's extended tour. Olivia's been professional and to the point, but recently, the amount of detail in her emails have made my head spin. The woman has reiterated the schedule so many times, I feel like I could recite it by heart, word for word.

After I get ready for the day and run some errands, I spend my afternoon working out, because staying in the best shape possible is necessary for my profession. I eat healthy, lift weights five times a week, and even run on most days too. One of my only requirements for this trip was for whatever hotel we stayed in to have a gym with weights because I planned to continue my workouts while on the road. Luckily, Rachel backed me on that one so Olivia couldn't argue it.

After I finish at the gym, I head home to take a shower and get ready to meet Olivia. She was dead set on going to a *public* place—a coffee shop not too far from the airport—and refused the invitation to come to my apartment. It's official, she's a prude, which I knew after the first time I spoke with her.

Once I'm out of the shower, I slip on a pair of jeans and a T-shirt and then step outside and schedule an Uber so I can catch up on some emails. Word has gotten out in the book world that my exclusivity expires after this summer, so photographers are desperately trying to book me. For the past few weeks, I've had an autoresponder send a message saying I will return all emails when I get back from traveling. Right now it's too overwhelming to deal with. Maybe I need an Olivia in my life too? If she can handle Rachel Meadows' intense schedule and attitude, the woman can pretty much handle anyone.

As the Uber pulls up, I hop inside and get lost in my phone. LA is a bitch to get through most of the time, so instead of struggling through bumper-to-bumper traffic, I prefer being in the back of a car so I can take care of business.

I read over the last email Olivia sent so it's fresh in my mind. She made it a point to stress we needed to meet at four on the dot, so I purposely arrive late just to test the waters from the get-go, regardless of first impressions and all that. Give me an inch, and I'll take a mile every single day.

When I walk into the coffee shop, I look around for an older, gray-haired woman and am pleasantly surprised when the only person in sight is a cute, uptight, sassy blonde with a scowl permanently fixated on her face.

Olivia Carpenter isn't eighty, which is shocking considering the way she acts.

I smile. She rolls her eyes.

And just like that, we're off to a good start.

Instead of rushing immediately toward her, I walk to the counter and take my time ordering a black coffee. Once the cup is handed over to me, I sit in front of her with a smirk. "Olivia?"

She looks down at her watch, then back at me unamused. "I said four. Not four twenty-five."

I chuckle. Studying her. Already noticing her quirks. She's the

Hermione Granger of author assistants with her planners stacked high in front of her, clothes perfectly pressed, and every button done up to her neck. Not a wisp of sandy blond hair is out of place from the bun tightly fixated on the back of her head, and she sits up straight as a board. I swear if the wind blows the wrong way, she'll tip over.

I glance down at the bottle of water she's drinking. "Who comes to a coffee house and drinks water?"

"I've had my daily allowance of caffeine already, thank you very much. Now, can we get down to business? I'm not one for small talk." *No kidding.*

I'm actually taken aback by the way she's treating me within the first thirty seconds of meeting me. Not many women blow me off like this, which makes me wonder if my charm is fading. It's true, some women are immune to it, and Olivia already seems like she's going to be a tough egg to crack. Then again, I'm always up for a good challenge.

I rub my hand across the scruff on my chin. "Sure thing. I'm ready to listen to you go over this *again*. But let me say this; when I close my eyes, all I can see is your three-page email detailing every second of my life for the next twelve days. But please, Miss Priss, continue."

She ignores my frustration and opens a notebook where she has everything written out in the neatest handwriting I've ever seen with bullet points, timelines, and dates. My phone vibrates as she starts reading off our insane schedule, and I check a text message and respond. Instantly, she stops and stares at me. It's actually the most attention she's given me since I sat down.

"Are you even listening to me?" Her green eyes bore into me.

"Are you hungry? Do you need a Snickers? You seem a little cranky." I tuck my phone in my pocket and give her a shit-eating grin.

She slams her notebook shut and glares at me. "This was obviously a huge mistake. I really hope I don't kill you before the end of this. I value my job, and a murder rap wouldn't look good for me."

I chuckle, which only seems to set her off even more. "I'm sure

Rachel and her raving fans wouldn't appreciate that. I'm willing to bet they'd go on a witch hunt if that happened."

Olivia huffs and interlocks her fingers together on the table. She looks like she wants to stand and strangle me but somehow shows great restraint. "Rachel expects you to be on your very best behavior during this tour because you're representing her brand, which she's worked very hard to establish over the last decade. That means you are required to arrive on time to all events. You need to be presentable and friendly to her readers. And you have to keep your dick in your pants. I know all this is going to be really hard for you, but those are the rules, and my job is to make sure you follow them. Understand? I've been voluntold to be your babysitter or truant officer—maybe both. So don't test me and everything will be just fine."

"Babysitter? That's hilarious!" I laugh and take a sip of coffee. "I don't need watching, though. I'm a big boy," I respond sarcastically.

"I've heard how some models act at these events. I've been made well aware of your kind, Mr. Playboy," she adds.

My eyebrows pop up. "Oh really? Please enlighten me then, Miss Priss. I'd love to know what preconceived notions you have about me so I can make them *alllllllll* come true in the next twelve days," I taunt, taking another swig of coffee.

"*Stop* calling me that," Olivia demands between gritted teeth. We've been around each other for approximately ten minutes, and I've already managed to permanently smash in her buttons. *Perfect.* This is going to be fun.

"Are you always this arrogant?" she asks.

"Are you always so uptight?" I fire right back.

She shakes her head. "This is an absolute nightmare. You're going to make me go crazy so we're done here."

Olivia stands up and grabs her notebooks and planners. She presses them against her chest and glares at me.

Instantly, I stand too. "Great talk."

She groans and walks toward the door, and I follow, checking her out in the process. Olivia is tall, though she's wearing heels. Her black skirt hugs her tiny waist and accentuates her curves. She looks like she just walked out of an episode of *Law & Order* with how put together she is. I chuckle at her expense and continue to follow her to the car that's perfectly parallel parked. As she unlocks it and sets her library of planners in the passenger seat, I stop.

"Please tell me you didn't rent a fucking Toyota Prius for a long road trip."

She turns on her heels and takes a step toward me. "Or what?"

"It's seriously one of the shittiest cars a person can rent for someone my size. You couldn't have gotten something more comfortable or spacious? I'm six foot two, for crying out loud."

"And when you're cramping, think about the amazing gas mileage we're going to get and the money we're going to save by going hybrid." For the first time all day, she smiles, but it's smug as fuck. Almost as if she gets some sick satisfaction out of the fact I will be tortured for the next two weeks. I'm pretty sure she does.

I swallow hard. I'm actually pissed. "Well then, I might have to call Rachel and let her know I won't be able to make it after all."

Olivia narrows her eyes at me, and I see a glimpse of panic flash across her face. "You wouldn't."

Tilting my head, I cross my arms across my chest. "Test me." I repeat her words from earlier, throwing them back in her face just to see if she'll combust with anger.

"If you did that…" She stops herself and bites her tongue, so she doesn't continue.

"What? What are you going to do?"

We stand there and stare at each other before Olivia relents. "Fine, whatever. Didn't realize we were using threats here. You have *no idea* what you just started, Maverick."

"Whatever it is, I promise you, I'll finish it, *Miss Priss*."

She shakes her head and climbs into the shitty Prius mumbling something under her breath, and I'm pretty sure I heard her call me an asshole. Before starts the car, she rolls down the passenger window but refuses to look at me.

"I'll be at your house at seven. Don't make me wait." As I watch her drive away and turn in the absolute wrong direction, I let out a laugh. I may have pushed Olivia's buttons, but she's managed to push mine right back. The next two weeks of my life are going to be a lot more interesting than I originally thought, and I'm sure she's thinking the same.

I look up at the cloudless blue sky, and a smile fills my face. Someone better say a prayer for Olivia because now I'm even more determined to wear her down to the bone, and I have a week and a half to do it.

Challenge accepted.

CHAPTER FIVE

OLIVIA

Maverick Kingston managed to get under my skin in less than an hour and then showed up in my dreams last night.

Not by choice.

Ugh! The man is infuriating. He doesn't take anything seriously and treats life like one big frat party. So, the next eleven days should be a blast.

After his not-so-subtle threat about not going on this road trip in a Prius, I had no choice but to replace the rental car. Driving with him will be painful enough. I don't need to hear him complain the whole time about the damn car.

Once I grab some coffee, I head over to Maverick's place and text him.

Olivia: I'm here. Use the bathroom before you come out. Our first stop isn't for five hours.

Maverick: Don't worry, babe. I'll bring a bottle of water and reuse it ;)

I groan, almost wishing I'd kept the Prius now.

Sipping on my coffee, I adjust the radio and play something mellow. It helps me relax, and if I'm going to be driving in LA traffic this early, I'll need to stay calm.

"Well, well, well…" I hear Maverick say in a singsong voice. He throws his luggage into the back and flashes me a victorious smile as he climbs into the passenger side. "Nice wheels."

"You didn't leave me much choice," I grind out. "Also, do you have something against being on time?"

"This is California, babe. We're a chill type of people here."

"Stop calling me babe," I tell him harshly as I pull onto the road. The GPS is already set, and it says we're twelve hours from our first hotel. This is going to be a long, miserable day. "I'm not *your* babe, and my name is Olivia."

"Well, *Olivia*. You aren't in Kansas anymore. You can lose the bitter, uptight attitude."

I scrunch my nose. I don't even know what that's supposed to mean. "I'm from Chicago."

He snorts, adjusting his seat and shifting it back to make room for his long legs. "That definitely explains it."

I roll my eyes though I'm not looking at him.

"Can I turn off this church music?" Maverick asks thirty minutes into our trip. He leans forward and starts messing with the knob.

"It's nice driving music," I argue, swatting his hand away.

"You can't be serious. This shit is gonna put you to sleep, and then we're going to crash and die. You really want that on your conscience?"

The corner of his lips tilts up just the slightest.

"Guess it wouldn't matter. I'd be dead." I flash a smug smile right back at him.

"Oh, I see how it is. You look all innocent and smart, but deep down, you have this morbidity to you."

I shoot him a look. "You're the morbid one with all your crashing and dying talk." I turn my music back on. "Now no more talking about it because if I don't get you to these events on time, Rachel *will* actually kill me."

"Why you so scared of her anyway? I could fit her in my pocket. She looks harmless enough."

Glancing at him, I shake my head, then force myself to focus on the road. "You know she's anything but harmless."

He chuckles, shaking his head. "Yeah, you're right. She's not a firecracker like you, though."

"I'm not even sure what that means, but you can't label me when you've just met me."

"Oh, like you haven't labeled me already?"

"I know your kind. I've heard plenty about you to form an opinion," I tell him with purpose.

"God, you're so hypocritical. You think you're the first prissy, stick-up-her-ass assistant I've met? Doesn't mean I know *you* just like it doesn't mean you know *me*."

He kinda has a point, but I don't tell him that. His ego is already taking up all the space in the car.

Ignoring his comment, I grip the steering wheel a bit tighter. We're in heavy traffic, and I'm not used to eight-lane highways.

"You better change lanes," he says.

"I'm trying." I look over my shoulder, searching for a spot to move into.

"Might wanna try the blinker. I heard it's a signal for other drivers to know you want to turn or move over."

I sigh and put it on. He's distracting me.

"Stay quiet so I can focus."

His chuckles are the last thing I hear from him as I attempt to move across the lanes. Finally, I make it, and we coast down the highway in silence until the city is behind us.

"When are we stopping for food?" He speaks up for the first time in hours. I look over at him and see he's sticking out his lower lip, making a pouty face. "I'm shriveling to nothing over here." He slightly lifts his shirt and pats his ridiculously cut stomach.

His eyes meet mine, and I quickly look away although he saw me staring. Swallowing, I look at the GPS to see how much farther until our first stop.

"We have about an hour left," I tell him. "Think you'll manage to stay alive for that long?"

He groans loudly, and it makes me laugh. I quickly catch myself and stop.

"You have a nice laugh. It's a pleasant change from your short fuse and snarl."

"I don't snarl!" I argue. "I just like having a plan and sticking to it."

He noticeably rolls his eyes. "Okay, Miss Priss. Letting your hair down won't kill ya."

"No, but your arrogant, self-absorbed attitude just might," I throw at him, holding back a smirk.

"Well, I think that's debatable. Most of the women I date think it's charming."

A loud snort bursts out of me, and I'm unable to bite my tongue. "I think that says more about *who* you're dating than anything. They must be desperate."

"Damn, what a burn." He chuckles. "Adding hostile to your personality resume."

I inhale a deep breath, realizing that was a really mean thing to say. "Okay, sorry. That wasn't nice. But I'm not taking back what I said about you. You're arrogant, and there's no denying that."

"Oh, well then, thanks, I guess." He smirks. "You say it like being arrogant is a bad thing, though. In my profession, I kinda have to be. I'm constantly selling myself to photographers and showing them I'm worthy of being in their magazines and advertisements. If I don't act confident and prove I'm the best guy for the gig, I'll lose it to the thousands of other people pursuing the job."

I think about his words for a minute. "Okay, well I can certainly understand that. But I think you're just naturally that way." I shrug, biting down on my lower lip so he doesn't see right through me. He has every right to be confident; there's no doubt about that. He's got it all—the body, the face, the perfect white teeth and smile. His abs are plastered all over Rachel's covers and book promo graphics. He even has that annoying muscular V that trails from his hips to down below his waistline. *Annoyingly sexy.* "However, that doesn't mean you can't be humble in other aspects of your life."

"That's a pretty big accusation for someone you just met. How do you know I'm not? You haven't been around me long enough to know anything about me. Don't you think?"

Damn. He's right. "Fine. Prove me wrong then."

An hour later, we're stopped at a little family diner for lunch, and I'm ready to suck down another gallon of coffee. At this point, I'm not even sure caffeine affects me, but I'm an addict, so I enjoy the taste too.

The hostess smiles wide at Maverick as soon as he walks in, and her demeanor changes when she sees me following behind him. She studies me hard, eyes lingering up and down my body as if she's disgusted a guy like him would be with a girl like me.

As we follow her to a table, I look down at my outfit and wonder what the judgmental snob was thinking about me. This is one of my favorite pantsuits, so she obviously has zero taste.

"Here you go." She places the menus down in front of us once we sit across from each other in the booth. "The lunch special is the turkey and avocado wrap, and the soup is French onion."

"Sounds great, thank you," Maverick says, giving her a million-dollar smile. I fight back the urge to groan loudly. She acts like I'm not sitting here and talks directly to him while smiling and giggling like a fool. No one is that excited about lunch specials.

"Your server will be right with you."

Maverick flashes her a quick wink before she trails off. I stare at him, dumbfounded.

"What?" He smirks.

I roll my eyes and grab a menu.

"What was that for?"

"Don't you think that was a tad inappropriate?" I ask, not looking up at him as I scan the menu.

"Inappropriate? How? You're gonna tell me how to act before we even get to the event?" His voice is gruff and laced with annoyance.

"Because I'm sitting right here, across from you, and she acted like I didn't exist. We could've been on a date for all she knows."

His brows shoot up, eyes widening.

"That didn't come out right. That's not what I meant. No, I mean like—"

"Olivia, stop." He chuckles. "You're cute when you're all flustered."

I narrow my eyes at his statement. "Don't call me cute. And I'm not flustered."

"And that's exactly how she knew we weren't on a date. Could probably smell the distaste you have for me the second you walked in." He smirks to tell me he thinks he's funny.

"Alright, but still. It's rude to ignore a customer and hit on the other one. So unprofessional," I assert.

Maverick shakes his head while smiling and lifts his menu. "She's a hostess with a low-cut top and six-inch platforms. I doubt she was aiming for professionalism at all."

Our waitress finally comes over, and we order. I'm so hungry, I ask for crackers while we wait for our food.

"You gonna eat that?" Maverick nods to the other half of my club sandwich twenty minutes later.

"No, I can't. I'm stuffed." I had soup before my meal because I was starving, but now I just want a nap.

"Sweet. Can I have it?"

My eyes widen, shocked he's still hungry after shoveling an entire steak into his mouth. "Are you serious?"

Maverick reaches over and grabs it from my plate. "Gotta feed those muscles." He shoots me a wink—to annoy me, I'm sure. He should know by now it has zero effect on me, yet he enjoys testing me.

"Sure," I say, laughing when he doesn't wait for my answer before taking a large bite. "I can't believe how much you eat considering how fit you are."

He reaches for his water and takes a long swig before setting it back down. "So you think I'm fit, huh?"

Rolling my eyes, I take my napkin and throw it at his smug expression. "That's like saying the sky is blue, so don't get any ideas in that big head of yours."

After paying, Maverick yanks the keys from my hand and says it's his turn to drive. I don't bother arguing with him this time.

"I'm going to use the bathroom again before we go," I tell him, so he doesn't wait for me. "You might want to as well."

"I went when we got here. So did you."

"I know, but it's better to be safe than sorry. We aren't stopping again for a few hours," I remind him.

"I'm fine. Meet you at the car."

Shaking my head, I drop the subject and go about my business. I told him earlier we were only making one more stop after lunch to fill up so we'll arrive at the hotel around eight tonight. Though I didn't want to be in the car for twelve hours today, it was necessary. As long as we stay on schedule, making it to Dallas on time tomorrow shouldn't be an issue.

"So since I'm driving, my radio now," Maverick says the moment I sit in the passenger seat.

"Is this where you tell me you're secretly into Ariana Grande and Avril Lavigne?"

"First off, no. Secondly, Avril is a killer punk singer, so joke's on you." He grins, fiddling with the stations.

"Yeah, clearly." I groan, buckling in and trying to mentally prepare myself for the next six hours with this man.

"AC/DC, baby!"

I furrow my brows and scowl, wishing I'd brought headphones with me.

An hour goes by, and instead of dwelling on his horrible music choices, I write in my notebooks and planner, making a list of the things I need to do in order of importance before this trip is over. Rachel has continued to pile on tasks, and if I can complete some of them during the next week and a half, that'll save me from being overloaded when we return.

Just as I'm writing down some notes about her next release, I see Maverick nearly dancing in his seat and looking over his shoulder to merge to the right lane.

"What are you doing?" I look around and see we haven't traveled very far since lunch.

"I need to piss. I saw a sign for an outlet mall coming up."

I look at the time. We don't need gas for a couple more hours.

"I told you to go at the diner!" I scold. "We don't have time to stop. We're already behind schedule since Miss Hostess with no shame chatted with you for an extra five minutes."

He turns his head and glares at me. "So you're going to punish me by making me piss myself?"

"Surely you can hold it for a couple of hours."

"Olivia."

"Maverick."

"I'm driving, and I'm taking this exit."

"No!" I hold my hand to stop him from turning the steering

wheel. "Those stores are probably packed. By the time we find a parking spot, you find a bathroom, and we drive out of the traffic, it'll waste twenty minutes!"

"Take your hand off the wheel, Olivia. You'll make us get into an accident."

"Fine," I grit between my teeth. "Keep driving then."

"I will as soon as I take a leak."

"Argh! Why are you so difficult? I just want to get to the hotel and take a hot shower and sleep before we have to do this all over again tomorrow."

"And you will, so stop being so dramatic."

"Maverick, seriously." I hold up my planner to show him the schedule. "We'll run right into the evening rush hour, and that'll fuck it all up."

He narrows his eyes as if he's actually reading it, and I'm so distracted by how close he is to me that I don't even see him moving to take it right out of my hand. He presses a button on his door, and the window automatically rolls down.

"What are you—"

"You wanna know how I feel about your fucking schedule?"

My eyes widen in fear. "You wouldn't."

"Wanna find out?" He quirks a brow, taunting me as he shifts it closer to the window. Watching the pages flutter in the breeze causes my heart to race. This can't be happening; my entire life is in there, and so is Rachel's.

"Give it back! That's my Bible!"

He laughs. Fucking *laughs*!

I know I'm not the easiest person to be around. It's probably why I don't have many friends or a social life, but this is just plain mean.

"I will junk punch you with no mercy if you don't hand it over, Maverick." I hold down my stare as I put one hand out for him to place it there.

"Damn, Miss Priss. Taking it to that level, huh?" He flashes a smirk, obviously not too worried about my threat.

My jaw drops open. "You started it!"

He shakes his head and chuckles as he tosses it on my lap, ignoring my hand.

Moments later, he takes the exit and finds a parking spot—which takes forever just as I suspected.

"Be back in a second," he says as he opens the door and steps out. When I don't respond, he leans into the car, and continues, "Let me know if you need help getting that stick out of your ass later. I'm assuming it's wedged pretty deep, so I'll buy some lube just in case."

Vibration at the back of my throat releases a deep growl. Gah! He's so infuriating.

I look up and see a wide, proud smile plastered on his chiseled face.

"Fuck off."

He chuckles loudly as if he accomplished what he was aiming for—riling me up.

"My offer to junk punch you stands," I remind him. "Hurry up."

"Ooh, I like it when you talk dirty to me." He winks and shuts the door behind him before I can respond.

Leaning back, I fall against the headrest and groan.

One day down, only eleven more to go.

CHAPTER SIX

MAVERICK

Olivia's knocking on my door before the sun rises, which only annoys the shit out of me because it's literally six on the dot. I understand being on a schedule and all, but she's absolutely relentless. I open the door wearing nothing but my boxer briefs, and she glances down at my morning wood, then back up at me.

"For crying out loud," she says. "It's time to go, and you're not even dressed."

I close the door in her face and hear her groans on the other side. I can just imagine her standing there, fuse lit, ready to explode as I throw on some jeans and a T-shirt. Considering we have all day to drive to Dallas and we're thirteen hours away means we don't have to really rush around just as long as we're there by tonight.

By the way she's acting, I can tell she's already wound up tight.

Last night after my shower, I packed everything, so I'm mostly ready to go, but I want her to sweat for a moment. After five minutes pass, I hear pounding on the door. I'm halfway surprised she waited out there that long.

I grab my suitcase, pop the handle up, and open the door. Olivia rolls her eyes and shakes her head, which only causes me to laugh. I follow her to the elevator. When we step in, she doesn't say a word to me.

"I need the keys. I'm driving." I hold out my hand, and at first, she hesitates but then places them in my palm. I'll take all the small victories I can get.

Before we leave the hotel lobby, Olivia stops at the front desk and hands over the key cards, then asks for her receipt. Instead of waiting, I walk to the car, pop the trunk, and throw my suitcase inside. Soon, she's walking toward me dressed in proper business attire and high heels, which I didn't notice earlier because I was too busy closing the door in her face.

"You're going to wear that to travel?" I look her up and down before taking her suitcases, pushing the handles down, and placing them in the trunk. I try to take her laptop bag, but she refuses to hand it over. I shrug and repeat my question.

"What's wrong with what I'm wearing?" she asks with her arms folded over her chest.

"It's too uptight for a road trip, don't you think?"

She doesn't say a word before she turns on her heels and climbs into the passenger seat. I take my time walking to the driver's side, climb in, adjust the mirrors, then find a rock and roll station on satellite radio, which will be a complete lifesaver when we're driving in the middle of nowhere Texas.

Olivia bends over and starts pulling notebooks from her bag, and when she flips to the daily itinerary she's laid out, I turn up the music because I don't want to hear about our stupid schedule today. Rock music screams through the car, and it takes all of ten seconds for her to reach over and turn it down.

"I can't concentrate with that crap blaring. I'd like to try to get some work done while you drive." She reaches and changes the station to her classical church shit.

I pull out of the hotel parking lot and put the radio back to my music. "When I'm driving, we listen to what *I* want to listen to and vice versa. Road trip rules 101." The Rolling Stones scream out about getting satisfaction. When she goes to turn it down, I lightly swat her hand. "I'm serious."

Olivia slams her planner shut and stares out the window as I pull into a gas station. We're a few miles from the New Mexico border, and I want to fill up now and get some water without her telling me when I'm allowed to drink. "We don't have time to stop right now. We can make it a little farther," she argues, but I don't listen.

Before I get out, she begrudgingly hands me her business credit card, and I fill up the car. She seems to be picking and choosing her battles today, which is pleasant in a way. I might actually start wearing her down. Who knows, by the time we make it to Dallas, we could be friends. I laugh at the thought. Before I get in the car, I run inside the gas station and grab a few bottles of water for us. When I open the door and hand her one, she gives me a smile, actually grateful.

"Thank you." She twists off the top and nearly drinks half of it.

"Dang, girl. Want me to go in and get you another one?" I grin.

She shakes her head, then goes back to her book, and the small moment we shared disappears. I get in the car and turn the radio just loud enough to drown out the road noise. Desert with patches of random green grass lines the road. I'm thankful the weather is nice and the sky is blue; it makes for easy driving. Soon we're leaving New Mexico and crossing the Texas border. Seeing all the brown really makes me miss the water in California.

Olivia looks around at the nothingness as we drive through El Paso and Van Horn. "Maverick. How much gas do we have?" she asks, going back to her planner.

I look down and see we're under a quarter of a tank, but closer to empty than not. "Enough," I tell her.

"Seriously. I had our gas stops planned out based on mileage, and you ruined that from the get-go. How much gas do we have?" I can tell she's starting to panic the farther we drive away from civilization.

"There's another town coming up. We'll make it there. Quit worrying. I've been road tripping since I was old enough to drive." I point at the GPS and show her the gas symbol in the next town. "There's a gas station in Toyah. We'll make it there, no problem."

Olivia relaxes, but only slightly. I watch the gas meter move closer to empty as we continue to drive. Glancing back at the GPS, I see the gas station is about a mile away and is located next to the post office on the main road. Almost sitting on the edge of her seat, Olivia glances around at the ghost town we're driving through. Old houses and empty buildings line the road. We inch closer to the gas icon on the screen, and I slow to turn into the parking lot only to see the station is closed with windows boarded. There's a faded *For Sale* sign nailed on the outside.

We're literally fucked, and we both know it.

"Now what are we going to do?" She turns to me, and I try to think of something, but I have nothing. So I do what any person would in this situation, and I continue driving until the small town is behind us. Thankfully, there's a pull-off in the distance, and I swing into the rest area which is more like a parking lot than anything considering there are zero bathrooms. Diesel trucks are pulled over with their engines running, the drivers most likely catching some sleep after a long haul. Metal windmills decorate the grassy area, and they spin fast in the wind, but other than that, nothing else is around us. I park in front of a big rig and pull my phone from my pocket and try to figure out our next step. Olivia grabs her phone too. I watch her turn it off and then turn it back on, annoyed with it.

"Please tell me you have cell service," she finally says, worry coating her voice.

"I do," I say, wanting to tell her I'll make this right, but instead, she gets out of the car, slamming the door behind her. Yep, she's pissed. Really pissed, and this time it's more than warranted. With some quick googling, I see there's a gas station twenty-three miles away, but there's no way we'd make it. It's not within walking distance, and I'll be damned if I try to bum a ride from anyone out here. *Texas Chainsaw Massacre* comes to mind.

I get out of the car and walk toward Olivia.

"Why didn't you just listen to me?" The words spew out of her mouth like venom when I get closer.

"I know this is totally my fault, and I'm sorry." I don't want to argue about this because no excuse I can give will even remotely fix this. We're going to be behind schedule now, and I'm grateful she doesn't throw that in my face even though I deserve it. Sometimes I can be too goddamn hardheaded for my own good.

"Apology accepted." She finally lets out a deep breath and checks her watch. "We're going to have to call roadside assistance. It's the only thing I can think of."

Olivia turns on her heels and walks back to the car. She leans over and pulls the rental contract from the glove compartment and reads through it. After a moment, she finds what she's looking for and shows it to me. It's the 1-800 number for roadside assistance. "I'm so glad I paid extra for this. Also, I don't have cell service, so…"

"I'll take care of it." I put in the number and am transferred to several different people before I'm sent to the right department.

"So where ya located again?" the woman on the line asks in a thick Southern accent.

"In the middle of nowhere." I laugh as I look around. "We're about two miles outside of Toyah, Texas, at a parking area. We're eastbound on I-10."

I hear clicking on a keyboard for a minute. "Ah, found you. Okay, hold, please. I'm gonna try to call around and see if I can get you some help. You weren't lying, sweetie. You really are in the middle of nowhere." She laughs. "Be right back."

I sit on hold for over five minutes, and I'm half worried that we're going to be stranded out here. Different horrible scenarios fill my mind. If we don't make it to Dallas tonight, Rachel will lose her shit, and neither Olivia nor I want that. We have one thing in common, at least.

"Sir, are you still there?" the woman asks, coming back on the line, pulling me away from my thoughts.

"Yeah, I am." I lean against the car and watch Olivia hold up her cell phone to try to find service. She should really loosen up. She's wound up so damn tight.

"So, I've got someone who can come out, but they're about ninety minutes away. This company is coming from Van Horn, and they're the closest."

"There's a gas station less than thirty miles away in Pecos. There's no one there who can help?" I'm already dreading telling Olivia how much time we're going to lose.

"No, sir. We've got companies we contract with, and they're the closest. I'm sorry. You'll need to make sure you have the rental agreement nearby when he arrives. If he's not there in an hour and a half, then you'll need to call back so we can check to make sure everything is okay. Do you have any more questions?"

"No. Thanks for your help."

She finishes explaining a few details, and then we say our goodbyes. Olivia walks over and gets in the car. I get inside too.

"So?" she asks.

I swallow hard. "An hour and a half."

She tucks her lips in her mouth and closes her eyes tight, and I have a feeling she's trying to control her emotions. Even just being around her this short amount of time, I've learned that she lives and dies by her schedule, so I actually do feel bad.

"We don't have time for this," she finally says, releasing a slow, agitated breath.

"I know," I say as she repositions the seat. I roll down the windows, allowing some sort of breeze to blow through, though it's hot as hell outside. Thirty minutes pass, and it feels like an eternity. My bladder is ready to burst on top of it all. Not able to hold it anymore, I get out of the car.

Olivia sits up. "Where are you going?"

"I gotta take a piss," I tell her, walking across the grass, trying to find some semi-secluded place where I can find relief. I walk across rocks and over patches of grass and find a few trees. What kind of rest area doesn't have a bathroom? Seriously. After I've pissed, I go back to the car and get inside. Olivia has hand sanitizer waiting for me.

"Are you a germaphobe too?" She squirts way too much in my hands.

"No. I just like being prepared."

That's the understatement of the year.

Another thirty minutes pass, and I see Olivia squirming as I scroll through my emails. "What?" I turn and look at her.

"I have to pee now too," she admits.

"There are a few trees over there. It's pretty secluded."

She squeezes her knees together. "I can't pee outside."

I burst out into laughter. "When you're desperate, you'll pee anywhere."

Five minutes pass, and she looks over at me. "Will you go with me and keep watch? I mean, what if someone walks up on me while I'm trying to squat."

I hold back my laughter. "Sure."

She digs in her bag and pulls out a travel size pack of tissues. I follow her across the gravel, and she's having a hell of a time walking in those heels. Instead of saying anything, I just chuckle.

"Shut up," she says, but I can tell she's smiling by her playful tone. Stopping, she looks around, then turns to face me. "I guess this is as good as it's gonna get."

I turn my back and can hear her struggling. Crossing my arms over my chest, I keep a lookout and laugh because she's dressed in business wear with pantyhose and all.

She groans behind me. "Great, now I'm pee shy!"

Eventually, she goes and lets out a sigh of relief. I hear her clothes rustling behind me as she tries to make herself presentable again, I'm sure.

"Finished?" I ask.

She comes up next to me and stumbles on her heel, causing me to catch her from falling. Olivia nervously looks up into my eyes.

"Next time, jeans, T-shirt, and Chucks when traveling for thirteen hours. Got it, Miss Priss?" I release my hold on her and smile. She smooths her skirt and runs a hand over her hair, then we head back to the car.

Thirty minutes to go and I'm growing more impatient with each passing second. Though I hate that we're in this situation, I can't say I hate being with her. I feel like the two of us are making headway, and her prissiness is beginning to grow on me.

CHAPTER SEVEN

OLIVIA

I LIVE in Chicago for a reason. Texas is hot as hell, and though it's not super humid, I'm pretty sure the sun is baking my skin, which is the last thing I need right now. As I sweat, I realize how bad of an idea it was to put on pantyhose this morning. I should've just worn something comfortable, but it's important for me to look professional on the outside regardless if I'm a hot mess on the inside. I try to control the things I can, and appearance is one of those things. You always dress for the job you want, not the one you have.

Just as I open my phone to check and see if I miraculously have service, I see an old beat-up Chevy truck pull up slowly next to the car. An older guy with a cowboy hat makes eye contact with me, then drives forward and reverses until the bumper is almost against the car. Instantly, I enter panic mode.

I look over at Maverick who's as calm as can be. "Is that the gas delivery?"

He glances at me, then back at the truck. "I have no idea."

My adrenaline spikes, and I realize this is how every horror movie starts. The truck is an older model, and there's no signage on it saying it's a company vehicle. I'm growing more anxious every minute the guy doesn't get out. Seriously, what is he doing? What's taking him so long? Is he busy sharpening his knife or loading his gun?

Eventually, the door swings open with a pop and a screech, causing me to jump. The man's wearing dirty blue jeans that are tucked into some tall worn cowboy boots. The button-up shirt is rolled to his elbows. Yep, we're going to die. I put my window up and buckle my seat belt just in case we have to hurry and drive away. Considering we're basically on empty, we won't get very far. Maverick glances over at me as the man walks toward us and leans against the car.

"Y'all waiting for some gas?" he asks, his voice rough and full of gruff.

"Yes, sir," Maverick says.

"Alright." He returns to his truck, pulls a gas can from the back, and Maverick gets out of the car to help. I let out a breath of relief, because holy shit, why did he feel the need to block us in like that? The whole situation is awkward as hell. I watch Maverick and the guy put the gas in the car from the side mirror. After Maverick signs a document and tips the man, he walks to his truck and pulls away. I suck in a deep breath, needing more oxygen.

Before Maverick walks around to the driver's side, I get out of the car.

"I'm driving the rest of the way." I hold out my hand, and after a moment of hesitation, he hands me the key. I refuse to run out of gas again on this trip especially after I've planned every single stop. I was too focused on my work to notice how far we'd gone, and by the time I did, it was too late. I'm somewhat pissed with myself for not saying something sooner. It's already late afternoon, and we've lost too much time, which means we'll arrive in Dallas well after dark. Not to mention, I have to be up at the butt crack of dawn to pick Rachel up from the airport.

We get in the car at the same time, and I take off down the road. The gas only filled the car up to a quarter of a tank, so as soon as we're in the next town, I fill up. Though I don't want to, because we don't really have time, we stop in Odessa and grab some food, then continue the rest of the way. Once we're back in the car, Maverick leans his seat back and instantly falls asleep for a few hours. Since he's out, I put on an audiobook and listen to it while I drive. I randomly glance over at him, noticing how peaceful he looks when he's sleeping. His chiseled jaw and pouty plump lips are enough to drive any woman crazy. I understand why women flock to him because he's attractive and has that arrogant charm. I've been warned about his type though. I'm determined to keep my eyes on the road and speed up, trying to cut as much time off our trip as possible. Once we get below a half tank, I stop and fill up again. Maverick is sleeping so hard he doesn't even notice.

Once we're back on the road, he lifts his seat, rubs his hands over his face, and looks around, noticing the sun is set. My audiobook is still playing.

He fucks me so hard, and I beg him not to stop. I want and need more of him, and he gives me exactly what I want. I feel as if I'm crumbling under his touch as he... I turn the radio off and am thankful it's dark so he can't see the blush on my cheeks.

"Damn. That's intense," he says. "What the hell were you listening to?"

I swallow. "Rachel's book that just released." I've already read the book half a dozen times during her revisions and listened to the audiobook for approval, but regardless of Rachel being a hardass, she tells a damn good story.

"Man. Y'all are dirty." He chuckles.

"And this is why all her readers want to meet you." I grin, though he can't see. "They envision you as the male character since you're on the cover. Another reason you need to be on your best behavior. They're fantasizing about Ian, the hero, when they look at you."

He yawns. "I'll take any advantage that I can."

I roll my eyes. As if he needs one.

"Do you want me to drive?" Maverick asks.

I shake my head. "I'm good. We only have an hour before we're there."

"Really? Wow. Good job." He pulls out his phone and scrolls through Facebook. "So what do you do for fun?"

I keep my eyes on the road. "I work a lot. There's no time for fun."

"Seriously? You don't have any hobbies or anything?" He seems shocked by this.

"I like to nap and read. Does that count?"

He shakes his head. "So you're telling me all you do is work, read, and sleep. That's it? You're such a party animal."

Wow, having someone repeat that aloud makes me sound lame.

"I take my job really seriously. I live and breathe Rachel's life and staying on schedule. There's no time for partying."

Maverick snickers, and I'm pretty sure he's laughing *at* me.

My grip tightens on the steering wheel. "What?"

"Nothing." He turns his head and bursts out into laughter.

"Seriously, what?" I ask.

He shrugs. "It's just unbelievable that you're so married to your job. If you don't live a little now, eventually, you'll wake up and wonder what you accomplished in life. From the moment I met you, I knew you were uptight, but this is crazy. I bet this road trip is the most fun you've had in ages."

"I wouldn't call this fun," I snap back, but I know he's right. It's just when Rachel releases a new book, she needs me more than usual, and considering this is the last book in this series that hit the charts for weeks at a time, there's no time for me to have a personal life. That's a part of the job, and I accepted it a long time ago. I'd try to explain myself to him, but there's no reason. We're only going to be together for the next ten days, and that's it. I'm not trying to be his friend.

"That's fair. But at least this is forcing you to live a little. Who knows, by the end of it, maybe you'll appreciate the adventure yo u experienced, even if you hate every minute of it."

I turn up the radio wanting this conversation to end and realize it's still a sex scene in the book and turn it back off. Rachel can write a chapter's worth of sex, and listening to the actors read it aloud makes it sound so much dirtier. Moans and pants are added in, and I cannot listen to that while he's sitting next to me and staring at me.

Eventually, we pull up to the hotel in Dallas, and I couldn't be happier to be here. I hand the car keys to the valet as they unload my bags and offer to take them up to my room. I allow them, knowing they're working for tips, but Maverick takes his own. Once I check into the hotel, I hand him his key card so we can go our separate ways for the night.

"Want to have a drink with me at the bar?" he asks. I can't deny how sexy he looks standing there with big puppy dog eyes. His tongue swipes his pouty lips, and I force myself to look away. If I weren't on the clock and he wasn't Maverick Kingston, I'd consider it. But no. Not now, not ever.

"Rachel has a strict no fraternizing policy," I tell him before turning and walking to the elevator, not waiting for him. "Good night, Maverick," I say as I step into the elevator alone.

The morning comes way too quickly, and I'm rushing around trying to get dressed. I slept like shit, just because I never sleep well in hotels. My back is aching, and my head is killing me, so I pop two Tylenol and get ready. Rachel is expecting me to be at the airport early waiting for her arrival. If I'm not, I'm sure she'll rip my head off all the way back to the hotel. I hurry and call for my car, make a cup of shitty hotel coffee, then brush my teeth before making my way to the elevator.

It's barely seven in the morning, and the Texas heat punches me in the face as soon as I walk outside. The valet opens the door for me and hands me the keys, and I speed off toward the airport. The traffic is total shit, because it's the time most people head to work, and I start to panic when I realize I need to be at the airport within the next twenty minutes when her plane is scheduled to land. Granted, she has to go to baggage claim, but she's traveling with Angel, so she'll be extra cranky.

My heart races and I quickly take an exit trying to divert traffic, which was luckily the right decision. I circle around and wait for Rachel to come out, and as soon as I roll up, I start receiving texts from her. Yep, she's in a mood. I can already tell.

My heart drops when I realize I didn't get her a coffee before heading this way. As soon as I see her step out of the double doors, I hop out of the car and grab her suitcase as she holds Angel securely in her arms. The little devil in disguise has pink bows on her ears, and her diamond collar is sparkling in the sunshine. I'd offer to take the dog, but screw that. She'd bite my arm off.

I put on a smile. "How was the flight?"

She lifts her sunglasses and gives me a look. "The worst."

I open my mouth and close it. "I got keys for you to go ahead and check in to your room early. The hotel is really nice. I think you'll like it."

It takes every bit of strength I have to put her suitcases in the trunk. I laugh to myself, knowing it would never happen, but damn, I deserve a raise.

"Did you get me a coffee?" Rachel asks, glancing down at my cup.

"No, Starbucks was out of soy, so I told them never mind." It's a lie, but it's better than the truth.

She groans. "They need to get their crap together."

We pull out of the airport and drive back to the hotel.

"So remember, I need you to take care of Angel for me. She needs to go out every three hours, minimum. Also, she'll need food. I like to make sure there are no additives or fillers in it, and she's to only drink triple filtered bottled water. I don't want my baby to have any impurities from the tap." Rachel looks at Angel as if she's the most perfect creature on the planet.

I beg to differ.

Nodding, I do my best to control my face, though all I want to do is roll my eyes. I memorize everything she says, but we've already been through this. Her dog eats and drinks better than me.

As soon as we pull up to the hotel, the valet opens the door for Rachel, and she steps out, instantly replacing her scowl with a smile. She knows how to act, especially when she's staying in a hotel where her readers will be. *You never know who's watching you*, she always reminds me, which I know is good advice. Her bags are removed from the trunk, and the bellman offers to take them to her room. I hand over the key, and she hands me Angel, who instantly snaps at me.

"She might need to potty. Bring her to my room when she's finished."

Forcing another smile, I reply, "Of course."

I look down at Angel who's growling, showing all her pointy teeth. She's such a small dog, but damn, her bites hurt. I lead her to the grassy area and wait for her to smell almost every blade of grass there is, and when I'm totally annoyed, she waits another minute, then finally goes.

"I hate you," I say to her, and she turns around and flicks her back foot toward me as if to say the feeling is one hundred percent mutual.

"Okay, that's enough. Now you're just playing." I tug on her leash, and she snaps at me. I glare at her and pick the asshole up regardless of her aggravation. The entire way to the elevator, she acts out, and we can't get to the fifteenth floor soon enough. We step off, and I knock on Rachel's door, and she swings it open.

I step in and hand her off to Rachel who already has the doggy dishes set up in the room.

"So how's it been traveling with Maverick so far?" she asks, studying my face.

"A nightmare. We ran out of gas yesterday because he refused to fill up when I told him to."

She half-snorts before covering her mouth. "Doesn't surprise me. Even more reason for you to watch him tonight with my readers. I do not want to hear about him sleeping with any of them, Olivia. I'm very serious about that."

I nod. "It won't happen," I assure her. We quickly go over our schedule for tonight, and I pull all her clothes from her suitcase and hang them in the closet. I explain how I've already confirmed reservations at the hotel restaurant downstairs. "I'll be back around six to make sure you're ready. You're wearing a blue blouse and black skirt with these shoes," I tell her, showing her.

"Perfect. I'm going to get some writing done, then take a nap," she says.

"Room service is scheduled for noon," I remind her.

"Fantastic." She stands, and I take that as my cue to leave. Rachel doesn't have to say much anymore. I can read between the lines, and her body language gives her away every single time. Or maybe our brains have finally synced.

Instead of going back to my room and catching up on the sleep I desperately need, I run through the itinerary again. I go to the front desk and have them bring all the boxes of swag items we ordered for her readers to my room so I can put the gift bags together. We had fifty people confirmed for the meet-n-greet dinner. Rachel is graciously paying for everyone's food, though they have no idea yet.

Twenty minutes later, a bellman delivers six huge ass boxes to my room. I spend the next five hours putting everything together, and my back hurts even more from slouching and working a one-person assembly line.

After that's all done, I neatly pack the goody bags in three boxes, then make my way downstairs to the cafe to grab something quick to eat for lunch.

As soon as I walk in, I notice Maverick on his phone drinking a coffee in the corner. I pretend not to see him because I don't have the energy to deal with him right now. After I order a wrap and a bottle of water, I pay, grab my food, and walk out.

"Olivia." I hear a deep voice behind me and turn around to Maverick standing in front of me.

"Yes?" My stomach is growling, and all I want to do is swallow this wrap whole.

"What time tonight? Eight?" His smug smile tells me he's purposely trying to push my buttons. I'm exhausted, and my patience is hanging by a thread.

"Six. And I'm warning you right now, don't make me track you down," I tell him, bluntly shaking my head and walking to the elevators. I'm pretty sure I can hear his laughter echoing behind me.

After I eat and take a shower, I do some work on my laptop, then finally get dressed for the evening. Time passes by so quickly because when I look at the clock, it's time to go downstairs and make sure the room is set up correctly, or Rachel will throw a fit. I call a bellman to bring a cart up for the boxes and deliver them to the reserved private room in the restaurant. As always, I feel like I'm rushing as I place the gift bags by each table setting. The bright pink tissue paper inside each bag perfectly matches Rachel's brand. After looking down at my watch to check the time, I hurry and go to Rachel's room and am pleasantly surprised when she's completely ready to go.

"I've already taken Angel out," she tells me and grabs her clutch. "Do I look okay?" She rubs her hands across her skirt. She's been stuck in the writing cave for so long, I haven't seen her in real clothes in months.

"You look perfect. Blue is your color. Ready to meet everyone?" I ask with a smile.

"I guess," she tells me, and I know she's nervous. Though she doesn't really like public events because she's an introvert, she's learned when she needs to put on an act. Rachel really does love meeting people who enjoy her words, though. That much I know is genuine.

We go downstairs, and as soon as she walks into the room, she's rushed by readers, and they surround her. The smile on her face is sincere as they discuss how much they love her characters and how excited they were about the release of the final book in her series. I look down at my watch and notice Maverick isn't anywhere around. We have fifteen minutes until the event officially begins, and he better pray to sweet baby Jesus that I don't have to hunt him down.

Thankfully, for him, he shows up right on time. The dinner goes well, and Rachel is in the spotlight. I try to keep off to the side, out of everyone's way and observe. Just as Rachel's readers are getting ready to leave, I see women crowd around Maverick, begging him for photos. He's being overly flirty and whispering in some of their ears. I watch as most of them undress him with their eyes, and he isn't doing himself any favors when he hugs them just a little too tightly. The numbers being exchanged isn't lost on me either.

When a woman decides to lift his shirt and place her hand on his abs, I walk across the room toward him. He's laughing, eating up all the attention. I pull him off to the side before his pants get torn off next.

"Best behavior," I tell him between gritted teeth. "I mean it."

"You need to chill out, babe. You've already got my number." He winks at me. Readers are calling him over, squealing over the wink and smile he flashes them as he tells them he'll be right back.

He takes me by surprise when he leans in, his lips softly brushing the shell of my ear. "If I didn't know better, I'd say you were jealous, Miss Priss."

My mouth falls open, and I'm two seconds from punching him in his abs of steel before he walks away, laughing.

CHAPTER EIGHT

MAVERICK

Last night was more fun than I anticipated. It was a low-key chill dinner with Rachel's readers who asked her questions about the series and what she planned to write next. Olivia mostly observed, making sure the staff was doing their jobs and occasionally barking demands at me.

I know she keeps telling me to *behave*, but I'm not the one who starts the grabby hands game. When women act that way, I know they're just having fun and goofing off, so I don't ever feel the need to scold them. Especially last night when I was supposed to be "on the clock" and entertaining Rachel's fans. Seeing Olivia heated and annoyed was just the cherry on top.

After the evening was over, I spent an hour in the gym, then took a shower and went to bed. Today's the first signing, and I'm not quite sure how it all works. I've never been to an author event before, but Olivia keeps informing me of all the things I'm "expected" to do.

A knock sounds out, and when I look at my watch, I smile. Right on time. *As always*.

I wait a few moments before slowly walking to the door and unlocking it. Once I swing it open, I'm taken aback by the Olivia in front of me. She's dressed in her normal business attire, always so damn proper, except she's wearing knee-high boots over her dark pantyhose. Her skirt is tight, showing off every natural curve, and her top is pale pink. It's almost see-through, but I'm not going to mention that.

"Are you ready?" Her voice snaps me out of my haze, and I blink at her.

"Yeah, I just have to change."

Olivia's face drops as she scans my body. "What?"

"Relax," I say with a smile, then place my hands on her shoulders. "I'm kidding. But you're tense. You need a drink."

"It's ten in the morning," she says, her body slowly relaxing.

"I'm ready. Do I look okay for my first signing?" I take a step back so she can see what I'm wearing.

"Unless your shirt buttons to the inside of your jeans, I'm not sure it's going to stop them from lifting it again," she says, biting her lip and releasing a small laugh. It's cute.

"I guess I'll take my chances then." I smirk. "Gonna grab my wallet and phone real quick."

As soon as I have everything, Olivia and I walk to the elevator, and after she hits the button for the third floor, she turns and faces me. "Okay, so I started setting up a little this morning, but we need to go down and finish. All her preorders are organized, but I need help with the swag items. There are tote bags, plastic mason jars, pens, bookmarks, candles, and lip balms."

"Holy shit."

The elevator doors slide open, and I follow Olivia down a long hallway.

"Yeah, I had to ask for an extra table so she has room to sign. There's a bookseller on site so we won't have to worry about dealing with taking payments."

"This sounds way too complicated for just a signing." The moment the words come out of my mouth, we approach a hallway already filled with anxious readers. I stand stunned for a second as I realize this won't be anything like the intimate dinner we had last night.

"C'mon," Olivia says, grabbing my hand and dragging me behind her. "Keep moving forward or—"

"Oh my God, it's Ian!" one woman to my left yells, and it causes a ripple effect. Women shift in line and wave their arms around, screaming in pure excitement. I continue forward, flashing them grins, but keep walking like Olivia instructed.

The hallway seems to go on forever, the long line of people is never-ending, but we finally make it to the front of the line. Olivia rushes me inside to a massive ballroom where dozens of tables are set up in rows around the perimeter.

"You could've given me a heads-up!" I scold her as soon as we're in private.

She gives me a look and shakes her head. "I've been warning you for days! Last night was just a small taste of what you should expect."

"So I'm just supposed to stand around like a piece of eye candy? A slab of man meat? Their sex on a stick?"

"Okay, back up." Olivia bursts out laughing. "I figured you'd like having your ego stroked, so what's the problem?"

"There's no problem," I quickly say. "I can take pictures and smile pretty."

She snorts, handing me a box. "You're basically an expert at that. Now place those mason jars on that table over there. Make sure her name and logo are facing out."

"So...how crazy are these readers?" I quietly ask Olivia about an hour after everything's set up. "Do I need pepper spray?" I half-joke.

"They aren't crazy. They're just...passionate. Rachel's readers are obsessed with the Bayshore Coast *series*, and you're the representation of the hero. They basically put you on a pedestal and bow down to you because of her character. For them, meeting you is the closest way to feel connected to Rachel's series, which is why so many of them like getting your autograph and taking pictures with you. It feels special to them, and it's something they will always cherish. So that's what you're doing here. This series means a lot to many of her readers for various reasons. Sometimes it's the emotional aspects, the funny moments, the family history, but Ian is who they ultimately fall for and root for throughout."

"Wow...that's the sincerest thing I've ever heard you say without disdain or disgust. Passionate and obsessed, that's how you are with your job." She gives me a look. "In a good way," I add. "But okay, I think I get it now. Channeling my inner Ian."

She smiles, then laughs. "Yes, which should be easy for you, considering Ian was a classic asshole. Arrogant, wealthy, full of himself."

"Women falling to their knees, begging for just one night," I add for her with a cocky grin.

Olivia rolls her eyes right on cue. "Focus, Maverick. Be polite, warming, and welcoming, offer to take pictures—some get too nervous to ask—sign their books or swag, and thank them for coming. Tell them it was a pleasure to meet them and move to the next person waiting to meet you, treating them each like they were the first reader in line."

"Like a pimp assembly line." I smirk.

Olivia groans, shaking her head. "Let's finish up, *Pimp Daddy*." I can tell she's holding back a smile, which I find amusing.

She turns around, and as she's fiddling with something, I stand behind her and press my chest to her back. The moment I lean in and my mouth closes in on her ear, her body tenses. "You can call me Daddy anytime, sweetheart." She shivers, though I know she'd never admit it. Her body reacts when mine is close, and I take that as a small victory.

An emcee interrupts our moment, and Olivia jumps, which puts space between us. The announcer lets everyone know the VIP ticket session is starting soon and the author photo will be in twenty minutes.

"Shit, Rachel better get here." She types away on her phone seconds later. "Lord knows I can't leave you here by yourself…"

And just like that, our special moment is gone.

"I'm a big boy, ya know? If you need to go check on her, I'll be fine."

Turning and looking at me, she contemplates my suggestion. She opens her mouth, but then her phone goes off, and she starts typing away again.

"She's ready. I'm going to meet her at the elevators. Be right back." Olivia takes a couple of steps forward, then stops to face me. "I didn't mean to imply you couldn't be here by yourself because I didn't trust *you*, but things are about to get really chaotic with eight hundred people in one room. You're my responsibility, and I just want to make sure you don't get bombarded or overwhelmed or kidnapped."

And there's another layer shredded off Olivia Carpenter. Damn. She almost sounds sincere.

I nearly close the gap between us. She tilts her head to look up at me, and while my eyes lock with hers, I grab her arms and softly squeeze. "I'll be fine, okay? Everything's going to be great. Stop worrying. You've got this."

Olivia looks at me as if she's never heard words of encouragement before. "Right." She nods, almost stunned. "Thanks."

After the authors huddle together and take a group photo, the room is buzzing with VIP ticket holders dragging their big ass carts and wagons behind them. People are waiting in long lines, squealing over their favorite authors and shouting in excitement. It's like a Black Friday sale for book lovers.

So far, I've taken pictures with Rachel at her table for readers and also stood and took some selfies with them. Rachel doesn't get up for photos, so they have to come behind the table and pose with her. I kinda don't blame her since she'd be getting up and down every five seconds, but I'd rather just stay standing at this point.

"The doors are about to open for the rest of the ticket holders," Olivia warns.

"There's *more* coming in?"

She chuckles slightly. "Yep. A lot more. So hold on to your shirt."

Rachel looks back and forth between Olivia and me, and I wonder what she's thinking. She's not said much to me since she arrived. Pleasant and kind, but just not with many words.

"I hope Olivia reminded you of the rules and expectations." Rachel speaks to me slowly, enunciating each word as though I'm incapable of understanding her.

"Of course she has. I'm well versed on what the expectations are," I say firmly.

"Good." Rachel turns to Olivia next. "I'll need another coffee."

Olivia looks at her watch and scrambles to her feet. "Of course."

"Don't you want to ask if Maverick needs anything? He's working hard today too." Rachel puts her on the spot, and if the space between us didn't feel tense and awkward, I'd be tempted to burst out laughing at Olivia's shell-shocked face at the implication that she's *not* working hard. It was a low blow because after a few days with Olivia, I know she busts her ass for that woman.

"Maverick," Olivia says slowly, swallowing as if waiting on me is physically painful for her. It makes me smile. "Can I get you anything to drink?"

"As a matter of fact, I'm kinda feeling a beer. Think you can get that for me, sweetheart?" I shoot her a wink only because I know it'll drive her crazy—and not in a good way.

"You shouldn't be drinking during the event. It's unprofessional," she tells me, crossing her arms, growing more impatient with me.

"Olivia," Rachel snaps, and Olivia instantly stands taller. "You'll get Maverick whatever he asks for. He's my guest of honor, and he'll be treated as such."

Olivia forces a smile and turns toward me. I smirk, because it's one small victory, though I know she'll ream out my ass for this later.

"Of course. I'll be right back." She grits her teeth and narrows her eyes at me. If looks could kill, holy fuck—Olivia would have buried me six feet under.

Most women would be more than happy to get me whatever I ask for, but not Miss Priss. No, she thrives on hating me and bossing me around. Not that I don't kind of like it, but I can't help but wonder why she loathes me so much. It has to be something on a deeper level than just my so-called reputation.

And I have eight days to figure out what it is.

CHAPTER NINE

OLIVIA

I LOVE MY JOB. I love my job. I love my job.

Maybe if I say it over and over in my head, I'll actually convince myself this isn't the most humiliating job right now. I love it most days, but this trip has definitely stretched me thin, and it's only the first city stop on the tour.

Lord help me.

After grabbing Rachel's coffee from the hotel cafe, I rush to the other side of the bar and order a bottle of Bud Light. There weren't many options, so Maverick better take it and love it.

By the time I make it back down to the ballroom, readers are being let in, and now I'm rushing through them to get back to Rachel's table before all hell breaks loose.

"What took you so long?" Rachel snaps, snatching her coffee out of my hand and taking a long swig. "The line is forming and blocking the walkway."

"I'll take care of it," I tell her, handing Maverick his beer. I hear a faint, *"Thank you,"* but I don't have time to reply because Rachel's right. Her line has reached across the walkthrough area, and I need to get them moved over.

"Hey, guys! Can I just ask that you please all shift a tad over here so we aren't blocking people or the other tables in?" I say loudly and cheerfully, directing them where to move. I know the event has volunteers who are supposed to help with this kind of stuff, but since the doors just opened, everything is hectic. "Thank you so much." I smile at them. "Don't forget to grab your books from the bookseller, and Rachel and Ian would love to sign them for you!" At the mention of *Ian*, readers start squealing all over again.

Most of Rachel's readers brought their own copies for her to sign. I can see them stacked high in their arms and carts. Since the last book in the series just released, they're eager to get them all signed by both of them.

Once the line shifts, I motion for the readers to start coming up, and as Rachel kindly greets each one, Maverick stands and gives them hugs and poses for selfies. They both make small talk with each reader, and even though the line seems never-ending, they handle it flawlessly.

Maverick is sweet and charming and really plays his part as Ian. Some of the younger women asked for group shots, so of course, I played photographer, and after snapping a couple of good ones, one girl yells out, "Silly pic now!" They all giggle and stick their tongues out; however, the one closest to Maverick actually swipes her tongue on his face and licks his cheek. Maverick's in a rocker pose with his tongue out and his hands in a rock-on sign. I snap the picture, and it's actually kinda cute, minus the cheek-licker.

"I feel like I need to bathe in sanitizer after all this." Maverick leans over and whispers in my ear when things start to slow down a tad.

"For your sake, you actually should," I fire back playfully. "That one girl probably gave you herpes of the cheek or something."

Maverick's head falls back as he bellows out a loud laugh. "Yeah, I didn't see that coming, but at least I didn't turn my head at that exact time. Would've turned things straight into Rated R territory." He winks as if that makes what he said any better. I pretend to retch at his implication and make a gagging noise.

The signing comes to an end, and although it was very successful for Rachel, I'm exhausted and ready to lay low the rest of the night. She has a dinner meeting in about an hour, which means after I take care of Angel, I'll finally get the night to myself.

"Do you need me to get you anything before you leave tonight?" I ask Rachel as she grabs her bag and stands. The signing has ended, and people are now just scrambling to clean up their tables.

"No, I'll manage just fine."

Rachel walks out without another word, and I'm left to deal with the aftermath of picking up her leftover swag bags and banners. I'm kneeling on the floor, packing up, and meanwhile, Maverick is surrounded by a crowd of women—no shocker there—but then I hear one of them invite him out to a bar tonight to eat and get drinks. I crane my neck to get a better look at who he's talking to, and I see it's a group of readers and a couple of authors.

Going out with them while being under Rachel's thumb is the exact scenario of what not to do, and he should know better too. But then I hear the idiot tell them he'd love to meet up with them.

Son of a bitch.

"Maverick." I say his name flatly, trying to grab his attention while making sure I remain professional around the group of people. "I could use your assistance, please, to get these boxes out of here."

A round of sad aww's linger at his departure, but he reassures them he'll be seeing them in the bar later.

"Just this box here?" he asks while I keep my head down, pretending to focus on the filthy floor I'm sitting on.

"Yeah, and those two banners." I nod my head toward the table behind him where I set them down and put them in their bags.

"Olivia."

His deep, firm voice forces me to look up at him. "What?"

"What are you doing?" He crosses his arms, looking confused.

"I'm picking up the mess I made with the tissue paper from the swag bags."

"You know they probably have a cleaning crew for after these big events. You picking up teeny tiny pieces of paper is doing nothing to help."

I look around and know he's right. I just needed a distraction from the fact all the attention he was getting from those women *annoyed* me, which in and of itself is annoying that it bothers me. This whole damn trip is annoying.

Lifting myself to my feet, I grab my bag and the second swag box and instruct him to grab the rest so we can get out of here before another tribe of women tackle him—except I leave that last part out.

"I just need to drop these off at my room quick then take out the devil dog," I tell him as we ride the elevator to my floor.

"The devil dog?" He pops a brow.

"Rachel's dog, *Angel*. She hates me and tries to bite me every chance she gets."

Maverick chuckles and shakes his head.

"How is that funny? She's a real terror!"

"She can probably smell fear and stress."

"I do not smell like fear and stress," I counter, scrunching my nose. "She's just an evil little shit."

Maverick walks behind me as I lead us to my room, and once we're inside, we drop off the boxes and banners. I sent a bunch of swag bags to each of the event hotels, so we'll take these with us as extras, just in case.

The moment I turn around, I walk smack into Maverick's chest, not realizing how close he was to me still. "Geez, boundaries." I snicker.

"You're the one who invited me into your room." He smirks, holding my shoulders with his large hands. Big and sturdy. *Oh God*. Not going there.

Not wanting him to see the blush creeping over my cheeks, I playfully smack him and laugh. "I did not invite you into my room. Why do you take everything so literal? I asked you to help me drop off the boxes so you wouldn't get swept away by that group of readers."

He steps back slightly, studying me. "You really gonna tell me I can't go hang out at the bar with some of the fans? Plus, I'm starving and need to eat. What's the harm?"

"That's exactly what I'm saying. And the harm is, it's not professional. They were already all over you, so you think having alcohol in their systems is going to help?"

"Well, if you're so worried, why don't you come chaperone then?"

He really is going to push every single button of mine before this trip is over.

"I don't have time to argue with you. I need to take care of

Rachel's stupid dog." I grab my bag so I can march out of there with my head held high, but of course, Maverick never makes anything easy on me.

"Okay, I'll meet you down there then," he shouts after me. I give him a one-finger wave over my shoulder before the door shuts behind me.

Thirty minutes later, I'm standing outside waiting for a ten-pound dog to finally take a shit so I can get to the bar and make sure Maverick behaves.

Ugh! I just wanted a quiet, relaxing night, and now I have to eat dinner in a noisy bar while keeping an eye on the hands of every woman who gets within a foot of Maverick.

"I will pay you a hundred dollars to just pick a damn spot, Angel!" I whisper-shout at her. "Think of all the amazing toys and bones you can buy with that? C'mon, just help a girl out!" Apparently, I'm not above begging a dog who has no idea what I'm even saying.

Ten minutes later, she's happy as can be and wagging her tail now that she's relieved herself. "It's about damn time." I pout, walking her back to Rachel's room. I bring her inside and lock the door behind me. Just as I'm about to get on the elevator and head to the bar, I decide to go back to my room and freshen up first.

I change into another outfit, something a bit dressier for night. I brush through my hair and dab more powder on my face. I don't even know why I care at this point, but I tell myself it's because even though Rachel has essentially given us the night off, people around the hotel could still recognize me as her assistant.

I make it down to the bar, and of course, it's already packed and loud with drunk people. At this point, I'm too hungry to care and weasel my way through the crowd. Just as I ask for a food menu from the bartender, a seat opens up, and I quickly take it.

"What can I get for you, darlin'?" a male bartender asks in a super friendly tone, and I'm convinced it's just the Southern culture.

"I'd like a glass of Chardonnay and the shrimp fettuccine alfredo with a Caesar salad, please."

"Of course. I'll go put your order in and be right back with your drink."

"Great, thank you."

I quickly scan the room for Maverick, wondering if he's actually down here. Just when I'm about to give up looking for him, I hear a bunch of ladies in the back scream-laugh and causing a commotion.

Looking over my shoulder, I finally spot him in a circle of women—*no surprise*—and they're all flashing him googly eyes.

Like he needs his ego stroked any more, ladies.

I mean, I see the appeal. I really do. He's the full package that most girls go crazy over, and if we had met under different circumstances, I might even say he has a decent personality. But even then, he's the exact type I stay away from.

My drink arrives, and I slowly sip it, only looking over my shoulder to check on Maverick a couple more times. I actually do trust that he will behave, but I don't always trust he'll know how to react if *they* don't behave.

Finally, my food arrives, and I don't hesitate to dig right in. About halfway through my pasta dish, I hear my name being called and look over my shoulder to Maverick waving me over.

"Join us," he shouts over the crowd, which causes me to blush with embarrassment. "They're telling me all about the dirty books you guys read." The ladies giggle and scoot closer to him. It makes me cringe.

I'm not about to yell in a bar and have a conversation, so I lift my salad bowl up and mouth, "*I'm eating.*"

"Oh come on!" he shouts again, this time even louder.

I force a smile and shake my head before turning back around. Looking up from my food, I immediately see the bartender standing in front of me.

"How is everything? Need a refill?" he asks, holding up my empty wineglass.

"Uh, sure, why not? Thanks!"

"You got it." He shoots me a wink, then pulls the bottle out and pours me another glass. "There you go, darlin'."

"Thank you."

"Either that pasta is giving you the best orgasm of your life, or you're just really hungry." Maverick's voice rings in my ear as he stands next to me. "I heard you moaning from all the way over there."

I quickly swallow and glance at his smug expression. "Are you sure you weren't hearing one of your groupies moaning for your attention?"

"You're sure hung up on who I hang out with."

I stare into his eyes and narrow mine, so he gets my message loud and clear. "It's my job, Maverick. Remember?"

"You're off the clock, Olivia. You're down here checking on me, *by choice*," he retorts, taking the seat next to me. I look over my shoulder to see his group is still there, obviously waiting for him to return. "I told them I had another fan to give my attention to," he says when he catches me looking at them.

His answer makes me laugh sarcastically. "A fan? That's a bit far-fetched."

"Oh come on. You said yourself you like this Ian character. So just pretend I'm him," he retorts with a stupid smile on his gorgeous face.

"If you knew me at all, you'd know you're preaching to the wrong choir."

"And why's that? Prefer the vagina?"

"Maverick!" I scold around a mouthful of food. His bold statement is forcing me to hold back laughter. Once I swallow it down and compose myself, I shoot him a disapproving look. "Do you just say the first thing that pops into your brain?"

"Well, no...not the first thing." He smirks with a playful shrug. "I mean, no judgment on my part. I'm a huge fan of vagina myself."

"Oookay, we're still on that. Just because I don't throw myself at you doesn't mean I'm a lesbian."

"I never said that. I only suggested it after you said I was preaching to the wrong choir."

"Meaning, I don't go gaga over book boyfriends and models. It's just not my...thing. I appreciate them, and I love reading about them, but I don't give myself a lot of time to dwell over the fantasy of the *perfect guy*. He doesn't exist, so I focus on my own life."

"You mean, *controlling* every aspect of it," he counters, leaning over to swipe a piece of my shrimp.

"Manners!" I swat at his hand, but it's too late. He shoves it into his mouth before I can stop him.

"I like having control. I don't feel the need to live a carefree, wild life. I don't judge others who prefer to live a different lifestyle than me either, so I expect the same respect in return," I say matter-of-factly.

"And where does that stem from?"

"What do you mean?"

"The need to control everything. I assume you didn't come out of the womb screaming for your planner bible."

That makes me chuckle, and I shake my head at him. "No, but I did appreciate being on a consistent schedule as a kid. I thrived on it." I find myself thinking about my childhood and force the thoughts away. Not right now.

"You need to learn to let go and live a little," he leans in and whispers softly. "You're going to wake up one day and realize that trying to control everything all the time isn't really living."

My mouth opens to disagree with him, but nothing comes to mind, so I clamp it shut.

"You think on that for a while." He shoots me a wink and pushes himself off the chair.

Fifteen minutes later, I'm still thinking about what Maverick said, and allowing his words to eat at me is frustrating. I finish my third glass of wine and wave at the bartender for my check.

"You're all paid up, ma'am." He sets down the receipt with Maverick's handwriting scribbled at the bottom.

What the hell? When did he do that? And why?

I reach for my phone and quickly send him a text.

Olivia: You didn't have to pay for my food. But thank you.

Maverick: A man should always pay. And you're welcome.

Olivia: That only applies during a date. We weren't on a date.

Maverick: I beg to differ. There was food, wine, good conversation. Best date I've ever been on.

His message makes me blush for real now. Who the hell is *this* guy?

Olivia: You're delusional. I'm going to bed now. We have that brunch in the morning.

Maverick: I'll walk with you. Stay right there.

Just as I'm about to tell him it's not necessary, I hear him telling the ladies good night and that it was a pleasure meeting and talking with them. Given the fact he didn't even have to be "on the clock" tonight, he sure made a lot of people happy.

"Ready?" he asks as soon as he's next to me, taking my hand and pulling me up from the chair. "You're a lightweight, aren't you?" He chuckles, tightening his grip on me.

"No. I'm fine. It's just these stupid barstools are hard to get out of."

I finally manage to land on my feet and look up to see Maverick smiling at me. "What?"

"I think I like tipsy Olivia. She's right up there with all-natural Olivia. I think I like her the most."

We walk toward the elevators. "What are you talking about?"

"Your different personalities. There's uptight Olivia—aka Miss Priss—then there's the Olivia under all those work clothes and makeup—all-natural Olivia—and now there's happy-go-lucky, tipsy Olivia."

I turn to face him as we wait for the elevator. "And what are your personalities, Maverick? You put this act on like you're this carefree, give-no-shits surfer boy, but that can't be all there is to you, is there?"

The doors swing open, and Maverick puts his hand on the small of my back to give me a small push to walk through. I watch as he hits the button for my floor.

"Also, you know what's really been chapping my ass?" I turn toward him again, and he's chuckling. "Why the hell don't you fly? Don't you know it's actually safer than driving? It can be a tad scary during turbulence, but the fly time is like a millisecond compared to the driving time." I can't help the word vomit spewing out of my mouth, but as soon as I look up and see Maverick's face, I regret it.

His face has dropped, his eyes low, and his shoulders slumped over.

"I think I should get you to bed if you're going to be on time for brunch in the morning." The doors open moments later, and he guides me out again and walks me to my room. I fiddle with the key, but the damn thing won't scan.

"Let me try." Maverick pulls a key out from his wallet and effortlessly opens the door.

"Wait. How'd you do that? Why do you have a key to my room?"

"Just a precautionary." He winks at me, but it's with a frown over his face.

"I'll be fine," I tell him, though I'm mostly trying to convince myself. "Brunch is at eleven. Don't be late."

"I know the drill." He smirks. "Good night, Olivia."

I look up and see him watching me. "Night." And for a split second, I almost ask him to stay.

CHAPTER TEN

MAVERICK

If I'm being truthful, I wasn't looking forward to this trip. I didn't know what to expect, considering I've never toured with an author before, but so far, it's been pretty cool. This morning, we had a brunch with Rachel's readers, and while many of them focused on asking her questions, others were too busy handing me their phone numbers. At this point, I'm pretty sure I have so many, I could use them like confetti. And yes, I know the rules. I don't plan on getting with any of them, but it's fun to watch Olivia squirm, just like she's doing right now.

One of Rachel's readers keeps leaning over and placing her hand on my thigh. She's beautiful but not my type. Then again, if I weren't on this tour, I'd probably go back to her room with her and show her a good time. Especially since she's throwing out all the signals. I know exactly what she wants, and by the look on Olivia's face, she knows too.

After the brunch is over, I'm standing around waiting for Rachel. A reader comes to me, talking too close, and Olivia smiles at the woman, thanks her for coming, then pulls me away.

"Your middle name should be Cockblock," I say as she pulls me onto the elevator and presses my floor along with hers since we're on different levels.

Her mouth is tight in a firm line. "We're leaving in thirty

minutes. We need to make it to Amarillo before dark. I have a lot of work to do."

The elevator stops on her floor, and she steps out. Before the doors close, she turns around and looks at me. "Do not be late."

And that warning is the reason I purposely take my time packing my things. I wish Olivia would stop with the act because I can see straight through it, though she'd never admit it. She's too concerned with her image to let her hair down and relax every once in a while. I can't imagine not ever being off the clock. Life isn't that serious or shouldn't be taken that way.

After I go to my room and get my stuff together, I wait until I'm supposed to be downstairs, then head toward the elevator, making sure not to rush. By the time I'm on the ground floor, Olivia is already in the car waiting. She pops the trunk, and I throw my suitcase inside, then climb into the passenger seat.

"You did that on purpose," she says, punching on the gas and pulling out of the parking lot. She gets up on the highway and drives through the city like she's a native or a maniac.

"You'll eventually learn I only need to be told to be somewhere one time," I tell her.

Once we're out of Dallas, she slightly relaxes. Something's streaming between us, and it's awkward. I don't really know what to say, and it shocks me that I'm tongue-tied for words. She sings along to an annoying pop song on the radio, and I laugh.

"Is this Justin Bieber?" I look down at the title on the screen to confirm.

"I love the Biebs," she tells me with a smile, going back to her lyrics.

I shake my head. "Don't you ever admit that in public."

"I like other music too. Especially the eighties and nineties. But my guilty pleasure is pop music and Taylor Swift."

"I'm trying really hard not to judge you right now." I grin.

We make small talk, and when we stop for gas, we switch places, and I drive the rest of the way. We're making good time, and I'm thankful no disaster has happened today. We got off to a bad start, but I think Olivia is beginning to soften up to me, or maybe my mind is playing tricks on me. I glance over at her while she works, and we exchange small innocent smiles before she goes back to scribbling in her notebook.

The GPS directs me to take the next exit, so I pull off the highway and travel down a few miles until we're pulling up to our hotel. We pull up to the valet, and I grab our suitcases. I stand back while Olivia checks in, which is taking much longer than it usually does. I walk up to the counter and stand next to her.

"Can you check again and make sure?" Olivia asks the woman in a panicked tone. She types on the computer then looks up.

"I'm sorry, Ms. Carpenter. We only have one room available for you."

I glance over at Olivia who's about to blow smoke out of her ears, she's so noticeably pissed.

"The hotel was overbooked. We tried to call you earlier this week to let you know there was an issue with your reservation, and one of them was being canceled so other arrangements could be made."

Olivia huffs. "I didn't get a call. My service has been in and out while I've been traveling."

"One room should be fine," I tell the woman with a smile. She instantly smiles back at me.

Olivia rolls her eyes. "I guess it will *have* to be."

The woman apologizes again, then explains where the elevators are and what time breakfast will be served. I take the key cards, wink at the receptionist, and then the two of us walk away. Olivia is raging, and I actually find it cute.

"I'm so livid," she seethes as we step on the elevator. "The review I'm leaving for this hotel…"

"It's only for one night," I remind her. "What could happen?"

She glances over at me. I give her a smirk, and she groans.

"Don't be nervous. I don't bite. Too hard." I chuckle as the elevator doors slide open.

Olivia leads the way to the room, and I study her from behind.

"I can only imagine the cheesy pickup lines you use on women," she says. "This is why I read so many romance books."

She swipes the card across the sensor, and the door clicks open.

"Reading those kind of romances can set unrealistic

expectations in a relationship," I tell her, locking the door behind us.

With one swift movement, she throws her suitcase and laptop bag on the edge of the mattress. "Great, one bed," she says to herself, groaning. "Or maybe it just sets the bar higher? When I do decide to get in a serious relationship, it's not going to be with just any man who can whisper sweet nothings in my ear. He'll have to be someone special, someone worth my time. Otherwise, I'm happy with how things are right now." She digs into her bag and pulls out some clothes. "Do you need to go to the restroom? I'm going to take a shower."

"Olivia, that man exists out there. And when you find him, you'll know. And no, I'm good. I'm probably gonna go work out. My muscles are stiff from sitting so long," I tell her before she walks into the bathroom.

She gives me a look, almost as if she's contemplating my words before walking to the bathroom. Something streams between us, but I try to ignore it, though it's hard. Once the door is locked and the water is running, I quickly change into some shorts and a dry-fit shirt, grab my headphones from my bag, and head to the gym.

Once I'm there, I do a few warm-up reps with the bar before I start adding heavy weights. I'm trying to focus, but I'm finding it a bit hard, and the only person to blame is Olivia. Though she's a prude and uptight and gets on my nerves more often than not, I can't help but be intrigued by her. It's refreshing how she doesn't fall at my feet. For the first time in a long while, I have someone determined to challenge me at every corner, and I kinda like it. Shaking the thoughts of her out of my head, I push myself to the limit. Once I've completed my reps, I make my way back to the room. As soon as I walk in, I can smell the sweetness of her shampoo and body wash.

I continue forward and am almost taken aback when I see her sitting with her legs crossed and laptop on the bed. Her wet hair is down, black-framed glasses on her face, and she's wearing a T-shirt and pajama bottoms. My mouth falls open, and I hurry to try to close it.

"Hi. My name is Maverick Kingston, and you are?" I hold my hand out to reintroduce myself to this stranger in my room. I'm not sure what I expected to find when I came back, but it wasn't Olivia looking so...normal. It's hot.

She swats at my hand and laughs. "Shut up, Maverick!" She dramatically rolls her eyes at me, then goes back to her computer.

I'm trying not to stare, but damn, it's so hard when she looks so naturally beautiful. Instead of standing there gawking, I force myself to go to the bathroom and run the water. Considering I'm sweaty as hell and need a distraction, I take a shower. Once I'm out of my clothes, I turn the water as hot as I can stand it and step in. The warmth feels good against my sore muscles, and I try to enjoy it, considering I've been sitting for most of the day. After my skin is pruned, I force myself to get out, and that's when I realize I didn't grab any clothes.

Shit. I'm used to staying in a room by myself, but I use this as the perfect opportunity to make Olivia squirm. I quietly chuckle just thinking about it as I finish drying off and wrap the towel around my waist, then walk into the bedroom.

I try to pretend as if I don't notice Olivia looking over her laptop at me. It gives me a rush, knowing her eyes are on my body. I make eye contact with her and lift an eyebrow as I reach for my suitcase, and that's when my towel falls from my waist into a pool on the floor. Instead of trying to hide, I just go with it. Olivia's eyes go wide as she checks out the full package, then her mouth falls open, which only causes me to smirk. I'm not a shy guy or embarrassed because I have a lot to be proud of.

"Maverick! Put on some clothes! Oh my God!" She picks up a pillow and throws it at me before covering her eyes.

I shrug, and dig out some pajama pants and slip them on. "Sorry, that was an accident."

She moves her hand from her face and glares at me. "I really doubt that. You were way too confident standing there. I mean, if you wanted to show off your dick, you could've asked first."

Laughter tumbles out of me. "Yeah right. You seem way too modest for that."

"I didn't say I'd say yes. Let me be very clear, I would've said hell no."

I nod at her. "Right. You're telling me you weren't even curious?"

When I sit on the other side of the bed, Olivia instantly stands. "Nope. No. No way. Totally inappropriate."

I snort. Always the professional. "Have you even seen a dick in real life before? You looked as if it was going to bite you." I know I'm crossing a line, but I can't help it. She's adorable when she gets all flustered.

"Probably does bite. Has to fight off all the women scrambling to jump on it."

I look at her, stunned.

"Shit, sorry. That was rude. You probably have a fine, satisfying dick. I just wasn't interested in seeing it."

Her words have my chest shaking with laughter. Not only is she as uptight as she looks on most days, but she's also socially awkward as hell. Though I actually find it refreshing.

"No worries. I've never had any complaints before." I grab my phone off the nightstand and start scrolling through my apps. When she doesn't sit back down, I glance over at her. Messy blond hair, glasses, wearing a baggy T-shirt with a coffee cup on it. She's stunning without her business costume on. It's the first time I've really seen her let her hair down, and there's an internal shift I can't deny. I swallow hard and look at her. "What?"

"We have to have some rules tonight," she tells me, but I can see the blush on her cheeks. Is it possible that I've broken through, made her nervous as hell? If so, mission accomplished.

"I'd expect nothing less, honestly."

She scoffs. "First, you need to put a shirt on too. The pants aren't enough."

I stand. "I work really hard for these abs." Yep, now she's staring.

She moves around the bed. "And we need a pillow wall between us when we go to sleep."

Now I'm laughing. "Why?"

"Because. I'm actually afraid of the anaconda in your pants."

Her words cause me to double over. "Anaconda? Well, I think you're safe. He doesn't just let himself out in the middle of the night and search for single women."

"You sure about that?" She lifts an eyebrow.

"Wow. You've got jokes. That's a first," I throw back at her.

"Trust me when I say I have no intentions of crossing the invisible line you've already drawn on the bed. I'll stick to my side, and you stick to yours. Unless you change your mind." I shoot her a wink.

In one swift movement, she picks up another pillow and chucks it at me as hard as she can. She's smiling and laughing, and she's finally releasing all the weight she carries around on her shoulders. This is the Olivia I want to get to know. Not the woman who wears tight skirts and button-up collared shirts. That version of her doesn't know how to have a good time or break out of a schedule. But the woman standing in front of me is someone totally different.

I smile at her. "I'm actually going to go to bed, I think. I'm exhausted."

"What about the rules?" she asks, sitting back on the bed.

Pulling the blankets down, I slip between the sheets. "If you learn one thing before this trip is over, Olivia, it's that I don't play by the rules."

I roll over on my side, where my back is toward her, and click off the lamp on the table. "Good night, Miss Priss," I tell her before I close my eyes.

"Good night," she mutters, but I can tell she's smiling.

CHAPTER ELEVEN

OLIVIA

As soon as my alarm goes off, I peel my eyes open. For a moment, I have no idea where I am, then I remember I'm in a hotel room with Maverick. Carefully, I slide out of bed and stand only to realize he's not here. I let out a deep breath and walk to the bathroom for my morning routine.

I'm surprised I got any sleep at all, considering each time I closed my eyes, all I could see was Maverick standing so confident, showing off his goods. Damn, that man is poison. With everything I have, I try to shake the image from my mind, but it's inconveniently plastered there.

After I wash my face and brush my teeth, I pack up my things because we'll need to leave soon. I stuff my toiletries in the suitcase and pull out my clothes for the day. After I've changed, Maverick walks through the door, sweating. I try not to make eye contact or stare as he pulls his shirt over his head.

"Mornin'," he says with a shit-eating grin plastered on his face.

I narrow my eyes at him, trying to keep my gaze above his chest. "What?"

"Did you sleep okay?" He's still smiling as he walks to his suitcase and pulls out a change of clothes.

"I did, why?" He's making me really suspicious by how weird he's acting, and considering I haven't had a drop of coffee yet, I'm not in the mood for his games.

"Has anyone ever told you how much you talk in your sleep?"

My heart begins to race, and my mouth goes dry. "What did I say?"

There's that panty-melting smirk again, and that's all he leaves me with before he goes into the bathroom and shuts the door. The water comes on, and I stand there holding my chest, trying to remember any of the dreams I had last night, but I'm drawing a blank. What the hell did I say? He's probably just fucking with me…right?

Instead of dwelling on it, I call a valet to have the car moved around. I knock on the bathroom door to let him know my plans before I leave.

"I'm going down to the car. You have ten minutes before I leave without you," I tell him, and all he does is laugh.

Shaking my head, I grab my stuff and head to the lobby, still trying to figure out what the hell I could've said in my sleep. Before the day's over, I will get it out of him, or it will be his ass.

When I walk outside, the car is parked and waiting for me. An older gentleman places my suitcases in the trunk and opens the driver's door. Considering how much they weigh, I tip him well. He thanks me, and I pull up to make more room for other cars as I wait for Maverick. Ten minutes pass and I'm so close to going back to the room and dragging him down here, but then I think maybe I'll just drive off to teach him a lesson. Just as I'm contemplating my options, he comes waltzing out of the double doors with a pep in his step. I pop the trunk, and he throws his suitcase in, then walks around to my side.

"I'm driving first," he bends down and says.

I shake my head. "Get in the damn car."

Crossing his arms over his broad chest, he just stands there. We should've already been on the road, so instead of arguing with him, I get out and switch places.

"See how easy it is when you listen to me." He flashes a victorious grin as we buckle our seat belts.

"Why are you looking at me like that?" I finally ask as I pull my laptop out of my bag and connect it to my hotspot.

He shrugs.

"Just tell me what I said. You're starting to irritate me." I huff.

Licking his lips, he sucks in a deep breath. I wait impatiently for him to speak, but he's taking his sweet time. "It's nothing really. You were just moaning my name over and over and *over* again."

My mouth drops open. "No, I wasn't. You're so lying right now."

Maverick chuckles. "Okay then. I may or may not have a video of it. It was dark, but I could tell by the tone of your voice that you were enjoying it. Must've been a really great dream although, if you ask me, real life is *much* better."

"I swear on your career, Maverick, if you recorded me, I'll–"

"Maybe I'll accidentally text it to Rachel and see what she has to say about it," he interrupts.

A groan releases from my throat. "You're determined to drive me crazy."

"Only six more days to make that happen. Though to be fair, I think you were already a little crazy."

I glare at him, but it doesn't faze him in the least. He turns on some music and goes into his little world, just as I go into mine. For an hour, I reply to emails regarding Rachel's next book release. Though we're still celebrating the grand finale of the Bayshore Coast series, Rachel is always a few books ahead, which means I never get a real break.

I've been texting my old boss, Vada, during this trip and giving her updates. When she first heard about Rachel forcing me to road trip with Maverick, she laughed her ass off—at my expense, of course. Then she begged me to give her all the juicy details so she could put it in a book.

Now every day she asks me for updates.

Vada: So, big? Or BIG BIG? :)

I hold back a chuckle because I don't want Maverick to know I'm texting about him.

Olivia: Why are you so interested in another man's dick? Don't think Ethan would approve.

Vada: Are you kidding me? He's asking for more details

than I am, and it's much worse! We're both quite invested and are placing bets.

Olivia: Placing bets on what?

Vada: …er, nothing. Never mind.

Olivia: VADA!! You better tell me, or I'm not giving you any more info.

Vada: You wouldn't do that to me! :'(

Olivia: …try me.

Vada: Gah! I forget how good you are at playing hardball. Fine! We placed a bet on how long until you two finally sleep together.

Olivia: OMG! Why would you bet that? Whoever placed that bet is going to LOSE!

Vada: So, he's small then? :(

I swallow down a laugh, though imagining her voice in my head is enough to send me over the edge and blow my cover. She was always such an introvert, all business and obsessed with her cat, Oliver. Now she's going to Saturday morning farmers' markets with her husband and new baby, London. Vada's a whole different person from when we first met, but regardless, I'm super happy for her. Her entire demeanor has changed, and I know she's the happiest she's ever been in her life.

Vada: Hey, Liv. It's Ethan. I've got a pretty good bet going if I win, so help me out, okay? If I win, I get blow jobs for a week. Don't let me down! :)

Oliva: Dude. GROSS. I'm not sleeping with him just so you can get some BJs.

Vada: Sorry about that. He thinks he's FUNNY. Don't worry, I smacked him for you.

Olivia: LOL, thanks. If it gets you two off my ass, I'll tell you this. Apparently, he was the star in my dream last night, and I said his name in my sleep. And of course, Maverick heard me too! I'm still embarrassed, and he obviously thinks it's hilarious.

Vada: OMG...that's amazing. Totally getting written in.

Olivia: Great. I'm glad my humiliation is inspiring you so much.

Vada: You should find out if he's a good kisser. Ya know, for the book's sake.

Olivia: Oh, of course, FOR THE BOOK I'll just throw all my dignity out the window.

Vada: Perfect, thanks!! :)

Olivia: I hate you.

She sends me a dozen kissy faces and hearts, and I roll my eyes and smile just thinking about her. I miss her a lot and wish we had more time to catch up and actually reunite.

Once we cross into New Mexico, I occasionally look out the window at the tall weed grasses and rolling hills. It's so damn green outside, and the setting is picture perfect. The sun is high in the sky, and I check the time against our itinerary. We're actually ahead of schedule for now, probably because Maverick doesn't know how to drive the speed limit on these country roads, though I'm not complaining.

As I stare out the window, the thought of Maverick naked fills my mind, which only annoys me because I don't want to think about him like that. It doesn't help that I've had to smell the light hint of cologne on his skin all morning either. I swallow hard, trying to push the thoughts away, but it's no help. The sexy V led straight down to his cleanly shaved…

"Hey," he says, and I nearly jump out of my seat. He hasn't said a word for hours.

I place my hand over my chest.

"You're jumpy as hell," he says, chuckling. "Are we stopping in Raton? We're about twenty minutes away."

"Yes. We'll need to fill up, and there's a really good steak house I want to try." I don't think I can eat any more fast food, so I did a quick Google search yesterday. The place has rave reviews.

"Perfect. You know how I love my steak," he says, speeding up.

Soon we're crossing the overpass and heading into Raton. The town is small with most businesses on the main strip. We stop and get gas, then continue to the steak house.

"K Bobs?" He pulls into the parking lot and turns off the car.

"The reviewers said it was awesome. I swear," I tell him, half-tempted to pull it up on Yelp. Instead, I get out of the car, and he follows. We walk inside, and I'm happy to see the restaurant is full of people. We're seated instantly, and our order is taken soon after. The silence draws on between us, and I don't really know what to say, considering I moaned his name all night after seeing his anaconda dick.

"So…" he says before drinking half of the glass of water that was set in front of him. "What's your favorite color? Fave TV show? Or maybe for you, favorite book?"

"Are we playing fifty questions now?" I give him a look that says I'm less than amused.

"My favorite color is red. Mainly because it symbolizes power and can convey many different emotions. Love. Hate. Anger. Passion."

I swallow hard, watching him. He's trying, so I decide to play along.

"I like the color black because it matches everything."

He chuckles. "Even your dark soul."

Before I can get a word out, our food is placed in front of us. Maverick is still smiling at me as he cuts into his rare steak. "Even like my steaks to be red."

"You're gross. It's basically still mooing," I say, fully content with my chicken salad.

He puts a piece of the meat on his fork and reaches across the table. "Don't knock it till you try it."

"Thanks, but no thanks."

The waitress walks over and asks us if we need anything before placing our check on the table. I look at the time, thankful we don't have to rush.

"So what's on the schedule today?" Maverick asks before scooping mashed potatoes into his mouth.

I smile. "You really want to know?"

He nods and continues chewing. I give him a thorough rundown, actually impressed when he listens. Only took close to a week to make that happen.

After we're both finished eating, I pay the bill, and we both stop to use the restroom before we go. I walk outside, and Maverick is waiting for me by the door. On the way to the car, I hold out my hand, and he gives me the keys. I'm starting to get used to this road trip stuff. Maybe one day I'll take one for pleasure. The thought of that makes me laugh.

We climb into the car, and I'm still smiling.

"What? Dreaming about me being naked again?" Maverick asks.

"No, that'd be a nightmare," I tell him as images of his abs and sexy V flash through my mind. *Ugh.*

"But you are now, aren't you?" His smug smile drives me nuts. I want to smack it right off his gorgeous, charming face.

I place the car in drive and try to ignore those thoughts. I glance at Maverick for a moment and see him watching me intently. Sometimes when he smiles, he has this small dimple in his cheek that's so damn cute. All I can do is shake my head as he sits there completely satisfied with himself for making me think about him naked all over again.

My mouth falls open as I try to soak in my surroundings as we drive out of Raton toward the mountains. The sky is so damn blue, and the grass is bright green. I follow the winding road until we're driving up in elevation through the pass and crossing the Colorful

Colorado sign. Every once in a while, I catch a glimpse of the snowcapped Rockies.

We drive through Trinidad, and I'm mesmerized by the mountains in the distance.

"They're beautiful," I whisper.

Maverick turns and looks at me with a small smile. "That peak over there is Pikes Peak. There used to be a cog train you could take to the top, but I heard it's closed indefinitely. It's one of the coolest experiences I've had. Though Colorado is beautiful during the summer, nothing compares to this place in the winter when everything is covered in white. It's unbelievable and steals your breath away. Every Christmas growing up, my family would fly to Aspen for a ski trip. It became my second home."

I look at him then back at the road. "Wow. I wish I could see it snowed over. And how lucky were you for getting to spend Christmas in the mountains? You must be spoiled or something," I tease.

Maverick gives me a cheeky grin. "I have an older brother and a sister who's a few years younger, so there was no room for me to be spoiled. My parents just believed in us all being together and creating memories and family experiences during the holidays instead of giving us gifts we'd break or lose or grow out of. So each year, we'd take a big trip because we all loved the mountains so much. Looking back at it, those times are some of the ones I cherish the most, and I'm so grateful for them. What about you?"

"No siblings. I'm an only child. You're lucky. I always wished I had a brother or sister, and you've got both."

A hearty laugh releases from his lips. "There were times when I would've happily given them away. It's not easy being the middle child. I've had to prove myself all my life. Probably why I'm so good at modeling. Lots of practice fighting to be in the spotlight." He goes back to staring out the window.

The mood shifts in the car. There's something more, something he's not saying, so I try to change the subject.

"So you said you used to fly to Aspen? Do you just road trip there now?" I let out a laugh, but he doesn't react. He seems too lost in his thoughts.

"We don't travel for Christmas anymore. Haven't for a long time now," he vaguely replies.

I give him a smile then bring my attention back to the road. "Well, why not?"

Maverick runs his bottom lip between his teeth before speaking, and I don't dare rush him.

"It's okay. That was rude of me to ask. You don't have to answer," I say, not wanting to make him feel uncomfortable.

"No, no. It's fine." Maverick runs his hand along the scruff on his jawline, looking torn. While he's usually clean shaven, the past few days he's allowed the stubble to grow. He sucks in a deep breath and exhales it slowly. "When I was seventeen, my entire world tilted on its axis. Olivia, this isn't something that I typically talk about, so go easy on me, okay?"

I nod, not saying a word because I realize the seriousness of the situation just by his tone. The smile that once played on his lips is long gone.

"All my life, all I wanted to do was prove myself to my father. To show him I was trying to make my own mark in the world and that I was special too. My brother was the starting quarterback for his university, and my sister was a child genius. Then there was me, Maverick, and I had the middle kid syndrome. I realize that now. Anyway, after I started driving, I'd volunteer my time on the weekends at a local senior citizen home, and that's when I was "discovered" in a sense. A photographer caught a shot of me helping an older woman walk to a car, and it was placed on the front page of a bigger newspaper. I basically went viral. Modeling agencies contacted my parents because they ultimately had to give permission for me to work since I was under eighteen. I was booked solid after school and on the weekends. My mother took it upon herself to be my agent, not allowing anyone to screw me over. Every penny I made, she put into a savings account for college. For the first time ever, I had my father's attention, and he was proud of me."

He glances over at me with sad eyes, and I give him a small smile of encouragement before he continues.

"My dad was a pilot and had been flying for nearly twenty years. He was doing private charter then, basically flying people back and forth like an air taxi. I had a meeting in New York with a big agency, and my dad was so adamant about flying me there, though he had clients he still needed to fly to Seattle. The plan was to fly from LA to Seattle, then take me to New York, but the plane was full, and there wasn't space for me to take the Seattle flight. I was so mad that I couldn't get on that plane. My mom booked our flights, paid a small fortune for them, and we flew commercial but ended up being delayed on our connecting flight due to weather. When we finally landed in New York, we got the call that my father was involved in an accident."

I swallow hard, and my mouth slightly falls open.

"He had clearance to fly to New York to meet us after he dropped his passengers in Seattle, and though the weather quickly shifted, he was certified to fly in those conditions. Due to mistakes he made, exhaustion, and other things, his plane went down." Maverick closes his eyes tight. "And I've blamed myself ever since."

Tucking my lips into my mouth, I try to get ahold of my emotions. I feel like such a bitch for saying anything about him refusing to fly. "I'm sorry. I'm so sorry."

I reach out and grab his hand and squeeze it. "And that's not your fault," I say, breaking our touch.

He lets out a stifled laugh. "Thank you. So needless to say, I haven't flown since my plane touched down in New York. The anxiety I experience in airports is too overwhelming, and getting on a plane is something I don't think I could handle. So, if people want me to go on tours like these, they have to take me like I am, broken and completely fucked up, or I don't go."

I fully understand now. "It totally makes sense, and I don't blame you. And you're not fucked up or broken, okay? It's just more personal than most people realize. I get it. And I'm sorry for giving you shit earlier."

Finally, he smiles. "This is the reason I try to live each day like it's my last, Olivia. I shouldn't be here right now because I was supposed to be on that plane. And I don't know what divine intervention had me going another path, but there's a reason. A lot of people ask me why I continue to pursue this career so hard, and the truth is, I want to continue to make my dad proud. He told me he knew I'd go far, and I'll spend every day for the rest of my life proving him right."

"I think you already have," I tell him and mean it.

When he looks into my eyes, that's when I feel the shift. There are unspoken words streaming between us, and it's almost too much for me to handle.

Thankfully, the GPS interrupts the moment and tells me to take an exit toward downtown Denver. The tall buildings steal our attention as we search for our hotel. People are riding bicycles and scooters while others are happily running on the side of the road. I lower the windows and allow the fresh mountain air to swiftly blow through the car.

I continue driving down 16th Street, pass the Tattered Covers Bookstore where Rachel's signing is, then make a right toward the hotel. It's walking distance from the bookstore, and I internally do a small victory dance because it's a bit closer than I originally thought. After I pull into the valet lane, I unbuckle and look at Maverick.

"Remember to be on your best behavior," I playfully remind him.

"What happens in Denver, stays in Denver." He chuckles.

"So, about that video you took of me sleep talking…"

Maverick gives me his signature smirk. "There's no video. I was just fucking with you."

My mouth falls open. "Was I really sleep talking then?"

He conveniently doesn't answer. "Just by the look on your face, I already know I was the leading man in your sexy dreams last night."

I let out a loud groan, and we're right back to where we were this morning, me imagining him naked. "Sometimes you're a real asshole."

I step out of the car and Maverick grabs our bags from the back and follows me inside. Just as we've done at every other hotel we've stayed at during this trip, I check in with the front desk as he waits for me off to the side. After the paperwork is signed, I hand him his room key, and we go our separate ways. But this time, if he would've asked me for a drink or dinner, I might've reconsidered.

Though I like spending my time alone, it's nice to have another person around, even if they only intend to annoy the shit out of me.

Maverick Kingston might not be the man I thought he was originally.

He might actually prove *me* wrong.

CHAPTER TWELVE

MAVERICK

I'D BE LYING if I said I didn't miss Olivia when she's not around. It gets lonely in the hotel room all alone. I actually liked sharing a room with her, but I won't admit that to her. Not yet anyway.

However, I wasn't lying about her moaning my name in her sleep. The first time I heard it, I thought I'd imagined it. A few moments later, she said it again, and that time I knew for sure I wasn't hallucinating.

Though I enjoyed giving her shit about it, I could see how embarrassed she was. It gave me a thrill to know she'd been dreaming about me. She pretends to hate my guts all day, but her subconscious betrayed her, and now I know I'm slowly breaking her down. She may live her life on a strict schedule, but I can see something deeper is going on in that head of hers.

I never expected to open up about my dad to her like that, but something felt right at that moment to tell her. I don't share that part of my life with many people, in general, but she's actually easy to talk to when she's not scowling at or scolding me.

The next morning, I woke up early to hit the gym and then enjoyed watching the sunrise from my balcony. Olivia found us a great hotel right in downtown Denver, and the view is incredible. The air is crisp, and the sun's warmth promises a great day.

Just as I'm getting out of the shower, a loud pounding on my door echoes throughout the room.

"Maverick!" *Bang, bang, bang.* "Let me in!"

Rushing to the door, I tighten my towel around my waist and quickly open it up to a frazzled Olivia.

"Please tell me your room has an iron? Rachel's shirt got wrinkled, and she's freaking out. The iron in my room is about a hundred years old, and reception said it'd take about thirty minutes for them to bring me a new one."

"Uh…" I smirk as my eyes gaze down her body. "Sure. I mean, let's go check if it works." I step to the side to let her in.

"Thanks. I'm sorry to be intrusive, but when Rachel is having a freak-out moment, it causes *me* to freak out."

"I never would've guessed. You're handling this so well," I say dryly, holding back a laugh.

Her face falls as she gives me a deadpan look. "You have no idea what it's like to work for a woman like Rachel. She is sweet as pie to you and everyone else, but when things don't go her way, I'm a punching bag."

"Olivia." I place my hands on her nearly bare shoulders. "Relax, okay? You can handle this. Deep breaths."

She actually listens, and I watch as her chest rises and falls a few times. Her luscious tits on display are making it hard to be a gentleman and not stare.

"There. Perfect. Now I'll get the iron for you."

"Thank you. Assuming this is even the shirt she decides to wear." She huffs. "She's been extra difficult today."

I return with the iron in hand and perk a brow at her. "Today just started."

Olivia grabs it from me and sighs. "Exactly. Not enough goddamn coffee or liquor in the world for this."

She starts walking toward the door and right before she opens it, she glances at the closet door with the mirror on it. Then I watch her do a double take and do my best to refrain from laughing.

"Oh my God!" She immediately tries to cover herself up with her arms.

"Not the worst way to start my day." I cross my arms over my chest and flash her a smug smile.

"You could've said something! Just letting me walk around

without a shirt on." She turns as if that's going to erase the image of her in a black lacy bra out of my head.

"I thought you were going for a new look," I tease. "Guess you weren't lying about black being your favorite color, though."

"Maverick. Shut up. I'm leaving now." I can see her reflection in the mirror, and she's squeezing her eyes tightly.

I walk up behind her and unwrap the towel from my waist. "Here, take my towel and walk back to your room." I drape it over her chest and around her neck to cover her up.

"Please tell me that's not the same towel you were just wearing." Her breathing picks up.

"Take a look for yourself," I say close to her ear with amusement.

A deep rumble echoes from her throat as she slowly peeks an eye open. She doesn't look in the mirror, though; she keeps her head up as if she's purposely not focusing on it.

"As considerate as that is, I think I'd just rather go topless down the hall."

Her nervous tone makes me laugh.

Leaning in closer, my bottom lip brushes right on the edge of her ear. "Just take the towel. You shouldn't be showing your gorgeous tits off to just anyone anyway."

Her breath hitches, and when I place my hands on her shoulders, I feel her entire body tense. "Now go, so we aren't late," I say in a light, playful tone. She's always on my ass about time, so it's only fair to turn the tables every once in a while.

I lead her to the door, and she carefully opens it, making every effort to keep her gaze on the ceiling. "See you soon," I taunt before shutting the door.

"That wasn't funny, Maverick!" she shouts from the other side.

"Really? Maybe you need to work on that sense of humor of yours!" I'm totally messing with her, but it's too easy. Olivia Carpenter, the self-proclaimed perfectionist, is a hot mess.

I hear her groan before storming off.

Today's event is a signing in downtown Denver at Tattered Covers Bookstore. I remember Olivia pointing it out when we arrived. It's a cute local shop, and I'm kinda curious why she picked this store, considering Rachel's high-maintenance status.

Olivia: Rachel's making me find her a gluten-free pumpkin muffin before she'll go to the event, so you're gonna have to meet us at the bookstore instead considering I'm going to have to walk a freaking MILE just to find one. She could have picked something easy like blueberry or chocolate, but NO! She thinks it's freaking pumpkin spice season or something! IT'S SUMMER!

I try not to smile at her outrage, but seriously, it's just too adorable. I can envision her voice as I read over her text, having a complete meltdown over this. The fact that she has to stress about the most ludicrous things makes me feel bad for her and a little guilty. I've given her so much shit for her obsessive need to be punctual that I haven't given much thought as to *why* she acts the way she does.

Given our bonding moment we shared yesterday, I'm curious to know more about her. What brought about her being an assistant? Where did she grow up? Why does she walk around like everyone she meets is going to hurt her or worse—leave her. She doesn't trust easily, that's a given, but there's more to her, and I want to know what it is.

Maverick: Deep breaths, Olivia! Why don't you let me help? I'm sure there must be a dozen cafes or bakeries around here.

Olivia: Yes, you would think! But pumpkin isn't as common apparently, and everyone keeps giving me weird looks as if I've lost my mind. Hell, maybe I have finally!

Sweet Jesus, this girl is going to pop a blood vessel if she doesn't calm down soon.

Maverick: I'm ready to go, so let me come and help you. Where are you right now?

Olivia: The corner of 16th and Wazee. Take a right out of the hotel.

Maverick: Okay, stay put. I'll be right there!

Grabbing my phone and wallet, I shove them both into my pockets and rush out of my room. Once I'm downstairs, I jog out the doors toward Olivia's location. Within a few minutes, I can see her pacing, pounding away on her phone.

"Hey," I say casually as I get closer.

"There's a place three blocks down that I haven't checked yet, and there's a bakery half a mile away." She finally looks up at me, and it nearly knocks the air out of my chest. Olivia has her hair all curled in loose waves, and it looks even blonder in the bright sunlight. Her plump lips are covered in a ruby red color, and I can smell the perfume lingering off her exposed collarbone. *Fuck me.* Olivia looks fucking gorgeous. "There's no way I can check both and get back to Rachel on time without her—"

"Olivia, I'm here to help, remember?" I step closer, demanding her attention. "I'll go to the bakery, and you go to the cafe. Text me if you find one, and I'll keep looking if neither have any."

She exhales a deep breath. "Okay, got it."

We part ways, and I shamelessly jog down the street until I see the sign for A Baker's Dozen and rush inside. The place is a sweets and carb addict's heaven, and if I weren't in a rush, I'd probably take a dozen for myself.

"May I help you?" a sweet, older woman asks.

"God, I hope so." I chuckle. "I'm hoping you have a pumpkin muffin? Gluten free."

"We do. We have twenty-six flavors available and—"

"Perfect, I'll take three please."

"Of course, sweetie."

As she bags my items, I quickly grab my phone and text Olivia.

Maverick: Maverick saves the day again! Meet you back at the hotel in five.

Olivia: OMG! I could kiss you right now! Thank you!

My eyes widen in surprise before another message comes through.

Olivia: But just for the record, I won't. So don't get any ideas, perv.

And there's the feisty, blunt Olivia I know.

Laughing, I shake my head and put my phone away so I can pay the lady.

"You got me a muffin?" Olivia asks as soon as she opens the bag. We're on the elevator to Rachel's room, and the smell is making my stomach growl.

"Uh, no. One for Rachel, two for me." I playfully pat my stomach.

Her face drops and she scowls at me. "Would it kill you to be pleasant, just once?"

I shrug, reaching into the bag and snagging a muffin. "It might." I flash her a quick smile before taking a large bite.

Once Rachel's muffin is delivered, I meet Olivia back down in the lobby so the three of us can walk together to the bookstore.

"Let me take that," I tell Olivia when I see she's carrying two large boxes. I don't wait for her to respond before taking them from her hands and holding them close to my chest.

"I was fine," she tries to argue, but I ignore it.

"Such a gentleman, Maverick," Rachel gloats.

"Always." I flash her a wink, and Olivia makes a show of rolling her eyes at me. "What? I am."

We're at the bookstore within ten minutes, and the aroma of old books hits my senses as soon as we walk in through the back. The front already had a line out the door of readers waiting to meet Rachel. It's a quaint little place, and as I follow Olivia's lead, I look around and see the endless rows of books and people walking around.

"You can put the boxes here." Olivia points to the floor next to a table. "I need to set out the little gift bags quickly," Olivia orders. I do as she says, but I take it upon myself to help unload them for her and put them in neat rows. There's a smaller table in the front with banners and signs of Rachel's picture and then another large banner with a picture of just me.

"Where did that come from?" I nod my head toward it.

She quickly looks over her shoulder to see what I'm referring to.

"Oh, you mean the Ian life-sized banner of you?" She chuckles. "The publisher sent it. Be prepared to take about a hundred pictures in front of it."

"Really? It's not even my best side."

Olivia throws a bag at my head, and hearing her laughter causes me to laugh.

Once the bags are all set out and organized to Olivia's liking, she starts instructing me on the plans. "Rachel will sit and sign, and you'll stand nearby to sign and take pictures."

"There's only one chair."

"Yep. Rachel will allow pictures at her seat, and to keep the line moving, they can stand and take a picture with you at the banner."

"Okay. So should I take my shirt off now or—" I grin.

"Don't even start," she says with a laugh. "I'm sure they wouldn't argue it, though." She quickly points a finger in my face. "But don't."

I snatch her finger in my palm and hold it. "Don't worry, I only reserve that for you now."

A deep blush surfaces on her cheeks, and our eyes lock, holding each other's gazes. She knows I'm teasing, but there's an undeniable spark between us that she refuses to acknowledge.

"Hilarious. We need to let them know we're ready now." Olivia steps back, our hands releasing in the process. I watch as she walks away, admiring how her tight skirt hugs her body. Olivia doesn't need to reveal a lot of skin or show off her best assets for me to know she's gorgeous, and it's not only skin deep. She definitely has more to her than she shows.

For the next few hours, Rachel woos fans with her big, bright smile and chats them all up as if she didn't just make her assistant go on a muffin search party. She plays the part well. I've only seen a glimpse of her demanding side through emails and calls, but to witness it firsthand is eye-opening.

Part of me wants to ask Olivia why she puts up with it, but I know better than to get involved. I'm sure it's just part of the job when you work with someone as well-known as Rachel Meadows. She's single, has no children, and is more attached to her dog than any other human.

I play the part while Rachel signs books, taking pictures and smiling when readers ask if I'll repeat a quote from the book with a Southern accent. Safe to say, I botch it completely, but they seem to appreciate the effort regardless.

"Can I get a picture with you and Julia?" one of the last fans asks, and I nod my head even though I don't know who she's talking about. I remain in front of the banner, waiting. "Can you get her attention for me?" She's pointing to the other side of the table where Olivia is standing, handing out the goody bags.

"Wait, who?" I ask.

"That girl with the blond hair over there," she persists, pointing aggressively at Olivia. "She looks just how I envision Julia, and getting a picture with the two of you would be amazing!" She squeals, nearly bouncing on the tips of her toes.

She looks so damn excited I don't have the heart to let her down. "Uh, sure. Let me get her attention."

"Olivia!" I whisper-shout, but she doesn't hear me. I step around the table and grab her elbow, pulling her toward me.

"What the—"

Olivia trips as I pull her and ends up smack against my chest. She swallows tightly and looks up at me with wide eyes.

I clear my throat. "A fan wants us to take a picture together," I try to explain, nodding my head toward the eager woman.

"What? Why?" She takes a small step back to look around me.

"She said you remind her of Julia?"

Recognition resonates in her face. "The heroine," she answers. "So she wants us to take a picture together?"

"Yep."

She bites down on her lower lip and looks uneasy.

"If you don't want to, I can tell her—"

"No, no. It's fine. It's just a picture," she says casually, walking around me to greet Rachel's reader. I furrow my brows in confusion at her hesitation one second and her willingness the next.

"Oh my God, thank you so much!" The fan hands her phone off to someone and then stands between Olivia and me.

We wrap our hands around each other's waists and smile at the camera. The other person takes at least a half dozen pictures and then the fan turns around and hugs us both.

"You two are so perfect for Ian and Julia! Can I get a picture of just the two of you?"

"Uh, yeah, of course," Olivia answers before I can.

The woman is bursting with excitement as she backs up a tad and motions for us to get close. Having my hands on Olivia and our bodies close causes all kinds of feelings to surface. She wraps her arm around my waist, and when I wrap mine around her shoulders, I pull her flush to my side. She looks up at me in surprise, and I just smirk back.

"Gotta give the fans what they want," I tease, giving her a wink.

She bites down on her lip again and looks down, but I can tell she's blushing. Even though we shared a bed the other night, we hadn't physically been this close before, but I'm not complaining. Olivia's small compared to me and she smells so goddamn sweet, I want to bury my face in her neck and inhale for days.

"Okay, ready?" The woman brings her phone up and starts snapping pictures. "Oh my God, you two are so damn adorable!"

Olivia and I look at each other at the same time, and when I smile at her, she smiles back.

"Thank you again so much!" She squeezes us one more time before walking away with her friend.

"Looks like you might have a career in modeling after all," I tease, both of us still posing although no one is taking our photo.

"Nah, I doubt there'd be enough room for me with your ego taking up all the space."

"Oh, I forgot you're already a comedian."

"It's not a joke if it's true," she taunts with a devilish smile, breaking apart and walking away, leaving me to wonder if she felt that same spark as I did or if it's completely one-sided.

...only one way to find out.

CHAPTER THIRTEEN

OLIVIA

Maverick. Maverick. Yesssss.

My eyes shoot open, and I feel the embarrassment the second I hear a knock on the door.

This time I *was* fantasizing about him while sliding my fingers under my panties.

Ugh, God. What am I even thinking?

"Olivia!" Rachel's voice on the other side of the door has me rushing to answer it.

"Hey," I say as soon as I whip it open.

Without a word, she shoves Angel into my arms and drops a bag at my feet.

"She needs to be fed and then walked exactly twenty minutes later. She likes to be brushed after her walk and then she takes her morning nap. Her food and things are in her duffle. Then I need my laundry done and ironed."

I swallow, scrambling to hold Angel without purposely dropping her. "Of course," I tell her.

"I'd also like a spa appointment for a massage and facial with the bonus package."

"Right, I'm on it. I'll call right now."

"Great." She starts to walk away then stops herself. "Oh and Olivia?"

"Yes?"

"I hope you haven't forgotten the rules regarding Maverick. I know you're working closely together, but the last thing I need is a breakup or scandal to ruin my business partnerships."

"Trust me, you have nothing to worry about," I remind her.

She purses her lips, tilts her head down, then scans her eyes up and down my body. "Good to hear. Text me when my appointment is set."

As soon as she walks away, I grab the bag and take Angel inside. I look at myself in the mirror and realize what she was looking at. I wore my silky shorts and tank top pajama set to bed last night, and now she probably thinks I have Maverick stashed away in my room somewhere. Considering she gave us an odd look when we posed for pictures yesterday, I can't blame her for reiterating herself, but honestly, that was just to make a reader happy.

When Rachel informed me last night that she'd need me to do some administrative errands today, I wasn't aware that was code for work bitch, although I really shouldn't have expected anything less. There's a packed scheduled tomorrow with the signing, but today there weren't any events. I was hoping to relax a bit and catch up on my work, but I should've known better.

When I finally have a second to breathe, I check my phone and all of Rachel's social media sites and emails. I follow a variety of hashtags on Instagram, so I don't miss anything that Rachel's books are tagged in, and just as I'm scrolling through them, I'm stopped by a picture of Maverick and me from the bookstore signing. My eyes linger over Maverick as his arm wraps around my waist and he holds me close to his side. I scroll to the right for a second picture, which is almost the same, except it's a shot of Maverick looking at me instead of the camera. Then I look down at the caption.

The real-life Ian and Julia! SQUEE! They are adorbs, for real! I love them so hard!

#ShouldBeARealCouple #HowCuteAreThey #IShipThem #SwoonyCouples #RelationshipGoals #CoupleGoals #BestLookingCoupleEver

My eyes widen as I read the hashtags, and then I click on the comments and start reading. There are dozens of them. The majority along the lines of *Ahhh OMG! I ship them so hard! If they aren't dating in real life, I'll never believe in love again! They are the perfect Ian & Julia!*

I make myself stop reading them after a few minutes because they're making my head spin. Maverick and I are so different. I never imagined we'd *look* like the perfect couple, but staring at our picture has me reconsidering. Julia has the same hair color as me, and she's described as petite, average height, with green eyes. I never realized it before now that I look like her.

I take a screenshot of the pictures before I close out of the app and get back to work. Angel needs to go out again, and if I don't finish Rachel's laundry, she'll have an aneurysm.

Four hours later, I finally complete everything on Rachel's list. I'm exhausted and hungry, and on top of it all, I haven't talked to Maverick all day and have this weird desire to know what he's up to. Today was *his* day off, so he probably worked out and then ravished all the local single ladies.

Rachel has dinner plans, so I put Angel back in her suite after taking her out again. This dog is higher maintenance than Rachel sometimes.

Once I'm back in my room, I lounge around for an hour, then I pace the small space between the door and the desk trying to decide if I should reach out to Maverick or not. I skipped lunch and am now starving for dinner. Should I ask if he wants to grab a bite with me? Or casually ask if he's eaten yet? Maybe just mention I'm going to go find something?

Ugh, why am I overthinking this? I'm an idiot.

I'll just go down to the bar and order something to eat from there and head in to get a good night's sleep. Lord knows I'll be up early tomorrow, running around like a chicken with my head cut off for Rachel again.

Deciding to go with that plan, I grab my things and take the elevator down to the lobby. The hotel bar is just off to the side, and it actually looks cozy with a fireplace in the middle and couches surrounding it. I find a stool and wait for a server.

Once I place my dinner and drink order, I settle in and look around. It's a nice hotel, and it's actually quite large and busy with people walking around. Just when I'm about to dig my phone out of my purse, I glance near the fireplace and do a double take when I notice Maverick sitting in one of the chairs.

What is he doing? I look around the bodies standing between us and...*is he reading a book?* What the hell?

Who reads a book in a bar?

Why the hell is Maverick reading a book?

I don't know why this amuses me so much, but I'm also impressed. Though I'm not going to let him know that. He could be using his time off to go drinking, clubbing, or worse—hooking up with single random locals.

Since I have to wait for my food anyway, I figure I might as well go say hello to him. I walk over and stand in front of him.

Maverick has one ankle propped on his knee, and he's leaning back slightly against a pillow, looking so relaxed, settled, and calm.

"You know you're blocking the only good light I had," he mutters without looking at me.

I hold back a laugh. "What are you doing?" I ask with my hands on my hips.

He finally looks up. "I *was* trying to read. Is that okay?"

"I'm just surprised." I shrug.

"That I'm reading a book?" He furrows his brows.

"That you *can* read," I tease, nudging his knee with mine.

"I'm not all muscles and good cheekbones, you know. I won the fifth-grade read-a-thon challenge and have a personalized blue ribbon to prove it," he replies with a smug attitude, and it causes me to chuckle.

"That's the most pathetic thing I've ever heard," I say, laughing. "So what are you reading?"

"Book three in the Mistborn series," he responds, flipping the book over and showing me the cover. "Always been a fan of the series and thought I'd do a reread."

I take the chair next to him and grab the thick paperback out of his hand. Turning it over, I skim over the synopsis and smile. "Sounds interesting. I'll have to add it to my TBR."

"Your what?" he asks when I hand the book back to him.

"My TBR," I repeat with a laugh. "My to-be-read list. It's about a mile long."

"Oh, didn't know there was such a thing."

"Are you kidding? They have a whole website dedicated to adding books to your TBR and reviewing them online. It's where an author's hopes and dreams go to die, but it's popular among readers."

"That sounds brutal," Maverick replies, chuckling.

"Yeah, it can be. I've had to check all of Rachel's early reviews for her before release because she refuses to go there herself. That way I can give her the sugary version and skip over the harsh shit."

"People really say that bad of things on there about her books?" He looks at me as if he can't comprehend anyone saying a rude thing about Rachel's stories.

"Oh my God! You wouldn't believe the reviews I've read over there. Not just for her books either. Reading is all subjective, and readers will experience the same book differently. There is no way to make them all happy, which sometimes means the hardcore fans will get really upset when a book in her series doesn't go the way they wanted. Rachel tells the story that needs to be told within her heart, and that doesn't always mean it's the way her readers expect."

"Wow...no wonder she doesn't go on there then."

"It's for the best. She's told me from the start that reviews are for readers—not for authors—so she understands that not all her readers will like every book she writes. She likes knowing what the early reviewers say, and then after that, she lets it go and moves on to writing the next. At that point, what's done is done, and it's not like she's going to go back and rewrite the book."

"Guess I could understand some of her hostility then," Maverick teases. "Wow, I had no idea there was so much involved in the publishing world. Kinda blows my mind."

"When I first started working in this field, I thought I was an expert in social media marketing and what it took to promote a book, but I had a rude awakening. It's so much more than just writing a book and trying to get the word out into the world. It's connecting with readers and bloggers and networking with other authors. It's finding a balance between life and work and managing deadlines. It's timing and luck and figuring out when to actually start promoting a book and when to post about it and *what* to post. Rachel gets emails weekly asking for interviews, Q&As, character interviews…you name it, she's done it. On top of all that, she plots a book for a week before she even starts writing it. She writes out their character profiles, outlines each chapter, lists all the secondary characters, prints out images of the setting, and sometimes makes Pinterest boards for inspiration. It's this whole week where she's taping pieces of paper all around her office, dozens of Post-it Notes everywhere, and she's muttering to herself for hours. By the time she actually sits down to write the first chapter, she can visually see the entire thing in her mind and just writes like crazy. It's actually a really neat process to watch—ya know when I'm not being yelled at for more coffee." I smile, chuckling. "It actually gives me a new appreciation for all she does to give her readers the best story she can. I know I complain about her a lot, but she's truly a genius in her craft."

"If I didn't know any better, I'd say you were a hardcore fangirl." Maverick's genuine smile has me smiling right back. He reaches over and tucks a piece of my hair behind my ear. My breath hitches as his fingers linger along my jawline before his hand drops back to his lap. "Don't worry, I won't tell anyone you kind of like your boss."

I snort, blushing. "Thanks. I'd like to keep that under wraps."

The bartender shouts at me that my food is ready, and it brings me out of my Maverick-induced haze. I wave a hand at him so he knows I heard him.

"Would you want to come eat with me? You probably ate already, but—"

"I'd love to," he interrupts. "Let's go."

He follows me to the bar and places his order with a beer. We drink and chat without skipping a beat. It's not forced or awkward. Maverick continues to surprise me during this trip, and I actually find myself enjoying his company tonight.

CHAPTER FOURTEEN

MAVERICK

THIS MORNING, I woke up early and had a cup of coffee at the hotel cafe downstairs. I sit smiling, thinking about last night. Olivia is something else. Not only is she beautiful, sassy, and smart, but she's sincere and funny too. Before this road trip, I never imagined myself settling down with anyone, but now I find myself falling for a woman who is my exact opposite. To say she's the whole package is an understatement. My heart knows, and while I'm trying to ignore it, eventually I won't be able to.

After I finish my cup of coffee, I get a bagel to go, then head upstairs and get dressed. Before I get a reminder text, I head out the door, not wanting to be late. I'm actually getting the hang of this signing thing. Of course, each venue is different, but the situations are the same.

Before the signing, we had an early lunch event with Rachel's readers. As I sat next to Rachel and listened to her answer the same questions she'd been asked a hundred times already, I found myself glancing at Olivia who was too busy to eat. If one weren't paying any attention, it'd be easy to gloss over her because she tries so hard to blend in with the background.

In this room, Olivia is the real MVP for running Rachel's life so flawlessly. What's disheartening is Rachel doesn't seem to appreciate anything Olivia does for her—only expects it all. Just because she's paying Olivia doesn't mean she has to continue to treat her like trash, regardless of her author social status. It's actually starting to irk me, but I know I'm walking on thin ice, so I find myself biting my tongue.

After the brunch, Olivia gives me a detailed rundown of what the rest of the day will be like. While I found it annoying in the beginning, it's actually helpful to know what to expect, though I still give her shit for it. She secretly likes it, though, whether she'll admit it or not.

When the main doors open, readers flood in. The line is so long, I don't see the tail of it, just the beginning. Picture after picture and the day seems to pass by in a blur. I've talked to so many people today that I don't remember many of the conversations.

Randomly, I catch sight of Olivia running around for Rachel, helping readers, and the smile on her face never fades. Occasionally, our eyes meet, and it causes my heart to lurch forward, which is confusing and exhilarating at the same time. While busting her ass, she moves around the room flawlessly, as if it's her own personal stage, following cues and giving rehearsed lines. Olivia deserves a fucking Emmy for her performance today.

Once the signing is officially over, a group of older women basically hold me hostage. They give me a rundown of the entire plot of Rachel's series and why they love Ian so much. I smile and nod and watch Olivia over their shoulders, hoping she'll save me, but she doesn't. While I enjoy chatting about Rachel's characters, I honestly have no clue what the hell they're referring to nine times out of ten, though I'm beginning to catch on now.

While I listen to them talk and try to make eye contact, I notice Rachel is reprimanding Olivia, who continues to act as if it doesn't bother her as she cleans off the table. Rachel eventually storms away, and Olivia rolls her eyes, which makes me chuckle. The ladies who I'm chatting with eventually ask for a photo and then offer to hook me up with their granddaughters. Laughter erupts from my core as I politely tell them no thanks.

"So are you in a serious relationship then?" one of them asks me. She's wearing a shirt that says, *COUGAR*. The ridiculousness of it actually makes me smile as the light reflects and shines off it. I've learned there are zero boundaries at these events. Zero. And if you have any, every single one of them will be demolished, then backed over a few times.

"Not at the moment," I say.

"But there's a special lady," the other adds with a cheeky grin. "I can tell. There's a sparkle in your eye."

I playfully shake my head.

"There's no reason to be shy about it. But just know, honey, if it doesn't work out, my Carley would be perfect for you." She leans in a gives me a hug. "Or maybe I would."

"Oh watch out!" I playfully tell her as she blows me kisses. Then, just like that, she takes a handful of my ass in her hand before they walk away. In any other industry, that'd be considered extremely inappropriate. At these events, though, I've learned it's just another friendly way to say goodbye. Luckily, I'm not easily offended, though I'm surprised Olivia didn't step in and shoo them away.

"Grandma knows best," I whisper under my breath as I walk toward Olivia who is obviously flustered and pissed. She's slamming bookmarks and bracelets around like they insulted her.

"Everything okay?" I grab a bucket of lip balms from the table and neatly place them in the box she's taking her aggression out on. "Okay then."

She stops in her tracks, and the look on her face is frightening as hell. "Do I *look* okay? Rachel is extremely pissed at me because she saw herself tagged on Facebook and there's red lipstick on her teeth. Apparently, it's *my* fault because I didn't tell her. Honestly, I didn't fucking notice because she rarely smiles that big."

I'm trying really hard to understand this because it's so childish. "There's not really anything that can be done about it now, though. Right? It's done. It's over with."

Olivia shakes her head. "I will never live this down. I even got the 'importance of paying attention to detail' speech. Detail is my middle name," she grits out.

I notice she's about to squeeze the life out of two heart-shaped stress balls that Rachel's series name is printed on. I take them from her hands and place them in the box, then turn to face her, placing my hands on her shoulders to force her to look into my eyes.

"You're so goddamn tense right now; you're going to snap in

two. Deep breaths. Shake off the bullshit. Okay?" My voice is soft when I speak to her, trying to bring her down from a level ten of angry. Just as the words leave my mouth, Olivia's phone starts dinging.

Not wasting a second, she pulls it from her pocket, unlocks it, and groans. "Great."

I search her face. "Now what?"

Olivia turns her phone around and lets me read the message.

Rachel: I'd like a slice of chocolate cake, gluten-free, low carb, with a side of sugar-free sprinkles. Also, Angel needs to be taken out and fed. I'm going to rest my eyes before my meetup tonight. So be quiet when you come in.

Olivia turns around and looks at the table that's still full of shit. She's about to have a meltdown.

"How about I take care of that, and you finish up here?" I tell her. We're standing so damn close to each other I can smell the sweetness of her skin.

I didn't expect her to agree with me, because that's just not in her character. "I'm sure Rachel wouldn't appre–"

I place my finger over her soft lips, and she immediately stops talking. "I'll handle her."

Green eyes bore into mine, and I smirk as Olivia swallows hard. Reluctantly, I remove my finger from her mouth. Her lips slightly part, and at that moment, before she can even mutter a word, I'm so tempted to kiss her.

"Okay," she whispers, then nods. "Please make sure it's gluten free, low carb, and sugar free. Just buy her chocolate-covered cardboard at this point and call it cake." Olivia finally smiles.

"With all this charm I have, she'll take whatever I give her and eat it with a grin."

Laughter erupts from her. "Don't flatter yourself. The woman can smell gluten from a mile away."

Olivia pulls her business credit card from her back pocket, along with Rachel's room key and hands them to me. "When you walk into her room, all the lights are going to be out, and the curtains will be shut. Don't say a word. Put the cake on the desk with some plasticware and grab that little shit stain of a dog and bring it outside. Trust me when I say Rachel will pretend you're invisible. She might not even notice it's you. Get in and out as quick as you possibly can, please."

"I can handle this. Just trust me," I tell her, giving her a wink of confidence.

"I do. And that's the scary part." She smiles.

"Ouch. Nothing like a compliment wrapped with poison. I'll be back. If she adds anything to her ridiculous fuckin' list, text me." For a moment, we hold eye contact and unspoken words stream between us.

"Thank you," she finally says, breaking the tension by walking back toward the table to finish packing.

I laugh. "You owe me. Like really, really owe me."

"Add it to my tab." Olivia smirks over her shoulder, and she looks so goddamn cute. I take a mental snapshot and walk out of the ballroom with a shit-eating grin plastered on my face.

Pulling out my phone, I do a quick Google search and find a place close by who conveniently has what Rachel wants, stupid sugar-free sprinkles and all. It takes all of ten minutes for me to get the cake that smells like sweet cardboard and head up to Rachel's room.

I swipe the key card, and the room is exactly how Olivia described it. I pull my phone out to see, place the cake on the desk, and see Angel who's wagging her tail at me. Quietly, I find the leash and snap it on her collar. This little dog is the sweetest thing in the world. I really don't know what Olivia is talking about.

As soon as I step outside and set Angel on the grass, she instantly finds a spot to go. Once she's finished, I pick her up and walk back to the elevator. The doors slide open, and I step inside, followed by a group of women. When I turn around with Angel, they all burst out into aww's.

"Her bows are so adorable," one woman says, petting her. Angel's little nub of a tail is wagging back and forth.

The elevator seems to stop at every floor on the way up to Rachel's, and eventually, I'm the only person left. Two more floors. Damn. The elevator stops once more, and Olivia steps in, which causes the air around me to evaporate. As soon as Angel sees her, she starts growling and barking like a maniac. I burst out into laughter because I swear it's like I'm holding two different animals when Olivia is around.

"Angel, shh. I was just complimenting your manners," I say between laughs.

"Isn't she the worst animal in the world?" Olivia asks, glaring at the dog.

My chuckles echo off the walls as the doors slide open, and we step out.

"I'll take her back, just in case." Olivia holds her arms out, and Angel is ready to bite her fingers off.

"No, I'll keep her. We can go together. I'm sure you need your arms for all the work you need to do. Did you get the boxes to your room?" I follow behind Olivia as she leads the way to Rachel's room.

"Yeah. The bellman took them for me." There's slight relief in her voice, and I'm happy she's a lot calmer than she was thirty minutes ago.

Pulling the key card from my pocket, I swipe it, and Olivia opens the door. The room is still dark. I take the leash off Angel as Olivia walks to her bowl with the flashlight on her phone activated and pours food into it.

"Olivia?" Rachel says from the black abyss. Olivia looks at me, places her finger over her mouth, and turns the flashlight off.

"Yes?" she asks quietly.

Rachel lets out an overdramatic sigh and takes her time before speaking up. My eyes are rolling so hard in the back of my head, but I honestly wish I could see Olivia's face right now.

"What do you need, Rachel?" Olivia asks her, flatly.

"Have you noticed how Maverick looks at you like you're a delicate flower?" Rachel asks.

Now I'm happy as fuck the lights are off.

"I think you're imagining things. The cake is on the table. I'll see you in the morning," Olivia quickly says.

Rachel doesn't say another word, and I hear Olivia walking toward me swiftly and nearly runs into me. I grab her by the shoulders and stop her, and we make our way through the suite. The two of us can't get the hell out of there quick enough. We step into the hallway, and Olivia is shaking her head. Annoyance is written all over her face.

"See how delusional she is?" she asks, walking toward the elevator with her fists clenched.

I nod and let out a nervous laugh, but I can't help but wonder if Rachel is right.

She actually might be.

CHAPTER FIFTEEN

OLIVIA

I'm forcing myself to walk in front of Maverick because I'm so damn embarrassed by what Rachel said. My cheeks are hot, and I'm flustered.

A delicate flower? I roll my eyes thinking about it. For someone who's so eloquent with words, she could've used a better descriptor. Me and delicate don't go together, and I take pride in having my shit together, regardless if I'm forcing it half the time. Not to mention, Maverick doesn't look at me any differently from the way he looks at Rachel's readers. I would know; I caught myself watching him a little too often today. He's an absolute natural around people, giving them the attention they desire from him. There wasn't one woman who left his presence feeling less than. So she's just looking into it too deeply, searching for shit that's not there.

I step inside the elevator and hold the door for Maverick. He joins me, and I press our floor since his room is actually somewhat close to mine. An awkward tension lingers between us, and I'm not really sure what to say or if I need to talk at all, but the silence draws on, and it's almost too much for me to handle.

"I'm sorry you heard her be like that. I'm sure if she knew you were there, she wouldn't have said that," I tell him. His hazel eyes meet mine, and my heart lurches forward, beating wildly, and I try to push it down. Maverick gives me a half grin which practically makes me melt before the elevator doors open.

"If it makes you feel any better, I don't think you're a delicate flower, Olivia. You're strong and fierce. You're a badass."

My breath hitches, and I'm so damn happy I'm walking in front of him again so he can't see the blush on my cheeks. That might be the sweetest thing anyone has said to me. "Thank you."

"What are your plans tonight?" he asks me as I stop at my room, then laughs because he already knows. "Right."

I'm doing what I do every night—working. "You can join me if you want. Not sure I'll be the best company, but..."

"Let me go back to my room and grab some things, and I'll be back."

My eyes meet his. "I really have a lot of work to do."

With hands held up, he grins. "I promise not to be a bother."

His tongue slides out and licks his bottom lip, and I find myself staring. The man is sexy as hell without even trying. "Okay. Good."

As Maverick walks down the hallway toward his room, I enter mine, shut the door, and lean against it. My heart is beating so hard in my chest. I understand why women go crazy for him, but he's more than his looks. At that moment, I find myself smiling thinking about him, but then Rachel's voice subconsciously screams at me. Shaking my head, I push it all away. First of all, there's no way a man like him would ever be with someone like me. We're complete opposites. I really don't know why she's so damn concerned about it.

I grab my phone and see I have a message from Vada, more than likely looking for an update. Too bad she'll be sadly disappointed.

Vada: Did you find out his girth yet?

Olivia: Like a Coke can.

Vada: REALLY?!

Olivia: No, you perv!

Vada: Bummer. So what? Like an uncooked hot dog then?

Olivia: Omg. I have no idea.

Vada: So you're saying you haven't slept with him yet? How's that possible?

Olivia: Willpower, self-control, the desire to keep my job.

Vada: Boring, boring, and double boring. Why are you keeping yourself from that delicious hunk of man meat? I already told Ethan he's my hall pass.

Olivia: I don't remember you being this weird. Was I just clueless back then or oblivious to your quirks?

Vada: Both, I'm sure. I'm sleep deprived, and my nipples feel like hardened pepperoni. Give your girl something over here!

I snort at her choice of words. Between breastfeeding, pumping, and diaper changes, I imagine Vada is completely unhinged.

Olivia: We've been getting along, and I'm enjoying his company.

Vada: Okay, Grandma.

Olivia: What? That's the truth! We've had some "moments" I guess you could say, but we both know the rules. Plus, I don't just sleep around. Even if he was attracted to me that way, nothing could come of it. We live worlds apart, and we're complete opposites. It'd just hurt in the end when reality hit.

Vada: Liv. You know I love you, but you, my friend, are using avoidance techniques to keep your distance. You come up with any excuse as to why you shouldn't instead of following your heart and listening to the list of reasons why you should. You figure if you never go for it, you can't get hurt. You're trying to control everything in your life when, in reality, you just can't.

Olivia: But they aren't excuses if they're the truth, right? Say I sleep with him and I get even more attached and then at the end of the trip, we go our separate ways because that's what's going to happen. I live in Chicago, and he's in LA. What's the point?

Vada: Do you think when you're old and on your deathbed, you'll be thinking of all the things you did and regret them, or will you be thinking of all the things you didn't do and regret not going for it? That's what you have to ask yourself.

I hate that Vada can outsmart me in two seconds flat. She's an old soul, and although I hate that she's right—she's right. Will I walk away thinking what if, or will I walk away heartbroken? Or both?

Once I get a grip, I kick off my heels and change into sweatpants and a T-shirt, then grab my laptop and place it on the bed. A knock sounds out on the door, and I rush to open it. Maverick steps in, looks me up and down, and gives me a nod.

"Hi, have we met before?"

"Stop saying that," I tell him with a playful eye roll.

A laugh escapes his throat, and it sounds like music. That stupid smile fills my face again. Is it possible that Rachel is right? Do I look at him a certain way too?

Maverick walks inside with his book from last night and has a small laptop with him. I plop down on the bed, and he sits on the other side. Looking over at him, he shrugs at me, then kicks off his shoes.

"Well, just get comfortable," I tease.

"You set the precedence here, not me."

Shaking my head, I unlock my computer and log in to my email and task manager.

Rachel's publisher sent an email reminding her of all the confirmed deadlines. I get up and grab my planners and notebooks and set them beside me. Glancing over, I catch Maverick watching me.

"I know it's serious when you grab your author Bible. So I had an idea. How about we ditch all this nonsense and go out on the town."

With wide eyes, I stare at him. "Are you serious?"

"As a heart attack. All this bullshit will still be here tomorrow. Get dressed, and let's go have some fun."

I look at him like he's lost his mind. "Not happening."

"It's Colorado. We should take full advantage and grab some special brownies. After we're good and relaxed, we can hit up 16th Street," he says with a smile. "Nothing like weed and pizza."

"Are you sure you haven't already had some special brownies? Now shhh. I have to concentrate."

The room grows silent, but only for a short time. "So if I wanted to hire you as my assistant, what would I need to do?"

I glare at him. "I only take on one client at a time. And you can barely handle me now, so I doubt you'd want me running your life."

"Perfect. So fire Rachel and come work for me. All these flagged emails need replies. It's people who want to book me for a shoot." He turns his laptop around, and his email inbox is a freaking nightmare. Pages of people need a response, and my mouth drops open in shock. I'm horrified by all the flags, and how there's zero organization.

"Maverick. Holy shit. I have no words."

He shrugs. "That's a first. So next time you're talking about something I don't care to hear, I'll just flash my inbox, and that'll show you."

When our eyes meet, he smiles, and I watch as his gaze moves down to my mouth. Quickly, I turn my head and go back to my laptop. I'm imagining things, and it doesn't help that Rachel's words are on repeat in my head about how Maverick looks at me.

"Are you hungry?" he asks. "You're bound to be."

"I could eat." Today was busy as hell, and I've only had a nasty protein bar that I packed for Rachel that tasted like prunes. I get so caught up in work that I often forget to eat. It's nice to have someone remind me while everything is still open.

Maverick begins typing away on his computer. "Done. Food is on the way."

"What did you order?" I ask.

He laughs. "Something that's got all the gluten, carbs, and sugar."

"Thank God." I smile.

The room grows silent again, and soon there's a knock on the door. Maverick gets up and answers it, and as soon as I smell the food, my mouth begins to water. The door clicks closed, and he comes into view holding a large pizza box with plates stacked on top.

"Little did he know, two people are eating this whooooole thing." He places it on the desk and opens the top. The aroma of the cheese and bread causes my mouth to water.

"Get ready to eat the best mountain pie ever. And you have to try honey on the crust."

I grab a plate and stack a few pieces. "Honey?"

"It's the best shit in the world. I dream about this pizza." He takes a huge bite and lets out a moan.

I take a bite of pizza and do the same. "Oh my God," I say while chewing.

"Right, told you. Beau Jo's will change your life." He finishes a piece and slaps another on his plate. It amazes me how he can make pizza look sexy.

We eat until we're ridiculously full, and I'm pretty sure this is what a carb coma feels like.

I try to get back to work, but it's impossible. Once I start yawning, Maverick takes notice. My eyes are heavy, and I think it's from all the activities from today. Signings exhaust me.

"You need rest," he says, closing my laptop and moving it out of the way. I slide under the covers, and Maverick stands to pack his things. My eyes feel like bricks, and I'm so comfortable that I feel myself drifting off. I hear his laughter when my eyes finally close.

"Good night, my delicate little flower," he says with a small laugh as the lamp next to the bed clicks off. "See you before the sun rises."

"Night," I whisper before I slip away to dreamland.

With a racing heart, I sit up in bed and glance around, making sure I'm alone. In my dream, Maverick was naked, walking toward me, and I was happily undressing for him. If I wouldn't have woken up, I know exactly where it would've led—the same place it's been going every night when he visits my dreams—his mouth on mine, my hands all over his body. Just thinking about it causes heat to rush through me, but I try to ignore it.

Unlocking my phone, I see I still have an hour before I'm supposed to be up, so I try to close my eyes and get more sleep, but it doesn't happen, which only frustrates me. I force myself into the shower to try to push the fantasies of him away. Though he doesn't make it easy for me when he wears clothes that hug him in all the right places. I let out a groan as I turn on the water and undress.

I try to busy my mind with the upcoming thirteen-hour drive and the signing in Vegas this weekend—anything that will lead me away from thoughts of Maverick—but somehow my mind keeps going back to him. Considering he appears in my dreams and my thoughts just makes me realize that I need to keep him at a distance. It's easy to pretend something's between us, but it's not reality. There are many reasons it would never work, regardless if my heart lurches forward each time I see him. I refuse to be another slash on his bedpost. Not to mention I need my job, and if Rachel suspects anything is going on between us, she'll fire me on the spot, and it's just not worth it. There's a line of people who'd die to be her assistant even though it's not full of glitz and glamour like they think.

After I'm dressed, I decide to read for a bit since I have time but realize I can't concentrate. Instead, I pull up my inbox only to find several emails Rachel's sent to her publisher about a summer tour she expects next year. Two weeks of my life on the road isn't so bad, but two months is pushing the line. I'm not sure I'd survive it. In reply after reply, Rachel has volunteered me to plan the entire thing and write up a proposal with the cost to be submitted by the end of the month. When I realize I'm grinding my teeth, I stand and try to shake off my annoyance, but it doesn't help. Thankfully, she gave me a year to plan it instead of three months, but damn, this might take a freaking village.

When my alarm rings out, causing me to jump, I realize I forgot to turn it off. I text Maverick and let him know when we'll be leaving, and I get a thumbs-up emoji in response. It's early, and I'm already in a shitastic mood. After I pack my stuff, I linger for another twenty minutes before I go to the lobby and wait for him. Surprisingly, he's right on time, which is impressive. Maybe I'm finally wearing on him.

I stand and wheel my suitcase outside.

"Well good morning to you too," he says, taking the keys from the valet.

After my suitcases are placed in the back, I get in the passenger seat. "Morning."

I flip open my planner for next year and try to nail down a practical schedule for a summer tour that doesn't interfere with any events Rachel already has planned. I'm so fucking frustrated and let out a huff.

"Everything okay?" Maverick turns down the music.

I glance over at him, then look back at my planner. "No."

"Want to talk about it?" He slows down at a stoplight, looks over at me, then yells, "Goat rodeo!" I'm so damn confused when he reaches for the handle, jumps out, and pretends he's riding a bucking bull as he runs around the car before climbing back into the driver's side. I burst out into laughter.

"Have you lost your mind?" I say between laughs as he gets back inside.

The light turns green, and he accelerates, then stops at another red light. Glancing over at me with the cutest smirk on his face, Maverick yells goat rodeo again. He does the same thing and gets back in the driver's side before the light turns green.

I'm laughing so hard, tears roll down my cheeks, and I can barely catch my breath. I glance over at a man in the car next to us, and he's shaking his head. Maverick waves at him with a grin.

"Better now?" he asks as he speeds up onto I-70. All I can do is smile and nod.

Soon the city is behind us, and I try to soak in the surroundings while I can, though I've heard the drive through this side of Colorado and through Utah is beautiful. The mountains disappear for a while, but then I see the top of the snowcapped mountains, and I can't keep my eyes off them.

"We should come back. You need to see Garden of the Gods. It's a must," he says as we drive through Grand Junction.

"Maverick." I look over at him. "You know good and well that after this trip we'll go our separate ways and never talk again unless it's about business."

His face slightly contorts. "Wow, that hurts. I thought we were getting friendship bracelets and all."

I snort, giving him a look. "We're two people who were forced to road trip together. I just don't want either of us to be confused about where we stand. You'll go back to California, and I'll go back to Chicago, and our lives will go on. Don't get me wrong, it's been fun, but this is all it is. That's the reality."

The car grows silent and stays that way until we're in Utah. I almost feel bad, but it's the truth, and sometimes the truth hurts. Once we're at the halfway point, Maverick pulls over, and we have lunch. Just as I'm about to take a bite of my chicken quesadilla, my phone starts ringing. *Mother* flashes across the screen. I reject the call and Maverick notices but doesn't say anything.

We pay, get gas, and I check the GPS before I put the car in drive and head toward Vegas. My phone vibrates again. I glance at it, then reject the call. I cannot talk to her right now.

"Why aren't you answering your mom's call?" he finally asks.

I swallow hard, not really wanting to discuss it, and stare out at the mountains. Maverick shared so much with me about his dad that I feel guilty about wanting to keep that part of my life from him. Sometimes it's better not to talk about my past because then it's almost as if it never happened. When I don't answer his question, he stares out the window, and I feel an invisible wall being built. Considering this trip is almost over, and we won't be hanging out again, I suck it up.

"It's because she probably wants money or something. I don't have the best relationship with my mother, and my father is nonexistent. My family life isn't the greatest. It's actually kinda fucked up."

He doesn't look at me with pity or sadness, and relief floods through me. "I don't know anyone who has a perfect family life. Everyone has skeletons."

I give him a small smile. "She's the reason I'm the way I am. It's important for me to have control of my life because for so long I didn't. It's why I live and die by my schedule. My father left us when I was a baby, and I don't actually remember him at all, and my mom struggled to keep a job for years. She's the type of woman who needs to be wanted by someone, and growing up, I witnessed that. My father leaving us ultimately destroyed her."

Maverick doesn't say anything; he sits there and listens.

"Eventually, she met the wrong man who introduced her to drugs, and it helped her push away the pain. At thirteen years old, I watched her destroy her life, one hit at a time. While love and that feeling of being wanted once ruled her, it was replaced with shooting up. When I was sixteen, she met someone who really cared about her. He was a stand-up guy and tried to get her help, but she refused. She chose drugs over him, and eventually, he left us too. This only caused her to enter another downward spiral. There were weeks when I didn't see her, didn't know where she was, but I kept it all inside while trying to finish high school."

"Wow, Olivia. I'm sorry," he offers, shaking his head.

"A week before I graduated high school, I came home and found her face down on the floor. I called 911 and did CPR until the ambulance arrived. That day, I thought she was going to die, and I'd be put into foster care until my eighteenth birthday. I was so scared and sad, because she was all I had, but I was never enough—I wasn't enough for her to stay clean. She needed companionship so much that she was willing to die for that. My entire life was chaos until I left home for college. So no, I don't always answer her calls because she usually wants something from me—which is the only time she ever reaches out—and I don't have time to deal with that right now. I have my own problems." My words come out harsher than I intended.

"I understand. I really do. Do you know where your dad is now?" he asks.

"Living in New York. He offered to take me in when shit got really bad, but I couldn't leave my mother. We have an okay relationship, but he was barely there for me. And any money he sent, my mother spent on drugs. I learned at a young age to take care of myself," I tell him.

"My opinion still stands. You're an absolute badass. I have so much fucking respect for you." His words are sweet and sincere, which I appreciate more than he'll ever know.

My phone vibrates again, and this time, Maverick rejects the call for me. The rest of the way we talk about things that aren't so personal—music, TV shows, Netflix series binges, and the beaches in California. Soon we're making our way into Las Vegas, and when I pull up to a stoplight, I look over at him and smirk.

"Goat rodeo!" I yell out and reach for my door handle. Maverick steps out and starts his bucking bronco movements, and I shut my door and accelerate. In the rearview mirror, I watch as he lifts his arms up in the air. I'm laughing so hard as he walks a block toward me. He opens the door and sits inside, and I'm huddled over, laughing my ass off.

"I owe you one for that! The woman at the light was so confused. She hurried and locked her door like I was going to rob her," he explains with a smirk.

"I know. I watched her mouth fall open when I drove off," I try to explain through my laughter.

"Just wait, I feel so sorry for you. I don't get back, Olivia. I get *even*," he playfully threatens.

I sarcastically nod. "Suuuure."

By the time we make it to our hotel, my face hurts from laughing so much. We get out, and I check in. I hand him his key, and he pretends to be mad.

"I'm going to get you when you least expect it," he warns as he walks toward the elevator.

I follow him. "Good. I look forward to it."

CHAPTER SIXTEEN

MAVERICK

I LOVE WATCHING Olivia finally loosen up and laugh until her face turns red. She's gorgeous without even trying, but when she stops overthinking everything and just relaxes, she's stunning. Simply beautiful.

"So what are you going to do on your first night in Vegas?" I ask her when we reach our floor.

"I'm exhausted, so I plan to order room service, take a hot bath, and go to bed." She drags her roller suitcase behind her, and I can't help but watch the sway of her hips rock back and forth. She stops at her room and turns to look at me. "What are you gonna do?"

"I have a couple of friends here actually and told them I'd hit them up once I arrived. Other than that, I'm not sure. Probably hit the Strip."

She bites down on her lip and lowers her head, scanning her eyes over my body. Even when she's trying to be subtle about it, I catch her every time.

"Well don't forget we have a very packed schedule tomorrow," she finally says, scanning her key card. "Rachel will—"

"I know, Olivia." I step forward, pinning her with my eyes. "I won't be late." I toss her a wink before walking to my room a few doors down. Just before I step inside, I lean back and see she's still standing in the hallway. "Good night, Olivia."

"Uh yeah, night. See you tomorrow." She scrambles to get inside as fast as she can with her luggage.

Waking up in Vegas is a complete experience all on its own. The sun is bright as fuck, the streets are filled with cars and people walking around, and it's as if no one even went to sleep. Everyone is still on the go, ready to keep the Vegas atmosphere alive.

According to Olivia's schedule, Rachel has a bookstore signing off the Strip and then a luncheon meet and greet with seventy-five VIP readers. After that, Rachel is meeting with some locals to gamble, which means Olivia and I will be on our own after dinner.

"Good morning," I say as soon as Olivia opens her door. I push off the wall and hand her a Starbucks cup of her favorite drink.

"Mornin'..." she replies slowly, narrowing her eyes at me suspiciously. "You're looking bright-eyed and bushy-tailed for this early."

"Don't I always?" I feign offense. She ignores me and sips her coffee as if it's her lifeline.

"You ready for today?" she asks as we make our way into the elevator.

"Ready as I'll ever be."

Olivia presses the button for the third floor where Rachel's private signing is being held. This event is different from the others because it's not in a bookstore or in a large ballroom with dozens of other authors. From what Olivia's told me, Rachel will participate in a Q&A, and then the readers will have the opportunity to get their books signed.

"You'll be sitting up there with Rachel, but the majority of the questions will be for her," she informs me.

"And you'll be doing what?"

"I'll be the emcee, asking the questions. After polling her reader group and Facebook page, I spent three months researching and narrowed the list of most frequently asked questions down to thirty. Her readers should enjoy it. Then if there's time afterward, I'll let the audience ask a couple of questions too."

"Wow...pretty intensive process," I half-joke with her, but honestly, I'm not even surprised anymore. Olivia doesn't do anything half-assed, and that's part of the reason I respect her so much.

I follow Olivia into the back way through a private room and am surprised to see Rachel is already there, talking to one of the hotel workers. There's a small stage up front with a table and chairs and a podium with a microphone. She's rambling off orders, demanding a beverage station, more chairs, and less of a "breeze," whatever that means.

"Olivia, about time." Rachel finally turns and acknowledges her. "Angel needs to be let out in about twenty minutes. I'd like a plain bagel with fat-free cream cheese, *not* toasted, and I've decided to have Maverick emcee the Q&A, so you'll need to give him the list of questions."

My head shakes to make sure I heard Rachel correctly. Looking at Olivia, she stands frozen in place, nodding as she listens to all her orders. I can't believe she's just taking it and not even arguing with her, considering Olivia just told me how much work it took to get this together. I wouldn't feel right taking her place, not to mention I wasn't even asked properly.

"I'm not sure that's a good idea," I finally blurt out, unable to hold back after seeing Olivia's face drop. "Olivia is more prepared. She knows the books. I-I'm just the image."

"Oh, that's why it'd be perfect!" Rachel singsongs, walking toward me with a bright smile. "They'll be glued to you and really take a lot from the whole experience."

I look over Rachel's shoulder and see Olivia's face. She gives me a tight head shake to tell me not to argue with her, though I'm really tempted. This is a shitty thing for her to pull at the last second.

I nod, giving Rachel my approval, and when I do, she squeals and nearly blows out my eardrums. After that's settled, Olivia and Rachel talk about the volunteers out front who are taking the readers' tickets and making final touches.

Four hours later, my throat is dry and raw after hosting the Q&A and then chatting with readers during the signing. As far as I know, everything went great, and Rachel and her readers left happy.

"Well, if your modeling career doesn't take off, at least you know you have a knack for hosting," Olivia says as we make our way back to our rooms. "Could be one of those TV game show hosts where they wear fancy suits and drink twenty-dollar bottled water." She forces out a laugh, but I see right through it.

"Olivia, stop." She turns but doesn't look at me. I bring a finger under her chin and tilt her head until our eyes meet. "Why did you let her walk all over you like that? I hated taking that from you."

She shrugs, and I reluctantly drop my hand. "Because it's my job to make her happy. It doesn't matter what I want or what I do on the side. Rachel always gets what she wants, and it's just easier to let her do things her way when she changes her mind."

"Just because it's easier doesn't mean it's right."

"Not in my world," she states. "What's it matter anyway? The readers were happy to listen to you talk and crack jokes, so that's all that really matters in the end."

"I wish Rachel knew everything you go through to please her. She takes you for granted. That's easy to see," I tell her sincerely. "We should go out tonight. You need a drink or ten." I flash her a smile, hoping she'll give in.

"I don't know. Rachel has that author reading tomorrow afternoon and…"

"Stop making excuses, Olivia. C'mon. Just one drink." I pout out my lower lip and make pathetic whimpering noises. "Don't make me get on my knees and beg because I will."

She snort-laughs and pushes against my chest. "You're full of shit."

Without missing a beat, I fall to my knees and put my hands out in a pleading hold, batting my eyes with the biggest frowny face I can muster. "Olivia, *please*!" I shout loudly, knowing she'll cave once I start embarrassing her. "Please! Please, please, please!"

"Oh my God!" Olivia squeals, pulling at my hands to lift me, but she's a weakling compared to me. "You're insane! Get up!" She's laughing now, and I know I have her on board. "Fine! Okay, let's go, you psycho!"

"Yes! Victory is mine!" I throw my fist into the air and celebrate.

"One drink! Got it?" she warns me with her puny little finger in my face.

Approximately six mixers and three shots of vodka later, Olivia and I are feeling every ounce of liquor. I'm not sure how many I've had or how many she's had, but the table between us is filled with empty glasses.

"Oh my God, I have an amazing idea!" Olivia shouts over the music, but she's close enough that I can hear her without her shouting. "We should find a karaoke bar!"

"A karaoke bar?" I question. "Are you finally going to serenade me?" I tease. I'm definitely not drunk enough to do karaoke, but Miss Lightweight passed tipsy and buzzed three drinks ago.

"We should do a duet! Oh my God, yes! Let's go!" Olivia bounces in her seat and is on her feet before I can comprehend exactly what she just said. I'm living for this version of her, knowing it's a side I'll probably never see again.

It takes us all of five minutes to find a karaoke bar, and as soon as we walk in, Olivia drags me to the DJ booth to sign us up. I have no idea what she told the guy, but it doesn't matter because he hands us two microphones and then Olivia pulls me up on the mini stage.

"Are you ready?" she asks with the biggest smile.

"That depends. What'd you pick?" I ask her, but as soon as the music starts, I immediately know. "Ah, good choice!"

"It's a classic! I love this song!"

Sonny & Cher's "I Got You Babe" plays loudly over the speakers as the lyrics flash across the little screen in front of us. We sing our parts and then come together for an off-key duet, but it doesn't matter because singing up here with Olivia is the best time I've had in a while. She's laughing and smiling, and even though her pitch is awful, at the same time, it's all perfect. She's not fidgeting with schedules or worrying about controlling anything, and I've never seen her so loose and happy.

We sing the last line, and I take her hand so we can give our audience of fewer than five people a proper bow. They clap with little amusement, and after we hand our microphones back to the DJ, I keep her hand in mine and drag her to a bar top table.

"You are amazing," I tell her sincerely, grabbing a piece of hair stuck to her cheek and tucking it behind her ear. "You were having the time of your life up there."

"I know." She laughs. "You're a good singing partner."

"I told you, I'm a man of many talents." I wink, but her eyes are locked on my mouth.

I swipe my tongue between my lips and watch as her chest rapidly rises and falls. She bites down on her bottom lip, and I bring my finger up to pluck it from her teeth.

"Olivia."

She blinks and brings her eyes to mine. We share a silent moment, but no words are needed to know what we're both thinking. I lean in and dip my head down and carefully brush my mouth against hers, swiping my tongue gently between her lips as I seek entrance. She doesn't pull back, so I take that as a good sign to continue. I wrap a hand around her neck and pull her body into my chest as I cover her mouth with mine. Olivia fists her hands in my shirt and slides her tongue against mine, and soon we're devouring each other, both begging for more.

The moment is getting heated, too heated for a public location, so I unwillingly pull back slightly. "Olivia..." I say between heavy panting. "We should go back to the hotel before—"

"I can't wait that long," she nearly purrs. "I want you right now."

This is definitely not the Olivia I've grown to know the last week and a half, and the last thing I want to do is take advantage of the fact that she's drunk.

"Olivia, we don't have to. You've been drinking and—"

"Maverick, I'm throwing myself at you, and you're going to tell me no?" She pulls back, giving me a look of shock and hurt. "I'm a big girl and can prove to you I'm just fine to make big girl decisions. Want me to walk a straight line and touch my nose? Or say the alphabet backward? ZYXWVUT..."

"Olivia, stop," I say, laughing at the fact that she would have the alphabet memorized backward. "Okay, I believe you."

"Good, now kiss me." She wraps both hands around my neck and pulls our mouths back together.

Fuck, she tastes so damn good. I want to lift her onto this table, push her legs apart, and slide inside her so goddamn deep she'll be feeling me long after this trip ends.

"Let's at least go somewhere private," I plead with her, grabbing her hand and leading her out of the middle of the bar. I have a feeling Olivia has never had sex outside of a bed before, and this wild side of hers is dying for something new. I find a hallway that leads to the restrooms and probably a storage room or two, but before dragging her down there, I turn around and make her face me. "Do you trust me?"

"I trust you not to murder me if that's what you're asking."

I laugh and pull her lips back to mine. "You're adorable. Good enough for me."

Luckily, we ended at a bar off the Strip, and it's not crowded, so I take her into the ladies' bathroom, figuring it'd be the cleaner of the two. As soon as we step inside, I pull her up until her legs are wrapped around my waist, and her back is pressed against the door. She squeals with laughter as I lock the door.

With Olivia's arms wrapped around me and mine holding her ass up, we devour and taste one another. I'm so fucking hard, I know she can feel it against my jeans. I press against her, and when she moans, it's like an electric current has a direct line to my dick.

"Olivia, tell me you want this," I demand. "I need to know you won't regret this in the morning."

"I want you, Maverick. But that doesn't mean I won't regret it. All that matters is I want you right fucking now."

I pull back slightly and set her down on her feet. "That's not good enough. Get out of that head of yours and tell me you won't hate me for this later."

"I promise, I won't hate you. But I really want you to fuck me, so if you don't, then I'll definitely hate you."

Laughing, I wrap one hand around my neck and pull my shirt over my head. "Fuck, you're even hotter when you're a demanding little vixen."

Scooping her up, I carry her to the counter that's actually semi-decent and start undoing her pants. She never changed out of her work clothes, so she's in one of those pantsuits.

"Is it weird I'm now oddly attracted to these business suit things you're always wearing?" I tease.

"Oh yeah?" She unbuttons her jacket and starts untucking her blouse. "Wondering what I was wearing underneath, weren't you?"

"Fucking always," I admit.

"Why don't you come find out?"

CHAPTER SEVENTEEN

OLIVIA

MAVERICK LOOKS at me with so much lust, I think I'll combust if he doesn't get inside me soon. I finish undressing to my bra and panties and watch as he makes a show of wiping the drool off his chin.

"I wish I had time to taste you right now, but that'll have to wait until later."

Later? I like the sound of that.

When he shoves his jeans and boxers halfway down his legs, and his massive erection bounces, it's so much bigger than I remember. Granted, it wasn't actually hard the last time I saw it but holy fuck. Maverick Kingston *is* the whole package.

"I think you're the one drooling now," he taunts, sliding his tongue up my chin and pressing a deep, heated kiss on my mouth.

"Well, you would be too if you saw how big you are," I tease. "I wish I had time to get on my knees and worship it like it deserves." I throw a version of his words back at him, but it's one million percent the truth.

I watch as Maverick reaches into his back pocket and grabs his wallet. He pulls out a condom and rolls it over his length. I've never had bathroom sex before—or sex outside the bedroom period—so I let him take the lead. He takes me by surprise when he leans in and slowly kisses me, cupping my cheek with one hand, then gently easing himself between my legs. I do my best to arch my hips with the awkward position I'm in, but my body quickly adjusts, and soon he's in so fucking deep, I'm panting and moaning with the best pleasure I've felt in my life.

He pulls back slightly before ramming back inside me. Everything between us is fire and electricity, and I almost beg for more. Maverick dips his head to my neck, feathering kisses along my jawline and shoulder as he increases his pace, making my world spin over and over again.

"Goddammit, Olivia...you're so fucking tight. You feel so good," he growls in my ear, squeezing my hip as he pins me harder against the counter and mirror. "Your pussy is fucking amazing."

"Don't stop, Maverick. God, yesssss…" My head falls back slightly, but his other hand catches it and brings our mouths back together.

"You need it, don't you, sweetheart?" he asks in a rugged, deep voice that has me panting for more.

I nod in response, and before I can ask what he's doing, he has me bent over the sink with my ass in the air and his cock deep inside me. His hand smacks against my ass once, twice, and then I'm moaning for more.

"That's it, baby. Arch that back for me." He slides his hand up my spine, pushing my shoulders lower and when he's satisfied, he grabs my hips and pulls me back on his dick. "I'm gonna go so fucking deep. Hang on."

Maverick's promise has me so wet that when he hits the right spot, I scream out his name and beg him to keep going. He pushes harder and faster, and soon I'm spiraling into oblivion. The buildup is fast and sudden, and when he reaches around my waist to rub my clit, it sends me over until my body is shaking with the biggest release I've ever had. I barely come down before he's sinking deeper into me and sending me off the edge once again.

"Oh my God, Maverick. I can't…" I pant, losing my breath as he chases his own orgasm.

"So close, baby...you feel so goddamn good. I don't want it to end," he admits, sliding his hand around my chest and squeezing my breast. "And fuck, your tits are amazing too. Go figure." I watch him in the mirror, and he's smirking at me.

"I bet you're dying to taste them," I tease, knowing when we're back at the hotel he'll take every opportunity to do just that.

"Fuck yes, I am."

I bite my lower lip just thinking about it and lower my eyes to where our bodies are connected in the reflection.

"Keep your eyes on me, Olivia. I want you to see what you do to me. What you've been doing to me. I want there to be no doubt in your mind." His words are so intense that my eyes are glued to his, and when his body finally goes rigid and shakes against mine, I watch him as he unravels inside me. His eyes squeeze tight, his jaw clenches, and his nails dig into my hips. It's fucking beautiful.

Maverick comes with a deep groan, and my body tightens around him as he fills me. Moments pass, and then he's pulling out and tossing the condom away.

"We better get out of here before someone catches us," he instructs as we layer our clothes on. "Then I'm taking you to my room and worshipping you all over again."

My phone alarm goes off, waking me out of a deep sleep. I roll over to turn it off and smack hard into a wall.

"Argh," I groan, feeling the immediate headache coming on. I drank more last night than I ever have before. I'm gonna need to find some meds stat.

"Mornin', beautiful." Maverick's deep, sleepy voice echoes out, and my eyes immediately shoot open.

Last night was definitely *not* a dream.

Wrapping an arm around my shoulders, he pulls me tighter to his body. Memories of our time together flash through my mind as panic starts to weigh on my chest.

What the hell did I do? I could lose my job over this. Rachel was adamant about her rules, and I just bulldozed over them. If she finds out, my career is completely over. Not only would she fire me, but she wouldn't give me the recommendation I'd need to find another job.

I'd be screwed.

"I can hear your thoughts racing a million miles an hour. Talk to me, Olivia." Maverick's tone is somehow smooth and rough at the same time, almost as if he's expecting me to freak out.

"I should go to my room before Rachel finds out I'm not there." I scramble to the edge of the bed, but Maverick grabs my wrist and holds me in place until he shifts his body behind me.

"Baby, wait."

Baby? Oh my God.

"Maverick, I can't. This...shouldn't have happened. I'm going to lose my job, everything." I jerk out of his grip and stand, taking the sheet with me to wrap around myself. Our clothes are littered all over the floor.

"Not if she doesn't find out," he tells me, which almost makes me laugh. Rachel's like a Russian spy. She finds out everything she needs to know, and the guilt written all over my face will be as obvious as Maverick's six-pack abs.

Leaning down to pick up my shirt and pants, I eye my panties and bra and scoop them up next.

"It doesn't matter either way. You and I both know this was a one-night thing. You're going home today, and I'll be praying I still have a job when I fly back to Chicago."

We still have one event left this morning, so I can plaster on a smile and fake it until it's over. Thank God the tour is coming to an end.

"You're overthinking this," Maverick tries to tell me, and when I look up at him, he's sitting on the edge of the bed pulling up his boxer shorts.

"No, I wasn't thinking—*period*." Taking my clothes, I walk into the bathroom and get dressed. I look at myself in the mirror, and my jaw drops. Maverick left bite marks on my neck and chest, and my hair is the exact definition of sex hair. Quickly, I change and try to fix my hair and makeup.

I can't chance running into Rachel before I can take a shower.

As soon as I open the bathroom door, Maverick is standing in the doorway, blocking my way out.

"Olivia, stay. Take a shower, and we can talk after. You don't need to rush off," he says. His words and voice are so genuine; if this were any other situation, I'd even consider it.

"I'm going to shower and change for the event in my room, and there's nothing to discuss. Last night happened, and there's nothing we can do about it now."

"Do about it?" His voice goes higher. "So last night meant nothing to you?" He stands tall with his arms crossed over his chest. "Is that what you're telling me?"

"I'm saying…" I linger, finally walking past him to gather my phone and shoes. "Considering the precedence our boss set, it shouldn't have happened."

"Fuck that, Olivia. Quit worrying about your job and just admit what you actually feel for once."

"I have to go." I find my purse, slip my shoes on, and head toward the door. Before opening it, I pause. "Rachel's reading is at noon. Meet me down in the lobby in an hour so we can go."

"I'm aware of the schedule, Olivia," he replies harshly.

"Good, just reminding you." I glance over my shoulder and see the pained expression on his face, and it kills me. "Please remember to act like nothing happened. Rachel will notice if something's off between us."

"Shouldn't be a problem for me. You're the one running away."

I part my lips to say something but decide against it and make my way out of his room. Once I'm in the hallway, I exhale a deep breath, feeling the emotions piling on top as I push away my pain.

An hour later, I'm showered and ready to go. Rachel has already texted me three times, and I'm trying to mentally prepare myself, so she doesn't suspect a thing, though I'm wondering if Maverick will be able to keep his word.

"Where's Maverick?" Rachel's voice booms behind me, and I jump. Her tone is short and cold.

"Uh," I start, feeling flustered.

"I just had to make a quick stop to the bathroom," Maverick chimes in before I can respond. I glance over and see he's wearing a big smile.

Today, Rachel will read the first six chapters of the first book in the Bayshore Coast series at a local Barnes & Noble. Afterward, she'll sign books that people bring or bought, and then the tour will be complete.

"Olivia," Maverick whispers next to me as we stand to the side.

Rachel is standing behind a podium with her book reading to her audience.

"What?" I ask without facing him.

"We need to talk."

I look over my shoulder at him and frown. "There's nothing to discuss."

"Like hell there isn't," he whisper-shouts, causing a few people to look over at us.

I scold him with my eyes to keep it down. He grabs my elbow and pulls me with him as he walks to a secluded part of the bookstore behind some shelves.

"What do you think you're doing?" I whisper-shout back at him.

"I want to know why you're acting as if last night never happened. I know you feel what I feel, Olivia. You might have this preconceived notion that I'm some kind of man whore, but we've been dancing around each other since day one. We have a connection, and there's no denying it. You aren't just some chick I picked up at the bar, and I'm not some guy you randomly met. So tell me how you can just pretend there's nothing between us?"

I meet his dark eyes, and I see the sincerity in them. His voice is deep and low, and I hate how pained it sounds.

"You know as well as I do that we could never work out, so I'm not going to live in a fantasy world and pretend that it could. I told you I could lose my career over this, so excuse me for not announcing it to the world that we slept together!"

"So that means you're going to erase last night from your memory? That's what you want? To act like we never happened and pretend our feelings don't exist?" He steps closer, narrowing the gap between us. I can smell his cologne, and it smells so fucking good, I want to drown in it.

"We have to, Maverick. Otherwise, we're just going to hurt more. Don't you understand? If I let myself fall for you, I'll end up with a broken heart. I'm married to my job. You're building a career in LA. You don't fly, so it's not like we could easily see each other. Last night was amazing, okay? But it can't ever happen again."

"I know the cards are stacked against us, but I also know that if

I let you walk away without putting everything out there, I'd regret it. Give us a chance." He cups my face and rubs the pad of his thumb along my cheek. I wish I could say the words he desperately wants to hear, but I just can't.

I inhale deeply, trying to hold back the tears. "I'm sorry, Maverick."

Stepping away, I walk back toward the reading without looking back.

Getting your heart broken is one thing, but breaking someone else's heart is torture.

CHAPTER EIGHTEEN

MAVERICK

Today is so fucking bittersweet, but it feels like a black cloud is hanging over me. Soon, I'll be back in Los Angeles, and it will be the end of Olivia's and my road, which she reminded me of at the signing. It passed by in a blur. I faked a smile and laugh, but her words fucking destroyed me. Olivia, in her typical fashion, put up a brick wall, and she won't allow me through. I'm hurt, and I'm pissed, and I wish for once she would just stop with the act. The way she kissed me last night meant something. We weren't just fucking. It was more emotional than that, and when I looked into her eyes, I know she felt it. I refuse to allow her to deny it and deny me.

After the signing, I go up to my room and pace around, wondering what I'm going to say. This isn't over. The smell of her body still lingers in my room, and I've got to escape it before I drive myself crazy. I pack my shit, then go downstairs to wait before she feels the need to send me a reminder text. At the beginning of this trip, I was ready for it to be over, but now I don't want it to end. And I don't think she does either.

I sit on a bench by the front door and wait for her, and I can't seem to shake this feeling. It's almost like an elephant is sitting on my chest. The days have been passing by so quick, and tomorrow when I wake up without Olivia, things will be different. And I'm not so sure that's a good thing. I've never felt this way about someone before. She's so fucking special, and forcing myself to forget her would be one of the greatest regrets of my life.

She eventually makes it downstairs but barely looks my way. I follow her out to the car, and the strain between us practically smothers me. Once we're on the highway, I randomly glance over at her, and she's paying zero attention to me as if I don't even exist. The tension is so thick it could cut through steel, and I hate it. Regardless of all my attempts to talk to her, she's purposely ignoring me. Olivia has already blocked me out, and it pisses me off because our time together is limited. It's not supposed to be like this. We shared something so intimate, and by the way she's acting right now, she's already erased it from her memory.

She's buried herself in her work, something I've learned she does when she's trying to avoid me. With one swift movement, I snatch her planner and roll down the window. I know I've already threatened her with this once, but I'm more serious than ever.

"Maverick. I swear to everything holy that if you let go of that planner, I will never forgive you."

I hear the pages fluttering in the wind and can tell she's overly annoyed, but it's the first time I've held her attention all day. I pull the planner inside and throw it in the back seat. When she turns around to grab it, I place my palm on her face and force her to look at me. With everything I am, I try to keep my attention on the road, but she needs to hear what I have to say.

"Olivia. Just stop for five minutes, okay?" I look forward and notice we're heading straight into standstill traffic. Just what I need to tell her what I have to say. Once we're stopped, I let out a deep breath. Taillights go on for miles, and while it's annoying, I'm thankful for the extra time I'll get to spend with her, even if she isn't. There's always traffic crossing the border to California, and it could take anywhere from thirty minutes to three hours to get through it, and by the look on Olivia's face, I know she wasn't prepared for it. Considering I drive everywhere, I was well aware, and for the first time ever, I'm happy to be waiting.

"After I lost my dad, I promised myself I wouldn't live my life with regrets, and that's why I take so many risks. But I know that if we head back to LA and go our separate ways without me telling you exactly how I feel or hearing you admit that our night together meant something, then I'll drown in the what-could've-beens. Olivia, I like you, okay? Like *really* like you. And I think you like me too." I look at her, and her eyes soften.

"I'm sure you tell that to a lot of women," she tries to joke, but I don't crack a smile.

"I don't. That's the thing. You have this made-up version of me where I'm this playboy who just wines and dines all these women and it's not true. There's not been anyone worth my time who has made me feel like this until you. Last night was something really fucking special. I'm not going to sit here and let you run from that. I refuse."

She swallows hard, and I watch as she tucks her bottom lip into her mouth. Gently, I place my thumb under her chin and lean forward, pulling that lip into my mouth and sucking on it. At first, she tenses, but not even she can deny how she truly feels. Olivia breaks down and kisses me back, pouring herself into me. Her tongue swipes against mine, and I want to devour her. As our kiss deepens, honking horns pull us apart, and we both laugh as I drive forward.

"If Rachel…"

"I don't give two shits about what Rachel thinks. We're consenting adults and can do whatever we want. It's not her business what anyone does behind closed doors, especially you. Stop letting her run your life outside of work. Stop using her as an excuse to run from your feelings, okay? I'm not ashamed of what happened, Olivia."

"I'm not either," she says, and I almost see her crack a smile.

"The difference between us is, I want the world to know how I feel about you, but you're okay with keeping me as a secret, tucked away to be forgotten as soon as you get on that plane to Chicago."

She shakes her head. "It's not like that, Maverick. I do have feelings for you, but we live a world apart. And who's to say, once we're not on the road, that things would even work out between us? I have my job and life in Chicago, and yours is in LA. So where does that leave us?"

Traffic begins to move more quickly, and soon we're crossing the border into California.

"It leaves us trying. Isn't what we have worth that, at least?"

She looks out the window, and I catch a glimpse of her reflection. Somber, it's the only way I can describe it. I don't push it any further, because I want to enjoy the time I have left with her. The clock is ticking, and with each passing second, I feel her slipping through my fingers.

Eventually, we make it to Los Angeles, two hours past when we were expected to arrive, which isn't surprising. I drive to my condo, and when I pull into the driveway, I look over at her.

"Well, I guess this is goodbye," she says, her tone flat.

I tuck a loose strand of hair behind her ear. "It doesn't have to be. Just one more night, Olivia. Please."

"But I have a hotel reserved already," she reminds me as if that matters. She's still trying to push me away, still trying to avoid what she's feeling. Her words can spew lies but her body can't.

I lean forward and whisper softly across her lips. "Cancel it." She parts her lips just slightly before closing her mouth again. "I'm only asking for one night. Say yes, Olivia." Her breath hitches before I close the gap between our lips.

"Okay," she says, breathlessly. "Yes."

The electricity streaming between us is so strong, I know she can't deny it. I turn off the car and pull the keys from the ignition. We both step out and grab our bags. I only asked her to stay one night, so this feels like a final goodbye, but I push the thoughts away. She grabs her laptop bag, but I take it from her hands and place it back in the trunk and shut it.

"Not tonight." I refuse to let her ignore me because of work.

She lets out a laugh. "I kinda like this side of you. Almost like a real-life Ian."

"Yeah? Well, hang on to your panties, sweetheart. There's more where that came from."

I punch in the code to my door, and we walk inside. She leaves her bags by the door and looks around.

"Shall I give you the grand tour?" I ask, smirking.

"I'd love one," Olivia replies with a grin. She follows me into the living room and looks at the photos of my family on the mantle. "This is your dad?"

I stand behind her and wrap my arms around her body, nodding. "Yeah. This is the plane we used for all our family trips."

"Wow. That would've been amazing." Her voice sounds so sweet.

"It was. Some of the best times of my life were in that plane."

She sets the picture down and picks up the next one. "This is your brother and sister?"

I glance at it, and we're all standing in front of a Christmas tree. "Yep. It was taken a few years ago."

"Holy shit! Is your entire family beautiful?" She laughs, glancing at the picture of my mom and all of us.

I set the picture down and spin her around until she's facing me, and I hold her close. "Are you hungry?"

"For you," she whispers. I pop an eyebrow at her before she stands on her tiptoes and steals a kiss.

"Hi there. My name is Maverick," I tease, and she playfully smacks my chest.

"If you introduce yourself to me one more time…" Olivia warns.

With one swift movement, I lift her into my arms.

She lets out a scream followed by a laugh as I walk us toward my bedroom. "Put me down!"

"No can do, sweetheart." I set her down on my bed. Blond hair cascades around her head, and at this moment, she's picture perfect. She props herself up on elbows and watches me as I unbutton my shirt. When it drops to the floor, she stands and walks toward me.

"Need some help?" she asks, unbuttoning my pants. I love it when she takes control, and I willingly allow her to.

I run my fingers through her hair and lean down to kiss her, wanting to inhale her—all of her. Pulling back, I peel her shirt off her body and toss it to the floor. My fingers brush across her soft skin as I reach around and undo her black lacy bra, causing goose bumps to surface.

"Fuck, Olivia. You're so beautiful." I lean down, taking her nipple in my mouth. Her head falls back on her shoulders as she runs her fingers through my hair.

"I need you," she whispers, and I smile as my lips memorize her body, loving her admission.

Carefully, I unzip her skirt and slide it down her body along with her pantyhose. She kicks off her heels, and I hook my fingers in her panties and help her step out of them. Olivia stands naked and confident, and I take a few seconds to soak in her flawless curves.

She reaches for me, scooting my boxers down my body and wraps her hand around my erection. A moan escapes me, and this only encourages her to continue stroking me. I'm putty in her hands, and she knows it.

Before I lose control, I move Olivia back to the bed. Her eyes flutter closed as I kiss up her calf, between her thighs, and find her sweet spot. Gasps and moans fill the room as my tongue twirls against her clit. Olivia rocks her hips against my mouth until her breathing increases.

"Not yet," I growl. She's a greedy little thing, and I love it. As I pull away, she releases an annoyed pant, and I chuckle, teasing her with flicks of my tongue. Pushing herself up on her elbows, she glares at me, which only causes me to burst out laughing.

"You're so damn sassy," I tell her.

"You're teasing the fuck out of me on purpose," she says with a sexy smirk. "Just wait. I'll get you back."

I hum against her clit, which only causes her to writhe against me. As she becomes greedier, I grab her ass cheeks and pull her closer to my mouth. I take all of her, licking and flicking and sucking her clit, watching her come undone beneath me. With arched hips, her body tenses, and within moments, she's losing herself against my tongue. I taste her, not wasting a drop as she rides her release.

Olivia is panting, her chest rapidly rising and falling, as I crawl onto the bed and hover above her. She leans up and kisses my lips, tasting herself.

Slowly, I enter her, filling her with my length. With sharp nails, she scratches down my back as I rock back and forth, enjoying the moment. We're slowly falling in the abyss together where the only thing that matters is us. Time makes no difference—only the right now. I need her as much as she needs me. We're two broken people mending together to create a whole, and I don't ever want to let her go.

Emotions roll through me, and it feels like an out-of-body

experience as I look into her hooded eyes. Is it too soon to have these types of feelings for someone I met only two weeks ago? I could love her if she'd let me. If she'd tear down her walls and let me inside, I'd give her everything.

Her body tenses and tightens as her mouth ravages mine. Our tongues twist together, and there's nothing in the world that I want other than her.

"More," she demands. I increase my pace and ram into her harder, giving her exactly what she needs. Soon, she's bucking beneath me, screaming my name for all of LA to hear. The orgasm builds so quickly that soon, I'm losing control too. I feel as if I'm free-falling straight into Olivia's heart as she holds me tight against her warm, soft body. I wish we could stay here forever, but I know that's not an option in her eyes.

After we clean up, I pull her into my arms as she lays her head against my chest.

"I'm really going to miss you, Maverick."

It feels like the end, but I refuse to let it be. "I'm going to miss you, too, Miss Priss."

She lets out a laugh as she playfully slaps my chest. I kiss her on the forehead, and we lie together in silence. The past two weeks flash through my mind, from the moment we first met until now, and a smile fills my face.

Eventually, I fall asleep with Olivia in my arms, and I hold her as tight as I can, almost afraid she'll disappear if I let go.

I sleep without dreaming, and when the sun peeks through my curtains, I roll over and reach for her. My eyes flutter open, and I realize she's gone. The bed is cold where her body once was, and I'm hurt she didn't wake me before leaving, but then again, I know it might've been too hard to really say goodbye.

After everything we shared during our trip, I just don't know how I'll be able to move on from Olivia—or if I'll ever want to.

CHAPTER NINETEEN

OLIVIA

"I NEED a tuna salad wrap to go, please," I tell the cashier, pulling out my card. "And a skinny vanilla latte."

Once I pay and grab my order, I rush down the street in a maze through the crowd of people. With my messenger bag slung over my shoulder, carrying my planners and shoes, I'm jogging back to Rachel's house before she scolds me for being late. I've already been working on her next year's book signing tour among a dozen other tasks. It's only been a week since I returned from LA, but it already feels like a distant memory.

Except for Maverick.

Everything about him is front and center in my mind. The way he smells, the taste of his lips, the sound of his laughter...

He texted me the day after I left to make sure I made it home safely. After I told him I did and thanked him for checking on me, I apologized for not saying goodbye because I didn't want to wake him so early. It wasn't a complete lie, but I also couldn't stand to see that hurt look in his eyes. I also knew if I had to say goodbye, I might change my mind. I couldn't risk hurting him.

Maverick said he understood and hoped we'd keep in touch.

I didn't text him back after that.

"Here you devil," I whisper, throwing Angel her treat so she won't bark at me as soon as I walk into the apartment.

I walk into Rachel's office, set her food and coffee down, then head back to my desk and start going over my to-do list.

When I'm finally able to check my phone, I see two new messages from Maverick. I don't know why I feel all giddy inside from just seeing his name on my screen, but my heart is racing as I anticipate what he said.

Maverick: Do you think my spray tan is too dark? I have a photo shoot tomorrow.

The next message is a picture of him holding up his shirt and showing off his too-perfect abs. I snort and shake my head at his obnoxiousness.

Olivia: Considering you're only showing a small part of your body, it's too hard to tell.

Maverick: Fair point. Hold on.

Oh God. What does that mean? He's not going to send me a nude, is he?

Would I want him to?

Maverick: What about now?

He then sends me a picture of a mirror shot of his backside, *naked*. Bare ass and all.

Olivia: Are you going to be showing that part of your body in the shoot?

Maverick: No. But I got a full body spray tan, so my question still stands.

I swallow, thinking how to respond. This is the playful side of Maverick I enjoy. Granted, he was usually poking fun at me, but I can't deny that he made that road trip an experience I'll never forget.

Olivia: I think it looks satisfactory. No complaints.

Maverick: Satisfactory? Okay, thanks, Grandma.

Olivia: What? It looks great. Better? I've never had someone show me their ass before to ask how their tan was, so forgive me.

Maverick: Apology accepted.

Olivia: So wait. You do spray tans naked? Like naked naked?

Maverick: Yep. Even my dick has a nice tan. Wanna see?

Olivia: No! Don't you dare send me a dick pic.

Maverick: Oh yeah, forgot you're a prude. Better delete my abs and ass picture just in case ;)

Olivia: Why do you live to make me crazy?

Maverick: I got so used to doing it every day, and now I'm going through withdrawals.

Olivia: Funny.

Maverick: I try. So how's it been back to work in the office? Missing my rock 'n' roll music, aren't you?

Olivia: Torture as always. Rachel's on my ass about everything, so nothing new. No actually. It's been stuck in my head for days, though.

Maverick: It's washing out your classical sleepy crap.

Olivia: I beg to differ.

Maverick: I like it when you beg.

Olivia: Maverick. Don't.

Maverick: If I recall when I had you bent over, it was "Maverick, don't stop."

Olivia: I'm going to smack you.

The next message is the same picture of his ass except now it's zoomed in.

Maverick: I'll be ready for it.

"Olivia!" Rachel's voice snaps me away from my phone, and she looks like she's about to pop a blood vessel. "Can you get me that email now?"

"Yes. Yes, of course." I scramble to my laptop and search for the email she told me she wanted earlier. I can't get the stupid, goofy grin off my face thinking about Maverick and his text messages. I can even hear his voice reading them, and it has me blushing all over again. "Just sent it to you."

"Pay attention next time, please."

You're welcome, I'm tempted to say but keep my mouth tight-lipped. Saying the words thank you might actually damage her throat.

I finish the day with an achy back and sore feet as usual, but I wait until I'm home to take off my shoes. Deciding to take a bath, I start stripping my clothes as I walk to the bathroom and turn on the water. I glance down at my phone to check the time and set it on the edge of the tub. It's been such a long week. Rachel has me working even longer days, so I've had zero time to recover since returning from the tour. I wish she would've given me a few days off, but that'd be too convenient.

Just as I'm sliding into my tub, I hear my phone ding, and my stomach flutters with anticipation. I didn't have a chance to reply to Maverick's last message, and I'm not convinced texting is a good idea, considering our feelings for each other.

Regardless, I grab the phone and smile when I see his name.

Maverick: What are you doing right now?

Deciding to mess with him, I send him a snapshot of my feet poking out of the bathwater.

Maverick: Are you seriously in the tub right now?

Olivia: Yep. Long day. Everything hurts.

Maverick: So you're naked?

I chuckle, knowing he's focusing hard on that very fact right now.

Olivia: That's typically how you take a bath.

Maverick: And I'm sorry you had a long, hard day. I'd rub your muscles for you if I could.

Olivia: I'm sure that's all you'd do.

Maverick: Well, I was trying to be a gentleman, but if you want to know the truth…

I bite my lip and send him another text.

Olivia: Okay, tell me…

Maverick: I'd give you a full body massage with some scented oils and make sure to cover every inch of your incredible body. I have big, strong hands, so you'd be moaning and begging for more—of the massage, I mean. I'd rub out all your knots and take care of all your soreness. Then I'd flip you to your back and take care of all your other needs.

Fuck, that sounds like heaven. I could really use all that right now.

Olivia: I like the sound of that. Too bad you're like a million miles away.

Maverick: That doesn't mean I can't help you relax in other ways.

Olivia: Oh yeah? Enlighten me.

Maverick: Slide your hand between your thighs.

Olivia: Are you serious?

Maverick: Do it, Olivia. Don't you trust me?

I sigh.

Olivia: Of course, I do.

Maverick: Then tell me how tight you feel. Slide your fingers inside. Are you wet?

Olivia: I'm in the bathtub. My whole body is wet.

Maverick: Funny.

Olivia: I thought so. *shrugs* Fine.

Maverick: Rub your clit.

Olivia: I am. It's really sensitive tonight.

Maverick: Good. I wish I could suck on it. Taste you. Slide my tongue inside your pussy and feel your body tighten around me.

Holy shit. How are his words making me so incredibly hot? Is this sexting? How does Maverick make me feel so damn comfortable in just a matter of hours? It's like no time has gone by, and we are right back to where we were before our awkward last day together.

Olivia: I'd like that, too.

Maverick: I know you would, sweetheart. But for now, just picture I'm there with you. Imagine it's my fingers inside you, fucking you and making you scream.

Oh God. Yes, I want *all* of that.

Olivia: I'm close, Maverick. My body is begging for it.

Maverick: Let go, baby. I'm right there with you.

My breathing picks up, and as I picture his hands and lips on me, I increase my pace until I'm riding a wave of intense pleasure. *Fuck.* That was definitely needed.

Olivia: Thank you.

Maverick: Are you seriously thanking me right now?

Olivia: Yes. Thank you for helping me relax.

Maverick: It was my pleasure. Let me know if I can help you with anything else.

Olivia: I'll talk to you later, Maverick. Good night.

Maverick: Night, Olivia.

That night, I go to bed feeling more relaxed than I have in months and with a big, stupid smile on my face.

Maverick: I can't believe you watch this crap.

Olivia: It's my guilty pleasure. Shut up.

Maverick: Kendall is seriously the dumbest chick I've ever seen. Cooper is a tool for even hooking up with her. This whole setup is crazy.

I can't help the smile on my face knowing Maverick is watching *Bachelor in Paradise* with me even though he claims to hate it. He secretly enjoys it, though he'll never admit it. This has been our Sunday night tradition for the past few weeks. We text during commercials, and he tells me how annoying everyone is.

Olivia: That's why it's called a guilty pleasure. Reality TV is always crazy! That's how they get their views.

Maverick: Well, it's killing brain cells. Also, Kendall's tits are totally fake.

Olivia: Obviously. They don't even bounce. That's how you know.

Maverick: They probably feel like bags of rocks.

Olivia: You'd probably know.

Maverick: Yours felt real to me. *Shrugs*

Olivia: Not me, asshole! Isn't LA full of fake boobs and nose jobs?

Maverick: Stereotypical.

Olivia: Not when I'm right.

Maverick: Isn't Chicago full of gangsters and sugar daddies?

Olivia: That sounds mostly right, though technically it's home to the best pizza in the world. Have you ever tried Chicago-style pizza?

Maverick: I have in LA, but I'm sure you're going to say it's not the same?

Olivia: Hell no! You need to experience it for real. In Chicago.

Maverick: Maybe someday.

Maybe someday. I know what that means.

It makes me sad when I think about how we'll probably never see each other face-to-face again. I don't plan to fly to LA anytime soon, and unless he plans to drive almost forty hours to Chicago, this is all we'll ever have. Even though it hurts to know that, I'd rather have his friendship like this than nothing at all. It's nice having someone to talk to who isn't barking orders at me all day long.

Olivia: I'd like that. OMG, Kendall just kissed Josh? WTF?

Maverick: Told you. She sucks.

Olivia: Hahaha... yeah she does.

Maverick: You owe me twenty bucks now!

Olivia: Ugh. Now you suck.

Maverick: Pay up, baby.

We make a bet every episode on who's going to "cheat" on their love interest, and I've lost every single week.

Olivia: How about I pay you another way?

Maverick: ...I'm listening.

Olivia: Take off your pants.

Maverick: It's cute you thought I was wearing pants this whole time.

Olivia: Argh. You ruined it.

Maverick: You're even more adorable when you get all flustered.

Olivia: I'm just gonna send you the money.

Maverick: Ha! There's my uptight city girl. I'm in my boxers... tell me what to do next.

Olivia: I want you to show me.

Maverick: I'm sorry. Have we met? I'm Maverick. And you are?

Olivia: Not funny.

Maverick: I'm laughing my ass off, so I beg to differ. Also, dick pic coming at you.

Olivia: Maverick, wait!

Too late.
And there he is in all his thick, hard glory.
I swallow then lick my lips, wishing I hadn't seen it.
Actually, that's a lie. I want all of it.

CHAPTER TWENTY

MAVERICK

Texting with Olivia has been the only thing keeping me going since she left. I'm not much of a texter, but I can't get enough of it with her, and I look forward to it every day. I know she told me things could never work out between us, but these past few weeks have me hanging on to the hope that she'll change her mind and we'll figure something out together.

Between shoots and trying to keep up with my emails, I check in with her to make sure she's having a good day, and I look forward to making her smile or laugh at night when it's just the two of us. I don't even mind watching her ridiculous TV shows if it means we have something fun to talk about.

Maverick: I had a dream about you last night. You were wearing a naughty nurse outfit.

Olivia: Was it Halloween?

Maverick: Nope.

Olivia: Then it was definitely a dream.

Maverick: A dirty fantasy.

Olivia: Keep dreaming.

Maverick: You're the star in all my dreams, so if I drift off...

Olivia: You're crazy.

Maverick: It's why you like me.

Olivia: Debatable.

Maverick: So I have a shoot this afternoon. Do you want to FaceTime after?

We've only strictly texted up to this point, but I want to see her face. I miss the cute little quirky expressions she makes. The way she bites her lip, wrinkles her nose, and scolds me with narrowed eyes. I wouldn't mind seeing her O face again either.

Olivia: Um... maybe.

Maverick: C'mon, Olivia. Don't you miss my adorable face?

Olivia: No, because it's normally talking and saying arrogant things like that.

Maverick: Can't turn the charm off, baby.

Olivia: So I've heard. What time do you want to chat tonight?

Maverick: How's 6 your time?

Olivia: I'll be here.

I smile victoriously when she finally agrees. I've loved texting back and forth with her, but nothing compares to actually seeing her gorgeous face. Olivia Carpenter is my girl, and I'm going to do whatever's possible to prove it to her.

"Maverick, shirt and jeans off. Mess up your hair a bit too," Jeannie orders five seconds after I walk into the studio.

"What? Not gonna even buy me dinner first?"

"Cute. I have thirty minutes, Mav." She waves a finger at me to start stripping.

I've done several shoots with Jeannie before, so I enjoy messing with her and getting her worked up. She's doing new shots for me so my agent can send them to agencies for magazines for their winter issues. I'd really love to be able to do another campaign for Calvin Klein or Levi's again, but that's part of the job. I'm never sure when my next gig will be, so I just keep going, hoping someone picks me up.

"Great, let's do some head shots. Put a shirt on and give me your best smolder," she directs after twenty minutes of full body shots in various angles and positions.

She reminds me a little of Olivia. Blunt and direct. Always to the point. It's so much hotter when it comes from Olivia, though.

Once we're done, I thank her and head out. I'm dying to talk to Olivia again. I've never been this lovesick over a woman before, but I know she isn't just "some girl."

Maverick: I'm gonna grab something to eat and then I'll be ready to chat. You?

I watch as the dots jump on the screen as she replies, but then it stops. Finally, a minute passes, and she replies.

Olivia: Sure, I can make that work.

Something feels off, and I'm not sure what it is, but either way, I'm excited. Not seeing her after a month has been way too damn long.

Maverick: You should eat with me. Are you hungry?

Olivia: What are you talking about?

Maverick: I want to eat with you. Have you had dinner yet?

Olivia: No. Been running around for Rachel all day. Just about to walk into my apartment.

Maverick: Perfect. Change into something comfortable, and I'll take care of dinner.

Olivia: Wait. What?

Maverick: Do you trust me?

Olivia: *Sigh* Yes. Fine.

Maverick: Good. I'll call you in twenty.

I do some Google searches on my phone and am soon placing an order for delivery. She never lets anyone take care of her, and I'm about to change that.

Before I head home, I pick up an order of Chinese food, and once I get the notification that Olivia's food has been delivered, I grab my laptop and call her.

"Hey," she answers with a smug grin. "You didn't have to do that."

"I wanted to. Plus, I knew you'd skip dinner if I didn't feed you," I reply, holding my plate up for her to see. "And now we can eat Chinese together."

"It's delicious. If you weren't watching me, I'd be stuffing my face right now." She chuckles, getting comfortable on her couch with a plateful of food.

"Uh, when has that ever stopped you before? I've seen you inhale a bacon double cheeseburger."

She laughs, and the sound is like music to my ears. "To be fair, that was a damn good burger."

"I love seeing you smile, Olivia. I've missed it," I tell her sincerely.

"It's definitely been a long time since I've felt like smiling. Rachel just finished going through the plotting and outlining phase, so she's not sleeping much, which makes my job even more hell than usual. She even called on my day off to ask if I knew where her coffee filters were. THEY WERE LITERALLY ON TOP OF THE COFFEEMAKER," she shouts, but the face she makes with it has me bending over laughing my ass off.

"Tell me why you put up with her again?" I ask, genuinely wanting to know. Olivia is amazing, and I hate that she gets treated like scum. "You're smart, babe. You could run your own PR marketing company."

She looks down and shrugs. "I know she means well. I can't afford not to have a job, and the pay is great. Rachel even offers full benefits and holiday pay. That's a hard thing to walk away from. I'd love to start my own company, but I'd never have enough to cover the start-up costs."

"Plenty of new business owners take out loans for that type of thing. I think you should do it. You have so much knowledge about publishing and that whole community that you'd have clients in no time. Then you'd have to start hiring people to help with the workload. I can see it now." I flash her a bright smile, wanting her to know I mean every word.

"I don't know," she says reluctantly, moving the food around on her plate. "That sounds wonderful in theory, but there's a lot of competition for that. There's a lot of reputable PR companies already out there who are established. I'd be a small fish in a huge pond."

"You're preaching to the choir, babe. I'm a model. Living in LA. Could I be any more cliché?"

That makes her laugh, and she agrees with a nod.

"How's your food? Is it as good as mine?" I ask, changing the subject to ease the tension.

"It's quite delicious. You picked good."

"I'm glad you approve."

"I was ready to beat the delivery driver with a plastic bat. No one ever knocks on my door," she tells me.

"And you were going to protect yourself with a kid's baseball bat?" I ask, chuckling in amusement.

"It was all I could find! Someone knocking on my door unexpectedly spooked me."

"You're adorable," I say, staring at her. I know she hates compliments like that, but I can't help it. I miss her so damn much. "So any plans for another trip soon?"

"Not until next year. She has this new series planned, and her publisher is going nuts over it. They want to send her all over and even to Canada. There's even been talk about her going to Germany and France."

"Wow...that's a big step from our road trip."

"Uh, yeah. Rachel lives for the high life. She'll probably complain the entire time but secretly love it. I'm clearly looking so forward to it." She rolls her eyes just like I've come to adore.

"I wish you were closer."

"I know. We already went down that road, Maverick. I live here, and you live there."

"But I want you here," I tell her, pouting out my lower lip. "It's warm and sunny year-round. We have the best food trucks, and as added bonus, I'm here." I wink at her, and she gives me a dramatic sigh.

"I like talking to you, Maverick. When you aren't threatening to throw my planner out the window or taunting me with your abs, I consider you one of my closest friends. Hell, aside from Vada, you're really my only friend. But that's all I can offer. You know this." Her words are soft and tender, but that doesn't stop it from feeling like a knife just pierced through my heart.

"A friend? I think you and I both know we're more than friends. You should know I want more with you. After waking up without you in my bed, I knew my heart was already yours. I'd never cared about a chick bailing on me. It was the first time I felt heartache. I understood why you did it, but it didn't stop it from hurting."

"Maverick..." She says my name with a sad tone. "Perhaps we should've just left whatever this is in LA. You're only going to get hurt again."

"I don't want to just forget everything that happened between us. If text messages and FaceTime is all we can ever have, then I'll take it. I'll take whatever you give me," I tell her, hoping like hell she'll say she can at least do that. I knew long distance would be hard, but I'm not giving up without a fight. "I'm falling for you, Olivia."

"Maverick—I'm sorry. I can't." She tilts her head back and looks up at the ceiling as if she's trying to keep herself from crying. I hate how upset she looks. I just want to hold her in my arms and never let go. "It's too painful for me. I'm sorry."

Before I can reply, she disconnects, and I'm left with a black screen.

I'm not giving up on her. *I won't.*

It's been three days since Olivia and I last talked, and I'm going crazy.

She won't reply to my text messages or answer my phone calls. I've left her voicemails, apologizing for pushing her too hard and that I'll respect her decision to keep us where we are—even if it kills me—but she hasn't called back.

Telling her I've fallen for her wasn't a lie—by any means—but perhaps she wasn't ready to hear it. Hell, maybe it scared her because she's fallen for me too.

Whatever her reasoning, I wish she'd give me a chance to fix it —fix *us*. I just want to talk to her, hear her voice, and see her beautiful face.

Maverick: Good morning, gorgeous. I hope you have a great day today.

Considering she didn't reply to my last eight text messages, I don't anticipate she'll respond to this one either. However, that doesn't stop me from sending them with hopes to brighten her day, because I know she's reading them.

Maverick: Good night, baby. I hope you get a great night's sleep.

I know she's pushing me away, thinking it's the best for both of us, but she's wrong. She's trying to control everything, and this time, I'm not going to allow it.

CHAPTER TWENTY-ONE

OLIVIA

It's the first time Maverick has visited my dreams since I stopped answering his texts and calls. Last week, I realized that I was falling way too hard—and he told me he was falling for me—and he'd become an integral part of my day. Things were moving in a direction that would only lead to heartbreak, and it was best to cut ties before things got even more complicated. My heart still flutters when I think about him, and that's frightening as hell.

I thought maybe my subconscious was mad at me for cutting him off, but then it presented me with the hottest sex dream I've ever had. I force myself out of bed and take a cold shower to rid my thoughts of him.

I know the statistics for long-distance relationships. Forty percent break up, and out of that, the split happens within the first four months—after the honeymoon phase and the real work begins. I care about him so damn much, but this is the best decision for both of us. He deserves someone who can give him what he wants and needs. Someone who doesn't live across the country, isn't married to their job, and can emotionally give him the relationship he deserves. I hate that I can't be that for him, and he might not agree with my reasoning, but I know it's for the best in the long run.

As I'm drying off, I hear my phone buzzing, and by the number of texts I'm receiving at once, I know it's Rachel having one of her early morning meltdowns. Not sure if I'm prepared for it today. I wrap the towel around my body, walk into my bedroom, and grab my phone from the nightstand.

> **Rachel: I ran out of my vegan protein powder. Can you stop and grab some before coming this morning?**
>
> **Rachel: The health store across town opens at 7AM.**
>
> **Rachel: Vanilla bean. If they don't have that, then chocolate will do.**
>
> **Rachel: Can you pick up some of those cookies & cream protein bars too?**
>
> **Rachel: Make sure to keep the receipt.**
>
> **Rachel: And be quick.**

I roll my eyes and shake my head as my hair drips water down my body. It's not even seven yet, and of course, there are no courtesy words used—please or thank you.

I need a truckload of caffeine before I can deal with her this morning.

Instead of replying, I send her a thumbs-up emoji because I don't trust myself with words yet. The way I really feel might leak out this early which would result in me being fired and left high and dry without a reference. Not that the job market is booming with positions anyway.

I walk to the kitchen and start a pot of coffee, because I forgot to schedule it last night, then get dressed. The sun leaks through my curtains, and I smile as it splashes across the floor. Considering winter will be here in a blink, I try to soak up as much of it as I can. It's going to be another beautiful day, one where I'm stuck inside listening to Rachel bitch and moan about how hard her life is. Her life isn't hard—she's living the dream—but she's spoiled as hell and doesn't appreciate much.

Once the coffee is finished brewing, I pour a cup, add some

French vanilla creamer, and take a sip. Before I can swallow, my phone starts vibrating again.

"Holy fuck," I whisper under my breath, hoping she doesn't send me on a scavenger hunt for a list of other things she wants because that's happened before.

I snatch my phone off my bed, but when I see it's texts from Maverick, my heart races.

Maverick: Good morning, gorgeous. Couldn't sleep. Thinking about you.

Maverick: Still ignoring me? :(

Guilt rushes through me, and I can't help but think I've led him on, that maybe he really thought this would progress into something more when he first texted me after our trip was over. Deep inside, I knew it wouldn't. It can't. Our lives are in two different places.

Maverick quickly became so much more to me than even he knows, and that scares the fuck out of me. Falling too fast and too hard reminds me too much of my mother, and I'll do anything I can to avoid that. Thankfully, we're thousands of miles apart, so it makes it slightly easier because he's not just going to show up on my doorstep, though it still hurts. This is exactly what I was afraid of from the beginning when our relationship began shifting. Ending it was the wisest and most logical decision.

Instead of replying, like I want to, I close out of my messages and open my Uber app to schedule a car. I haven't responded to any of his texts, and a part of me wonders how long he's going to keep this up. He's setting himself up for heartache, and it kills me in the process. His messages are what keep me going through the day, and even though I'm a total ass for not replying, I know that if I do, it'll just start a constant texting back and forth situation again.

Even though Rachel is a pain in my ass most days, I'm happy for the distraction today because my heart hurts. If I could, I'd stay locked up in my apartment and binge watch Netflix and eat ice cream. All while feeling sorry for myself. But I won't do that. I can't let myself go down that self-loathing path.

When my ride is close, I grab my laptop bag and head downstairs to wait. Once I'm inside the car, we head across town toward the health food store. I rush inside and grab the shit Rachel wants, say a little thank-you prayer for them having vanilla bean, then head back to my ride, who graciously waited.

On the way over to her apartment building, I feel a pressure weighing on me. I stare out the window and watch the people walk by on the street and can't help but wonder about their lives. Are they happy? In love? Sad? The Uber slows in front of Rachel's, and I thank him, grab my laptop bag, then head upstairs. The elevator is waiting, as always, and I give Sam a small smile, and that's when I realize I left Rachel's stupid protein powder in the car.

"Holy shit," I yell out and rush off the elevator toward the street. By the time I make it outside, the car is long gone. I stand on the sidewalk, pinching the bridge of my nose, trying to suck in air before I lose it. Like clockwork, my phone vibrates.

Rachel: Where are you? What's taking you so long?

I don't even know what to say.

Oh, I'm downstairs because I'm too busy daydreaming than paying attention?

Sure. That will go over really well, and I don't think I can handle being told to pay attention to detail today. Instead of saying anything yet, I open my Uber app and report a lost item, put my phone number in, and pace back and forth on the sidewalk as I wait for a return phone call. If this is an indication of how the rest of my day will go, I'm totally fucked.

My phone vibrates, and I'm so happy I might cry when I answer it and hear my driver's voice. After I explain what happened, he finds my plastic bag in the back seat and lets me know he's about ten minutes away. Relief floods through me. I might live to work another day. After I've got a solid timeline, I text Rachel back.

Olivia: I'll be there in about fifteen minutes.

Rachel: Why?

I let out a breath and suck in another one. Luckily, she's not the only one good with words.

Olivia: Just waiting on my Uber.

It's not the whole truth, but it's close enough to make her happy, or rather, make her not text me with any more questions. Soon I see the Toyota Corolla pulling up. The man hands me my stuff, and I give him a twenty because he saved my sanity. He tries to hand the money back, but I insist with a smile. My day might be shitty, but hopefully, his isn't.

I finally breathe when I'm back on in the lobby. Sam looks at me.

"Rough day, already?" He half-grins, then glances at his watch.

All I can do is smile. They all know Rachel is an absolute terror.

"Good luck," he says sweetly as the elevator doors slide open.

I step in and nod. "I'll need it."

Quickly, I pull my keys from my bag and step inside her apartment. I smell coffee and see Angel eating in the kitchen. Before Rachel can even ask, I prepare a protein shake and deliver it to her in her office. She's typing away and stops and looks up at me when I set it down with a smile.

"I need you to meet with Presley today since she's in town. We had a meeting last week, and I forgot to get copies of my contracts. You know exactly how I feel about that."

I nod. She's such a freak and doesn't trust scanned copies of anything. She wants all originals. It's not the first time I've had to chase them down.

"I also made a grocery list, so I need you to hit the store on your way back. Then go to the post office and mail out last month's signed paperback giveaways for my reader group and check my PO Box."

I bite the inside of my mouth, and I might actually taste blood when I see a hundred signed books that need to be individually packaged and mailed. "Sure."

"Presley will be at her studio around ten. So." That's her passive-aggressive way of telling me I need to hurry. Just as I walk over to the books to get started, she takes a sip of her protein shake and practically spits it out.

"Oh my God, Olivia. Did you put any banana in here? This tastes like shit!" Rachel stands, snatches the protein shake from her desk, and storms into the kitchen like a two-year-old who got milk instead of juice. The blender goes off, and I know she's remaking it. One day, she's eating bananas, and the next, she's not. How the hell am I supposed to know when those carbs are okay?

While she's busy making her point in the kitchen, I open my laptop, connect to the wireless printer, and try to make some order out of her madness. Books are signed, and I'm forced to open each one to figure out who it's personalized to and try to find the person's address on the list. Clusterfuck doesn't give this catastrophe justice, and I have two hours to make it happen.

After the first hour, my back hurts so bad from bending over to stuff envelopes with books and postcards. By some miracle, I figure it out. Close to the two-hour mark, everything is packaged, labeled, and placed in huge totes for me to take to the post office. If she would've thought of this yesterday, I could've scheduled a pickup, but I'm pretty sure "inconvenience" is her middle name. It takes me four trips to carry everything to the bottom floor, and thankfully, Sam helps me as I schedule a ride.

Before my Uber arrives, Rachel texts me her grocery list, and if I didn't know better, I'd say she's stocking up for the winter because there's no way one person can eat all of this. The car pulls up, and the driver gets out and helps me load the totes into the trunk.

"Jesus, what're in these bags? Bricks?" She laughs.

"Close. Books," I say as I climb into the back and we take off. Instead of having the driver wait around for me, I let her leave because the line at the post office is longer than I anticipated. Rachel insists she get the receipt that shows they've been mailed, so instead of just dropping them in the cart, I'm forced to wait.

After an hour, the packages are finally mailed, the PO Box is checked, and I'm scheduling a ride across town toward Presley's rented studio. I try to cheer up because I really like Presley, but I'm in such a sour mood that I'm not sure I can shake it. She's dealt with Rachel for the past five years, so I know she understands my frustration.

I'm dropped off in front of a brick building with large windows. There's nothing too fancy about the outside of it, but the inside is gorgeous. There's a backdrop set up in one area, hardwood floors, and the most perfect natural lighting. The space was made for photo shoots, especially with her eye. She's one of the most creative people I know.

As soon as I walk in, I tuck Rachel's fan mail under my arm. Presley peeks up from her makeshift office space with a smile. "Hey, you!"

I let out a breath, and it's the first time today since Maverick's text this morning that I've genuinely smiled. The heels of my shoes click against the wood floor as I walk toward her.

"You look like hell," she says when I move closer.

I narrow my eyes at her. "Do I even have to explain why?"

She snorts. "No. It's because you work for the devil incarnate." Presley can barely get her words out before laughing.

Though I want to join in on bashing Rachel, I don't because it's too easy. "Where're the fingerprints, blood samples, and DNA results?"

Presley stands and grabs a manila folder. I open it and see the original signed contracts, and I hold on to them tightly. If I lose these, it will be my head.

"Have you eaten lunch yet?" she asks. "It's about that time." She looks down at her watch and grins at me.

Shaking my head, I smirk. "There's no time for food, Pres. I still have to go grocery shopping. Though, with the list she gave me, it might just be easier to buy the whole store."

"No offense against you, but I'm actually surprised you've lasted this long with her. You're her assistant, not her maid, housekeeper, or dog sitter. I hate to say it, but you need to set some boundaries. If not, she's going to continue to walk all over you because you've allowed it for so long."

She's right. I know she's right. Maverick even said the same thing. However, I need this job like I need air. "I know." Glancing down at my phone, I realize I've already wasted too much time.

Presley stands and gives me a big hug and a smile. "I'm sorry."

Pulling back, I narrow my eyes at her. "For what?"

A door closes in the studio, and I hear footsteps on the wooden floor behind me. I turn around to see who's coming, and when my eyes meet Maverick's, I feel as if I'm falling. Quickly, I turn and glare at Presley who shrugs and goes back to her computer. "Told you I was sorry."

"How did you know?" I whisper, wondering how she knew about Maverick and me. Seeing him standing so damn sexy, wearing clothes that hug him in all the right places, makes me forget every reason I've been avoiding him. The need I have for him is too damn powerful to ignore.

She just grins. "I have my resources."

CHAPTER TWENTY-TWO

MAVERICK

THE MOMENT my eyes meet hers, it's as if time stands stills. She's just as beautiful as the last time I saw her. My heart lurches forward, and though my feet feel frozen to the floor, I force myself to walk toward her. The fact that she's shocked, with her jaw dropped, makes not telling her I'd be here worth it. I wanted to surprise her but wasn't sure if this would be a good or bad surprise, considering she hasn't been talking to me. Distance is hard, but for her, I'd try anything. The only way to tell her how I really feel is in person.

"Maverick. What are you doing here?" she finally asks, blinking hard as if to make sure I'm real.

I don't immediately answer, and Presley raises her hand, temporarily bringing the attention back to her. "I booked him for a shoot. Wanted to show him around the studio first." By the look on Presley's face, I know she's bluffing. She must know about our history and planned this somehow.

Olivia turns and looks at Presley, shaking her head. All I want to do is pull her into my arms and kiss the fuck out of her, but I know Olivia prefers discretion and privacy. I'm not one to kiss and tell, mainly because Olivia doesn't want anyone to know. The truth is, I don't want Olivia to be my best-kept secret. I want the fucking world to know how I feel.

"Surprise?" I smirk with a shrug, hoping she doesn't push me away again. I don't know if I could handle being rejected by her in person.

As she walks forward, her heels click on the wood floor. "Surprise? Surprise?! You're in Chicago. Here. Right now. And that's all you have to say?"

I nod and close the gap between us. She places her hands on her hips, giving me all sorts of sass, and I pull her into my arms. Though Olivia is reserved, and Presley is around, I don't care. I can't wait any longer. Ever since I signed the contracts for the shoot, I've been thinking about this very moment, what I would say to her when we were face-to-face and how this would all play out. I just didn't expect her to be here when I arrived, so I'm somewhat shocked as well. Divine intervention wins again.

Not another minute can pass without me knowing if my feelings will be reciprocated. There's no rushing when I pull her close. My lips softly press against hers, and she sinks into me, the kiss growing deeper. It's as if no time has passed at all, and I'm so damn happy that when we pull apart, a grin fills her face.

Olivia reaches back and smacks my arm.

"Hey!" I playfully say, rubbing the area as if it actually hurt.

"You deserve that!" she responds.

"Why?" I chuckle. "You're the one who's been ignoring me."

Presley stands, smiles, and then makes her way across the studio. "I'll see you two lovebirds later," she announces, and then I hear the door click closed.

As soon as she's out of sight, Olivia wraps her arms around my waist. "I'm really glad you're here. I know I have a lot of explaining to do."

"Have you eaten yet?" I ask, knowing she probably hasn't.

Before she can respond, her phone goes off. She groans as she pulls it from her pocket. "Shit. I have to go. I'm so sorry. I still need to go grocery shopping for Rachel and work for a few more hours before I'm released from prison. Will you be around later?"

I take her phone from her hand. "Rachel can wait. We're having lunch."

She opens her mouth to argue, but I place my finger over her lips. "Say yes, Olivia."

"You know I can't deny you when you look at me like that," she admits with a pouty face.

"Like what, like you're a delicate flower?" I laugh, reminding her what Rachel once said. Instantly, Olivia rolls her eyes.

"Okay, fine. Lunch. Then I really have to get back to work."

I smirk. "I'll take what I can get."

We walk outside, and Olivia bursts out into laughter when she sees the Toyota Prius parked on the street.

"Are you kidding me? I thought you didn't do Prius?" she asks with her hands placed on her hips.

"They don't bother me that much. I just wanted to see how far I could push you. I won, didn't I?" I unlock the car and walk toward it.

"You asshole!" She chuckles getting inside. "Do you have any idea what I had to do to get rid of that car in LA?"

"Sell your kidney?" I glance over at her, and it almost feels like we're getting ready for another adventure, and in a way, we are.

"Basically. I promised my firstborn and had to slip the guy a fifty."

When I laugh, she scolds me for being a douche when we first met. I almost apologize, but then don't, because I don't regret anything that led us to where we are right now.

"Where do you want to eat?" I ask, pulling out onto the street.

"Chicago pizza. The real kind, not that bullshit you eat in LA." She glances at me, and I see the blush hit her cheeks.

"Perfect." I let her plug in the address and have the GPS guide me. After we park and get out, I place my hand on the small of her back as we walk in. She looks over at me and smiles. I'm relieved she welcomes my touch.

After we order the biggest pepperoni pizza on the menu, we find a table outside on the sidewalk. The city noise creates a relaxing ambiance. For a moment, I don't even know how to start the conversation, because there's so much I need to say.

We both open our mouths at the same time, then close them.

"Go ahead," I tell her.

"No, you go first," she says.

"I've missed you so damn much." I search her face and watch her lips turn up into a genuine smile. Before she can respond, her phone starts ringing, and she rejects it.

"I've missed you too, Maverick," she admits.

The phone rings again. I glance down and see it's Rachel, and I'm so annoyed because we have important things to discuss, things that can't wait, unlike her groceries. When the phone rings again, I answer it.

"Olivia's phone."

"Who is this?" she instantly asks.

I don't have time to be friendly right now. "What do you want, Rachel?"

"Maverick?" she asks, shocked.

"Yep. What do you need?"

"I need to speak to Olivia," Rachel demands.

I look at Olivia sitting on the edge of her chair. I put the phone on speaker so Olivia can hear the rest of the conversation.

"Olivia isn't available for the rest of the day. She will not be picking up your groceries or doing whatever else you need her to do. It can wait. You have run her ragged for the past year, and enough is enough. For once, you need to treat her with the respect she deserves and like a human. You need to learn to treat her better than you treat your goddamn dog, Rachel. Learn how to say thank you and please every once in a while. Learn how to be appreciative of everything she does for you. Otherwise, you're going to lose someone who's running your entire fucking life. Now, do you need anything else or are we done here?"

The line is dead silent.

Olivia sits in front of me with wide eyes and her hands covering her mouth, completely stunned.

"Excuse me?" Rachel finally speaks up.

"You heard every word I said. Olivia will see you first thing Monday morning. She's taking the rest of today, Friday, and the weekend off. She's due for some vacation time after traveling, and you'll be perfectly fine without her for a few days," I tell her, imagining her face and how she's probably internally losing her shit. The thought makes me smile.

"Okay then." Her voice is flat with zero emotion.

"Alright. Nice chatting with you." I hang up, not waiting for her to respond.

The color drains from Olivia's face. "I can't believe you did that.

I mean, I should've said those words to her ages ago, but I'm probably going to get fired on Monday. I just know it."

Shaking my head, I grab her hands. "Rachel knows her entire life will fall apart without you. She can't afford to fire you. You run the show, not her."

Olivia lets out a breath. "Okay. I just hope you're right, but I trust you." Her eyes meet mine. "Thank you for sticking up for me. I don't think anyone has ever done that for me before."

"Honestly, I should've done it in Dallas, Denver, or Vegas," I admit. "I hated watching her treat you like that, but it was hard to know my place and if I could say something to her. But enough is enough," I tell her. "But now I have you all to myself without any interruptions." I grab her hand and place a soft kiss on her knuckles. "So what would you like to do for the rest of the day?"

"You have a photo shoot," she reminds me as the most glorious pizza I've ever seen is set on our table. It smells delicious and makes my mouth water.

"Actually..." I linger, grabbing a piece of pizza and trying not to moan out how amazing it is when I take a bite.

Olivia laughs between bites. "It's good isn't it?"

"The best fucking pizza I've ever had," I admit. "Also, the shoot isn't until tomorrow. Presley booked it for Friday, but I decided to come a day earlier. I was hoping to see you. I didn't know you'd be at the studio, though."

She sets her pizza down and looks at me. "Presley knows something's going on between us. She knows all the drama. You really can't tell her anything or even give hints. She's like Scooby Doo and picks up on any sort of clues." She chuckles. "But I'm really happy you're here."

"Me too."

After we've finished the entire pizza, we head back to the Prius.

Once we're inside, I hesitate before starting the car. I turn my body and face her.

"Olivia," I say, grabbing her hand. "I didn't just come here for the photo shoot. I came here because I needed to see you. I'm not giving up on us even if you have or believe it's the right thing to do. I know why you stopped responding to my messages, but I haven't been able to stop thinking about you. Texting with you every day made me feel a happiness I didn't know existed. Just getting to be a part of your life somehow, in any way, felt special to me. I know this whole long-distance thing will be difficult, but I want to try because I want to be with you. Those two weeks we spent together have forever been imprinted on my heart. I let you into a piece of my life that I don't share with anyone. You told me things that I'm sure you don't tell others either. There's something between us, and I don't want to let it go. What we have is special, and I'd be dumb to let you slip through my fingers. On the road, I fell in love with you, Olivia. No amount of distance can change that."

"Maverick," she whispers, squeezing her eyes tight before looking at me. "I'm scared."

I move closer to her. "I know. I am too. But I'm more scared of losing you. Scared that if I don't take a chance, I'll never know what we could've been. Maybe I'm crazy, but I love you, Olivia. I love you so damn much."

She leans forward and greedily kisses me. She doesn't hesitate when she repeats those four words. "I love you too, Maverick. As crazy as it sounds, I already knew I was falling for you before I left LA."

"It's not crazy. Well, maybe a little." I chuckle. "But I don't care. I know what I feel and that what we shared together was real."

"It was real," she confirms. Her tone is low and daunting, which starts to scare me. " I'm sorry. I'm so sorry for what I did."

I can see she's upset. "What do you mean?" I ask.

"For pushing you away, ignoring your messages, trying to pretend we were better off without each other. I thought that if I stopped talking to you, I'd just be able to forget anything ever happened between us. I tried to get on with my life and stupidly thought it would go back to how things were before I met you. But it was impossible. The more I ignored you, the more I thought about you. It hurt so much, but I was afraid of falling for you, Maverick, even though I already had. I'm afraid I'll end up like my mother." Her voice cracks at the end, and I notice she's tearing up, though she somehow holds herself together. "I've never felt this way about anyone before. It's a foreign feeling for me, and I'm afraid when the newness wears off, you'll no longer be interested."

"Olivia." My voice is soft. "I will love you for as long as you'll let me. I promise you that."

"Forever then?" She slightly smiles.

"Yes, sweetheart. Forever." And when I say those words, they feel so deeply ingrained in my soul that I know what we have is special. No other person has made me feel so alive, not since my dad passed away.

"I want to bring you home with me," she adds, and I don't argue. "But I'm driving us there."

I tilt my head at her, and we switch places. "I like a woman who takes control." A smile touches my lips because it reminds me of our road trip.

As we're heading through downtown Chicago, I roll down the window. It's not my first visit here, but being with Olivia, makes it feel new and exciting. After she parks on the street, she gets out, and I follow her up the stairs. She unlocks the door and steps aside to allow me to enter. Looking around, all I can do is take it all in. I imagine her walking around in her T-shirt with her hair down working and drinking coffee. This place fits her with the small kitchen, cute living room, and big windows that overlook the street. Everything is neat and perfectly in place, which doesn't surprise me.

I turn around and see her staring at me. "What?" I ask with a half-smile.

"I just..." She shakes her head. "I can't believe you're here right now. Feels like I'm dreaming. Am I?"

Within five steps, I close the space between us and barely pinch her arm. "Nope. I'm really here."

Our mouths violently crash together, and we're ravenous for one another. I've thought about this very moment every day since I planned my trip to Chicago. I was worried she'd reject me, push me away, but as her tongue glides across mine, I know it was a useless concern. She fists my T-shirt in her hands, and it's all the approval I need as I undress her. She's so damn greedy, rushing to take off her clothes, but I stop her.

"I don't want to rush," I admit.

Her eyebrows shoot up. "You pop up out of the blue, and now you want to take it slow?"

I smile with a laugh. "Yeah?"

She lets out a humph and grabs my hand, leading me to her bedroom. "How was the drive? Did you get into any bad weather?"

I chuckle, brushing the hair from her shoulder, kissing the softness of her neck. "It was quick."

"Quick?" She pulls back, slightly confused.

When she looks up at me, I tuck loose hairs behind her ear and dip down to paint my lips across hers. "I flew here."

Her mouth falls open, and I give her a side grin. Shocking her is way too pleasing.

"Wait. You flew? Like on a plane?" Olivia searches my face as if she's waiting for me to say I'm joking.

I chuckle, then nod. "I'd fly to the end of the Earth if that means being with you, Olivia. It was time I faced my fears—all of them."

"Oh my God. I can't believe you flew. I feel awful for ignoring you. I thought I was protecting you from a broken heart. I never imagined you'd come out here," she says.

"I love you, Olivia. I couldn't wait two days to see you, so I booked a flight. The only thing that kept me sane on that plane was the thought of you, the thought of us, together. You were the light at the end of the tunnel."

She pulls me close, holding me in her arms, and smiles. "Thank you for coming here. I missed you more than you'll ever know." She wraps her arms around my neck. Olivia kisses me so passionately, she steals my breath away.

"Baby, I'll do anything to make this work. Long-distance, texting, FaceTime, phone calls. Weekend flights. I'm not giving up on us."

"Me either. I'm all in," she confirms, and it makes me the happiest man in the world to hear those words.

We make love until the early morning, losing track of time, and only stopping to eat dinner. I feel like I'm in a dream state with her, appreciating every inch of her body. Time almost stands still when we lose ourselves together.

Eventually, we fall asleep, holding each other as if we'll never let go, and this time, I know when I wake up, she'll still be here.

Olivia Carpenter is mine.

CHAPTER TWENTY-THREE

OLIVIA

ONE YEAR LATER

AFTER DOING the whole long-distance relationship thing for the past year, I finally took the leap and packed up my life in Chicago to be with Maverick. Being away from him and having to fly back and forth wasn't the easiest task in the world, but we learned to cherish every moment we had together. Though it never felt like enough. We knew that if we really wanted to see where things could go, we had to be together. So we decided to buy a condo and start in a new, fresh place. It's been the scariest, riskiest, and most exciting thing I've ever done. In his typical Maverick fashion, he's surprising me, and I've only been here for twenty-four hours.

"I don't know why you insist on this stupid blindfold." I laugh as Maverick interlocks his fingers with mine and kisses my knuckles.

"It's because I know you'd peek." I can tell he's smiling. "I know it's hard for you, Miss Priss, but have a little patience. We're almost there."

We've been in the back of an Uber for at least thirty minutes. Several months ago, I finally set some boundaries with Rachel, and she realized she no longer had permission to control my life. She decided to join a yoga class where she surprisingly met someone. This caused her to demand more private time, and once Douglas moved in with her, my shackles were officially removed. Rachel—the micromanaging, needy-as-hell author—no longer needed me the way she once did. I was able to do my job from home like I did for Vada when she'd take her writing retreats. Douglas doesn't allow Rachel to do as she pleases, and he freely puts her in her place and calls her out for being rude, which is what she needs. I need to send him an expensive Christmas gift because the man is a saint for dealing with her day in and day out. It just proves that there's someone out there for everyone—even high-maintenance Rachel.

Telling Rachel I was moving was a bittersweet moment. I didn't want to leave her empty-handed, so I trained a new assistant before I left. I still plan to do administrative duties for her, and we'll do conference calls in between. My goal is to eventually open my own PR and marketing firm. Maverick's career has taken off significantly, and I plan to help him keep up with all of it as well. I'm so excited about this new journey and this next chapter in our lives.

I've never been this happy before, but I know it's because of Maverick more than anything. He's supportive and sweet and everything I need. I squeeze his hand three times, and he leans over and steals a kiss.

The car finally rolls to a stop, and the door cracks open. Maverick gently guides me out. The cool breeze brushes against my cheeks, and I smile.

"The anticipation is almost too much," I tell him as we walk for a little while, then stop.

I feel his body move behind me, and his hands fiddle with the material. Before he undoes the blindfold, he leans in and pulls my earlobe between his teeth. "Ready?"

I keep my eyes closed and pop them open quickly. I gasp as I notice we're standing in a hangar with a plane. I turn and look at Maverick, and he's grinning ear to ear.

"What are we doing?" I ask, somewhat confused.

He twirls a set of keys around his pointer finger. "Going for a ride."

My eyes go so wide they might fall out of the sockets. I look around and realize the car is long gone, and it's just us standing around. "In that? Is that the plane from the photo on your mantel?" I ask, pointing. That picture of them all together and happy is ingrained in my mind.

He nods. "Yeah. It was my dad's private plane, and I found out recently that my mom never sold it. She said she couldn't bring herself to do it, even after all these years, but we thought she had. Instead, she rented it out and stuff to keep it up. Anyway, I had trained when I was younger to be a pilot but never finished getting my license. After doing some research, I realized it wouldn't take much to get certified. So...I did. My dad would be so fucking proud." He's smiling so big that it causes me to smile too.

"Maverick, this is a huge deal." I'm shocked and proud. A tad speechless too.

He shrugs me off and smirks. "I was going to tell you sooner, but I thought it would be more fun to shock the shit out of you. It was worth it."

My jaw is practically on the pavement as he walks to the plane and pulls it out of the hangar.

"Is this real life?" I ask as I follow him around like I'm his shadow as he checks the outside of the plane.

He pulls me into his arms. "Better believe it, baby."

Maverick opens the door and climbs in, then leans over and holds his hand out for me. I follow his lead and step on the wing then sit in the passenger seat. There are so many dials and knobs that I'm completely overwhelmed. He hands me a headset and tells me to put it on, and he puts one on too. We fasten the seat belts, and my heart is pounding so hard in my chest that I swear Maverick can hear it.

"Do you trust me?" he asks.

"Yes, always," I tell him.

"Okay, we're going to do our pre-check. It's required before every flight." I can tell he's being patient with me, probably because I'm nervous as hell.

He reads the list of things out loud and makes sure everything is done before starting the engine. When he turns the key, the propeller comes to life, creating a hum. I look over at him with his headset on as he uses pilot lingo to talk to the tower. My heart is so full right now, I feel like it might burst. This is huge, following in his dad's footsteps after everything that happened, but I get it. It's a way for him to be close to his father in a different way while also facing his fears.

He glances at me and does this cute little scrunchy thing with his nose that's so fucking adorable. I'm listening to Maverick talk back and forth with someone, and it doesn't seem like English other than being cleared for takeoff. I suck in a deep breath and feel my body go tense. I've never been in a plane so small before.

Maverick looks over at me and grabs my hand. "The weather is perfect for flying. It's going to be like glass up there, smooth as can be."

I nod as he positions the aircraft on the runway. Soon we're speeding down it until the plane lifts off the cement and we're in the air soaring above the ground. Looking down, I see a golf course and then the beach.

"Right there is the Santa Monica Pier," Maverick says, pointing as we fly over it. Specks of people are below us, and I can make out the Ferris wheel, roller coasters, and restaurants.

"Wow," I whisper as he turns the plane, and we head toward LA. In the distance, I can see the tall buildings and highways. It's almost unrecognizable from above. Sure, I've flown into LA a dozen times in the past year, but this is more intimate, closer. Once we've been in the air for an hour, I turn and look at Maverick, and he's smiling.

"Okay, where are we going?" I finally ask.

"Thought we'd go on a sky trip." He shoots me a wink.

I smirk. "Do we have enough gas?"

"We better," he adds. "There's no roadside assistance in the sky that's going to deliver us any."

The thought of being stranded in Texas comes to mind. Actually, the whole road trip does. I'm mesmerized by looking out the window, and eventually, Maverick circles around, and we land on another runway. After the wheels touch ground and the plane comes to a complete stop, I'm so ready to straddle his lap and take him.

"Whoa girl," he says between kisses after he turns off the engine.

I giggle. "Pilots are hot."

"If that's all it took…" He trails off, and I need him like I need air. My fingers brush through his hair, and it's hot in the cabin because there's no air conditioner like in a car. By the time we pull away, my lips are throbbing, and his are swollen. Eventually, we climb out of the plane and walk toward a building in the distance. Looking around, I notice we're surrounded by desert. Texas, maybe? Lower Colorado? I try to put the pieces together, but I'm falling short.

After we go inside, Maverick checks in and grabs some keys to a rental car, and we walk out and get inside.

"You've thought about everything, haven't you?" I smile, buckling my seat belt.

"You're just mad because you didn't plan it all," he playfully throws back.

A chuckle escapes me. "You're right. I need to sit back and enjoy it."

As he places the car into drive, he turns on the radio and glances over at me.

"I wasn't going to say anything!" I protest.

"My radio," he reminds me, blasting out Aerosmith.

I look around for anything familiar so I can figure out where we are, and that's when I see the Las Vegas sign. My mouth falls open for the hundredth time today. "Vegas?"

"What gave it away?" He glances over at me with a grin.

"Ha, don't be a smartass," I tell him as we head toward the Strip. When we make it to our hotel, Maverick gets out and hands the keys over to the valet, then goes to the front desk and checks us in. I stand back and wait, and that's when it clicks that we're staying the night. Just as I open my mouth to ask about clothes and everything else, I realize that I'm micromanaging this trip. As he walks up, he notices the color drain from my face and tilts his head at me.

"What's wrong?" he asks as he wraps his arm around my shoulder and we walk toward the elevator.

"I think Rachel has rubbed off on me," I say, which causes him to erupt into a big, hearty laugh.

"That would never happen. You're too compassionate and

caring. Pretty sure she sold her soul to the devil in exchange for selling millions of copies of her books."

Now *that* makes *me* laugh.

"I realized I was going to ask you a slew of other questions. So, for the rest of the night or weekend or however long we'll be here, I solemnly swear not to ask about anything else. You're in control," I say just as the elevator comes to a stop at the top floor.

"I kinda like the way that sounds. Me being in control. No questions asked." Maverick unlocks the door, and when I step in, I cover my mouth. The room is bigger than my apartment was in Chicago and even has a fucking chandelier. Champagne is in a bucket, rose petals are sprinkled across the floor, and chocolate-covered strawberries are next to the bed. There's even a suitcase with clothes. He really has thought of everything.

When I turn back around to face him, he's down on one knee with a little black box open.

"Olivia," he says, clearing his throat. I can tell he's nervous by the way his hand is shaking, and I take steps forward to close the space between us. Maverick swallows hard before he continues, but when I look into his eyes, I know exactly what he feels because I feel it too. As much as I didn't want to admit it, I have since the first time I met him.

"You are my sunrise and my sunset. The dust jacket to my favorite book, the send button on an important email, and the caffeine to my coffee," he says, chuckling. "On a serious note, I once told you that I didn't know why I'm still here or what my purpose was in life after losing my dad. After I met you, I knew it was to protect, to care, and to love you. For years, I didn't know what living was truly like and then we went on that road trip, and it changed my life. *You* changed my life, Olivia. Love was like a dream, and something everyone else experienced. Something that only happened in books or movies. I never thought I'd find it, but I fell so madly in love with you that my head is actually still spinning. I can never get enough of you, and any time we've been apart, it's like I'm missing my other half, and I'm so glad I don't have to anymore. Being able to kiss you good night and have you in my arms every morning is a dream come true. You've already made me the happiest man in the world by just giving me a chance and having faith in us. I don't ever want that to end. I want to spend the rest of my life making you laugh and loving you. I know we just made a huge step in our relationship, but I want it all, Olivia. My life is nothing without you. So, Miss Priss, will you marry me?"

I topple him over, kissing him as happy tears stream down my face. I can't be close enough to him, and at this moment, nothing else in the entire world matters. It's like we're the only two people on the planet, and time stands still. My tongue grazes against his, and soon I'm straddling him. All I know is I need him, and I need him right now.

"So," he draws out, laughing and reaching for the box he dropped because we got so caught up in the moment.

"Yes, yes, of course." He slips the gigantic diamond on my finger, and I look at it sparkling in the light. "But…there's one condition," I add with a sly smile.

Maverick searches my face, waiting for my next words.

"Let's get married here. *Today.* You said you didn't want to wait. I don't either." I lean forward and kiss him as his thumbs dig into my hips. He's hard as a rock, and I can feel him through his jeans. "I don't have any family who'd attend anyway. There's really only you and some friends, and I wouldn't be surprised if there's a running bet on when we'll get married."

He laughs, holding his palm to my face. "If I could've married you last year, I would've."

Butterflies swarm in my body. "I've never wanted anything more than to be with you, Maverick. You're my everything. My best friend. My lover. My family. You've seen me at my best and worst. I can't imagine my life without you."

Maverick sits up, pulling me into his arms, and we hold each other for a moment. "Okay. Let's do it. But we're going right now."

I let out a laugh. "I'm calling your bluff."

"There's no bluff, sweetheart. When I make love to you next, you'll be my wife." His lips softly touch mine, and soon we're both on our feet—standing.

My face hurts from the smile that's permanently there. Maverick grabs his phone and does a quick Google search, and after ten minutes, we're using walking directions to one of the dozens of drive-by wedding chapels in Vegas. Nothing has ever felt so right in my life.

As we walk up to the little chapel, I thought I'd feel nervous, but instead, my heart, body, and soul are happy and content, knowing this is how it was always supposed to be. Me and Him. Together forever. He glances over me as if to ask if this is what I want to do, and I don't hesitate before I pull him inside.

After some paperwork is signed, I'm changed into a white wedding dress, and Maverick is fitted into a tux. They even had rings for sale, so then I could slip one onto Maverick's finger until we can go shopping. Strangers are brought in from the street to watch and celebrate. The woman up front gives me quick instructions, which I take like a pro, considering, and soon the "Wedding March" is playing.

As Maverick stands in the front of the room, it's like everything else around us disappears, and I practically glide toward him. An Elvis impersonator comes out and gives us all the cheesy lines until we're pronounced man and wife. The kiss leaves me breathless, and it's as if our hearts permanently meld together at that very moment.

The crowd cheers, and we're quickly moved to a photo area where hurried snapshots are taken of us so we can remember this forever. But the truth is, my heart will never forget.

Soon we're changed from our faux wedding gear into our street clothes and are walking out. I stop and look up at the little chapel, down at the paper in my hand, and then at Maverick.

"I love you." I stand on my tiptoes and paint kisses across his lips.

"I love you, too. Now it's time to consummate our marriage," he adds with a wink, picking me up and carrying me down the sidewalk for at least three blocks. People who pass us don't give us a second glance because we're in Vegas, and weirder things are happening. When we make it back to the hotel and step onto the elevator, I'm practically bursting with happiness.

"We really did it," I say, glancing down at my ring, then at him.

He pulls me into his arms and swipes a piece of hair out of my face. "It's official now, Mrs. Kingston. *I've got you, babe.*"

That damn karaoke song comes to mind, along with all the

special moments we've shared. I nod my head, not taking a moment for granted, realizing how lucky I am to have someone love me and to feel the same way.

"You're right," I tell him with a smirk. "And I've got you, too. Forever."

EPILOGUE
MAVERICK

"Olivia! We've got to go," I shout at her for the third time. So much for my schedule-enforcer wife staying on time.

"I had to pee! Stop shouting," she scolds as she waddles down the hallway.

"Again? Didn't you just go?" I chuckle, knowing she's going to glare at me.

"It's not my fault! Your child is using my bladder as a trampoline," she says, groaning.

I bend down and rub her belly. "It's okay, baby girl. Your mama and I still love you." Looking up, I give Olivia a wink, then kiss her bump. Standing, I cup her face and kiss her softly. "She'll be here before we know it."

"Only ten more weeks," she says excitedly.

"Which is why we need this little babymoon getaway." I smile and press a kiss to her forehead. "You've been working nonstop, and I need some alone time with my wife," I add.

"If only you'd tell me where we're going." She lifts a brow, annoyed that I want to surprise her.

"Not a chance."

I'm so damn proud of her, but she works herself until she's falling asleep at her keyboard, and I have to carry her to bed. A few months after she moved here and we got married, she got serious about starting her own PR and marketing firm. She was able to walk away from Rachel once her replacement was completely trained, and while she helped me with my career, it was time for her to finally do something she was passionate about. I knew how much she loved her job before—even on the bad days—and watching her do something that excites her and has her bouncing on her feet every morning has been worth it. I love seeing her determination and hard work pay off.

I take her hand and lead her to the car. Our bags are already in the back, and although she's begged me to tell her where we're going, I won't budge.

"We're flying?" She gasps when I pull into the airport.

"I told you we were going on a vacation, didn't I?" I look over at her and grin. I've taken her on several trips since I got my license, but I'm most excited about this one because it's a surprise she won't be expecting at all.

Once we're in the air, I look over at my beautiful wife with her growing belly and feel so blessed that our lives have led us here. Never in my wildest dreams would I have imagined a road trip two years ago would bring me the most amazing woman I've ever met. Spending that year flying back and forth was hard, but it's safe to say we definitely made up for it during our first year of marriage.

Hours pass and Olivia falls asleep shortly before we land. I can't wait for her to see where we are. It's gorgeous here, especially in summer. I haven't been to the Carolinas in years.

"We're landing, baby," I tell her through the headset.

"Where are we?" She looks around for clues. "It's so green and beautiful."

"You'll find out in just a minute." I smile, feeling anxious and excited.

Once we're on the ground and the plane is parked, I grab our bags and help Olivia off the plane. She's looking around, trying to put the pieces together, but it's not until she sees Vada standing in the hangar that she realizes exactly where we are.

"No way! Oh my God!" Olivia squeals as Vada runs and nearly lunges at her. She pulls back and hugs her again.

"You look adorable!" Vada gushes.

"I can't believe this!" Olivia turns and faces me. "You brought me to Vada?"

"I know how much you've missed her and figured we could babymoon on the beach."

Olivia closes the gap between us and wraps her arms around my neck as best as she can with her bump in the way. "Thank you. I can't even express how much this means to me."

"It's nice to finally meet you, officially," I say, holding my hand out to Vada. Instead, she pushes it away and gives me a big hug.

"I'm a Southerner now, and in the South, we hug," she explains playfully.

"Where's Ethan and London?" Olivia asks as we walk to Vada's car.

"Waiting for you at the house. They're so excited!"

The surprises aren't over, but I don't tell her that just yet.

Vada drives us to her house where I meet her husband, Ethan, and their son, London. They give us the tour of their house and property, which is pretty awesome. I love the cozy and modern feel to it.

"I can't believe you have a rooster," I say, trying to get the guy to eat food out of my palm.

"That's Henry, and he's an asshole," Vada says dramatically.

"You love him," Ethan protests.

"I remember the stories you told me when you first got here," Olivia says, laughing. "I about died."

"Yeah, it's all fun and games until a cock is trying to bite your ankles!"

Olivia snorts, and I love watching them together. I wish we were closer so she could have a friend like Vada nearby, but I know she's slowly been making new friends in LA.

"Maybe we should've bought a condo here instead," I tease.

"I'm afraid there aren't many modeling opportunities here," Vada jokes. "But maybe a summer house?"

"Don't give him any ideas!" Olivia shouts. "He'll be looking in the homes for sale ads before we go to sleep tonight!"

We all laugh at her outburst, but I don't deny how right she is. Though I'm not surprising her with a summer house, I did find us an awesome rental for our vacation.

After Ethan and I drink a few beers and the girls set dinner on the table, we have a nice, relaxing evening together. Their son is a cutie, and I had fun playing with him too. It has me even more excited for our little girl to arrive.

"We should get going, babe. The Airbnb is about twenty minutes from here, and I have another surprise for you there."

"If it's in your pants, you can save it. I've had that surprise, and it's how I ended up like this," she says, pointing at her big bump.

"You're the one who couldn't fall asleep," I retort.

Ethan and Vada burst out laughing, and Olivia gives me a look that says she's going to pay me back for that one later.

"We better see you guys before you leave," Vada says when our Uber driver arrives.

"You will," I say with a reassuring smile.

"If you hadn't already run to Vegas to marry him, I'd tell you to marry that man. He's pretty awesome," I hear Vada tell Olivia. They both giggle and hug, and I love seeing her like this.

"So I'm dying to know what else you have planned," Olivia says as we make our way to the rental.

I take her hand and kiss her knuckles twice. "You'll see very soon." I flash her a wink, and she doesn't push for more. I know it's hard for her to give up the control sometimes, but I'm actually impressed by how much she's let go lately. She does so much for her clients that I love being able to spoil her anytime I can.

The driver pulls up, and I watch as Olivia's jaw drops. "Oh my God, what did you do?"

Laughing at her silly outburst, I grab her hand and help her out of the car. Once our bags are out, I tip the guy and lead Olivia to the twenty-foot-tall deck that leads to the beach house. It's on stilts and sits right on the edge of a private beach. I can see the waves hitting the sand behind it as the sun is setting.

"Do you like it?"

"Are you kidding me?" She wraps her arms around my waist. "It's a dream!"

I give her the grand tour, and she kisses me in every single room, thanking me. This getaway was definitely needed for the two of us before the next chapter in our lives begins, which is in less than three months.

"Let's go watch the sunset," I tell her, leading her out to the deck.

We spend the night staring out at the water, and I even talk her into christening the jet bathtub. It's not easy with her belly, but as a man of determination, I made it work.

"So what are we doing today?" she whispers first thing the next morning.

"I thought you were going to let me surprise you…"

"I am. I was just asking!"

I smile and kiss her forehead. "Let's get ready and dressed, and then you can have your surprise."

"Ugh, fine!"

An hour later, I finally manage to get Olivia up and ready while I make sure everything is set to go without a hitch. She has no idea what's about to happen, and I'm living for the fact that she's not able to guess.

"Are you ready?"

"Hold on. I have to pee. Again!"

I stifle a laugh, knowing she can't help it. Though she did just go fifteen minutes ago.

"Okay, I'm ready. This is really what you want me to wear?" She sways her hips and the dress moves back and forth. She's a goddamn a goddess.

"You look gorgeous," I tell her for the third time.

She flashes me a deadpan look. "I look like a beached whale."

I close the gap between us and bring her into my arms. "My gorgeous beached whale."

"Always the charmer." She wrinkles her nose and chuckles.

"You ready?" I press my lips to her neck and feather kisses along her jawline, loving the way she tastes. No matter how many times we make love, it's never enough. She makes me feel insatiable.

"I guess." She laughs. "What are we doing?"

I pull back to give her a smartass answer, but the doorbell rings right on time.

"Who's here?" she asks.

"Go answer it."

She walks to it and opens the door, and the next second she's squealing.

"Presley, oh my God! What you doing here?" Olivia pulls her inside and wraps her arms around her the best she can.

I walk up behind Olivia and greet Presley. "She's here to take our maternity pictures on the beach."

"What?" Olivia looks at me, then turns to Presley. "Really?"

"I knew you wanted them done, and you said it was hard to coordinate with our schedules, so I planned it for you. Presley squeezed us in before her trip to Texas and said she could meet us here."

"Why are you so amazing?" Olivia turns and is nearly in tears as she wraps her arms around my neck. "I can't believe you did all this."

"When are you going to realize I'm the perfect man?" I tease. "That's what you get for pegging me as a playboy."

She laughs. "Ha! You *were* a playboy! One who makes me crazy."

"Presley, help me out…"

"I'm not getting in the middle of this. You two are sickly adorable and it makes me want to throw up."

"Oh come on! You'd find the perfect guy, too, if you'd sit still long enough to meet someone," Olivia tells her.

"She is going to Texas next week," I add.

"Ooh! Find yourself a hot cowboy to ride and then tell me all about it," Olivia encourages with eagerness. "Seriously, I expect some juicy details. I've read some cowboy romances, and if there's one thing those cowboys are good at—"

"Okay, I don't need the details." Presley stops her with a laugh. "I'll be staying at a B&B on a ranch. If I meet any real-life cowboys, I'll jump at the opportunity. Happy now?"

"Very." Olivia smiles victoriously.

"You ready to get your pictures done? The view is amazing," Presley says.

"Yes, let's do it!"

The three of us head toward the beach and step in the shallow part of the water. Presley poses us and has us look at each other and facing different directions while she snaps away. Olivia looks so damn happy, I can't wait for her to see these shots.

My hand is over her bump, and I feel a kick against my palm. "I think she's dancing in there," I say, placing both hands over her stomach. "She's having fun." Feeling our baby girl inside her never gets old.

I kneel in front of her, and I can hear Presley taking more snapshots. "I can't wait to meet you, baby." Looking up and seeing my gorgeous wife with her golden hair blowing in the wind and her eyes bright with happiness causes my heart to burst with the love I feel for her and our little one. "Thank you for marrying me."

"What?" she asks softly.

"Seriously. I can't imagine my life without you. Thanks for giving me the chance to prove you wrong."

"Prove me wrong?" She arches a brow.

"That I wasn't just looking to get into your pants." I wink. "And that you were more than just an uptight, prissy know-it-all."

"That was almost romantic until you ruined it." She grins.

I stand and steal a kiss. "I love you."

"You're lucky I love you too."

He smirks. "So fucking lucky."

Read Colton & Presley's story in *Make Me Stay*

MAKE ME STAY

make me series

USA TODAY BESTSELLING AUTHOR
KENNEDY FOX

CHAPTER ONE

PRESLEY

THE FLIGHT from Los Angeles to San Antonio is nothing special, but I enjoy stealing glances at the clouds out the window. Stuck between a snoring man and a coughing woman, all I want to do is spray myself with Lysol, but I settle for rushing off the plane once we land. Even though I travel a lot for my job as a photographer, I still get anxious about flying and dealing with everything that comes with it. Once I get the keys to the rental car and place my suitcases and camera gear in the back, relief takes over. As I pull out of the parking lot, I breathe easy. That is, until I hit midday traffic.

Growing up in LA, I dealt with bumper-to-bumper traffic no matter the time of day, so even though this is still annoying, it doesn't faze me. Over the years, I've learned to aggressively cut people off and drive like I have better insurance. That mentality seems to work in every city I visit, and San Antonio is no different. After a few middle fingers, curse words, and honks, I'm zooming down the highway toward Eldorado where I've rented a room at a bed and breakfast for the next ten days.

Eventually, the cityscape is behind me, and I smile as I make my way onto I-10. After only three more hours on the road, I'll be at my destination. From the photos, the B&B looked like paradise with lots of land, horses, and a huge white house with a wraparound porch. It should be on a movie lot at Universal Studios; that's how perfect the photos were. Considering I need cowboy-themed photos for a big publisher to post on my Instagram account, I thought I'd find more inspiration by being on a real ranch. It's just one of the many perks of my job.

Traveling is in my blood and sets my soul on fire, but it sits behind my passion for photography and books. My mother always said you find the road to success by doing something you love, and I figured out what I loved in high school. Now I'm living the dream of a freelance photographer and get to travel often. Working directly with publishers, I take photos for book covers and am often hired as the primary photographer for book signing events. This job is everything I've ever wanted in life, and I'm so grateful.

Admiring the vast land in all directions causes a smile to touch my lips. Texas is so different from California. Instead of electric cars and scooters, cowboys drive lifted trucks with mud tires. Even though the speed limit is eighty, everyone around me drives at least twenty over, so I step on the gas to keep up with the flow of traffic. As the hours pass, I'm surprised to have cut nearly thirty minutes off my drive.

The GPS directs me to take Exit 388, so I slow to veer onto the off-ramp. The directions the B&B gave me when I confirmed my reservation included driving straight after the stop sign, then taking a right past a pump station. I'll eventually see an old barn, so I need to slow down because apparently, the GPS directions will bring me to the end of a dirt road that leads to nowhere. Gotta love country road driving.

Once I see the barn, I do as directed, and the wrought iron Circle B Ranch sign comes into view. Excitement streams through me as I turn down the long driveway. Over the past few months, I've been staying in big cities, where the constant noise drones on, but as I roll down the window and smell the fresh air, I hear nothing but silence. It's divine. As soon as the B&B comes into view, I realize I desperately need this change of scenery.

I park the car and get out, staring at the giant house. Next to the front steps of the porch is a flowerbed with a B&B sign. I can't wait to capture this picturesque scene with my camera.

Before I grab my bags from the trunk, I decide to check in first. As soon as I step inside, my mouth falls open. The pictures didn't do it justice. The hardwood floor perfectly complements the off-white walls decorated with Western-themed portraits. A sitting area surrounds a large fireplace, and I see an older woman quietly reading a book. I smile at her as I walk through the house, pass the stairs, and head to the check-in desk.

"Howdy, ma'am." A man with dark hair and blue eyes greets me. His sleeves are rolled up, showing off his muscular arms.

"Um," I say, swallowing hard. He caught me off guard because I don't think anyone has called me ma'am before and meant it. "Hi."

"Are you checkin' in?" He gives me a smile, and what they say about the Southern charm is true. I glance down as he pulls a scheduling book out from under the counter, and that's when I notice the wedding ring on his left hand. All I have to say is if all the men look this good in Texas, I might never leave.

"The reservation is under Presley—"

"Williams," he interrupts. "I spoke with you on the phone and confirmed your reservation last week. I'm John Bishop." He holds his hand out to introduce himself, and I shake it. "Nice to meet you, ma'am. How was your flight?"

I smile at his genuine kindness. "It was…well, it sucked. But the drive was nice."

"Probably a lot different than what you're used to." He gives me a sincere grin. I nod and chuckle. "Here are your room keys," he says, handing them to me. "I just need you to sign a few documents. Well…" He looks around. "I have to print some more. Sorry. I'll be right back."

"No problem," I say as he walks off.

I turn and take in my surroundings, making notes of where the natural afternoon light streams in through the windows. The back door swings open, and I see John wearing a cowboy hat and different clothes.

"Howdy, ma'am," he says, giving me a smirk.

My mouth falls open, and I look toward the office where I just saw him enter. "Weren't you…?"

"What?" he asks. "Wearing something else?"

I nod. "I must be drained from traveling. Sorry."

He lets out a booming laugh just as John comes back carrying the papers in his hands. All he does is shake his head. Yep, I've officially lost my mind.

"Sorry, Presley. This is my brother Jackson."

I let out a laugh and exhale a deep breath. "I knew I was tired, but wow. Identical twins. Didn't see that one coming."

"I've been telling him we need a wall with all the employee photos, but he refuses to take any of my suggestions. It's nice to meet you, Presley," Jackson says, walking through the house to the dining area, and I turn my attention to John.

"He does that to everyone, thinking it's so funny to pretend to be me. I'm pretty sure he's the only one who laughs," John says, handing me a pen and pointing at where I need to sign.

Clinging and clanging rings out from the dining area. "We're out of coffee," Jackson shouts.

"Then make some! You know how to!" John yells, then glances at me. "Sorry about him."

"It's fine," I say with a laugh.

"Yours always tastes better," Jackson says, walking with an empty cup in his hand. John completely ignores him.

"So your room is up the stairs on the left-hand side. It's the Violet room, and when you walk in, you'll know why. Breakfast is served between six and nine. Afternoon cookies are ready around two, and dinner is served at six. If you need extra towels, just let me know. And you can call the number on the bottom of your agreement at any time if you need anything at all. Okay? Any questions?" He smiles, continuing to annoy Jackson who is tapping his foot loudly behind me. "Oh yeah, you had a few boxes of what felt like bricks arrive yesterday. They're already in your room waiting for you."

"I don't have any questions at the moment and thank you so much. I really appreciate you letting me ship my things here," I tell him.

"Do you need any help with your suitcases?" he asks.

I shake my head. "No, thanks. I got it."

He gives me a nod before making his way toward a swinging door where I'm sure the coffee is kept.

As I turn around, Jackson just looks at me. "So where you from? Not these parts."

"From California. Los Angeles," I respond.

"Really? My sister lives in Sacramento. Been out west a few times. Not my cup of sweet tea. Too busy and weird," he says with a chuckle.

I smile. "Yeah, it's different. But so is Texas."

"So you're single?" he asks bluntly.

My eyes go wide, and I'm sure he can see the confusion on my face.

"Oh, I'm not asking for myself." He proudly shows me his wedding ring. "I'm married. Just had our third baby. My wife is home taking care of the little angel now. But just wanted to warn ya that some men moseying around the ranch think they're some real-life cowboy Casanovas if you know what I mean. You're a pretty girl, and I'm not one to usually warn women, but—"

I feel my cheeks heat. "Okay, okay. I get it. Thanks for letting me know." But all I'm really wondering is if they look as good as these two and if they'd sign a waiver for me to take some pictures. My mind wanders. *Do all cowboys have abs of steel?* My thoughts are totally in the wrong place.

I almost laugh but somehow hold it in when John comes back. "Coffee is brewing, jackass."

I snort and shake my head, then thank him again before going to my car to grab my bags. Though I know John offered to help, I'm not used to gentlemen and manners and can handle it myself. So being the independent woman I am, I carry my bags up the stairs. By the time I make it to my room, I'm exhausted. Pulling the keys from my pocket, I unlock the door, and when I step inside, I'm shocked to find the room isn't purple. Instead, I see a little plaque in memory of one of their family members.

Southerners. I already love them.

Once I'm unpacked, I check out the scenery from one of the many large windows in the room. I have a direct view of a barn and a horse corral and can even see the rolling hills in the distance.

The sunrise and sunset must be beautiful here, and I make it a point to remember to catch both so I can take photos of them.

My exhaustion takes over, so I take a quick shower to wash off the travel stank and lie down for a nap before dinner. As I close my eyes, all I can do is smile because I'm really in Texas, and so far, it's checked all my boxes. Including the one marked finding a real cowboy even though it seems cliché.

CHAPTER TWO

COLTON

THE MORNINGS COME WAY TOO QUICKLY, ESPECIALLY when I stay up late. Working on a ranch means every day is an early one, but it's brutal when I don't go to bed until after two a.m. Braxton, one of my best friends who's also a ranch hand, wanted to go to the Honky Tonk bar last night, and since I owed him one, I agreed. That meant drinking past our personal limits, having Jake, Braxton's roommate, drive us home, and me riding a four-wheeler to work before dawn. Luckily, I was able to rent a house from Jackson's wife, Kiera. When she moved in with him, she needed to find a tenant, so I hopped on the opportunity. With a cleared half-mile trail leading straight to the B&B, it's easy for me to ride a horse or take a four-wheeler to work.

Jackson's family owns the Bishop ranch. And since he's now helping Kiera with her horse training business, I'm in charge of the horseback riding lessons and leading the trail rides, which I love. Riding has been my passion since I was a kid, and now I get to share that with other people.

Once I'm parked near the barn, I walk toward the doors to start my day. Though it's early summer, it's still brisk in the morning, and the fog lingers. The horses know the drill as soon as they see or hear me. Most go to their stalls while others continue to sleep, but once the feed hits the buckets, they're all up and impatiently waiting.

Over the past two and a half years since I took over Jackson's job, I've learned how to get through my morning duties quickly. While I've worked on the ranch for over four years, I've been promoted from ranch hand bitch to the stable bitch. Feeding the horses, cleaning up their shit, checking the water levels, and then going over my schedule are how every day starts—come rain or shine. Just because I have a day off doesn't mean my tasks sit. Ranch life means the job must get done whether I'm here or not. Luckily, Braxton can cover for me. He usually helps Alex, one of the Bishop brothers, take care of the working horses used in the pastures to herd the cattle among other things. Since he has a lot of experience with horses, when I get sick—which basically never happens—or go on vacation—which also *never* happens—or have a day off throughout the week, he's my backup. But truthfully, I've grown to really love and appreciate my job and don't even care if I have a break away. I couldn't ask for a better life, and I owe the Bishops so much for giving me the opportunity to prove myself.

After I feed the horses and fill the water troughs, I go inside to keep Jackson's tradition of stealing coffee from the B&B alive. The sun is still sleeping, but John isn't. He's at the B&B at five a.m. every morning to make coffee, ensure breakfast is being prepared, and then double-checks the reservations. He's anal most of the time about things being right, but so am I, so we work well together.

"Mornin'," John says from his office when I walk in. "Coffee's ready."

I grab a cup and fill it to the top, hoping it will help this impending headache. I try hard not to make a mess with the sugar packets and creamer like Jackson does. I want to stay on John's good side so he doesn't boycott my morning routine.

"I don't have anyone signed up for lessons this afternoon," he tells me as I open the drawer and grab the bottle of ibuprofen. "But I think Jackson might need some help with training if you're caught up. Since training is now a part of the family business, we all gotta pitch in." His eyes meet mine, and he continues to sip his coffee. "I think he just wants to sleep late. You know how Jackson gets on Fridays."

"Lazy," we say in unison and laugh. John nods.

"I just have to go over to the hay barn and load the trailer because we need more bales in the loft. Yesterday afternoon, I noticed it was pretty empty."

"Sounds good. Might be able to get Braxton to help you so you don't have to make so many trips. Just text Jackson when you're done and see if he still needs help."

I finish my coffee before throwing the Styrofoam cup in the trash. "Will do. If something changes, let me know." I grab the keys to the old ranch hand Chevy as I head out the door, then back it up to the lowboy trailer. Before I make my way across the property toward the barn where the hay is kept, I text Braxton and let him know my ETA.

Braxton: I already got the damn memo.

I chuckle and lock my phone, not even giving him a courtesy reply. When I pull up to the barn, I see him leaning against his parked truck. Yep, he's not in a good mood, but honestly, it was his fault we went out last night. After two ibuprofen and a cup of coffee, I'm good. Learned that little trick from Jackson during his single days.

I roll down the window and catcall Braxton. "Hey, good lookin'," I say with a whistle. He flips me off, which only encourages me to give him more shit.

All the ladies wanted to go home with him last night. Shoulda sold tickets to ride the Buckin' Bronco. Once I'm parked, I get out of the truck, and he walks toward me.

"Can we hurry and get this over with? I was right in the middle of helpin' Alex change a tire on one of the Jeeps."

I laugh. "So you were supervising him? Because seriously, how many people does it take to do that?"

Braxton rolls his eyes. A few years younger than me, he's from Alabama and has one of the thickest accents I've ever heard. We teased him about it when he started working on the ranch a few years ago, but it drives the ladies wild. When I lived at the ranch hand sleeping quarters, we'd get into so much damn trouble. But then again, even though I moved out, we still do.

"Holy shit!" I shout. "Is that a hickey on your neck?" I move the collar of his shirt. "Damn dude, was her mouth a vacuum? That shit looks like it hurts."

He waves me off, pushing me away. "Enough about me. Where the hell did you go last night?" He climbs up the wooden ladder that leads to the top area of the barn.

"I had Jake drive me home. My truck's still at the bar. Wanna take me there later to get it?" I ask. "Oh, throw fifty bales over if you can."

He smirks, puts on his leather gloves, just as I do, then starts tossing the hay over the edge. "I thought you went home with that redhead who was eyeing you all night. Actually placed a bet you did."

"Then you lost, *again*," I tell him. Slipping my hands under the twine bundling the hay, I walk it to the trailer and load it. "You'll go broke betting on me bringing a woman home. I'm cleaning up my act. Regardless if they're redheads."

"That's true. Your dick might fall off from lack of use before that happens." He chuckles.

"And yours might fall off from overuse or herpes. Hell, maybe both," I taunt, making my rounds back and forth. Eventually, he climbs down from the loft and helps me finish loading the rest of them.

After a good three hours, the sun shines in the sky, and the trailer is packed. Braxton hops in his truck and leads the way so I won't have to take him back to his truck after we unload. I drive slowly through the pasture until I hit the dirt road, continually checking in the rearview mirror to make sure I don't lose any hay on the way. As I pull up to the barn, I see Braxton flirting with a woman leaning against the horse corral. I'm not sure he can turn it off.

I back the trailer into the large opening and whistle at Braxton as soon as I get out of the truck.

"You ruin all my fun." He groans, and I see the woman trailing him. She smiles wide, looking me up and down.

"Howdy, miss." I tilt my head at her. By the way she's peeling off all my clothes with her eyes, I almost feel the need to tell her I have a strict personal I-don't-sleep-with-the-guests policy, but I don't. Braxton whips around, throwing her one of his boyish grins before happily putting on his gloves and carrying the hay bales into the barn. I chuckle at him trying to show off as she stands around, making small talk.

"You've lived here all your life?" she asks in a thick accent. I can't tell if she's from Boston or Jersey because I'm horrible at picking up on those things.

"Yes, ma'am. Born and raised," I reply, helping Braxton. He's basically flexing as he carries the hay over his head. If I would've known that all it took to motivate him was the presence of a pretty lady, I would've had a line of women out here watching him every day.

"I grew up in Alabama," Braxton adds.

"Really?" She sounds intrigued, and I'm happy he takes the attention away from me as he lays the charm on thick.

Eventually, the trailer is unloaded, the hay is put up top, and the woman goes back to the B&B while Braxton smiles like an idiot.

"What?" he asks, guilty as sin.

All I do is shake my head. "If Mama Bishop finds out you're getting guests' phone numbers…"

"The only person who knows is you. So keep your mouth shut," he says, and a throat clears behind us.

"And me," Jackson adds, and I chuckle.

"Fuck," Braxton whispers.

Jackson lets out a booming laugh. "And I've been known to have the biggest mouth in the South, so there's that." Jackson holds out his hand. Braxton pulls the woman's business card from his pocket, placing it in Jackson's palm, and he proceeds to rip it into confetti. "I'm doing you a favor. Trust me."

Jackson looks over at me. "I don't need any help training after all. Got it all situated. Mama took the babies, and Kiera is helping. She's been dying to do more since Kaitlyn was born, and the weather today is gonna be perfect."

"Good. That means this jackass can take me to my truck." When I look at Braxton, he has his arms crossed over his chest and his lips pulled into a firm line.

"Fine. Let's go," he tells me, turning and walking away.

"What crawled up his ass and died this morning?" Jackson asks.

I shrug. "Might be all the whisky he drank last night combined with the Hoover vacuum that practically sucked his neck off, I suppose."

Jackson shakes his head. "Been there."

Not even a minute passes before Braxton is laying on the horn.

I lift my arms up at him, and yell, "I'm coming. Damn!"

I turn and look at Jackson. "He has the patience of a two-year-old."

"Accurate, considering I've got two of them at home," he adds, walking past me toward the B&B. "Try not to murder each other."

"No promises." As soon as I get into the truck, Braxton starts bitching about the phone number. All I can do is laugh at him. He basically has a Rolodex full of women's numbers in his phone. You'd think he was playing a Collect Them All game.

After we make it into town, Braxton fills up his gas tank, then we head over to the grocery store to pick up a few things. "I just need to get a steak for dinner tonight. Since I'm already here."

"Alright, whatever," I say, considering I'm on his watch. I follow him through the aisles, and as we're leaning over to look at the fresh-cut meat, I hear my name being called from behind me.

"Colton?" It's a woman's voice.

I turn around, and the color drains from my face. "Mallory," I say behind the knot lodged in my throat.

"How have you been? It's been…"

"Five years," I finish her sentence, then look down and see a little girl with blond ringlets standing beside her. Mallory notices me glance at her, and my heart drops.

"Julia, this is Colton," she tells her. The little girl politely smiles and then hides behind Mallory.

"Nice to meet you, Julia," I greet with a grin even though I've known her since before she was born. My eyes narrow in on Mallory. "What are you doing here?"

"Moved back last month," she explains. Being around her is awkward as hell, and I'm not really sure what to say.

Braxton, being the perfect distraction, walks up beside me, holding the biggest steak I've ever seen. He looks at Mallory, then looks at me. A smile touches his lips, though this isn't a happy moment.

"Good seeing you," I quickly say before introductions can be made. "Take care."

All the air escapes my lungs, and I walk past Braxton, out the door, and wait by the truck. A few minutes later, he's unlocking the door, and we climb inside.

"So that was her?" he asks, starting the truck.

"Yep. That's the woman who destroyed my fucking heart."

CHAPTER THREE

PRESLEY

PEOPLE AREN'T LYING when they say Texas heat is an experience all its own. Waking up in the gorgeous rustic B&B won't get old anytime soon; however, this humidity is causing a hair-tastrophe. California has low humidity this time of year, so imagine my surprise when I wake up with a new 'do. Well, everything is bigger in Texas, right?

Deciding not to fight it, I throw my hair into a ponytail after my shower. I'm a natural redhead, but I also have blond highlights from being in the sun. Too bad my body doesn't take to the sun like my locks do. If I don't slather myself with sunscreen, I'll burn in less than five minutes. So as a precaution, I put some on.

As soon as I'm ready, I grab my large duffle bag of photo props and books and head downstairs to the dining room. The scent of fresh coffee hits me as soon as my foot hits the bottom step, and I inhale.

"Good mornin'," John greets me with a pleasant smile. "Did you sleep okay?"

I drop my things on a chair and roll my shoulders. "I did, thank you! The room is very charming."

He chuckles. "Decorated by my mother, so yes, charming is a good way to describe it."

I laugh in return. "It smells amazing in here."

"Please, help yourself. There's plenty."

"Thank you." I make my way to the table piled with pastries and grab a muffin, bagel, and some dessert looking thing. Then I pour a cup of coffee and add milk and sugar. I have a lot to do today, and caffeine is a must if I'm going to accomplish it all.

Just as I walk back to my table, someone bumps into me, and my coffee spills down my V-neck shirt on my chest.

"Oh shit." The guy who nearly knocked me over holds my waist to keep me on my feet. He releases his hold on me to swipe a few napkins off the table.

"Oh my God!" I squeal, immediately pulling my shirt away from my body.

He hands the napkins to me, and I try to wipe the coffee from between my breasts and dab the liquid from my shirt.

"Are you okay?"

I look up and see a guy who's too good looking to be real, but considering hot coffee was spilled on my skin, I know for certain he is. "I have second-degree burns on my boobs now. What do you think?" Attractive or not, I'm pissed. I loved this shirt, too.

He stumbles, pulling back to study me, and I watch his eyes lower to my chest. My shirt isn't extremely low-cut, but it still shows off my chest. I'm not on the small side either, so pulling my shirt away from my body exposes more of myself than before.

"I'm really sorry. I wasn't paying attention. It's this jackass's fault." He nods his head over his shoulder to a man wearing a cowboy hat and a smirk.

"Who is that?"

"Braxton. He's a ranch hand and holds the title for the number one asshole around here."

My eyes flick to where Braxton is standing near the kitchen.

"And you just stole his title." I grimace, glancing down at my coffee-covered shirt, then back at him.

Raising his brows in surprise, he clears his throat. "I'm Colton, by the way. I am really sorry. Can I get you a cold towel or anything?"

He sounds sincere—hell, he even looks it—but I'm not in the forgiving mood, considering I haven't had any caffeine and now I need to change.

Instead of answering his question, I reply, "How is it his fault?"

Colton clears his throat as he leans back on his heels. Looking down, I see dark faded jeans tucked inside cowboy boots. His messy brown hair peeks out from his ball cap, and his T-shirt looks like it's painted on. It's clear he's rock solid underneath, but I can't let that distract me.

However, he'd make one hell of a cover model.

"He sent me in for coffee and food and then called my name. When I looked over, I didn't see you, and well, you know the rest." Colton pinches his lips together and shrugs. "Are you sure I can't get you anything? I feel awful." He places a hand on his chest over his heart in sincerity.

"No, forget it. I add a lot of milk to my coffee, so luckily, it wasn't too hot."

The corner of his lips tilts up just the slightest. "I thought you said you had second-degree burns on your..." He swallows. "Chest."

"Well, it doesn't feel great. Why don't you let me pour coffee on yours, and you can see for yourself?"

He chuckles. The bastard.

"Colton! Hurry up!" Braxton shouts, and two seconds later, John walks over and smacks him on the shoulder to be quiet.

"I didn't get your name," he says.

"I didn't give it to you." I walk around him, set my plate down on the table, then march back upstairs. As tempted as I am to look over my shoulder to see if he's watching me, I don't. He can't use his Southern charm to erase the fact he ruined my favorite shirt.

Once I've changed clothes and reapplied my lipstick, I go back to my food and refill my mug, carefully mixing a perfect concoction of cream and sugar. Colton and Braxton are long gone, so I actually get to drink my coffee instead of wearing it.

After checking my email and scrolling through my Instagram, I decide to go outside for some inspiration. I open the back door, suck in the fresh Texas air, and walk along the gorgeous white wraparound porch. The whole place is a dream; something out of a *Country Living* magazine. There are fans on the ceiling of the porch, which I find amusing, along with rocking chairs and wooden benches on the porch. Hanging plants swing from hooks in the light breeze, and flower beds surround the railings.

I pull my camera from my bag and take snapshots of the house in the distance. Walking around, I capture different angles of the B&B with the sun high in the sky. I stop to review the images on the tiny screen of my camera and smile.

"Gorgeous," I mutter to myself. I take pictures of the B&B sign and some with the hills behind it in the distance. The images on their website are great, but no picture will be able to do it justice, not even mine.

Once I've taken a variety of photos to double-check the outdoor lighting, I find a spot on the back porch to set up a mini photoshoot with a few of the southern romance books several publishers sent me. The scenery from the back of the B&B will make a perfect backdrop too. I brought a variety of props with me, and once I pull them out of my bag and lay out some fake flowers, an old pair of worn cowboy boots I bought from a secondhand shop, and some rope, I'm nearly ready to start. I always take pictures of the book with props and then some with me holding it or pretending to read it. Staging different items that are true to the theme of the book is my favorite part, but sometimes it's difficult to be creative and to keep things original, especially with the competition on Instagram. I'm always trying to stay fresh and relevant with my photos in the book world.

I pull down my high ponytail and brush my fingers through my hair. Once I've smoothed it enough to twist my hair into a low braid, I place the cowboy hat on my head. Standing in front of my camera, I take a few test shots. After I'm positioned perfectly in the frame, I mark a spot on the ground, then I click on the timer for ten seconds. I press the button, hurry to my mark, and face the opposite direction as I hold the book above my shoulder with both hands. The photo will be of the back of my hat, fully showcasing the book cover, the blue sky, and the pastures in the background. The camera clicks and snaps a set of pictures. I set it up for another shot so the book remains in focus and the surrounding area is blurry.

After a few more shots, I review the images and smile with pride.

As I glance around, I decide to do a flat lay with a few of the books and take out the rest of the props from my backpack. The worn white wood makes for an authentic backdrop, and I get excited just imagining how the pictures will turn out.

"Hmm…" I think aloud, repositioning some of the items. "Let's try this."

I place five books side by side with the spines facing up, and after a few failed attempts, I finally get them to stay. Carefully, I set the fake flowers, candles, and rope around them. I'll have to shoot from above, but keeping my shadow out of the shot is relatively easy with my tripod. It's a tedious process, but my followers love my pictures, and it makes me happy.

Editing the pictures is one of my favorite parts of the process, and sometimes I manipulate the lighting so every image I post matches my aesthetic. I also enjoy playing with different filters in my editing software to enhance or add elements that aren't really there. In LA, everyone talks about movie magic. However, in my world, it's photo magic.

Once I have the layout exactly how I want it, I position my tripod and camera. Typically, I take five to ten shots and then change a few things around and take more. It's quite a process especially when I'll only post one or two pictures out of each shoot on my feed. However, I love it so much I don't mind how long it sometimes takes to get the perfect picture.

I take a few shots, and when I kneel to reposition one of the flowers, the door swings open and a cowboy boot steps right into my setup, nearly kicking me in the face.

"What the hell?" I shout, quickly leaning back. I lose my balance and fall backward onto my ass. My hat falls off, and when I look up, it's none other than Colton. *Again*. "Seriously?"

"Fuck. What are you doin' on the ground?" He holds his hand out for me, but I ignore it and manage to get on my feet by myself.

"You knocked me down!" I scold. "Don't you ever watch where you're going? You could've broken my camera."

Colton looks down and sees what he's standing on. It makes me see red.

"And you stepped on my books and props. Wow, you're two for two. Good job." Grabbing my tripod, I move it away from him and start picking up my things.

"I'm sorry. I didn't see you down here." He kneels to help me gather my items. "I was looking out at the view, and it was like you came out of nowhere."

He holds out a candle, and I snatch it from his hand. "Well, most people look in front of them when they walk."

"Look, I said I was sorry, okay? Don't need to keep yelling at me." He stands and crosses his arms over his chest. His broad, muscular chest.

Damn him.

He looks just like the cowboys on the covers of these books. Or hell, even better.

I don't reply and stack my things on one of the chairs near me.

"What are you doing anyway? Why all the books?" he asks.

"I'm a photographer," I reply in a short tone, grabbing my bags.

"Really? That's impressive."

"Yeah. I travel a lot and take pictures of books for publishers," I respond as I remove my camera from the tripod.

I glance over at him and notice he's intently watching me with a smile. "Take pictures of books? For what?"

"You wouldn't understand. I'm going somewhere else now that you've slowed me down *twice* today."

Colton sighs, and when I look up, he takes off his baseball cap and rakes his fingers through his hair before putting it back on. "C'mon, I said I was sorry. What else do you want me to do?" He gives me a little pouty face, but I'm not giving in that easy.

"Just stay out of my way," I say with a forced smile.

When I go to walk around him, he gently grabs my elbow and stops me. "Gonna tell me your name at least?"

I inhale a deep breath before speaking over my shoulder. "It's Presley. Watch where you're going from now on. Think you can handle that, Cowboy?"

CHAPTER FOUR

COLTON

"If that's what you want, Red," I mock, throwing an obvious nickname right back at her. "Though I can't be held responsible if your beauty distracts me again."

She snorts before taking a step out of my grasp and turns to face me. "That Southern charm won't work on me. I've been warned about your charisma already."

My brows lift. "Is that so? Enlighten me." I wave a hand in front of me for her to continue.

"I've read my fair share of romance novels," she replies.

I scrunch my nose and scoff. "That's your credible source?"

"Well, aside from friends who have visited Texas before, Jackson warned me that the guys around here are…what'd he say?" She taps a finger on her lips. "Oh right. Cowboy Casanovas."

I burst out laughing, but she doesn't crack a smile. "Seriously? Jackson has *no* room to talk. Trust me."

"That just confirms it even more then. Southern men are swoon-worthy, charming, and will say whatever it takes to get a woman into bed."

"That's presumptuous."

"I doubt it." She shrugs as if she doesn't care one way or the other. "Just was telling you to save it for someone who'll willingly fall to her knees at your sweet talk."

Fuck. I'd love to see her fall to her knees in front of me, but I don't say that aloud. I'm afraid she'd actually junk punch me for that kind of comment. As a feisty firecracker, Presley lives up to the redhead stereotype. The moment I set her off with the coffee, she put me on her shit list. I don't typically give a damn when women get angry with me, but for some reason, it bother me that she won't accept my apologies.

Presley's curvy in all the right places. Her chest was on display right in front of me, and I'm a man with only so much willpower, so I definitely took a peek. She has gorgeous tits; there's no denying that or the instant attraction.

"Let me make it up to you," I offer, hoping for some kind of truce. "I feel awful and want to make it right." I flash her a toothy smile, hoping she'll take the bait.

She licks her full lips, and I can't help but stare. Presley's skin is pale, and tiny freckles cover her cheeks. When she walked away from me earlier, I noticed her ass and how tight her jeans hugged her round globes. I want to grip them in my callused hands and feel her softness against my roughness.

"Fine. I have something you can do for me." She grins as if she's plotting my death.

"By the look on your face, I'm scared to ask."

"You pose and model for me so I can get some genuine cowboy shots, and I'll forgive you for fucking up my day."

"*Fucking up your day*? That's harsh. And wait…you want me to do what?" My head is spinning. Presley's going to be the one woman who'll knock me on my ass.

"I told you, I'm a photographer. I take a wide variety of pictures, and you ruined the ones for my Bookstagram, so I need replacements."

"What the hell is that?" I ask, more confused than before. "A booksta-what?"

"Bookstagram," she repeats, slower. "It's a book community on Instagram. People post images of the books they're reading or have read or want to read. Some pose with the books and some post flat lays, which is what I was doing when you so recklessly stepped into my photo setup."

"And what in the world is a flat lay?" I'm completely lost.

"Pictures taken on a flat surface with a pretty backdrop. It's where I create a scene by laying out the books with props, and once I arrange everything perfectly, I take pictures from above. The items I use are typically related to the book somehow. It's just a creative way to display novels and give subtle hints about the plot. There are many ways to pose them for Bookstagram, and that's part of what I do as a photographer." The passion and excitement are evident in her tone as she explains it to me.

"So people just post images of books on social media? For what?" I ask, needing clarification.

"Because they're passionate about reading," she explains. "It's how a lot of people find new authors in various genres, and publishers often send early review copies so Bookstagrammers can share before its release. A marketing strategy to help spread the word."

I blink, trying to wrap my mind around this. "I've never heard of that in my entire life."

"Yeah, well, I'm not surprised." She purses her lips and looks away.

Pretty sure that was a diss, but considering I "fucked up her day," I let it slide. "Alright so tell me what I need to do."

"Meet me back here around six. That's the golden hour. The sun casts a warm glow, and it almost looks like early morning, so it's the perfect lighting for outside photos. Oh, and wear dark jeans, a cowboy hat, and boots," she orders.

I furrow my brows and cross my arms over my chest. "Anything else?"

"And something flannel."

"You just assume I have a flannel shirt because I'm Southern?"

She raises a brow in challenge. "Am I wrong?"

No. "I'll see if I can find something to your liking."

"Good," she says victoriously. "And for the record, it's not because you're Southern. It's because you have that stereotypical cowboy look. But being that we're in Texas doesn't help your case either."

I grin, not sure if I should laugh or call her out for assuming. Though I do have a few flannel shirts and maybe even a jacket or vest, I'm still going to give her shit for it.

"So does that mean you're going to wear booty shorts and a bikini top?"

Presley pops her hip out and places a hand on it. "What's that supposed to mean?"

"It's obvious you aren't from around here, darlin'," I say. "Let me guess. West Coast? Am I right?"

She exhales through her nose as if she's annoyed with me. "Maybe."

"Well, there ya go. California is known for its beaches, so if we're going to make assumptions, you should come dressed as the stereotype too."

"That's not even the same thing." She dismisses me with a wave of her hand. "Whatever. I just need a cowboy model, which means you need to look like one. Can you do that or not?"

"I'll do my best." I grin, rubbing a hand across the stubble on my jaw.

"Great," she replies with fake satisfaction. "Don't be late."

When I finish my work for the day, I head home to shower and change. Presley and I might've gotten off on the wrong foot, but I'm determined to fix it. If being a model in her little photoshoot is gonna make her happy, then I'll suck it up and do it.

"You're late," she scolds the second I step onto the porch. She doesn't even look up while she fiddles with her camera.

"Actually, I've been inside." I walk toward her and wait for her orders. "Well? Do I fit the mold?" I ask, holding out my arms.

She finally looks up, and when our eyes meet, I'm worried she's going to tell me off again. Except for her jaw slightly drops, and when her lips part, she licks them.

"Ripped jeans, nice touch," she says.

"Well, you said you needed a sexy model." I grin.

Presley snorts, and I'm actually growing to like the way it sounds. Though it means I'm getting under her skin, it's progress. "I didn't say that, but let's get started." She puts her camera strap around her neck, and I watch as it falls between her large breasts.

She clears her throat, and I blink as if I wasn't just looking at her tits again. "Position me where you want," I tell her, using the sexual innuendo on purpose.

"Calm down, cowboy. Let's start small. Lean up against that

post and tilt your head to the side so I can get a profile shot," she instructs, pointing at the railing.

"Like this?" I position myself just like she said, but she looks over at me as if she's contemplating her next move.

"Look to your left and tilt your hat down just enough so I can't see your eyes," she explains, moving closer and adjusting my shirt. "Yes, like that. Don't move."

She steps away, and it's followed by the sound of her camera snapping. "Tilt your chin out just an inch," she says. As soon as I do, more clicking. "Good." She pauses a moment. "Not bad." I glance over without moving too much and find her looking at the images on the camera screen.

"Okay. So I need you to unbutton your shirt."

My head pops up. "What?"

"Abs," she says. As if that explains it.

"If you wanted to see my abs, all you had to do was ask." I smirk, unbuttoning my shirt like she demanded.

"Ha, you're hilarious." She puts her hands on her hips. "Looking at abs is in the job description. Yours aren't any more special than the last guy I photographed."

"You wound me, Red." I rest a hand over my chest, feigning heartbreak. "I thought we had something special."

"You're pathetic," she says but laughs. "Open your shirt up a bit and roll up the sleeves."

"So demanding." I do it as she intently watches me. "Anything else?"

"Let's try this one with a book. Think you can handle that?"

I scoff. "Handle what? Holding a book? Yeah, I think I'm capable." I hold out my hand, and she places a paperback in my palm. Looking at the cover, I chuckle. "Seriously?"

Presley rolls her eyes and takes a few steps back. "Just hold it to your left. Down by your hip. Yes, there." She continues taking pictures as she tells me to move an inch this way or that, and when she's not satisfied, she closes the gap between us and literally poses me like a doll. "Now don't let this get to that big head of yours, but I need you to unbutton your jeans."

I look up, and our eyes meet. The tiniest of smiles hints on her lips. "Excuse me?" I ask with raised brows. "If you wanted to save a horse and ride a cowboy, all you had to do was say so in the first place."

She pushes a hand against my chest, making me stumble back a step. "That's the cheesiest line I've ever heard."

"But you were thinking it, right?" I give her a smug grin.

She audibly groans and turns around. "Never mind. There has to be someone else around here who won't drive me insane."

"Fine, fine. No more sexual innuendos," I promise. "But if you ask me to strip naked, I might not be able to contain myself."

She turns around with a death glare. "Trust me. I'm not that desperate. Now are you going to stop wasting my time?"

Fuck. Red's a firecracker, and I'm living for it.

I hold my hands up in surrender. "I'm all yours."

For the next hour, Presley poses me in various positions that include standing, sitting, and holding books. She leaves my shirt open and jeans undone. I stand out in front of the hills and pastures as she takes shots from different angles. After a while, she explains she also takes stock images for book covers that are completely different from her pictures for social media.

"I think that should do it for now," she says while she reviews the images. There have to be hundreds by now. "The lighting looks so good." The way her eyes light up brings a smile to my face. "Can you do a few more without your shirt?"

"You're the boss," I tell her with a smirk. Having a body crafted from hard work and tedious labor, I have nothing to be ashamed of and don't mind showing it off to her in the least. Though she acts all tough, I don't miss the slight blush on her cheeks when I bare my chest and abs.

Presley glances around as if she's trying to decide where to place me next. "Stand over there, turn around, and then look over your shoulder. Keep your hat angled down and your fingers in your belt loops."

"Seriously? That sounds corny as fuck."

She flashes me a look, and I almost regret questioning her.

"Fine." I chuckle, feeling like an idiot. This pose is ridiculous.

"Move two inches to the right and cock your hip," she instructs in the distance. "I'm going to kneel so I can get a really cool shot with the sun behind you."

Moments pass as she continues to take photos, and then I hear laughter.

"Lookin' good!"

"Hot damn!"

"Sexy cowboy!"

Catcalls. Whistles.

What the fuck?

I turn around and see Braxton, John, Jackson, and Alex.

Assholes. They're all smirking and laughing, watching me.

Glancing over at Presley, she snickers and isn't trying to hide the fact she knew they were around.

I walk toward her and rip my shirt from her hand. "Very nice."

"Now we're even," she says smugly. I'm sure she doesn't feel an ounce of guilt.

I chuckle at her boldness. "Not in the slightest, Red. I'll get you back," I promise.

CHAPTER FIVE

PRESLEY

I WAKE up wearing a smile and feeling as though I slept on a bed of clouds. The photos I took of Colton yesterday turned out so well. I can't wait to edit and post them. After I got back to my room last night, I uploaded them to my computer and picked out a handful of good pictures. Honestly, there weren't any bad ones. He's a natural behind the lens.

Though he did an amazing job, I wouldn't dare tell him as much because he already seems to have an ego the size of Texas. The man is perfect for the camera—chiseled jaw, high cheekbones, messy dark hair, and blue eyes—and I'm not sure Colton has a bad angle because I looked. While I tried not to stare, I did catch myself ogling his bare chest, abs, and the happy trail that led down to his noticeable package. Which—after seeing how tight his pants were—I know isn't tiny. I find something ridiculously sexy about a man who earns his abs from hard manual labor.

Trying to push my thoughts of him out of my head, I get out of bed and open the curtains to take in the morning sunshine. Texas in late May is beautiful.

After I go through my morning routine and get ready, I make my way downstairs for breakfast. Everything smells so good, but I rush to the caffeine first. Carefully, I pour my coffee and look over my shoulder to make sure no one is around to bump it from my hand before I place it on the small table by the window and make a plate. The sausage, bacon, hash browns, and eggs have my mouth watering. After I put a little bit of everything on my plate, I grab my coffee and head to the back porch with everyone else. The early morning weather is too lovely to pass up.

Just as I sit and take a bite of a sausage patty, I look out at the land, taking in the rolling hills and how the fog billows on the ground. The scenery is beautiful, but I know there has to be more to this place, considering the ranch sits on over a thousand acres.

As I'm about to dig into my scrambled eggs, I see Colton walking from around the house, smiling about something. I study the food on my plate, trying to pretend I'm completely intrigued by my bacon. From my periphery, I see him walk up the steps and feel his eyes on me, but I stay focused on ignoring him. That is, until he plops down in the chair in front of me.

"Hey, Red. How's it goin' today?" he asks in a playful tone.

I glance at him. "Considering I didn't have my boobs scorched with hot coffee, it's better than yesterday." I pop a piece of food into my mouth, acting disinterested in anything he has to say.

"Oh, we're on that again?" He chuckles. "Do I need to remind you what you did to me yesterday?"

I groan and roll my eyes. "It's not my fault they all showed up. I just didn't tell you right away." I shrug as if it was completely harmless.

Colton snickers but doesn't keep arguing about it. "How'd your bookstastuff pictures turn out anyway?"

"Bookstagram," I correct "Have lots of work to do today still." I take a bite of my bacon, and he snags the other piece off my plate. "Hey!"

"Thanks." He points the piece at me and shoots me a wink, then stands. "See you around, Red."

He doesn't wait for me to respond before walking off the porch. As I find myself staring at his tight ass, he turns around, looking over his shoulder at me with an eyebrow popped. Heat rushes through my body, and I quickly glance down at the hash browns on my plate. Suddenly, I don't have an appetite for food anymore. Once he's out of sight, I release the breath locked tight in my chest.

"Those cowboys are some lookers, aren't they, honey?" an older woman says, sipping a cup of coffee. I'm pretty sure I've seen her around the B&B in passing. "They're the only reason I book this trip each year. Makes me feel young again after my husband passed away." She has to be in her late 60s, early 70s and doesn't have a gray hair out of place.

"Sorry about your husband," I offer.

"Oh, don't be. He was an asshole most of the time." Her tone is sweet as she pours sugar in her coffee. "But I gave him the best years of my life, and he rewarded me with a pretty large savings, so I have no complaints. Loved the man until his last breath, still do." She grins at me, picks up her coffee, and sips it with a pinky in the air as she looks out in the distance.

I place my napkin on my plate and stand. "It was nice speaking with you. I'm Presley," I tell her.

"I'm Sadie. Nice meeting you, dear. Watch out for those cowboys, though. They'll rope your heart with one end, then tie you up with the other," she playfully warns, and I feel the blush over my cheeks return. I like her. She's sassy. But I can't seem to get away quick enough.

"Nice meeting you too! I'll see you around, I'm sure." I wave as I walk away.

"I'm sure you will. I booked the next month too," she tells me with a friendly wave as I open the screen door and walk in. I set my plate inside the dish tub, then take the stairs to the second floor, trying to calm my racing heart. Once I'm in my room, I glance around and see the stack of books I had shipped here.

My schedule has been so tight lately with cover shoots that I haven't had much time to read. So to take my mind off tight jeans and shit-eating grins, I grab the top book off the stack. As soon as I pick it up and see the cowboy on the cover, my thoughts are right back to where they were. I read the first page, and it starts off with a woman arriving at a ranch and having an altercation with a sexy cowboy. Instantly, I roll my eyes and close the book. Nope.

Just as I let out a frustrated huff, my phone vibrates in my pocket.

When I see Olivia's name on the screen, I snort-laugh. Olivia and I have been friends for years. Considering she assisted one of the biggest authors around, we ran into each other often and grew close. Her publisher hired me to take photos for an entire series, which ended up selling millions of copies and becoming a worldwide hit. It helped put me on the map too. Before I came to Texas, I was asked and honored to take Olivia's maternity photos with her husband at a beach house in South Carolina.

Olivia: So did you find yourself a hot cowboy yet?

I send her an eye roll emoji.

Olivia: Oh, come on! There has to be at least one.

Presley: All the men in Texas are good looking. But most of them are taken. Like always.

Olivia: Texas is huge. I'm sure there's at least one single guy.

Presley: Maybe. I'll keep you updated.

Of course, Olivia reads between the lines. She's a smart one. Nothing gets past her.

Olivia: So…who is he?

Presley: Don't know what you're talking about.

Olivia: The hell you don't. Is he hot at least?

I look up from my phone and find myself smiling as I think about Colton, then my lips transform into a firm line.

Presley: They're all hot. TRUST ME.

And they know it too.

Olivia: Send me pics! Also, I'm trying to live vicariously through you, so have tons of kinky sex. K? In the barns. Under the stars. On a horse. Please and thanks.

Presley: OMG, Liv! I am NOT going to have sex in a barn! Or on a horse! What is wrong with you?! Plus, I doubt those things happen in real life.

Olivia: I've read all the cowboy books. IT HAPPENS.

I laugh at the thought of Olivia begging me to give her sex updates. I doubt she and Maverick are going through a dry spell of any kind, but she's also very pregnant, so she's probably hornier than usual.

I look at the time and realize I should really get some work done. As I glance at the books piled on the table that I still need photos of, I realize I still have a lot to do, so there'll be no free time for reading today. I tell Olivia bye, and she sends me kissy face emojis. If something happens—even though I highly doubt it will—she'll be the first to know. *Maybe*.

Most of the time, I feel like a therapist for the people in the book community. I know all the drama because people confide in me. I don't look for it and definitely don't get involved. Considering I stay on the straight and narrow most of the time, it'd be a change of pace for me to have something to tell someone. But if I'm being honest, I haven't dated much, and I don't always make an effort to meet men. My true passions are traveling, photography, and books, so there's not a lot of time for much else.

Though I book photoshoots with sexy men throughout the year, their good looks and washboard abs don't faze me. I've always felt as though I'm in a different league anyway. I'm not stick skinny like the models they're used to spending time with, though I don't allow it to hold me back. I embrace my curves as best as I can and am all about body positivity and loving myself the way I am. However, I sometimes feel that others don't see me. The *real* me. They only see the chubby girl with a pretty face.

I quickly check the time and realize I've sat around texting Olivia for way too long. After I scroll through the pictures I took of Colton and my flat lays before he ruined my setup, though I'm not complaining too much, ideas start coming to me in full force. I hurry and grab my backpack and stuff the books and small props in my bag. After I slip blank memory cards into the front pouch of my bag, I pick up my camera, put in new batteries, and go downstairs.

Once my foot hits the bottom stair, I see John sitting in his office.

"Hey," I say, grabbing his attention.

He stands and approaches the counter, flashing me a grin. "Hey. Everything okay?"

"Yeah, it's great so far. I just have a question. I read online about how big the ranch is, and I think I could get some really awesome pictures off the beaten path. Maybe something out in the middle of nowhere, secluded, with tall grasses or an old barn or something. Do you have any place like that? I want to take photos where no one else has."

His smile widens. "Actually, have you ever been horseback riding before?"

Nervous laughter escapes me. "Um. No."

"There's availability on the schedule in thirty minutes, and it would actually be a great opportunity for you. I think you'll find exactly what you're looking for." He glances at my camera, then back at me. "It would be a one on one, so you could take your time."

I contemplate it. "But I have no idea how to ride a horse."

"Our trainer is great. By the time you go through the first few steps, you'll feel like a professional rodeo star."

I glare at him.

"Okay, well, maybe not a professional, but you won't be let out on your own. The trainer will make sure to lead you around. The horses are gentle enough for my daughters to ride them."

Nodding my head, I let out a deep breath. "Okay, okay. You convinced me."

He chuckles. "Perfect. I'll just need you to sign a waiver really quick, then you can meet out at the barn in about ten minutes."

"A waiver? That puts me at ease." I snort.

John chuckles, handing the paper over. "It's just a formality."

Once I sign my life away and promise not to sue the ranch, I stop by the restroom really quick, then walk out to the barn. The fresh Texas air brushes against my face, and excitement rushes through me. I walk past the corral and mosey into the barn. A man stands brushing a horse tied to a post.

But as soon as I see that ass, I know exactly who it is. And when Colton turns around, I try to swallow the knot in my throat.

"Hey, Red. You my lesson for today?"

My mouth falls open, and I hurry and close it.

"You're the horse trainer?" I ask, confused. I'm not sure what I thought he did around here, but it wasn't this.

"Yes, ma'am. But I've been known to train women too." He winks and smirks, and I want to smack it right off his damn face.

I shake my head. "Yeah, I'm not doing this. Changed my mind."

Within five steps, he closes the gap between us. "I promise to be a professional in all aspects. I'd never allow you to get hurt. Ya trust me?"

My eyes meet his, and I notice just how blue his eyes are. "No."

He bursts out laughing and shrugs. "If you don't do it, that just means you're a chicken."

Licking my lips, I pick up my camera and take a shot of him acting all smug before I smirk. "No one calls me a chicken."

CHAPTER SIX

COLTON

THE DETERMINATION in her step causes laughter to erupt from my core. I turn toward the stall where Snickers is, and I can hear her following me.

"So…" She lingers. When I stop and turn around, glaring at her with a smirk, she swallows hard. "You can guarantee I won't get hurt?"

I take a few steps toward her. "My main job is to ensure you make it back in one piece."

Her eyebrow shoots up. "Ensuring isn't the same as guaranteeing."

The next step I take makes her breath hitch. Her eyes soften before she breaks our gaze.

"I *guarantee* it, Red."

A moment passes between us, and the silent draws on. Her tongue darts out and licks her plump bottom lip, and I long to pull her into my arms and kiss the fire out of her.

"I'll take your word for it then," she adds with a small half-grin.

I somehow force myself to turn away, breaking the electricity crackling between us, and go to the stall. Before entering, I pull a lead rope from a hook close by and snap it on Snickers's halter. The kids love this chocolate and caramel-colored horse, mainly because he loves to gallop.

"He looks huge and scary," Presley says as I walk him past her and place him next to Ghost, the horse I ride when I guide tours.

"He's not." I shoot her a grin as I tie him to a hook. Feeling her eyes on me, studying me, I grab the pad and saddle, then place them on Snickers. I explain what I'm doing along with the importance of each piece. She stands back, listening intently as I walk her through the basics of a saddle.

"So you've never ridden before?" I ask.

"Not a horse," she quips. Instantly, the thought of her riding me enters my mind, but I try to push it away. I can't help imagining my fingers digging into her thick hips as she takes me whole. Fuck. Just thinking about it makes me rock hard. I excuse myself to the tack room to grab the bridle, but I really need to adjust myself before my dick rips right through my jeans. I take a few seconds to get ahold of myself before I return.

"You okay in there?" she finally asks, and that's when I realize I've taken way too much damn time.

"Yep, fine. Just looking for the correct rein length for you," I tell her, but I'm making shit up. I suck in a deep breath, grab what I need, and walk out. She's busy taking shots of the horse from different angles, which makes me happy to see.

When she pulls the camera from her face, she stares at her screen and walks toward me. "Look how awesome these are."

"You're so talented," I say, glancing at her, then back at the pictures.

"Thanks." She drops the camera between her breasts and places her hands on her hips. "Alright, cowboy. Let's get this show on the road. I have a ton to do today."

I chuckle at her sass, putting the bridle in Snickers's mouth and moving the reins back to the horn of the saddle. "You're the boss, boss."

As she watches me, I tighten the cinch so the saddle won't slide, then turn and hold out my hand. "Give me your camera and backpack. You're about to climb on."

She hesitantly removes it from over her head. I loop it over my shoulder, then she hands me the backpack, which I hang on a hook. I'll wear it when we ride so she doesn't have to worry about her balance with these bricks attached to her body. I point out all the pieces of the saddle again. "You're gonna put your foot right here in the stirrup, grab the horn, then pull yourself up and loop your leg over the other side. Got it, Red?"

Confidently, she takes a few steps forward and places her foot in the stirrup. In one swift movement, she's sitting on top of the saddle. But not before I get a nice view of her luscious ass in those jeans. Presley looks down at me, and I give her a nod, thinking how good she looks sitting up there. I hand her the camera, and she places it around her neck as I unhook Snickers and walk her around outside so she can get used to the motions in the saddle.

"Your hips naturally rock when you're on the saddle. Be one with the horse, holding the reins in one hand, and try to relax. Pull the reins right to go right and left to go left. Barely kick with your heels to make him go faster. Pull back to stop. Super easy. Hold yourself in place by tightening your thighs against the horse. Easier than riding a bike." I take her into the corral so Snickers can't run away with her and place the lead rope around the horn. "Okay, you're on your own now."

Presley follows my instructions and walks around the corral, and the smile from her face doesn't fade as she practices turning and stopping. "This isn't so bad," she admits.

"It's because you have an amazing teacher," I gloat, leaning against the metal of the corral.

"I wouldn't say amazing." She laughs, fucking with me.

As she continues guiding Snickers, she periodically glances over at me. I'm mesmerized by her on top of the saddle. I love a confident woman who knows what she wants and goes after her dreams. As I'm lost in my thoughts, I catch her biting her bottom lip when she looks over at me. Damn, she's as hot as flames right now.

I push off the railing and walk toward her. "Feelin' good?"

When Presley nods, I lead her back to the barn and tell her to stay put. I grab Ghost, put on her heavy-ass backpack, and quickly climb on, then meet her outside. Within a minute, we're heading down the Green Trail toward one of the lookouts that will be perfect for taking pictures.

"I've got to say, I'm a little disappointed," Presley jokes. She's riding so close beside me, I could reach out and touch her.

"About what?" I look over at her, meeting her green eyes.

"I thought you'd wear a cowboy hat to teach lessons, really playing up the whole cowboy cliché. But instead, you're wearing a baseball cap."

I reposition it on my head. "Sorry to disappoint, ma'am. But the hat isn't what makes a man a cowboy."

"It's the pants, isn't it?" She chuckles.

I hold back a smirk. "You better hold on, Red."

"For what?" she asks.

Seconds later, I'm digging my heels into Ghost's flanks, and we're trotting, then galloping. Snickers follows along, and when I look back, Presley is bouncing all over the saddle. I can't stop laughing as we speed down the trail. She's screaming at me, calling me every name under the sun.

Glancing back at her over my shoulder, I see her hair is blowing in the wind, but she's doing a good job holding on. Fight or flight. I pull back on the reins to slow down, then head over to our first stop. Snickers follows because he's used to trail riding. I slip off Ghost, and my face hurts from smiling so much. Presley scowls, and it only causes me to laugh.

"What the fuck!" she scolds as I tie Snickers to the post.

"What?" I shrug, pretending nothing happened.

"I could've gotten hurt! I could've fallen off! You promised to be nice!" She holds the horn and loops her leg over to climb off, losing her balance, but I'm there to catch her before she falls. I set her on the ground, and she turns and looks up at me. We're so damn close I can smell the sweetness of her skin. Her breasts are rising and falling because she's so worked up from riding.

I place my hand under her chin, forcing her to look into my eyes. "But did you die?"

She smacks her hand against my chest, groaning as she walks around me to unzip the backpack on my back. "But I *could* have. And then it would've been your ass."

"I actually kinda like the sound of that," I tease as she rezips the backpack. I cinch Ghost on the post next to Snickers and then lead her to a lookout point.

Presley places her hands on her hips, glaring at me. "You owe me."

"Add it to my tab," I tell her, chuckling.

"You're impossible!" She growls.

I snort. "Not the first time I've heard that one."

Presley moves toward me with the books held against her chest. She narrows her eyes at me, continuing past me. I stand back and watch her work her magic as she places the books next to a cactus and rocks. She stacks them, takes pictures one at a time, then reviews them. Her hair is a mess on her head, and she tries to smooth it down, but it's helpless. I actually chuckle, remembering how her red hair blew in the breeze as we galloped because it now looks like sexy bed hair.

"Will you take a picture of me holding these?" she asks, but the attitude is still in her tone, and I love it.

"Did it kill you to ask for my help just now?" I shoot her a wink, just trying to see how far I can push her.

"Never mind! I knew I should've brought my tripod."

I laugh and hold out my hand. "I'll help you. Just do all the fancy shit you do so all I gotta do is push a button."

Presley hesitantly hands me the camera and gets in place, holding the books so the spines are showing. Her back is toward me, and I stifle a laugh while I zoom in and take a few perfectly framed photos of her plump ass.

"Did you get the shot?" she asks over her shoulder, and I take another photo. The sunlight creates a soft glow around her face.

"No, not yet. Get back in place." I twirl my finger in a circle for her to turn around so I can take a few normal pictures so she doesn't murder me. "Got it."

She walks toward me.

"You should hop on Snickers and get some photos in the saddle. It would look cool. We could even stack the books on the saddle pad and have you turn toward them and kinda lean against this huge ass pile."

Presley's head tilts as if she's trying to imagine it, then her eyes widen, and she nods. "Yeah, we can try it."

And just like that, the attitude fades away.

I grab Snickers and bring him over to the lookout. Presley hands me the books, and I hold Snickers still as she climbs on. I put the books on the saddle pad behind her and have her twist her body. "Okay, now put your elbow on top of the stack."

Once she's in place, I put the viewfinder up to my eye. "Okay, now smile like you're actually having fun."

As soon as Presley bursts out laughing, I hold down the button and get several shots of her as happy as can be. "Perfect, Red."

She playfully rolls her eyes at me and holds the books in different ways and bosses me around while I take pictures of her from different angles. After an hour of taking photos, I tell Presley we have to head back. We've already gone over time for the lesson, and though I'd spend all day out here with her, I have to help Jackson unload a few horses around three.

"I have tons more to do today anyway, so that's perfect." She stuffs the books back in her backpack before zipping it up, then scrolls through some of the photos and her face twists. "Why are there pictures of my ass?" Her attitude returns, and I can't help smiling at the way she's busted me.

"My finger slipped," I say dryly, though I know she's not convinced by the eye roll she gives me.

Before Presley climbs on the saddle, she hands me the camera and backpack. "The other pictures turned out nicely at least." I smile, knowing that probably hurt to admit. Once she's situated, I hand the camera back to her.

"You know, cowboy. If this whole horse riding thing doesn't work out for you, you might consider becoming a photographer. You have a natural eye," she says. I tighten the backpack, then get on Ghost and lead the way down the trail.

As we slowly ride back, I can hear her snapping photos of trees we pass. After she puts the camera down, I look over at her.

"Ready?" I ask.

She starts shaking her head. "No, Colton. Don't."

I shoot her a wink, then tell her to hold on before Ghost bolts into a sprint. Snickers stays right next to me, and she hunkers down, holding on to her camera.

"I hate you!" she screams. "You're such an asshole!"

We make it back to the barn in record time, and I bend over, laughing so damn hard because she looks like a hot mess with hair everywhere and wearing that sassy scowl. My voice reverberates off the walls of the barn, and she's steadily cursing me as she climbs off the saddle.

With annoyance in her step, she stomps toward the B&B.

"I will never trust you again!" she yells, not turning and looking at me.

I slide off the saddle and tie Snickers and Ghost to a post, allowing her to walk away.

"Hey, Red?" I shout after her.

She turns and narrows her eyes at me.

"Forgetting something?" I lift the backpack full of books as if I'm holding them for ransom. She storms toward me, and I swear she's going to punch me in the face as she snatches the backpack from my hand.

"You're a dick, Colton," she says, but as she turns to walk away, I grab her arm and gently pull her back to me.

"I think you like it. Also, told you I'd get you back."

She searches my face, bites her tongue, then forces herself to walk away. As I'm taking mental snapshots of her ass, she looks over her shoulder, catching me. "Back on my shit list you go."

"As long as I'm on your list, that's all that matters, Red."

I hear her growl as she picks up her pace. I amble back to the barn with Snickers and Ghost in tow wearing a grin on my face as I unsaddle them.

The way Presley looks at me isn't lost on me. The attraction and electricity that streams between us are undeniable. I've never felt this way about anyone who's stayed at the B&B—or any woman since Mallory—and while she should be off-limits, I find myself wanting to break all the rules.

CHAPTER SEVEN

PRESLEY

Opening the large window in my room, I look out at the vastness. Staring at the cloudless blue sky inspires me to head out and find more areas to stage shots. Even though Colton helped me take some great ones yesterday, I'm here to take full advantage of the scenery and to stock up on pictures. With land for miles and the breathtaking views, I almost don't know where to start. If only I could find a couple more models—ones who won't torment me with their devilish good looks and snarky smart mouths.

Once again, my hair can't handle the humidity. Instead of trying to maintain it, I throw it in a messy bun. I also don't bother with a lot of makeup since it'll melt right off, so I just put on some lipstick and waterproof mascara. My eyelashes and eyebrows are so blond that if I don't wear mascara or eyebrow liner, they don't exist.

You know what else really sucks in this weather? Having thick thighs. I want to wear shorts, but considering how hot it is, I'm afraid they'll ride up my legs and get stuck, causing an unbearable heat rash. Against my better judgment, I opt for a maxi sundress. It'll hopefully be easy to work in, and I won't die from the heat.

"Mornin'." John greets me as soon as I sit down with my coffee and a plate of food.

"Good morning," I reply, giving him a smile. "I'm gonna have to agree with Jackson on this one." I hold up my Styrofoam cup. "You make it the best."

John chuckles. "Yeah, there's really no comparison. You'd think by now he'd learn the right proportions, but then again, he'd still find a way to fuck it up."

That makes me laugh. It's fun to watch them give each other shit. "I bet he was fun to grow up with."

His head falls back as a rowdy laugh bellows from his throat. "You have no idea. We might be in our thirties, but he's still basically a big kid at heart. He has three kids, but his wife has four—including him."

I chuckle, and it's easy to see why people love the Bishops so much. "Sounds like it would've been fun growing up here. I have three sisters and three brothers, but we struggled a lot living in LA."

He pinches his lips together as if he's sorry to hear that. Though it sucked at the time, it helped shape me into who I am.

"Growing up here was great but still a lot of hard work. Lots of wonderful memories. I hope to pass them down to all our kids too," John adds.

"Yeah? How many kids do you have?" I ask, genuinely curious. While he gives off this serious and down-to-business persona, I could definitely see him being a softy with his own children.

"I have two girls. Maize and Mackenzie. They keep my wife and me *very* busy."

I snicker at the way his eyes widen with his words. "I bet. I was smack-dab in the middle of my siblings."

"Ah, middle child syndrome?" John smirks.

"Something like that," I say, exhaling slowly. Picking up my fork, I shovel more food into my mouth.

"Oh, how did your lesson go yesterday?" He swiftly changes the subject, which I'm grateful for because I don't like talking about my childhood.

I slam my fork down for affect. "Considering you forgot to mention Colton would be giving me the lesson, I should really be mad at you right now," I say with a little bitterness in my tone.

John chuckles and shrugs. "Did I forget to tell you that little tidbit?"

"Yeah, you did. He gave me the worst horse ever!" I shout a little dramatically.

"There are no bad horses," John tells me.

"Uh, I beg to differ. This horse kept running even with me pulling back on the reins. And did Colton help me? No, he just let me flail around while we galloped."

"Sounds like Colton," a thick accent says. Once I turn around, I see Braxton, the cowboy Colton pointed out on the first day we met. He's busy helping himself to the breakfast buffet, and John gives him a look.

"What? I gotta do bitch work today. I need fuel," Braxton tells him, but John barely budges his stance.

"You do bitch work every day." John deadpans.

"Exactly. Plus, Mama Bishop told me I was welcome anytime." He flashes a smile as if he knows that'll get him off the hook.

At the mention of that, John's shoulders relax. "Of course she did."

"Mama Bishop?" I raise my brows. "Your mother, I take it?" I ask with a grin.

"Yep. The real boss around here." He chuckles. "Love her to death, but she'd feed the entire county if she could."

"She sounds sweet."

"She's the fuckin' best," Braxton adds, taking a seat across from me.

"Yeah, well, you have exactly seven minutes to eat and get your ass back to work," John demands.

"Yeah, yeah." Braxton groans, loading up his fork.

John waves him off and tells me to have a good day before he walks toward his office. I love how down to earth and hospitable he's been. It really makes a difference because I knew I'd be an outsider staying on a ranch, and I worried about that.

"So you're Red, huh?"

"Actually, it's Presley. I assume you've heard things about me." I don't hide my annoyance at the thought of Colton talking about me.

He's focusing on his plate, but I see the smile spread across his face.

"I take that as a yes."

"Colton's mentioned you," he says casually. "Called you a spitfire."

"Well, that's rude, considering *he's* a jackass."

Braxton lifts his head and chuckles. "Somethin' we agree on."

He finishes his food well before I do, which is crazy considering how much he had stacked on his plate.

"See ya 'round, Red," he tells me before leaving. I suppose John's seven-minute countdown was real. As soon as I finish eating, I go back to my room and grab the books I want to shoot today. There have to be some neat secluded spots here, and I'm determined to find them.

Walking outside, I quickly realize it's hotter than it was an hour ago. And since I'm wearing a backpack filled with books, I'm already sweating. The gravel driveway to the parking lot of the B&B has several trails leading off it, including one I know heads to the horse barn where Colton gives lessons. Deciding to take one of the others, I start walking, and after a while, I stop to snap some pictures. With my camera pressed to my face, I slowly walk backward as I find the right angle to get the sun shining against the barn in the distance.

"Oh, hi." I hear a woman's voice directly behind me, catching me off guard. I quickly spin around and apologize.

"Sorry, I hope I didn't get in your way." If she hadn't spoken up, I would've quite possibly toppled over her. My chest alone has been known to take people out.

"No, no! You're fine! I was walking to the B&B and saw you, so I thought I'd introduce myself. I'm Mila. Hope I didn't interrupt." She holds out her hand, and I take it with a smile.

"You totally didn't. I'm Presley. I'm actually a guest at the B&B."

"Yes, my husband mentioned a photographer was staying."

"Your husband?"

"John Bishop. I'm his wife," she explains.

"Oh! That makes much more sense." I chuckle. "He's been so nice. He mentioned you and the girls this morning actually. Well, until Braxton showed up and started eating everything."

Mila and I both laugh, and I already love her. "Sounds like

Braxton. And Colton. And Jackson. Everyone loves the B&B food. It's Mama Bishop's personal recipes." She shrugs as if she can't even blame them for it.

"I can definitely see why. Truthfully, I was a little nervous coming here. It's quite different from where I'm from and the places I usually visit, but I guess it's true what they say about Southern hospitality," I say with a smile.

"I understand completely. I'm originally from Georgia, and Texas has a culture of its own. Especially around here. The Bishops are amazing. They're why I couldn't leave." When she laughs, I'm sure there's more to the story, but I don't want to pry. "So John said you take special pictures. He had a hard time explaining it to me."

That makes me laugh, considering most people don't quite understand unless I show them. "I'm a freelance photographer, so I travel a lot. I do anything from book cover shoots to maternity to social media pictures. I'm really passionate about reading, so I started posting pictures of the books I was into, and it turned into having a dedicated account just for Bookstagram." Before she can ask what it is, I explain it to her.

"Oh wow. That's so cool! I love the whole idea and concept. Plus, you get to travel! What a cool job." The genuine excitement in her voice has me smiling from ear to ear.

"It really is. Publishers send me copies before the book releases, and that's basically why I'm out here. Thought it'd be cool to get some authentic shots. Plus, I love being somewhere new."

"You'll have to show me some of your pictures. There are endless places around here. At the heart of Eldorado is your traditional small town with rustic street lamps and a small café. Not to mention, everyone knows everyone."

She sighs, which totally makes me chuckle. Mila Bishop is a sweetheart.

"Oh totally. Let me give you my card with all my info and my Instagram link. I also take pictures for magazines, and I sell stock images too."

"Wow, you do it all." She takes the card from my hand and studies it.

"I get inspired a lot, I guess." I smile. She and John are the kindest people I've ever met.

"Talking about my abs again, I hear?" And just like clockwork, Colton shows his face. We were so busy discussing things that I didn't even hear him approach.

"Colton!" Mila scolds, giving him a dirty look. "Don't be rude."

"I don't think he knows how *not* to be rude," I say before Colton can speak.

"Oh, so you two have already met." Mila takes a step back and smirks.

"Unwillingly," I say dryly, glaring at Colton.

"Oh c'mon, Red. You can't really hate this face." He sticks out his lower lip and gives me a pathetic little pout. Mila bursts out laughing, and I have a feeling she's used to the men around here trying to get their way.

"I bet Colton would love to show you around the ranch. Or even take you into town!" Mila exclaims. "I'd offer to help, but I have to get back to work."

She walks around me and offers a little wave, then winks.

"I don't need your help," I tell Colton before he can say anything else. "Don't you have another victim to nearly kill?" I say, walking away so he gets the hint.

He doesn't.

"I only have one lesson this afternoon, so I'd be happy to show you around till then."

"I'm good." I deadpan.

"You're going the wrong way." His footsteps stop, and I turn around. "I know a great place if you want me to show you." He flashes me a toothy grin as if he's trying to be sincere.

"How far is it?" I ask suspiciously.

"Fifteen-minute walk or five minutes on a four-wheeler."

I inhale and exhale slowly. I really do need to get more pictures, and with the sun beating down on me, his offer sounds appealing.

"On one condition," I say, stepping closer toward him.

"Does it involve me stripping off my clothes again?" Colton smirks as if that'll really work on me.

"Trust me, I've been scarred for life." I groan to emphasize my point.

"Why must you break my heart, Presley?" He puts on a sad face, but I don't buy his act. Though the sound of him saying my name instead of Red sends butterflies to my stomach. I have no idea why the hell it does, but I ignore it.

Well, try to anyway.

"You must be a gentleman. No driving me out there and then leaving me off to fend for myself or something. No mocking me or sabotaging my photos. Do we have a deal, Colton?" I hold out my hand, pinning him with my gaze.

He takes it and shakes a truce. "Deal, Red."

As I follow him to the four-wheeler near the horse barn, it dawns on me I'm going to have to sit behind him—in a dress. *Shit, shit, shit.*

Colton hops on and starts it up. Damn, he looks good today too. He's even wearing a cowboy hat. Argh.

"Gettin' on?" he shouts over the rumble of the engine, raising a brow.

Carefully, I lift my dress just enough to swing my leg over and settle in behind him.

"Might wanna hang on," he yells before the four-wheeler jerks forward, and the weight of my backpack has me falling backward. Quickly, I wrap my arms around his waist and tighten my grip as he speeds up and turns on the trail, climbing the little hills.

I take in the scenery as we cruise and am in awe of my surroundings. California is beautiful too, but in a much different way.

"We're here," Colton announces, then parks and shuts off the four-wheeler. I look around and see bales of hay circling a fire pit. Even though trees surround us, we have a stunning view of the ranch from this distance.

"It's perfect," I say, swinging my leg up and around so I can jump off. "What is this place?"

Colton hops off and rubs his fingers over his scruffy jawline. "Jackson used to bring his wife here as kids, and it became something pretty special for them. Ever since they got together, he makes an effort to keep it in good condition. They bring their twins out here for little campfires, and now the entire family uses it."

"Wow, that's so cool. I didn't realize Jackson had twins. How old are they?"

"They just turned two a few months ago."

Hmm...I wonder if he'd let me borrow them for a shoot. I'll have to ask him or John about it later.

"So he's a twin and had twins? That'd make one badass photo."

Colton chuckles. "I guess."

"Alright, well I'm going to set up and see what I can come up with. I may need your help, though," I tell him, then continue before he gets any ideas. "With the camera, I mean. I need to get a few pictures of myself, but I might need you to make sure I'm in focus and set the timer."

"So now we're working together?" The amusement in his tone is too damn obvious.

"You owe me!" I tell him. "For nearly trying to get me killed on that horse."

"Damn, girl. You're never gonna let me live that down, are you?"

I flash him a smug smile. "Nope. Now let's get to work."

Opening my backpack, I pull out my camera and tripod, then a few of the hardbacks I brought with me. After I prop the books on the hay bales, I take some pictures, making them the focus while blurring the sky and trees in the background. I try different angles and positions. Next, I stack them on top of the hay with the firepit in the background.

"This would be a super cool shot at night with the fire going," I say mostly to myself, but Colton overhears me.

"I'm sure we could come back out here if that's what you wanted." His voice is sincere, which isn't something I expected.

"Maybe," I say, keeping my eyes on the screen of my camera as I look through the images.

"Okay. For this next one, I'll need your help. I'm going to sit on the hay with a book, and I need you to make sure I'm in focus and then hit the button to start the timer. I want to get a side profile first and then a back shot. Then I'm going to stack the books in my palm and take a few with me holding them."

"How do you think of all that so quickly?" Colton asks as if he's impressed.

I shrug modestly as I set up the camera on the tripod and get it into position. "I don't know. Experience, I guess. Once I get inspired, the ideas just flow."

"That's pretty cool, ya know? You have a vision, then bring it to life." Colton approaches me, and goose bumps form along my arms when he steps closer, brushing his body against mine. "So show me what I need to do. I haven't done the timer thing with this camera yet."

I give him a quick lesson and settle into my spot with one of the books. Thank God I picked a long dress today because this shit itches.

"You look like you're about to break out in hives," Colton says, chuckling. "The hay won't bite."

"No, but it's prickly!" I complain.

"Let me know when you're ready," he calls out.

I pose for a lot of my own pictures so my followers can get a taste of who's running the account, but I still feel awkward doing them. Especially in front of an audience.

Or maybe it's because every time Colton looks at me, I feel him undressing me with his gorgeous blue eyes.

"Okay, you can press it," I tell him, knowing I only have ten seconds before the picture takes. Once it does, I tell him to do it again and adjust my pose. This goes on a few more times before Colton says I'm missing something.

"What?"

He walks toward me and places his hat on top of my head. "You gotta look the part." He winks, then goes back to the camera and pushes the button again.

Ten minutes and various poses later, I'm all pictured out and decide to take more shots of the view.

"So I have a favor to ask," I say as I pack up my things.

"Of course you do." He snickers.

"Do you have a humble bone in your body?" I grimace.

"Well, if you really wanna find out…"

I hold up a hand. "Forget I asked." I place my bag on my back.

"I'm just messin' with ya, Red." He flashes me a perfect smile, and I groan. "You ready?"

Colton starts the four-wheeler, and as soon as I walk toward him, he guns it. I stop and glare at him. "Not funny."

"What?"

I take another step toward him, and he moves again.

"Colton." I growl.

"What are you waiting for? Hop on." He smirks when I furrow my brows.

I take a step forward, and he does it again. "Screw it, I'll walk!"

Walking around him, I march past and stomp my way through the grass.

"Red, come on!" Colton chuckles as he steers the four-wheeler behind me. "Presley!"

"Leave me alone, asshole," I shout.

Moments later, Colton's standing in front of me and lifts me up over his shoulder, which is impressive. I've never had a man pick me up or attempt to carry me over his shoulder before, but he makes it seem effortless. "You gonna be stubborn, then I'm gonna treat you like a stubborn animal."

"Put me down, you caveman!" I kick my feet, but it's no use. Colton's rock solid from head to toe and doesn't even flinch.

"Presley, sit." He plops me down on the four-wheeler and pushes my shoulders down. "Wanna drive?"

"Do I wanna dr—? What? You're a lunatic!" I scoot up on the seat, and before he can sit behind me, I give it gas just like he did.

"You aren't that slick, Red!" I hear him shout, and then I feel a thud as he jumps on the back. His arms wrap around my waist, and my breath hitches at the closeness of our bodies and the way his large hands feel against my stomach.

"You gotta be faster than that," he says in my ear. His lips on my skin send a shiver down my spine, and when he chuckles, I know he felt it too.

CHAPTER EIGHT

COLTON

FEELING PRESLEY'S body react to my touch has put a permanent smile on my face. As much as she pretends to hate me, I know she can't deny the attraction sizzling between us. We might've gotten off to a rocky start but pushing her buttons has been the hottest foreplay I've ever experienced.

Too bad Jackson and John would have my head if I messed around with a B&B guest. It's their one strict rule, and the one I've personally refused to break.

"You're gonna have to do better than that, Red," I tease the moment we arrive at the B&B as I reach around her to shut off the engine.

"Don't worry, cowboy." She swings her leg over the seat and stands tall. "I plan to." She flashes a smile, and I wonder if I should be worried.

"If you say so," I singsong.

"You're so annoying." She groans, spinning around, and just as she starts to walk away, I reach out and grab her arm.

"Presley, wait." I pull her closer as I sit back down. "You aren't really mad at me, are you?" I search her face with a half-grin.

She rolls her eyes at me and crosses her arms over her chest as if she's really trying to be upset. "Yes, I am. You could've broken my camera with that little stunt of yours."

Placing a hand on my chest, I frown. "Okay, you're right. I'm sorry. Will you ever forgive me?" I ask sincerely, holding her gaze with mine and hoping she'll give in.

Presley groans audibly as she drops her arms. "On one condition," she states.

"Whatcha got this time?" I ask.

"I need a model."

I snort, removing my hat and brushing a hand through my hair before putting it back on. "I already did that for you."

"Right, but I need you for a different kind of shoot."

"Like what?"

She bites down on her lip and looks away before making eye contact with me. "I need some pictures for my Bookstagram hashtag challenge."

"You're speaking a different language, darlin'." I arch a brow, just as confused as I usually am when she talks about her bookstastuff.

Presley inhales slowly through her nose as she tries to find the patience to explain it to me. "I come up with daily picture challenges each month. It normally involves a specific theme. I take them in advance so I can schedule them along with my other Bookstagram shots."

"Okay, so you come up with these hashtag challenges and then post them?" I ask, making sure I understand correctly.

"Right. So I still need the Late Night Bedtime Reads hashtag. I envision myself lying in bed surrounded by books while I hold one in my hand as if I'm reading it. Then maybe do one with me holding a stack of them in my hand. Maybe add a cup of coffee or stacks of pillows." I smile as she continues to ramble off her ideas, and it's pretty adorable to see how passionate she is about it. "Okay, well anyway. I can usually do the pictures myself with my timer. However, I need someone to place the books around me, so…"

"So it's a two-person job," I finish for her.

"Yes."

"So how does that equal me being a model?"

"Well, I wanted to try it for my other photo challenge with the Steamy Bedtime Reads hashtag, and that's where you come in…" She holds out her hand. "Sound doable?"

I make a fist and pound it against my chest like a gorilla. Presley laughs, then rolls her eyes.

"Can you come around four? Or do you have lessons this afternoon?" she asks.

I purse my lips before responding. "I'll make it work."

"Great, thank you." She turns to walk away but quickly stops and spins around again. "I mean this in the nicest way possible but…come looking decent."

My eyebrows rise. "Decent?"

Her shoulders slump as she gives me a knowing look. "Like shower and look clean."

Scoffing, now I'm the one to roll my eyes. "I'm sure I can make that happen. Anything else, Red?"

She points a finger at me and grins. "I'm staying in the Violet room. Don't be late."

After finishing my chores, I head home and clean up. I'm not entirely sure what Presley wants me to do, but I want to help her. Teasing her and hearing her laughter make me smile, and I've thought about her way more than I care to admit over the past few days. When things happened with Mallory, I never wanted to get close to a woman again. Relationships were a thing of the past, and one-night stands became my new norm.

Presley makes me want to reconsider my rules. Even if her being here is only temporary.

"What are you doing here?" John asks as soon as he sees me walk into the B&B. He's been pulling long or split shifts since his assistant went on maternity leave. Being that we're in the middle of nowhere, finding long-term help isn't easy.

"What? I can't pop in to say hey?"

John walks around the counter toward me with his arms crossed over his chest. "You never come in to say 'hey.' You're here to see a specific guest, aren't you?"

I shrug. "I'm just doing her a favor."

"Mm hmm."

"Seriously. She asked me to help take pictures," I tell him, walking toward the staircase.

"Better not be any funny business, Langston!" he shouts.

Taking the steps two at a time, I yell over my shoulder, "You're not my boss, Bishop!"

Once I reach Presley's room, I knock and wait. Moments later, she opens the door and nearly takes my breath away.

"Uh, hi," I say as my eyes roam down her body, taking notice of her lingerie. The see-through material over her chest leaves nothing to the imagination, exposing the top of her breasts. Her curves are even more delicious than I fantasized about. The bottom of the dress lands just below her panty line, and my dick gets rock hard just looking at her. "Why are you wearing…?" I lick my lips, bringing my eyes back to hers. Her amused look tells me I'm totally busted for gawking.

"I probably should've warned you." She steps aside to let me in. "I dress for the photo theme too."

She shuts the door, and when I look at her again, my throat goes dry. Presley stands so confidently and bold, and I'm absolutely certain she's doing this to me on purpose.

"The theme?" I barely manage to say and clear my throat. "I thought this was for your bookstapage."

"Bookstagram," she corrects. "And it is. The challenge is for the Bedtime Reads hashtags so…" She waves a hand down her body. "The books will cover most of me anyway."

So she's wearing it just to kill me, I want to say but hold back.

"Alright, so what do you need me to do?" I look away, needing to calm down my dick before I toss all my rules out the window, press her against the wall, and claim every inch of her gorgeous body.

"I'm going to get into position on the bed, and then you can cover me in books. John let me borrow some from downstairs, so there should be plenty," she explains, then lies on the bed. She angles herself so she's half propped up with pillows and bends one leg underneath her. "Hand me the first book on top please." She points over at the dresser.

"*A Cowboy for Christmas*?" I say with a grin as I bring it over to her. Presley reaches for it, but I quickly pull it back to take a second look at the cover. "This sounds really cheesy. Isn't it a little early for holiday books?"

She snatches it from my grip and glares at me. "Shut up." She chuckles. "It releases this winter, and readers love her cowboy romances."

Laughing, I surrender and walk behind her camera already set up on the tripod. "The lighting looks great."

"Well, you better hurry and cover me before it gets darker," she tells me. "All those books on the dresser and desk."

It takes me fifteen minutes to pile them on the bed and her body, and it takes all the willpower in the world not to let my fingers linger on her bare skin when I place them over her leg. The stack ends up two to three books high, and by the time I'm done, I can't help laughing at how adorable she looks buried like that.

"Now what?" I ask, adjusting a few of the books while being extra careful not to wreck anything.

"Hand me the mug and sleep mask please."

She puts the mask over her head and pushes it above her eyes to her forehead. The way it messes up her hair a bit looks fucking adorable. She curled it, and I love how it cascades down her back. I've always had a thing for redheads—which all my guy friends love to tease me about—but that's not why she's pretty. Presley's beautiful on the inside and out, and I knew that from the moment I ran into her.

I watch as Presley opens her cowboy book and grips it in one hand while she holds the coffee cup in the other. Carefully, Presley gets herself situated, and when she's in position, she announces she's ready for the pictures.

"This might go faster if we skip the timer."

"So you want me to just click and take the pic?" I ask, suddenly worried I'm going to fuck it up for her. Sure, I've used her camera before, but we have limited time to get the right shot.

"Yeah, I'm going to pretend to drink my coffee and read my book. I'll shift a little so I get some different angles. Just start clicking and I'll tell you when to stop," she explains. "Got it?" She smirks.

I grasp my fingers together and pretend to crack them as I stretch my arms out. "I think I can do it."

Once I'm behind the camera again, I look at the screen and grin. "You look great," I tell her. When Presley's eyes meet mine, she smiles sheepishly as if she wasn't expecting the compliment. If I were being completely truthful, I'd tell her she looks fucking gorgeous, and I want to rip that thin material she calls clothes off her luscious body.

But somehow, I restrain myself.

"Okay, ready? Five, four, three, two…one." Presley immediately poses, and as I continue to press the button, she shifts slightly from one shot to the next. She angles her face and body and pretends to sip her drink. Her smile is beautiful and contagious, and soon, I'm smiling right along with her. "This is the weirdest thing ever. Who knew about all the behind-the-scenes stuff it takes to get photos like this?" I'm amazed.

Presley laughs at that, and I keep snapping. The candid shots are by far my favorite.

Ten minutes later, she tells me to stop and finally rests her arms.

"Think you got some good ones?" she asks with amusement.

"They're all good," I reassure her, and she rolls her eyes with a grin. "Now what?"

"Well…" she begins, slowly pulling her leg out from the stack on top. "You help me out of here."

I laugh at how she's stuck, and instead of taking her hand and helping her out like she probably expected, I grab her around the waist and lift her. Carrying her in my arms, she squeals as she quickly wraps her arms around my neck.

"Colton!"

Reluctantly, I set her down on her feet and try to remind myself to keep my eyes above her neck.

Though it's a *very* hard task.

"Okay, cowboy. It's your turn."

I pretend to groan but smile anyway. "Okay, but I'm not wearing lingerie."

"Har, har. No, but I do need you to take off your shirt again." She licks her lips, then lowers her eyes as if she doesn't want me to see the way my body affects her. It's crystal clear we're at a truce here, but that doesn't mean I can't taunt her as much as she's been taunting me. Especially while wearing close to nothing.

Once I've stripped off my shirt and unbuttoned my jeans as ordered, she instructs me to lie on top of the books. "Be very careful!" she tells me as I slowly sit on the stack and lean back.

"You know books are hard, right? Not exactly a soft landing," I tease.

She sighs. "I know. It won't take long. I promise."

"Now what?" I ask once I'm in position.

"I'm going to set the timer for ten seconds," she says, moving her tripod to the side of the bed. "The light coming in from the window will make a stunning backdrop."

"What do you need me to do?"

"Just lie there. Very still, Colton. Got it?" Her tone has me worried about what she's planning. "Put your hands behind your head and close your eyes."

"You fuckin' with me or something?" I do as she says anyway.

"No, I lost my remote, so I have to do this another way. Promise me you won't move. Got it?"

"Alright, alright. Now what?" I ask as I close my eyes.

"Timer is set. Don't move or talk," she says in a rushed tone. A second later, her hand rests on my leg as she straddles my hips. "Stay still," she whispers.

I swallow, willing myself to keep my hands to myself, but fuck, it's hard.

Presley climbs on top of me and rests her head on my chest. I feel every inch of her body against mine, and there's no way she can't feel the erection poking her in the stomach. *Fuck.*

As she lies on top of my body and the camera shutter clicks, I stay completely still as I wait for her next move. I'm not sure what the hell she's doing, but I know if she doesn't say or do something soon, I won't be able to control myself much longer.

"Going to do a few more," she whispers. I feel the weight of her move, and when she climbs back on, she settles into my side and rests her arm over my waist. The camera clicks again.

Presley changes position, climbing on and off, three more times as I helplessly lie still. Feeling her rapid breathing against my bare skin drives me insane.

"Last one," she tells me. "When I say your name, open your eyes and look at me."

"Okay," I manage to say.

I hear her counting down, and then she says, "Colton." Doing exactly as she instructed, I peel my eyes open and find her looking at me with a lust-filled expression. I know she's a professional photographer, but this kind of chemistry can't be faked. The camera goes off, but neither of us looks away.

Moments pass between us, and I can't take it any longer. Presley leans up on her elbow, and I do the same. Our faces are mere inches apart.

"Thank you," she says just above a whisper. "I think these will turn out really well. A little steamier than my usual stuff, but it fits the Steamy Bedtime Reads hashtag and genre I love to read."

"It's my pleasure," I tell her, keeping my eyes locked on hers.

Presley leans toward me just barely, but when I close the gap between us, needing to taste her and feel her lips against mine, she suddenly turns away. My forehead presses against the side of her head, and I pull back to study her expression.

"I should start editing these pictures," she blurts out before sliding off the bed. "And clean up this mess."

"Uh, sure. Right." I carefully climb out, adjusting the noticeable growth in my jeans, and walk around the bed to where she's standing. "I can help pick up if you want," I offer, hoping she'll invite me to stay.

"No, no. You've done enough. Plus, I'll probably take some prop photos and flat lays so…" She lingers, lowering her eyes to the floor before looking at me. "And I should probably change now that I've scarred *you* for life." She chuckles, but I hear her insecurity. Presley has no problem speaking her mind and giving me shit, but I see the worry in her expression when she tries to cover up her beautiful body.

I button my jeans and put on my shirt. The last thing I want to do is make her feel self-conscious or embarrassed by overstaying my welcome, but honestly, I'm having a hard time looking away from her.

"Thank you again," she says when she opens the door, and I step out into the hallway. "I really do appreciate your help even though you've tried to kill me twice now." I know she's trying to lighten the mood, so I laugh with her, wanting her to feel comfortable around me.

"I beg to differ, Red." I flash her a charming smile. "It wasn't so bad. It's kinda cool seeing what goes into taking the perfect picture."

"It's a lot of work, but I really love it. I've always had a creative mind, so I'm pretty lucky to be able to do what I love for a job."

"For what it's worth, Presley…" I take a step closer because I can't stand the distance between us. "I think you're gorgeous. You have *nothing* to be ashamed of, and admittedly, I can't take my eyes off you."

I watch as she swallows hard, and I can only imagine the thoughts swirling in her mind. Before she can respond, I grab her hand and kiss her knuckles.

"Good night, Presley. Sweet dreams."

CHAPTER NINE

PRESLEY

When Colton leaves, I lean against the door to slow my racing heart. I don't know what came over me, but I don't regret it. Being close to his hard, warm body did things to me I didn't expect. I felt him, *all* of him, and to know I made him hard as a rock gave me the confidence I needed. With bated breath, I waited for him to make a move, but when he tried, I panicked. The reality of me leaving in a few days hit me like a ton of bricks. As I stand against the cool wood, I try to tell myself rejecting him is for the best. Right?

Changing out of the lingerie I wore just to drive him wild, I put on some pajama bottoms and a T-shirt. After I reorganize all the books and clear them off the bed, I decide to take some flat lays with the portable ring light I brought with me. I place the books on the white sheet, using it to my advantage, and put dried flowers next to them. I continue to change out the props, hoping to keep my mind busy. Two hours later, I go downstairs and grab something to eat. Once my belly is full, I lie in bed and try to force myself to sleep, though it seems impossible with my thoughts. All I can see are Colton's piercing blue eyes. I replay the way his lips parted accompanied by the feel of his warm breath against my skin. It's all too much, and I'm a bag of mixed emotions—confused and exhilarated—all at once.

Somehow, I eventually fall asleep, but I'm awake as soon as the first hint of sunrise peeks over the horizon. Restlessness hits me like a brick, but sleep evades me. Instead of fighting it, I pull my hair up into a ponytail, put on my slippers, and walk downstairs feeling like a zombie.

John greets me with a warm hello, and I eat my breakfast with few interruptions. I find myself glancing toward the barn, hoping to catch a glimpse of Colton, and I wonder if that's wrong of me. I'm not one to do a one-night stand or have a vacation fling, but I'd be lying if I said the thought hasn't crossed my mind more than once in the past few days.

Once I've finished eating, I set my plate on top of the other dirty dishes in the tub and fill my coffee mug to the brim. I carefully take the stairs to my room, making sure not to spill a drop of the caffeine heaven. As I take small sips, I quickly go through my to-do list for the day. First up is to edit the photos from the past few days, then schedule posts to my Instagram feed. Wasting no time, I grab my laptop and memory cards and settle in at the small desk close to the window.

While some may say going through the over a thousand pictures is the most daunting part, it's what I enjoy the most. Like going on a treasure hunt and finding the prize because I don't remember every shot or angle I took.

Once I've successfully downloaded everything from my camera, I sort through and separate the pictures based on their category—landscape, Bookstagram, or stock. Just as I'm searching through the plethora, I come across a picture of my ass, zoomed in, perfectly framed. While I want to be mad, I burst out laughing because somehow Colton was able to capture my best angle. Shaking my head, I stare out the window and look at the wisps of clouds moving across the horizon. After I review the pics of him shirtless, while trying not to ogle too much, I find the perfect one. I already know the comments are going to be priceless. Abs make my followers go wild.

I place all the photos of him in a folder, then go through and edit each one. Keeping the same aesthetic among my photos is important because it makes my feed cohesive. Considering it's summer, I've been using bright filters and increased lighting to make the image pop. After a few hours of editing, one picture resonates with me the most. I'm mesmerized by how he's standing with his head tilted down, and the way the cowboy hat shields his face. I snort when I realize the book he's holding is titled *My Mysterious Cowboy Lover*.

Muscles cascade down his stomach and go on for days. Then I notice his unbuttoned pants and lose all focus. My mouth goes dry, and I know if I react like this, others will be dying over it. This shot has the perfect combination of sex appeal and mystery. Typically, I schedule photos a week in advance, but I've fallen behind with travel, so my last post was yesterday. It's important that I stay on schedule and get something up today. I make sure it flows with my other photos on my feed, then live post, which means uploading it directly. After I tweak it, I send it to my phone and then open Instagram. Typing up a witty caption, I insert my usual hashtags along with some extra funny ones before posting it. An evil smirk spreads across my face because I just know everyone will love this.

After it's posted, I refresh a few times and reply to the first few comments, then set my phone down and get back to work, considering I need photos ready for the rest of the week. I continue scrolling through the sessions, and when I come upon the pics we took last night, my chest instantly tightens. Colton's intense stare nearly takes my breath away. With our gazes are locked, I can see the invisible threads pulling us closer. No words can describe the way he made me feel, and I know he felt it too. The large bulge in his jeans made that obvious. I hurry and push those dirty thoughts away, then glance at the time in the corner of my laptop. It's barely ten in the morning, and it feels like I've worked an entire day already. With heavy eyes, I drift off, but the only thing I think about is Colton.

My phone's constant vibrating startles me awake. I pick it up, open one eye, and see it's my older sister Callie calling. Out of my six brothers and sisters, we're the closest. She always took care of me when we were kids, and besides Olivia, she's one of my best friends.

"Yes?" I answer, rubbing a hand over my face.

"*Yes*? Yes? That's all you have to say to me right now? Are you freaking kidding?" She sounds mad. "I take it you made it to Texas okay."

"Um. I did. Sorry for not texting you when I got here. I've been super busy. And what time is it?"

Callie loudly huffs on the other line, and it sounds like she's pacing. I pull my phone from my face and see it's just past two in the afternoon. Dammit. I'm almost pissed at myself for wasting so much time today.

"Wait." Callie's voice drops. "Are you seriously sleeping right now? You need to get your ass up and look at Instagram right now. Because you're way too calm for this!"

What the hell is she even talking about?

I immediately sit up in bed, looking around for my phone, and it takes me a moment to realize I'm talking on it. I need more coffee. "I'm going to put you on speaker real quick."

I click out of the call and open the app, and my jaw nearly falls to the floor. "What the…?"

"Yes. I know. What the fuck. My exact reaction. This post is insane, Pres. Look at how many likes it already has and the number of comments. The comments…oh my God." She laughs. "Just read them. All I have to say is that man needs to be put in witness protection stat."

"Holy fuck." I gasp, scrolling through them all. There are hundreds of them. "All the sexual favors being offered." I chuckle at the insanity. "Phone numbers even. This is crazy. And the likes keep coming." I'm in shock. Complete shock. My phone is vibrating nonstop. Direct messages are flooding in, comments popping up by the dozens, and likes jumping by the hundreds. I can't even wrap my head around this. Normally, I average a couple of thousand likes or so, but going viral of this magnitude has *never* happened.

"Um, have you seen him?" Callie mocks. "He's going to be my future brother-in-law, right? Because seeing him during the holidays wouldn't be so bad." She chuckles, but I'm trying to ignore her jokes. Next, I check my email and find hundreds of messages in my inbox. It's overwhelming considering it's only been live for four hours.

"Shit. I tagged the location of the B&B. This might possibly be the stupidest thing I've ever done," I admit, mentally facepalming myself. Out of habit, I always tag my locations when traveling. I couldn't have anticipated this kind of reaction, though.

"The *smartest* thing you've ever done," she corrects. "One woman said she's only a few hours from the B&B and plans on heading that way this weekend to find her Mystery Cowboy. Thankfully, no one can see his face, but with abs like that along with that happy trail—"

"Callie. You really need to stop." I groan, knowing Colton is going to fucking freak.

A laugh escapes her. "Well, with men like that walking around, maybe I'll pack my bags and move to Texas. Lord knows the men here all suck."

"He has no idea I posted that. Then again, it's not like he has anything other than Facebook. So I might be safe." I chew on my bottom lip, contemplating it all.

"No chance." Callie snorts. "People are already asking if you're doing a shoot with him and when they can buy his photos. They want more of that hot Cowboy Casanova—accurately nicknamed, by the way—lots more!" Her voice goes up an octave with excitement.

"I'm seriously stressing, Callie." The likes are coming in nonstop and so are the messages. It's to the point where I'm forced to turn off my notifications, which I've never done.

"The caption was my favorite part. '*This super-hot Cowboy Casanova is waiting for you to pre-order your copy of* My Mysterious Cowboy Lover, *and who knows, maybe he'll even special deliver the book to you. Remember ladies: save a horse, ride a cowboy. Who's ready to saddle up?*' He's pretty much in big trouble if anyone ever finds out his name," Callie informs me as if I hadn't already thought about that.

I let out a ragged breath and frown. "Why are you reading it aloud to me? I know what it says! And he kinda deserves it. For spilling coffee on me, making me nearly fall off a horse, and—"

"Oh my God," she squeals, interrupting me. "You like him! You totally have a thing for him. I can hear it in your voice."

I stand and try to carefully formulate my words because I know whatever I say, I won't live it down, ever. "He's attractive. But no. I travel too much. I have a career. It would never ever, ever work."

"I didn't ask if a relationship could work between you two. I said you have a thing for him, and since you didn't deny it, that's all the answer I need." She laughs as if she's won a one-sided argument. "You're so doomed."

"Do *not* jinx me," I beg, pacing the floor.

"I say it takes all of three days before something happens," she tells me.

"I hate you so much right now. I gotta go." I try to end the call, but she continues to poke at me. I have no desire to discuss this with her.

"I'm hanging up now." I try not to listen and force the thoughts of my body on top of Colton's rock-hard…

"Okay, fine. Good luck. Wear protection. Or don't. Basically, just do it. I can't wait to be an aunty. Also, call me when you get back into town, or I'll track you down. Love you. Bye!" The line goes dead before I can say a word. I love my sister, I really do, but sometimes, she can be a bit overprotective or pushy. But maybe she's right. Maybe I really *am* doomed.

I continue to read through the comments until my growling stomach pulls me away. I need to eat, and I'm hoping I can scrounge something up, considering I missed lunch. Grabbing my phone and changing into some jeans and a T-shirt, I head downstairs.

As soon as my foot hits the bottom step, John hangs up the phone and rushes over to me.

"So you gonna tell me what you did?" He crosses his arms over his chest and stands tall.

I open my mouth and close it, feeling the knot in my throat. I try to play dumb. "What do you mean?"

"The phones and emails have been nonstop since this morning. Everyone wants to know who this Cowboy Casanova is, and somehow, I think you're responsible. I keep hearing something about Instagram, and I don't even know what that is really. No offense, ma'am, but you got some explainin' to do." He shoots me a grin, then looks over his shoulder as the phone continues to ring.

I pull my phone out of my pocket and click on the Instagram app just as the back door slams open.

"And I imagine this is our very own Cowboy Casanova?" John

glances at me, then shoots Colton a shit-eating grin. I hand John my phone, and he looks at the photo and begins scrolling through the comments.

He lets out a hearty laugh, then hands it back to me. "Because of you, we're booked for the rest of the year, and the waitlist is five pages long now. Keep them coming, Cowboy," he says directly to Colton, who looks confused as hell. Yep, I definitely have some explaining to do because his face says it all.

I walk over to Colton, grab his arm, and lead him outside.

"What's going on?" He folds his arms over his chest and searches my face. "Just spit it out, Red."

"So. Um. Yeah. Remember those pictures I took of you with your shirt off and holding some of my books?" I actually feel nervous telling him about this.

"The one where you forced me to unbutton my pants?" He flinches at me as if remembering it causes him actual physical pain.

I nod and hand him my phone, showing him the photo.

He begins reading the post. "What's with these hashtags? Rideitmypony, rideacowboy, saveahorse, saddleiswaiting, cowboycasanova, southerngentleman, giddyup." He narrows his eyes at me, but all I can do is shrug.

"It shows the B&B up top; what does that mean?" He waits for me to answer.

"That...they know I was here. It's a location tag. It gives them a GPS coordinate."

His mouth falls open slightly, and I can't help but study his full bottom lip. "Wow, Red. You've really done it this time."

"I'm sorry. I didn't realize—"

He interrupts me and reads some of the comments out loud. "Give me his name. I'll be his cowgirl all night. Cowboy Casanova call me 930-555-1476. Maybe I should give some of them a call? They're all so willing." He gives me a deadpan look.

My cheeks begin to heat, and I smack his arm. "No. You can't encourage it. Some of these women are stalkers, for real. I never said your name. I never mentioned who you were or if you worked here or anything personal like that, and your face wasn't shown. So you're safe right now. You heard what John said. The B&B is booked, and the waiting list is full. You'll just need to keep your shirt on going forward."

"So should I be scared of a bunch of thirsty women who want to jump on it? Maybe I should be thanking you instead?" When he laughs, a pang of jealousy creeps up that I can't explain.

"These women will study the pattern of your happy trail. The shape of your muscles. They'll find out who you are. One model whose face was hidden in a shoot was identified just by the freckles on his shoulders."

Just as he goes to open his mouth to likely say something snarky, his phone rings, and he answers.

"No. No. Do *not* come here. No. Seriously, Everly. Don't you listen? It's a bad idea. I—"

He looks down at his phone, and I see the call ended. Glaring at me, he presses his lips into a tight line. "Well, fuck. Now my sister is on the way here. Word apparently is already getting around."

I give him a sheepish smile and hold out my hand for a truce. "So you forgive me for all this, right?"

Colton shakes his head and shoves his hands in his pockets, then throws me a smirk. "No way, Red. You just started a war."

CHAPTER TEN

COLTON

Presley acts shocked that her photo gained traction, but I'm not. Most of the Instastuff is over my head until she hands me her phone and shows me the comments. She's talented, there's no doubt about that, but I'm standing here with my jaw on the floor as I read the responses. I've been getting shit about it from John since the phone calls started this morning, but I had no idea it was at this level.

The comments have me laughing more than anything, and I can't help but notice the way Presley narrows her eyes at me when I crack jokes about it. If only she knew me a little better, she'd realize I'm fighting way too many demons to seek out random women on the internet who want to "ride me like a pony."

"So you don't forgive me?" She looks up at me with wide eyes. Her pouty face is absolutely adorable, and I'm almost tempted to kiss her—right here, right now.

Instead, I shoot her a half-smile. "I'll think about it." I walk back into th B&B and she follows behind, begging.

She clasps her hands together and steps up her game. "Please? Pretty please with cherries on top?"

"That's pathetic," I tease, and she sticks her bottom lip out farther. "Okay. I forgive you. For now." I open my mouth to say something else when I hear my sister yelling my name as soon as she enters the B&B.

"Over here." I groan, rolling my eyes, but when I turn around to face her, I smile. Though Everly can be a little shit most of the time, I still love her. She's barely twenty-one, loves to read books and ride horses, and is known for her attitude. She was born without a filter and speaks her mind. Before I can say anything, she gives me a hug.

"It's a shame I have to come all the way out here to see my big brother," she scolds. "So this is her?" Presley's eyes go wide, and within a few seconds, Everly has enveloped her in a big hug.

"I am a huge fan of yours! I've been following your Bookstagram for the past two years," Everly tells her.

"Wait, you know what Bookstagram is?" I ask, feeling as if I'm really behind on the times.

Everly playfully rolls her eyes at me.

"It's nice to meet you," Presley says, sweetly. "Thanks for following me."

"Like, you're a huge deal. When I saw you tagged the B&B and then recognized my brother, I about died. I'm not even kidding. Seriously, I don't even know if my heart is beating right now. I might be a ghost." She laughs.

I place my hand on Everly's shoulder. "That's enough."

Presley shakes her head and smiles. "No, she's fine."

"Yeah!" Everly turns and looks at me, swiping my hand from her. "Anyway. If you need any help or anything, I will clear my schedule in two point five seconds. I'm such a huge fan. HUGE!"

Carefully, Presley takes her phone out of her pocket. "I always love meeting other booklovers who understand my obsession. We should take a selfie together and put it on my Instastories."

Everly's eyes go wide. "No. Way."

"Yeah, it'll be great." Presley unlocks her phone and opens the camera. She pulls Everly in close to her and holds her phone up in the air, and they both smile. In the background, John photobombs them, holding up a peace sign, which makes me chuckle. I look over her shoulder as she reviews it.

"Good one, John." Presley opens Instagram, clicks a button, then adds the picture. "What's your handle so I can tag you?"

"BooksandBoots," Everly says with a proud smile.

"Oh, that's super cute! And posted," Presley says. "It was really nice meeting you! I'm going to follow you back."

Everly covers her mouth with her hands. "I think I'm in shock right now. I need a minute."

Presley scrolls through her pictures. I honestly had no idea my sister was into all this. "Your photos are adorable. This picture with sweet tea is really creative."

"I love you," Everly tells her. "You inspire me so much. All the traveling you do. All the amazing books you get to review. Not to mention *all* the hot guys. Those things are what book nerd dreams are made of."

Just the mention of other guys makes my heart beat a little faster. They continue to discuss books, but I stand over to the side, giving them space as I get lost in my thoughts. Presley does travel a lot and is known for her photos of cover models. Is it possible this is just business to her? Does she treat everyone she meets the same way she treats me?

I somewhat feel like a fool, but I know I didn't imagine the other night. Though it stung when she pulled away just as I was about to kiss her, I felt the electricity sizzling between us. There's no denying that. Or maybe I made it all up in my head? Well, fuck. I want to talk to her about this, but I know she won't be here forever. Eventually, her stay will end, and she'll be on the road to her next destination. I don't really know what to think about that, so I don't.

Everly's phone starts vibrating like crazy, and her loud shriek pulls me back to their conversation.

"Hey, you can't be loud like that in here. You'll interrupt the guests. Okay?" I look back and forth between them.

"I just got twenty new followers from being tagged!" Everly practically yells.

I walk over to them. "You gotta go. Red has stuff to do, and I have to get back to work."

"Red?" Everly looks at Presley.

"It's a stupid nickname he gave me." Presley glances at me and smiles. All I can think about is how pretty she looks when the afternoon sun leaks through the window, making her hair look more red than usual.

"So original, Colton." Everly looks at me with a pointed glare. "But yeah, I should probably get going. It was *so* nice meeting you. Maybe we can meet up again before you leave?" Everly asks.

"I'll DM you if I get some free time." Presley gives her a side hug, they say their goodbyes again, and Everly walks toward the front door. I follow her outside.

As soon as my feet hit the parking lot, she turns around with a devilish grin. "So can you please date her? Marry her? I'd love to have her as my sister. Thanks." Everly goes to her truck and climbs inside.

"Sometimes, you're so embarrassing," I joke.

"Keep it up, and I'll name drop you on Instagram." She cranks it and buckles up.

I cross my arms over my chest. "You wouldn't."

"You could be my claim to fame," she taunts, knowing it'll annoy me even more.

My face contorts. "I'd never speak to you again."

"Yes, you would." She laughs. "See you at breakfast next week."

As she backs out of the driveway, I wave and watch as she travels down the long dirt road. When I walk inside, Presley is at a table in the breakfast area eating a sandwich with some chips.

"I missed lunch…again," she says.

I sit down in front of her. "Shoulda told me. We could've gone to the small café in town. They've got the best chocolate cake on this side of the state."

"Yeah?" Her eyes light up. "I love chocolate cake."

It grows awkward between us, and I'm not really sure what to say. Although I want to bring up the almost kiss, I don't even know how to start the conversation, so I decide not to.

"Don't you have work to be doing?" John asks, grabbing my attention.

I stand. "Yeah, I do."

He walks away, and I look at Presley. "You'll be around later?"

"Yep. Sure will. Have a billion emails and messages to sort through, some more editing to do, then I want to try to take some photos before the sun sets. Plus, I need to schedule my posts for the week." She looks up at me and bites her lower lip, and it drives me wild. Damn, she's gorgeous.

"Well, be careful out there, Red. Lots of crazy fans waiting for you."

"Shut it!" She laughs. "You're the one who should be careful." One of her eyebrows pops up.

I stand and playfully shake my head. As I walk toward the back door, I glance over my shoulder and catch her watching me. She hurries and averts her eyes back to her plate, making me chuckle as I step outside. But that soon fades when I hear Jackson catcalling me.

"Woohoo. Over here, big boy!" He shouts over Braxton's laughter.

I pick up my pace, and when my feet hit the ground, I take off running at a full sprint.

"Save a horse, ride a cowboy. Ooooh, I'd put a saddle on him and ride his wild stallion." Braxton just adds fuel to the fire. Boots pounding against the ground, I rush toward Braxton. Eventually, he notices I'm coming right for him, and he takes off running in the opposite direction.

"You better not trip and hurt your pretty face," Jackson continues to tease, and that's when I stop and turn toward him. Instead of moving, he just crosses his arms over his broad chest, calling my bluff. Even though I know I should stop my charge, I don't, and when I'm mere inches from him, he takes one step to the left, causing me to lose my balance. I topple to the ground, dust and dirt rising, and I just lie there looking up at the blue sky.

Jackson comes to stand over me. "Do you have any idea who my brothers are? You have no chance against me, Casanova. I've been dealing with douchebags worse than you all my life." He gives me a wide smile and holds out his hand to help me up. "You dumbass."

As I stand, I try to brush the dirt and hay from my clothes, but it's no use. Braxton walks up with a big grin. "Did you get it out of your system?"

"Shut the hell up," I mutter as I follow Jackson to the barn. He pulls out some paintbrushes and buckets along with rollers.

"What're those for?" Braxton asks.

Jackson smirks and overexaggerates his words. "This right here is called a paintbrush, and this is paint."

I add, "And this is the barn we're going to paint. Do you know what painting is?"

Braxton rolls his eyes and snatches a brush from Jackson's hand. "Both of ya are assholes."

"I think we can finish painting the barn before dark. Each of us needs to take a side, though, and then we'll meet back at the front and finish up there," Jackson directs.

"I bet I can finish my side first," Braxton says.

"How much you wanna bet?" Jackson smirks.

"Five hundred bucks," Braxton immediately says, turning toward me.

I shake my head. "I'm not betting shit."

"Good. I'll put five hundred on Colton," Jackson tells Braxton, then they shake on it.

I groan. "I don't want to play this damn game!"

"Too late, Casanova. Now don't make me lose my money," Jackson tells me, grabbing a bucket of paint and a brush and heading around the back of the barn. "You both have the same square footage to paint, so get ready. I'm gonna give you a fair start."

As I grab my supplies, I call over my shoulder to Braxton. "I hate you for this."

"You're going down."

I make sure to flip him the bird as I walk away. Jackson steps back where he can see us on each side of the barn.

"Pour your paint," Jackson yells. I pop the top of the can and pour the red liquid into the metal pan, then dip my roller inside.

"On your mark, get set, go," Jackson calls out, and I just know Braxton is rushing around on the other side to beat me. Though I'm not a super competitive person, it does actually light a fire under my ass to work faster, which might not be a bad thing.

After about an hour, Jackson leans a tall ladder against the barn, and I know he gave one to Braxton too.

"How far along is he?" I ask, curious, but he just shrugs and goes back to painting.

After I've painted half the barn, I climb the ten-foot ladder to get the top area. It's a perfect day to be doing this because there's a slight brisk breeze, though the sun keeps me warm. Days like this make me love early summer.

I climb down the ladder, move it over, then climb back up, and repeat until my side is complete. With zero paint drips, this is some of my best work. I walk around the back of the barn where Jackson's sleeping on a bench. Within three steps, I sneak up on him, bending down until I'm in line with his face. Light snores escape him.

"Fire!" I yell as loud as I can. Jackson freaks, rolls off the bench, and lands right on his ass.

Jackson rubs his face, and I burst out laughing.

"I've dealt with douchebags like *you* most of my life, so I know how this works." I hold out my hand to help him up, and he takes it. "Now we're even."

"What's on fire?" he asks, not completely awake.

"Nothing. But I finished painting."

Jackson walks over to Braxton's side where he's still frantically working.

"I'd like to be paid in hundreds," Jackson tells him with a smirk. "Five hundos!"

"There's no way he's finished," Braxton argues. Climbing off the ladder, he stomps over to my side and is shocked when he sees it's done.

"What the fuck! You cheated. Jackson must've helped you."

I narrow my eyes at him. "I ought to beat your ass for even insinuating I'd cheat. I give you my word, and that's more than enough. And you know Jackson's lazy ass ain't helping anyone. He was too busy sleeping."

Jackson laughs and shrugs. "Basically."

"See. Now can we finish this shit up? It's the last thing we have to do today. That should be enough motivation for you," I tell Braxton.

When he nods, I grab my roller and paint, and he meets me up front. It takes us no time to finish the front because of the large sixteen-foot double opening. Once we're all done, Jackson walks around both sides and gives us his approval.

As we're walking back toward the B&B, Jackson turns to

Braxton. "I'm not gonna make you pay up, Brax. Colton used to earn money every summer painting barns. I knew he had an advantage over you. I just didn't want you lollygaggin' all afternoon."

"Seriously?" He looks at me.

"It's how I saved money. I could've painted the whole barn in two hours by myself."

"Dicks!" Braxton says. "The both of ya."

Jackson howls with laughter as we walk up on the back porch. As soon as we enter, I see Mama Bishop rushing toward me.

"There you are, son!" She comes and gives me a big hug. "I don't know if I should be askin' for your autograph or not."

"Not you too, Mama B." I shoot her a wink. Mama Bishop treats all of us ranch hands like we're her own, like we're family because, in a roundabout way, we are. She's a fierce woman and rules the ranch as if it's her kingdom.

"And see, that's why all these ladies want to meet you, or that's what I've heard from John. But there's something special to be said about a Southern gentleman with Southern charm. So…" She looks around. "Where's the famous photographer?"

It's almost as if Mama Bishop called her because a moment later, Presley conveniently walks down the stairs. A smile touches my lips. "Well, she's actually right here."

I walk over to Presley, happy to introduce her to one of the most generous women I've ever known. "Red, this is Mama Rose Bishop, Jackson and John's mother. Mama B, this is Red, I mean Presley."

Presley smiles and holds out her hand. "It's nice to meet you."

Mama Bishop pulls her into a big hug. "It's lovely to meet you, darling. I wanted to come over here and meet the woman who's done so much for us in just a few short days. Oh, I brought you something too." Mama B snaps her fingers, and John comes over with a Tupperware container and hands it to Presley.

"Oh? What's this?" She pops open the container, and I immediately smell the sugar.

My mouth falls open. "That's her super special, insanely delicious homemade divinity. I'd trade a kidney for a piece."

Presley holds them close to her body. "Nope. You better keep out."

Mama Bishop laughs. "Honey, we appreciate everything you've done for us so much, and I felt it necessary to come over here and personally show my gratitude. If you need anything while you're here, please don't hesitate to reach out to me. I'd be happy to feed you or take you to church with me."

"Thank you. I love this place so much. It's everything I've ever dreamed of. This has been one of the best workcations I've had in a long time." Her genuine smile is contagious.

After clearing her throat, Rose looks at me. "I think you owe Presley a thank you as well, Colton. Because of her, you'll have no problem finding a woman so you can start making some grandbabies for your mama."

My mouth drops open, but she stands with a hand on her hip, waiting for me to show some gratitude. If I've learned anything over the past decade, it's never to argue with a Bishop, especially not the head honcho of them all. So I do as she says and shows some manners.

I look into Presley's eyes and watch her face soften. "Thank you ever so much for *everything*, Presley." I grab her hand and place a chaste kiss on her knuckles, not taking my eyes from hers. Heat hits her cheeks, and she tucks her lips into her mouth. For a moment, it's only us. When I pull away, I'm so tempted to wrap my arms around her and kiss her the way I wanted to the other night.

"There we go," Mama finally says, breaking the tension. "Nice meeting you again, Presley. See you, Colton. Or should I say… Cowboy Casanova?" Mama B giggles and makes her way toward the door, but my eyes are still on Presley.

"Sorry about that," I tell her.

"About what?" She acts as if nothing happened, but I can see right through it.

"Nothing," I tell her, knowing we're eventually going to have to talk about what's going on between us. "Nothing at all."

CHAPTER ELEVEN

PRESLEY

My brain is already overloaded, and it's barely six in the morning as I scroll through the emails on my phone. I wanted to get an early start on tackling all these notifications because, with each passing hour, it becomes more overwhelming. One after another asks about the "Cowboy Casanova" and whether he's available for book covers and other kinds of shoots. Sure, only half his face was in the frame, but their focus was on his abs of steel and the defined V that goes from his hips down below his jeans anyway. It takes a lot to embarrass me, but the comments alone have me blushing, and I wasn't even in the picture!

I get up to open the container of divinity Mama Bishop gave me yesterday and pop a piece in my mouth. Now I understand why Colton would've traded his kidney for a piece; it's sweet and creamy and practically melts in my mouth. I smile, thinking about how nice she was, and feel the heat rush through me as I remember Colton's lips on my knuckles. For a moment yesterday, everyone around us disappeared, and we were the only people in the room. I swallow hard, pushing the thoughts away, and open my Instagram. As I sit here, the comments continue to flood in.

Colton loves the attention, of course, though the guys give him shit for it. As if he needed a bigger ego boost, his smile reached from ear to ear as he skimmed the comments that ranged from asking for a ride on the cowboy to where they can find their very own. Many of the posts included cliché sayings, and most weren't even original.

The fact that Colton enjoys this shouldn't bother me, but it does. In fact, I should be ecstatic that a picture of mine went viral. Overnight, my Bookstagram account has grown like crazy with thousands of new followers and a ton of new likes on my previous photos. My DMs are out of control, and my email is overflowing with messages. This is everything I've ever wanted, but for some reason, I don't want to share him with the world.

Even the publisher reached out to tell me how happy they were with the response. I'm not sure if people even read the description of the picture or noticed the book Colton was holding since it wasn't the main focus, but I'm glad they're pleased with it.

My text messages have been nonstop since the photo blew up, and while I've neglected to open them, Olivia just sent her ninth message, so before going downstairs to grab breakfast, I decide to read them.

Olivia: OH MY GOD! YOUR COWBOY PIC IS HAWT!!

Her first one came shortly after I posted the picture yesterday.

Olivia: HOLY CRAP, PRESLEY! Your Cowboy Casanova has officially BROKE the internet!!

Olivia: Please tell me you're not responding because you're riding that cowboy to honky tonk town!!

Olivia: Seriously?! I need updates! Give me something! I'm fat and pregnant and can't see my vagina anymore. I need juicy gossip!

Then her latest message…

Olivia: Okay, I've given you enough time to roll in the hay with Mr. Rodeo, but Mama's getting anxious over here! I need ALL THE details!

I inhale a deep breath and decide to go ahead and text her back regardless of how early it is in California. The woman rises before the sun.

> **Presley: Calm down, woman!! My phone has been blowing up for 24 hours straight! It's been a little nuts, so I apologize for not getting back to you sooner. I did NOT expect that picture to do that. It's crazy! I mean, I knew it was a great photo but damn. Also, he isn't used to that kind of attention. Sure, he's good looking, so obviously he's used to chicks pining over him, but all this is out of his comfort zone.**

> **Olivia: Ooh, so he's totally humble and charming? Is that what you're saying?**

I send her back a rolling eyes emoji, and she responds with a crying laughing one.

> **Presley: He doesn't need an ego boost, so I'm not saying a damn thing. He's helped me with some of my shoots, but THAT'S IT! So before you even insinuate anything, I have no time for a messy fling right now.**

> **Olivia: How'd I guess you'd say something like that? BORING. What happens in Texas, stays in Texas, just like Vegas…except you'll tell me because I need to live vicariously through you while I wait for this baby.**

> **Presley: Ha-ha! No. I won't deny that we've grown close, but I can't get involved. I'm leaving in less than a week.**

> **Olivia: Are you saying something almost happened?!**

I sigh, not wanting to think about the almost kiss from a couple of days ago.

> **Presley: No, not really. Well maybe. Kinda. I'm not sure! I**

think he was going to kiss me, and at the last second, I pulled away. Then it got awkward and weird, and before we could talk about it, the photo went viral and distracted us.

Olivia: You know I adore you, right? And I care about your happiness. But maybe you should just see where it goes. You never know if you don't put yourself out there. Take it from ME! I know firsthand!

Presley: You know I can't do that. I'm not worried about getting hurt or being sad about leaving as much as I am about hurting him. Plus, I hardly know him.

Olivia: Well, you still have five days, right? Make 'em count! ;)

The fact Olivia is giving *me* advice is kind of ironic, considering she met her husband through her old boss and hated him the second they met. When they were forced to road trip to book signings together, I knew it was only a matter of time before one of them cracked and gave in to temptation. After doing the whole long-distance relationship thing for a year, Olivia moved to LA, and Maverick proposed. They got married, and the rest is history.

My life isn't a storybook, though. I don't settle in one spot for long. It's not that I'm unable to maintain a relationship, but most guys don't like their girlfriend traveling more than being home. Not that I can really blame them, but I saw the way my mother settled when she was younger. Though I know she loves us kids and my father, I always felt she slightly resented the fact she was never able to pursue her true dreams. She was a stay-at-home mom until my youngest sibling started school, and then she worked part-time so she could still take care of us in the evenings. My father worked various jobs, and it was always a struggle, living paycheck to paycheck. I saw the stress it put on their relationship, so when I decided to pursue photography and travel the world, I promised myself I'd never settle for anything less than what my dreams could give me. Maybe it's just a phase in my life, and eventually, I'll be ready to stay in one spot, but that time is definitely not now. I love what I do, I love reading and being involved in the book community, and I love discovering new places. That doesn't leave a lot of room for relationships or falling in love. It'd only lead to heartbreak and pain. My stomach grumbles, and I can't put breakfast off any longer. I hurry and dress, throwing my hair into a bun, and then head downstairs. I make my plate and open my phone to check my emails and DMs, hoping to get through as much as I can while I eat. I'm the multitasking queen.

"Hey, Red."

Speak of the devil himself.

Colton takes a seat across from me with a plate of food and a cup of coffee. I didn't even see or hear him come in.

"Good morning," I reply, grabbing my coffee and taking a sip. "You look chipper today."

"I'm always chipper! It's just your attention remains glued to your phone, and you don't always notice." He flashes a smug smile.

"Har, har." I roll my eyes. "How ya doing with your newfound fame?" I tease, knowing he was quite embarrassed when the guys found out.

"Well, I created an Instagram account to scroll through the new comments."

I raise my brows. "Why?"

Colton shrugs, and I take a bite of my food. "It was like a meat market."

I nearly spit my eggs out and start choking.

"Geez, Red." Colton laughs as he stands up and leans over the table to pat me on the back. "Don't die on me now."

Once I finally stop hacking and take a drink of water, I scowl at him. "Don't say things like that when I'm eating!"

"Thought you'd be used to it, considering your job and what you read." He takes his fork and stabs a piece of my sausage link.

"Do you always have to steal *my* food? Get your own sausage!" I place my hand over my plate, covering my food, and move it toward me so it's out of his reach.

"Did I just hear you tell Colton to eat his own sausage?" Braxton pops up out of nowhere with a muffin in his hand.

"I said to *get* his own sausage! He keeps eating mine," I explain.

Braxton cracks up and takes a seat next to Colton. "Yeah, he digs the sausage." Braxton cups his hand on Colton's shoulder and shows off his pearly whites in a smug grin.

"Shut the hell up." Colton growls, shaking Braxton's hand off him.

Braxton and I both laugh, and I'm thankful for his intrusion so things don't get awkward between Colton and me again.

"So since pretty boy over here is getting famous on the internet, think you need a new cowboy to be your next model? I'd be willing to take it *all* off for you…"

Before I can respond, John walks up and smacks Braxton right across the head. "What the hell is wrong with you?"

Colton stands and does the same to Braxton. "Idiot."

"I was just askin'!" Braxton holds up his hands in surrender with a mouthful.

"It's not all that it's cracked up to be, so calm down." Colton groans and sits.

"Guys still giving you shit?" I ask.

"Jackson enlarged the picture and printed it. Then Alex framed it and hung it up in the barn." Colton deadpans.

I can't help laughing at his less than amused expression, and Braxton joins in too.

"Sorry, man. But that shit was hilarious. Seeing it in person is nothing compared to reading the comments, though. There're some dirty old birds on there."

Colton groans.

"Some nasty old ladies too," Braxton adds.

"Shut your muffin hole and eat your damn food," Colton sneers.

"Don't worry, I won't out you," I reassure him. "Though I have about a thousand more emails asking about you and wanting you on book covers." I hold my phone up and show him all the emails I have yet to even open.

"Emails about Colton?" Braxton asks, arching a brow.

I scroll through my endless messages and show him. "I had no idea it would be like this, or I would've never tagged the location. Now some are saying they're going to show up, and that's just creepy."

"I still can't believe you tagged the freaking B&B." Colton shakes his head.

Braxton starts clapping. "That was fuckin' brilliant."

"I always do! It's out of habit." I cringe, feeling guilty. "Don't worry, I won't tag it in the next picture."

"The *next* picture?" Braxton asks, popping his brow.

"Is there a reason you're still here?" Colton turns and scowls at him. Neither of us has mentioned the intimate photoshoot or the *almost* kiss. I definitely don't want to bring it up with other people around either.

"Damn. Fame has changed you already." Braxton shoves the rest of his food in his mouth and finally gets up.

I snort at his ridiculous comment as he walks away.

"I know you didn't ask for this. I'm really sorry. I don't plan to release your name or anything, so don't worry about that." I try to reassure him.

Colton keeps his head down as he stares into his coffee. "Nah, it's fine." He finally looks up at me. "I know you didn't do it on purpose. Or did you?" He pops a brow and smirks.

I throw the last of my sausage link at him, and he catches it. "Thanks." He pops it into his mouth like it's nothing.

Colton is dressed in his usual work attire of tight shirt, tight jeans, and a cowboy hat. He'd honestly look good in anything though or, hell, *nothing*. After feeling his muscular chest against me, it's not hard to imagine him completely naked.

Shit. I blink a few times, forcing the visual out of my brain.

"So you'd be okay with me posting the Steamy Bedtime Reads hashtag picture? If not, I'll totally understand. I can show it to you first if you prefer, though." I know I'm rambling now, and my cheeks feel hot. I was just thinking about him naked, and now I probably sound and look like a crazy person.

Colton looks right, then glances to his left before leaning over the table closer to my face. His elbows rest on either side of my plate as he brings his mouth closer. "You made me lie on a pile of books while you laid on top of me practically naked," he whispers as if he's telling me a secret. "So I'd hate to see it go to waste." He winks before pulling back and sitting down.

I swallow hard, feeling the pounding of my heart in my chest. Why does he do this to me? He obviously knows his closeness affects me, but does he really have to taunt me?

Asshole.

"Great, thanks." I place my silverware on my plate and stand. "I should get going. The pictures won't edit themselves, and I still want to do more flat lays."

"Whoa, wait." Colton grasps my wrist gently, holding me in place. "How much longer are you here?" He looks at me as if he's afraid of my answer, but it was inevitable he'd ask.

"I fly out Thursday for an event next weekend," I reply, gauging his reaction.

"Oh gotcha," he says as if we're talking about the weather. He releases his grip on me and leans back. "Well, if you need my help before then, I'd be glad to."

I narrow my eyes and cock my head. "Really?"

"Why are you lookin' at me as if I'd be anything other than sincere?" He flashes a crooked grin, and that's exactly why.

"Colton!" Before I can respond, I hear his name being yelled from the front door. Turning my head, I see three women all walking in this direction.

"Oh hell," he mutters before standing up and turning to them. Butterflies swarm my stomach as I wonder who they are and watch them engulf Colton in a bear hug. "What're y'all doin' here?"

"Well, we heard you're Instafamous now and wanted to meet the photographer who made it happen." They all simultaneously turn their heads and look at me. "Is this her?" one of them asks.

Colton looks uncomfortable as he adjusts his hat before waving a hand at me. "This is Presley Williams. Red, this is Kiera, Emily, and River, aka the Bishop wives." He chuckles slightly as all three of them approach me. I hold my hand out to them, but they all ignore it and wrap me in a hug.

"We don't shake hands 'round here," one says as they squeeze me tighter. "We hug like family."

"I've started to notice that," I say, chuckling when they finally release me.

"I'm Kiera," the blonde one introduces. "You're so pretty. You should be in the shots with Colton. I bet your followers would die over them." She smiles wide.

"Oh, um, well...I have a couple I might use."

"Seriously?" she shrieks. "Oh my God, you must post them. I bet they're super adorable."

"You're scaring the poor girl," one of the dark-haired women interrupts. "I'm Emily, by the way. Don't let Kiera freak you out."

"I'm River," the other brunette says. "Don't let either of them freak you out. I'm a Southern transplant from Wisconsin, so it's okay to tell them they're overwhelming and crazy."

"Hey!" Emily and Kiera say in unison.

"I think you're *all* overwhelming her," Colton interrupts.

Smiling at how sweet they all are, I chuckle. "Don't worry. I'm used to meeting new people. Comes with the job. However, I didn't anticipate this photo getting so much attention, so it's been a little shocking, to say the least."

"I almost died laughing at the comments," Kiera says. "Seriously, Jackson and I were crying from laughing so hard."

"Oh, I read them to Evan during our break yesterday. Soon the entire locker room was filled with doctors listening to them," Emily says.

"Oh, for fuck's sake." Colton groans.

"Alex..." River starts, then clamps her mouth shut.

"Yeah, I know what the prick did." Colton crosses his arms over his chest. "Asshole's just jealous."

"Hey, I didn't do a damn thing," John chimes in as he walks over to our little group. "However, people have offered kinky promises for insider info on you, so you should be thanking me. I could've given out your address and phone number by now." He chuckles, and I shake my head in embarrassment. I feel so damn bad, but at the same time, it's been really impressive that one of my photos is getting so much attention as well as the rest of my feed.

"Do it, and you'll wake up in the castration stall," Colton threatens, though John looks amused.

"So what photos are you taking next?" River asks, thankfully changing the subject.

"I was thinking of getting some sunset or sunrise shots,

hopefully both. Set up a few of my books with the sun in the background. I think it'd look stunning, especially on the ranch," I explain.

"That sounds amazing!" Kiera says. "There are plenty of horses and cowboys to model for you too."

"Yeah, I'm sure everyone's scared of me now," I say, laughing.

We talk for a few more minutes before John tells us we're making too much noise and he needs to get breakfast cleaned up.

"It was great meeting you all," I tell them before they head out.

"You know, I could help you out with those shots if you wanted," Colton says once we're alone.

"What do you mean?" I ask, furrowing my brows.

"You know that spot we went to on the four-wheeler? Jackson's spot on the hill."

I nod. That was only a few days ago.

"Well, we could camp out there tonight so you can get your sunset photos. Then we'll be out there in the morning for your sunrise shots. I can bring a tent, sleeping bags, food, water, whatever."

His offer takes me by surprise, but he sounds genuine, and it makes my stomach clench even tighter than before. Damn him for being so sweet and charming—when he isn't giving me shit, that is.

"Don't you have to work? I'd feel bad for taking you away from your duties."

"Nah, I have off on Sundays." He shrugs casually.

I think about it for a moment, really liking the idea of getting those shots but also nervous that Colton and I will be alone again. The last time, he nearly kissed me, and things got weird. However, I still can't fight the fact I want to be alone with him.

"Okay, sure."

"Great. I'll build a fire, and we can make s'mores." He flashes a boyish grin, and damn, it's so adorable.

"Oh! Bring stuff for pudgy pies too! I love those!"

"What the hell is that?"

"Seriously?" I gasp. "You've never heard of a pudgy pie?"

"Uh, no?"

"Well, I hadn't either until I started traveling. We don't have it in California, but you're seriously missing out! You butter two pieces of bread on the outside, place them in the pudgy pie maker, and then put pie filling inside. You close it up and cook it over the fire, rotating it back and forth. Then when it's done, it's a pie-filled sandwich! All hot and gooey. It's amazing."

"That is the weirdest thing I've ever heard," he says, chuckling at my enthusiasm.

"You can make other things in it like grilled cheese, stuffed mini pizzas, or PB&Js. Basically anything that you can make with bread," I explain.

"That sounds badass. I'll have to see if I can find one in town," he says. "Meet me back here at seven?"

I smile. "Sounds good."

Colton nods, tipping his hat. "Oh and Red?"

"Yeah?"

"As much as I enjoyed seeing you in see-through lingerie, you're gonna want to pack something a bit warmer for tonight." He winks, then walks away before I can think of a comeback.

Though it wouldn't matter because his words leave me speechless.

CHAPTER TWELVE

COLTON

ASKING Presley to camp out tonight wasn't a completely selfless move on my part. Getting her alone might've been my main incentive, but I also want to help her with her photos. After being deemed the "Cowboy Casanova" on Instagram and reading all those comments, I'm ready for a social media break and getting out of cell phone reception range.

Plus, I think it'll be good for her too. She's so damn worried about the effect this has had on me. Even if the guys have given me shit nonstop, it hasn't really been all that bad. The public doesn't know it's me, and as long as it stays that way, I'm glad it helped Presley.

I'll be the first to admit the whole idea behind a Bookstagram confused me and made no sense, but after scrolling through the images and reading some of the posts, I can confidently say I understand a bit more now. It's not just about the images, but about the story she tells through the lens and the descriptions she uses under the pictures. She replies to most of the comments on every post, which shows how dedicated she is to her followers. That's something I can appreciate about her.

Even though I'm the one who asked her to go tonight, I can't deny I'm a little nervous about it. Getting close to Presley is a risk, and the better part of me tells me to stay away because I know she won't be here much longer. But I can't deny how I want to spend time with her, get as close as she'll let me, and hell—not think about the aftermath yet. She's the closest I've let a woman get since Mallory, and that means something.

"You can't be serious," Braxton grumbles when he sees me loading my truck with gear. "You're going camping?" He stands next to me with his arms crossed over his chest as if his disapproval will stop me. I needed to borrow a cooler, which is why he's at my house in the first place.

"What? It's going to be a decent night." I shrug, not making eye contact with him because I know he sees right through my bullshit.

"Mm hmm. I'm sure it is." He snickers, then leans over the truck bed to examine my supplies. "Firewood, tent, sleeping bags, blankets, food…just missing the condoms and lube."

"Fuck off," I snap. "I'm not taking her out there to bang her."

Though I can't say the idea hasn't crossed my mind. Presley is fucking gorgeous even if she walks around as if her curves are a curse.

"Right, sure," Braxton mocks, pursing his lips and nodding as if he believes me. "You know you could if you wanted to."

I look at him, and he shrugs.

"She's not Mallory," he tells me as if he's interpreting my thoughts.

"I know she's not," I snap.

"What the hell is this thing?" Braxton points, confused.

I smirk when I look at it. "It's a pudgy pie maker," I explain. "Something Presley mentioned earlier. I went into town to look for one, and the woman at the store looked at me as if I was crazy when I tried to explain it to her."

"Like how I'm looking at you now?" He laughs.

"Pretty much, but luckily, River had one and is letting me borrow it. Apparently, it's a thing in the north, and she bought a set online a while ago."

"Hm, interesting." Braxton examines it as if it's a medical device or a weapon.

"Alright, well I have everything I need." I slam the tailgate and walk to the driver's side. "I'll have my cell if you need anything, but the reception sucks up there, so don't need me."

"Yeah, yeah." He rolls his eyes.

Opening the door, I hop in and start the truck. As I drive away, I roll down the window and wave to him with my middle finger.

"Asshole!" I hear him shout in the distance and laugh when I see him huff in the side mirror.

I try not to overthink this whole thing as I drive over to the B&B to pick up Presley, but I can't help it. Something interesting always happens when I hang out with her, and perhaps that's why it's so exciting. Presley's one of a kind and different from any girl I've known. She's smart, beautiful, creative, and witty. Everything about her makes me want to be around her that much more, which scares the ever-living hell outta me.

"Hey!" she greets as soon as she steps off the porch. I've barely parked and got out of the truck before she skips toward me. "Thanks again for your offer. I'm excited."

The camera hangs around her neck on a strap, and I can't help but notice the way it bounces between her breasts when she walks. "No worries. It's gonna be a beautiful night. I bet you'll get some great shots."

I take her bag and lift it over my shoulder, then lead her to my truck. "How many books did you bring this time?" I say, only half-teasing because of the weight.

"Only eleven."

I snort at her admission.

"What? Too heavy for you, cowboy?" She arches her brows at me.

I flash her a look and snicker. "Please. I could lift you over my shoulder with a broken wrist, so don't even imply that I'm weak."

"You better not lift me again!" She points her finger at me, and I snap my mouth at it as if I'm going to bite it. "Colton!" She laughs, pushing me away. "Let's go, *Casanova*."

"Hey, you're the one who gave me that nickname!" I remind her once we get into the truck.

"Yeah well, it was because of Jackson. I didn't know it would catch on like wildfire!" she rationalizes.

She plays with the radio as I drive us toward the spot. "We don't have many options out here," I tell her, noticing her frustration.

"Well, that's annoying. You're missing out on a lot of great music."

"Nah. We're not that superficial out here."

She makes a show of eyeing my body. "I can tell." The corner of her lips tilts up, and she's trying hard not to laugh at her joke.

"Something wrong with my clothes?" I try to sound offended, but she doesn't fall for it.

"You mean your ripped jeans and plaid shirt? No, it's totally retro."

"You mean country," I correct, chuckling at her accusation.

She laughs with me, and I love the sound. It's so natural and sweet.

"Different from LA that's for sure. I much prefer a minimalistic style, but it's just not a thing out there. Even when I'm traveling to events, I'm on the clock, so I dress professionally. I don't mind sundresses and shorts while I'm here, but people are so judgy back home."

"Yeah, I'd stick out like a sore thumb there just like you do here," I tease.

"I do not!" She laughs. "Okay, maybe a little."

Ten minutes later, I park and unload the back of my truck. Presley looks over everything I brought. She helps me set up the tent, and I tease her when she struggles to get the rods in the correct position. Before it gets dark, I build a fire and set out the fresh hay bales and a blanket so we can sit comfortably. After I check the time, I realize we have an hour before the sun sets, so I ask her to show me how to make pudgy pies.

"You bought like every flavor of pie filling!" Presley's eyes light up like a kid on Christmas morning. "You're a godsend."

Laughing at her expression, I'm glad I bought one of each option. "Which one should we start with?"

"Apple! My favorite."

While I open the can, Presley butters the cast iron mold and places a slice of bread on each side. She puts filling on both pieces of bread before closing it up and locking the handles together.

"So question, where the hell did you find one of these things here?" She sets it in the fire.

"Not everyone who lives on the ranch is from Texas." I shoot her a wink.

She lets out a laugh and shakes her head, but I can tell she's impressed.

"We have to cook it for a couple of minutes on each side before we check it. Once the bread is toasted, it's done and ready!" she explains with a smile painted on her face.

I can't stop grinning at her as she makes the first pudgy pie, but I really can't wait to eat it. The fire keeps us warm, but I know as soon as the sun goes down, the air will get cooler, and we'll need to stay close.

"This is crazy good," I tell her after taking my first bite. Once Presley checked it and said it was ready to go, we put it on a paper plate and cut it in half. "We gotta make another one," I say around a mouthful of apple pie filling.

Presley laughs and smiles as if she's proud she's converted me. She makes a cherry filled one next, and it's just as delicious.

"Damn, woman. You can cook," I tease.

"You learn a lot when you're traveling," she says. "Food is a common denominator no matter where you go. Someone always wants to teach you about their local cuisine."

"I bet you have a lot of good stories."

She stares blankly at the fire with a smile as if she's thinking of them all. "It's why I love taking pictures. They're worth a thousand words. My other Instagram has lots of photos of landscapes and some random travel shots. Scrolling through them brings back all those memories and hopefully tells the stories of my adventures. I don't write long posts for them because I don't want to take away from the actual image. It's part of why I care so much and take it so seriously."

"It's not hard to see that you're very passionate about it, Presley," I say with sincerity. "I've only known you for five days, and I could tell that early on. It's evident in everything you do."

"Thank you. That means a lot to me." She finally looks up at me. "Even if you tried to sabotage me."

I laugh at her expression, enjoying how easy it is to just sit and chat with her. "For the record and *the people in the back*, it was an accident!"

Presley cracks up laughing so hard at my dramatics, she snorts loudly and then tries to cover her mouth with her hand, ultimately losing control.

"You're a mess," I tell her, laughing too.

"I know," she says when she finally catches her breath. "Ooh! I should start setting up."

Looking out at the sky, I realize we're cutting it close to sunset and almost forgot the whole reason we're here.

"Can I help with anything?" I ask, standing.

"Well, I'm going to set my camera on the tripod and see where the best angles are first. However, I might use you as a silhouette shadow if I can find the right spot."

"I literally have no idea what you're talking about so put me where you need me."

She chuckles and nods. A few moments later, she's leading me where to stand. Presley has me moving to different areas before finding the right place.

"Okay, now turn so you aren't facing me. Good. Tilt your head down a tad more. Oh, that looks awesome. I see the outline of your hat just right. Now move your legs apart a couple more inches. Yep, like that." I stay still as I wait for more orders. Once I hear the camera shutter click a dozen times, she tells me to move to the side just slightly and tilt my head away from her. This continues for five more minutes before she directs me to switch places.

"I'm going to hold up a book, and I just need you to make sure it's in focus. I'll be in the background, so you'll have to tell me to move either left or right until the book is clear."

"Got it," I tell her and do just that. I can't help smiling as I take her picture, admiring how natural she looks in front of the lens. "Looks great."

"Okay perfect!" She jogs toward me and reaches for the camera. I hand it to her, and she immediately scrolls through the images. "I'm going to set up some of the books around the hay to get the fire in the background with the sunset."

Thirty minutes later, the sun has completely set, and Presley looks happy and content with the images she was able to capture. "Thank you so much again. I really do appreciate your help even if I give you shit for being an ass."

"That was the most backward sincere apology I've ever heard," I tease. "But you're welcome. It's been surprisingly fun and not that awful."

Presley chuckles and shakes her head at me.

"You cold? I brought a heavy blanket."

"Yeah, a little."

I quickly grab it from the tent and cover us as we sit on the hay in front of the blazing fire. The flames cast a soft glow on Presley's face. I love her red hair and how she pulled it up into a messy ponytail with a few loose strands. She's beautiful with freckled, pale skin and a bright smile. Kissable is the only way I can describe her naturally plump lips, and I can't help glancing at them every chance I get.

"So tell me about working on the ranch," Presley says after staring at the fire in silence for a while. "What made you want to work here?"

I brush my hand over the stubble on my jawline as I think about what and how much to tell her. I don't have anything to hide, but discussing what brought me here isn't something I like to think about.

"Well..." I begin, contemplating how to start this conversation. "I kinda fell into it, if that makes sense. I had just gotten out of a long-term relationship and wasn't getting over it. Deciding to get completely shitfaced, I went out to a bar and ran into Jackson. He's older than me, so we didn't go to high school together, but everyone knows the Bishops. Jackson sure liked to drink and party back then, which is just what I needed to get my head out of the deep end of pityville, so we started hanging out. Soon after that, he said they needed some help on the ranch, which was perfect because I loved horses anyway. I grew up closer to town but being out here around the animals is where I feel most at home."

"I totally see Jackson being a party animal," she comments, and it makes me laugh.

"Oh, you have *no* idea. That's a story for another time, though."

"His wife seems very nice at least, so I guess it all worked out."

"Yeah, fifteen years in the making." I snort. "So now I've been here for almost five years and really enjoy it. I started helping more with the horse lessons and training when Kiera got pregnant with the twins. When they found out they were having a third baby, I took on even more responsibility, and now I can't see myself doing anything else. Honestly, I really love the ranch, the people around here, the workers, and the guests. I moved into Kiera's old house, so I'm not far away. Town is only a fifteen-minute drive."

"Sounds like you're really settled," she says, but I don't miss the hint of sadness in her tone. "I've never really felt that before, but it's hard to when I'm constantly on the go."

"But you love traveling, right?"

"Yeah, I do, but sometimes I feel like I'm always chasing the next thing. I have to remind myself to live in the moment instead of dreaming about what's to come. It's a blessing and a curse, I guess." Presley shrugs as if she even doesn't quite understand it.

"I think you don't give yourself enough credit, Red. You're doing what people wish they could do their whole lives. Not many go after their dreams so boldly like you do. There's always a reason they can't, or they put it off until the time is right, but you just went for it. You're fearless, and there's no shame in that. In fact, I admire the fuck out of you because of it."

"You do?" she asks as if she's surprised that I'd say that.

"Fuck yes, I do! I used to have dreams and goals. In one day, they were all ripped away from me, and every day, I used it as an excuse to hold myself back. But you…you didn't let anything get in your way."

"What do you mean?"

"Huh?"

"Yours were ripped away? What does that mean?"

I inhale sharply, not realizing how much I let slip or how much she caught. Shit.

"Well, as I said, I was in a long-term relationship. We were engaged. We were so young, and my entire life revolved around her. When I found out she'd been cheating on me, my whole world stopped. I didn't know how to function or breathe or even live life without her."

"Wow. Colton, I'm so sorry. It was obviously her loss."

"Unfortunately, that's not the worst of it."

She cringes. "Oh man, I'm afraid to even ask."

I pull my hat off my head and rake a hand through my hair,

stalling as I try to think of how to explain this. Jackson and Braxton only know because I told them while I was drunk, but I never talk about it otherwise.

"I started dating Mallory in high school. We were about fourteen."

"Wow, super young."

"Oh yeah. Young and dumb." I chuckle lightly. "Engaged at eighteen."

Presley's eyes widen in shock, but she doesn't comment.

"I was one hundred percent devoted to her. Madly, crazy stupid in love with her. So much that I stayed here after graduation to get a job and save money while she went off to college four hours away. She wanted to get an education so she could get a decent job, and we could be financially stable. I worked and put money away for our wedding and a down payment on our future house. I even sent her money when she needed it because she wasn't working. We had planned to get married once she graduated, but during her junior year…"

I pause, not realizing how tight my throat is or the pain that's stiffening my spine.

"Colton…" Presley takes my hand under the blanket and squeezes it. "You don't have to continue."

I glance at her and give her a small smile, appreciating her understanding. However, I want to share this part of my life with her even if it's painful.

"I'm okay. It's just been a while since I've talked about this."

She keeps her hand in mine, and I link our fingers together, giving me the courage to continue. "During her junior year, she came home one weekend and told me she was pregnant."

"Oh wow," she whispers.

"I was shocked but also excited. I wanted kids and a family with her. The timing wasn't ideal, but still, I was over the moon." After inhaling a deep breath, I continue. "Nine months later, I learned she'd been cheating on me for the past three years, and that the baby girl I'd fallen in love with throughout her pregnancy wasn't…*mine*."

CHAPTER THIRTEEN

PRESLEY

"Oh my gosh," I whisper in shock. Instinctively, I cover my mouth with my hand. That was the last thing I expected to hear, and now I feel guilty for asking. "I'm so sorry, Colton."

He glances over at me and rests his hand on my knee, then squeezes. "I was devastated. I was for a really long time."

"How long ago was it?" I ask.

"Five years. She stayed in San Antonio and raised the baby there. I heard it through the grapevine that she ended up marrying the father, so I tried my best to move on. However, after being together for so long and being so head over heels in love with her, I didn't process not having her in my life very well." He bows his head as if he's embarrassed to admit that, which is the last thing I want him to feel.

"You were young. No one in your position would know how to properly react." I do my best to reassure him. "Shame on her for cheating in the first place, but to not even tell you until the baby was born is unforgivable."

"Trust me, I was *mad*. So goddamn angry with her for betraying me like that, but also mad because, in the blink of an eye, I'd lost everything. I didn't know how to function after that, so I drank to numb the pain. Drank so damn much that I'd wake up and not even remember what happened the night before or how I got home. Shamelessly enough, I wouldn't even remember who the girl in my bed next to me was. Those were some of the lowest points of my life."

I turn my body to face him because I don't want him to feel alone. Taking his cheek in my hand, I make him look at me so he stops hiding. "No one would fault you for how you responded to a shitty situation. Especially me. I really appreciate you sharing that with me. I know it couldn't have been easy."

He shrugs as if it's no big deal. "I should've talked about it a lot sooner, to be honest. Perhaps then I would've been able to get over it quicker."

"I've never allowed myself to feel that kind of love, so even though I'm sorry you went through that, I also envy you. My parents had seven kids, and though I knew they loved each other, I could see the loneliness in my mother's eyes. She basically went through the motions, and I grew up realizing I wanted more for myself. Though I absolutely love what I do, at times, I feel that same loneliness I saw in her. Life isn't worth living if you have no one to share it with."

"I totally agree, Red." He smiles sweetly at me. "So you said you got into photography in high school and wanted to travel, but what made you share your pictures online? How did you start up your bookstapage?"

I laugh and turn toward the fire to warm my hands. "Booksta*gram*," I correct him once again. "It was something that just kinda happened. I wanted to see if I could make some extra money from my photos, and once I started sharing them, people asked for more, so I designed a website. That led to creating an Instagram account to find models for shoots, and I stumbled across the book community. After learning about the world of romance readers and authors, I made a Bookstagram page for that so I could keep my photos separate. Authors hired me to take pictures of models for their book covers, and it basically exploded. Publishers now send me books to review and post; authors and their publicists send me copies too. So when I'm not taking pictures, I'm reading. Though I admit I haven't exactly read a lot this past week." I smirk, hinting that he's the reason.

Colton laughs when he catches my implication. "If it's cowboy romance you want, babe, then you're living the real thing anyway." He winks at me, causing me to burst out laughing.

We continue talking and decide to make s'mores. Colton burns his marshmallow until it's a gooey blackness, so I dare him to eat the entire thing. Of course, he doesn't want to back down from a dare, so he does it, but I can see the regret on his face when it crunches.

"How many marshmallows can you fit in your mouth?" he asks as he puts another one on the stick.

"Uh...probably three before I gag and throw up," I admit, laughing. I've already eaten one s'more, so I'm only making another to prove to him that he sucks at roasting marshmallows.

"Wanna see who can fit the most in their mouth without having to spit them out?" He flashes a smug grin at me as if he's already done this challenge before and knows he'll kick my ass.

"That sounds like a horrible idea!" I blow lightly on my marshmallow that's evenly melted and perfect.

"What? You scared you'll lose, Red?" he taunts, holding up the bag of marshmallows. Of course, they're the jumbo too.

"Why do you enjoy being an ass?" I jerk the bag out of his grip and grab a handful. "You go first, cowboy." I hold open my palm so he can take them.

"You're on!" Colton opens and closes his mouth as if he's stretching his jaw.

"You're a freak." I giggle when he repeats the motions.

"Start countin'." He grins and reaches for the first one.

"One. Two. Three. Four. Five." I count as he shoves them into his cheeks and can't hold back my laughter when he faces me. "You look like a chipmunk." His ridiculousness has me tickled to death.

"Muh," he says.

"What?" I chuckle, unable to understand what he's saying.

"*Muh!* Gim-me muh!" He points at my empty palm.

"More?" I ask, and he nods. "You're insane!"

Grabbing more marshmallows, I hold out my palm, and he snatches two more. Colton holds them up as if he's doing a magic trick before shoving them into his mouth at once.

"You're going to choke!" I tell him with a smile. He holds up a finger. "One more? Are you crazy?" I do what he says. Of course, he makes a show of moving his mouth like he's making room for the final one before stuffing it in.

Colton holds up his arms in a victorious motion and fist pumps the air.

"Do you have a humble bone in your body?" I tease, rolling my eyes at him. He continues gloating, and when I smack a hand against his rock-hard abs, he starts chuckling, and the marshmallows fall out. I'm bent over with tears rolling out of my eyes at the look on his face as eight large marshmallows roll to the ground.

"Sabotage!" He points a finger at me when he's finally able to talk. "That's cheating!"

My cheeks hurt from laughing so much, but I don't even care. This is the most fun I've had in a long time, and although Colton is sex on a stick and his looks are literally the first thing I noticed about him, his outgoing personality makes him even sexier.

"Alright, it's your turn, Red. Think you can beat the record?" he taunts, holding the bag and preparing to hand them over one by one.

"Well, I'm not used to having so much in my mouth at once like you, so I doubt it," I say evenly, and when I see the shock on his face, I start giggling.

I only end up with six marshmallows before Colton tickles my side, causing me to spit them out just so I can breathe.

"That's way worse sabotage!" I push him away. "Worried you were going to get shown up by a girl, weren't you?" I taunt.

"Pfft, please."

As the fire dies down, Colton adds wood to keep the flames going. Even though I'm wrapped in a blanket, the heat feels nice, especially next to him.

"Wow…" I say hours later as I see the peek of the sun rising. "We stayed up all night."

Colton looks up at the sky, and his eyes widen in surprise too. "Yeah, we did." He smiles at me, and it makes me want to break all my rules about not getting involved. He looks at me so intimately as our gazes lock and our shoulders touch. We've been close all night, and the urge to cross that line gets stronger and stronger.

"Guess you can take the rest of your photos now," he says, breaking the connection, and I immediately feel the loss of it.

"Oh, right," I stammer, removing the blanket and reaching for my camera. "Could I get a shot of you on the small hill? When the sun rises, you'll be nothing more than a silhouette as the bursts of yellows and oranges surround you. I think it'll make a stunning picture."

"Yeah, of course. You're the boss."

I gather my tripod and a few books so I can take shots of them as well. Colton puts on his cowboy hat. Him in tight jeans wearing that hat is becoming my new favorite look. Most guys can't pull off this look, but he does it so effortlessly. No wonder he's quickly found a way into my fantasies.

"So when are the other shots of me going up on your Instagram?" he asks as I look for the right angle of him on the hill. "Just so I can prepare and all." He chuckles.

Smiling, I snort at the irony, considering he had no idea what Bookstagram even was a week ago. "I'm thinking this weekend. I have to double-check the exact date for that hashtag," I tell him. "Don't worry, no tagging will be done."

"I trust you, Red."

My heart warms at the sincerity in his voice. Without a doubt, my time here wouldn't have been as fun or productive if we'd never met. I feel lucky and cursed at the same time—because we're growing closer, and I'm leaving in a few days.

I spend the next half hour taking as many book photos as I can while the orange, red, and yellow hues paint the sky. It's so gorgeous here, especially without all the city noise and pollution. These shots are going to be breathtaking.

When I've taken enough pictures for my Bookstagram, I get some for my stock portfolio. Colton takes the tent—that we never ended up using—down. He packs the food and blankets, and as soon as I'm done, I spot him sitting on the tailgate of his truck.

"All finished," I say, walking toward him. "Thanks for doing this. I really appreciate it," I tell him with a smile. "Some of the best shots I've taken I think."

"You're welcome. It actually didn't suck."

I smack his arm and glare at him. "Rude!"

"Just kiddin'!" He holds up his hands. "Pudgy pies, s'mores, and a gorgeous woman near a blazin' fire. What else could I ask for?"

Butterflies immediately swarm my stomach as shiver courses up my spine. How does he manage to do that in just seconds? From taunting me to saying the sweetest things, my heart beats rapidly at his words, and I can't help wanting to hear more.

"I'm sure you take all your conquests here," I deflect, shooting him a sly grin.

"You should know better than that by now, Red." He reaches for my hand and holds it between both of his. I swallow, waiting with bated breath as he brings it up to his mouth and presses his lips softly against my knuckles. "Thank you for an unforgettable night."

Kiss me. Please.

Consequences be damned, I want those lips on mine, and the way he's respecting my boundaries makes me want him even more.

"Well, let's get you home, Red. I'm sure you'll need some sleep before tonight." He hops off the truck and shuts the tailgate.

I furrow my brows as I follow him to the passenger side door. "What's tonight?"

Colton motions for me to get inside, and after I hop in and buckle up, he flashes me a smug smirk. "Tonight I'm making you dinner at my place. You can't live off pudgy pies and marshmallows." Then he winks and shuts the door.

Oh my God.

I can't contain the smile on my face as he drives us back to the B&B. Just knowing I'll get to see him later has me all jittery and excited. I'm already anxious about what I'm going to wear, which is something I never get worked up about.

Colton parks, gets out, and walks around to open my door. "I'm gonna come in and grab a quick cup of coffee before I go check on the horses."

The blood drains from my face. "Wait. I thought you're off on Sundays?" Now I'm concerned he stayed up all night with me and has to work all day.

"I am. Well mostly. Horses still need to get fed and need fresh water. Then I clean their stalls and look over the schedule for my lessons. Another ranch hand does them today, but I still like to check everything over."

"Oh my gosh, I feel so bad now."

We walk into the B&B, and the heat feels nice against my cheeks.

"Nah, don't. I've worked on worse terms before, believe me. I'd rather pull an all-nighter sober than try to work with a hangover." He flashes me a wink as he walks toward the coffee.

"Well, I hope you get some rest later then. If you aren't up for dinner later, I'll understand."

"You aren't getting out of it that easily," he teases. Grabbing my wrist, he pulls me toward him. "I'll pick you up at seven." I look up into his eyes, and he presses a chaste kiss to my cheek before walking out the door, leaving me breathless.

CHAPTER FOURTEEN

COLTON

I'VE NEVER FELT SO nervous about a woman coming over. Not that I've cooked for many, but I guess there's a first time for everything. After I fed the horses this morning, I stuck around and cleaned the stalls, then drove to town and bought the groceries for dinner tonight. By the time I made it home, my eyes were so tired I could barely keep them open, but somehow, I found the strength to take a shower before I crawled in bed for a quick nap.

Eventually, my alarm wakes me up, but I feel as though I could sleep until tomorrow. Then I remember my plans for the night, so I get up. I quickly pick up my dirty clothes off the floor, then light a few candles so it doesn't smell like a bachelor pad—or a barn. After that, I head to the kitchen and start dinner before I pick Presley up at the B&B.

What Presley doesn't know is I could essentially outcook anyone within a five-mile radius—well except for Mama Bishop. I pull out the homemade tomato sauce I keep in the fridge because the jar stuff doesn't begin to compare to my recipe. A smile touches my lips thinking about it. All the guys know I'm a pro in the kitchen, and I even helped Jackson cook for Kiera the first time. Mainly because I was scared she'd be forced to eat a burnt microwaveable pizza or, even worse, the box.

As I stand here prepping, I'll never forget how worried he was in almost the same position as I am now. Except Jackson has known

Kiera since they were kids, and I've known Presley for a week. I have so many questions about her past and her future plans, and I want to know it all. Being alone with her last night was everything—more than I could've asked for—and I didn't want it to end. I haven't felt those feelings for someone in over five years, and it both excites and scares me.

I pour the sauce in a large pot, add fresh minced garlic for taste, then let it simmer while I set the table with a stark white cloth and candles. Taking a step back, I rub my hand over the scruff on my chin, wondering if it's too much. I've thought of everything, so hopefully, she'll be impressed.

Once the sauce is simmering, I turn the burner on low, then go to my room to find something date-worthy to wear. Instead of going for my typical plaid button-up, boots, and worn jeans, I choose slacks with a navy button-up shirt rolled to my elbows. I even wear my nice church shoes for the special occasion. As I study myself in the mirror, nothing I'm wearing says "saddle up," which will probably surprise her. Tonight, the cowboy suit is staying in the closet. I want to show her there's another side to me too.

I go back to the kitchen, rewash my hands, then chop and brown the chicken. I begin boiling the water for the pasta. My house smells as good as the food's gonna taste. Time is ticking, and I grow more anxious with each passing minute. I try to focus on grating the parmesan cheese and cutting the veggies, but it's almost useless. I desperately want tonight to be perfect because I only have this one opportunity to make it right. It's now or never because her days here are limited, though I'm trying not to think about that too much.

As I'm pouring the sauce in the cast iron skillet with the chicken, I can't help but think how it's just my luck to find the perfect woman who inconveniently lives in a different state. I'm forcing myself to focus on the *right now* and enjoy all the time I can with her, as hard as it is.

After sharing my past with her, I felt as if my heart was somewhat on the mend. I've spent years trying to forget what Mallory did to me, but it's been difficult. Everything around this town reminds me of her and all the memories we made together. I'm a broken man because of her, and maybe that's partially my fault because I never tried to move on. It's been too hard to trust someone, but talking to Presley, I feel as though I could tell her all my secrets—hell, I already did. She understood me in ways I didn't expect. I haven't allowed myself to willingly open up to another woman until her, and that means more than she'll ever realize.

After I check the time, I see I have less than an hour before I need to pick her up. Once I put the extra cheese on top of the dish, then place it in the oven, I drop the noodles in the pot. I turn around and look at the table, and all my insecurities are on the forefront. Is it too much? What if she thinks this is way too cheesy? I'm overthinking this. It's just dinner. I run my fingers through my hair and go back and forth with it all just as my phone vibrates in my pocket.

Braxton: I'm on my way over with some beers.

"Shit," I say under my breath. Granted, it's been hectic after that picture was posted, but I totally forgot to tell him I'd be busy tonight. I hurry and text him back, but the bastard must've been driving down the dirt road when he texted because I hear his truck come to a stop outside. I open the door, and he grabs the six-pack of beer. As soon as he sees what I'm wearing, he lets out a roaring laugh. Before I can say anything, he walks past me and steps inside.

"Oh God. Please tell me you didn't do all this for me, honey pie." He shoots a wink my way and blows ridiculous kisses toward me.

Now I'm laughing. "Get the hell outta here."

"So who's the special lady?" He sets the beers on the counter, opens one up, and takes a swig. "Ahh. Red."

"You have to promise not to tell a soul." He knows the rules around here just as much as I do, though he breaks them most of the time.

He sets down his beer. "Don't get your panties in a knot, Casanova. I ain't gonna say shit to anyone. I know about the 'no fraternizing with guests' rule, but I think it's good for you to step outta your comfort zone a bit," he says. "I think she's gonna like it. Looks fancy as fuck."

"You don't think it's too much?" I ask. "Like she's not gonna run for the hills when she walks in?"

"She'll probably be impressed. Whaddya cook?"

I walk over to the oven and grab a mitt and pull it out, then drain the noodles.

"She's gonna have an instant orgasm when she eats your chicken parm. That shit is delicious." He makes a show of inhaling the scent.

"You sure have a way with words," I tell him, lowering the heat of the oven and placing the skillet back inside.

"That's why the ladies love me." He finishes his beer and throws it in the trash.

I grab two wine glasses and set them on the table, then take a step back.

Braxton stands beside me, places his hand firmly on my shoulder, and then squeezes. "Quit worryin' 'bout it. She's gonna be really impressed with all this. It's top-notch."

I nod. "Yeah, yeah, you're right. Just don't wanna fuck this up."

Braxton becomes more serious. "It's obvious the attraction is there between the two of ya, so what do you really have to lose?"

"Her." There's way too much truth in my statement.

"I get it. But at this point, I think you could serve her ramen noodles and wear the shit-stained clothes you had on this mornin' and she'd be happy. Don't be so damn hard on yourself."

"Thanks, I appreciate it." The timer on the oven goes off and Braxton takes it as his cue to leave.

"You got this, man," he tells me over his shoulder as he grabs his beers and goes toward the door.

"I hope so." I cover the top of the skillet with foil, make sure the oven's off, then head to my truck.

After I start it, I sit there for a moment, trying to get a hold of myself before I drive over to pick up Presley. I can't remember the last time I cooked for a woman or brought someone home without first drinking myself into oblivion.

As I make my way down the shell road and toward the B&B, a stupid smile fills my face, and I wonder if she's just as nervous as I am. Eventually, I'm turning off the winding road and parking on the side so no one sees me because I don't want to be caught breaking the rules. I send her a text letting her know I'm here. I'm happy the sun will set soon, so my truck won't stick out like a sore thumb.

Presley sends me a short text back telling me she's on her way down, so I hop out of the truck and walk around to the passenger side. It feels like an eternity passes as I wait for her. Soon, I hear the front door click closed and see her face lit by her phone's screen. She's pulled her hair half back, and she's wearing a sundress.

As she steps off the porch, I whistle, and she smirks, walking toward me. When she comes closer, I stop her, getting a good look. Thankfully, the sun gives me just enough light to see how absolutely fucking beautiful she is.

"Wow, you're so damn pretty," I tell her.

She licks her lips, then bites the corner. "Thanks," she says shyly.

"I mean it." I open the door and help her climb into my truck.

"Southern gentleman. I like that," she compliments.

A laugh escapes me. "I got more where that came from, sweetheart." I shut the door and then walk around to the driver's side and climb in. All I can think about is how she smells sweet like apples and cinnamon.

"Oh my God." She leans over and turns up the radio. "Is this a real song? 'She Thinks My Tractor's Sexy.' I must've missed that one growing up." She gives me a look and smirks.

"Yes, ma'am. That's how we roll around here. We live the life, then we listen to songs about it on the radio." She chuckles as I put the truck into reverse and pull out of the parking lot. We travel the short distance to my house, which puts me on edge. The conversation stays light, but I can feel the awkwardness building between us, and I find myself becoming tongue-tied.

"Nervous?" she jokes as I park.

I let out a breath. "Actually, I kinda am."

She unbuckles and tilts her head at me. "Why?"

"Because I'm obviously in the presence of a celebrity."

She scoffs and gets out, waving me off. "Pretty sure you're more of a celebrity than I am these days."

We take the steps up the porch, and I turn and look at her over my shoulder. The sweet smile on her face is just for me, and it's enough to settle my nerves for now. I step aside after I unlock the door, and she walks in. I barely hear her gasp as she comes to a stop, looking around. Maybe it wasn't too much after all.

She turns and looks at me. "Colton. You didn't have to—"

Within a few steps, I'm standing in front of her. "You deserve all this and more, Red."

I'm so tempted to press my lips against hers, but somehow, I find the strength to go to the kitchen. "I hope you're hungry."

"Starving, actually," she says right behind me, trying to see what I made. I step to the side and peel the foil from the top and show her the chicken parmesan with zucchini.

Her mouth falls open. "You cooked this? Like, by yourself? It looks like it's from one of those cooking shows on the Food Network or something."

I chuckle and nod. "You're adorable, but lemme know what you think after you eat it."

She looks up at me, and I place my finger under her chin. I know I shouldn't kiss her, I shouldn't make a move, but when she licks her lips, I can no longer deny the way I feel. I slowly lean in and watch her eyes flutter closed, and it's all the permission I need. Our lips softly touch, and I become lost in the moment as she pulls me closer to her. Quickly, we become more greedy, no longer holding back as our tongues twist together. I need her. I need her more than sunshine or rain, and the way she holds on to me tells me she feels the same. Presley melts into my chest, and we lose ourselves in the kiss. Somehow, I force myself to pull away, both of us gasping for air, for relief, but neither of us finding it.

"I'm sorry," I say, knowing we probably shouldn't have done that.

Presley clears her throat and smooths her hair down. "Don't be."

The room grows silent. Though all I'm thinking about is her, and what that moment between us meant, I quickly change the subject. "Speaking of, we should probably eat."

She nods. Her full lips are noticeably swollen from our kiss, and I already want to kiss her again.

I place my hand on the small of her back and lead her to the table. After pulling the chair out for her to sit, I light the candles and pour two glasses of white wine.

"This is so fancy. I'm really impressed," she says. "This setting would make an awesome Instagram picture."

"So you like my aesthetic?" I place the chicken and veggies on two plates, then shred fresh parmesan cheese on top. Picking them both up, I walk over to the table and set one in front of her and then sit with mine. Carefully, she picks up her fork and knife and cuts into the chicken. I watch her, hoping she likes it. She lets out a long, exaggerated moan, which causes me to nearly choke.

"Sorry." She looks up at me.

"No, don't be. Braxton actually said…uh, never mind." I stop, figuring it's probably not appropriate to mention what he said earlier about orgasmic chicken parm.

She takes another bite. "This is the best meal I've ever had."

"Really?" I shoot her a skeptical look and grin. "Well, you're in luck because I love to cook, and I have a plethora of recipes I want to make. You can be my test subject."

Presley looks up at me with sad eyes. "Colton."

I don't want her to speak her next words. I know what they're going to be.

"You know I'm leaving Thursday morning." The sadness in her tone is obvious. "I wish I had more time, but I have another commitment next weekend."

I nod in understanding, my expression mimicking hers. "I knew the day was coming. I'd be lying if I said I didn't want to ask you to stay, but it's not my place. I'd never hold you back, Presley. You have big aspirations and things going on in your life; that has always been obvious to me." I shoot her a wink so she knows I'm not upset with her, and her shoulders relax.

"I wish I could offer you more than this—more than what we have right now—but I can't. Let's enjoy the time we have left without my leaving looming over us and without worrying about the future. Just the right here and right now." Her eyes soften as she looks at me, then takes a sip of wine.

"You're right," I agree. Shooting her a grin, I change the subject as we continue eating. It doesn't seem like enough time, and it's the only thought that fills my mind as we make small talk about the weather and things that don't matter. After we're finished eating, I pick up our plates, and Presley meets me at the sink. She touches my arm, and I stop and look at her.

"If circumstances were different—"

"Hey," I interrupt. "We're focusing on the right now. Don't dwell on the what-ifs, okay?" I remind her softly.

She swallows hard, and her lips turn up as she sucks in a deep breath. "Okay."

I slowly lean in and take her bottom lip into my mouth. She melts into my kiss, and it's so hard for me to pull away. I lean my back against the counter and watch her.

"Wow," she whispers before her eyes flutter open.

I search her face with a grin. "What?"

"It's stupid." Her cheeks flush, and she playfully walks away.

I follow her, then pull her into my arms. Her back rests against my chest, and I lean in and nuzzle the crook of her neck before I take her earlobe into my mouth.

"Tell me," I whisper.

Quickly, she turns and faces me. "You have to promise not to laugh."

"No can do, sweetheart. I don't have a good poker face."

Crossing her arms over her chest, she makes the zipper movement over her mouth and shakes her head.

"Okay, okay, fine." I hold up my hands in surrender. "I promise to *try* not to laugh."

Narrowing her eyes at me, she smirks. "I guess that's as good as I'm going to get."

"Basically. Now spill it." I take her by the hand, and when we sit on the couch, she turns her body toward me.

"There are times when you do things that are just like one of the heroes I read about in romance books. I know it sounds stupid, but I've been reading a few cowboy Southern-themed novels, and all I have to say is I feel as though I'm living inside one. Every day has been a different adventure with you." She smiles, then lowers her face as if she's embarrassed by her admission.

I take her hand and hold it in mine, wanting her closer. "So tell me, Red. What happens in these books?" I ask, already having my suspicions.

She immediately starts chuckling, and I lift an eyebrow.

"Let's just say it's not exactly PG-13." She shrugs as if it doesn't faze her.

"Ooooh. Say no more." I tuck loose strands of hair behind her ear as she tucks her swollen lips in her mouth. "You want dessert?" I ask. "I have pie."

"Pie?" She lifts her brows excitedly. "Yes, please!"

I head to the kitchen and prepare our plates with apple pie. I warm them up for a minute before adding whipped cream on top, then carry them back to the couch where Presley is waiting.

"Thank you. Smells so good."

"I can't take all the credit on this one, unfortunately, but Mama B's pies are undeniably the best around." I take a bite and watch as she scoops a large piece on her fork.

"Mmm." She closes her eyes as she releases the fork from between her lips. "This is heaven."

"It sure is," I agree. Except I'm not talking about the pie.

We continue to talk while we finish our dessert. Presley is so easy to talk to that I don't even realize how late it's getting. I want to push her down on the couch and kiss her all night long, but I know that would only complicate things further.

"I should probably head back, Colton." The mood turns serious, and I know the night has to end eventually.

"Sure thang. Did you get some sleep after you got back to the B&B?" I stand and grab my jacket and keys as she follows me.

"Hardly. I was too pumped from all the sugar we ate and way too excited as I went through the pictures. I maybe got a few hours." She shrugs as if it's no big deal, but I can see the exhaustion in her eyes.

We walk outside, and I open the door to the truck so she can climb in. "Ahh, I know. Same. I'm actually super tired too, but it was totally worth it. I'd do it a million times over again." It was one of the best nights of my life.

"I haven't had that much fun in ages," she tells me as I climb inside, and we head toward the B&B. The headlights guide us in the darkness, and within five minutes, the Circle B Ranch sign comes into view. When I see the sign, signifying the end of our night, I can't help but feel like our time together is slipping through my fingers.

After I park, I get out and walk her to the door. The porch light is on, and I know people are probably still awake inside.

I lean in and kiss her on the cheek, but when I pull away, she wraps her arms around my neck and pulls me back to her. She softly traces my lips with hers until she's practically devouring my mouth. Her tongue wrestles with mine, and I try to hold back, but it's hard when I'm this close to her. At first, we take it slow, but when she becomes more ravenous, the kisses intensify, growing into greed and need.

"Colton," Presley says against my mouth, her palms resting on my chest.

Our breathing is erratic, and if we were back at my house, I'm sure we would've lost all self-control. Maybe that's why she suggested we leave.

"You make me want to stay. I'm afraid of falling for you," she admits in a soft whisper. I can hear the vulnerability in her voice.

I'm afraid I already have, I want to reply, but I think better of it.

"If that happens, I'll be there to catch you." I look into her eyes, the warmth of the porch light casting a glow on her red hair, and I take in the moment. As she looks up into my eyes, I lean forward and softly kiss her again, and I'm pretty sure she actually melts into me this time. Somehow, we manage to pull apart for her to head inside. I wave goodbye through the screen door, and when she walks away, I know she's taking my heart with her.

CHAPTER FIFTEEN

PRESLEY

THE NEXT MORNING, my body is still buzzing from finally crossing that line with Colton. I can still taste him on my lips, and being here with him is like living in a romance book. How could this really be my life? I don't date. I've never been kissed with such fervor that my breath was literally taken away, but each time Colton kissed me, my emotions were ready to bubble over. There were zero doubts about how he felt as he poured himself into me, and though I'm scared to admit how I feel, denial wasn't an option with his lips pressed against mine.

I try to push the thought of him away, but it's impossible. All I can see when I close my eyes is how good he looked in that navy blue button-up shirt and slacks. I'm a sucker for the cowboy garb, but last night? *Damn*. I'm tempted to pinch myself to make sure it all really happened because it seems unreal. Colton is one of the good guys, and I have no doubt when I leave Texas, he'll find someone who's a much better fit for him and forget about me. But until then, I'm going to enjoy the time we have left and try to forget I'm leaving in three days.

It weighs heavily on my chest, but so does the fact that this seems too good to be true. My insecurities are leaking through. I've never been the girl who guys flock to, especially ones who look like Colton. I've just always stood in the background, hiding behind my camera, because it's my safe place. As long as I'm taking pictures of other people, the focus isn't on me, and I like it that way. Somehow, he sees past all that, and I'm not used to the attention. My eyes flutter closed, and I let out a sad sigh. I don't want to hurt him, though I have a feeling we're both going to get hurt regardless.

After I go through my morning routine, I throw on some jeans and a T-shirt and decide to text Olivia before I go downstairs. Out of everyone I know, she'd understand my situation the most. Checking the time, I see it's barely past eight here, and she's two hours behind me. Then again, she's an early bird by nature, so I'm sure she's awake.

Presley: So I might need you to talk me off the ledge.

Olivia: Good morning to you too!

A smile touches my lips. Olivia in the morning can be a little much to handle.

Presley: Good morning. ;)

Olivia: That's better. Tell me what's going on. Cowboy Casanova playing hard to get?

Presley: No and that's the problem. He's perfect. Everything about him is perfect.

I feel as if I can hear her laughter all the way from California. I'm so screwed. While I'm usually one to keep my love life to myself, I feel like if I don't talk about it with someone, I might lose my mind.

Olivia: And that's a problem because why again?

Presley: Because I'm leaving. Last night, he cooked me dinner at his place, and it was amazing. It was something straight out of a romance book, and if I would've had my camera and a studio, there would've been an entire shoot

of him. He wore a button-up shirt rolled up to his elbows. Do you even understand how hot that is?

Olivia: Have you met my husband? Of course, I understand. I swear they dress that way on purpose. And the cologne. Playboys. Please tell me y'all did it at least? I'm still living vicariously through you.

I chuckle at her message and replay each sweet moment of last night. It could've easily happened, and just the thought makes my blood pump quicker. I'm not marking it off my list entirely but won't push it because sex *always* complicates things. Though I know my fantasies won't even touch the real thing, especially if his kisses are any indication of what it'd be like with him.

Presley: No. That didn't happen.

Olivia: I get it. I really do. You're scared. The odds are stacked against you. But sometimes, the risk is worth the reward. Just putting that out there…

I take in her words, and I know she's right.

Olivia: The only advice I have is to live the next few days as if you're not leaving. And whatever happens, happens. (Then tell me all about it).

Presley: Thank you. I owe you.

Olivia: I still owe you for the maternity pictures. ;) Have fun! That's what it's all about. If you're too focused on the future, you'll forget to live in the now, and these are the times we'll reminisce about one day. If you need to talk again, I'm here.

Presley: Thanks, girl. Means a lot to me.

Olivia: **NOW GO HAVE HOT COWBOY SEX! BYE!**

My laughter echoes throughout the room as I shake my head, but a lot of what Olivia said is true. I do need to live in the moment and quit worrying about leaving.

After I set up my computer to download pictures from my camera, I make my way downstairs and grab some breakfast. After I tell John hello, I take my plate and eat on the back porch so I can take in the view. I'm really going to miss this place when I'm gone. California tranquility has nothing on Texas.

As I bite down on a crunchy piece of bacon, I open my Instagram and reply to a few dozen messages. I'll need to schedule my posts for the rest of the week and post the Steamy Bedtime Reads hashtag photo. My to-do list is forever long, but I find myself looking toward the barn, hoping to catch a glimpse of Colton working. No such luck. I finish breakfast, then head upstairs to start my tasks.

The day passes by in a blink, and by the time I look at the clock, I realize it's close to four, and I lost track of time again. After hours of organizing photos, editing them, then scheduling, I'm exhausted. It's crucial that every picture flows together nicely on my Instagram feed, so I rearrange the photos until they're just right. I can't help but smile as I scroll through what's scheduled, and I can't help but think about what Olivia said this morning.

Right now, I really am living the best moments of my life, and I have to enjoy every second I can.

I stand and stretch and notice how bright it is outside. Instead of wasting perfectly good daylight, I tighten my ponytail before I stuff my backpack full of books, then grab my tripod and camera. I'm a woman on a mission as I go downstairs, step off the back porch, and make my way toward the barn.

Not sure why, but I grow more nervous with each step I take, knowing I could run into Colton. As I walk past the barn, I slow and look inside. When I don't see him, I feel a little disappointed but know he's probably busy or giving a lesson.

I look at the barn and realize the freshly painted exterior will pop in my photos once I edit them. Bending over, I dig in my bag and try to find a book that will match the barn.

"What's up, Red?" I hear as I make it to the other side.

Just the sound of his voice makes my breath hitch. His footsteps come closer, and I turn to look at him, but instead, I'm at eye level with his crotch. When he clears his throat, I straighten up and meet his baby blue eyes. They're the color of the ocean when the sun is shining down on the water, and I find myself drowning in them.

"Lookin' for somethin'?" He shoves his hands in his pockets, and I want him to touch me. I've felt that need since last night on the porch when he kissed me good night.

"Nah," I joke, propping a book up against the side of the barn. The red text on the cover looks amazing against the fresh paint. I pull my camera from my shoulder and kneel to get almost eye level with the book and take different angles of it. Colton stands back, allowing me to work, and I love the way it feels when his eyes are on me.

After I take several pictures, I move to stand but don't realize how close he is and stumble forward. His strong hands land on my waist, steadying me. When I look up at him, I study his plump lips and the layer of scruff over his jawline. My mouth parts slightly, desperate to taste him again.

As he leans forward, my eyes flutter closed, and his lips quickly brush against mine.

"I'm sorry. I can't," he whispers and pulls away.

Rejection floods through me, and I swallow hard, feeling a knot form in my throat. Just as if he could read it on my face, he takes my hand in his and kisses my knuckles.

"You have no idea how much I want to fucking kiss you right now, but I can't right here. John will flip his shit. It's too dangerous," he whispers, and I feel better knowing it's not because of me but rather the risk of getting caught. Which makes it even hotter, if that were possible.

"I understand," I say, taking a step back to create space between us. I'd never do anything to compromise his job at the ranch.

"Do you wanna get out of here?" He flashes me one of his devilish grins, and I can't stop my smile at how this feels like we're two teenagers sneaking around.

Though I have tons of pictures to take, I can't deny I want to spend more time with him.

I nod, and he beams. "Meet me at my truck in about fifteen minutes. I'm parked on the side in the front."

"Okay!" I tell him as he walks away.

"Oh, and Red?" he says over his shoulder.

I begin to put my stuff away so I can drop it off upstairs. "Yeah?"

"Bring your books and camera with you." He gives me an amused look, and I'm pretty sure it's because I'm taken aback by him. Butterflies swarm inside as I wonder what he's planning. The first time a guy has ever told me to bring my books, but hell, I like it.

I swing my backpack over my shoulder and rush to the B&B to grab a few more books, extra batteries, and a few memory cards. Before I leave, I go to the bathroom and adjust my ponytail and put on some lip gloss.

Somehow, I'm able to make my way out of the B&B without running into John, which is a small miracle because I'm terrible at lying. It's obvious Colton wants to keep what's going on between us private, which will make this easier when I have to leave. At least he won't be wearing his emotions on his sleeve once I'm gone. It would be too obvious for everyone.

I make my way across the front of the B&B and walk over to the side where Colton said he'd parked. Soon, he's striding toward me with a shit-eating grin and unlocking the truck.

"You thought I was someone bustin' ya for sneaking off with the ranch hand, didn't you?"

I snap a picture of him as he puts the truck in reverse and drives out of the parking lot. His messy hair peeks out from under his baseball cap. Colton is a country boy through and through. Though he's been working all day, I love how he smells like fresh leather, horses, and hay. This is exactly how I'll remember Texas.

As he pulls onto the main road, I take pictures of the narrow highway that seems to go on for eternity. Colton lowers the window as he slows, then pulls over on the shoulder.

"Go ahead, it's picture perfect," he tells me with a grin.

I hop out of the truck and go to the fence line, making sure the composition is just right with the blue sky and fluffy white clouds in the background. After I've taken as many pictures as possible, I climb back into the truck.

"You got it?" He pulls onto the main road.

I review the pictures. "They're beautiful. Like they should totally be in a calendar or in a magazine."

"Kinda like you." Colton shoots me a cute wink.

"You're just saying that to be nice." My cheeks heat.

His face contorts, and he shakes his head. "No, I'm not. You're beautiful. Too bad you don't see what I do. You're really missing out, Red."

"Well, thank you," I reply shyly. "I think Cowboy Casanova was the best nickname for you after all." I snicker.

The downtown area of Eldorado is cute and has that true small-town vibe only found in remote areas like this. Among the many brick buildings in the center of town are the post office and city hall next to a church and feed store. I chuckle as Colton clicks on his blinker and parks in an empty parking lot.

"Where's the McDonalds?" I jokingly ask as we get out of the truck, and I grab my camera and backpack.

"About forty-five minutes that way." He points behind us.

My mouth practically falls to the sidewalk. "Forty-five minutes? Holy crap. Though their salty fries just might be worth it." Being from California means everything is within reach. Hell, I don't even have to leave my apartment now that apps allow you to order food and have it delivered.

"We have a diner and a grocery store. If you can't find food there, then you starve. Welcome to real life country living, sweetheart." He chuckles, and I follow him as he starts walking.

"No wonder you guys are all so fit. There's no terrible food to tempt you late at night."

Being a size twelve in a city like LA makes me an outcast among all the size two women, and the insecurity I feel about that doesn't always stay hidden. Even though I'm healthy and mostly happy with my body, it's hard not to compare myself to all the tiny women surrounding me in the big city. Even here, every girl I've met has been petite and adorable. It's impossible not to feel incompetent when I have curves for days. My ass isn't exactly on the small side, and I have stretch marks on my breasts from when I nearly developed overnight. It's probably why I'm not viewed as a threat when the cover models bring their girlfriends to a shoot. I prefer to be behind the camera but take them for my Bookstagram page when I need to.

"Yeah right. Our mamas are always tryin' to fatten us up. All the five-course meals and homemade pies and cakes are a million times worse than a cheeseburger and fries. Not to mention we couldn't leave the table until our plates were empty." He rounds a corner, and I literally stop walking.

A beautiful painting decorates the side of a building. The bright colors flow and splash together in one of the largest murals I've ever seen. I'm almost shocked to see it go from top to bottom without an inch of space wasted.

"When you were talkin' 'bout places to take pictures, I knew I had to bring you here." Colton beams, and I appreciate how much he cares about my passion.

My mind races with all the possible poses that could be taken in different sections of the painting. It's so large, one would have to go the next block over to capture it all in one frame.

"It's huge," I say, looking over it.

"Haven't you heard? Everything's bigger in Texas."

"I think I've heard that a time or two," I muse.

I take my camera from over my shoulder and set my backpack on the ground. Golden hour is sneaking up on us, and I'll have a short period to get the photos, but I've got the best model, even if he doesn't yet know he'll be the star of the show again.

"What does all this stuff mean?" I ask, handing Colton the books from my bag.

"It's all a part of Texas heritage. Symbols that represent the great state. The bluebonnet is our flower, the longhorn is our animal, the Lone Star flag doesn't even need an explanation, and a monarch butterfly is our insect," he explains. I back him up against the wall, posing him, though he's too distracted to notice.

"But what about the stars?" I look up at them, noticing how many there are.

"The stars at night," he says in melody.

"…are huge and bright," I add to the song, taking a few steps back.

He tucks the books under his arm and claps three times. "Wrong lyrics, but it'll do." He smirks, and it makes me laugh.

"Of course. I suck at lyrics." I shrug. "Then again, 'Deep in the Heart of Texas' isn't really a song we sang as kids in California."

"I almost feel sorry for y'all missing out on all the Texas awesomeness."

I walk up to him and remove the hat from his head and place it on my own. "I don't want the shadow on your face this time."

As I go to walk away, he pulls me back to him and kisses me like there's no tomorrow. Because right now, there isn't one. He sinks into me, his hard body pressed against mine, and I don't want him to pull away. I want to devour him, all of him, right here, right now, against this building. Catching my breath seems impossible as his tongue slides against mine, and it takes everything not to moan against his lips. He tastes like coffee and mints, and the smell of him envelops me. If I could stop time, I'd do it now. Eventually, we break apart, and I feel the immediate loss.

"Where do you want me to place these books?" He tries to hand them back to me.

I look up at the sky and see the warm glow splashing across the building. "In your hand. Lean against the wall by the Texas flag."

I take so many pictures of him, I almost feel like the paparazzi. Because I know the time is ticking, I hand him several different books and direct him on how to pose as I place him in front of distinct parts of the painting. Honestly, Colton is a natural at this and listens better than most of the models I've worked with over the years. After an hour and a thousand pictures later, I think I've gotten every pose I could ever need. I scroll through and review what I took while Colton places all my books in my backpack and swings it over his shoulder. He stands beside me and looks at some of the shots I got.

"Wow, I never would've thought it'd look like that. The colors really pop." He smiles at me, and I smile back.

"I'm impressed by them too. Probably should've had you take off your shirt, though," I kid, but just as I do, he slowly lifts his shirt, revealing his washboard abs. Damn.

"You're a tease," I say, turning off my camera and swinging it over my shoulder.

"Anytime you want this shirt off, sweetheart, you just let me know. I'll make it happen in a snap."

Laughter escapes me. "Don't tempt me."

"I wish I could." He grabs my hand and interlocks his fingers with mine. It's such a small gesture, but it feels so intimate to walk with him back to the truck like this. If I close my eyes, I can almost imagine this transforming into something more than what it is now. The thought alone makes my heart drop, and that imaginary countdown clock appears in my mind.

After we're in the truck, Colton cranks it, but before we pull away, he turns to me. "You hungry?"

"I think I'm always hungry," I joke, but then remember I didn't have lunch…again.

"Good 'cause we're gonna eat some of the best beef tips and mashed potatoes around. And you've gotta try the pie." He pulls onto the main road, and within a minute, we're parking at the diner. Through the large windows in the front, I can see booths. Just thinking about food makes my stomach grumble.

I follow Colton out of the truck, and he holds the front door open for me. The smell of fresh baked desserts and coffee fills my nose just as an older woman with white-gray hair walks up. Her name tag reads Betty, and she looks like she could easily be a television grandma with her cute smile and soft eyes.

"Hey, darlin'. Table for two?" she asks, looking back and forth between us.

"Yes, ma'am. A booth please," Colton tells her so politely I almost melt at his natural charm. The Southern drawl makes the simplest thing sound hot.

She places our menus down in front of us and takes our drink order. As soon as she walks away, I lean over.

"This place is the best already," I whisper with a grin.

"Wait until you try the food."

Betty walks up with our drinks and makes small talk with Colton before we order.

"How's your mama? She doin' okay?"

"Yes, ma'am. Been doin' real good lately," Colton tells her. "Dad is doin' good, too. Keeping busy."

"And your sister?" Betty pulls a notepad from her apron.

"Everly's stayin' out of trouble," he says, then adds, "for now." Betty laughs, then asks for his order.

"The regular. You know how I like it."

She gives him a wink, then turns to me. "For you, honey?"

"I'll have what he's having." I smile really big, not knowing what the hell he ordered, but I know it's bound to be good. Plus, he's local, so I trust his decision is the right one. I just hope it's not some insane portion of meat. She gives me a small nod and walks away. I turn my camera on and take a picture of Colton sipping his coffee.

"I'm gonna have to start chargin' for those," he teases, but it causes me to snort.

"You actually should, considering three publishers and ten authors all want your photos. You could be a rich man."

Colton rolls his eyes as if I'm kidding. "I like my simple life. I don't need all the attention unless you're the one givin' it to me."

His words leave me speechless, and I don't know what to say. As if he notices, he quickly changes the subject.

"So you have any idea what you just ordered to eat?"

Shrugging, I lick my bottom lip. "I'm praying it's not something weird like oxtails or cow tongues. I've heard about some of the Texas cuisines."

His laughter when I say that scares me.

"Oh man. All of a sudden, I'm not feeling very confident about my choice now," I tell him. Ten minutes later, Betty walks up carrying two huge plates. My eyes go wide as she sets down enough food to feed an army, and that's just my plate. My mouth drops as I take in the tower of mashed potatoes, brown gravy, and huge chunks of beef.

Colton smirks, then takes a big bite of potatoes. "I told you the beef tips were the best."

I pick up my fork to see if it's as good as he says, and it definitely is. The potatoes practically melt in my mouth, and the meat is so tender, I barely have to chew. We don't talk while we devour our food, and when we're done, Colton tries to order pie to go, but I refuse. I'm so full, he might have to carry me to the truck, but I don't mention it because I know he would. After he introduces me to all the regulars sitting at the counter, Colton gives Betty a hug, and we leave. I snap some photos of the sunset before I hop in the truck.

On the way back to the B&B, I can't help but laugh at the stories Colton tells me about Braxton. I can tell they're good friends, but after hearing some of the shit they get themselves into, I'm surprised they're still alive.

"Then there was this one time he stumbled into the wrong hotel room and crawled into bed with this woman, and her husband came back to the room. Braxton got the shit kicked outta him, then the guy pulled a gun on him—because it's Texas and everyone has guns—and I basically had to come to his rescue. Long story short, Fireball is dangerous," he says between his laughter.

I'm basically crying as he recounts all these stories, and soon we're turning into the parking lot. I've never smiled as much as I do when I'm with him. Colton really brings out the best in me. After he parks, we get out of the truck and walk toward the B&B.

He opens the door for me, and I step in, waiting for him to come to my side. Colton takes a few steps with me, then immediately stops, growing silent. I turn to look at him, but his eyes are focused on the woman in front of us. I glance at her, then turn back to him to see the color has drained from his face as if he's seen a ghost.

With a ragged breath, he exhales. "Mallory."

And I know exactly who she is.

CHAPTER SIXTEEN

COLTON

What the fuck? It's the only thought that comes to mind the second I see *her*. Mallory. The woman who broke my heart and shattered me. I knew she was back in town, but why the hell is she *here*?

Anger runs through my veins as I look at her, and all those memories of her betrayal hit me full force. The cheating. The lies. The baby who wasn't mine.

Rage heats my skin as I shoot her a look of disgust.

"Hey, guys," John says. "This is Mallory, my new assistant. Mallory, this is one of our ranch hands—"

"She knows who I am," I bite out. Presley looks over at me, and I know she's putting two and two together. I hate that she's here to witness this. "And what do you mean she's your new assistant?" I dart my eyes to John.

"I've been looking for one for months, and she's more than qualified. What's your deal?" John asks, narrowing his eyes as he studies my expression with his arms crossed over his chest.

I see Presley out of the corner of my eye step toward Mallory and hold her hand out. "Hi, I'm Presley. It's nice to meet you."

"You too, thanks. I'm excited to be working here," Mallory replies, purposely dragging her eyes over Presley, which gets my blood boiling even more. "Do you work here too?" she asks her, and for some reason, the insinuation that Presley would only be seen with me if she works here has me cutting into their conversation.

"No, she doesn't." My tone is harsh, but I can't help it.

"So…you two know each other then?" John intervenes, looking at Mallory and then me. "Maybe you can give her the grand tour then."

"Oh, I'm not sure—" Mallory starts, but I cut her off.

"Not happening," I grind out with a scoff. "John, I need a minute with you." I walk toward his office without waiting for his response. I hear him apologize to Mallory and excuse himself. I feel bad for leaving Presley out there, but seeing as she knows the backstory, I hope she'll be able to deflect her way out of answering any questions.

"Dude, what's with you?" John asks once he's followed me and closed the door. "You're being rude as hell."

I turn and face him. "You can't hire her. There's no way she can work here."

He crosses his arms over his chest, waiting for me to explain further.

"She's my ex that I haven't seen in five years, well minus a week or two ago when I ran into her at the store. I was shocked then, but this…" I brush a hand through my hair, frustrated and shocked. "I don't know if I can deal with her being here."

John gives me a look that tells me he sympathizes with me, but I have a feeling it won't change things. "I didn't know, but I need the help, and she needs the job. She has a five-year-old daughter."

"I know." I exhale. "I thought she was mine until the day she was born, and then Mallory told me I wasn't the father."

"Holy shit." John's jaw drops. "That's some heavy shit."

"Yeah, well it was a long time ago, and I took this job after it all happened, so only a couple of people here know. It's just…she caused a lot of pain in my life and having her back brings all that up again when I thought I was over it. I mean, I am over it. I don't have feelings for her anymore, but it's still painful. I thought we were going to be a family, get married, have the whole shebang."

"I can understand that more than you know," he says with sad eyes. "I wish I could tell you she's out of here, but—"

"You need the help, and she needs the job," I finish for him.

"Yeah, I got it. I probably overreacted anyway, considering you had no idea. I just hope she didn't apply for the position knowing I worked here."

"Well, your picture *has* been all over the internet, so it wouldn't take much for her to put two and two together," he points out and shrugs.

"Shit, you're right." I inhale deeply, trying to calm myself. I don't want Presley to see me lose my temper either.

"She has a daughter to support, so I'd hate to kick her out on her ass," John continues. "Maybe it's time you two dealt with it and moved on?"

I scoff. "Pfft. There's nothing to deal with."

I walk out and head back toward Presley who's being way too kind to Mallory. I hear her talking about the ranch and how beautiful it's been for her pictures.

"So you're the famous photographer?" I hear Mallory ask, and the distaste in her tone isn't lost on me.

"Um..." Presley stammers, nervously, and my suspicions are confirmed. Mallory saw the picture or at least heard about it.

Fuckin' small-town perks.

"Hey," I interrupt before Presley can respond. She doesn't owe Mallory anything, and I want to end the conversation now. "I gotta get back to work." Grabbing Presley's hand, I pull her aside so we can have some privacy. "I'll text you later?"

"You okay?" she asks.

"Yeah, thanks." I give her a smile and squeeze her hand since I can't kiss her.

I walk out without looking over my shoulder. Seeing Mallory on my turf after all this time has my blood boiling, and I need to cool down before I go off on her. Even if she deserves it.

Just when I reach my truck, I hear my name being called behind me, and when I look, I see Mallory running toward me.

What the fuck?

"Colton, wait! Please," she begs.

I turn around with my arms crossed. She's the last person I want chasing after me.

"What is it, Mallory?"

"I'm sorry. I didn't know you worked here."

I snort. "I'm sure."

"No, seriously. I saw your Instagram picture and the B&B location after I had already applied. When John called me for an interview, I was desperate. I need this job."

"Why? What happened to your husband?" I ask harshly.

She swallows hard, then looks down at her feet. "Things didn't work out. I took Julia and left, then came to my parents' house."

"I'd say I'm sorry, but the truth is, I don't feel bad for you," I snap, pushing myself off the truck to get inside.

"I know I hurt you, Colton—"

"Hurt me?" I turn back around, my blood pressure rising by the second. "That's the fucking understatement of the fucking century!" I shout, and her breath hitches as she leans back. "I gave you everything," I seethe. "You didn't *hurt* me. You fucking destroyed me and everything I believed about love and relationships. You made me believe we were having a child together. I fell in love with her before she was even born. We were starting a life, making plans, planning a fucking wedding! You didn't hurt me. You broke me *for years*. That's something *you* have to live with, so don't expect me to help you feel better about yourself for what *you* did."

Five years of pent-up anger spills out of me, and I'd say I feel bad about it, but the truth is, I feel nothing.

"Colton, I'm so sorry," she stammers around the tears falling down her cheeks. "I know I fucked up, and there's nothing I can say or do to change what I did to you. I was a dumb kid, and I regret hurting you in that way. You have no idea how much I wished Julia was yours, but I couldn't let you think she was when I knew I had cheated, and there was always that chance."

"Well, thank God you had some morals," I retort sardonically.

I turn and hop into my truck, slamming the door and ending the conversation. My tires spit up gravel as I race out of the parking lot, and when I look at my rearview mirror, I see Mallory's still standing there. I decide not to give it another thought as I drive home, leaving the past in the past for good.

Tense and unable to clear my mind, I take a long, hot shower, then decide to go for a walk. I don't want Mallory ruining the time Presley and I have left. Although I spent the afternoon with her, I miss her like crazy already. I need to work off my frustration, so I hop on a four-wheeler and drive back to the B&B to take care of some tasks in the barn. Even though I worked most of my shift, there's always stuff to do.

Colton: Hey, wanna meet me in the barn?

I see her reply bubbles pop up immediately, which makes me smile.

Presley: Sure. I just need to clean up my mess quick. Be right there!

As I'm fumbling around the tack room, I hear footsteps and wait to see if it's her. I smell her perfume before I see her, and when she snakes her arms around my waist, my shoulders fall in relief.

I wrap a hand over her wrist and pull her around to face me. No words need to be exchanged as I see the lust in her eyes, and I can no longer hold back. I step into her space, and she backs up to the wall before I cover her mouth with mine. My hands wrap around her waist and pinch into her hips, needing her impossibly closer.

Presley melts into my chest as her head falls back, opening her mouth for me as I slide my tongue between her soft lips. Every part of me comes to life, and when she releases a throaty moan, and it vibrates against me, I nearly lose control. My hands roam down to her ass, and when I cup her round globes in my palms and lift her, she automatically wraps her thighs around my waist.

I walk us over to one of the empty saddle racks and set her down. Her legs stay around me, and when my cock bulges in my jeans, she lifts her hips and rubs against my groin. By the way she looks at me, I know for certain she can feel how hard I am. I let her rock against me as my fingers slide up her thighs, bringing the material of her sundress up to her hips. Feeling her thin panties against my fingertips has my dick straining even more.

"Sweetheart," I murmur against her lips. "Are you wet for me right now?"

"Yes," she says with a breathy whisper. "Achingly wet." Her confirmation has me growling against her neck. I fucking love the taste of her.

"Fuck, Red. I'm trying to be a gentleman, but it's taking all the goddamn willpower in the world."

When I look into her eyes, they're pleading. She wants this as badly as I do.

"What do you want, baby?"

Presley licks her lips, keeping her gaze on mine. "Touch me. Please."

I can't deny her, and when she begs me, there's no way I'd say no. My fingers slide over her panties until I feel her pussy under the fabric. When my finger runs over her slit, her wetness is unmistakeable against my skin. "Damn, Red. You're drenched."

Sliding her panties aside, I brush the pad of my thumb over her and nearly come in my damn jeans when I sink a finger inside her wetness.

She releases a moan, edging me further. I finger fuck her like my life depends on it as I rub her clit and capture her whimpers with my mouth. When I deepen the kiss, I add a second finger and curve them in as deep as she can take. Presley rocks her hips against my palm as she climbs closer to the edge, and I'm determined to get her there.

My lips trail down her jawline, and when she drops her head, my mouth moves to her neck and sucks the skin there. Her arms are tight around my neck, and her body stiffens as her pussy squeezes my fingers. I rub circles over her clit, faster and harder.

"Oh my God…" she breathes out, lifting her hips, and her legs tremble around me as she rides out her orgasm.

"So fucking perfect, Presley," I whisper in her ear. "So goddamn beautiful."

Her heavy breaths are all that can be heard as I kiss her neck, up her jaw, and back to her mouth. I adjust her panties back into place as I cup her face and devour her with my lips and tongue.

"I can feel your heart pounding so hard," I whisper against her mouth. "Are you okay?"

She chuckles, and when I lean back slightly and look at her, I see her cheeks are flushed, and her lips are swollen from me.

"Better than okay," she confirms. "Just a little winded."

I smile, bringing my two fingers to my mouth and slowly sucking and tasting her sweet juices. "I knew you'd taste good but come the fuck on."

"Oh my God, stop." She blushes, and I love when her cheeks redden. It's obvious with her pale skin and light coat of freckles.

"I'm serious, sweetheart." I dip my head down and press my lips to hers, then kiss her slowly. "See?"

"No." The seriousness of her tone has me cracking up.

"You're too damn precious, aren't you?" I give her a wink, then help her down. Brushing pieces of her hair behind her ear, I look into her eyes and wonder what she's thinking. "I hope you don't think I asked you to come out here for this. I didn't plan for that to happen."

"I'd never think that, Colton. I wanted you to touch me, remember? Plus, after the way you left, I wanted to distract you."

The corner of my lips tilts up. "So it was out of pity?" She knows I'm teasing but doesn't call me on it.

"Well, I mean…" She shrugs with a mocking grin. "Would any guy say no to pity sex?"

"We're not having sex out here but, for the record, probably not."

Presley chuckles, and it's music to my ears. "Prude."

"Sassy!" I reach around and give her ass a little smack.

It's dark out, and with the barn lights on, it's only a matter of time before someone comes out here to check on things. "We should probably get out of here before we garner an audience."

"I think we already gave that horse a show." She points at the stall behind me.

"Whoops." I laugh.

"Will I see you at breakfast tomorrow?" she asks.

"You know it, babe. You're the only reason breakfast is the most important meal of the day." I take her hand and press a kiss to her knuckles.

"I don't think that's the reason, but it was sweet nevertheless." She flashes an amused grin.

Pulling her back into my arms, I press my lips to hers for one final kiss. "I'll see you then. Have sweet dreams."

"I will now." She gives me a wink, which is freaking adorable because both of her eyes blink. I watch as she walks away, and when she looks over her shoulder, she catches me staring at her ass. "Down, boy."

I clench a fist to my chest and pretend to weep. "You wound me, Red!"

"Good night, Cowboy!"

CHAPTER SEVENTEEN

PRESLEY

The moment I saw Mallory storming out the door after Colton, I knew shit was about to go down. I didn't want to intervene, so I didn't follow, but moments later, I heard him shouting. It echoed through the B&B, and I'm pretty sure John was about to have a stroke. He was tempted to go out there and break it up, but luckily, it didn't come to that since Colton drove off shortly after.

I wanted to text him and make sure he was okay, but I didn't really know what to say or how to offer him any comfort. I was glad when he texted and wanted to see me.

I hadn't expected anything when I walked into the barn, but I sure as hell didn't want it to stop. Everything about Colton is sex on a stick, and I want everything he gives me.

The next morning, I wake up with a smile. I slept like a baby, and every thought started and ended with Colton. His lips. His hands. His body. I want him and more.

Those thoughts alone have me smiling ear to ear. I know the closer it gets to me leaving and the closer I get to him, the harder it's going to be. Yet I've convinced myself not to think about that. I don't want to have any regrets, so I'm following my heart on this one, even if it absolutely terrifies me.

Once I'm dressed and ready to go, I head downstairs for breakfast, excited to see Colton again even if it's been less than twelve hours since I last saw him. He's like a drug because I'm completely and irrationally addicted to wanting more of him.

"Good morning, Presley," Braxton says as soon as he sees me. I look around for Colton, who's generally with him. I'm piling pastries, fruit, and of course, bacon on my plate.

"Morning," I reply, happily. When I look at him, he's giving me a suspicious look. "What is it?" I ask.

"Nothing." He shakes his head. "You just look like you have a coat hanger in your mouth."

I nearly choke at his words and burst out laughing. "That's mildly inappropriate."

"Well, you're the one who can't stop smiling. I was just stating a fact." He grabs a handful of pancakes and stacks them on his plate.

"I can't be happy?" I deflect. "It's a beautiful day."

"Yeah, I'm sure it's the weather that has your face lit up like the Fourth of July." He smirks, then shoves a sausage link in his loud mouth.

I groan and give him a look. It's obvious he knows about Colton and me and is trying to get it out of me.

"The weather is suspiciously nice this morning." A familiar voice comes up behind me and squeezes my hip.

"Oh look. He has a coat hanger in his mouth too," Braxton blurts out.

I shake my head at him, then look over at Colton who's beaming.

"Don't mind him." Colton leans in. "He's just a jealous fucker."

"Heard that, asshole," Braxton says.

I laugh at their banter. I find a table and wait for him to join me. Instead, Braxton comes and sits next to me.

"Move it, tool bag." Colton nods his head to the other side of the table, and Braxton reluctantly gets up and sits across from me instead.

"I love the little pet names you two have for each other," I tease once Colton takes his seat.

"Don't even get me started," Colton says.

The three of us eat and chat, and when the door opens and a tall brunette walks in, Braxton gets awkwardly quiet.

"Mornin'." I watch as she greets a few of the guests and see she's carrying a pastry box. "Oh hey, Colton." She walks toward us. "Hi, asshat." She directs her gaze to Braxton, and my eyes widen, wondering if this is playful banter or not.

Braxton looks up at her with fury.

Guess not.

"What are *you* doin' here, Katarina?" He says her name with disgust as if it tasted like horse shit.

"Kat," she corrects him with edginess in her tone. "John asked me to bring in some samples of my pastries for the fall season. So I brought some of my pumpkin cream cheese muffins, mini apple cider pound cakes, caramel-pecan pumpkin bread pudding, and my famous caramel-glazed monkey bread," she explains with a sugary sweetness in her tone. I sense hostility between her and Braxton, and I'm eager to find out why.

"Hell yeah, I'll try one of each." Colton immediately reaches for the muffin.

"They're gluten-free, sugar-free, and completely organic," she tells him as he takes a large bite.

Braxton grabs the other half of his muffin and takes a bite, making a face. "I think you forgot to mention flavor-free. Pass."

A hand flies to my mouth, shocked at his rudeness. I don't know this Kat girl, but still, that was a rude thing to say even with the weirdness between them.

"Braxton!" I scold since Colton's mouth is full. "That's not nice."

"Don't worry," Kat says to me with a smug smile. "His opinion matters to me just as much as the dirt on my shoe."

"Kat, this is Presley. Presley, Kat. She's Mila's cousin and owns a bakery in town." Colton finally introduces us, though I'm sure he's just trying to redirect the conversation.

"Mila's cousin? It's awesome to meet you. Mila's a sweetheart."

"Nice to meet you too. You aren't from around here." She pops her hip and puts a hand there as if she's trying to figure it out. "West Coast?"

"Yep, California. I'm here for a work trip," I explain, giving her the short version.

"Presley's a photographer," Colton tells her, and two seconds later when Kat's eyes light up, I know she's about to ask if I'm "the" photographer. When Colton confirms that I am, she squeals.

"Love, love, love your photos!" she gushes.

I smile and thank her. Moments later, John comes out of his office, and Kat runs off to greet him with her basket of goodies.

"Okay, someone needs to spill the tea," I say as soon as she's out of earshot. "What's the deal with you and her?" I direct my question to Braxton. "You were anything but pleasant to her, so I know there's a story."

"Short version, they hate each other," Colton says, laughing. He's finished his half of the muffin, so I know Braxton was just being rude about it not tasting good.

"What? Why?" I look at Braxton, waiting for an explanation.

He scoffs. "She's a spoiled rich girl with an entitled attitude."

"Regardless of your history, you *still* wanna fuck her." Colton grins.

"Colton!" I elbow him.

"Trust me, he does. Hate sex is hot," he adds.

"Been there, done that. Not impressed." Braxton scoffs.

"Oh my God. I knew it!" I point at Braxton. "You're both pigs."

"I'm just stating facts!" Colton tries to defend himself. "Not saying I agree with him."

"Fine," I give in. "Braxton's the pig."

Instead of arguing, Braxton makes a pig noise and snorts.

I laugh at his crude attitude and finish my plate of food. Braxton gets up and heads out first, knowing Colton and I want to be alone. John is still in his office with Kat, which gives us a couple of minutes of privacy.

"What do you think about sneaking me into your room tonight?" he asks, flashing me a devious grin.

"Ooh, I like the sound of that. You wanna come up through the window? Want me to lasso down a rope for you?" I tease.

"She's got jokes." He deadpans, and it makes me burst out laughing at his pathetic poker face. "John should be gone by the time I come, so when I do the secret knock, you'll know it's me." He winks.

"The secret knock?" I ask, and he does it against the table for me. Smiling, I repeat it, and he nods his approval. "Okay, got it."

Colton drops his hand to my thigh and squeezes. "See you then, Red."

He stands and grabs his plate. I stare at his backside, appreciating all the taut muscles and how hard he must work every day to maintain them. Even after staying here, I have no idea what all his job entails, but knowing he's up at dawn and works ten hours straight makes me appreciate that he wants to spend any of his downtime with me.

Once I finish eating, I head to my room and begin my routine of checking emails, DMs, looking over my scheduled posts, writing captions, and editing more pictures. Then I flip through my planner and jot down notes about the future posts I still need. Publishers don't always give me a heads-up of when or what books they're sending, so I always have a few float days in a month for anything unexpected.

I have a Most Authentic Props hashtag I still need a picture for and wonder if I could find some innovative ideas around the ranch. The horse barn stores a lot of equipment, so perhaps I could talk Colton into letting me borrow some for a flat lay picture.

It's just after ten in the morning when I decide to head out to the barn with my camera. I'm not even sure if he'll be there, but hopefully, he won't mind me snooping.

I can't help but feel disappointed when I don't see him inside, but I know I'll see him later. Looking around the room we were in last night, memories of his hands and mouth on me flood in, and my cheeks heat even though I'm alone and shouldn't feel embarrassed. Colton makes me not care about the consequences, which can be both good and bad.

Bales of straw are in one corner, so I grab a fistful and set it on one of the empty stools. Next, I grab one of the lead ropes, a thing I know snaps to the horse's halter, and a whip. Hmm...I could use a hat too.

I start digging around, and just when I'm reaching for something I dropped, I hear a deep voice behind me.

"Hands up where I can see them, ma'am."

I spin around so fast, I nearly trip over my own feet. "Jesus, you scared the shit out of me!" I scold and swat at his chest when he closes the gap between us and wraps his arms around my waist.

Colton's laughter echoes off the walls, and I love the sound of it. "And what exactly are you doin'? Stealing all my equipment?" He raises his brows.

I snort. "Hardly. Just getting some props for a picture. Hey! Can I use your hat?"

"Uh, sure." He grabs it and hands it over.

"Hm…I need your boots too."

"Uh…" He nervously chuckles. "I kinda need those, Red."

"Just for a minute," I say and stick out my lower lip. "I just need to get one pic."

Colton leans back, exhaling an exaggerated groan. "Okay, okay fine. But I draw the line at taking my shirt off. Unless you need my jeans too?" He flashes a devilish smirk, and I know he's messing with me.

"Oh yes. Everything off." I snap my fingers at him. "Chop, chop."

"Hilarious." He glares. "Not that I'd be against rolling around in the hay with you."

"And who says cowboys aren't charmers?" I snicker.

Once his boots are off, I position the hat next to one of them and lay the other items close. I take the stool and step on it so I'm high enough to get everything in the frame. I take about a dozen shots and decide one of them will be good enough to use.

"Okay, got it," I tell him, stepping off the stool.

"Can I see?" he asks, looking over my shoulder.

I flip through the images. "I need to crop and edit them, but I think it'll turn out super cute."

"Nice. Glad my boots and hat could be of service."

I look over my shoulder at him and see him grinning. "So humble, Casanova."

He chuckles, then helps me put the items away and puts his hat and boots back on.

"Thanks for your help, again."

"So on a scale of one to ten, how lost would you have been during your trip without me?" Colton flashes me his infamous smug grin, and I know he thinks he's so sly. He's leaning against the wall with his arms crossed looking like a tempting meal.

Just to mess with him, I play along with his little game. "Uh, zero. Braxton would've had no problem stripping for me."

"Just for that…" He pushes off the wall and charges for me. I laugh as he grabs me and lifts me. My arms wrap around his neck, holding on to him and never wanting him to let me go. He walks us to the other side of the room and presses my back against the wall as his mouth stays glued to mine.

He presses his hard bulge between my thighs, taunting me with his dick for the second time. When he pushes harder against me, it's more than evident his erection aches for release.

"Colton…" I whimper against his lips. "Set me down."

For a moment, his eyes look panicked as if he did something wrong, but then I drop to my knees. My fingers fly to his jeans, and I eagerly unbutton them. I want this man, and I'm done depriving myself.

"Presley, what are you doin'?" he rushes out in a whisper.

"Taking advantage," I taunt with an evil smile. We both know he's not opposed to what I'm doing. I unzip him, then slide his jeans down until I can get to his boxers. Instead of teasing him like I want, I know we're living on borrowed time out here. I pull his shorts down, and when his cock bounces free, I immediately wrap my fingers around it and stroke his impressive length. He's thick and glorious, and I thank the gods above me for this.

"Holy fuck, Red." He presses his hand on the wall and leans toward me. I cover my lips around his tip, then run my tongue along his shaft. "Jesus Christ."

Looking up at him, I love watching his expressions. From his clipped tone, it's almost as if he's in pain, but I know the intensity he's feeling right now. I felt the same last night, and I wanted to touch him so badly, but I knew we could be caught at any minute if someone walked in—just like now if we aren't careful.

I pull him into my mouth and continue stroking him as I keep my eyes locked on his. Colton puts a hand around my head and directs me exactly where he wants me. I eagerly comply and watch as his face contorts the deeper I go. Bringing my other hand up, I cup his balls and work them while I stroke his cock into my mouth. He tastes so damn good, I don't want to stop.

"Fuck, you look so beautiful with my cock in your mouth, Red."

The intensity of his gaze has me clenching my thighs, wishing I could reach down and touch myself.

My eyes widen at his words, loving the filth he's spewing. It makes me increase my pace, stroking and licking and deep throating him as far as I can.

"Red…" His breathing picks up, and I know he's close. "Baby, back up."

I shake my head and pull him closer.

"Seriously, Red…I'm gonna—"

I pump him one more time, and when the hot spurts hit the back of my throat, I swallow them down. Licking up his shaft, I wrap my lips around his tip once more and clean him.

When I see he's fully sated, I pull back and smile. He shakes his head with a grin and pulls his boxers and jeans back up. Reaching his hand out to me, I take it and stand. He pulls me against his body and immediately plants his mouth on mine.

"You're a naughty girl," he muses between his kisses. "But now I'm going to feel like a jackass because I have to get back to work."

"No, don't," I protest. "I have things to finish up anyway. I'll see you tonight?"

"Bet that ass you will," he teases, rounding a hand to playfully smack my ass.

"You have an ass fetish, don't you? And all this time, I thought you had a thing for tits." I shake my head in fake disapproval.

"You're my exception. That perky ass caught my attention the first day I ran into you, and it's distracted me ever since."

My head falls back, and I belt out a laugh at his confession. "You blamed Braxton!"

"Which I still stand by," he says. Colton leans down once more and gives me a quick kiss. "I'll text you when I'm on my way."

"I'll be waiting, Cowboy."

CHAPTER EIGHTEEN

COLTON

THE SHIFT between Presley and me happened when I said fuck it and decided to finally kiss her. We haven't been able to keep our hands off each other since then, which I know will only complicate things. However, I couldn't let her leave without at least expressing how I felt. It was a risk, but I'm glad I took the leap because she feels the same.

Last night after I snuck back into the B&B and up to Presley's room, I memorized every inch of her lips and neck. I didn't want her thinking that was the only reason I wanted to see her, so between our mouths fusing together, I held her in my arms, and we just talked. It was really nice, but inevitably, Presley fell asleep, and I didn't have the heart to wake her. She looked so breathtakingly beautiful and relaxed. Getting up and leaving was hard as fuck, but I knew I had to sneak out before John came in for the early shift.

As I make my way back to the B&B for my morning coffee, my mind is a clusterfuck of emotions. I'm still on a high from the past few days and being able to spend those tender moments with her, but I woke up after a couple of hours of sleep feeling dreadful because tonight will be our last time together. She'll fly out to Florida tomorrow morning, and I have no idea if I'll ever see her again. The thought alone cripples me.

"Late night?" Braxton smacks his hand on my shoulder as I eagerly sip my coffee. Being so lost in my head, I didn't even hear him approach. I could've never imagined she'd become such an important part of my life in her short time here. A smile touches my lips as I think about how I bumped into her and she basically hated me from the start.

From fucking up her day to finding any reason to see her, Presley has carved herself into my heart, and I know I'm doomed for heartbreak. I never thought I'd be able to let another woman in after Mallory, but somehow, I did. Knowing I don't have any lingering feelings for her means I'm more than ready to move on. I just wish Presley was the woman I'd move on with.

And even though Presley has the potential to destroy me all over again, I know she's worth it. I'd fight for her if I knew it wouldn't simultaneously hold her back. She's a traveler, and that's been clear since day one.

"When isn't it a late night?" I groan. "Long day, long night."

"Well yeah, that's easy to say when you have some sweet tail," he says much too loudly.

"Sit the fuck down," I growl, not wanting to disturb the B&B guests who are enjoying their early coffee and breakfast.

Braxton chuckles before heading to the kitchen to make a plate. Moments later, he returns and knows to keep his mouth stuffed with food rather than give me more shit. I know Presley should be coming down soon per her usual, so I waited until after I fed and watered the horses before coming in for breakfast. I got my early morning chores out of the way so there'd be no interruptions while we eat.

"I'm surprised you're working today," Braxton says casually.

"I wish I didn't have to," I say honestly. "But I have a lesson this afternoon, and then I'm leaving early."

"Do you have something special planned?"

I shrug, not wanting to think about it, but at the same time, I can't wait to spend tonight with her. "I thought I'd invite her over for dinner and a movie."

"A movie?" He raises his brows.

"Yeah, I want to keep it simple. I've already made her a fancy meal, camped out for the night at Jackson's spot, took her to the diner and around town, went horseback riding…" I linger, wondering if my plan is stupid after all. "I don't know. I just want to hang out and spend uninterrupted time with her before she has to go."

"I'm sorry, man." I look up and see a look of pity on his face. Though he's an asshole twenty-three hours a day, I appreciate his concern.

Before I can reply, Mallory walks into the room and comes over. "Good morning."

Braxton and I both look up at her and freeze. "Uh, I was just seeing if you guys needed anything. Today's my first official day so…"

"Don't worry about those asshats." John walks up behind her and interrupts. "They're moochers."

"Hey, we earn our keep 'round here!" Braxton protests.

Chuckling, I shake my head. "I do at least. Can't say the same for him."

"So you just come in and eat the B&B's food?" Mallory asks, and the amusement in her tone isn't lost on me. I hate that her smile brings back those memories from years ago, but it no longer has the same effect it once did.

"Hell, they all do," John tells her. "You'll see Alex, Dylan, and Jackson all in here at some point."

"Well, they are outside working all day," Mallory defends with a grin.

"Don't encourage them," John warns. "You worry about the *paying* guests and let them fend for themselves. As long as they clean up, I don't kick them out," John mocks while giving Braxton a side-eye.

"Duly noted." Mallory laughs. I keep my gaze focused on the stairs, hoping Presley comes down before I have to go back to the barn.

"I gotta grab something from my office quick, then I'll meet you in the kitchen to go over the checklist tasks," John tells her. I have nothing more to say to her, but I can't exactly ask her to go away without coming off as a dick.

"So Mallory, you're originally from here?" Braxton asks, and I stand. Taking my plate and empty coffee cup, I set them in the tub and awkwardly leave the two of them.

As if she knew, Presley walks down the stairs looking

absolutely stunning in yoga shorts that accentuate her fit legs. She's wearing an oversized sweatshirt, but I know exactly how soft and sweet her skin feels underneath.

"Well, good mornin'." I make a show of running my eyes up and down her body with a devilish grin, so she knows exactly what I think about what she's wearing. "Don't you look fuckin' adorable?"

A smile splits her cheeks as I take her hand and press a kiss to her knuckles.

"Apparently, I fell asleep last night before I could set my alarm." Heat hits her cheeks in embarrassment. "And I didn't wanna miss you before you went back to work," she explains with a wave of her hand down her body. "So I haven't showered or anything yet."

"If this is what you look like first thing in the morning, then you have nothing to be sorry about, Red."

"I'm just glad I made it on time. I promise to wash my hair and wear clean clothes later, assuming you want to see me tonight," she teases, letting me hold her hand as we walk to the food area.

I pull her to me until she's flush against my chest. "First thing, fuck yes I want to see you tonight. I'm leaving work early so I can shower and clean up. Second thing, you could be naked, and I wouldn't even judge you." I flash her a wink, and she immediately starts laughing.

"Wow, how kind of you." She rolls her eyes.

"I'm nothing if not considerate." I place a finger under her chin, and since I know John is in the kitchen, I tilt her mouth up and sneak a kiss. "Mm...I don't know if I can wait until tonight."

She rests a hand on my chest and leans in with a devious glimmer in her eyes. "I promise it'll be worth the wait, Cowboy." Her voice is low, almost a whisper, but I hear her promise plain as day all the way down to my dick.

Groaning, I lean back on my heels and curse before moving back toward her. She's smiling wide, clearly proud of herself for causing me agony. "You're gonna fucking kill me, Red. Now, I'm gonna walk around all day with a raging hard-on."

Presley bites her bottom lip like a goddamn temptress. Her eyes lower to my groin, and I know she's enjoying torturing me way too much.

"Laugh all you want now, sweetheart. Your mouth will be busy later." I shoot her a wink and chuckle when her cheeks turn beet red.

"Good mornin'," Mallory interrupts at the worst fucking time.

I look over at her and glare. A deep growl escapes me, and she flinches when she realizes what she just walked into.

"Hello," Presley replies, sweetly.

"Did you sleep okay?" Mallory asks, and the tension between us is awkward.

"She slept fine, just like the past ten days she's been staying at the B&B," I blurt out harshly. Mallory grimaces, and Presley takes my hand, squeezing it hard.

"Sorry, didn't mean to interrupt you guys. Just trying to get to know the job." Mallory purses her lips, lowers her eyes, then walks away.

"I'd ask how things are going with her working here, but I think I have an idea…" Presley says, trying to ease the tension with her sarcastic tone. "You going to be okay sticking around with her here while I eat?"

I brush a hand through my hair and take a deep breath. "Yeah, I gotta get used to her being here anyway. Not much I can do about it."

Presley grabs a plate and starts stacking food on top. I make her a cup of coffee, knowing how she likes it, and meet her back at a table.

"So what do you want to do tonight?" I ask, reaching for a piece of her bacon.

She pretends to think about it for a split-second before she blurts out her answer. "You."

I nearly choke on my food at her response because it was unexpected. Presley laughs at my expense, and it's hard to even be mad when I very much agree with her idea.

"Okay, so I'll pick you up after lunch then?" I tease.

"I need to pack and say goodbye to everyone too," she reminds me.

I narrow my eyes at her and shoot her a look. "Screw everyone else."

Presley throws a piece of fruit at me, and I catch it before popping it into my mouth. "Fine, I'll give you a few hours. Be ready by four, okay? We'll have dinner and then take it from there."

"Sounds good, Cowboy. As long as you show me a real Southern farewell."

I snort, shaking my head at her. "You've been reading too many romance novels, Red."

"True." She nods. "I read probably twenty a month, sometimes more."

"Damn. How do you read so fast?" I ask, impressed.

"I've always been a fast reader, I guess. My family didn't have a lot of money to take us anywhere, so books helped me pass the time. As I got older, I started reading romance and got sucked in and couldn't read them fast enough. Now I inhale them like I'd die without them."

"So I know your passion is photography, but have you ever considered writing? I mean, if you need a muse…" I pause with a smirk. "I might know a guy."

"I think all your Instafame has gone to that big head of yours." She snickers.

We continue chatting while she finishes her food and coffee. I love this part of our day. It's meant a lot to me, and I hate that this is the last time.

"Alright, I better get back to work so I can get done early," I tell her, wanting to lean over and kiss her, but I know John could walk in at any minute. "I'll text you." I flash her a wink, and she smiles back.

"See you then, Cowboy."

The day drags on more than usual, and I know it's because I'm so damn anxious to finish and go home to shower. I want to make her something special, but I also just want to hang out too. After a moment, I decide on homemade pizza and figure she might actually enjoy making it with me, so I text her as soon as I'm home.

Colton: I'm going to hop in the shower if you wanna come

over in about twenty? You can help me make my famous homemade pizza, so come hungry :)

Presley: No worries. I'm famished ;) I just need to change... be there soon!

God help me. This woman will be the death of me.

As I shower, Presley completely consumes my thoughts and how I wish she were in here with me. One night with her will never be enough, but I'll take whatever she has to offer. Even if it means my heart breaks the second she leaves.

I hear a car pull up, and nerves instantly fill my chest. She's the only woman in years who's had my body responding this way, and it scares the shit out of me every time I think about it.

Wanting to greet her before she comes up the steps, I whip the door open and lean against the frame with my arms crossed as I watch her park. I can't help the smile that covers my face when she jumps out of the car and runs straight for me.

I'm quick to catch her in my arms the moment she leaps off the stairs. We're both laughing and smiling when I have her securely against my chest. With her legs wrapped around my waist, I know she can feel the effect she has on me.

"What the hell are you doing, crazy woman?" I walk us into the house and kick the door shut behind me.

She frames my face with her hands and pulls our mouths together. It's heated and intense, her tongue sliding between my lips to reach mine. I squeeze her ass cheeks in my palms and press her against my erection.

"Presley..." I breathe out when our lips part slightly. I want this so goddamn badly—she has no idea—but I don't want her to think it's what I expected when I invited her over tonight. "We don't have to, Red. I'm okay with just spending time with you."

She leans back slightly and gives me a sultry look as she pulls in her bottom lip that I plan to suck on later. "This is our last night together, Colton. Let's make it count." The fire in her eyes, the seduction in her tone, and the way she lifts her hips to tell me exactly what she has in mind are all the permission I need to give her what she's begging for.

My mouth returns to hers seconds later. I walk us into the living room and sit on the couch, and soon, she's straddling my lap. I bring my fingers to the hem of her shirt and pull it up and over her head before tossing it to the floor. Her breasts are on full display, and I can't deny wanting to suck them into my mouth and taste her nipples around my tongue.

"Fuck, Red…" I growl, then reach around her neck and pull her against me. She rocks her hips against my dick, knowing exactly what she's doing to rile me up. "I want to do so fucking much to you, but I also want to take my time too," I admit, groaning.

"We have all night," she tells me. "I want you, Colton."

Presley moves and latches her mouth to my neck, licking her tongue up to my ear. "Take off your shirt," she demands just above a whisper. I grab the fabric behind my head and pull it up and over before throwing it. She climbs higher on my lap, rubs herself against my rock-hard cock, then presses a kiss to my chest.

With her ass in my palms, I grind her back and forth on me, and I grunt when she threads her fingers through my hair.

"I can't wait to taste you," I tell her and bring my mouth to her chest. The cups of her bra are in the way, so I wind my arms around her to unhook it.

"Wait, no," she says in a rushed tone. My head immediately snaps up to meet her gaze.

"What's wrong?"

Presley lowers her eyes as if she's embarrassed, and I hate that she's shutting down around me. "Don't hide from me, Red." I tilt her chin up and press a soft kiss to her lips. "To me, you're beautiful. You have nothing to be ashamed of because I already think you're the most stunning woman I've ever had the privilege to look at."

"You have no idea what that means to me," she whispers. "I feel so flawed and not worthy of you."

"Presley, I hate that you think that. Your smart mouth, your curves, your luscious tits, and round ass—I fucking love it all. I thought you were beautiful the second I laid eyes on you, and nothing will ever change that. I mean that. More importantly, your heart is why I wanted to spend time with you. Everything else is just a bonus."

When she blinks up at me, and I see the tears in her eyes, I wipe them away with my thumb. "I'm going to spend all night worshipping you and your gorgeous as fuck body, Red. I'm going to prove over and over how I feel about you, so I hope you're ready."

Before she can respond, I unhook the clasp of her bra, and as soon as her tits are revealed, I palm and suck on them. Presley leans back, pushing them right into my face where I cherish the hell out of them with my mouth and tongue.

"I can't wait to watch them bounce as you ride my cock, Red," I tell her, moving my hand down to her shorts and undoing the button. "But first, I want to see how wet you are for me."

Presley leans forward so I can pull her shorts down and eventually get them off. She's on top of me in just her panties, and I want to tear my own jeans off and slide inside her so goddamn badly. Instead, I slide my hand up her thigh and press between her legs. My thumb slides over her pussy, and her juices coat my fingers as soon as I push a finger inside her tight body.

"Fuck, Red." I groan into her throat. "Your cunt is so wet and tight. So fuckin' sweet, like honey."

"Mm, yes." She purrs, rocking her hips against my palm.

"You need it, baby? Fuck my fingers. Yes, just like that. Take it all." I growl, pressing my lips to her neck and feathering kisses to her ear. "You ready for me, Presley?" My voice is deep and thick with desire, and I can no longer hold back my need for her.

"Yes, Colton. God, yes." The want and lust in her tone have my cock aching even more.

Pulling back slightly, I reach for my wallet and grab a condom. She lifts her brows and gives me an amused look. "A Boy Scout is always prepared."

"So it's been in there a while?" Her teasing tone has me laughing. Yet another reason I adore this woman.

"Actually, wait. I should check the expiration date." I pretend to read the wrapper when she snags it out of my hand and rips it open.

"Time to saddle up, Cowboy." She wiggles her body off mine and helps me pull my jeans and boxers down. My cock bounces the moment it springs free. Presley leans forward, and I assume she's going to sheath my erection, but she takes me by surprise when she wraps her hot lips over my dick.

"Presley, fuck." My back arches the second her tongue slides up my shaft, and she teases the tip. "I'm not coming in your mouth again, baby. Not this time."

"I love the way you taste," she admits, her cheeks slightly pinking. "I just wanted one more lick." The seduction in her voice has me nearly unraveling underneath her, so I reach for her head to pull her back.

"As much as I want you on my cock, I need inside you more. I'm not busting a nut before that pussy tightens around me. Got it, Red?" I grab her wrist and pull her back on top of me.

"So bossy." She finally takes the condom and slides it over my hard length. The slow movement of that alone nearly has me exploding.

"Fucking right I am." I cover her mouth with mine before she can respond. "I want to see all of you, Presley. Touch you, taste you, kiss every inch of your body."

"I want you inside me, Colton." With her low, desperate plea, our gazes lock, and a mutual understanding passes between us. "No hiding. I promise."

"Good girl." I smile, grabbing her hips and positioning her body over me. "Let me know if I hurt you, okay?"

She nods, then I cup her face and bring her mouth back to mine as she eases on top of me. My cock slowly slides into her, and it's everything. For the past two weeks, the heat, passion, and desire for her are all wrapped up in this very moment. I feel so much for her that it's almost painful. I know this could be the last time I ever see her, kiss her, and feel her body against mine, so I want to soak in every second of it.

"Fuck. You're so beautiful, Presley. You feel so goddamn amazing," I tell her when she takes all of me. She's filled to the hilt, and I'm worried I'll hurt her, but then she starts rocking against me and bouncing her perfect ass. "Shit, Red."

I lean back when she places her hands on my shoulders. Reaching up, I palm her breast, and when I play with her nipple, her head falls back with a deep, loud moan.

Goddamn, she's stunning. Riding my cock and groaning like she's a fucking pro have me finding it hard to stay calm.

"Look at me, Presley," I say in a desperate tone. "Can't you see how good we are together? Do you feel this?"

I lower my hand down her stomach and rub my thumb against her clit.

"Yes…" she hums and nods. "So good."

"You feel it too?" I keep my eyes locked on hers, unable to stop watching her and how blissful she looks with her bottom lip between her teeth.

"Colton." She says my name in a soft plea. "I feel it too…" she admits. "I don't want it to stop."

My hands fly to her hips, and I squeeze, guiding her body to grind harder and faster against me. "I'm not stopping anytime soon, baby. Hang on."

Presley locks her hands around my neck as I drive fast and hard inside her, and when her pussy tightens around my dick, I know she's close.

"Let go, Red. Come on my cock, baby," I encourage her in ragged breaths. "Fuck, you feel so goddamn amazing…come, Red." I rub circles over her clit again, and when her head falls back on her shoulders, I increase my speed and press harder. "Yes, yes. That's my girl." Her body shakes and spasms, and she screams out. It's the most glorious sound I've ever heard.

As much as I want to come too, I'm not anywhere near done with her.

"Fuck, that was hot." I smile when she brings her eyes back to mine. "Gorgeous."

"That was…" She releases a breath. "Intense!"

I laugh at her surprised tone. "Lock your ankles around me, sweetheart. I'm just getting started with you."

Before she can question me, I lift our bodies and flip her over on her back. I lift both of her legs and place her ankles on my shoulders. She raises her arms and presses her palms against the arm of the sofa, and as soon as I start moving inside her again, her head falls back with another loud, exaggerated moan.

My hips pummel into her over and over again, her pussy contracting against my dick and making every swift move feel like heaven. I palm her breasts, squeezing and massaging them as I continue driving deep and hard inside her. I love the way she looks at me when I hit that spot that has her seeing stars.

"Colton…oh my God. I-I-I…"

"You're so tight, Red…I don't know how much longer I can last. I wanna feel you come again, baby."

"I'm so close…" She can barely say the words between her ragged breaths. She arches her back as if she's trying to climb inside me. I know she's close; I can feel it with every movement. Presley's wet and glistening, and I want to devour her with my mouth.

With a flick of her clit, I rub circles over her, and she unravels underneath me once again. It's pure fucking perfection.

"Yes, baby. That's it." I could watch her come a million times.

I know she's sated and tired, but there's no way we're stopping here.

Standing, I grab her hand and pull her up. I wrap my hand around her head and claim her lips. "Bend over," I demand. "Put your hands on the back of the couch and stick your ass out for me."

She obeys without question. "Spread your legs, Red."

She does.

"Fuckin' perfection." I kneel behind her, palming her ass and spreading her cheeks apart. I bring my mouth to her pussy and slide my tongue over her slit before sinking deep inside her. I lick, suck, and devour Presley until her knees begin to buckle. "Goddamn, you taste amazing."

Grabbing her hips, I spin her around and let her taste how sweet she is on my lips. "I'm addicted, Presley."

"Colton…" She squeezes her eyes shut. "I'm sorry."

I tilt her chin up. "Look at me. Please."

She blinks, finally looking up at me and I see the sadness in her eyes.

"Don't be sorry. I'm not. I'd take any amount of time with you and cherish it because no matter what, it'd never feel like enough. You've made me want *more* for the first time in years. If this is all I can ever have, I'll never forget it."

She nods but lowers her eyes. "I'll miss you, Colton. I tried really hard all week not to think about leaving, but the truth is, it's breaking me."

Instead of replying, I tell her exactly how I feel with my mouth. Nothing more needs to be said because we both know how hard this is. I want to make love to her so neither of us walks away not knowing how the other feels.

I guide her into my room, place her on my bed, and show her over and over again how much she means to me, how much these past two weeks have meant to me, and how fucking much I'm going to miss her sassy, smart mouth.

When we've used our last ounce of energy, I drive into her one last time before letting go and releasing inside her. My body trembles on top of hers, and her legs shake around my waist as she holds me tightly to her.

"Fuck. That was so intense," I murmur into her neck. "You drained everything out of me." I chuckle, and she laughs.

Once I get rid of the condom and clean us both, I wrap the covers around us and hold her. "I have a weird question for you."

I grin. "Okay."

"If I'd never come here and we hadn't met, do you think you and Mallory would've reconciled, considering your history? I mean, second chances happen all the time, and sometimes after years apart, couples get back together."

"I wish there were a bigger, better way to say *hell no*, but that's all I've got since the blood is still rushing back to my head."

That makes Presley snort. "I think she's hoping."

"If that's the case, she's delusional. I can't even say we'll eventually be friends at this point."

"People can change a lot in five years."

I roll over and face her. "Are you trying to set me up before you leave?" I arch a brow at her. "Because let me say this once so it's loud and crystal clear. Whether you showed up here or not, nothing would change the fact that I have absolutely zero feelings for Mallory. In fact, her showing up after all this time has proved that to me even more. I loved her with my whole heart, and she was my life, but the woman I was in love with never existed. That was apparent after what she did. Recently, I realized I mourned the idea of us and not actually being with her if that makes sense."

"I hate how she hurt you so badly. Makes me want to march over there and slap some sense into her." Her words make me smile and laugh. As I hold her in my arms, I realize how much she means to me.

"You're not jealous, are you?" I raise a taunting brow at her.

"No!" She scowls at me. "Well, maybe a little. I'm jealous of the fact she had years with you. Not just days, but months and months, and she didn't even appreciate it. I'd do anything to have that time with you and when I think about everything you two must've shared together—that makes me jealous. Then she hurt you and it makes me wanna rage. But then I remember I'm not any better because I know I'm going to hurt you too."

She closes her eyes as if she's trying to hold back her emotions.

"Presley, please look at me." She blinks and meets my gaze. "I'll admit there were horrible days. I wanted to hurt her as much as she had hurt me. I wanted to hurt anyone who dared to piss me off. I wanted to hurt myself. I was certain she'd broken me for good when shit went down, but eventually, I learned to breathe on my own again. The days weren't so dark, and I found the light. However, it wasn't until *you* that I wanted to breathe again. You sparked life back into my soul, and it wasn't just because of your sexy-as-hell curves. It was your give-no-shits attitude and ability to consume my every thought while simultaneously taunting me. I never cared what a woman thought about me, especially if she clearly showed no interest, but I wanted your attention. You made me work for it, and I knew you were special. It wasn't the chase that drew me to you; it was all *you*. Your fun and witty personality, your sweet side, and your deep-rooted passion for photography. You're not only chasing your dreams, but you're also living them, and I respect the fuck out of that. Those qualities along with dozens more are why it wasn't hard to fall for you, Presley. As much as I want to make you stay, I know I can't."

"You make me want to stay so damn badly." I see the tears in her eyes, but I know nothing more needs to be said for her to know exactly how I feel. Bringing our mouths together, I slide my tongue between her soft lips and devour her as if it'll be the last time I ever taste heaven—which it very well may be.

"Just so you know, Red, I would welcome you here, in my life, if you decided to ever come back. Even if just for a visit. I'll never resent you for leaving to do what you love and staying true to your passion. Plus, I have a great pull-out couch."

She bursts out laughing, then gives me the sweetest and sincerest look. "I'll keep that in mind, Casanova."

CHAPTER NINETEEN

PRESLEY

The morning has felt like a dream, or rather a nightmare, as I drive to San Antonio. Last night was amazing and being with Colton so intimately will forever be imprinted in my heart.

Once I return the rental car and walk through security, I'm hit with the full force that I'm leaving. After spending so much time trying to force it out of my mind, it's hard to believe the day has arrived.

I try to busy myself as I wait for my flight, but I can't shake the overwhelming anxiety that overcomes me as I board the plane. My heart is heavy and it just doesn't feel right even though I know I have to go. I never imagined saying goodbye would be this hard. If someone would've told me this trip to Texas was going to change my life, I would've laughed in their face. I crave adventure—I *need* it—and it's what drives me to work so damn hard. But as the plane lifts into the air, and I look out over San Antonio, I know I left a piece of my heart at the ranch.

As soon as the flight attendant passes by, I order a glass of wine to numb the pain. I don't typically drink on flights, but at this point, I need the whole damn bottle to calm my nerves. After she delivers my drink, I can't get the booze in me quick enough. I down half of it even though I know the wine won't fix this. The emptiness runs too deep, which I knew would happen. Once I've drunk two glasses, I somewhat relax enough to fall asleep.

By the time I wake up, the plane is making its final descent into Orlando. Soon we're touching down, and since I was one of the first to board, I'm able to grab my carry-on with my camera equipment and deboard quickly. People wearing Mickey Mouse ears and Disney shirts are commonplace as they navigate the crowded airport to their gates.

I finally make my way to the carousel to wait for the rest of my bags, and I turn on my phone. Notifications immediately start flooding in from Instagram, and I have no idea what's going on until I go to my most recent post.

I tuck my lips inside my mouth, hoping my emotions don't seep out. I totally forgot I'd scheduled the Steamy Bedtime Reads hashtag picture of Colton and me on the bed with all the books to post today. Since I've been so preoccupied trying not to take a second of my time for granted, it slipped my mind. So much has changed since the day we took that picture, and it seems like a century ago. At that point, I thought I'd found nothing more than a hot cowboy to pose in my pictures, but instead, I found a man who'd rope the moon for me if he could.

The likes are happening so fast I can't even keep up, and the comments I skim make my heart skip a beat.

You two make the cutest couple!

OMG...please tell me you're a thing now!

Cowboy Casanova can lie on my bed any day of the week.

IS THERE A HEA TO THIS STORY?!!

I typically reply to each comment on my photos with a personalized response, but I don't have it in me to say anything about Colton's and my relationship. So instead, I send heart emojis and thank yous. It's all I can offer anyone right now.

I'm so lost in my own world, I don't even notice people hovering around the conveyor belt until I lock my phone and stuff it in my pocket. My suitcase makes its way around, and I'm forced to push my way through. I barely grab it in time before it passes me by. Though I love to travel, I don't like airports. Too many inconsiderate people in one area makes me get a tad ragey.

Once I have my luggage snapped together, I make my way to ground transportation and schedule an Uber to take me to the hotel. Considering Eldorado was four hours from the airport, on top of having to arrive two hours early, and not including the three-hour flight, I've been traveling most of the day. Now it's nearly five, and I'm hungry and tired.

After five minutes of waiting, my driver arrives. She places my suitcases in the trunk, and we make our way to the hotel. My phone continues to vibrate in my pocket, and I turn the notifications off again, but before I do, I take another look at the likes and comments. I'm barely caught up from replying to everyone from the last one, and I still have a handful of emails I need to answer. This picture is just as popular as the first one I posted of him. My audience adores Colton, maybe just as much as I do, but now I want to keep him all to myself. I don't want to commercialize him in any way, and once publishers got a hold of him, they would. He enjoys the simple life working on the ranch and doesn't crave attention or fame, which is so damn respectable, considering he could be the next big thing.

I squeeze my eyes shut and try to think of something else. Luckily, we pull into the hotel parking lot, and when the car comes to a stop, I'm quick to jump out. After getting my luggage, I hand the driver a tip and a thank you and head inside.

I'm exhausted and mentally drained. Luckily, it takes no time for me to check in. I grab my room keys and hurry to the elevator, hoping I can make it to my floor before I run into anyone who recognizes me. Ever since that photo went viral, people have been talking about me, and while it's increased my popularity, that was never my intention, so it's still a strange sensation.

The elevator stops, and when the doors slide open, I step out and walk to my room. As soon as I'm inside, I plop on the bed, lean back, and close my eyes. My body is sore from last night—a delicious ache—leaving me with the reminder of our night together. The thought of his hands on my bare skin and his lips against mine causes a wave of sadness to rush through me because it's over. We both knew we had limited time together, but it doesn't hurt any less. His words continue to repeat in my mind.

Just so you know, Red, I would welcome you here, in my life, if you decided to ever come back. Even if just for a visit. I'll never resent you for leaving to do what you love and staying true to your passion. Plus, I have a great pull-out couch.

Wouldn't I be imposing on his life? I'm like a hurricane, arriving on short notice and wreaking havoc on everything he knows. The guilt almost destroys me because if I feel this way, like I've lost something special, then I know he feels it too. I'm tempted to text him, but I don't want to give him false hope. This is all so fucking complicated.

As I roll over, my phone feels like a brick in my pocket. I take it out and text my sister, letting her know I made it to Florida. The last thing I need is her calling me right now and hearing the sadness in my tone. I set my phone down and stare up at the ceiling, wishing I were back in Texas.

The thought catches me off guard because I've never wished to be somewhere else when traveling. Never. This is crazy.

My phone vibrates, and I hurry and pick it up but find myself disappointed when it's Callie. I don't know why I thought it'd be Colton, but I wished it were.

Callie: I know you're probably tired from traveling. Call me tomorrow. Miss you!

Presley: I will. Miss you too! :)

I add a smiley face in for good measure, so there isn't a red flag to how I really feel.

Callie: Oh, HOT pic, btw! OMFG. That's all I've got to say. JEALOUS AF!

I'm pretty sure there's a list of women who are jealous right now, including myself. I wish we would've had more time, and I know it's going to take a while for me to get over this because that's what I'm supposed to do, right? Move on. Forget it ever happened? Regardless if he's the kind of guy who's unforgettable.

> **Presley: Thanks! I'll have to tell you more later. Gonna eat then go to bed. Headshots start early tomorrow.**
>
> **Callie: Really? How early?**
>
> **Presley: Six. Sucks! But it was the only way to get everyone in.**
>
> **Callie: So proud of you! Anyway, get some food and rest. Chat later. LOVE YOU!**
>
> **Presley: Thank you. Love you too. Night!**

My stomach growls, but instead of going out for food, I decide to order room service. As I look over the menu, nothing sounds appetizing, but I order quesadillas because it's almost impossible to mess them up.

As I wait, I try to prepare for tomorrow. I grab my laptop and pull out the file folder I've kept tucked in my bag since I left California. I reviewed the confirmed and paid list and realize I have at least forty authors scheduled for headshots. It's imperative I stay on schedule tomorrow because as it stands, I'll be working for twelve hours straight to get through everyone. While I'm dreading being on my feet for that long, I'll also welcome the distraction.

Just as I close the folder, a knock rings out on the door, and room service enters with my tray of food. I've never been so happy to see food, probably because I haven't eaten since I left the B&B before sunrise. I find myself going through the motions of eating, and once I finish, I take a quick shower, then climb into bed.

The morning comes early, and I'm running on caffeine and adrenaline. As soon as I make it downstairs, I set up and immediately get started. The hair stylists and makeup artists keep a tight schedule throughout the day, and I usher the authors through the sessions like they're cattle. I don't have time to think about anything except head angles and taking pictures. By the time I photograph my last author, I'm almost shocked by how quickly the day flew by. After I pack up my things, I proceed to my room and collapse on the bed. As if Callie knew I was done for the day, I get a call from her.

"Hey, sis! Mom and Dad said hey. Told them I was calling you today."

"Really? How are they doing?" I ask.

"They're getting over their summer flu. Brought them chicken noodle soup today and they both seemed in better spirits. I practically walked into the house wearing a hazmat suit and carrying a can of Lysol."

I giggle because she's always been a germ-a-phobe. As soon as a person coughs, she starts freaking out, which always gave me an advantage when we were kids. Callie always hated playing doctor. Sick people aren't her thing.

"I can't believe you were around people with the flu." I snort. "I'm kinda shocked. It's like you're evolving or something."

"They haven't had a fever in seventy-two hours. I think I'm okay, but I did disinfect my entire body. So." I can tell she's smiling, but I also know she's not joking. "Everything okay?" she asks.

"Yeah, why?" I offer, but she knows me so well I might as well just spill the beans now.

"You sound...different. Down almost. I know you worked your ass off today, but usually, you're so full of energy and excitement after a long shoot like this."

I let out a breath. "Yeah. I'm not feeling like myself."

"Because of Cowboy Casanova? So...I saw that pic. Did y'all, you know?" There's a distinct hint of amusement in her voice as if she's hoping I'll give her the answer she wants.

BINGO. Of course, she'd nail it.

"Yes and guilty," I tell her, squeezing my eyes tight, and she lets out a loud squeal. I don't have the energy to deny anything. "I miss him so much that my whole body literally hurts. I've never fallen for a man like this, and it's just, I don't even know how to describe it. I probably sound stupid right now." I kick off my shoes and tell myself as soon as I get off the phone, I'm jumping in the tub and soaking until my skin wrinkles like a prune.

"You don't sound stupid. You sound like you're in love, that's all." She says it so casually as if falling for a man in less than two weeks is completely normal.

"It scares the shit out of me, Callie. What am I supposed to do? California is really far away. I can't move. Long-distance relationships hardly ever work, so the odds are already stacked against us. We agreed to move forward with our lives after I left. So this is me moving on, and twenty-four hours in, I'm already failing miserably. I'm not happy right now, and I don't even want to be here—which never happens when I'm on work trips. I literally feel broken." I miss him so damn much. I miss his laughter and how he jokes with me. I even miss hearing him call me Red.

"So you're just going to walk away and wash your hands of it? Pretend like Texas didn't happen?" she asks with a stern voice. "I've always admired you, Presley. You're strong, and you don't take shit from anyone. You're a risk taker, and you've never allowed anything to hold you back, so I'm trying to figure out why this is so different. Where the hell is my strong-willed sister who fights for the things she wants in life?"

I sit silently while trying to find my words. "The difference, I guess, is that my heart is on the line here. What if—"

"Don't you dare give me some hypothetical bullshit, Pres," she interrupts before I can finish. "That's just an excuse, and you know it. It's obvious you care for him and have fallen hard. Don't wake up ten years from now with five hundred cats and realize you've made a mistake. He seems like a nice guy, and someone's going to snatch him up if you don't. He'll eventually move on, and you'll be left to wonder what could've been. And don't even get me started on how sexy he is either. Like seriously? I think I would've proposed to him before I left."

She's dropping so many truth bombs, and in my heart, I know she's right. But the last part has me snorting. Gah, I love my sister so much. She's the only person in the world who can make me smile like this when my world is burning down.

"Listen. I'm sorry if I'm being harsh, but someone has to be truthful because too many people are worried about your feelings. I'm not. I'm more concerned with your overall happiness, and honestly, I think you're making a mistake by ignoring how you feel and walking away."

Her words drive a stake right into my excuses. No matter what I say, Callie will have a rebuttal waiting.

"Do you know how much I hate it when you're right?" I tell her as I contemplate what I'm going to do after I take photos of the signing tomorrow. My flight leaves out early on Sunday, and I don't have any travel scheduled for a month. I've got time, but what if Colton can't handle my schedule or the attention my page gets? Or what if the honeymoon phase wears off, and I'm no longer the woman he wants? I shake my head, knowing I'm being ridiculous. There's no way he was faking anything, not when his eyes told all his truths.

"Come home, pack up your shit, and go back to him. You already sublet your apartment anyway since you're never freakin' there. Then if things don't work out, you'll know that at least you tried, but you'll never know until you put yourself out there. You have to give you and him a chance. So figure your shit out and let me know what you're gonna do."

"I will. Promise. And thank you. Thank you for being you and for always being the voice of reason," I tell her.

"Always. Call me later. Kay?"

"I will," I agree and end the call.

As soon as I toss my phone on the bed, I take deep breaths to hold back the tears threatening to spill over because I know what I have to do. At this moment, it all seems so clear. A piece of my heart is back in Texas, and I won't be whole again until I'm there.

I have to take a chance, but I know Colton's worth it.

CHAPTER TWENTY

COLTON

IT'S BEEN one week since Presley left—the longest week of my life—and it's taking everything I have not to text or call her. We agreed to go on with our lives, but I haven't stopped thinking about her. Sunrises and sunsets, the tack room, and even my couch remind me of her. I just want to hear her sweet voice and boisterous laughter. It was always music to my ears even when she was laughing *at* me.

I kick off my boots and stretch out on the couch. Picking up my phone, I go to our last texts. I try to type out a message to send to her, but everything sounds stupid as hell and makes me look desperate. It was very clear that once she left, it was over. That was always the plan, though I wonder what would've happened had I pushed for more. I stop myself from hitting send and toss my phone aside. Considering our short amount of time made things tense between us, texting her now wouldn't help either of us. Thinking back to just a few days ago, I was scared and didn't want to believe it'd actually end.

I should've told her how ridiculous it'd be to give up on something as incredible as what we have, knowing it was so damn special. I know everything happened fast, but just like that, it was gone in the blink of an eye. Sometimes, I feel as if she were nothing more than a dream. But each time I'm called Cowboy Casanova, I know it was real.

Red has the whole world to conquer, and she'll do it one picture at a time. I'm here in Texas, and I refuse to be the man who holds her back from her dreams and aspirations. It would destroy me to know that she stayed and settled to be with me, so in a twisted way, I'm happy she left. Of course, I didn't want her to go, but only for selfish reasons, because I've never felt this way about a woman before. Not even Mallory. Regardless of the bad timing, what Presley and I had was real. I now know that nothing in life worth fighting for is gonna be easy.

I pick my phone back up and find her number. I'm two seconds away from pressing call when my front door swings open. Braxton comes barreling through the door with a bottle of booze in his hand, and I sit up.

"Are you still actin' like a love-sick puppy?" he taunts, taking a swig.

"Holy shit. You're drunk," I tell him. "I hope to hell you didn't drive over here."

"Yeah. And no, I didn't drive. Got dropped off by Jake." He stumbles. "It's time to go to the Honky Tonk. They're havin' a dancin' contest, and Jackson bet me I wouldn't enter."

My eyes go wide. "Are you serious right now?"

"As serious as a damn heart attack. I need you to take me, *please*." He sets the booze down on the table and sits on the chair.

"Even when you're drunk, you got manners." I chuckle at the irony. "But I really don't wanna go."

"You need to. Look, I just need to enter. It'll take one hour. That's all I need. And you ain't got nothin' goin' on other than moping around here with your dick tucked between your legs. It'll do ya some good to get out."

I roll my eyes, but I do need a distraction, even if that means I'm gonna babysit Braxton tonight. "Okay, give me ten. I need to change."

"You're bein' timed," he tells me. I get up and put on some clean clothes, but I'm not trying to impress anyone. I just don't feel up to it.

After I walk back into the living room, Braxton pops up, ready to go. I grab my keys, force Braxton to leave the booze on the table, then we both get in the truck. The smell of alcohol oozes from him, and I have a feeling he's going to regret all this tomorrow.

"You're gonna make a fool outta yourself."

"Maybe. But what if I win? If I get a trophy or something, I'll carry it around every day next week just to prove I'm a badass to Jackson."

"I hope you do," I say as I pull into the parking lot. "Tonight we need a game plan. Okay? No getting into fights. No flirting with married women. And no leaving with anyone."

He whips his head over to look at me and grunts. "I didn't realize I was bringing Buzz Killington with me tonight."

"Ha, I just don't want to have to save you from destruction later."

"The only person who needs savin' right now is *you*," he tells me over his shoulder as he stands in front of me, scouting out the place. Maybe he's right. The last week has been rough, and as much as I've tried to keep it to myself, I can't pretend everything is okay because it's not. I've been known to wear my heart on my sleeve, and this time is no different.

The full parking lot kinda surprises me, but then again, there's not much to do in this little town besides go to bake sales, church, and drink. Right by the door, a woman sits at a table asking people to sign up for the dance contest. Braxton beams as he puts his name on the dotted line, and the woman hands him a number like he's signed up for the rodeo.

"Take a picture of me as proof," he tells me with a cheesy grin.

I pull my phone from my pocket and do as he says.

"Now you gotta post it on your new Instagram." He chuckles.

"Don't you dare joke about it. I'll do it," I warn as I make my way to the bar. I'm too sober for this. I sit on a stool and order a drink, then send the picture to Jackson.

Colton: I'm blaming you for this.

Jackson: HAHAHAHAHAHA!!!!

I insert an eye roll emoji.

Colton: I'm calling you when I need a designated driver tonight. Might need to drink enough to forget the memory of all of this.

Over my shoulder, I hear Braxton hooting and hollering, and I don't even wanna turn around and look. Thankfully, my beer is set in front of me, and I take a long pull of it.

Jackson: How 'bout this? I'm gonna text Jake and tell him to pick y'all up around 2, so then you don't have to worry about gettin' home safely since it's my fault.

Colton: Have him show up at 1. Might take us an hour to get Braxton in the truck.

Jake is Braxton's roommate, and one of the ranch hands who's overeager to help anyone out. He's driven me and Braxton home several times already. It also helps that he's a night owl, so I don't feel so guilty.

Jackson: Deal. Good luck. I bet him he wouldn't sign up. Then he bet me he would. So I upped the ante and told him if he won, I'd pay him $500. He swore he could dance as well as Magic Mike.

Colton: Wow. A warning woulda been nice.

Jackson: Nah, you need to get out of the house. Sittin' home thinking about how ya miss Red ain't gonna do you no good.

I don't know what to say, so I don't reply at all. Soon, a woman comes over the loudspeaker and introduces herself, then lists the rules of the contest. "And we have three judges over here who will rate your performance with a number. At the end of round one, the top five will move to the final round."

I look at Braxton and shake my head.

"We'll get started in about thirty minutes," she says, moving the mic from her mouth and telling the contestants something. Braxton walks over to her, and she writes something down on a notepad, then he comes to the bar.

"I need a shot. Want one?"

I don't answer quick enough, and he orders four.

"Four?" I turn to him.

"Two for you, two for me." The bartender sets the shots down, and Braxton hands me two. "Let's drink to having a good ass time." He clicks his glass against mine, and we down the liquid gold. Drinking whisky straight typically gets me into trouble, so it's been a while. I order another drink just as the contestants are all called back over.

While I wait for this ridiculous contest to start, I sip my fresh beer. Pulling my phone from my pocket, I find myself scrolling Presley's Instagram account. Damn, she's so beautiful even without trying. I stop when I see the photo we took at the B&B on the bed with all the books surrounding us. I'll never forget how I wanted to kiss her that night.

It quickly becomes hard to swallow, and I miss her so damn much it hurts. Instead of tucking my phone in my pocket and trying to forget the way I feel about her, I decide to really send her a text this time. Over the past week, I've written and deleted messages so many times I've lost count, and I can't continue like this. She has to know that I haven't forgotten about her, and I never will.

Colton: Hey Red. I've written this message about a thousand times already, but I want you to know how much I miss you. I can't stop thinking about you and us.

I send the message and wait for a minute. It's just after nine here, which means it's around seven in California. So it's not too late or early. I stare at the screen as if it'll make a message from her appear, but one doesn't come. She's probably busy—or that's what I tell myself—and if she doesn't reply, at least I know I put myself out there and made an effort.

Before I get too caught up in my head, Braxton takes the stage, and the ladies in the room go wild as he dances around to Def

Leppard's "Pour Some Sugar on Me." I finish my beer and order another and can't stop laughing at Braxton as he pulls a woman up on stage with him. He's absolutely ridiculous, but the judges seem to love his antics. The song ends, and after three more contestants compete, the emcee announces the names of those who'll be going to the next round.

"So make sure you give the DJ your song for your next dance," she orders. "You have ten minutes." Braxton points at the bar, and somehow, I know exactly what he wants. So I order a shot of Fireball, knowing it's his kryptonite, and have the waitress deliver it to him.

Once he takes the shot, his eyes go wide, and I give him a head nod. Fireball makes him crazy; well, it makes the crazy inside him come out and play. The woman calls his name because he's first up to perform. The song of choice this time is "Let's Get It On" by Marvin Gaye, and I feel as if I'm watching a strip tease as he slowly unbuttons his shirt for a group of women huddled around the dance floor.

Braxton twirls the shirt around his head, then drops it to the floor. I almost spit out my drink when he drops it like it's hot. I swear he's been practicing this. Just as he begins to unbutton his pants, the song ends, leaving all the thirsty women hanging. I glance over at the judges, who give him a perfect score of tens all the way across the board. I think he might actually win this, which shocks the shit outta me. I didn't know he had it in him. If ranching doesn't work out, he should move to Vegas and audition for Magic Mike, for real.

After the remaining four contestants perform, the emcee comes to the stage with a huge grin on her face. "So the judges have made their final decision. The winner is...drum roll, please...Braxton Harper!"

He looks surprised, but I think it's all an act. He walks to the stage, winking and waving at his adoring fans, and takes the microphone to accept his small trophy and $100 gift card.

"Thanks, y'all. Just want to say thank you to my best friend, Colton, for bringing me here tonight." Some of his words slur together.

The women go crazy.

"Oh, and he's single, ladies!"

I instantly groan until another woman yells out at him. "But are you?"

"Yes, ma'am. Single and ready to mingle! Thanks again!" He walks off the stage, and a hoard of ladies follow him as he admires his trophy. Any one of them would take Braxton home, but instead, he collects their phone numbers like playing cards. Pretty sure at this point, he has enough for a phone book.

"I didn't know you had it in you," I tell him as he plops down on the empty barstool next to me.

"Jackson should've never bet me. This time, he lost his ass! Celebratory drinks?" he asks but then orders before I can answer again.

A few hours pass, and I've had way too much to drink. I keep pulling my phone from my pocket to see if Presley responded, but nothing. Maybe I shouldn't have sent it at all. Perhaps she regrets us and wants to forget we ever happened. The thought pretty much destroys me, but I keep it tucked deep inside.

As my world crumbles around me, Braxton continues to flirt with the bartender. Jake shows up right on time, and when I look at him and can barely focus, I'm glad he's here because I'm in no shape to drive. Thankfully, tomorrow is Sunday so I can sleep in later than normal.

"Y'all are so fucked." Jake snickers, looking over us as we stumble to the truck.

Braxton gives him a sarcastic thumbs-up and waves his trophy around. "At least I won. Jackson's gonna pay big time."

"Winner, winner, chicken dinner," I say, but I'm yelling. I'm at the point in the night when I can't control my volume.

After Jake unlocks the truck, we all pile in and buckle up. He starts the truck, and it feels as if we're flying down the road. In no time at all, he's pulling up to my house and dropping me off. I trip up the step and somehow get the door unlocked and stumble to my bedroom. After I kick off my boots, I empty my pockets on the nightstand, then crawl into bed and pass out.

The sound of footsteps on the hardwood floor wakes me from my deep sleep, and I know it's Braxton. He can get shitfaced one night and then be chipper as fuck the next morning. I don't know how he does it, but I'm not amused with him right now. I roll over, pulling the blankets over my head and hoping he makes coffee, then leaves because my head is pounding. My bedroom door swings open, and I pretend to be asleep until I feel his touch.

"Go away, Braxton. Seriously," I mutter, but when I hear a woman chuckle, I rip the blankets from over my head.

Standing over me is Presley wearing a mischievous evil grin on her face.

"I must still be drunk and hallucinating." I deadpan, trying to blink the fog away.

"No, you're not." She leans over and crawls in bed with me. I wrap my arms around her warm body, and that's when I know I'm not dreaming.

I look at her, completely shocked. "What're you doin' here, Red?"

"Well..." She opens her mouth and closes it. I can tell she's nervous and hesitates. "I couldn't be away from you any longer. This past week sucked and not having you in my life didn't feel right. I'd already decided leaving was a big mistake when I got your message, but I thought it'd be better if I told you how I felt in person."

I swallow hard, my emotions ready to boil over. I know she wouldn't come all this way to tell me I need to get over her and let her move on, but unless she confirms my biggest fear, I stay silent, admiring and holding her.

Presley looks up at me with her big, bright eyes as she holds me around the waist. "I know what we have is special, and I've never felt this way about anyone, ever. And I can't walk away from that and forget we ever happened. I want to stay here with you forever." She smiles up at me, and my entire chest wants to burst. "You're unforgettable, Colton Langston. I'm ready for one more adventure...if your couch is still available," she adds with a smirk.

I pull her closer, wanting and needing to breathe her in. My mind is reeling at what this could mean for us, for our future. The fact I'm even contemplating a future with Red excites and scares me all at the same time. However, the heart wants what it wants, and I'm not about to deny that. Part of me still can't believe she's here, and I wonder what I did to deserve such a kind and amazing woman.

"You're not sleeping on the damn couch," I say matter-of-factly, painting my mouth against her lips and pulling her on top of me. I need and want all of her as she straddles me. I grip her ass in my hands as she gently rocks against my cock, causing it to grow harder with each movement. Her fingers lightly trail down my bare chest, and she leans over and kisses me with soft, plump lips. The fire in her eyes and the eagerness in her kiss tells me everything I need to know.

I tug on the hem of her shirt, and she playfully slips it over her head and unsnaps her bra, allowing her gorgeous tits to bounce freely. Fuck, she's going to be the end of me.

Laying her down on her back, I trail kisses over her body and unsnap her jeans and slip her panties off in one swift movement until she's naked in my bed. Instead of rushing, I stop and look over her.

"You look good enough to eat," I say with a chuckle, causing her eyebrow to pop up with amusement. I move down her body and kiss her sweet spot, allowing her to melt against me. "Enjoy it, sweetheart," I whisper against her pussy. Presley is a greedy little thing as she writhes against my mouth, and I want to give her the relief she seeks. With white knuckles, she grabs the sheets and allows soft moans to escape from her lips. The sound has me needing her more than she'll ever know.

"*Yessss*, Colton," she says in a needy whisper as I slide two fingers inside. "Yes, yes."

I kiss her inner thigh. "Tell me what you need, Red."

"All of you," she breathes out desperately as I swirl my tongue against her clit. Presley rocks her body against my mouth, and soon, she's losing herself. Before she can fully relax, I quickly remove my clothes, and moments later, I'm hovering above her. She has me so damn hard I can barely wait. Presley leans up and kisses me as I push inside her. Taking my time, I enjoy filling her with my length. As we rock together, I devour her lips. Knowing she's mine and here to stay is like a dream come true. Something I wanted but didn't think would happen.

"I missed you so fucking much."

Presley scratches her nails down my back, creating a delicious mix of pleasure and pain. "I couldn't stop thinking about you. I needed you," she breathlessly confesses.

As her body begins to tense, I give her everything I have, pumping deep and hard.

"More," she begs. "I'm so close."

"Yes, baby. Me too." I don't know how much longer I can last, but I do as she says because I want to please her. Presley gasps as the orgasm takes over, and her pussy clenches so tight as she rides the wave that it sends me over the edge seconds later. As we're coming down from our high, I'm transfixed, completely mesmerized by everything about her. She smirks as if she's reading the thoughts running through my mind at full speed.

"I've been dreaming about that all week," she admits after we clean up.

"I was worried I'd never see you again." The thought of what-if almost destroys me as I lie next to her, pulling her back into my arms. She rests her head against my chest, and I lightly brush my fingers against her arm as she listens to my rapidly beating heart.

My heart is so damn full as I hold her, never wanting to let her go, and I'm pretty sure the smile on my face is permanent. She props herself up on one elbow and looks up at me with big green eyes, and I can't believe I almost lost her forever.

"I'm falling in love with you, Presley," I admit with my whole heart as I tuck loose strands of messy red hair behind her ear.

"I already fell, Cowboy." A smile plays on her lips. "Guess that means we're *finally* even."

I chuckle, thinking back to all the things we did to get back at each other. "You're mine, sweetheart, and I'm never letting you go." I squeeze her tighter.

"Good because I'm not letting you go either."

CHAPTER TWENTY-ONE

PRESLEY

THREE MONTHS LATER

"Colton, faster," I demand as he bends me over, thrusting hard. As the warm shower grows tepid, I know I'm going to be late for work since he decided to sneak in here and seduce me.

Squeezing his fingers over my hips, he digs deeper as he pounds roughly. He removes a hand, then I feel a wet slap against my ass.

"Colton!" I squeal, nearly falling into the wall, but he's quick to catch me. His hand wraps around my center, then slides down between my legs where he plays with my clit.

"That's it," he praises when my pussy clenches around his dick. "Come on my cock, Red."

And I do just that because my body responds to everything he demands, even when I want to be disobedient to taunt him. He works me like an expert violinist, and when his orgasm hits, he pulls out and pumps himself all over my back, then rubs it over my ass cheeks.

"You have a weird fascination of rubbing your sticky sperm on me." I snicker and turn around to face him. "You're lucky we're in the shower."

"I'm just marking my territory," he says innocently.

"You act as if there's a threat of someone taking me," I say, reaching for the body wash with a smirk so we can clean up. Though deep down, I know he still has a sliver of insecurity from when Mallory cheated and he lost everything that was important to him at the time.

"Have you seen you? There's always a threat!" He pounds his chest with a fist and growls like a caveman.

"You're insane." I chuckle, turning around to rinse off. He smacks my ass again before wrapping his arms around my body and cupping my breasts. "You're also insatiable."

"Can you blame me? You have these beautiful curves, luscious breasts, and biteable ass cheeks. It drives me insane." He moans, and it sends tingles down my spine just thinking of how amazing being with him is and how it never feels like enough.

"Biting my ass was cute the first time, but the teeth marks are starting to leave bruises." I laugh when he makes a show of lowering himself and scraping his teeth along my backside.

Another ten minutes go by before he finally lets me out of the shower. It's not easy to leave him, but when I look at the time, I know I have to finish getting ready and quickly head to the studio.

"I'm meeting with Kat today to do a photoshoot of the bakery for her website. She wants to get new shots on her social media ASAP, and I don't want to be late, so stop giving me those bedroom eyes!" I scold when he attaches his lips to my neck. "Shouldn't you be working anyway?" I remind him.

"I skipped the B&B to have breakfast at home," he tells me with amusement.

"Well, time for you to go back out into the wild, Cowboy. I have work to do, and you're distracting me." I turn around and playfully scold him.

He groans, then pulls back with a frown. "Fine."

I pat his cheek, then kiss his lips. "I'll see you tonight. Kat wants pictures of her in front of and inside the bakery, and then some shots of her food. Shouldn't take me too long actually, but then I have some Bookstagram pics to take and edit. I should be done before dinner, though."

"I'll be anxiously waiting." He sneaks another kiss, and I laugh at his eagerness.

Colton heads back to the ranch, and I finish getting ready for my day. Ever since I packed up all my belongings and moved to Texas a few months ago, things have been a whirlwind of an adventure—the very best kind. It sounds crazy when I think about it all, but I followed my heart, and it led me to the greatest man I've ever met. Of course, he wanted me to move in right away, which I had no problem with since we both stay busy with work during the day.

Shortly after I settled in, I decided to open a photography studio in town so I didn't have to depend on traveling gigs to pay my bills, but also because I wanted to soak in as much time with Colton as possible. We both work so much as it is, so we use every moment we can to be together. Now I do engagements, bridal, newborn, and family pictures on top of my Bookstagram images. However, I still plan to travel to the book events I confirmed months ago before I met Colton.

"Hey, Kat!" I greet as soon as I walk inside the bakery and see her behind the counter. It always smells so damn good in here, and I usually leave with a large box of goodies.

"Presley! Hey! I'm just trying to pick a few of the best pastries for the photoshoot." She contemplates a few muffins on top of the counter. "I'm so excited! My website has needed a revamp for months, so I'm happy we're doing some new pictures."

I reach into my bag and pull out my camera. "It's gonna be great, Kat. Don't even worry. Once I edit these babies, you can pop them up on your site and watch the customers flood in," I tell her with a big smile. Not that Kat needs the encouragement. Her bakery is consistently jam-packed, and she's always selling out. In fact, her website doesn't even look that bad, but when she begged me to help her with some new shots, I couldn't say no.

"Where do you want to start?" I ask, and she directs me to the part of her bakery where she wants close-ups. I start right away, knowing I have a long checklist of things to get through today.

"Any chance you want to take a bite of that cupcake?" I ask, angling my camera on her face. "That'd be a cute shot for your Facebook page."

"I mean, I guess." Kat playfully rolls her eyes. She's a gorgeous brunette and would make a great cheeky model for my Bookstagram page too.

"Any chance you want to pose with a book too?" I bite my lower lip, anticipating her response.

"Why am I not even surprised you have a book with you?" She laughs, shaking her head at me.

"Technically, it's just a plain white one that I photoshop covers onto, and depending on what I need to feature that day, I'll add the cover image over it. It's a necessity in my purse." I shrug with a smirk.

"So just pose with it?"

"Yeah! I mean, in your cute apron and with a muffin or cupcake."

"I'm not paying you to take pictures of me for *you*." She gives me a look, but I know it's all for show. She obsesses over my Instagram feed.

"That's okay. We'll call it a freebie," I tease.

"That's not what I meant!" She laughs.

I pose her in front of one of the bright white walls with bookshelves filled with cute merchandise. She has a table with one of those cupcake towers on it too that I use for the shots as well. I take what I need, and twenty minutes later, I'm satisfied.

"Thank you. Don't worry, when I post them, I'll tag the bakery for extra exposure. Maybe you'll be my next Instagram sensation." I playfully grin, knowing she'd probably love that although she'd pretend not to.

"Only if it comes with a hunky cowboy like you ended up with," she retorts. "I'm starting to think they're all taken."

"Braxton isn't," I blurt out, knowing their messy history.

She blinks, giving me a dirty look for even mentioning his name.

"Well…he's not." I shrug, then focus on the screen on my camera.

She shoots me a glare, and I know the conversation about him is over.

"Alright, let's get some shots of you behind the counter with your wall logo," I direct, knowing I need to change the subject. Kat's a natural, and though she tries to act as if she has a hard exterior, she has a soft, sensitive side she doesn't let many people see. From what I've gathered over the past year, she's from a super wealthy family who own half of Eldorado. I think she's had trouble trusting people in general, never knowing if they were only getting close to her because of her family's money.

"These are great," I tell her, taking a few more snapshots before pulling the camera back to look through them. "Let's take some close-ups of your muffins and cupcakes so you can feature them on your social media."

I watch as Kat pulls a variety out of the display case, and I'm tempted to ask her if I can eat them afterward.

"You're looking at my muffin like it's your last meal." Her voice is filled with amusement.

"How you can bake so many delicious goodies and be around them all day and still look like a supermodel blows my mind," I tell her. "I look at a buttercream cupcake, and I gain a third ass cheek."

"Well, from what I heard, Colton's a fan of your ass, so it probably wouldn't be the worst thing in the world."

Her comment makes me snort, then smile as I think about us in the shower this morning.

"That look on your face right now is all the confirmation I need." She chuckles.

"I plead the fifth."

"Mm hmm." Kat nods. "Try this one," she says, handing me a cupcake. "It's one of my newer creations."

It looks like something out of a Martha Stewart magazine with chocolate chips in the frosting, and if I wasn't trying to act like a professional, I'd shove the whole thing in my mouth at once. Instead, I keep my dignity by taking a decent-sized bite.

"Oh. My. God," I say around a mouthful. Looking inside the muffin, I see what I bit into. "Is that cookie dough inside?" Kat answers with a proud smile. "This is the most amazing thing I've ever put in my mouth."

"I'll be sure to let Colton know you said that," she blurts out.

I nearly spit out the delicious dessert and cover my mouth with my hand. "Please don't. It'll wound his ego." I chuckle, knowing exactly what he'd say if he heard this conversation.

Once I've finished the incredible cupcake, I reluctantly lead us back to work. "Let's do a few more just for good measure, then we can head outside and take some of you in front of the bakery," I direct.

"Sounds good. I just need to check a few messages first about the pick-up orders." She grabs her phone and starts typing away, so I take the opportunity to go outside and figure out where to place her without the sun blazing down on us.

It's a gorgeous spring day, and the lighting is near perfect in my test shots. Moments later, Kat meets me outside with a wide smile. "Ready for me?"

"Yep. Let's start with you just standing in front of the bakery on the sidewalk. Then I think I'm going to have you walk toward me and stand on the road. I can get a good shot with the building blurred behind you."

"Sounds good, boss."

She poses, and I snap more shots, moving around and shooting various angles as she changes her position. The sun looks good on her skin too, so I know she's going to love these.

"Come check these out and tell me what you think," I tell her, waving her over.

She looks over my shoulder as I scroll through the images and grin. "Wow, they look pretty good."

"They're gonna look even better when I edit them to really bring out the colors. Your cute sign looks so good too. I love the new design."

"Oh totally." Kat looks around as if she's trying to find another spot.

"Do you want more?" I ask, worried she's not happy with them.

"No, well yes. But not of me."

I furrow my brows. "What do you mean?"

"Well, I'd like to post some shots for my Facebook page of customers too, not just me. So maybe you could stand in front of the bakery with a box filled with pastries looking all happy and excited to eat your healthy treats?"

"Of *me*?" I question. She never mentioned this beforehand.

"Yeah!" she replies. "I mean, if you wouldn't mind? I could take the shot, and then you can look them over and let me know if they're good?"

I pinch my lips together and move my head from side to side. "Sure, I guess? I didn't really dress for the occasion," I say self-consciously, looking down at my faded capris and plain T-shirt. I dressed for comfort, considering I'd be working all day.

"Really? I think you look great! Plus, the sun really makes your hair sparkle."

"Well, it's red, so the sun gives it some natural highlights along with burning my pale skin like a lobster." I sigh.

Kat chuckles, then reaches for my camera. "Give me a quick lesson."

I give her a skeptical look and raise my brows. "I'll make it simple," I say with a laugh. "I'll leave the setting as it is. Make sure it's in focus and then press this button." I show her and have her do a few practice shots. It's pretty easy when you're outside with natural lighting.

"Got it! Can I position you and all? Let me play photographer!" She squeals with excitement.

"Uh, sure! I'm your canvas." I smirk.

Kat takes it to heart and poses me in front of the bakery before taking a few shots. She tells me to smile and look excited to be eating a healthy, gluten-free muffin. Then she tells me to imagine what it'd taste like eating it off Colton's cock. It makes me laugh so hard that she ends up getting a candid shot of me that turns out so awesome, I might actually post that one on my Instagram feed.

"You're a natural, Pres! I totally knew it, too." She's scrolling through the images and smiling. "Okay, I have one more idea I want to do."

"Sure, but then we have to get back to doing some shots with you!" I follow her lead into the middle of the street. Luckily, the downtown is small, so there's little to no traffic. Kat looks around as if she's trying to find the best angle and finally decides on a position.

"Okay, ready? I have the best view right now!" She smiles wide, almost devilishly, and then takes a bunch of shots. "Hands on hips," she orders, then takes a few more pictures. "Great, now I want you to turn around and face the bakery."

"What?" I furrow my brows. "I give up my camera for ten minutes, and now you're a professional?" I tease but do it anyway.

"No booty though allowed on your—Oh my God! Colton!" I shriek so loudly, my voice echoes off the buildings. He scared the shit out of me, but even more so because he's down on one knee.

"Hey, Red." He flashes that gorgeous smile of his that had me smitten with him in the first place just a few months ago. I'm speechless when I see he's holding a ring box with a large diamond ring inside. My hand flies to my mouth, and I want to blurt out a million questions, but I have no words.

Footsteps echo behind me followed by a rapid shutter sound as I realize what's really happening.

The whole thing was a setup, and the man of my dreams is kneeling in front of me with the biggest grin on his face, reaching for my hand and looking at me as if I'm his whole world.

"Colton," I whisper when I finally find my voice. "What are you doing?"

"Give me your hand, Red," he orders, and I comply. The pad of his thumb rubs over my ring finger on my left hand, which makes my heart beat even faster. My chest tightens, and it's as if the air is being sucked out of my lungs. My hand shakes as he tightens his hold, and I anticipate his next words.

"I hope by now you know how much I love you, how much you mean to me, and how I'd do anything in this world for you. If, for some reason, you don't grasp the magnitude of my love, let me break it down." He smirks, and I realize he's not dressed in his regular jeans and a T-shirt. He's not even wearing a hat, which is uncanny. He's wearing nice dress clothes that he'd wear to church or a wedding. "From the moment we met, I knew you were special. It wasn't always clear or obvious as to why, but my gut instinct told me you were meant to be in my life. Not only are you funny, gorgeous, smart, witty, sweet, and kind, but you also have this goddamn sexy determination. When you had to leave, and I thought I'd never see you again, my entire world tilted. I wanted to fight for you, but I also didn't want to keep you from your dreams. When you came back for *me*, I knew I'd never let you go again. This might seem fast, but there's no one else I'd rather spend the rest of my days doing life with, and I don't see any reason to wait because when you know, you know."

I lick my lips, feeling my heart squeeze with every confident word he flawlessly speaks. I want to reach into his soul, wrap my arms around it, and never let go. The love I feel for him seems impossible to convey.

"So Red, the love of my life, my everything—will you make my life complete and be my wife?"

I see Kat in my peripheral vision and realize Colton set this up because he knows how important photography is to me, and that I'd want something this special captured. Though she's walking around us and whispering soft, "Awws," when I hear Colton's words, I feel like we're the only two people in the world.

"I can't believe this, Colton." My eyes fill with tears as I grasp this moment. "Of course I'll marry you!" He immediately stands and cups my face, fusing our mouths together. When he finally lets me up for air, I try to catch my breath with his strong arms wrapped around me. "I love you so much," I tell him. "Never had a doubt in my mind."

CHAPTER TWENTY-TWO

COLTON

When Presley looks at me as if I'm her entire world and repeats the words she's said to me each day for the past few months, something comes over me that I can't control. My eyes swell with tears of happiness, and my only instinct is to kiss the hell out of her.

"You have no idea how happy you've just made me," I tell her, pressing another kiss to her lips. "The luckiest SOB on the planet!"

Presley chuckles, and it's music to my ears.

"I love you, Red. I promise to always love you no matter what."

I grab her left hand and slide the ring on her finger.

"It's a perfect fit!" Kat gushes, and I almost forgot she was here.

"Just like us, babe." I give Presley a wink. She laughs and takes a closer look at the diamond.

"This is gorgeous, Colton." Her eyes widen as she inspects it. The minute I saw it, I knew it was perfect for my Red.

"I got some amazing shots of you two," Kat tells us. "The way you two look in each other's eyes…" She releases a dreamy sigh. "Sickly sweet. Pretty sure I got a cavity."

Presley turns and smiles at Kat. "You lying little shit," she quips. "Behind this all along, weren't ya?"

"Well of course! Just because I don't have my own dreamy cowboy doesn't mean I don't want to help two lovebirds!" She grins, but I hear the bitterness in her tone. Whatever back and forth arguing she and Braxton are doing is being kept tight-lipped. He refuses to give details about what happened. I only know about the one-night hookup because I was called to pick him up when she kicked him out the next day. Though Kat doesn't really know that, and I'm not mentioning it. It's obvious there are underlying feelings that neither of them wants to admit.

I thank Kat for helping before sweeping my new fiancée away and dragging her to my truck a block away. Unable to keep my hands and lips off her, I help her into the truck and tell her to buckle up.

"What do you have up your sleeve, Cowboy?" she asks skeptically.

"You just let me romance my future bride, got it?" I shoot her a wink, and as usual, she groans when she doesn't get her way. I think it's adorable that she pretends to hate surprises, but deep down, she loves them. No one has ever treated her the way she truly deserves, and I plan on showing her every single day of my life how incredible she is and how much she means to me. Every. Damn. Day.

Adapting to life with Presley has been a smooth and flawless adjustment. I wanted us to come home to each other and wake up every single morning with her in my arms. Considering she moved here for me, I wasn't about to let her live anywhere else and am so grateful we're taking this next step in our relationship. I know it's fast, but I've never been more sure of anything before.

I spent years with Mallory, thought she was the one, and was ready to make the sacrifices to provide for our family, but then after five years together, she destroyed it. So whether it's three months or three years, there's no reason to wait when I know without a doubt Presley's the one. People may think we're crazy, but the only thing I am is crazy in love with her.

Even though Mallory is back and those feelings I once had for her are completely gone, we've managed to tolerate each other. I knew if I had to see her every day, I was going to have to put in the effort to forgive her in order to properly move on with my own life with Presley. Her daughter, Julia, has even come for riding lessons a few times, and she's a pretty sweet kid.

"The B&B?" she asks as soon as we pull into the driveway.

I park and kill the engine, then turn toward her. "You trust me?"

She tilts her head and smiles. "You know I do."

Taking her hand, I bring it to my lips and press a kiss to her knuckles just as I have dozens of times before. The way she smiles at me and melts into my touch never gets old. "Then let me surprise you, babe."

"You already have. Since the first day I met you."

I walk around to the other side of the truck and help her down. Leading her up the porch, I stop her right before she can open the door. "Ready?"

Presley bites her bottom lip and bobs her head back and forth as if she's contemplating it. "Don't even pretend." I cup her cheeks and steal a quick kiss. "Close your eyes now."

My heart pounds harder, the excitement from this day fueling my adrenaline. I can't wait to show her this surprise, knowing she has no idea what's about to happen.

Opening the door, I lead her inside and bring her into the dining area. Everyone's smiling and bursting at the seams. I hold my finger up to tell them to wait one more moment. Once I'm standing behind Presley, I lean into her and whisper in her ear. "Open your eyes, Red."

"*Oh my god!* No way!" Presley leaps into her mother's arms, and her siblings rush over. They're all passing her around like a doll and hearing their excitement makes me smile.

Since she moved here, she's mentioned wanting to fly her parents in to meet me and visit the ranch. I already knew I wanted to propose weeks ago, so I contacted them myself, booked them rooms at the B&B, and flew them all in.

"Colton!" Presley rushes toward me and wraps her arms around my neck, then pulls our mouths together. "I can't believe you did this! How? When?"

I love how shocked she is because it means I managed to do it all under the radar and truly surprise her.

"Well, you wanted them to come here, and what better time than after getting engaged?" I grin. "I knew you wouldn't want them to miss this."

"You're amazing, Colton Langston. Seriously. How am I so lucky?"

"I ask myself that same question every single day, babe."

Presley's family arrived early this morning, and I helped get them settled after I formally introduced myself. I've spoken to her parents on the phone a little, but meeting them in person at this level of our relationship was important to me, and I knew it'd be important to Presley too. John and Mallory have been making them feel at home and taking care of all their needs.

When I told John about my plans to propose and bring her family here, he had no reservations about telling me how happy he was for me. He understands what it's like to be so crazy in love, you want nothing more than to start a life and family together.

"Don't you just love the B&B?" I hear Presley ask her mother. "I stayed here for ten days and fell in love with it." She tilts her head and meets my gaze, blowing me a kiss. "Fell in love with a sexy cowboy too."

"Ew," her sister Callie interrupts. "I hear enough over text. I don't need to see your PDA in person."

Presley laughs and swats at her. Her family is so sweet and loveable; everything I'd imagine, considering what kind of person she is.

Her siblings ask about the proposal and to see the ring, and after a round of awws and congratulations, John pops in and lets them know lunch is almost ready. I plan to take everyone on a ranch tour later, but right now, I want to get my new fiancée home and worship every inch of her gorgeous body.

"So…you already have a wedding date picked out?" she taunts when I'm driving us to the house.

"Tomorrow too soon?" I glance at her and smirk.

"I think I have plans, actually."

"Oh, bummer. Well, I'm sure we can find a date. But I'm not waiting long to make you my wife, just so you know…" I kiss her hand and shoot her a wink. "I plan to knock you up right away too."

Her eyes immediately widen, which causes me to laugh. "I can't even imagine the amount of love I'd feel for our child, but I know that I love you so deeply that I want to make babies with you for years to come."

"I think I'd be okay with that," she mocks, then inches closer to me. "But why wait? Let's start practicing now."

"Red…" I growl when she lowers her hand to my leg and begins rubbing my crotch. "You're going to make me drive into a freaking tree if you don't stop that."

"Then you better pay close attention to the road, Cowboy."

She lowers her head and undoes my buckle. Instinctively, I part my legs and adjust my hips to give her access. The zipper goes down, my pants open, and then she pulls out my cock.

"We're almost home, babe," I warn but don't pull away when she puts those soft, beautiful lips around the tip. Uh, fuck me.

She works my dick like a goddamn pro. Licking up my shaft, she wraps her mouth around my tip, then pulls me all the way to the back of her throat. Her palm wraps around me as she pumps and strokes and teases me.

"Red," I warn, pulling into our driveway. "We're home."

Shifting the truck into park, I pull at her shoulders, but she refuses to budge. My fingers tangle in her hair as she bobs up and down on my dick, sucking it as if her life depends on it. Her cheeks hollow, and I can't take it any longer. I push her head down to take more of me, but when she gags, I quickly release her. I expect her to stop, but instead, she brings me back down as deep as she can. The sensation is intense as fuck, but there's no way I'm going to come in her mouth when I want to be inside her.

"Inside, Red. Let's go," I demand, but when she finally looks up at me, I see a devious twinkle in her eyes. She's totally up to something.

"Move the seat back, Colton. I'm about to ride you hard and fast."

My head leans back with a deep groan. "Fuck, I think I came already."

Presley bites her lip and giggles, knowing she's getting a rise out of me. She's a little vixen, always getting me worked up and shocking the shit out of me when something like that comes out of her mouth.

She helps me out of my slacks and orders me to remove my

shirt. Presley shimmies out of her bottoms and panties and straddles me with her sweet breasts in my face.

"Have I told you lately how much I love your tits?" I cup one and bring it into my mouth over her shirt. "Tonight, I'm going to slide my dick between them and watch as they fuck me, then I'm going to come all over your face."

"Yes," she whispers, slowly sliding on top of me.

"And then, you're going to sit on my face as I devour that sweet pussy of yours. You're going to come over and over on my lips, baby."

Presley rocks her hips, and soon, we're rocking in a frantic rhythm of need and desire. She has me so goddamn riled up, I thrust inside her harder and deeper and cup her ass cheeks in my hand as I direct her body to grind on top of me. "Fuck, Red. You feel so tight. So fucking amazing." I end my sentence with a slap to her ass, which I know she loves. She squeals, and it encourages her to move faster.

"That's it, Red. Fuck me just like that." She locks her hands behind my neck and rocks so fast on top of me, I'm actually worried she'll snap my dick in half. But at this point, I want everything she's giving me. The way I feel when we're together doesn't compare to anything else in my life, and I cherish these moments. Though we've been intimate for months now, each time feels special. My heart beats a little faster. My love for her is overflowing, and my life feels more complete every day I get to call her mine.

"I love you, future Mrs. Langston," I tell her when I know she's close. Seconds later, her body shakes and tightens, and she's holding us together as she rides out the intense waves of pleasure. I reach down and rub her clit, knowing it's always so sensitive after she orgasms. It doesn't take long to get her off again, and that's when I release with her, growling deeply as it takes over my senses.

"I can't believe I get to experience that for the rest of my life," I tell her softly, pushing the stray strands of hair out of her eyes.

"Yeah," she breathes out. "You're a lucky bastard."

I burst out laughing, not that I should be surprised by now. Presley always makes me laugh, even when she's trying to be serious or telling me off. It's another reason I'm crazy about her.

"Trust me, I know, babe. That fine ass is mine forever." I give her a swat for emphasis. "Who knew one Bookstagram photo would change our lives?"

"Considering you didn't even know what Bookstagram was," she says, chuckling.

Smiling, I laugh too, knowing she's right. "Well, whatever reason brought you to me, I'm just so thankful it did."

Her smile is so broad, it reaches her eyes, and when she leans in for a kiss, I grab around her neck and pull that sassy mouth to mine.

"I love you. Thank you for asking me to marry you." She leans her forehead against mine, our heavy pants the only sound in the cab of the truck.

Tilting her chin up so I can gaze into her beautiful green eyes, I say, "Thank you for saying yes."

EPILOGUE
PRESLEY

TWO YEARS LATER

"Being pregnant in the summer is hell," I whisper under my breath as I try to pull my hair in a ponytail.

Colton stops at the bathroom door. "Did ya say somethin', sweetheart?"

"Just ready for summer to be over. I'm sweating in places I didn't even know I *could* sweat." Though I've spent two full summers here, I'm still not used to the heat, and being pregnant makes it a hundred times worse.

"You almost ready, Mrs. Langston?" He walks inside and wraps his arms around me. "You know Mama doesn't like tardiness."

"I know, I know. Just need to change into my dress really quick."

Colton follows me through the house as I pretend to give him a striptease.

"Oh man, don't stop now." He chuckles, grabbing his chest over his heart.

"That, right there, is what got us into this mess in the first place." I meet his eyes before I slip on the cute slinky black dress with a pink ribbon that laces under my boobs to really accentuate my growing tummy.

He shrugs and walks to me, kissing my neck before finally

meeting my lips. "Not my fault you're so damn sexy. And having you carrying my baby? Damn girl, you better watch out."

"Me? You're the one who decided to walk around shirtless the entire first year of our marriage," I tell him. "This is mostly your fault."

His lips meet mine one last time. "Just remember, you chose it!"

"I sure did, and I'd do it over a million more times." I shoot him a wink as he leaves the room. I sit on the edge of the bed and slip on my shoes, and I think back to the ceremony. It was small and beautiful, exactly how I always imagined it would be. My family flew to Texas to be a part of my special day and have been super supportive of my decision to start my life here. Out of all of them, Callie has been my number one fan. She absolutely adores Colton and has been over the moon ever since I told her I was pregnant. Randomly, she'll text me and say she's moving to Texas too. Of course, she's kidding, but I wish she would consider it. I'd love to have her here, and plus, she wants to be close to the baby.

After I took my tenth pregnancy test, I was nervous as hell to tell Colton, but I don't know why. He was so elated and happy and couldn't wait to tell the whole state of Texas. Sometimes I wake up and can't believe this is my life. I'm so lucky to have found a man who'd do anything for me and loves me wholeheartedly. And to know we're starting a family together and will be raising our baby girl here fills me with joy.

"We need to get going soon," Colton says from the kitchen.

"Almost done," I answer, standing to take one last glance in the full-length mirror. I actually look cute, which makes me happy because I know a million pictures will be taken today especially considering how proud Mama Langston is. She and Everly planned the shower with the help of Mama Bishop, so I've been warned it's going to be super extra. Every family from here to San Angelo was invited, which makes me nervous because I don't like being the center of attention.

I walk into the living room where Colton is patiently waiting for me with a grin. "If we're late, we're gonna have two mamas to answer to. And two isn't always better than one in this situation."

"I know, I know. Just stalling," I admit as he opens the front door, and we walk out to the truck together. Colton stands by to help me step up into the truck because the bigger the belly becomes, the harder that is. Once I'm settled and buckled, he gets in, and we make our way downtown. The shower is being held in the old bank building where Mama Bishop hosts a lot of events for the community. Apparently, so many people RSVP'd to the shower that the church reception hall couldn't fit everyone.

We roll into the parking lot, and Colton turns off the truck and glances over at me. "Don't be nervous, Red. You're gonna do just fine. And you look absolutely stunning."

As if he reads my mind, Colton leans over and gives me a kiss of encouragement because I need one. I look at all the cars in the parking lot, and my heart beats like crazy. "Can we get a rain check on this?"

He shakes his head. "Only if you wanna be disowned. Forever. Mama will hold a grudge so hard."

"Okay, yeah, not an option." Southern mamas can be really scary sometimes. They're not known for their subtly if they don't like something.

Colton grabs my hand and kisses my knuckles. "It's showtime, baby!"

A nervous laugh escapes me as I release a long breath. "Okay, let's do this."

Colton wraps his arm around me as we walk toward the building, giving me just a sliver of his confidence. As soon as we enter, my mouth falls open. Pink streamers hang from the ceiling, and big pink balloons decorate every table. A giant cake sits in the corner, and there are tables and tables of presents. Before I can even turn to Colton, my mother wraps her arms around me.

"Mom! Oh my gosh! I didn't think you were going to make it," I say, trying not to get emotional, but as soon as I see Callie, happy tears start falling.

"No one else could get off work. They tried really hard but told us they send their love. And they're mailing gifts," Callie tells me with a hug.

"I know it's not easy traveling and doing all that, so I completely understand," I say, wiping my face. That is until I spot Olivia and Maverick with their toddler between them.

Olivia comes to me and wraps her arms around me, squeezing

me so tight. "I'm so happy for you two! Pregnancy looks great on you." Olivia rubs my tummy, and Maverick gives me a side hug. I kneel down and tickle their girl. She pretends to be shy, which makes me laugh.

"Hey, hope you've been doing well," he tells me, then shakes Colton's hand. They officially met at the wedding and instantly became friends. As I look around the room, I'm trying hard to internalize the way I feel, but I'm so full of happiness it's becoming hard for me to keep it all in. The Bishop girls rush over to me, trying to talk over one another, and soon, I see Mama Bishop and Colton's mom, Beth, waving us over.

I've hugged so many people that my head is spinning, and I've smiled so much my face hurts, and the shower hasn't even started.

"I thought we'd play a few games, eat cake and drink punch, open gifts, then call it a day," Beth says sweetly. "Can't have you and my grandbaby gettin' too tired."

"Thank you," I say just over a whisper. Colton told her I didn't want to be the center of attention, which is why we made it a co-ed shower. This way, he can take some of the spotlight.

Everly comes over to me and rubs my baby bump. "How's my favorite niece doin'?"

I give her a smile. "She's doing well. Other than using my bladder as a mattress."

"She's going to be so loved. I can't wait for her to get here. I'm gonna spoil her so much! Fill her up with candy, then send her back home to drive my brother nuts." She snickers. "I owe him for annoying me when we were kids."

I shake my head just as Mama Bishop tells me we're going to start playing the games. Colton and I sit in the front of the room, like a king and queen, as our friends and family compete to try to see who can drink liquid out of baby bottles the fastest. Watching the Bishop boys drink from bottles is the most ridiculous thing I've ever seen. Just as Braxton finishes his bottle and does a victory dance around the room, Everly announces the next game.

"So hold your pants, y'all. The next game is called What the Poo," she says with a chuckle as baby diapers are being passed around with melted chocolate in the center. "And the first person to guess the correct candy in each diaper is the winner."

Colton's face contorts as he watches the girls and guys try to figure it out. "Gross."

"Just wait until it's the real thing," I lean over and tell him with a smirk. "You're on poop duty for the first six months."

"We'll see," he scoffs, then grins. "Oh my God, did Jackson just eat some?" His eyes grow wide, and I turn and look at Jackson taste testing the chocolate in the diapers.

"This is hysterical." I'm laughing so hard that I'm scared I might pee myself.

"This is the best poop I've ever eaten," Jackson yells out. The room fills with laughter as the game ends with Kiera and Jackson winning because they have zero shame.

Soon, Colton and I are ushered to pose next to the cake that Kat made for us. It's baby pink with embellishments that look like real pearls, but it's all edible. I know it's going to be delicious, but it's so gorgeous. It's almost too pretty to eat, but that doesn't stop Colton's mama from cutting into it and handing us a piece. The cake practically melts in my mouth, and I overhear Kat telling someone it's gluten-free. Of course, it is. She's a magician in the kitchen, creating healthy versions of cakes and cookies that taste like the real deal.

After we finish chatting and eating, we're moved to the front of the room to open gifts. I'm shocked by everyone's generosity. I feel like we unwrap presents and take pictures for over an hour. The room fills with oohs and awws, and I'm so grateful we won't have to buy diapers or clothes for what seems like years. Everything we could ever possibly need or want we received, and even things I didn't think about. This is all too much, and I'll never be able to show my gratitude.

As the party wraps up, my emotions finally get the best of me because I'm so elated by all the love and support surrounding our growing family. I begin to wipe tears—damn pregnancy hormones—and Colton notices. He stops talking to John and Braxton and comes to me. Pulling me into his strong arms, he holds me tight. I look up at him and can't believe this is my life. It's a dream come true, one that I never imagined could really be mine.

Before we leave, I try to thank every person who showed up as our family loads the gifts into the truck. There are so many I watch

Everly and Callie stuff several cars to the brim as well. As I cross the parking lot, Everly lets me know they'll be over after she helps clean up the hall.

"Thank you so much for everything," I tell her again, though I can never say it enough.

"Anything for my sister," she says with a hug, and Callie clears her throat.

"Just remember who's the OG sister," Callie jokes with Everly. They get along so well, and I know if Callie lived closer, they'd be best friends.

I make sure to find Maverick and Olivia before I leave.

"Mama Bishop said she's hosting a big lunch at her house in your honor tomorrow. So I better see you then." Olivia smiles. "I love Southerners! She said she was gonna fatten me up!"

I tilt my head at her and grin. "She will. They all will."

"See you tomorrow then?"

I nod. "Yes, see you then!"

Exhaustion takes over, and Colton walks over. He knows me better than I know myself sometimes. "Ready to go?"

"Yep."

On the ride home, Colton interlocks his fingers with mine, and I steal glances of him as he drives. After we pull into the driveway, we walk in and plop on the couch, letting out a long sigh. Sometimes peopling is hard. Colton moves closer, pulling me into his arms, and kisses me with so much fervor he takes my breath away.

"I love you so damn much," he says between kisses. "Thank you, Red."

"For what?" I pull back and search his face, still loving that he calls me that.

"For coming back when you did," he adds with a smirk. "And staying."

"I'm happy I did. I love you more than you'll ever know."

Our lips crash together, and we become more greedy and breathless. He moans against my mouth, and I giggle because I know exactly where this is heading.

"How much time do we have until your sisters show up?"

"About an hour," I answer quickly, growing more desperate for him with each passing moment.

"Good. That's all the time I need," he says, carefully lifting me in his arms and carrying me to the bedroom.

If you want more cowboys, start with *Taming Him* of the Bishop Brothers series, then continue with the Circle B Ranch series.

AVAILABLE NOW

**Start the Bishop Brothers series
with *Taming Him***

Alex Bishop is your typical cowboy.
Charming, sexy, and wears a panty-melting smirk.

Working on the ranch helped build his solid eight-pack and smoking body. He's every girl's wet fantasy and he knows it too. Alex doesn't follow the rules of your typical playboy bachelor. After wining and dining his dates and giving them the best night of their lives, he always sends flowers and calls the next day—even if it's to say, *let's just be friends*. His mama taught him manners after all and his southern blood knows how to be a gentleman. Still, that isn't enough to tame the wildest of the Bishop brothers.

River Lancaster has finally met the man of her dreams. Too bad after six months of romantic bliss, she finds out he's married. With a broken heart and blind rage, she books herself a ticket to Key West, Florida. Tired of cheaters and liars, she's set on escaping to forget he ever existed. Who needs a man when there's an all-you-can-drink margarita bar, anyway? That's what she tells herself until she bumps into the right guy who can make all those bad memories disappear.

Even if it's only temporarily.

Two weeks on the beach is what they both need. No strings attached, no expectations, no broken hearts. Too bad the universe has other plans—one that'll change the entire course of their lives in just nine short months.

ABOUT THE AUTHOR

Brooke Cumberland and Lyra Parish are a duo of romance authors under the *USA Today* pseudonym, Kennedy Fox. Their characters will make you blush and your heart melt. Cowboys in tight jeans are their kryptonite. They always guarantee a happily ever after!

CONNECT WITH US

Find us on our website:
kennedyfoxbooks.com

Subscribe to our newsletter:
kennedyfoxbooks.com/newsletter

- facebook.com/kennedyfoxbooks
- twitter.com/kennedyfoxbooks
- instagram.com/kennedyfoxduo
- amazon.com/author/kennedyfoxbooks
- goodreads.com/kennedyfox
- bookbub.com/authors/kennedy-fox

BOOKS BY KENNEDY FOX

DUET SERIES (BEST READ IN ORDER)

CHECKMATE DUET SERIES

ROOMMATE DUET SERIES

LAWTON RIDGE DUET SERIES

INTERCONNECTED STAND-ALONES

BISHOP BROTHERS SERIES

CIRCLE B RANCH SERIES

BISHOP FAMILY ORIGIN

LOVE IN ISOLATION SERIES

ONLY ONE SERIES

MAKE ME SERIES

Find the entire Kennedy Fox reading order at
Kennedyfoxbooks.com/reading-order

Printed in France by Amazon
Brétigny-sur-Orge, FR